SKETCHES OF THE CRIMINAL WORLD

VARLAM SHALAMOV (1907–1982) was born in Vologda in western Russia to a Russian Orthodox priest and his wife. After being expelled from law school for his political beliefs, Shalamov worked as a journalist in Moscow. In 1929, he was arrested at an underground printshop and sentenced to three years of hard labor in the Ural Mountains, where he met his first wife, Galina Gudz. The two returned to Moscow after Shalamov's release in 1931; they were married in 1934 and had a daughter, Elena, in 1935. Shalamov resumed work as a journalist and writer, publishing his first short story, "The Three Deaths of Doctor Austino," in 1936. The following year, he was arrested again for counterrevolutionary activities and shipped to the Far North of the Kolyma basin. Over the next fifteen years, he was moved from labor camp to labor camp, imprisoned many times for anti-Soviet propaganda, forced to mine gold and coal, quarantined for typhus, and, finally, assigned to work as a paramedic. Upon his release in 1951, he made his way back to Moscow where he divorced his wife and began writing what would become the two-volume *Kolyma Stories*. He also wrote many books of poetry, including *Ognivo* (Flint, 1961) and *Moskovskiye oblaka* (Moscow Clouds, 1972). Severely weakened by his years in the camps, in 1979 Shalamov was committed to a decrepit nursing home north of Moscow. Following a heart attack in 1980, he dictated his final poems to the poet A. A. Morozov. In 1981, he was awarded the French PEN Club's Liberty Prize; he died of pneumonia in 1982.

DONALD RAYFIELD is Emeritus Professor of Russian and Georgian at Queen Mary University of London. As well as books and articles on Russian literature (notably *A Life of Anton Chekhov*), he is the author of many articles on Georgian writers and of a history of Georgian literature. In 2012 he published *Edge of Empires: A History of Georgia*, which has recently come out in an expanded Russian edition, as have his *A Life of Chekhov* and *Stalin and His Hangmen*. He was the chief editor of *A Comprehensive Georgian-English Dictionary*. He has translated several novels, including Hamid Ismailov's *The Devils' Dance* from the Uzbek and Nikolai Gogol's *Dead Souls* (an NYRB Classic), as well as Varlam Shalamov's *Kolyma Stories* (an NYRB Classic).

ALISSA VALLES is the author, most recently, of the poetry collection *Hospitium*. Her translations include Zbigniew Herbert's *Collected Poems* and *Collected Prose*, Ryszard Krynicki's *Our Life Grows* (NYRB Poets), and Józef Czapski's *Memories of Starobielsk*, forthcoming from NYRB Classics in 2020.

SKETCHES OF THE CRIMINAL WORLD
Further Kolyma Stories

VARLAM SHALAMOV

Translated from the Russian by
DONALD RAYFIELD

Introduction by
ALISSA VALLES

NEW YORK REVIEW BOOKS

nyrb

New York

THIS IS A NEW YORK REVIEW BOOK
PUBLISHED BY THE NEW YORK REVIEW OF BOOKS
435 Hudson Street, New York, NY 10014
www.nyrb.com

English publishing rights acquired via FTM Agency, Ltd., Russia in 2015.
Originally published in Russian in *Sobranie sochineniĭ v 6 + 1 tomakh* (Collected
Works, vols. 1–7) by TERRA-Knizhnyĭ klub in 2013.

The publication was effected under the auspices of the
Mikhail Prokhorov Foundation TRANSCRIPT Pro-
gramme to Support Translations of Russian Literature.

Library of Congress Cataloging-in-Publication Data
Names: Shalamov, Varlam, author. | Rayfield, Donald, 1942– translator, writer of
    introduction.
Title: Kolyma stories / by Varlam Shalamov ; translated and with an introduction
    by Donald Rayfield.
Other titles: Kolymskie rasskazy. English
Description: New York : New York Review Books, 2018. | Series: New York
    Review Books classics
Identifiers: LCCN 2017046693 (print) | LCCN 2017049306 (ebook) | ISBN
    9781681372150 (epub) | ISBN 9781681372143 (alk. paper)
Subjects: LCSH: Political prisoners—Soviet Union—Fiction. | Kolyma
    (Concentration camp)—Fiction.
Classification: LCC PG3487.A592 (ebook) | LCC PG3487.A592 K6413 2018
    (print) | DDC 891.73/44—dc23
LC record available at https://lccn.loc.gov/2017046693

ISBN 978-1-68137-367-6
Available as an electronic book; ISBN 978-1-68137-368-3

Printed in the United States of America on acid-free paper.
10 9 8 7 6 5 4 3 2 1

CONTENTS

BOOK SIX: THE GLOVE, OR, KOLYMA STORIES II

INTRODUCTION

"EVERY story of mine is a slap in the face of Stalinism," Varlam Shalamov wrote to his friend Irina Sirotinskaya in 1971, "and like any slap in the face, has laws of a purely muscular character." He returns to the idea a little later in the letter, contrasting his own ideal of prose to the expansive "spade work" of Tolstoy: "A slap in the face must be short, resonant."[1] Most of Shalamov's stories are indeed short, some extremely so, and constitute an argument both with the great nineteenth-century Russian novels and with the wretched ones of the Stalinist era that sought to pour the pap of socialist realism into a pseudo-epic form. The slap works simultaneously as a figure for aesthetic form and political protest, and in Shalamov's late essays and letters, it functions as a motto of sorts, a creed of laconic defiance echoing, distantly, the Russian futurist manifesto *A Slap in the Face of Public Taste* and—more intimately and immediately—the famous opening of Nadezhda Mandelstam's memoir *Hope Against Hope*: "After slapping Aleksey Tolstoy in the face, M. immediately returned to Moscow."

Mandelstam sent the manuscript of her memoir about life with the poet Osip Mandelstam to Shalamov in 1965, and while neither could hope to publish their prose in the Soviet Union at that time, the two established in the correspondence that followed a shared sense of purpose. He writes: "If I had to give a literature course on the second half of the twentieth century, I would start by burning all the textbooks on the podium, in front of the students. The link between eras, between cultures has been broken; the exchange has been interrupted and our mission is to pick up the ends of string and tie them back together." She replies: "I don't think we should burn textbooks: it's too classical a gesture ... Let's just not use any"; her main concern, too, she writes, is "the link that connects one era to another, the only thing that allows society to be human, a human being to be human."

The task Shalamov took on as a writer was what Osip Mandelstam in the celebrated and chilling poem "The Age" ("Vek") figured as piecing together the broken back of an animal.

> My age, my beast, who will look you
> straight into the eye
> And with his own life blood fuse
> Two centuries' vertebrae?

Shalamov conceives of his writing not only as an act of witness (to a crime) but also as an act of healing or at least of treating an illness or injury. The crimes of Stalinism were committed by a country against itself, in a self-consuming process by which each generation of executioners soon became the next group of victims. Giving an account of the Gulag means finding a form for a suicidal cycle of alienation and death. What is being documented has no end, either logically (since to rid the Soviet state of all its possible "enemies" Stalin would have had to exterminate every single citizen) or historically (there was no liberation of the camps, no formal end to the system, even after Stalin's death and Khrushchev's denunciation). The literary means to find an escape from a vicious cycle is necessarily elliptical. A narrative slap in the face, as opposed to a physical one, is the opposite of mimetic violence: it is a transformation of pain into artistic form—a form that, like a set fracture, makes the bone stronger than it was before.

But the Stalinist years brought with them—along with the torture, starvation, and destruction of millions of human beings—an assault on language that systematically subverted and diminished the power and viability of words. To resurrect the dead in living memory Shalamov had to bring words back into an organic relation with reality. He found help in the Acmeist movement to which Mandelstam had belonged, the work of a group of poets reacting against the mystical vagaries of symbolism and striving to plant poetry firmly back in the soil of the physical, perceptible world. The essays that Shalamov wrote alongside his stories in the 1950s and '60s—including one titled "Diseases of

Language and Their Treatment"—are his continuation of that struggle. In their polemical, battle-ready tone and their call for a "new prose" equal to the new crisis conditions of Soviet life, they bring to mind the manifestos of the prewar avant-garde. Challenge and disputation are methods of "tying the ends together" no less than reverence and emulation.

Shalamov's insistence on the direct participation of literature in life has its roots in the 1920s, when he was a student and, briefly, a journalist in Moscow. Few environments in modern history can have been more exciting to an aspiring writer than the Moscow of those years, a revolutionary city teeming with artistic movements, publications, performances, and quarrels. The futurist movement, the radical formal explorations of the journal *LEF*, and slightly later *Novyi LEF* and its promotion of "factography," all had a profound appeal for Shalamov, who sincerely believed in the aim of raising millions out of illiteracy and out of the poverty he himself had known growing up in Vologda. Inclined to believe in the place of art in that struggle, he spent several years exploring the contending ideas of art as political instrument and the work of art as a sovereign creation.

In 1925, the year Shalamov arrived in Moscow, the critic Viktor Shklovsky published his *Theory of Prose*, and in the years that followed Shalamov eagerly read the publications of OPOYAZ, the Society for the Study of Poetic Language, a group that in addition to Shklovsky included the critics Boris Eikhenbaum and Yuri Tynyanov. Although Shalamov didn't develop into an exemplar of the formalist program, it is hard not to see an affinity between the stony reality of the Kolyma stories and the kind of prose Shklovsky argued for in his *Theory*: "And so, in order to return sensation to our limbs, in order to make us feel objects, to make a stone feel stony, man has been given the tool of art. The purpose of art, then, is to lead us to a knowledge of a thing through the organ of sight instead of recognition."[2] It was also Shklovsky who gave, in *Knight's Move* (1923), a brutal description of hunger in Civil War–era Petersburg that is already more than halfway to the long drawn-out starvation in the Gulag that sounds the ground tone of Kolyma in Shalamov's stories.

In 1958, drawing from his own experience of near starvation and his passage (a year earlier) through the same transit camp near Vladi-vostok where Osip Mandelstam died, Shalamov wrote the story "Cherry Brandy"[3] about the poet's last days hovering between life and death, a narrative of the end of a life permeated and animated by a poetic consciousness (reminiscent in some ways of Hermann Broch's magisterial novel *The Death of Virgil*, but condensed into six pages). The later story "The Resurrection of the Larch" (1966), included in this volume (and lending its title to Shalamov's fifth collection), enacts an oblique resurrection in the form of a larch branch sent from Kolyma to the poet's widow. Aided by the woman's "passionate will," the branch miraculously returns to life standing in an empty food can with dirty Moscow tap water, growing fresh green needles and exuding the vague odor of turpentine, which is "the voice of the dead." Only a living culture can remember and mourn. In bringing the branch back to life, both sender and recipient resurrect for a moment "a memory of the millions who were killed and tortured to death, who are laid in common graves to the north of Magadan."

The story invokes the great age of the dahurian larch, which is still maturing at two hundred years and achieves maturity at three hundred. The Gulag alters not only the measures of human life—emotion, ethical choice, and spirit—but also the scale of historical time. The natural world, on the other hand, even in the hostile climate of Kolyma, can sometimes be enlisted as an ally of art against the prisoner's extremes of deprivation and erasure. The larch can be called as a witness not only to the fate of a prisoner in the Far North under Stalin but also to the journey Shalamov invokes of the eighteenth-century writer Natalia Sheremeteva-Dolgorukova, who as a young wife followed her husband into exile in Siberia, where he perished: "[The larch] can see and shout out that nothing has changed in Russia, neither men's fates, nor human spite, nor indifference."

In the story "Graphite," the marks ("tags") made by topographers on notches cut in trees connect the twentieth-century dwellers in Kolyma with the vast time span of the geological earth. The author follows this observation with the unsentimental comment that dead prisoners go into the earth each with a tag of their own tied to one toe and marked with graphite—a product of millennia of compressed organic matter. In "The Resurrection of the Larch" and "Graphite" Shalamov reminds the reader that the bodies of the dead do not decay in the Arctic permafrost: they endure in an icy immortality that is a terrible inversion of heroic glory and also a powerful metaphor for the Soviet inability to mourn the victims of Stalin. (By the same token, the current signs of thaw in the Arctic permafrost as a result of climate change may bring the dead back to press their claims on a world that denied them.)

Nothing has changed: yet elsewhere, Shalamov insists on contrasting the conditions of earlier prisoners with those he himself experienced in Kolyma. In the story "Grishka Logun's Thermometer," he marks the distance between the prisoner-narrator and the prisoner Dostoyevsky by pointing to the novelist's many "miserable, tearful, humiliating but touching letters to his seniors for all of the ten years he spent as a soldier after the 'House of the Dead,'" even his "poems to the empress." The narrator writes a petition on behalf of his immediate boss, Zuyev, a mining inspector and a former prisoner, who is trying to get his conviction annulled by the authorities. The narrator agrees to the job in order to spend a day indoors, out of the lethal cold, but he fails to produce a letter of sufficient rhetorical power because he is so depleted and damaged that "the repository where I used to keep grandiose adjectives now had nothing in it except hatred ... There was no Kolyma in the 'House of the Dead.' If there had been, Dostoyevsky would have been struck dumb."

To Shalamov, Dostoyevsky is a genius and an example of artistic integrity, but he is also to be judged severely for his failure to reveal the true depths of depravity in penal camp life. In "What Fiction Writers Get Wrong," an argument against nineteenth-century literary romanticization of criminals, Shalamov claims that Dostoyevsky mistook the accidental criminals he came across during his imprisonment for gangsters, for the professional class of criminals who live by their own brutal code of law and have dominated camp life for generations. Shalamov is willing to allow for the possibility that "Dostoyevsky never knew them," because "if he did see and know them, then, as an artist, he turned his back on them." Tolstoy and Chekhov also failed in this regard, in Shalamov's view, although he felt Chekhov had undoubtedly come across real criminals on his journey to the prison island of Sakhalin; in "Crooks by Blood" he is pleased to be able to correct Chekhov on a fragment of gangster cardplayers' slang misheard on Sakhalin.

Shalamov considered swashbuckling portrayals of criminal outlaws by twentieth-century writers like Babel to be frivolous. In the letter to Sirotinskaya quoted earlier, his censure also falls on Babel's prose style (to many a model of concision): "If I practically never thought about how to write a novel, I thought about how to write a short story from early on and for decades...I once took a pencil and crossed out of Babel's stories all their beauty, all those fires like resurrections, and looked at what was left. Of Babel not much was left, and of Larisa Reisner, nothing at all." As for poets, Sergei Yesenin, despite his great lyrical gifts, was fatally compromised in Shalamov's eyes by sucking up to the criminal world and by the fact that criminals had adopted him as their bard, tattooing lines from his poems on their bodies. "The gangster...is not wholly without aesthetic needs, however little he may be human. His needs are satisfied by prison songs...usually very sentimental, plaintive, and touching" (this from "Apollo Among the Criminals"). Yesenin caters to that taste.

Written in the late 1950s, the stories in Book Four, "Sketches of the Criminal World," are a merciless indictment of this corrosive, brutal criminal subculture but also of the ideological delusions Shalamov saw at work in popular attitudes toward it. Soviet propaganda put forward a model of punitive labor as moral transformation: Shalamov more than once refers contemptuously to the primary ideologue of labor in education, Anton Makarenko, whose 1930s hit novel *A Pedagogical Poem* was made into a popular Soviet film in 1955. Shalamov writes of the "fashion for 'reforging'" by labor as a paltry smoke screen for extreme exploitation, which allowed criminals to manipulate themselves into positions of power in the Gulag. Another connoisseur of Soviet prisons, the Polish poet Aleksander Wat, recalls in *My Century* his own bewildering contact during his wartime odyssey with the "immense para-republic of criminals...a dense network covering Stalin's tsardom" and remarks on the close sympathy between the gangs of juvenile delinquents he observed in prison camps and the NKVD officers overseeing them, many of whom he rightly assumed had emerged from gangs in the first place. Traditions of criminal organization predating the revolution (and manifest in slang that Shalamov knew well) were themselves preserved and absorbed into the culture of the new Soviet state—institutionalized, just when the prerevolutionary traditions of the Russian intelligentsia were being systematically destroyed. His stories show better than anything written about the Gulag how these processes were parallel and inseparable.

It should be said that features of the Gulag endure in the current Russian prison system. In an important 2017 book titled *Imperiya FSIN* (FSIN is an acronym for the Federal Service for the Implementation of Punishments), the Russian human rights advocate and researcher Nikolai Shchur writes that *blatnye* (gangsters, though not necessarily direct descendants from Gulag gangsters) still hold a great deal of power over political prisoners and, with the collusion and often encouragement of the authorities, are able to exert influence on important aspects of prison life, like the number of visits or packages a political prisoner is allowed to receive in a given period. Although during the period of Dmitry Medvedev's presidency tentative moves (most likely motivated by a transient wish to improve Russia's international image) were made to de-Gulagize the Russian penal system, with Vladimir Putin's return to the highest office in 2012 all such reforming gestures were abandoned. The system retains the main features of the Gulag: pretrial facilities in metropolitan areas and "correctional colonies" mostly in remote locations, with terrifying transports that are an integral part of the punishment. Judith Pallot's work based on interviews with women prisoners in Russia also throws up grim parallels with Shalamov's stories.[4]

Shalamov is rare as a writer on camp life because he refuses to provide any variety of redemptive narrative, whether by portraying death in the Gulag as martyrdom or by finding heroism in survival or in acts of witness. Survivors have no aura of courage or strength, just qualities of luck or cunning that do not reflect particularly well on their character. Nor does Shalamov participate in the process by which the state, having lost the ability to justify its killing by keeping its victims within a zone of exception, chooses to portray them as tragic sacrifices of a cruel but rational strategy.[5]

In order to resist the inscription of meaning on what is to him, strictly speaking, meaningless suffering, Shalamov employs radical ambiguity and inconsistency. The same stories are given in slightly differing versions; an incident is rendered in such a way as to have contrary meanings. In the story "Brave Eyes," a geologist's senseless shooting of a weasel, spilling unborn cubs from its belly, is a whimsical, wasteful killing that echoes how people die in the Gulag; on the other hand, the geological excursion is an escape into a wilderness where the dying animal's eyes have a proud dignity that moves the broken-spirited prisoners. In "The Nameless Cat," a Gulag driver who "wasn't a spiteful man" breaks a cat's spine and ribs with an industrial drill bit. It crawls to shelter and, adopted for a time by a paramedic in the psychiatric department of the camp hospital, somehow gives birth to a litter of kittens, one of which survives and works alongside a prisoner attempting to supplement his starvation diet with freshly caught fish from a stream near the camp. After a time it just as unaccountably disappears. Has it been caught and cooked by thieves, like its mother and her other kittens, or has it found a freedom superior to the cowed and humiliated life of men? The question, and its pendant, as to whether this or any life is worth living, is left like an unresolved chord, a snatch of subversive "formalism." Animals are the repositories of virtues—courage, strength, care—that have fled from human lives.

Alert to the aura of martyrdom that attached itself to the hosts of Gulag victims, Shalamov refuses to sanctify them. He repeatedly declared himself an atheist, though the Orthodox Christian culture of his father shaped his imagination in unmistakable ways. Christian symbols, when he discovers them, are irrevocably altered like parts of the human body after exposure to frostbite, to employ one of his central metaphors. They are unhealing wounds rather than trophies. In the story "Graphite," the larch's "wounded body is like a newly revealed icon, the Chukotka Mother of God, if you like, or the Virgin Mary of Kolyma, expecting a miracle and declaring a miracle." In "The Path," the mere sign of the intrusion of another, anonymous person is enough to curtail the brief spiritual freedom that allows the narrator to compose poems in his head, and the path itself proves resistant to his attempts to turn it into poetry.

Shalamov himself left a body of poetry that, as Donald Rayfield has said, belongs to an earlier century than his prose. Jorge Luis Borges and Ivan Bunin are other examples of twentieth-century authors of innovative prose whose poems for the greater part read like imitations of their fin de siècle predecessors. Shalamov's stylistic ideals are "early Pasternak and late Pushkin," and it is Pushkin above all who in his eyes provides a moral and aesthetic antidote to the nineteenth century: to its sentimentality, its distended forms and messianic delusions. Shalamov's critical essays on poets show him to be an acutely sensitive reader and rigorous analyst of the poetic form, notably patterns of sound repetition and intonation. Svetlana Boym wrote incisively about Shalamov's use of intonation in prose to counteract the wooden speech, the *novoyaz* or newspeak of his era.[6] His own poems are well built, honest, and relentless, but it is in his prose that Shalamov's ear is most exquisitely employed in catching living speech rhythms, desolate cadences of event and emotion in which the pitch patterns of the speaker's voice, moving against the warp of *novoyaz*, expose the false harmony imposed in the camp universe.

In 2007, on the centenary of Shalamov's birth, an exhibition devoted to his life and work took place at the Memorial Society in Moscow. During a discussion organized as part of the commemoration, the critic Ilya Kukulin spoke of the distance between Shalamov's prose and poetry in terms of the author's discovery in prose that the formal harmony and order he sought in his poems existed in the world of the Gulag only in a malignant form; in Mandelstam's words, "In the undergrowth a serpent breathes / The golden measure of the age." In the final story in this volume, "Riva-Rocci," we read that "even third-class camps need flowers and symmetry." Where poetry appears as a natural, even vital human impulse, as in the story "Athenian Nights," it is interrupted by the incursion of a vindictive superior. This story begins with a curious presentation of what Shalamov cites as "man's four basic feelings," listed in Thomas More's *Utopia*, "that, when satisfied, provide the highest form of bliss": eating, sex, urinating, and defecating. It is these urges men are prevented from satisfying properly in the camp. To this list Shalamov adds poetry, also a physical need that manifests itself as soon as the immediate threat of death recedes slightly.

In fact More does not sum up human needs in quite this way; in a chapter titled "Of the Travelling of the Utopians" we are told that they "divide the pleasures of the body into two sorts—the one is that which gives our senses some real delight, and is performed either by recruiting Nature and supplying those parts which feed the internal heat of life by eating and drinking, or when Nature is eased of any surcharge that oppresses it, when we are relieved from sudden pain, or that which arises from satisfying the appetite which Nature has wisely given to lead us to the propagation of the species." Significantly, More also includes in the top Utopian pleasures the enjoyment of music, which "strikes the mind with generous impressions." But Shalamov's argument for poetry is different: it is as vital to prisoners as food, so that even if gathering for recitations in the bandaging room of the camp hospital exposes them to the danger of discovery and punishment, they continue to meet until they are prevented by the imposter "Dr. Doctor." They recite Pushkin, Mandelstam, and Akhmatova to one another not because they are sublimating or rising above their physical needs but because poetry can aid the return of "goners" to the world of the living.

The stories in this volume are an astonishing achievement in a tradition of high art that surprises by surviving and describing the very conditions created to destroy it. In Shalamov's own account, when he wrote he paced and raged in his room, weeping and shouting, saying every story aloud. Most of his best stories, he told Sirotinskaya, "were written in one go, or rather, copied from a draft only once." They were intentionally left unpolished, in a conventional sense unfinished, meant to retain the rough edges that proved they had been torn whole from real experience. How Shalamov found the strength to carry out this arduous labor after almost two decades of crippling prison life and exile, in impoverished isolation and recurrent physical and mental pain, with no hope of recognition or publication, without the slightest compromise with a timid post-Stalinist literary establishment and without allowing himself to be used as a pawn in the Cold War, is one of the miracles of modern literature.

—ALISSA VALLES

BOOK FOUR

Sketches of the Criminal World

WHAT FICTION WRITERS GET WRONG

FICTION has always represented the criminal world sympathetically, sometimes sycophantically. Deceived by cheap and tawdry ideas, it has given the world of thieves a romantic aura. Fiction writers have been unable to see through the aura to the actual revolting reality of that world. This deception is a pedagogical sin, a mistake for which our young people are paying a high price. You can forgive a boy of fourteen or fifteen for being thrilled by the "heroic" figures of the criminal world, but you can't forgive a writer. Yet even among great writers we cannot find any who are able to discern the thief's true character and to reject or condemn him, as all great artists should condemn that which is morally bad. Moreover, historically the most enthusiastic preachers of conscience and honor, for example, Victor Hugo, have often used their gifts to praise the criminal world. Hugo was under the illusion that this world was a part of society engaged in a strong, decisive, and public protest against the false world of power. But Hugo didn't bother to examine what the position that this community of thieves adopted to struggle against the state authority entailed. Quite a few young boys have tried to befriend real *misérables* after reading Hugo's novels. Even today Jean Valjean is a popular nickname among gangsters.[1]

In his *Notes from the House of the Dead*, Dostoyevsky avoids giving a direct, categorical answer to the question of real criminality. All his Petrovs, Luchkas, Sushilovs, and Gazins were, as far as the criminal world of real gangsters was concerned, just "suckers," *freiers*,[2] "pushovers," "oafs"—in other words, the sort of people the gangsters despised, robbed, and trampled on. Gangsters saw murderers and thieves like Petrov and Sushilov as resembling the author of *Notes from the House of the Dead* more than they resembled themselves. Dostoyevsky's thieves were as likely to be attacked or robbed as the hero Aleksandr Gorian-chikov and his equals, however wide the chasm that separated this criminal gentry from the ordinary people. After all, a thief is not just someone who has stolen something. You don't have to be a gangster to belong to that foul underground order, to steal something or even to thieve systematically. Apparently, when Dostoyevsky was doing hard labor, this category of the gangster didn't exist. Gangsters are not usu-ally punished with very long terms of imprisonment, for most of them are not murderers. Or rather, in Dostoyevsky's time they weren't. There weren't too many people in the criminal world who were prepared to "whack" anyone, whose hands were "brazen." The basic categories of crooks or cons, as the criminals called themselves, were "cracksmen," "filchers," fences, pickpockets. The phrase "criminal world" is an expres-sion that has a specific meaning. Crook, con, cove, gangster are all synonyms. Doing hard labor, Dostoyevsky did not encounter any of them, and if he had, we might very well have been deprived of the best pages in his book, pages where he affirms his faith in human nature. But Dostoyevsky did not encounter gangsters. The convict heroes of *Notes from the House of the Dead* are just as peripheral to real criminal-ity as the main hero Gorianchikov. For instance, was stealing from one another, something that Dostoyevsky dwells on several times and emphasizes in particular, really possible in the gangsters' world? They went in for robbing *freiers*, sharing the loot, playing cards, and then finally losing possessions to various master criminals, depending on the outcome of their games of poker or pontoon. In *Notes from the House of the Dead*, Gazin sells alcohol, as do other "barmen." But gangsters would have instantly taken Gazin's alcohol, and his career would have been nipped in the bud.

Traditional "law" dictated that no gangster ever worked when in prison: the *freiers* had to do his work. Dostoyevsky's Miasnikovs and Varlamovs would have been called by the contemptuous criminal name "Volga dockers."[3] None of those sneaks, louts, and pilferers have any-thing to do with the gangster world, the world of recidivist convicts. They're just people caught up in the negative side of the law, entangled by chance, or overstepping some limit in the dark, like Akim Akimo-vich,[4] a typical "*freier* fool." The gangster world is a world with its own laws; it is eternally at war with the world represented by Akim Akimovich or Petrov, as well as the eight-eyed deputy commandant.[5] In fact, the deputy commandant is closer to the professional criminals. He's their God-given boss, so that their relationship with him is as simple as with any representative of authority: anyone like him will hear a lot of talk from a gangster about fairness, honor, and other lofty subjects. And it has been going on for centuries. The pimply, naïve deputy commandant is the gangsters' declared enemy, but the Akim Akimoviches and the Petrovs are their victims.

None of Dostoyevsky's novels contains a single gangster. Dostoyevsky never knew them, and if he did see and know them, then, as an artist, he turned his back on them.

Tolstoy doesn't have any memorable portraits of this sort of person either, even in *Resurrection* where the external and illustrative descriptive brushwork is done in such a way that the artist cannot be held responsible for his criminal characters.

Chekhov did come across this world. Something in his journey to Sakhalin changed the way he wrote.[6] In a few of his letters after Sakhalin, Chekhov clearly indicates that everything he'd written before the journey seemed to him to be trivia unworthy of a Russian writer. Just as in *Notes from the House of the Dead*, the stupefying and debauching foulness of the prisons on the island of Sakhalin inevitably destroys anything pure, good, or human. The criminal world horrifies the writer. Chekhov senses that this world is the chief battery of the foulness, a sort of atomic reactor that creates its own fuel. But all Chekhov could do was wring his hands, smile sadly, and point out this world with a mild, albeit insistent, gesture. He, too, knew it from reading Hugo. Chekhov was in Sakhalin for too short a time, and until the day he died he lacked the boldness to use this material for his fiction.

One might think that the biographical side of Gorky's work would give him a reason to show the gangster world truthfully and critically. His Chelkash[7] is undoubtedly a gangster. But this recidivist thief is portrayed in Gorky's story with the same forced pretense at fidelity as the hero of *Les Misérables*. Gavrila, of course, can be interpreted as something more than just a symbol of the peasant soul. He is the pupil of the old crook Chelkash, perhaps by chance, but nevertheless inevitably: a pupil who might the next day have become a "gutless wannabe" rises one rung higher on the ladder leading to the criminal world. For as one philosopher, who also happened to be a criminal, said, "Nobody's born a criminal; they become one." In "Chelkash," Gorky, who came across the criminal world in his youth, was just paying his dues to that ill-informed delight at what appears to be that social group's freethinking and bold behavior.

Vaska Pepel (in *The Lower Depths*)[8] is a very unlikely criminal. Just like Chelkash, he is romanticized and exalted, instead of being exposed for what he is. A few superficial, well-rendered features of this figure, and the author's obvious sympathy, mean that Pepel, too, serves an evil cause.

Such are Gorky's attempts to portray the criminal world. He too was ignorant of this world and had apparently never really encountered gangsters, for such encounters are generally difficult for a writer. The gangster world is a closed, if not particularly secretive order, and outsiders who want to study and observe it are not allowed in. No gangster would open up to Gorky the tramp, or to Gorky the writer, for Gorky is just another *freier* in the gangster's eyes.

In the 1920s our literature was swept by a fashion for portraying robbers: Babel's "Benya Krik," Leonov's *The Thief*, Selvinsky's "Motke Malkhamoves," Vera Inber's poem "Vaska Svist Behind Bars," Kaverin's "The End of the Hide-out," and, finally, Ilf and Petrov's Ostap Bender.[9] Every writer appears to have frivolously paid tribute to a sudden demand for romantic criminality. This unbridled poetization of criminality was greeted as a fresh new current in literature, and it led many experienced literary writers astray. Although all the authors I have mentioned, as well as others not mentioned, show an extremely weak understanding of the essence of what they were dealing with in their works on this theme, they had great success with readers and consequently did a significant amount of harm.

Things got even worse. There was a prolonged period when people were carried away by the notorious fashion for "reforging," the reforging that gangsters laughed at and are still laughing at just as loudly today. The Bolshevik and Liuberets communes were opened, 120 writers contributed to a "collective" book about the White Sea–Baltic

Canal, and the book was published in a design that made it look like the New Testament.[10] The literary crown of this period was the play by Pogodin *The Aristocrats*, where the playwright repeated the old mistake for the thousandth time, not bothering to give any serious thought to the living people who gave a very elementary live performance for the benefit of a naïve writer.[11]

Many books, films, and plays about reeducating members of the criminal world have been published and staged. Alas!

Ever since Gutenberg began printing, the criminal world has been a sealed book for writers and readers. Writers who have tried to tackle this theme have dealt with it frivolously; they have let themselves be carried away and deceived by the phosphoric glare of criminality, they have disguised it with a romantic mask and thus reinforced their readers' utterly false idea of what is in fact a treacherous, revolting, and inhuman world.

Fussing over various sorts of reforging has given many thousands of professional thieves a break and has been the salvation of gangsters.

So what is the criminal world?

1959

CROOKS BY BLOOD

HOW DOES someone stop being human?

How are criminals made?

People can enter the criminal world from outside: a collective-farm worker serving a prison sentence for petty theft then decides to throw in his lot with the gangsters; former hoods commit criminal actions that lead them to do things they only knew about secondhand; a factory metalworker is short of the money he needs to go on a spree with his pals; someone without a profession wants to live a good life; and people who are too ashamed to ask for work or to beg, whether in the street or from the government, it doesn't matter which, prefer taking things to asking for them. It comes down to character, or often to the examples others set. Asking for work is agonizing for a sick man, or for a prideful man, especially an adolescent, who has stumbled. Asking for work is just as humiliating as begging. Wouldn't it be better...?

An adolescent with a shy, unsociable character can reach a crossroads that he simply doesn't yet have the strength or ability to evaluate. At some time or other in life, everyone finds themselves at an important crossroads and must tackle their fate head-on; most people find themselves in this situation in their youth, when they have little experience and are very likely to make mistakes. But this is also a time when their boldness and determination are greater than any established routine for their actions.

Faced with a difficult choice, deceived by literature and by a thousand widely believed legends about the mysterious world of criminals, an adolescent takes a terrible step, after which there is often no turning back.

Then he gets used to the situation, becomes embittered, and in turn begins to recruit other young people into the ranks of this accursed order.

There is one important but subtle aspect to the workings of this order, and not even specialized literature has noticed it.

The fact is that this underground world is ruled by hereditary thieves, men whose relatives—fathers, grandfathers, and, very likely, uncles and elder brothers—were old crooks; men who were raised from early childhood in gangster traditions, in the gangsters' merciless hatred of the whole world. These are people who for obvious reasons cannot adapt to any other situation, they are people who are "crooks by blood" and of whose pure blood there can be no doubt.

Hereditary thieves, in fact, form the ruling core of the criminal world; it is they who have the decisive vote in any consideration of the rules, in the dealings of the gangsters' "courts of honor," which constitute an essential and extremely important basis of this underworld life.

During the so-called dekulakization the criminal world expanded greatly. Its ranks were swollen by the sons of those who had been declared kulaks. It was the state's ruthless disposal of those who had been dekulakized that led to this increase. All the same, nobody who had been dekulakized ever played an important part in the criminal world.

They were the best at robbery, they took the loudest part in orgies and wild sprees, they belted out criminal songs louder than anyone, they cursed in filthy language, excelling more than any professional criminal in the subtle and important science of foul obscenities, in the precision with which they imitated professional criminals: nevertheless they were only emulators, imitators.

These people were not allowed into the inner core of the gangster world. There were occasional individuals who distinguished themselves not so much by their heroic exploits in committing robberies as by their adoption of the rules of gangster behavior, sometimes taking part in the kangaroo courts held by the highest circle of thieves. Alas, they didn't know what to say during these kangaroo courts, whereas at the slightest hint of a conflict—and gangsters erupt easily—the outsiders would be reminded of their outsider status.

"You're half-baked! And you dare to open your mouth! Call yourself a thief? You're just a Volga docker, not a thief! You're a real dumb animal!"

"Half-baked" meant a half-baked *freier*, a *freier* who had stopped being a *freier* but hadn't yet become a gangster. ("This isn't a bird yet, but it's no longer a quadruped," as Jules Verne has Jacques Paganel say.) The half-baked patiently put up with the insult. The half-baked cannot, of course, be the keepers of the criminal world's traditions.

To be a good thief, a real one, you have to be born a thief: only those who have mixed from their earliest years with thieves, and moreover with good, well-known ones, who have completed many years of study of prison life, an education in criminality and theft, are allowed to decide important questions of criminal life.

However prominent a thief you may be, however successful you have been, you will always remain a lone outsider, a second-class citizen among the hereditary thieves. Thieving is not enough: you have to belong to the order, and that requires more than thieving and murdering. Not every heavyweight, not every killer, just because he is a robber and a murderer, has a place of honor among gangsters. These people have their own guardians of pure morals: important thieves' secrets, having to do with the enactment of the general laws of their world (which, like their lives, change) and with the development of the thieves' language, "criminal cant," are reserved for the godfathers, who consist of hereditary thieves, even if they were only pickpockets.

The gangster world will pay more attention to the opinion of a mere boy or adolescent (the son or brother of some prominent thief) than to the arguments of the half-baked, even if the latter are as skilled as the folk epic hero Ilia Muromets in the robbery business.

Even the Marys, the women of the criminal world, are shared according to the reputation of the boss. The first to have them are those with "blue blood," and the last to get them are the half-baked.

Gangsters devote considerable concern to preparing their replacements, to bringing up worthy men to continue their business.

The terrible, tawdry cover of criminal romanticism attracts young men and boys with its fancy-dress brilliance, and then poisons them with its venom forever.

This is the false brilliance of a glass bead that pretends to be a diamond, and it is reflected by a thousand mirrors in fiction.

It can be said that fiction, instead of exposing criminality for what it is, has done the reverse: it has prepared the ground for poisonous plants to flourish in the inexperienced and untried souls of young people.

A young person hasn't got the strength to discriminate, to see through to the true face of crooks and cons: afterward, it is too late, for he will be helping thieves if he has even the slightest brush with them. He will then be branded by society and, for life and until death, he will be bound to his new comrades.

The key fact is that personal resentment will now be building up in him, that he will have a personal score to settle with the state and its representatives. He will think that his passions and personal interests are in irreconcilable conflict with society and the state. He will think that he is paying too high a price for his misdeeds, which the state calls not misdeeds but crimes.

He is lured on by the usual youthful longing for cloak-and-dagger games. But now the game is no joke; it is real and bloody, and its psychological tension is not to be compared with *The Disciples of Christ* or *Timur and His Gang*.[12] Doing evil is far more entertaining than doing good. The boy enters this underground den of thieves, his heart pounding, and sees standing next to him the very people his daddy and mommy are afraid of. He can see their apparent independence, their false freedom. He takes their boasting and their lies to be the honest truth. The gangsters seem to him to be people who challenge society. Instead of earning an honest penny by hard work, the youth sees the thief's generosity in stylishly throwing banknotes around after a successful robbery. He can see the thief drinking and celebrating and he is anything but put off by the spectacle of this wild life. He compares his parents' dreary everyday modest work with the "labors" of the thieves' world, where all you need to be, it seems, is bold . . .

The boy doesn't think how much his hero has robbed and squandered other people's labor and human blood without giving it a moment's thought. There's always vodka, hash, and cocaine: they give the boy drink, and he is overcome by the joy of emulation.

The boy notices that his peer group, his former comrades, are somewhat alienated from him, as well as afraid of him: in his childish naïvety he takes this reaction to be a form of respect.

Above all, he can see that everyone is afraid of the thieves, afraid that any one of them could cut your throat or gouge out your eyes...

The thieves' den is visited by some Ivan "No Front Teeth" from prison, who brings thousands of stories about whom he's seen, who's been convicted of what, and what sentence they got: all that is dangerous and seductive.

The youth can see people living without having to bother with the constant worries that his family has.

By now he's thoroughly drunk; soon he's beating a prostitute—you have to know how to hit a woman, that's one of the traditions of the new life.

The youth dreams of becoming fully trusted, of finally being accepted into the order. That means prison, which he has been taught not to fear.

The older thieves take him "on a job": the first time it will mean standing somewhere as the lookout. By now the grown-up thieves trust him, and then he can do his own thieving and make his own arrangements.

He quickly catches on to the mannerisms, the sarcastic smile of unspeakable brazenness, the gait; he has his trousers specially cut to fit over his boots, he puts a cross around his neck, he buys a fur hat for winter and a seaman's cap for summer.

During his very first spell in prison he has himself tattooed by his new friends, who are expert tattoo artists. This is the identifier that shows he belongs to the professional thieves' order; it is the mark of Cain, permanently etched on his body in blue ink. Afterward, he will regret these tattoos many times: they cause a lot of friction between gangsters. But that will come later, much later.

He has by now mastered the thieves' cant, the secret language. He eagerly does the senior thieves favors. When he acts, he's more afraid of underdoing things than of overdoing them.

The gangster world opens its uttermost depths to him door by door.

Now he's taking part in bloody kangaroo courts, courts of honor, and he is being made, like all the others, to sign his name on the corpse of someone strangled after being sentenced by a criminals' court.

Someone thrusts a knife in his hand and he sticks it into the still-warm corpse to prove his solidarity with his teachers' actions.

Then he does the killing himself of a traitor or "bitch" whom his seniors have sentenced and pointed out to him.

There probably isn't a single gangster who hasn't at some point become a killer.

This is the curriculum for a young gangster, recruited in his youth from another world.

Those who have blue blood in their veins get a simpler upbringing: these are hereditary gangsters or people who have never known, and do not intend to know, any life other than that of a thief.

There is no cause to think that these people who are to become the ideologists and leaders of the gangster world, these crooked princes of the blood royal, get some special, hothouse upbringing. Certainly not. Nobody protects them from danger. It's just that there are fewer ob-stacles on their path to the heights, or rather, the deepest pits of the gangster lower depths. Their path is simpler, quicker, more guaranteed. They are trusted earlier and are sent out to rob earlier.

But even if a young gangster's forefathers were the most influential lords of the thieves' society, he has to mix for many years with the adult bandits whom he deifies, running to fetch them cigarettes, giving them a light, relaying sick notes and messages, and doing all kinds of menial jobs for them. Many years will pass before he is taken on a robbery.

The thief steals, drinks, parties, goes in for debauchery, plays cards, cheats fools, refuses to work, whether in prison or not, spills blood when he eliminates renegades, and takes part in kangaroo courts that sort out important questions of underground life.

He keeps gangster secrets (there are quite a few), helps his fellow members of the order, and sees to it that the thieves' law is preserved in all its harsh purity.

Their code is not complicated. But over the centuries it has accu-mulated thousands of traditions, sacred customs that have to be observed to the letter, and their observation is carefully monitored by the guard-ians of the thieves' testaments. Gangsters are very much like Talmud scholars: from time to time, to make sure that the thieves' laws are implemented in the best possible way, they organize grand universal underground meetings where decisions are made dictating the rules of behavior that apply to any new conditions in life, and in which changes in the eternally changing thieves' vocabulary, the thieves' cant, are made, or rather, confirmed.

All the people in the world, according to the gangster way of thinking, are divided into two groups. One group consists of "people": crooks, the criminal world, cons, gangsters, professionals, and so on.

The other group is the *freiers*, which means "free people." *Freier* is an old word that originated in Odessa. In gangster music of the nineteenth century there are a lot of Yiddish-German slang words.

There are other words to describe *freiers*: fools, peasants, gulls, coves, devils. There are "rookie gulls," who are close to the criminals, and there are "beaten *freiers*," people familiar with the doings of the criminal world, who have some insight into them, who are experienced. A beaten *freier* means someone experienced, and the phrase is respectful. These are different worlds and they are separated by more than prison bars.

"They tell me I'm a bastard. All right, I'm a bastard. I'm a bastard, and a swine, and a killer. But so what? I don't live like you, I have my own life with its own laws and different interests, different honor," is what the gangster says.

Lies, deceit, provocation whenever he meets a *freier*, even if it is a man who has saved a gangster's life, are not only in the natural order of things; they represent the special valor of the criminal world. They are its law.

When Lev Sheinin[13] calls on us to trust the criminal world, he is being worse than naïve: that trust has already been paid for by far too much blood.

There is no limit to gangsters' mendacity, for as far as *freiers* are concerned (and the whole world consists of only *freiers* and gangsters), the only law that applies is the use of deceit in any possible way—by flattery, by slander, by false promises...

The *freier* exists only in order to be deceived; any *freier* who is on his guard, who has already had the bitter experience of dealings with gangsters, is called a beaten *freier*, a special group of devils.

There are no limits or boundaries to the oaths and promises. A fabulous number of all kinds of bosses, official and unofficial educators, policemen, and interrogators have been caught by the simple bait of "the honest word of a thief." Probably every single one of those employed to be in daily contact with the crooks has been caught many times with this bait. They get caught twice, thrice, because they can't understand that the morality of the criminal world is a very different morality, that what is called Hottentot morality, with its criterion of immediate gain, could not be more innocuous, compared with the gangster's grim practices.

The bosses (or the little men at the top, as the gangsters call them) have constantly shown themselves easy to deceive and fool.

And yet, Pogodin's thoroughly false and harmful play[14] has been revived with incomprehensible persistence in various cities, so that new generations of little men at the top become imbued with ideas of the honor of Captain Kostia.

All the attempts to reform thieves, on which millions in government money has been wasted, all these fantasy reforgings and other legends of the White Sea canal, which have long been the talk of the town and the subject of the criminals' casual jokes, all this edifying work was based on something as ethereal as the honest word of a thief.

"Just think," says some expert on the criminal world who's read too much Babel and Pogodin, "it's not as if Captain Kostia gave his word of honor that he would reform. I'm an old hand, and you can't pull the wool over my eyes. I'm not such a *freier* that I don't understand that when they give their word of honor it means nothing." But Captain Kostia gave the honest word of a thief. Of a thief! That's the whole point. That's a promise he really can't break. His "aristocratic" pride wouldn't let him. He'd die of contempt for himself if he broke the honest word of a thief.

Poor, naïve boss! For a thief to give his word of honor to a fool, to deceive him and then crush that oath underfoot and break it is a thief's idea of valor, a reason for boastful stories on some prison bunk.

Many escapes were facilitated and prepared, thanks to the honest word of a thief given at the right time. If only every boss knew (and the only bosses who do know are those who have been made wise by many years of dealing with the "captains") what a thief's oath was and if they gave it the credence it deserved, then there would be far less blood and far fewer atrocities.

But are we perhaps wrong to try to connect the two different worlds, the world of the *freier* with that of the old crook?

Perhaps the crook's world, with its laws of honor and morality, operates in a different way and we simply have no right to judge the gangster world by our own moral criteria?

Perhaps the thief's word of honor when it is given to a "godfather" and not to a *freier* really is a word of honor?

That is precisely the romantic element that excited youthful hearts, that appears to justify and introduce a spirit of some moral decency, albeit an odd decency, in the way thieves live, in the relationships of people within that world. Perhaps dishonesty has different meanings in the world of *freiers* and the world of gangster society? Let's say that old crooks' instinctive urges are governed by their own law: then only by taking their point of view will we understand and even recognize de facto the special nature of thieves' morals.

The cleverer gangsters are quite inclined to think along these lines; they are quite inclined to pull the wool over the eyes of simpletons.

Any dishonesty and bloodshed that affects a fool is justified and sanctified by the laws of the gangster world. But when dealing with his comrades, the thief, you might think, has to be honest. The gangster commandments demand that he should be, and anyone who breaks the laws of the guild can expect merciless punishment.

All this is theatrical posing and boastful lying from beginning to end. You only have to take a look at the behavior of the dictators of gangster fashions when they are having difficulties, when they lack plentiful supplies of *freiers*, when they have to stew in their own juices.[15]

The major thieves, the most authoritative (the word "authority" is a favorite among thieves—"he got himself some authority," etc.) and the strongest, keep their position by oppressing minor thieves, who bring them food and look after them. If any thieves are forced to work, then the major thieves send their weaker comrades off to labor for them, and the leading gangsters then demand that these comrades do what was once demanded of *freiers*.

The terrible saying "You die today, I'll die tomorrow" is beginning to be repeated more and more often in all its gruesome reality. Alas, that gangster saying has no figurative sense, it is quite literal.

Hunger will make a criminal take and eat the rations of his less authoritative friends, will make him send them off on expeditions that have very little to do with the proper implementation of thieves' laws.

Threatening notes, "docs," are sent in all directions, asking for help, and if there is a chance of earning a piece of bread but there is no chance of stealing it, then it is the petty thieves who go off to work, to "plow." They are sent off to work in the same way as they were sent off to murder. It isn't the chiefs who have to pay for murders: the chiefs only issue the death sentences. The men who actually kill are petty thieves, acting out of fear of being killed themselves. They murder or they gouge out eyes (a very widespread sanction against *freiers*).

When in trouble, thieves also denounce each other to the camp bosses. Denouncing the *freiers*, the four-eyed eggheads, and the "politicals"[16] is normal. These denunciations are a way to make the gangster's life easier, and they are a subject of special pride for him.

If you removed the chivalrous cloak, all that is left is the pure swinishness that imbues the gangster philosophy. It is only logical that in difficult circumstances this swinishness is turned on fellow members of the order. That is not in the least surprising. The underground criminal kingdom is a world where the aim of life is a greedy satisfaction of the basest passions, where interests are bestial, worse than bestial, for any wild beast would be scared of the actions that criminals will undertake without hesitation.

("The most frightening animal is the human being" is a widespread criminal saying, and once again, it is meant literally, it is reality.)

A representative of that world is incapable of exhibiting moral firmness in any situation that threatens him with death or with prolonged physical torment: he simply will not show any firmness.

It would be a great mistake to think that their concepts of drinking, partying, debauchery are just like similar activities in the *freier* world. Alas! Anything a *freier* does looks like the height of chastity when compared to the feral scenes of criminal life.

A tattooed prostitute or "city girl" is summoned or uses her own initiative to get into a hospital ward to see the sick gangsters (who are malingerers or exaggerators, of course); that night, after threatening the male nurse on duty with a knife, a company of criminals gathers around this apparition of Saint Teresa. Anyone with crook's blood can take part in this "pleasure." The woman, when she's detained, explains without embarrassment or blushing that "I came to help the boys out, the boys asked me to."

All the gangsters are pederasts. Every major gangster in the camp has young men with swollen, lackluster eyes hanging around him. These Zoikas, Mankas, and Verkas[17] are fed by the gangster, and he sleeps with them.

In one of the camp sections (where there was plenty of food) the gangsters tamed and debauched a bitch dog. They fed it, caressed it, then slept with it as if it were a woman; they did so openly, in front of the whole barracks.

People don't want to believe that such cases occur all the time: they seem too monstrous. But that is the way they live.

There was a women's camp, a mine; it had a lot of prisoners who did heavy stone work and were starved. Liubov, a criminal, managed to get a job there.

"Hey, I had a great winter," he recalled. "Obviously, you can get anything for bread, for a bread ration. And the rule, the agreement was: you give her the bread ration and she has to eat it. While I'm with her she has to eat that bread ration, and if she doesn't finish it, I take it back. One morning I got a bread ration and threw it in the snow. If I froze the ration, how much frozen bread could the woman gnaw off?"

Of course, it's hard to imagine that a human being can think of such a thing.

But there's nothing human about a gangster.

Prisoners in the camp are handed a little money, whatever's left after deductions for communal services such as the guards, the tarpaulin tents in temperatures of minus sixty, the prisons, the transit camps, the uniform, food. What's left is a pittance, but it's still money in a spectral form. The scales are reversed, and even negligible pay of twenty to thirty rubles a month arouses prisoners' interest. For twenty to thirty rubles you can buy bread, and a lot of it: that, surely, is an important dream, a very powerful stimulus during the many hours of heavy labor at the pit face, working in freezing temperatures, hungry and cold. People's interests are no weaker for being pared down, when people have become only half human.

The wages, the handout, is paid once a month. On that day the gangsters patrol all the *freiers'* barracks and make them hand over their money; how much depends on the racketeers' conscience—half or all of it. If prisoners don't hand it over voluntarily, then violence is used: beatings, crowbars, pickaxes, spades.

Apart from the gangsters there are many other people out for these wages. Often the brigades who have good food rations, who are better nourished, are warned by their foreman that the workmen will not be getting any money, that the money will go to the guard or the norm setter. If they don't agree, then their ration cards will be worse and the prisoners will thus sentence themselves to die of starvation.

Taxes taken by the "little bosses"—the norm setters, the foremen, the warders—are a universal phenomenon.

Robberies committed by gangsters happen everywhere. Rackets are considered legitimate and don't surprise anyone.

In 1938, when there was virtually an official concordat between the authorities and the gangsters, when thieves were deemed to be "friends of the people," the top bosses tried to use the gangsters as a weapon in the struggle against "Trotskyists" and "enemies of the people." There were even propaganda sessions for the gangsters in the Culture and Education Section, where cultural workers explained to the gangsters the authorities' sympathies and hopes and asked for their help in exterminating Trotskyists.

"These people have been sent here to be exterminated, and it's your job to help us do so" were the actual words used by Sharov, the culture inspector of the Partisan mine: he said it to them at one of their "sessions" in early 1938.

The gangsters responded with total agreement. Of course they did! This helped save their lives, it made them useful members of society.

When they saw the Trotskyists, they encountered the intellectuals they already heartily hated. In any case, in the gangsters' eyes the intellectuals were little bosses who had gotten into trouble, bosses due for a bloody revenge.

With the full approval of the authorities, the gangsters set about beating up the "fascists"—that was the only term used in 1938 for those convicted under article 58.

Major figures, such as Eshba, who had been the secretary of the North Caucasus Party District Committee, were arrested and then shot at the notorious Serpantinka,[18] while the others were finished off by the gangsters, by the guards, and by starvation and cold. Gangsters took a major part in liquidating Trotskyists in 1938.

I'll be told, "There are, however, cases when a thief, if a favor is done for him, will keep his word and behind the scenes will help keep order in the camp."

"It's more useful for me," says the boss, "to have five or six thieves not working at all, or working where and when they like, so long as the rest of the population in the camps, provided that they're not oppressed by the thieves, works well. Especially since I'm short of guards. The thieves promise not to steal and to make sure that all the other prisoners work. True, the thieves don't guarantee that these other prisoners will fulfill the norm, but that's of minor importance."

Cases of such contracts between the thieves and the local bosses are not so rare.

The boss doesn't have to strive to see that the rules of the camp regime are observed to the letter; his own task is being made easier and significantly so. Such bosses don't understand that they have been "hooked" by the thieves, that they have him on a lead. He has already ignored the law by giving concessions to thieves on a false and criminal basis, because the *freiers* who populate the camp have now been doomed by the boss to be ruled by the thieves. Of the *freiers*, only the non-politicals, convicted of crimes in employment or domestic crimes—thieves of state funds, murderers, and bribe-takers—will find any protection. Those convicted under article 58 will find no protection.

This first concession to the thieves easily leads to the bosses having a closer relationship with the criminal world. The boss takes bribes in gundog puppies or in money, and things are decided by the skills of the giver and the greed of the taker. Thieves are experts at bribing. The bribe is all the easier and more generous because whatever is handed over is funded by theft and robbery.

The bribe could be a thousand-ruble suit (professional criminals wear and keep very good "outside" things as potential bribes when the need occurs), or some wonderful footwear, a gold watch, a significant sum of money...

If the boss won't take it, they "smooth over" his wife and put all their energy into making the little boss take a couple of things. Those are gifts. They don't ask him for anything in exchange. They'll thank him as they give him things. Later they'll ask for something in return, once the little boss is nicely tangled up in the thieves' nets and afraid of being exposed to the top authorities. Exposing a boss is a weighty threat that's easy to carry out.

So the honest word of a thief that nobody will ever find out anything is just a thief swearing something to a *freier*.

Apart from anything else, a promise not to steal is a promise not to steal openly, not to commit robbery: that's all. No boss will let thieves go off on thieving expeditions (although there have been such cases). Thieves will steal regardless, for that is their life, their law. They may promise the boss not to steal from their own mine, not to rob the camp support staff, not to rob the camp shop or the guards, but all that is mendacious. There will always be senior thieves who will happily release their comrades from such oaths.

In camp sections where the thieves dominate the work organizers, the cooks, the warders, and the bosses themselves, the prisoners live worse, with fewer rights, with more starvation and fewer earnings, and with worse food.

The camp escort guards follow the example of their bosses.

For several years guards who escorted prisoners to work were answerable for the fulfillment of the plan. This liability was not really genuine or serious: it was like a trade unionist's responsibility. Nevertheless, the guards would observe a military order by demanding work from the prisoners. "Get a move on, get a move on" was the usual outcry not just from the foremen, warders, and mine guards but also from the escort guards. For the escort guards this was an extra burden beyond their purely escort duties: they were not particularly overjoyed by these new, unpaid obligations. But orders were orders, and so their rifle butts were used more and more often as they beat the production percentages out of the prisoners.

Very soon—I'd like to think empirically—the escort guards found a way out of their situation, which had been somewhat complicated by the insistent production orders of their bosses.

The guards would lead a group of prisoners (always a mix of politicals and thieves) to work and lease this group out to the thieves. The thieves enjoyed playing at being voluntary foremen. They would beat up the prisoners (with the guards' blessing and support) to make old men, half dead from starvation, carry out heavy labor at the gold-mine pit faces; they used their sticks to beat the "plan" out of them, that plan including the part of the overall production targets assigned to the thieves themselves.

The mine guards never interfered with such minor details; all they wanted was to step up overall production by any means.

The mine guards were almost always bribed by the thieves. These were outright bribes, in kind or in money, with no preparatory softening up. The mine guard was expecting a bribe. This was a constant source of considerable extra income.

Sometimes the mine guard was worked over with the help of "gambling for cubics," playing cards for cubic meters of dug ore.

A foreman-thief would sit down to a game with the guard and in return for the "rags" he staked—suits, sweaters, shirts, trousers—would demand payment in "cubics," cubic meters of earth.

If he won—and he almost always did, except when an "elegant" bribe was required (a tribute to a French marquis who played cards with Louis XIV)—the lost cubic meters of subsoil and ore were paid for with real labor, and the brigade of criminals, without having to work, received big earnings. The more sophisticated guards tried to keep things balanced by cheating the Trotskyist brigades.

Credited work, selling cubic meters, was a disaster at the mine. The mining surveyor's measurements would establish the truth and expose those guilty of manipulation. Corrupted mine guards were only demoted or transferred elsewhere. And they left behind the corpses of starving men from whom they had tried to beat out the cubics gambled away by the guard.

The depraved spirit of the professional criminals penetrated every aspect of life in Kolyma.

You cannot understand the camp if you don't have a precise understanding of the essence of the criminal world. The professional criminals make places of imprisonment look the way they do, and they set the tone for life there, starting with the top bosses and ending with the half-starving workmen at the gold-mine pit face.

The ideal gangster, the real thief, the criminal Cascarilla,[19] never robs "private persons." That's one of the criminal world's "legends in the making." The thief robs government property—depots, tills, shops, if pushed, then "free" apartments—but a good thief won't take away a prisoner's last possessions. They'd have you believe that stealing underwear, forcibly swapping good clothes and shoes for bad ones, or stealing gauntlets, fur jackets, scarves (which include government-issue), and sweaters, jackets, trousers (from the outside world) was done by the rabble, by delinquent children, by opportunists, by casual thieves.

"If we had real thieves here," sighs the man in the street, "they would stop all the burglaries that the petty thieves do."

The poor fool believes in Cascarilla. He refuses to understand that it is the serious criminals who send the petty thieves to steal linen, that the reason authoritative thieves are seen wearing the ill-gotten two-pieces and fancy pants is not because these more powerful thieves do their own thieving of jackets and trousers.

The *freier* doesn't know that the thieves who do break-ins are mostly petty pilferers who've been told to become old hands in their trade, and that they are the last ones to get a share of the proceeds. If the job is a more difficult one, then the adult thieves will also participate in the robbery, using methods of persuasion—"Hand it over, what do you need it for?"—or by their notorious swaps, when they force a *freier* to squeeze himself into some old garment, something that has long been just a symbolic garment, just good enough to be handed in when the inventory is taken. That is why, a day or two after new sets of clothing are issued in the camp to the best brigades, it turns out that the new fur jackets, pea coats, and hats are owned by the thieves, even though they weren't issued to them. Sometimes a swap is accompanied by the offer of a cigarette or a piece of bread, but only if the gangster is "decent" and not naturally spiteful, or if he is afraid that his victim will "squawk," will make a fuss.

To refuse a swap or a "gift" will lead to a beating, and if the *freier* is stubborn, to a stabbing. But in most cases things don't reach the knife stage.

These swaps are no joke in conditions where men work for hours on end in temperatures of minus fifty, are deprived of sleep and food, and suffer from scurvy. To hand over felt boots that you were sent from home means getting frostbitten feet. The rough cloth boots offered as a swap won't allow you to work for long in the freezing cold.

In the late autumn of 1938 I received a parcel from home: my old pilot's boots with cork soles. I was afraid of bringing them back from the post office; the building was surrounded by a crowd of gangsters hopping about in the white evening twilight, waiting for victims. I sold the boots there and then to Boyko, a guard, for a hundred rubles; in Kolyma the boots would have cost about two thousand. I might have gotten as far as the barracks in those boots, but they would have been stolen on the very first night; they would have been pulled off my legs. In exchange for a cigarette, for a crust of bread, the men who slept next to me would have brought the thieves to our barracks and would have "pointed" the robbers immediately. The camp was full of such "pointers." The hundred rubles I got for the boots, however, was a hundred kilograms of bread. It was far easier to keep your money by tying it to your body and by not giving yourself away when you bought anything.

That's how the gangsters go about in felt boots with the tops folded down in the criminal fashion so the snow doesn't get in; they get themselves fur jackets, scarves, and hats with earflaps, not ordinary ones but stylish, criminal, proper cossack fur hats.

A peasant boy, a young worker, or an intellectual is so stunned by unexpected things that his head spins. The young man sees the thieves and murderers in the camp living better than anyone else, enjoying a relatively prosperous material life, and demonstrating a definite firmness of views and an enviable reckless, fearless behavior.

The bosses take the thieves seriously. Thieves determine who lives and who dies in the camp. They are always well-fed; they can always "get" things, when everyone else is hungry. Thieves don't work; they get drunk, even in the camp, and the peasant boy is forced to "plow." Thieves will even make him plow: they have their clever ways of seeing to that. Thieves always have a bit of tobacco, so the camp hairdresser comes and gives them an army-style haircut in their "home" in the barracks, and brings his best scissors. Every day the cook brings the stolen canned food and sweets from the kitchen. For lesser thieves the kitchen gives out better portions, ten times bigger than the usual ones. The bread cutter never refuses them bread. All the free men's clothing is on the gangsters' backs. Gangsters get the best bunks, by the light, by the stove. They have their own quilted blankets and quilted covers, whereas the young collective farmer sleeps on beams split lengthwise with an ax. The peasant begins to think that gangsters are the bearers of truth in the camp, that they are the sole force, both material and moral, in the camp, apart from the bosses, who generally prefer not to quarrel with the gangsters.

The young peasant boy begins to do favors for them, to imitate their cursing and behavior, and he dreams of helping them, of being lit up by their fire.

It will not be long before he is instructed by gangsters to contribute his first theft to the kitty: then a new rookie thief is made.

The poison of the gangster world is terrifying. Exposure to it corrupts all that makes a man human. Anyone who comes in contact with that world breathes this stinking, poisonous exhalation. What gas mask can protect against it?

I knew a man with a doctorate, a free contract doctor, who recommended to his colleague to be especially attentive to a certain patient: "He's a major thief, after all!" You might have thought that the patient had at the very least sent a rocket to the moon, so strong was the tone of the recommendation. This doctor wasn't even aware how degrading such comments were for himself, for his own person.

Thieves quickly identified the weakness of Ivan Aleksandrovich (the doctor). In the section he managed there were always perfectly healthy men resting in bed. ("The professor's like a father to us," the thieves said, laughing.)

Ivan Aleksandrovich kept falsified patients' notes. He didn't grudge his night's rest or his labor: he made daily notes, he ordered analyses and examinations.

I once happened to read a letter addressed to him by a group of thieves from a transit camp requesting that their colleagues, whom they alleged needed a rest, be admitted to the hospital. And all the gangsters on the list were eventually admitted.

Ivan Aleksandrovich was not afraid of the gangsters. He was an old Kolyma hand, he'd been around, and threats would have gotten the gangsters nowhere. But their friendly slaps on his shoulder, their gangsterish compliments, which he took to be sincere, and his fame in the gangster world, a fame whose essence he did not and would not see through—all of this brought him close to the gangster world. Like many others, Ivan Aleksandrovich was hypnotized by the gangsters' monopoly of power, and his will became theirs.

After many years of mixing with thieves, society's most damaging element, which has never ceased to poison our youth with its stinking breath, the harm is immeasurable and boundless.

The theory of reforging arose from purely speculative hypotheses, and it has led to tens and hundreds of thousands of extra deaths in prison; it has led to a prolonged nightmare in the camps created by people who do not deserve to be called human beings.

*

Gangster slang changes from time to time. Changes of cryptic words are not part of a process of perfection but instead a means of self-preservation. The gangster world is aware that police detectives study its language. Someone who joins a gang and thinks he can express himself in the "crook's music" of the 1920s, when the terms "on alert" and "on the zinc" were in use, would arouse gangsters' suspicion in the 1930s, when the usual expressions were "on the water," etc.

We don't understand the difference between thieves and ruffians. Obviously, both groups are antisocial, both are hostile to society. But we are rarely able to assess the true danger posed by either group, to evaluate it properly. Certainly, we are more afraid of a ruffian than of a thief. In everyday life we very seldom come into contact with thieves, and such contact always occurs either in a police station or in a detective's office, where our role is that of victim or witness. Ruffians are far more terrifying: a frightening display of drunkenness, a violent thug suddenly looming up on the street, or in a club, or in the corridor of a communal apartment. We are all familiar with the traditional behavior of Russian youth—drunken binges on church holidays, drunken brawls, pestering women, filthy swearing—and it seems far more terrifying than the mysterious world of thieves, of which we have only the vaguest concepts. That is the fault of fiction writers. Only people who work in criminal investigation know the true nature of ruffians and thieves, but the writings of Lev Sheinin tell us that this knowledge is not always applied properly.

We don't know what a thief is, what an old crook is, what a professional criminal, a recidivist thief is. Someone who steals the clothes off a cottage clothesline and then gets drunk in the nearest station bar is considered by us to be a prominent burglar.

We fail to realize that a man can steal without being a thief, a member of the criminal world. We don't understand that a man can kill and steal and yet not be a gangster. Of course, gangsters steal: that's their living. But not every thief is a gangster, and it is absolutely essential to understand the difference. The criminal world exists alongside property theft and alongside hooliganism.

True, it makes no difference to the victim who broke into his apartment and stole his silver spoons or his Navarino smoke-and-flame[20] suit—a gangster thief, or a professional nongangster thief, or the man in the next apartment who had never stolen before. He'll say that this is a job for the detectives.

We are more afraid of ruffians than of thieves. It's clear that no "people's vigilantes" will cope with thieves when we have, unfortunately, such a perverse understanding of them. It is sometimes thought that mysterious gangsters are hiding out in some deep underground den under false names, that they only rob shops and tills. These Cascarillas don't take the wash off the line, and the ordinary citizen would even be glad to help these noble crooks—such citizens sometimes hide them from the police, either for romantic reasons or because, as they say, "I was afraid": it's fear more often than not.

A ruffian is more frightening. A ruffian is someone you see every day, easy to understand, close by. He's frightening. So we look to the police and the people's vigilantes to keep us safe from him.

All the same, ruffians, every single one of them, are still within the bounds of humanity. A thieving gangster is beyond human morality.

Any murderer, any ruffian is nothing compared with the thief. A thief can also be a murderer and a ruffian, plus something that is hard to put a name to in human language.

People who work in prisons or criminal investigation are not inclined to share their important memories. We have thousands of cheap detective stories and novels. We don't have a single conscientious book about the criminal world, one written by someone employed to do battle with it.

This is a permanent social group, which could be called more aptly an antisocial group. It poisons our children's lives; it fights our society and sometimes wins, because people treat it with trust and naïvety, while it uses quite different weapons in its battle—the weapons of unprincipled lying, treachery, and deceit—and survives by deceiving one person in authority after another. The higher the rank of such a person, the easier it is to deceive him.

Gangsters themselves show outright hostility to ruffians. "He's no thief, he's just a ruffian"; "That's the sort of thing a hooligan would do, no thief would stoop so low"—such are the phrases uttered in the criminal world's inimitable accent. You constantly come across such examples of thieves' hypocritical arrogance. The gangster wants to draw a line between himself and the ruffian, to place himself far higher; he insists on ordinary citizens discriminating between thieves and ruffians.

Young gangsters are initiated in this way of thinking. A thief must avoid being a ruffian: the image of the gentleman thief is testimony to the novels that criminals have listened to, as well as to their official creed. This image of the gentleman thief shows the thief's longing for an unattainable ideal. Likewise, in their world great value is placed on elegant and sophisticated manners. Such phrases as "the criminal world," "moving in circles," and "dining" enter the gangsters' vocabulary and become a part of it. These expressions are not felt to be pretentious or ironical; they're definitive and much used.

The thieves' "lines" require that a thief differentiate himself from a ruffian:

> Modestly dressed, a flower in his lapel,
> Wearing a gray English coat,
> At exactly seven thirty I left the capital,
> Not even looking through the window.[21]

This is the classic ideal, the classic portrait of a safecracker, a gentleman thief, Cascarilla from the film *The Three Million Trial*.

Hooliganism is too innocent, too chaste an activity for a thief. Thieves have other amusements. Killing someone, ripping open his belly, spilling his guts, and strangling another victim with those guts: that's a thief's way of doing things; such cases have happened. Quite a few foremen were murdered in the camps, but only a gangster, not a human being, had a brain capable of such dark inventiveness as sawing right through a living man's neck with a two-handed cross-saw.

The foulest hooliganism looks like an innocent child's joke compared with a gangster's everyday amusement.

Gangsters can go on a spree, drink, and act like hooligans somewhere in their gang's hangout: partying without debauchery, showing the limits of their recklessness only to their comrades and to reverent neophytes whose entry into the thieves' order is just a few days away.

Hooliganism and opportunistic thieving are on the periphery of the gangster world; it is a border area where society meets its antipodes.

Young or new thieves are seldom recruited from hooligan circles. The exception is only when a ruffian gives up his debauchery and, his reputation stained by prison, rises into the ranks of the gangster world, where he will never play a big part in its ideology or lawmaking.

The ruling thieves are the hereditary ones, those who have taken the entire course of criminal science since boyhood, have run errands to fetch vodka and cigarettes for their elders, have been the lookout or "on the water," have climbed through skylights so as to open the door for burglars, have steeled their spirits in prison, and then gone out on independent jobs.

The gangster world is hostile to authority in any form whatsoever. Gangsters, the thinking ones, understand this well. The heroic times of "old squads" and penal servitude under the tsars doesn't seem glorious to them in the least. "Old squaddies" is the nickname for prisoners who served in the tsar's prisoner squads; "hard laborer" applies to those who did penal servitude in Sakhalin or at Kolesukha, the prison on the Amur River. In Kolyma it was normal to call central Russian provinces "the mainland," although the Chukotka peninsula is not an island. This term "the mainland" has entered the language of literature and the newspapers, as well as official correspondence. This image and word also originated in the gangster world, thanks to the sea route linking Vladivostok to Magadan and the disembarkation on deserted rocks, which was very much like the pictures of the past, when prisoners were disembarked on the island of Sakhalin. That is how the term "mainland" came to mean Vladivostok, even though nobody ever called Kolyma an island.

The gangster world is the world of the real, authentic present. The thieves understand only too well that some legendary Gorbachevsky, the subject of song—"The thunder roared that Gorbachevsky had been nabbed"[22]—was no more a hero than Vanka Chibis from a nearby gold mine.

No foreign country has any attraction for gangsters, who are made wise by experience; the thieves who were abroad during the war didn't have a good word for foreign countries, especially not for Germany, because of the extremely harsh punishments for thefts and murders. Thieves could breathe a little more easily in France, but there, too, ideas of reforging hadn't caught on, and thieves had a tough time. Our Russian conditions seem relatively agreeable to criminals; our trust is so extensive and we have these frequent and ineradicable reforgings.

Among the gangster world's legends in the making is the boastful assertion that a good con tries to avoid prison and curses it, that prison is just a sad inevitability of the thieves' profession. This assertion is an affectation, a pose. It is as mendacious as anything that comes from a gangster's lips.

The burglar Yuzik Zagorsky (a Pole), putting on airs, used to boast that in his twenty-year career as a thief he had spent only eight years in prison. Yuzik insisted that he never drank or went on a spree after a successful burglary. He went, would you believe it, to the opera, where he had a box, and only when his money ran out did he go back to burglary. It was all just like the song:

> It was there at the concert, in the garden that I met
> A miracle of earthly beauty.
> The money melted very quickly, like snow,
> I had to go back.
> I had to dive deep beneath the waters
> Of sullen and evil Leningrad.[23]

But this lover of opera couldn't recall a single title of the operas he had listened to with such enjoyment.

Clearly, Yuzik was singing from the wrong sheet: the conversation broke off. Yuzik had, of course, taken his taste for opera from the novels he had heard told in prison so often in the evenings.

Even when talking about prison, Yuzik boasted, repeating someone else's phrase, uttered by a more serious gangster.

Gangsters say that during a theft they experience a special kind of thrill, a vibration of the nerves that makes the act of theft inspired, like a creative act; they undergo a peculiar psychological state of nervous excitement and uplift that can't compare with anything, being so alluring, full, deep, and strong.

It is said that a person stealing lives a far fuller life at that moment than a cardplayer at the baize table or, rather, at his pillow, the traditional card table in the gangster world.

"You get your hand into his glad rags," a pickpocket was telling us, "and your heart races ... You die a thousand deaths and you resurrect by the time you've pulled out that damned wallet, in which you might find only two rubles."

There are thefts that incur absolutely no danger, but the creative excitement, the thief's inspiration, is still present: the feeling of risk, fervor, life.

The thief doesn't care at all about the person he's robbing. In the camps thieves sometimes steal rags they don't need at all, simply for the sake of stealing, so as to experience that "lofty disease"[24] of theft one more time. "Infected" is what the professional criminals call such thieves. But there are not very many practitioners of theft for theft's sake in the camps. Rather than theft, most of them prefer face-to-face robbery, brazen, unconcealed robbery, in which they tear a jacket, a scarf, sugar, butter, tobacco—anything edible and anything that can serve as hard currency in a game of cards—off somebody in full sight of everyone.

A railway thief told us of the special excitement he feels when opening a stolen suitcase (which he calls a "corner"). "We don't pick the locks," he said. "We bash the lid with a stone, and the corner opens."

This thief's excitement has nothing to do with human boldness. Boldness is the wrong word here; it's pure brazen insolence without limits, which can be stopped only by erecting the strongest barriers.

A thief's actions have no basis in his psychology or his emotional experiences.

Cards play a very important part in the gangster's life.

Not every gangster plays cards on all-night benders, like sick people, losing their last pair of trousers in the battle. To lose everything like that is not considered disgraceful.

Nevertheless, all gangsters know how to play. Of course they do!

The ability to play cards is part of the "code of chivalry" in the gangster world. There are just a few games of chance that every gangster is obliged to be able to play and that he learns as a child. Young thieves are constantly being trained to manufacture cards and to learn the art of raising the stakes, "transport plus couche."[25] Incidentally, Chekhov in his *Sakhalin Island* mistakenly wrote down the cardplayers' phrase "transport plus couche," which means raising the stake, as "the transport is eaten"(!),[26] and he identified the phrase as a card-playing term used by convicts. This mistake has migrated through all the editions of *Sakhalin Island*, including the academic one. The writer misheard a very common set phrase in card playing.

The gangster world is slow to change. Its traditions endure. Card games that have long vanished from normal life are still preserved in the criminal world. State Councilor Shtoss from Gogol's "The Portrait"[27] is still a reality today. The game of shtoss, or faro, is at least a hundred years old and now has the easier-to-pronounce name of shtoss. In one of Kaverin's stories, street urchins sing a well-known romance, shortening a word to something they can understand and relish: "Black rose, 'blem" (for "emblem") "of sadness."

Every criminal has to know how to play shtoss and how to double the stakes, like German or Chekalinsky in Pushkin's "The Queen of Spades."[28]

The second game, the most widespread, is a sort of pontoon, bura, what the criminals call thirty-one. Similar to blackjack, thirty-one has survived as a game played by gangsters. Blackjack is not a game thieves play with each other.

The third, most complicated game, which requires a score to be kept, is terzo, "three in a row," a sort of bezique, and a variation of the game five hundred and one. This is a game for experts, generally for the senior criminals, the aristocracy of the gangster world, its sophisticates.

All the criminals' card games are remarkable for their extraordinary quantity of rules. These rules have to be committed to memory, and the player who remembers them best wins.

A game of cards is always a duel. Criminals don't play in big groups, they always play one-on-one, separated by the traditional pillow.

If one loses, another one takes his place to face the winner; as long as a player has something to "answer with," the battle of cards goes on.

According to the rules, which are unwritten, the winner has no right to end the game, as long as there is an answer—whether it be a pair of trousers, a sweater, or a jacket. The value of the stake is usually determined by mutual agreement, and the item can be lost just like a monetary stake. All scores have to be memorized; players have to know how to defend themselves, to not let themselves be cheated or deceived.

Cheating at cards is considered to be glorious. The opponent has to notice the cheating, expose it, and by doing so win the "rubber."

All gangster players are cardsharps, but that is as it should be: you should know how to expose, catch, and prove a cardsharp...That's how they sit down to play, trying to deceive each other, exercising cardsharps' tricks under each other's watchful eyes.

A card battle, if it is taking place somewhere safe, is an endless torrent of insults, of obscene curses; the game is played to the sound of mutual swearing. Old criminals say that when they were young, in the 1920s, thieves didn't curse each other so foully and obscenely as they do now when they play cards. The gray-haired old gang leaders shake their heads and whisper, "O times, o morals!" The criminals' habits worsen with every year.

Cards are manufactured in prison and in the camps with fabulous speed. The experience of many generations of thieves has worked out a method for making them: in prison, cards are made using the most rational and easiest method. To do so you need a paste, which is bread, the ubiquitous bread ration that you can quickly chew into a paste. You also need paper: newspaper, wrapping paper, pamphlets, and books will do. You need a knife: but what prison cell or what group of camp prisoners can't produce a knife?

The main thing is that you need an indelible pencil to color the cards, which is why criminals are so careful to hang on to the lead of an indelible pencil and protect it during any searches. This bit of pencil has two uses. If you are in a critical situation, you can stick the splinters of the pencil in your eyes, which will force the paramedic or doctor to send you as a patient to the hospital. Sometimes the hospital is the criminal's only escape from a difficult or menacing situation.

Woe to you if medical help is delayed. Quite a few professional criminals have gone blind after this reckless operation, but quite a few have escaped danger and found safety in the hospital. That is the emergency use of an indelible pencil.

The young little bosses think that an indelible pencil is necessary for forging seals, stamps, documents. Such a use for it is extremely rare; obviously if documents are being forged, the forger will need more than an indelible pencil.

The main reason for getting hold of and keeping indelible pencils, the reason they are valued much more highly than ordinary pencils, is that they can be used to color, to "print" playing cards.

First of all, a "stencil" is made. This word is not part of criminal slang, but it is very common in prison language. The suit's pattern is cut using a stencil: criminals don't distinguish red and black, rouge and noir. All suits are the same color. The jack has a double pattern, because international convention allots two points to a jack. The queen has a combination of three patterns. The king—four. The ace has a complex of several patterns in the middle of the card. Sevens, eights, nines, and tens are made in the usual pattern, just like the cards issued by the state's card monopoly.

The bread, once chewed, is squeezed through a rag; this excellent paste is used to glue together sheets of thin paper, which are then dried and cut with a sharp knife into the required number of cards. The indelible pencil is wrapped in a rag and wetted: the printing machine is ready. The stencil is laid over the card and rubbed with purple until it leaves the required pattern on the face of the card.

If the paper is thick, as in Academy editions, then it is just cut up and cards are printed directly onto it.

It takes about two hours to make a pack of cards (including drying time).

This is the most rational way to make playing cards; it is a method evolved from age-old experience. The recipe works under all conditions and anyone can follow it.

Whenever there is a search, and whenever parcels arrive, indelible pencils are very thoroughly looked for and removed. There is a strict order to do so.

It's said that thieves lose free-worker girls to each other when they play cards: something like that happened in Pogodin's play *The Aristocrats*. I rather think that this is one of those legends in the making: I never chanced to see any scenes from Lermontov's *The Treasurer's Wife*.[29]

It's said that an overcoat a *freier* is currently wearing can be lost at cards. I never happened to come across this sort of loss either, but there is nothing improbable about it. I suspect, however, that this was a loss "on credit," when someone had to "produce"—take or steal—within a limited time an overcoat or something equal in value.

There are moments in a game when luck switches sides and favors one player by the end of the second or third day of play. Everything is lost, and the game is ending. Mountains of sweaters, trousers, scarves, and pillows are piled up behind the winner. But the loser pleads, "Let me try to get it back, give me another card, give me credit; I'll produce tomorrow." If the winner has a generous heart, he agrees, and the game goes on, the winner's partner having to answer with his physical possession. He may win, luck may change, he might win back one garment after another and resurrect himself to become the winner . . . Or he may lose . . .

A game is played on credit, to produce, just once, and the sum agreed on stays the same; the time limit for producing is not extended.

If a garment or money is not produced by the allotted time, the loser is declared "played out," and he has few options: either suicide or trying to escape from his cell, from the camp, fleeing to the devil. He has to pay his card debts on time; it's a matter of honor!

That's how other people's overcoats change owners, still warm from the heat of a *freier*'s body. What can you do? A thief's honor, or rather, a thief's life, is more precious than a *freier*'s overcoat.

We've already discussed even baser needs, their nature and their extent. These needs are peculiar and very far from anything human.

There is one more way of looking at gangsters' behavior. It's said that they are psychologically sick people and therefore, in a way, insane. Certainly, almost all gangsters are hysterical neurotics. Their notorious spirit, their ability to throw a tantrum, is a testimony to their shattered nervous system. It is extremely rare, but not unheard-of, for a criminal to have a sanguine or a phlegmatic nature. The famous pickpocket

Karlov, whose nickname was the Contractor and who was written about in *Pravda* in the 1930s, when he'd been caught at Moscow's Kiev station, was a stout, rosy-cheeked, potbellied man who loved life. But he was an exception.

There are medical scientists who consider any murder to be a sign of psychosis.

If gangsters are psychiatric cases, then they need to be kept in a madhouse for life.

But we believe that the criminal world is a special world of people who have ceased to be human.

This world has always existed, and it still does, and its exhalations bring depravity and poison into the lives of our young people.

The thief's whole psychology is based on a longstanding, age-old observation by gangsters that their victim will never do, and cannot even think of doing, what a thief will happily do any day, any hour, with a light heart and a calm soul. That is the criminal's strength: unbounded insolence in the absence of any morality. The phrase "too far" does not exist for the criminal. If a thief's law does not let him consider it honorable or valorous to write a denunciation of a *freier*, he is not in the least reluctant, for his own advantage, to compose and hand the authorities a political character reference against any *freier* who happens to be near him. In 1938 and later, up until 1953, we know of literally thousands of visits paid by thieves to the camp bosses, giving statements to the effect that they, as true friends of the people, are obliged to denounce "fascists" and "counterrevolutionaries." This activity took on mass proportions, and the subject of the thieves' special hatred in the camps was always the intellectual prisoners, the four-eyed eggheads.

Once upon a time pickpockets were the most highly qualified group in the thieves' world. Experts in "attic" thefts, as pickpockets were known, even underwent a sort of training to master their trade, and they took pride in their restricted specialty. They would go on long journeys, and from start to finish, as they did their "tours," they stuck to their skill and didn't diversify into burglary or passing off fake jewels. The light punishments for pickpocketing, the convenient loot—just cash—were the two circumstances that attracted thieves to pickpocketing. The ability to hold your own in any society and not to stand out was also an important merit of an expert pickpocket.

Unfortunately, the government's currency policies reduced the pickpocket's "earnings" to an income that was wretched, compared with the risk and the liability if caught. The vulgar snatching of wash from the line turned out to be "more profitable and more charming." Washed clothes fetched a bit more money than the contents of any wallet hooked on a bus or a tram. You'd never find a thousand rubles in a pocket, but any glad rags, even after the discount for stolen goods, were worth more than the money you could find in most wallets.

Pickpockets changed their specialization and merged with the ranks of housebreakers.

All the same, crook's blood is not a synonym of blue blood. Even a *freier* can have crook's blood, "a drop of crook's blood," as long as he shares some of the gangster's convictions and helps "people" and shows some sympathy with the thieves' law.

An interrogator, too, can have a drop of crook's blood if he understands the soul of the gangster world and secretly sympathizes with it. Even a camp boss (and this is not so rare) can, unbribed and unthreatened, make major concessions to criminals. A drop of crook's blood can be found in all the world's "bitches," that is, informers: it is significant that these men were once thieves. People with a drop of crook's blood may be of some help to thieves, and thieves need to keep this in mind. All those who've gotten "tied up," those who have broken with the criminal world, stopped thieving, and gone back to honest work, still have a drop of crook's blood. Such people exist, and they are not informers: the tied up are by no means hated. At a difficult moment they may possibly even be able to help, and then the crook's blood will come into action.

"Fences" (those who sell stolen goods) and the landlords of thieves' dens are almost certainly people with a drop of crook's blood.

Any fool or *freier* who gives help of one kind or another to a thief has, as the professional criminals say, a drop of crook's blood.

That phrase is the gangster's vile, condescending praise for anyone who sympathizes with the thieves' law, anyone whom the thief deceives and then repays with this cheap flattery.

1959

A WOMAN FROM THE CRIMINAL WORLD

AGLAYA Demidova was brought to the hospital with false papers. It wasn't her personal file or prisoner's ID that was forged: that side of things was all in order. It was just that her personal file had a new yellow cover, which showed that her term of punishment had begun all over again, and recently. She came under the same name she used when she had been brought to the hospital two years earlier. Of her identifying data nothing had changed except her sentence. It was now twenty-five years, whereas two years earlier her personal file was in a blue folder and her sentence was ten years.

As well as the double-digit figures entered in ink under the section "Article of Criminal Code," another figure, a three-digit one, had been added. But all that was completely genuine. It was her medical documents that were forged: a copy of her medical file, her health assessment, the laboratory analyses. These had been forged by people with official posts who could lay their hands on the right stamps and seals, and such corrupt people had a reputation: whether good or bad was irrelevant. The head of the health section at the mine had had to work for many hours to concoct false medical notes and create a fake medical document, one that demonstrated real artistic inspiration.

A diagnosis of tuberculosis of the lungs appeared to be the logical deduction from the ingenious daily notes. A thick packet of temperature recordings with diagrams showing the typical tuberculosis curves and forms filled in with every possible laboratory analysis all showed ominous indicators. For a doctor, creating this file was like a written examination, one in which you are asked to describe the progress of tuberculosis as it develops in an organism to the point that the only outcome is an urgent hospitalization of the patient.

Such a job might be done out of purely sporting motives: an ability to prove to the central hospital that even at a gold mine the doctor was not born yesterday. It would simply be pleasant to remember everything in the right order, as you once studied things at a medical institute. Of course, you'd never have thought that you would have to apply your knowledge in such an unusual, "artistic" way.

The main thing was that Demidova had to be given a hospital bed, come what may. The hospital could not, and had no right to, refuse to admit a patient like her, even if the doctors had a thousand suspicions.

Suspicions were immediately aroused, and while the question of admitting Demidova was being decided at the highest local level, she herself was sitting in the enormous area that was the hospital's admissions room. In any case, she was alone only in the Chesterton sense of the word.[30] The paramedic and the hospital porters in reception clearly did not count. Nor did her two escort guards, who never moved an inch from her. A third guard, who had the papers, was wandering around somewhere in the jungle of the hospital offices.

Demidova hadn't even taken off her hat; she'd just unbuttoned the collar of her sheepskin jacket. She was unhurriedly smoking one cigarette after another, throwing the ends into a wooden spittoon that was filled with sawdust.

She rushed about the admissions room from the big bow windows to the doors, and her guards dashed after her, copying her movements.

When the third guard reappeared with the duty doctor, it had already gotten dark—quickly, as always in the north—and the lights had to be turned on.

"Will they give me a bed?" Demidova asked the guard.

"No, they won't," the guard said sullenly.

"I knew they wouldn't. It's all Kroshka's fault. She knifed a woman doctor in the belly, and I'm paying for it."

"Nobody's making you pay for anything," said the doctor.

"I know better."

Demidova went out ahead of her guards and slammed the exit door, and the truck's engine roared into life.

At that moment an inner door opened silently, and the head of the hospital, followed by a whole suite of officers from the special section, entered the admissions room.

"Where is she? Was that Demidova?"

"She's been driven away, sir."

"Pity, pity that I didn't take a look at her. It's all because of you and your stories, Piotr Ivanovich . . ." The boss and his followers then left the admissions room.

The boss wanted to have at least a glimpse of Demidova, the famous female thief: her story was, in fact, rather unusual.

Six months earlier Aglaya Demidova, sentenced to ten years for murdering her labor organizer—she'd suffocated the overenthusiastic labor organizer with a towel—was being taken to the mine after her trial. There was just one escort guard, since the journey didn't require an overnight stay: it was only a few hours by truck from the administration settlement where Demidova had been tried to the mine where she worked. Space and time in the Far North are identical forms of measurement. People often measured distance by time, as do the nomadic Yakuts, who say, for example, six days' journey from one hill to another. Everyone living by the main artery, the paved highway, measures distance by what a truck can cover in a day.

Demidova's guard was one of the young "old men," those who stayed on after serving their term of duty; he had gotten used to the liberties of life as an escort guard, and to its peculiarities, which meant that a guard was completely in charge of the fate of his prisoner. This wasn't the first time he had escorted a woman: such journeys always held the promise of familiar amusements, which rather seldom come the way of the average musketeer in the north.

In a wayside refectory all three—guard, driver, and Demidova—had dinner. For Dutch courage the guard drank alcohol (in the north vodka is drunk only by the very top bosses) and led Demidova off to the bushes. There were plenty of willows and young aspens around any settlement in the taiga.

Once they were in the bushes the guard put his automatic on the ground and turned his attention to Demidova. She tore herself free, grabbed the automatic, and with two rounds of fire put nine bullets into the body of the libidinous guard. She then threw the automatic into the bushes, went back to the refectory, and left on a passing truck. The driver of the other truck raised the alarm, and the guard's corpse and automatic were very soon discovered; Demidova herself was detained two days later a few hundred kilometers from the scene of her encounter with the guard. She was tried again and given twenty-five years. She refused to work, as she always had, and robbed the women in the neighboring barracks. The mine bosses decided to be rid of this criminal woman at all costs. They hoped that after a spell in the hospital she wouldn't be returned to the mine but would be sent elsewhere.

Demidova had been a shoplifter and a burglar, "a shopper-dropper," as the old crooks termed it.

The gangster world distinguishes two classes of women: actual thieves, whose profession is theft, just like the male criminals; and prostitutes, the gangsters' girlfriends.

The first class is considerably smaller than the second, and among old crooks, who consider women a lower order, they enjoy a certain amount of respect—because their merits and active qualities have to be recognized. Usually, a woman who lives with a thief (the word "thief," male or female, is constantly used in the sense of belonging to the underworld order of old crooks), a female thief, often takes part in devising plans for a theft as well as the theft itself. But she does not take part in the courts of honor. Life itself has dictated this rule: men and women are kept apart in prisons, and that has made a difference in their ways of life, in the habits and rules of both sexes. Women are, after all, softer, and their courts are not as bloody and their sentences not so cruel. Murders committed by female criminals are less frequent than in the male half of the criminal house.

It is out of the question for a woman thief to live with any *freier*.

Prostitutes are the other and the larger class of women linked to the gangster world. A prostitute is a thief's recognized girlfriend and she earns a living for him. Naturally, prostitutes take part in thefts when needed, and act as pointers and as lookouts, as well as concealing and disposing of the loot. But they are not in the least equal members of the criminal world. They are indispensable participants in orgies, but they cannot even dream of taking part in courts of honor.

A hereditary old crook learns from the earliest age to despise women.

Theoretical, pedagogical lessons alternate with real-world examples from his seniors. As a baser creature, woman is created only to satisfy the thief's physical passion, to be a target for his coarse jokes and the object of public beatings, when the criminal is on a spree. She is a living thing that the gangster takes for temporary use.

Sending your girlfriend-prostitute to your boss's bed, if that is required for the good of the cause, is a normal technique, approved by everyone. She too shares that opinion. Any talk about this topic is always extremely cynical, laconic to an extreme, and expressive. Time is precious.

The thieves' ethics make jealousy and deceit irrelevant. The sacrosanct ancient custom is that the leading thief, the most authoritative in any given thieves' company, has the right to choose his temporary wife, the best prostitute.

Even if the day before a new leader appears the prostitute was sleeping with a different thief and was considered his property, which he could lend to his comrades, all those rights are now transferred to her new owner. If he is arrested the next day, the prostitute will go back to her former boyfriend. And if that boyfriend is arrested, she'll be told who her new owner is: the owner who decides whether she lives or dies; the owner of her fate, her money, her actions, and her body.

What room is there left for a feeling like jealousy? There's no room for it in the professional criminal's ethics.

It's said that a thief is human, and that nothing human is alien to him. Possibly he is occasionally reluctant to hand over his girlfriend, but laws are laws, and the guardians of the "ideological" purity of gangsters' morals will immediately point out his mistake to the thief, should he show signs of jealousy. And he will submit to the law.

There are cases when the untamed temper and the hysterical nature common to almost all criminals will push one of them to stand up for his woman. That now makes the question one for the kangaroo court to settle, and the criminal prosecution, appealing to the authority of decisions made over a thousand years, will demand that the guilty man be punished.

Usually, however, things don't get as far as a quarrel, and the prostitute obediently sleeps with her new master.

In the criminal world there is no sharing of women, no ménages à trois.

Men and women are kept apart in the camps. But in prisons and camps there are hospitals, transit camps, outpatient clinics, clubs, where men and women can still see and hear one another.

One can be amazed by the ingenuity of prisoners, by their energy in achieving the goals they set for themselves. The colossal amount of energy spent in prison is astounding when it is a matter of getting a piece of crumpled tin and turning it into a knife, a weapon with which to commit a murder or suicide. The warder's attention is always weaker than the prisoner's, as we know from Stendhal, who in *The Charterhouse of Parma* said, "The warden thinks about his keys less than the prisoner thinks about escaping."

In the camps a gangster's energy when he wants to see a prostitute is enormous.

It is important to find the place where the prostitute is going to come: the gangster never doubts that she will come. A vengeful hand will strike down any guilty woman. So she changes into men's clothes, does the boss or labor organizer a favor by sleeping with him, so that she can slip off at the appointed hour to wherever her completely unknown lover is waiting for her. Lovemaking takes place hurriedly, like the summer flowering of plants in the Far North. The prostitute goes back to the women's zone, is spotted by the warder and put in a concrete cell, and is sentenced to a month of solitary confinement before being sent to a punishment mine. She puts up with all this without complaint, and even with pride, for she has carried out her duties as a prostitute.

In the big northern hospital for prisoners there was a case of a prominent criminal, a patient in a surgical ward, who managed to have a prostitute brought to his hospital bunk for a whole night. There she slept in turn with all eight thieves in the ward at the time. The hospital porter on duty, himself a prisoner, was threatened with a knife; the duty paramedic, a free contract worker, was given a suit that had been ripped off of somebody in the camp. (The owner of the suit recognized it and registered a complaint, so that a great deal of effort was expended to hush the whole matter up.)

The girl wasn't in the least abashed when she was found the next morning in a ward of a men's hospital.

"The boys asked me to help them out, so I came," she calmly explained.

It doesn't take much imagination to guess that the criminals and their girlfriends almost all have syphilis, if not chronic gonorrhea, even in our penicillin era.

There is a well-known classic expression: "Syphilis isn't a disgrace; it's a misfortune." Here syphilis is even less of a disgrace; it's considered good fortune rather than a misfortune for a prisoner: yet another example of the reversal of scales.

First of all, every criminal knows the compulsory treatment of venereal cases is enforced. He knows he can put on the brakes, that is, get some rest, that with his syphilis he won't end up somewhere in the sticks but will live and receive treatment in some relatively well-equipped settlements where there are doctors who specialize in venereal diseases. All this has been so well considered and understood that even gangsters whom God has spared from the four or three crosses of the Wasserman test[31] still declare themselves to be syphilitics. And the unreliability of a negative result from this test in the laboratory is something that gangsters are also well aware of. Fake sores and mendacious complaints are just as common as the genuine sores and well-founded complaints.

Patients requiring treatment for venereal diseases are put together in special zones. Nobody in these zones worked, and this temporary arrangement was the "Monrepo refuge"[32] that suited the criminals best. Later, these zones were set up at special mines or lumberjack stations where, apart from getting Salvarsan[33] and a special bread ration, the prisoners had to work the usual norms.

But in actual fact there was no real demand for work in these zones, and life there was much easier than at any ordinary mine.

The zones for male venereal patients were always places from which the gangsters' young victims were admitted to the hospital: they had been infected anally with syphilis. Almost all criminals are pederasts, and in the absence of women they debauched and infected men, who would more often than not have been threatened with knives, or who would, less often, have submitted in exchange for rags or for bread.

When speaking of women in the criminal world, we cannot ignore the army of Zoikas, Mankas, Dashkas, and other creatures of the male sex who'd been baptized with women's names. What was striking was that the bearers of these female names responded to them as if it were perfectly normal, and didn't see anything disgraceful or degrading in doing so.

To live on a prostitute's earnings was not considered demeaning for a thief. On the contrary, the prostitute was supposed to highly value her personal contact with the thief.

On the other hand, pimping is one of the attractive aspects of the profession that young criminals very much like.

> Soon, soon, we will be sentenced,
> They'll take us to Pervomaiski court,
> The staff girls will see us,
> They'll bring us a food parcel.

This is what's sung in the prison song "The Staff Girls," whose subjects are in fact prostitutes.

But there are occasions when whatever feeling replaces love, plus a feeling of pride and of self-pity, pushes a woman in the criminal world toward illicit acts.

Of course, more is asked of a woman thief than of a prostitute. A thief who lives with a warder is committing treason in the view of the criminal dogmatists. She is liable to be beaten to show her the error of her ways, or she might just be knifed, as a snitch.

If a prostitute does such a thing, it won't be held against her.

When a woman goes against the laws of her world, the problem is not always dealt with in the same way: it depends on personal qualities.

The thief Tamara Tsulukidze, a twenty-year-old beauty, was once the girlfriend of a prominent Tbilisi criminal. In the camp she became intimate with the head of the Culture and Education Section, Grachiov, a fine thirty-year-old lieutenant and a handsome bachelor.

Grachiov had another mistress in the camp, a Pole called Leszczewska, one of the famous performers in the camp theater. When he took up with Tamara, she didn't insist that he drop Leszczewska, and the latter had nothing against Tamara. That fine young man Grachiov was living at the same time with two "wives": he inclined toward Muslim customs. Being a man of experience, he did his best to divide his attention equally between the two, and he succeeded. Not only love but its material expression, too, was shared: Grachiov got two specimens ready of each gift of food. He did the same with lipstick, ribbons, and perfume: Tsulukidze and Leszczewska received completely identical ribbons, bottles of perfume, and handkerchiefs, and on the same day.

This looked rather touching. Moreover, Grachiov was a very presentable and fastidious young man. Both Leszczewska and Tsulukidze (who lived in the same barracks) were delighted by the tact that their common beloved showed. But they did not become close friends, and when Tamara was suddenly called to account by the hospital thieves, Leszczewska felt a secret schadenfreude.

Once, Tamara fell ill and spent time in the hospital, in the women's ward. At night the ward doors opened and an envoy from the old crooks crossed the threshold, banging his crutches. The long arm of the criminal world had reached Tamara.

The envoy reminded her of the laws that applied to a criminal's ownership of a woman and suggested she should appear in the surgical department to carry out "the will of the man who sent him."

According to the envoy, she was going to be seen by people who knew the Tbilisi criminal whose girlfriend Tamara Tsulukidze was considered to be. The Tbilisi man was now replaced by Senka Gundosy. Tamara had therefore to immediately accept his embraces.

Tamara grabbed a kitchen knife and threw herself onto the lame criminal. It was all the hospital porters could do to get him away from her. With threats and obscene curses against Tamara, the envoy left. The next day Tamara discharged herself from hospital.

Quite a few attempts were made to bring the prodigal daughter back under the banners of the criminal world, and they all failed. Tamara was knifed, but the wound was slight. When the end of her sentence came and she married some warder, a man who had a revolver, she finally escaped the criminal world.

The blue-eyed Nastia Arkharova, a typist from Kurgansk, was neither a thief nor a prostitute: when she bound her fate with the world of thieves forever, it was not of her own free will.

Ever since childhood, Nastia had been surrounded with dubious respect, the ominous respect of people she had read about in detective stories. This respect, which she noticed while she was still on the outside, existed in prison and in the camps, wherever gangsters were to be found.

There was nothing mysterious about this: Nastia's elder brother was a prominent "cracksman" and ever since she was a child Nastia had basked in the glory of his criminal fame, his fate as a successful thief. Imperceptibly, Nastia found herself in criminal circles, sharing their interests and activities, and she didn't refuse to help hide their loot. Her first three-month sentence strengthened and toughened her, and made her ties with the criminal world much closer. While she lived in her hometown, thieves were afraid of her brother's anger and decided not to use Nastia as gangster property. Her social position meant that she was closer to the women thieves, and she was certainly no prostitute: so it was as a thief that she was dispatched on the usual long-distance journeys at government expense. Here she had no brother, and in the first town she found herself after her release, the local gang leader made her his wife, infecting her with gonorrhea in the process. He was soon arrested, and as they parted he sang Nastia the thieves' song: "My pal will take possession of you." Nastia lived for just as short a time with this pal, or comrade; he was put in prison, and another owner laid claim to Nastia. Nastia found this man physically repulsive: he was always drooling, and he suffered from boils. She tried to use her brother's name as protection, but she was told that even her brother had no right to break the great laws of the criminal world. She was threatened with a knife, and she stopped resisting.

In the hospital Nastia meekly turned up to any summons for love: she was often in the cells, and she wept a lot. Either she cried easily or she was terrified by her fate, the fate of a girl of twenty-two.

Vostokov, an elderly hospital doctor, was touched by Nastia's situation, which by the way was the same as thousands of others. He promised to help her get a job as a typist in the office if she agreed to change her way of life. "That's not up to me," Nastia wrote in her fine handwriting, when she replied to the doctor. "I can't be saved. But if you want to do something for me, then buy me some nylon stockings, the smallest size. Ready to do anything for you, Nastia Arkharova."

The thief Sima Sosnovskaya was covered in tattoos from head to toe. An incredible sexual scene, all intertwining and of the most intriguing content, covered her whole body in very ingenious lines. Only her face, neck, and lower arms were without ink. Sima was well known in the hospital for her bold theft: she had taken a gold watch off an escort guard's wrist while they were traveling and the guard decided to take advantage of Sima's favors. Sima's character was far more peaceful than Aglaya Demidova's, otherwise the guard would have been lying in the bushes until the second coming. She regarded what had happened as an amusing adventure and considered that a gold watch was not too high a price for her love. But the guard nearly went out of his mind; he never stopped demanding his watch back and he searched Sima twice but found nothing. The hospital wasn't far away and there were a lot of prisoners in the group; then, the guard hesitated to start a fight in the hospital. Sima kept the gold watch. Soon she sold it and spent the money on drink, and all traces of the watch vanished.

The gangster's moral code, like the Quran, declares that women are contemptible. Woman is a despicable creature; a lower animal who deserves to be beaten and is unworthy of pity. This applies to all women regardless: any female representative of a world that isn't the gangsters' is still despised by them. Gang rape is not all that uncommon in the mines of the Far North. The bosses transport their wives in the company of guards; no woman ever goes anywhere alone, on foot or by vehicle. Little children are guarded in the same way: raping little girls is what every criminal constantly dreams of. And that dream doesn't always remain a dream.

The criminal is brought up from infancy to despise women. He beats his prostitute girlfriend so often that she is said to stop feeling love to the fullest unless she gets a regular beating for some reason or other. Sadistic inclinations are nurtured by the very ethics of the gangster world.

The gangster must have no comradely or friendly feelings for a woman. He must have no pity, either, for the object of his underworld entertainment. There can be no fairness in his attitude toward a woman of his world: the woman question is well outside the criminals' ethical "zone."

But there is one unique exception to this grim rule. There is just one woman who is not only is guaranteed against any attempts to dishonor her but also raised onto a pedestal. A woman who is poeticized by the gangster world and who has become the subject of gangsters' lyrics, the heroine of criminal folklore over many generations.

This woman is the thief's mother.

The gangster's imagination constructs a malicious and hostile world, encircling him on all sides. In a world populated by his enemies there is just one bright figure worthy of pure love and respect and worship. That is his mother.

The cult of the mother, despite an embittered contempt for women in general, is the criminal world's ethical formula for dealing with the woman question, and the formula is expressed with a special prison sentimentality. A lot of rubbish has been written about prison sentimentality. In reality this is the sentimentality of a murderer who waters his bed of roses with the blood of his victims. It is the sentimentality of a man who will bind an injured bird's wounds, yet an hour later is capable of tearing that living bird into pieces with his own hands, for the spectacle of a living creature's death is the best of spectacles for a gangster.

You have to know the true face of the authors of the mother cult, a cult that has a poetic haze wafting over it.

With the same uncontrolled theatricality that makes the criminal sign his name with a knife on the corpse of a renegade he has killed, or rape a woman in public and in daylight so that everyone can see, or force himself on a three-year-old girl, or infect a male Zoika with syphilis, and with just the same expression, the criminal poeticizes the image of the mother, deifies her, makes her the object of the most refined prison lyrics, and forces everyone to show her every kind of respect, even though they can't see her.

At first glance, a thief's affection for his mother seems to be the only human aspect surviving in his grotesque and distorted feelings. The criminal would always appear to be a respectful son, and any coarse talk about someone else's mother is invariably cut short in the criminal world. Mother is a lofty ideal, and at the same time something completely real, something which everybody has. A mother who forgives everything, who will always take pity.

"Mommy worked so we could live. But I quietly began to steal. 'You'll be a thief, like your daddy,' my mother used to say, as she shed tears."

Those are lines from "Fate," a classic song of the criminal world.

The thief understands that only his mother will stick with him through his short and stormy life until the end, and so he spares her his cynicism.

But this apparently unique bright feeling is as mendacious as all the impulses of the gangster's soul.

Glorifying the mother is a camouflage; praising her is a form of deceit and, at best, only an observed expression of prison sentimentality.

In what you might think to be an exalted feeling, the thief is lying from beginning to end, as in everything he says or thinks. None of the thieves ever sent his mother so much as a penny; they never helped her even in their own way; they spent the thousands of rubles they stole on drink and women.

There is nothing but pretense and theatrical lying in this feeling for mothers.

The cult of the mother is a peculiar smoke screen that covers up the unprepossessing world of the thieves.

The cult of the mother is a pretense and a lie, since it is never transferred to a wife or to women in general.

The attitude toward women is the litmus test for any system of ethics.

This is the place to note that it was the poet Yesenin who created the cult of the mother, which coexists with cynical scorn for women: thirty years ago, Yesenin was a very popular author in the criminal world. But more about that when the time comes.

A woman thief or a thief's girlfriend, any woman who has directly or indirectly entered the criminal world, is forbidden to have any sort of romance with *freiers*. If she does, however, she won't be killed or "done over." A knife is too noble a weapon to be used on a woman: a stick or a poker will do for her.

Things are quite different when it comes to an affair between a male thief and a free woman. That is honor and valor, the subject of boastful tales by the lucky man and secret envy from the others. These cases are quite common. But such a mountain of fairy tales is piled up around them that it is very hard to discern the truth. A typist turns into a female prosecutor, a messenger girl into the director of an enterprise, a shopgirl into a minister. Fantasy drives truth into the darkness, somewhere at the back of the stage, and there is no prospect of making sense of the show.

It goes without saying that a number of gangsters have families in their native towns, families long ago abandoned by the gangster husbands. Their wives and small children all battle with life the best they can. Sometimes the men return to their families from imprisonment, but they usually return for only a short time. "The restless spirit" draws them on to new wanderings, and in any case the local criminal investigation department eases the criminal's departure. So children are left behind in families for whom the father's profession does not seem horrible; instead, it arouses pity and, worse still, the desire to follow in their father's footsteps, as in "Fate":

> If you have the strength to fight with fate,
> Continue the fight to the very end.
> I'm very weak, but I shall still be compelled
> To follow in the path of my dead father.

The gangster has little to do with questions of fatherhood or bringing up children, although these questions are not excluded from the criminal's Talmud. The future of his daughters (should he have some somewhere) seems to a thief completely assured if they choose to be prostitutes or the girlfriends of famous thieves. Generally speaking, there is no moral burden (even of the specific criminal kind) weighing on a gangster's conscience in this matter. The fact that his sons will also grow up to be thieves seems utterly natural to a thief.

1959

THE PRISON BREAD RATION

ONE OF the most popular and cruel legends of the criminal world is that of the prison bread ration.

Just like the fairy-tale gentleman thief, the legend is a piece of advertising, the facade of criminal morality.

The essence of the legend is that the official prison ration is in prison conditions sacred and inviolate, and that no thief has the right to infringe on this official source of existence. Anyone who does so is supposedly cursed from then on for all eternity. It doesn't matter who he is, a distinguished criminal or the lowest kind of wet-behind-the-ears *freier*, what they call "a skeleton from Bataisk."

You can keep your prison ration without fearing for its safety if you have a bedside table in the cell, and under your head if you don't have a table or a shelf.

Stealing that bread is considered shameful, unthinkable.

The only thing that can be confiscated from *freiers* are their parcels, no matter whether they contain clothes or food. That is not forbidden.

Although it is clear to everybody that it is the prison regime itself, not the merciful criminals, who see that the prison ration is protected, all the same not many people harbor any doubts about the thieves' magnanimity.

Such people argue that the administration can't, after all, save parcels from the thieves' clutches. Which means that, if it weren't for the gangsters . . .

The administration does not, in fact, protect parcels. The ethics of the cells demand that a prisoner share his parcel with his comrades. The gangsters present themselves as the prisoner's "comrades" when they come out with open threats and claim a parcel. The more farsighted and experienced *freiers* immediately sacrifice half their parcels. None of the thieves takes any interest in whether a *freier* is destitute or not. For them, a *freier*, whether in prison or outside, is in all cases a legitimate prey, and his parcels and clothes are the gangster's battle trophies.

Sometimes the parcels or clothes are the subject of wheedling: the victim is told, "Hand it over; you'll need us on your side." And the *freier*, whose standard of living outside was half that of a thief's in prison, hands over the last crumbs his wife put together for him.

How else could it be? It's the law of the prisons! But at least he's kept his good name, and Senka Pup himself promised to look after him and even let him have a cigarette from the packet his wife sent in the parcel.

Stripping the *freier* of his clothes and robbing him in prison is the gangster's prime job, and he enjoys it. This robbery is done by the "puppies," the young ones frolicking about . . . The older criminals lying in the best corner of the cell keep an eye on the operation; they are ready at all times to intervene if the *freier* puts up any resistance.

Of course, the *freier* could yell out, call the guards and the commandant, but what good would that do? Just to get beaten up at night? Or later, when traveling, to get your throat cut, too? To hell with the parcel, anyway.

"On the other hand," the poor devil is told by a gangster, who is hiccupping from overeating as he claps his victim on the shoulder, "you don't have to worry about your ration. That's something sacred, brother . . . we'd never touch it."

A young thief is sometimes puzzled about why he can't touch the prison bread, if the owner has now eaten his fill of white bread from home, sent in a parcel. The owner of the white bread is equally puzzled. Both of them get explanations from the grown-up thieves: this is a law of prison life.

God help the naïve hungry peasant who doesn't get enough to eat in his first days of imprisonment, should he ask the gangster next to him to break off a piece of prison bread that is drying up on the shelf. The dressing-down he'll get from the gangster about the sacrosanct nature of the prison bread ration!

In prisons where not many parcels are received and there are few new *freiers*, the concept of "prison ration" is restricted to the bread, while anything cooked—soup, porridge, beetroot, and potato salad—however poor the item offered, is not considered inviolate. The gangsters always do their best to control the distribution of food. This wise rule costs the other inhabitants of the cell dearly. Apart from the bread ration, they scoop the dumplings out of the soup, and the second-course portions are, for some reason, reduced. A few months of living with the controller of the prison rations has the most negative effect on a prisoner's nutritional state, to use the official term.

All of this takes place before the camp, in prison where the pretrial prison regime applies.

In a corrective labor camp, where everyone does manual labor, the prison ration question becomes a matter of life and death.

There are no surplus pieces of bread here: everyone is starving and having to do heavy labor.

Here, being robbed of your prison ration is a crime, a form of slow murder.

The thieves, who do not work, get their claws into the cooks in the kitchen and grab most of the fats, sugar, tea, and also meat, should there be any (that is why all the "simple people" in the camp prefer fish to meat: the weight norm is the same, but the meat gets stolen). Apart from the thieves, the cook also has to feed the camp support staff, the foremen, the doctors, and sometimes the duty warders in the guardhouse. So the cook feeds them all: the thieves simply threaten to murder him, while the prisoners who have authority in the camp (the gangsters call them the "cretins") can at any moment dismiss a cook and have him sent to the pit face, which is a terrible fate for the cook, and not just for the cook.

Deductions from prison rations are made at the expense of a large army of ordinary workmen. These workmen receive just a small part of their "scientifically based norms of nutrition," and it has little fat and few vitamins. Grown men weep when they get a watery soup, since all the solid content has been taken out for various Senkas, Kolias, and other thieves.

To bring about at least a minimum of order, the authorities have to be not only personally honest but inhumanly and constantly vigilant and energetic in their struggle with the plunderers of food, above all with the thieves.

That is the situation with prison rations in the camps. Here nobody thinks about the gangsters' propaganda declarations anymore. Bread becomes bread with no ifs or buts or symbolic value. It becomes the chief means of staying alive. Woe to anyone who, by some supreme effort, saves a bit of his ration for nighttime, only to wake up in the middle of the night and to experience the taste of the bread, even the crunching in one's ears, in an empty mouth.

His bread will have been stolen, simply grabbed, taken by the hungry young gangsters who carry out searches every night. Any bread issued has to be eaten immediately: that's the practice at many mines where there are a lot of thieves, where these noble knights are hungry and want to eat, even though they don't work.

It's impossible to swallow five or six hundred grams of bread instantly. Unfortunately, the human digestive tract is different from that of a boa constrictor or a seagull. A human esophagus is too narrow, and a piece of bread weighing half a kilo can't be pushed down at one go, especially not with a crust. So the bread has to be broken up before it is chewed, and valuable time is lost doing so. When a workman is doing this, the criminals tear the rest of the bread from his hands, by bending back his fingers and hitting him.

In Magadan transit camp there used to be a system of issuing bread: the ration for twenty-four hours was given to a workman under the eyes of four guards carrying automatics. These guards kept the mob of hungry gangsters at a decent distance from the place where the bread was issued. Once a workman got his bread, he started chewing and chewing, and in the end he managed to swallow it all. There were no cases of gangsters ripping open a workman's belly to get hold of that bread.

But all over the place there was something else. Prisoners receive money for their work. It isn't much, a few dozen rubles (for those who exceed the norm), but still, they get it. Those who don't fulfill the norm get nothing. These dozens of rubles allow the workman to buy bread, sometimes butter, in the camp shop or stall: in other words, to improve his nutrition a little. Not all brigades get money, but some do. At the mines where gangsters work, this payment is purely fictitious: they take the money by "taxing" the workmen. For failing to pay them you get a knife in your side. These unthinkable "deductions" went on for years. Everyone knew about this blatant racket. If, however, the gangsters weren't doing it, then the deductions would have gone to pay the foremen, the norm setters, and the labor organizers.

This is the reality behind the concept of the prison ration.

1959

THE WAR OF THE "BITCHES"

THE DUTY doctor was summoned to the admissions room. On the freshly washed floorboards, which were faintly bluish after being scraped with a knife, a tanned tattooed body was writhing: a wounded man had been stripped naked by the hospital porters. His blood was staining the floor, and the duty doctor gave a malicious laugh, for it would be difficult to wash off. Anything bad that this doctor chanced to encounter or see made him glad. Two men in white gowns were leaning over the wounded man: the admissions paramedic, who was staunching the flow with bandaging material, and a lieutenant from the special squad, who was holding a document.

The doctor realized straightaway that the wounded man had no papers and that the lieutenant from the special squad was trying to get at least some information about him.

The wounds were still fresh; some were bleeding. There were a lot, more than a dozen, all tiny. The man had recently been stabbed with a small knife or a nail, or some similar tool.

The doctor recalled the last time he was on duty two weeks ago: a shop assistant had been killed, murdered in her own room, suffocated with a pillow. The murderer hadn't managed to slip away unnoticed; a hue and cry was raised, and the murderer, his dagger drawn, leapt out into the frosty mist of the street. Running past the shop, where there was a line, the killer stabbed the last person in line in the buttock—out of sheer hooliganism, or the devil knows why.

But this time was different. The wounded man's movements were becoming less jerky; his cheeks were turning pale. The doctor realized that this was due to internal bleeding, for the belly also had small, alarming stab wounds that were not bleeding. The wounds might be internal, in the intestine or the liver.

But the doctor was reluctant to interfere with the sacrosanct procedure of the records service. Cost what it may, he had to find out the "identifying data"—surname, name, patronymic, article of conviction, sentence—and get an answer to the questions put to each prisoner ten times a day at checks and roll calls.

The wounded man tried to reply, and the lieutenant quickly wrote down on a piece of paper what he was told. He now knew the surname and the article of conviction, which was article 58, paragraph 14. The main question, to which everyone—lieutenant, admissions paramedic, and duty doctor—was waiting for an answer, was still outstanding.

"Who are you? Who?" the lieutenant appealed excitedly, as he kneeled by the wounded man. "Who?"

Then the wounded man understood the question. His eyelids quivered, he parted his bitten, caked lips, and he breathed out in a drawl: "A bi-i-itch . . ."

Then he lost consciousness.

"A bitch!" the lieutenant cried out with delight, as he got to his feet and brushed his knees off with his hand.

"A bitch, a bitch!" the paramedic repeated joyfully.

"Take him to ward seven, surgical ward seven!" said the doctor, bustling. They could start bandaging him. Ward number seven was for the "bitches."

Many years after the end of the war, in the criminal world, at the bottom of the human sea, the submarine waves of blood still hadn't been stilled. These waves were the consequence of the war, an astounding and unforeseen consequence. Nobody, not the gray-haired criminal lawyers nor the veterans of the prison administration, could have foreseen that the war would divide the criminal world into two mutually hostile groups.

During the war, criminals, among them numerous recidivist old crooks, were taken out of the prisons where they were locked up and sent to the army, where they served in temporary units at the front.

Rokossovsky's army won its fame and popularity because of the criminal element that served in it.[34] The professional criminals turned out to make cunning scouts and bold guerrillas. Their natural fondness for taking risks, their determination and lack of inhibitions, made them valuable soldiers. At the time a blind eye was turned to looting and the urge to commit robbery. True, the final storming of Berlin was not entrusted to these units. Rokossovsky's army was deployed elsewhere, and it was Marshal Konev's professional units, regiments of the purest proletarian blood, which headed for Berlin Zoo.

The writer Vershigora, in *People with a Pure Conscience*,[35] assures us that he knew a criminal called Voronko who turned into a good guerrilla (just as in Makarenko's books).[36]

In short, criminals left the prisons for the front where they fought, some well, some badly. When Victory Day came, the heroic criminals were demobilized and returned to their peacetime activities.

Very soon postwar Soviet courts encountered their old friends in court sessions. It turned out—and was not hard to foresee—that the recidivists, the old crooks, the thieves, the "people," the criminal world, had no intention of stopping the activities that before the war had provided them with a living, not to mention creative excitement, moments of real inspiration, as well as a position in society.

Bandits went back to killing, safecrackers went back to breaking into safes, pickpockets to studying the pockets of people's rags, thieves to robbing apartments.

War, rather than teaching them to be good, had strengthened their brazen inhumanity. They took murder less seriously; it was even more straightforward than before the war.

The state tried to organize a fight with the increasing criminality. In 1947 decrees appeared "on protecting socialist property" and "on protecting citizens' personal property." These decrees meant that a relatively minor theft, for which thieves used to pay with a few months in prison, was now punishable by twenty years in jail.

Thieves who had fought in World War II were now loaded by the thousands onto ships and trains and sent under strict guard to numerous labor camps, where activity had not slowed down for a minute during the war. By now there were very many camps: northern camps, northeast camps, northwest camps; in every province, at every large or small building site, there were camp sections. Along with the dwarf organizations, which barely exceeded a thousand men, there were giant camps whose population, in the years when they were at their peak, was several hundred thousand men: Baikal-Amur camp, Taishet camp, Dmitrov camp, Temniki, Karaganda...

The camps quickly began to fill up with criminals. Two big remote camps, Kolyma and Vorkuta, were filled with special care. The harsh climate of the Far North, the permafrost, the winters of eight or nine months, combined with a carefully designed regime, created the right conditions for liquidating criminality. Stalin's experiment with the Trotskyists in 1938 had fully succeeded and was well remembered by everyone.

Trainload after trainload started to arrive at Kolyma and Vorkuta, bringing men sentenced under the 1947 decrees. The gangsters were poor labor material and unlikely to be of any use for colonizing the area, but escape from the Far North was almost impossible. The problem of isolating these people was thus reliably solved. Incidentally, the geographical peculiarities of the Far North gave rise in Kolyma to a special category of fugitives who never escaped anywhere but just went into hiding along the two-thousand-kilometer road (the colorful criminal term was "gone on the ice") and robbed passing trucks. Such fugitives were not usually charged with actual escape, nor with highway robbery. Lawyers viewed escape as evasion of work and treated it as counterrevolutionary sabotage, as a refusal to work: the chief crime in the camps. The combined efforts of lawyers and other great minds in the camp administration managed at last to squeeze the criminal recidivists into the frame of the most terrible article in the Criminal Code, article 58.

What is a thief's catechism? A thief, a member of the criminal world—the term "criminal world" having been invented by the thieves themselves—must steal, deceive *freiers*, drink, party, play cards, evade work, take part in kangaroo courts, that is, courts of honor. Prison might not be a thief's home, or his "house" or "bed of roses" or "den," but it was where the thief was compelled to spend most of his life. The important conclusion that follows is that criminals in prison had to look after themselves—by force, by cunning, by insolence, by deceit—and that they had important, if unofficial, rights, such as the right to a share of other people's parcels or property, the right to the best sleeping place, the best food, etc. In practice, all this was achieved as long as there were several thieves in a cell. They would then obtain everything that could be obtained in prison. These traditions allowed the thief to live better than anyone else in prison and in the camps.

Short terms of imprisonment and frequent amnesties had given thieves the chance of spending time in prison without working and with no particular problems. The only ones who worked, and then only from time to time, were the ones with skills: metalworkers, mechanics. No thief ever did dirty work. He would rather be in a concrete cell in the camp's solitary confinement.

The 1947 decrees with their twenty-year sentences for minor crimes presented the thieves with a new problem of "occupation." If a thief might once have hoped, by hook or by crook, to get through a few months or a year or two without working, now he would have to spend virtually his whole life in prison or at least only half alive. And a thief's life is short. There aren't many elderly gangster bosses among the old crooks. Thieves don't live long. Their mortality rate is much higher than the country's average.

The 1947 decrees presented the criminal world with serious problems, and their best minds strained to find a workable solution to the question.

The thieves' law states that a thief must not occupy any administrative posts in the camps, if those jobs are allotted to prisoners. He had no right to be a labor organizer, or a barracks elder, or a foreman. If he was, he would effectively enter the ranks of those with whom he had been at daggers drawn all his life. A thief who took on such an administrative post stopped being a thief and was deemed to be a "bitch," to have "bitched himself"; he was declared an outlaw, and any gangster would think it an honor to take the first available opportunity to cut this renegade's throat.

The criminal world's fastidiousness about such things is very great: their orthodox interpretations of some complex problems remind one of the subtle convoluted logic of the Talmud.

For example, a thief passes the guardhouse. The warder on duty shouts to him, "Hey, please hit the rail, make it ring, since you're passing." If the thief does hit the rail (the signal for reveille and roll calls), he will have broken the law and become "a bit of a bitch."

Kangaroo courts, or courts of honor, where people insist on their rights, are mainly concerned with examining actions and misdemeanors connected with such betrayals of their banner, and with a "legal" interpretation of some suspicious act. Guilty or not guilty? A guilty verdict from a court of honor usually and almost immediately leads to a bloody reprisal. It is not the judges, of course, who do the killing: that is entrusted to the young thieves. The chief gangsters always considered such "actions" beneficial for a young thief: he gets experience; it hardens him.

The thieves who had been convicted after the war began to arrive by ship and train at Magadan and Ust-Tsilma. The "war lot" was what they later became known as. They had all taken part in the war, and they would not have been convicted had they not committed new crimes. Alas, there were very, very few like Vershigora's Voronko.[37] The overwhelming majority, an enormous number of thieves, had gone back to their old profession. Strictly speaking, they had never left it: looting at the front was fairly similar to that social group's basic activity. Among the "warrior" criminals there were some who had won medals. Criminal war invalids found themselves a new and very good source of income as beggars on suburban trains.

Among the war lot were many major old crooks, prominent active members of this underworld society. After several years of war and freedom they were now returning to familiar places, buildings with barred windows, camp zones entangled with ten rows of barbed wire; they were coming back to familiar places with unfamiliar thoughts and undisguised alarm. They had already discussed a few things during the long nights in transit camps, and they all agreed that they couldn't go on living the way they used to live. The bosses of the war lot wanted to get together with their old comrades, who had been saved, or so they thought, only by luck from taking part in the war, with old comrades who had spent the entire war in prisons and camps. The bosses of the war lot imagined joyful reunions with old comrades, scenes of unbridled boasting by both "guests" and "hosts," and, finally, help in solving the very serious questions that life now presented to the criminal world.

Their hopes were to be dashed. The old criminal world refused to accept them into its ranks, and the war lot wasn't allowed to take part in kangaroo courts. It turned out that the questions bothering the new arrivals had long before been considered and discussed in the old criminal world. But the decision reached was quite different from what the warriors thought it would be.

"You were in the war? You picked up a rifle? That means you're a bitch, a thoroughgoing bitch, and you should be punished according to the law. What's more, you're a coward! You didn't have the strength of will to refuse to serve in the temporary squads: you should have taken a sentence or even died, but not picked up a rifle!"

That was the answer the new arrivals got from the "philosophers" and "ideologists" of the criminal world. The purity of criminal beliefs, they were told, came first. And nothing should be changed. If a thief was a "man" and not a milksop, then he should be able to carry on living, whatever decrees the government made: that's what being a thief meant.

It was pointless for the warriors to hint at their past merits or to demand that they should be allowed to take part in courts of honor as equally qualified judges and men of authority. The old crooks, who'd put up with living on a few ounces of bread in a prison cell during the war and endured a few other things, were adamant.

Nevertheless, among the thieves who had returned there were a lot of persons who'd been important in the criminal world. They had plenty of their own philosophers and ideologists and leaders. Being excluded so unceremoniously and ruthlessly from an environment that was home to them, they could not accept the status of pariah that the orthodox old crooks had doomed them to. The leading representatives of the war lot tried in vain to point out that, because their situation was due to bad luck and to special circumstances requiring them to go to the front, they should be spared such a negative response. Of course, the criminal world never had any patriotic feelings. The army and the front were pretexts for getting out of prison, and nobody was bothered by what came next. For a short while the interests of the state coincided with their personal interests, and that was why they were now being called to account by their former comrades. Moreover, the war fell in with some of the professional criminal's feelings, such as love of danger and risk. They had never even thought of being reforged or of breaking with the criminal world. The hurt pride of authorities who had ceased to be authorities, an awareness that they had nothing to gain from having taken a step that was now declared treason against their comrades, their memories of the hard slog of war: all this put relations on a knife's edge, and heated the atmosphere in the underworld to an extreme. Among the thieves there were those who had gone to war out of moral weakness: they had been threatened with the firing squad, and they would have been shot at the time. The weaker ones followed their leaders, the authorities: life, man, is always life.

The major criminals, the leaders of the war lot, were puzzled but not dismayed. Well, if the old law didn't include them, they'd declare a new one. The new thieves' law was declared in 1948 at the transit camp in Vanino Bay. The port and settlement of Vanino were opened during the war, when Nakhodka, the bay's port, was destroyed in an explosion.

The first steps toward this new law were linked with the semi-legendary name of a criminal called the King, a man of whom the godfathers, who knew and hated him, would many years later say, respectfully, "Well, whatever you say, he had guts..."

Spirit, guts are concepts peculiar to thieves. They include boldness, pushiness, a tendency to shout, an idiosyncratic sort of recklessness, and firmness, combined with a certain hysterical and theatrical quality.

This new Moses possessed these qualities in full.

The new law stated that criminals were allowed to work in the camp and in prison as elders, as work organizers, as guards, and as foremen, to take on a whole series of many other camp posts.

The King negotiated a terrible agreement with the chief of the transit camp: he promised to impose complete order on the transit camp, to use his forces to deal with the godfathers. If in the end it came to bloodshed, he asked that no particular attention be paid to it.

The King reminded the chiefs about his war service (he had been given a medal during the war) and made it understood that the bosses were facing a crucial moment when the right decision could lead to the disappearance of the criminal world and of criminality in our society. He, the King, was undertaking to carry out this difficult mission, and he asked to be allowed to do so without interference.

Presumably, the chief of the Vanino transit camp immediately informed the top authorities and then received approval for the King's operation. Nothing happens in the camps without an arbitrary decision from the local bosses. Moreover, the rules state that everybody spies on everybody else.

The King was promising to go straight! A new thieves' law! What could be better? This is what Makarenko had dreamed of; it was the realization of the deepest wishes of the theoreticians. Finally the criminals had been reforged! At last they had a long-awaited practical confirmation of many theoretical exercises on this subject, starting with Krylenko's "rubber band" and ending with Vyshinsky's theory of retribution.[38]

The camp administration had been taught to regard the nonpolitical criminals, the article 35 convicts, as friends of the people, and it had paid little attention to the invisible processes that had been going on in the criminal world. It didn't detect any worrying information from that world: the camp authorities' net of spies and informers worked in quite different areas. Nobody was interested in moods or in the questions that excited the criminal world.

That world was supposed to have gone straight a long time ago, and finally the hour had come. The proof was, the bosses said, the King's new thieves' law. This was the beneficial effect of the war in action: even among the criminals a feeling of patriotism had been awoken. We, they said, have been reading Vershigora and we've heard about the victories of Rokossovsky's army.

The bosses who were veterans and whose hair had turned gray in the camps were probably skeptical: "Can any good thing come out of

Nazareth?" But they considered, though they didn't say so, that any split, any hostility between two groups of thieves, could only be good and advantageous for everyone else, the ordinary people. "A minus times a minus is a plus," they reminded themselves. "Let's give it a go."

The King got consent for his experiment. During one short northern day the entire population of Vanino was lined up in pairs.

The head of the transit camp recommended their new elder to the prisoners. He was the King. His trusted henchmen were appointed as commanders of the squads.

The new camp support staff didn't waste any time. The King walked up and down the ranks of prisoners, giving each one a penetrating look, and peremptorily called out: "Step forward! You! You! And you!" The King's finger kept moving, often stopping, and never made a mistake. Life as a thief had taught him to be observant. If the King had any doubts, it was very easy to check up, and everyone—the criminals and the King—was well aware of this fact.

"Undress! Take off your shirt!"

Tattoos are the identifying mark of the order, and they played a lethal role. Getting tattooed was a mistake of the young criminals. These indelible designs made the work of criminal investigation very easy. But their deadliest significance was only now revealed.

Reprisals began. With feet, cudgels, brass knuckles, and stones, the King's gang crushed the adherents to the old thieves' law, and with the full support of the law.

"Will you accept our rules?" the King shouted triumphantly. He would now test the spirit of the most obstinate "orthodox" thieves, who had been accusing him of being too weak. "Will you accept our rules?"

A ceremony, a theatrical procedure, was invented to mark this conversion to the new thieves' law. The criminal world loves to be theatrical in life, and if only Yevreinov or Pirandello knew that fact, they wouldn't have missed the chance of enriching their stage theories with these arguments.[39]

The new ceremony was as impressive as the well-known initiation into knights' orders. It's perfectly possible that Walter Scott's novels were the origin of this solemn and grim procedure.

"Kiss the knife!"

A knife blade was put against the lips of a criminal who had already been beaten up.

"Kiss the knife!"

If the godfather agreed and put his lips to the steel blade, he was considered to be a convert to the new faith; he now lost any rights he had in the thieves' world by becoming a bitch forever.

This idea of the King was truly royal. And not only because initiating men into the chivalrous order of criminals was a promise that his army would have plenty of reserves—it was unlikely that the King was thinking of tomorrow or the next day when he introduced this knife ceremony. But he had certainly considered something else! He would impose on all his old prewar friends the same terms—life or death—that he, the King, had been too afraid to face, in the view of the orthodox thieves. Let them now show what they could do! The terms were the same as before.

Anyone who refused to kiss the knife was murdered. Every night new corpses were dragged up to the locked doors of the transit barracks. These victims had not been merely killed. That was not enough for the King. Their former comrades, those who had kissed the knife, signed their names with knives on all the corpses. The criminals were not simply murdered. Before they died they were "put in the bilge," which meant trampled, beaten, and disfigured in every possible way. Only after that were they killed. A year or two later, when a party of prisoners came from Vorkuta and several prominent Vorkuta bitches (in Vorkuta it had been the same story) got off the ship, it became apparent that the Vorkuta men disapproved of the Kolyma men's excessive cruelty. "We just killed them, but as for putting them in the bilge . . . why do that?" The Vorkuta procedures must have been somewhat different from those of the King's gang.

News of the reprisals by the King at Vanino Bay quickly crossed the sea, and in Kolyma the thieves who observed the old law set to defending themselves. Total mobilization was declared; the entire criminal world armed itself. All the forges and metalworking shops in Kolyma secretly labored to make knives, short daggers, and bayonets. The blacksmithing was, of course, not done by gangsters but by real craftsmen on the camp staff who'd been threatened with "something fearful," as the gangsters put it. Long before Hitler, the criminals had known that frightening a man was far more reliable than bribing him. And cheaper, too, obviously. Any metalworker, any blacksmith, would have agreed to sacrificing a percentage of his target production if it meant staying alive.

Meanwhile the energetic King persuaded the bosses that it was essential for him to do a "tour" of the Far East transit camps. Accompanied by seven of his henchmen, he visited all the transit camps as far as Irkutsk, leaving behind him in the prisons dozens of corpses and hundreds of newly converted bitches.

The bitches couldn't stay at Vanino Bay forever. Vanino was a transit camp, from which prisoners moved on. The bitches went overseas, to the gold mines. The war was transferred to a wider area. Thieves murdered bitches; bitches murdered thieves. The figures in Archive No. 3[40] (the dead) leapt up, nearly reaching the record heights of the infamous year of 1938, when whole brigades of Trotskyists were executed.

The bosses grabbed their telephones to get through to Moscow.

It turned out that the most important part of the alluring formula of the new thieves' law was the word "thieves," and reforging had nothing to do with it. Once again the authorities had been made fools of by the cruel and clever King.

Since the beginning of the 1930s, making skillful use of the widespread ideas of "reeducation through labor," criminals had been saving their key personnel by not hesitating to give millions of words of honor, by exploiting both Pogodin's play *The Aristocrats* and the hard-line instructions from the authorities about the need to show trust in the recidivist criminal. Makarenko's ideas and the notorious reforging had in fact allowed the gangsters to use these ideas as a cover for saving and strengthening the position of their key personnel. The official line was that only corrective sanctions, and no punitive ones, were to be applied to the poor criminals. In reality this seemed like a strange concern for looking after the criminal world. Anyone who was not a theoretician—for instance, a camp employee—knew, and always had known, that any reforging or reeducation of a recidivist criminal was out of the question, that all this was a harmful myth. The thief's idea of valor was to deceive the *freiers* and the bosses; you could swear a thousand oaths to a *freier*, a thousand words of honor, so long as he took the bait. The shortsighted playwrights like Sheinin or Pogodin went on, for the greater benefit of the gangster world, preaching the need to trust gangsters. If there was one Captain Kostia who was reformed, then there were tens of thousands who were released early from prison and then committed twenty thousand murders and forty thousand robberies. That was the price paid for *The Aristocrats* and for *Diary of a Criminologist*. Sheinin and Pogodin were far too ill-informed to deal with such an important question. Instead of exposing criminality for what it was, they romanticized it.

In 1938 the criminals were openly called upon in the camps to deal physically with the Trotskyists; gangsters would murder and beat up helpless old men and starving goners. Counterrevolutionary agitation was punishable by death, but the gangsters' crimes had the authorities' protection.

No signs of any reforging were ever discovered in either the criminals' or the bitches' world. The camp morgues merely accumulated hundreds of corpses a day. What seemed to be happening was that the authorities, by accommodating the criminals and the bitches together, were deliberately subjecting both groups to deadly danger.

The instructions not to intervene were very quickly canceled, and separate special zones were set up everywhere for the bitches and for the godfathers. The King and his followers were hurriedly, but belatedly, removed from all their administrative posts in the camps and turned into ordinary mortals. The expression "ordinary mortal" took on an unexpected, special, ominous sense. The bitches were not immortal. It turned out that setting up separate special zones in the territory of the same camp had not done any good. Blood was being shed at the same rate as before. Separate mines had to be set aside for the thieves and for the bitches (these mines, of course, also had, as well as professional criminals, men convicted under other articles of the Criminal Code). Expeditions were mounted: raids by armed bitches or thieves on "enemy" zones. Yet another organizational step had to be taken: entire mine administrations that governed a number of mines had to be assigned to thieves and to bitches. So the Western Administration, and its hospitals, prisons, and camps, was left in the hands of the bitches, while the thieves were concentrated in the Northern Administration.

In the transit camps each criminal had to inform the authorities whether he was a thief or a bitch; depending on his answer, he would be included in a party that was being dispatched to a camp where he would not be in danger of being killed.

The term "bitch" might not properly reflect the real situation and may be terminologically inexact, but it caught on straightaway. However hard the leaders of the new law tried to protest against such an offensive nickname, a better-sounding or more appropriate name could not be found, and they were recorded in official statistics as bitches, a term that they very soon began to apply to themselves. For clarity's sake; for simplicity's sake. Any linguistic argument could rapidly lead to a tragedy.

Time passed; the bloody war of annihilation still raged. How might it end? "How?" mused the sages in the camps. The answer was: in the murder of the leaders of both sides. By now the King had been blown up at some remote mine. (When he slept in a corner of the barracks he was guarded by armed friends. The criminals smuggled a charge of ammonal under the corner of the barracks, which was powerful enough to send the corner bunks flying into the heavens.) By now the majority of the warriors were in the camps' mass graves with wooden tags (that wouldn't rot in the permafrost) on their left legs. The most prominent thieves, One-and-a-half Ivan Babalanov and One-and-a-half Ivan the Greek, had died: they had refused to kiss the bitches' knife. But others who were just as prominent, such as Chibis and Mishka from Odessa, had kissed the knife and were now murdering criminals to the greater glory of the bitches.

A new important factor marked the second year of this fratricidal war.

How? Could the ceremony of kissing the knife change a criminal soul? Or had the notorious crook's blood changed its chemical composition in the veins of an old crook just because his lips had touched a steel blade?

Of those who had kissed the knife, by no means all approved of the new bitches' testament. Many, very many, remained at heart faithful to the old laws, for they had personally condemned the bitches. A number of these criminals, the weak at heart, did try, when they had an opportunity, to go back to the law. But the King's royal idea once again showed how profound and strong it was. The "lawful" thieves threatened the newly converted bitches with death and refused to make any distinction between them and the longstanding bitches. It was then that a few old thieves, who had kissed the bitches' steel, thieves who could not get over their shame and therefore nurtured hatred in their souls, took another amazing approach.

A third thieves' law was declared. This time the criminals of the third law lacked the theoretical powers to work out a program of ideas. Their only guiding principle was anger and the only slogan they had to offer was one of vengeance and bloody enmity toward both the bitches and the thieves equally. They set about physically exterminating both. At first such a surprising number of old crooks joined this group that the authorities were forced to designate a separate mine for them, too. A series of new murders, which the authorities had failed to foresee, thoroughly bewildered the minds of those who ran the camps.

The third group of criminals was given the expressive name of "mayhem men." The mayhem men were also know as Makhnoites, for one of Nestor Makhno's aphorisms during the Civil War, about his attitude toward both Reds and Whites, which was very familiar to the criminal world.[41] More and more new groups began to appear, and they adopted a wide variety of names, such as the "Little Red Hats." The camp authorities were run off their feet trying to find separate accommodation for all these groups.

As time passed, it became clear that the mayhem men were not so numerous. Thieves always operate in company: a lone gangster is unthinkable. In the thieves' underworld the public nature of their orgies and kangaroo courts is essential to both big- and small-time thieves. You have to belong to one of their worlds, to seek and find help, friendship, and a common cause.

The mayhem men had, essentially, a tragic fate. In the bitches' war they had too few on their side; they were a striking psychological phenomenon, their psychology being the most interesting aspect. The mayhem men were also to undergo many particular humiliations.

The fact is that official orders stated that cells for prisoners in transit and under guard had to be of two kinds: one for godfathers, the other for bitch thieves. The mayhem men, however, had to beg the authorities for a place and had to spend time explaining things, had to seek shelter in corners, among *freiers* who had no sympathy for them at all. Almost all the mayhem men were solitary travelers; a mayhem thief had to make a request to the authorities, while the thieves and the bitches demanded their rights. That was why one of the mayhem men, once he was discharged from the hospital and before he was sent off, had to spend three days under the sentries' tower, the safest place, since in the camp he could have been murdered: he refused to enter the zone.

In the first year the bitches seemed likely to end up on top. The energetic measures taken by their chiefs, the corpses of thieves in all the transit points, the permission to send bitches to mines where nobody had risked sending them before—all this hinted that the bitches had gained the upper hand in the war. The ceremony of kissing the knife as a way of recruiting bitches became widely known. The Magadan transit camp was solidly in their hands. As winter came to an end, the godfathers eagerly waited for the shipping season to start. The first ship would decide their fate. What would it bring: life or death?

The ship brought the first lot of hundreds of orthodox criminals from the mainland. There were no bitches among them!

The Magadan transit camp bitches were quickly sent to their own Western Administration. After receiving reinforcements, the thieves came back to life and a bloody struggle flared up with new strength. From year to year, the leading thieves kept being reinforced by newly arrived thieves from the mainland, whereas the ranks of the bitches were increasing through the familiar method of kissing the knife.

The future was no longer as predictable as it used to be. In 1951, Ivan Chaika, one of the most authoritative representatives of the godfather thieves at the time, was included in a party of prisoners to be dispatched. He had just spent a month being treated in the central hospital for prisoners. Chaika hadn't been ill in the least. The chief of the health administration in the mine where Chaika was registered had been threatened with reprisals if he didn't send Chaika for a rest in the hospital; he was promised two suits if he did send him. The health chief did as he was told. Hospital tests didn't show any threat to Chaika's health, but people had already had a chat with the head of the therapy department. Chaika spent a whole month in the hospital and then agreed to be discharged. But when he was being sent from the transit point at the hospital, Chaika was summoned by the labor organizer, who had a list. Chaika asked where the party was heading. The labor organizer thought he would have a joke at Chaika's expense and named one of the Western Administration mines, where godfather thieves were not to be sent. Ten minutes later Chaika declared himself sick and asked for the boss of the transit point to be summoned. The boss appeared with a doctor. Chaika put his left hand, his fingers spread out, on a table; holding a knife in his other hand, he struck at his own hand. Each time the knife cut through down to the wood; then Chaika jerked it free with a sharp movement. The whole action took about a minute or two. Chaika explained to the alarmed boss that he was a thief and knew his rights. He should go to a thieves' place, the Northern Administration. He was not going to the Western Administration to his death; he'd rather lose his hand. The boss was thoroughly cowed and at the same time couldn't make head or tail of what was happening: after all, Chaika was being sent exactly where he wanted to be sent. So, thanks to the labor organizer, Chaika's monthlong rest in the hospital was a bit ruined. If he hadn't asked the organizer where he was being sent, everything would have turned out fine.

The central hospital for prisoners had more than a thousand beds: it was the pride of Kolyma's medicine. It lay in the territory of the Northern Administration. Naturally, the thieves considered it to be their district hospital and not a central hospital. For a long time the hospital authorities tried to rise above the conflict and pretended that it treated patients from any administration. This was not entirely true, for the thieves considered the Northern Administration to be their citadel and insisted on their special rights to its entire territory. The thieves were trying to stop bitches from getting treatment in this hospital, where the conditions for treatment were far better than anywhere else, and, above all, as the central hospital, it had the right to "documentize" invalids so that they could be sent away to the mainland. The thieves tried to get their own way not by written applications nor complaints, not by verbal requests, but by using knives. A few murders witnessed by the head of the hospital were enough to tame him: he grasped what his real position was in such subtle questions. The hospital didn't try for very long to stick to purely medical criteria. When at night a patient has a knife stuck into his belly by the man lying next to him, that has a very convincing effect, despite all the authorities' declarations that this civil war in the criminal world was no concern of theirs. The stubbornness of the hospital administration and its guarantees of safety did at first deceive a few bitches. They agreed to treatment that was offered to them at their workplaces (at the workplace any doctor would agree to "fill in" the medical documents, as long as that would rid the mine at least for a time of the criminal element). The escort guard would bring them to the hospital, but no farther than the admissions room. Here, the bitch would realize where he had landed and demand to be sent back immediately. In the majority of cases, the same escort guard took him away. There was a case when the hospital refused to admit some prisoners and the chief of the escort guards then threw a bundle of personal files into a nearby ditch, abandoned the patients, got into his truck with the other guards, and tried to get away. The truckload of guards had managed to travel about forty kilometers when soldiers and officers from the hospital's guard caught up with it in another truck: their rifles and revolvers were cocked. The fugitives were returned to the hospital under guard, their prisoners were handed back, and everyone parted.

Only once did four bitches, important old crooks, dare to spend the night inside the hospital. They barricaded the door of the ward that had been set aside for them and took turns standing by the door with knives at the ready. In the morning they were sent back. That was the only occasion when weapons were brought openly into the hospital: the hospital tried to turn a blind eye on weapons in the hands of bitches.

Usually, there was a very simple procedure to remove weapons in the admissions room: patients were stripped naked and taken to the next building for a medical examination. After the arrival of each party, the abandoned daggers and knifes were left on the floor and behind the benches. Even bandages were unwrapped and casts removed from fractures, since knives could be bandaged to the body or hidden under dressings.

As time passed, fewer bitches came to the central hospital: the thieves had in effect won their argument with the authorities. A naïve boss who had read too much Sheinin and Makarenko and was secretly, or openly, enchanted by the romantic world of criminality (the words "You know, he's an important thief" were spoken in such a tone that you'd have thought they were talking about some academician who'd discovered the secret of the atomic nucleus), would get it into his head that he was an expert on gangster customs. He'd heard of the Red Cross, of the thieves' attitude toward doctors, and awareness of his own personal contact with thieves tickled his vanity pleasantly.

He'd been told that the Red Cross, meaning medicine and medical workers, and above all, doctors, held a special position in the eyes of the professional criminal world. They were invulnerable, "extraterritorial" as far as thieves' operations were concerned. Moreover, in the camps doctors were protected by the criminals from any misfortunes. Many people fell for, and still fall for, this crude, coarse flattery. Every thief and every doctor in the camp is able to repeat the age-old fairy tale about thieves returning to a doctor a watch (a suitcase, a suit, a pocket watch) as soon as they find out that the victim of the theft was a doctor. That's a variation on "Herriot's Pocket Watch" by Sheinin.[42] There was also a popular story about a starving doctor in prison who was nourished by the well-fed thieves (using parcels taken from others in the cell). There are several similar classic story subjects that, like openings in a game of chess, all follow a definite set of rules.

Is there a core of truth here, and what is it? It all comes down to the gangster's cold-blooded, strict, unprincipled calculations. The truth is that the prisoner's only defender in the camps (and this applies to thieves, too) is the doctor. Neither the camp chief nor the culture organizer can give a prisoner any regular and effective help: only the doctor can. The doctor can admit him to the hospital. The doctor can let him rest for a day or two, which is very important. The doctor can send him off somewhere else, or not send him: any sort of transfer requires a doctor's sanction. A doctor can have someone assigned to light labor and can reduce a man's "labor category": in this most important area, on which lives depend, a doctor is almost entirely free to make his own decisions and, at the very least, the local bosses cannot overrule him. A doctor keeps an eye on the prisoners' food, and if he himself does not take part in plundering that food, then that's all to the good. He can prescribe a slightly better diet. The doctor has major rights and duties. And however bad a doctor he may be, he still remains a moral force in the camp. It is far more important to be able to influence the doctor than to get your claws into the camp chief or to bribe the culture organizer. Doctors have to be bribed very skillfully, and care must be taken when intimidating them; probably doctors do get back things that have been stolen. Not that there are any concrete examples of that happening. More often, you see camp doctors, including the free contract ones, wearing suits or nice trousers that the thieves have given them. The gangster world maintains good relations with the doctor as long as he (or any other medical worker) carries out everything demanded by that insolent gang, and the demands increase as the doctor gets more and more deeply entangled in what he might think are innocent ties with gangsters. After all, sick people, exhausted old men, are left to die on their bunks because their places in the hospital are occupied by healthy criminals having a rest. If the doctor refuses to carry out the criminals' demands, then he is certainly not treated like a representative of the Red Cross. The mine doctor Surovoi, a young Muscovite, refused outright to carry out gangsters' demands to have three of their number sent to the central hospital for a rest. The next evening he was murdered while he was admitting patients: the pathologist counted fifty-two knife wounds on his corpse. An elderly woman doctor, Shitsel, working at a women's mine, refused to exempt a female gangster from work. The next day the woman doctor was hacked to death with an ax: the sentence had been carried out by her own ward assistant. Surovoi was young, honest, and hot-blooded. After he was murdered, he was replaced by Dr. Krapivnitsky, an experienced head of the health section at punishment mines, a free contract doctor who had seen a thing or two.

Dr. Krapivnitsky simply announced that he was not going to treat or to examine anyone. Any necessary medicines would be issued daily by soldiers guarding the hospital. The zone was to be locked down, and the only people who could leave it were the dead. Two years after he was appointed, Dr. Krapivnitsky still held the job and was flourishing.

The closed zone, surrounded by machine guns, cut off from the rest of the world, had its own terrible life. The criminals' grim imagination set up here, in broad daylight, proper courts with sessions, speeches for the prosecution, and witnesses giving evidence. The thieves broke up some bunks and erected a gallows in the middle of the camp; they hanged two exposed bitches on those gallows. All this was done not at night but in broad daylight while the authorities just watched.

Another zone at this mine was considered to be a working one. The lower-ranking thieves came out of it to work. After criminals had been placed there, the mine, of course, stopped producing anything of importance. The influence of the neighboring nonworking zone was always palpable. It was from the working barracks that an old man, an ordinary offender, not a professional criminal, was brought to the hospital. As the criminals who accompanied him said, he had been seen "talking disrespectfully to Vasechka."

Vasechka was a young gangster, a hereditary thief, and therefore one of the leaders. The old man was twice Vasechka's age.

Vasechka felt offended by the old man's tone ("still snarling"); he ordered someone to fetch a length of explosive fuse and a percussion cap. The percussion cap was put in the old man's palm, and his hands were tied together—the old man dared not protest—and the fuse was lit. Both the old man's hands were blown off. Speaking disrespectfully to Vasechka had cost him very dearly.

The war of the bitches was still raging. Inevitably, what some of the cleverer and more experienced bosses had most feared came to pass. Now that they were thoroughly skilled in bloody reprisals—and there was no death penalty at the time for camp murders—both the bitches and the gangsters began using knives on any pretext, even if it had nothing whatsoever to do with the war of the bitches.

If someone thought the cook had given them too little soup, or that the soup was too watery, then the cook would get a dagger in his side and thus give up the ghost.

If a doctor wouldn't release someone from work, he'd get a towel wrapped around his neck and be suffocated.

The head of the surgical department at the central hospital reproached a prominent gangster because doctors were being murdered and the Red Cross had been forgotten. How, he asked, can the earth bear to have people like you on it? Gangsters are very impressed when the bosses discuss such theoretical questions with them. The gangster replied, putting on airs and getting his words out with an inimitable criminal accent, "It's the law of life, doctor. Circumstances vary. One case goes this way, another goes in a completely different direction. Life changes."

Our gangster was pretty good at dialectics. He was an embittered gangster. Once, when he was in solitary confinement and wanted to get to the hospital, he ground the lead of an indelible pencil to powder and put it in his eyes. They did let him out of solitary, but he got proper medical help too late and was permanently blinded.

But being blind didn't stop him from taking part in discussions of all the questions of gangster life, or from giving advice and pronouncing authoritative and enforceable judgments. Like Sir Williams from Ponson du Terrail's *Rocambole*,[43] the blind gangster got on with a life of criminality. His guilty verdict was enough to settle any investigation into the deeds of bitches.

Since time immemorial, the word "bitch" was used for anyone who betrayed the thieves' cause, for any thief who crossed the line and collaborated with the police. But in the war of the bitches things were different: this was about a new thieves' law. All the same, the derogatory term "bitches" was permanently applied to the knights of the new order.

After the first months of the bitches' war, the camp authorities had no fondness for the bitches. They preferred to deal with the old-fashioned type of gangster whom they found easier to understand.

The war of the bitches met the thieves' dark and powerful need for the sensual pleasure they derived from murder; it quenched their thirst for blood. This war was a copy of events that the criminals had witnessed for a number of years. Episodes from real war were reflected, as in a distorting mirror, in the events of criminal life. The breathtaking reality of bloodshed aroused the leaders' enthusiasm to an extreme. Even a banal pickpocketing crime, which was only worth three months in prison, or a burglary was now committed with a sort of creative excitement. These crimes were now associated with what the criminals called an incomparable spiritual tension, a tension of the highest order, a stimulating nervous vibration that made the thief feel he was alive.

How much more acute, sadistically acute, was the feeling to be gotten from murder and bloodshed: the fact that your opponent is a thief like you makes the experience even more acute. The feeling of theatricality so typical of the criminal world finds an outlet in an enormous bloody spectacle that goes on for many years. Now everything, the present and everything in it, is a game, a terrible, lethal game. As Heinrich Heine put it, "people ate flesh, / And the blood was human."[44]

The gangsters' game was an imitation of politics and war. Leading gangsters occupied towns, sent out reconnaissance squads, cut the opponent's lines of communication, condemned and hanged traitors. It was all both reality and a game, a bloody game.

The history of the criminal community goes back many thousands of years and it records many examples of bandits' bloody internecine battles—for robbers' territory, for domination in the criminal world. But many peculiarities of the war of the bitches make it a unique event.

1959

APOLLO AMONG THE CRIMINALS

GANGSTERS don't like poetry. Poetry is totally irrelevant to this overwhelmingly real world. What secret needs or aesthetic demands does a thief's soul have that poetry can meet? What requirements of the professional criminal would poetry satisfy? Yesenin knew a bit about this and guessed at a lot of things. But even the most educated criminals shun poetry: reading rhyming lines seems to them to be a shameful pastime, foolishness as offensive as it is incomprehensible. Pushkin and Lermontov are far too complicated to any man who comes across poetry for the first time in his life. Pushkin and Lermontov require a certain amount of preparation, a certain aesthetic level. You can't use Pushkin, any more than Lermontov, Tiutchev, or Baratynsky,[45] to introduce people to poetry. But there are two authors of classical Russian poetry whose verse does have an aesthetic effect on the un-initiated listener: if you want to teach people to love poetry and understand it, then you have to begin with these authors. They are, of course, Nekrasov and, especially, Aleksei Tolstoy.[46] "Vasili Shibanov" and "The Railway" are the most reliable poems for this purpose, a fact that I have tested many times. But neither of them made any impression on gangsters. It was obvious that they could follow only the plot of any piece, and that they would prefer a prose version or, at least, Aleksei Tolstoy's *The Silver Prince*. In the same way, a landscape description in any novel that was being read aloud said nothing to the souls of the criminal audience, and you could see they wanted to move on as quickly as possible to a description of action, movement, or, at the very least, to dialogue.

The gangster, of course, is not wholly without aesthetic needs, however little he may be human. His needs are satisfied by prison songs, and there are a lot of those. There are epic songs, like the now nearly defunct "Smash and Grab,"[47] or stanzas in honor of the famous Gorbachevsky and other similar stars of the criminal world, or the song "The Solovetsky Islands."[48] There are lyrical songs that express the criminal's feelings, with a very specific coloring: they differ sharply from ordinary songs in their intonation and themes, as well as their outlook.

Prison lyrical songs are usually very sentimental, plaintive, and touching. Despite frequent deviations from normal spelling and grammar, the prison song is always full of feeling. This is also achieved through the melody, which is often idiosyncratic. It may be primitive, but in performance the song's effect is intensified: the singer is no actor, he is a real live participant. The author of a lyrical monologue doesn't need to dress up in theatrical costume.

Our composers haven't yet gotten around to criminal musical folklore: Leonid Utiosov's attempts, such as "From the Odessa Jail,"[49] don't count.

One very widespread song with a memorable tune is "Fate." Its pathetic melody can sometimes bring tears to the eyes of an impressionable listener. It won't do that to a gangster, but even he will listen to "Fate" with solemn and profound gravity.

It begins like this:

> Fate plays a major part in everything
> And you can't get far away from it.
> Everywhere it controls us,
> And you meekly go where it tells you.

Nobody knows the name of the "court" poet who composed the text. "Fate" goes on to tell a very realistic story of the thief's inheritance from his father, his mother's tears, the tuberculosis he catches in prison, and it expresses his firm intention to continue on the path he has chosen in life until the day he dies.

> Whoever has the strength to fight with fate,
> Carry on the fight to the very end.

The gangster has no need for theater, sculpture, or painting. He takes no interest whatsoever in these muses, these forms of art: he is too much of a realist, and his aesthetic emotions are too bloodthirsty, too bound up with real life. It's not a question of naturalism: it's impossible to draw a boundary between art and life, and the exceedingly realistic spectacles that the criminal stages in real life frighten off both art and life.

At one Kolyma mine gangsters stole a twenty-milliliter syringe from the outpatient clinic. What did they want a syringe for? To inject morphine? Perhaps the camp paramedic had stolen a few ampoules of morphine from his boss and had sycophantically offered the drug to the criminals?

Or was it because any medical instrument is extremely valuable in the camp and the doctor can be blackmailed, so that the syringe can be ransomed in exchange for a rest for the godfathers in the barracks?

Neither explanation is correct. The criminals had heard that if you inject air into a vein, the air bubbles will block the brain's blood vessels, forming an embolism. And the victim will die. They had decided to test the truth of this information they had from an unidentified medic. Their imaginations pictured a series of mysterious murders that no chief detective, no Vidocq, no Lecoq or Vanka Kain,[50] could solve.

One night the criminals grabbed some starving *freier* from the solitary cells, tied him up, and gave him an injection by the light of a smoking flare. The victim soon died, and the talkative paramedic was proved right.

Criminals can't understand ballet at all, but dancing, especially Gypsy dancing, has long been a part of the criminal's "honest mirror of youth."[51]

You can always find expert dancers among the criminals, just as they have plenty of lovers of such dances and people who will stage them.

This dance, a Gypsy girl's tap dance, is not as primitive as it may seem at first sight.

Among the criminal "ballet masters," one used to come across extraordinarily gifted virtuosos, who could have set a speech by Akhun Babayev[52] or a headline from yesterday's newspaper to dance.

I'm very weak, but I shall still be compelled
To continue the path of my dead father.

There's an old lyrical romance, of which the criminal world is especially fond, with a classic lead-in:

The mirrorlike waters were lit by the moon—

where the hero complains of being separated and asks his beloved:

Love me, my child, while I'm still free,
While I'm still free, I am yours.
Prison will part us, I shall live in captivity,
My pal will take you over.

The rhythm demands "someone else" instead of "my pal," but the criminal who sings this romance wants to break the meter, to syncopate the rhythm, as long as he can preserve a particular sense, the only one required, of the phrase. "Someone else" would be too ordinary, too much from the *freier* world, whereas "my pal" fits in with the laws of criminal morality. The author of this romance seems not to have been a gangster (unlike the song "Fate," for which there is no doubt that the author was a recidivist criminal).

The romance continues in philosophical tones:

I'm a crook from Odessa, a son of the criminal world,
I'm a thief, it's hard to love me.
Wouldn't it be better, my child, for us to part,
And forget each other forever?

It goes on:

I shall get a sentence, I'll be sent far away,
Far away to Siberian parts.
You will be happy and, perhaps, you'll be rich,
But I shan't: never, never.

There are a great number of epic criminal songs.

> These golden points, these lights
> Remind us of the Solovetsky camps.
>
> (from "The Solovetsky Islands")

The very old "Smash and Grab" is a peculiar hymn of the criminal world; it is widely known and not just in criminal circles.

One classic work of this genre is the song "I can remember a dark autumn night."[53] There are many different versions, later adaptations, of this song. All the later additions and substitutions are worse and coarser than the original version, which gives us a classic image of the ideal criminal safecracker, his job, his present, and his future.

The song describes the planning and execution of a bank robbery, breaking open a safe in Leningrad.

> I remember the drills, steel and strong,
> Buzzing like two bumblebees.
> And now the iron doors were open, where
> The long-awaited money in neat packets
> Was looking at us from the shelves.

The participant in the robbery, after getting his share, immediately leaves town, just like Cascarilla.

> Modestly dressed, a posy in my lapel—
> Wearing a gray English coat,
> At exactly seven thirty I left the capital,
> I didn't even look through the window.

The "capital" is, of course, Leningrad, or rather, Petrograd, which allows us to date the first appearances of this song to sometime between 1914 and 1924.

The hero leaves for the south, where he meets a "miracle of earthly beauty." It is clear that

> The money, like snow, very quickly melted.
> I had to go back,
> I had again to dive deep into
> Sullen and vicious Leningrad.

Then comes a "case," arrest, and the last stanza:

> Along a dusty road, under strict guard
> I'm off to criminal court,
> I'm now getting ten years' strict,
> Or a pass to the next world.

All these are works with specific themes. At the same time, other excellent songs, such as "Open the window, open it: I haven't long to live," or "Don't cry, my girlfriend," especially in its original version from Rostov, are popular in the gangster world and find plenty of people to perform them and to listen to them.

The romances, "How good you were, blue night" or "I remember the little garden and the avenue," don't have anything specifically gangsterish about them but are still popular with thieves.

Every criminal romance, including the famous "It's not for us that the accordions will be playing" or "Autumn Night," has dozens of different versions, as if the romance has undergone the same process as the "novel," being reduced to an outline, a skeleton for the performer's own effusions.[54]

Sometimes *freier* romances are subjected to significant changes as they become imbued with a criminal spirit.

Thus the romance "Don't talk to me about him" has been turned by the criminals into a very lengthy (prison time is lengthy time) "Murochka Bobrova." The original has no Murochka Bobrova. But criminals like things to be called by a name. They also like detailed descriptions.

> The carriage drove up to the courthouse.
> A voice called out, "Get out,

This way, up the steps and around,
Don't look to either side."

The key places are listed tersely.
A blonde, eyes burning,
Bowed her head meekly,
And she went all pale,
And covered her face with her scarf.

The court chairman says to her,
"Listen, Murochka Bobrova,
Are you guilty of this, or not,
You'll have to say a few words."

Only after this detailed "exposition" does the usual romance text follow:

Don't talk to me about him,
What's happened is not yet forgotten—

Etcetera.

Everyone says that I'm sad,
That I've stopped trusting people,
Everyone says that I'm ill,
But perhaps I'm just tired of life.

Finally comes the last stanza:

Hardly had she finished
Than a horrible shout came from her chest,
And their sentence at the trial
Was broken off before it was read.

The fact that they didn't finish reading the sentence always moves the criminals greatly.

*

The dislike gangsters feel for songs sung by choirs is very typical of them. Even the universally known "The reeds were rustling, the trees were bending, and the night was dark" hasn't managed to touch the criminals' hearts. "The reeds were rustling" is not popular with them.

Gangsters don't have any choir songs, they never sing together, and if *freiers* start singing one of the immortal songs, like "There used to be merry days" or "Khaz-Bulat," the thief will not only refuse to join in but he'll leave rather than listen to it.

Gangster singing is exclusively solo, sitting somewhere by a barred window or lying on a bunk with his hands under his head. A gangster will never sing when invited or asked to; every time he starts unexpectedly, because he feels the need to. If he is a good singer, the voices in the cell will fall silent and everyone will listen to him. The singer enounces the words quietly and carefully as he sings one song after another, with no accompaniment, of course. The absence of an accompaniment seems to increase the song's expressiveness: it is certainly not a defect. There are orchestras, brass bands, and string ensembles in the camps, but all that is the devil's work: gangsters almost never play instruments, even though gangster law does not expressly forbid such activity.

It's completely understandable why prison vocals have only been able to develop as solo singing. This is a necessity that has its origins in history. No choral singing would have been allowed within prison walls.

All the same, even in their dens outside of prison, gangsters do not sing choral songs. Their parties and orgies dispense with choral singing. This is yet more evidence of the thief's wolfish nature, his dislike of anything collegial, which may have its source in the habits of prison life.

There are few lovers of reading among the professional criminals. Of tens of thousands of criminal personalities, I can recall only two for whom books were not something inimical, foreign, and alien. The first of these was the pickpocket Rebrov, a hereditary thief: his father and elder brother followed the same calling. Rebrov was a philosophically minded young man who could pretend to be anyone he liked and could maintain with understanding a conversation on general topics.

In his youth Rebrov had managed to get some education: he studied at a technical college for cinematography. His much-loved mother fought a constant battle in the family for her youngest son, as she tried at any cost to save him from his father's and brother's terrible fate. But the crook's blood turned out to be stronger than love of his mother: Rebrov left college and never did anything but thieve. His mother continued fighting for her son. She married him off to a friend of her daughter, who was a village schoolteacher. Rebrov had once raped this girl, but afterward at his mother's insistence he married her and lived with her happily, on the whole, always going back to her after numerous spells "inside." Rebrov's wife bore him two little daughters, whose photographs he kept on him all the time. His wife often wrote to console him as best she could; he never bragged, he never boasted of her love and never showed anyone her letters, although women's letters were usually common property to a gangster's pals. He was now over thirty. Later on, he converted to the thieves' law of the bitches: he had his throat cut in one of the countless bloody battles.

Thieves treated him with respect, but they disliked and distrusted him. They were repelled by his love of reading, his literacy in general. Rebrov's comrades found him a complex and therefore incomprehensible and worrying character. They were irritated by his habit of setting out his thoughts briefly, clearly, and logically: it made them suspect there was something alien about him.

Thieves think it right to support their younger colleagues, to "feed them up"; each "big" gangster has a number of adolescent thieves he feeds.

Rebrov suggested following a different principle.

"If you're a thief," he told an adolescent, "you should be able to fend for yourself: I'm not going to feed you, I'd rather give the food to a hungry *freier*."

At the next kangaroo court, where this new heresy was discussed, Rebrov managed to prove that he was right and the decision of the court of honor was in his favor, but his behavior, which had broken the thieves' traditions, met with no sympathy.

The second reader among thieves was Genka Cherkasov, a hairdresser in one of the camp sectors. Genka was a genuine booklover: he would read anything he got his hands on, and he read day and night. "I've done it all my road"—by "road" he meant life, he explained. Genka was a housebreaker, a burglar, who specialized in breaking into people's apartments.

"Everyone steals," he would say noisily and proudly, "all sorts of rags"—he meant clothes—"but I steal books. All my pals used to laugh at me. Once I robbed a library. I took the stuff out on a truck; I swear to God it's true."

More appealing to him than being a successful thief, was Genka's dream of a career as a prison "novel-writer," a storyteller; he loved telling anyone who'd listen all sorts of stories, such as *The Viazemsky Princes* or *The Jack of Hearts Club*,[55] which were classics of prison literature. On each occasion Genka would ask for any remarks about faults in his performance; he dreamed of telling stories "in different voices."

Those were the two men of the gangster world for whom books were something important and necessary.

But the mass of thieves recognize only "novels," which satisfied them in full.

I noticed, however, that not everyone liked detective stories, even though you'd think they would be a thief's favorite. But a good historical novel or a romance was listened to far more attentively. "You see, we know all that," Seriozha Ushakov, a railway thief, used to say, "it's all about our life. We're fed up with detectives and thieves. As if we weren't interested in anything else."

Apart from novels and prison romances, there were films, too. All gangsters are fanatical cinema lovers: this is the only form of art that they deal with "face-to-face": they see movies not less but more often than the average townsperson.

In films their clear preference is for detective stories, foreign ones in particular. Criminals are taken only by the cruder comedy films, where the action is funny. Witty dialogue is not for them.

Apart from movies, there is dancing, tap dancing in particular.

There is one other thing that feeds the criminals' aesthetic feelings. This is "exchanging experience" in prison, telling each other about their "cases," tales told on prison bunks while waiting for trial or deportation.

These stories, exchanging experience, occupy a prominent place in a thief's life. They are by no means a waste of time. They are summings up, training, and education. Each thief shares the details of his life, his ventures and adventures, with his comrades. A lot of a gangster's time in prison, and in the camps, is spent on these stories (which are only partly a way of checking up on and examining a thief who is a stranger).

These stories are a self-composed reference: "with whom did you run around" is shorthand for "with whom did you run around the lights," which means, with which well-known thieves (even if the criminal world has only heard of them but not met them) did you work?

What "people" know you? This question is usually answered by a detailed account of one's exploits. This is a "legal" requirement: the story helps gangsters straightaway to make a fairly accurate judgment about a stranger; they know what can be discounted and what can be taken as the absolute truth.

Recounting a thief's exploits is always done with embellishments, to glorify the thieves' laws and behavior: this is extremely dangerous, as it becomes a romantic lure for younger thieves.

Every fact is embroidered with seductive and attractive colors (gangsters don't spare the colors), so that any boy who finds himself among thieves (say, after his first theft) and is listening gets carried away and is delighted by the gangster's heroic behavior. Such stories are entirely fictional fantasies. ("If you don't believe it, take it as a fairy tale!")

All these "neat packets of long-awaited money," diamonds, orgies, women especially, are gestures of self-assertion: lying in this case is not considered a sin.

Even if the grand orgy in the den was just a modest mug of beer, drunk on credit in the Summer Garden, the lying accounts are unstoppable.

Once a storyteller has been "checked out," he can lie as much as he likes.

Other people's exploits, which the storyteller has heard at some prison transit point, are appropriated by the inspired fantasist, who puts ten times as much coloring into it as he presents someone else's adventure as his own.

That's the way criminal romanticism is created.

It turns the head of any youth or boy. He is enthusiastic; he wants to imitate his living heroes. He runs errands for them, looks them in the eye hoping for a smile, hangs on their every word. Actually, such boys have nobody else to attach themselves to, since fraudsters and peasants who have broken farm laws stay clear of young thieves aiming to become recidivists.

There is no doubt that this boastful exaggeration of one's own person conceals a certain aesthetic sense of the same order as literary fiction. If the criminal's literary fiction is the "novel" as an oral work, then such conversations are a form of oral memoirs. What is being talked about is not the technical questions of operational thieving; it is an inspired narration of how "Kolia the Laugh whacked a cop and left no clues," or "Katia the Girl Burglar seduced the prosecutor": in a word, these are memoirs narrated at leisure.

Their power to deprave is enormous.

1959

SERGEI YESENIN AND THE WORLD OF THIEVES

> They are all murderers or thieves,
> As fate allotted them to be.
> I've grown to love their sad eyes
> And their sunken cheeks.
> There's a lot of evil from joy in murder,
> Their hearts are simple,
> But on their blackened faces
> Blue lips are twisted.

THE PARTY of prisoners on its way north through the villages in the Urals was a party straight out of a book, so similar was it to what you might read in Korolenko, Tolstoy, Vera Figner, and Nikolai Morozov.[56] This was in the spring of 1929.

Drunken escort guards with crazed eyes, punching prisoners in the back of the neck or slapping them in the face; every minute the click of rifle bolts; a Fedorov-sectarian,[57] cursing the "dragons"; fresh straw on the dirt floor of sheds that served as housing for prisoners on the march; mysterious tattooed men wearing engineer's caps; endless checks and roll calls; and counting, counting, counting...

The last night before the prisoners' journey on foot: a night of salvation. Looking at their comrades' faces, those who knew Yesenin's poetry—and in 1929 very many did—wondered at the poet's utterly exact words:

> But on their blackened faces
> Blue lips are twisted

Everyone's lips really were blue, and their faces were black and twisted from pain and from the many bleeding cracks on their lips.

Once, when for some reason walking was easier, or the distance covered was shorter than usual—so much so that everyone settled down for the night when it was still light, and they all rested—in the corner where the thieves were lying, you could hear quiet singing, more like a recitative with an improvised tune:

You don't love me, you have no pity...

A thief finished the romance and, when he had gotten a lot of listeners, he said solemnly, "It's banned."

"It's Yesenin," said someone.

"Suppose it is," said the singer.

Already, just three years after the poet's death, his popularity in criminal circles was very great.

He was the only poet who was accepted and consecrated by the criminals, who generally disliked poetry altogether.

Later, the gangsters made him a classic, and to refer to him respectfully became a sign of good manners among thieves.

Every knowledgeable criminal is familiar with such poems as "Spill the notes, accordion," "Again they're drinking, fighting, and weeping here." Yesenin's "Letter to Mother" is very well known. His *Persian Motifs*, his longer poems, his early verse are completely unknown.

What is Yesenin's affinity to gangsters?

Above all, an unconcealed sympathy for the gangsters' world can be traced throughout Yesenin's verse. Several times it is expressed openly and clearly. We remember well:

Everything that lives has a special mark
Noticeable from early on.
If I weren't a poet,
Then I'd surely be a crook and a thief.

Gangsters remember those lines well, too. Just as they remember the earlier (1915) "In the land where the yellow nettles," and many, many other poems.

But there is something else besides the open statements. It's not just in the lines of "The Man in Black" where Yesenin gives himself a purely gangster's assessment:

> That man was a risk-taker,
> But one of the highest
> And best sort.

The mood, the attitude, and the tone of a whole series of Yesenin's poems are close to the gangsters' world.

So what familiar notes do gangsters hear in Yesenin's poetry?

Above all, they hear notes of anguish, everything that arouses pity, everything related to "prison sentimentality."

> I never hit wild animals on the head,
> They are our younger brothers.

The verses about a dog, a fox, about cows and horses, are understood by criminals as the word of a man who is cruel to human beings and kind to animals.

Gangsters are capable of stroking a dog and then ripping it apart alive: they have no moral barriers, but they are very inquisitive, especially as to the question, "Will it survive, or won't it?" They begin in early childhood observing the torn-off wings of a butterfly they've caught and a bird with its eyes gouged out; then, when they grow up, they gouge out a man's eyes, out of the same pure curiosity that they had as children.

Yesenin's poems about animals make gangsters think they have found a kindred soul. They don't take these poems with tragic seriousness. They think they're just clever rhymed declarations.

The criminals are sensitive to the notes of challenge, protest, doom, all elements of Yesenin's poetry. They're not interested in any "Mare's Ships" or "Pantocrator": criminals are realists. There is a lot in Yesenin's poetry that they don't understand and therefore reject. The simplest verses in the *Moscow of the Inns* cycle is taken by them to be a feeling akin to their souls, to their underworld life with prostitutes and grim underground orgies.

Drunkenness, orgies, celebrations of debauchery all find a response in the thieves' souls.

The criminals make bold cuts, however, in the poems they know and, in their own way, love: so in the poem "Spill the notes, accordion" the criminals' scissors have removed the last stanza, because of the words:

> Darling, I'm crying,
> Forgive me ... Forgive me ...

The foul language that Yesenin incorporates into his verses always arouses delight. Of course it does! The speech of any criminal is laced with the most complex, multistoried, highly developed foul curses: that's their lexicon, their life.

And now they have a poet who has not forgotten this side of things, so important to them.

Poeticizing hooliganism also raised Yesenin's popularity among the thieves, although you might think that this side of him would find no sympathy in the thieves' world. After all, thieves try hard, in the eyes of the *freiers*, to draw a sharp distinction between themselves and hooligans: they actually are something quite different from hooligans, for they are far, far more dangerous. In the eyes of the man in the street, however, a hooligan is even more frightening than a thief.

The hooliganism that Yesenin celebrates in verse is seen by the thieves as something that happens in their dens, their underworld sprees, their reckless and grim orgies.

> I'm as doomed a person as you are,
> I can no longer go back.

Each poem in *Moscow of the Inns* has notes that echo in the criminal's soul. What do they care about the profound humanity or the radiant lyricism that lies at the heart of Yesenin's poetry?

What they need from it are different lines that accord with them. And Yesenin has these lines, this tone of a person with a grudge against the world, a man insulted by the world.

There is one other side of Yesenin's poetry that brings him close to the dominant concepts of the gangsters' world and its code of morals.

I mean the attitude to women. Gangsters despise women; they consider them to be a lower order. Women deserve nothing but taunts, coarse jokes, and beatings.

The gangster doesn't give children a thought: his morality has no duties or concepts that bind him to his "posterity."

What will his daughter be? A prostitute? A thief? What will his son be? The criminal doesn't care in the least. And doesn't the thieves' law require a thief to surrender his girlfriend to a more authoritative comrade?

> But as for my children,
> I've scattered them over the world.
> As for my wife,
> I lightheartedly handed her to someone else.

Here too, the poet's moral principles are in complete harmony with the rules and tastes sanctified by thieves' traditions and life.

> Drink, you ugly bitch, drink!

The criminals know Yesenin's verses about drunken prostitutes by heart: they've long since made them a weapon. Just like his "The nightingale has one more good song" and "You don't love me, you don't pity me," which have been included with an improvised tune in the golden treasury of criminal folklore. So has:

> Don't snort, troika running late.
> Our life has passed, not leaving a trace.
> Perhaps tomorrow a hospital bunk
> Will give me peace forever.

The criminal singers replace the hospital bunk with a prison one.

A cult of the mother, side by side with a coarse, cynical, contemptuous attitude toward wives and other women, is a typical mark of the thieves' way of life.

In this respect, too, Yesenin's poetry reproduces the concepts of the gangster world with the utmost subtlety.

For a gangster his mother is the subject of sentimental wonderment, she is his "holy of holies." This is also part of a thief's rules of good behavior, his "spiritual" traditions. Combined with a thuggish attitude toward women in general, this sickly-sweet sentimental attitude toward the mother looks fake and dishonest. But the cult of the mother is the gangsters' official ideology.

Literally every gangster knows Yesenin's first "Letter to Mother" ("Are you still alive, my old woman?"). This is the gangster's equivalent of "God's bird" from Pushkin's *The Gypsies*.[58]

In fact all of Yesenin's other poems about his mother, even if their popularity doesn't compare with the "Letter," are also well known and approved of.

Certain aspects of the mood of Yesenin's poetry coincide with an amazingly well intuited fidelity to the concepts of the gangster world. This explains the poet's great, special popularity among thieves.

When gangsters try to emphasize their closeness to Yesenin and show the whole world, as it were, their connection to the poet's verses, they tattoo their bodies with quotations from Yesenin—a typically theatrical gesture. The most popular lines that you often find on very many young criminals, mixed with sexual depictions, playing cards, and cemetery epitaphs, are:

> How few are the roads I've walked,
> How many the mistakes I've made.

Or:

> If I must burn, then let me burn entirely.
> Anyone who's burned out, can't be set fire to.

I put my money on the queen of spades,
And played an ace of diamonds.

I don't think any other poet in the world has yet been publicized in such a way.

Only Yesenin has been accorded this peculiar honor of recognition by the gangster world.

Recognition is a process. It took two or three decades for a cursory interest at first acquaintance to result in the inclusion of Yesenin's poetry in the compulsory library of the young criminal, with the approval of all the leaders of the underworld. Those were the years when Yesenin was being published rarely or not at all (even now, *Moscow of the Inns* is no longer published), which only increased the trust and interest that the poet aroused among criminals.

The gangster world dislikes poetry. There is no place for poetry in this gloomy world. Yesenin is the exception. It's worth noting that his biography and his suicide have played no part whatsoever in his success there.

Professional criminals don't know what suicide is: the percentage of suicides among them is zero. More-educated thieves have explained Yesenin's death as the result of the poet not being a proper thief; he was a sort of "halfway thief," a "spoiled *freier*," capable, in their eyes, of anything.

But Yesenin had, of course, as any gangster, educated or not, will tell you, a drop of crook's blood.

date unknown

HOW "NOVELS" ARE "PRINTED"

PRISON time is time prolonged. Prison hours are infinite because they are monotonous and have no story to tell. Life, displaced into an interval of time from reveille to end of work, is strictly regulated: it conceals an inner musical element, a certain even rhythm of prison life, which organizes a stream in the flow of individual mental shocks, personal dramas that have been imported from outside, from the noisy and varied world outside the prison walls. This prison symphony also includes a starry sky, divided into grids, and a flicker of sunlight bouncing off the rifle barrel of the sentry who is standing on the guard tower, a tower whose architecture resembles that of a skyscraper. This symphony also includes the unforgettable sound of the prison lock, its musical ring, like the noise made by ancient merchants' chests. And many, many other things besides.

There are few external impressions in prison time, which is why time in prison later seems to be a black abyss, a vacuum, a bottomless pit from which your memory can only with a reluctant effort retrieve any event. That's inevitable: after all, nobody likes to remember bad things, and memory, obediently carrying out its master's secret will, pushes unpleasant events back into the darkest corners. Were they events, anyway? The scales of concepts have been changed, and the reasons for a prison quarrel that ends in bloodshed seem quite incomprehensible to an outsider. Later that time will seem to be blank and empty: time will seem to have flown by quickly, flying by all the quicker for the slowness with which it was dragged out.

But the clockwork is still something absolute. It is the source of order in the chaos. It is the geographical grid of meridians and parallels against which the islands and continents of our lives are mapped out.

This rule applies to normal life, too, but in prison its essence is more exposed and more undeniable.

It is these long prison hours that thieves try to shorten by their "memoirs," and not only by mutual boasting, monstrous bragging, when they colorfully describe their robberies and other adventures. Those stories are fiction, artistically simulated events. Medicine has the term "aggravation": exaggeration, when a trivial illness is presented as serious suffering. Thieves' tales are like this aggravation. A pennyworth of truth is turned into a silver ruble to be exchanged in public.

A gangster talks about whom he ran around with, where he used to steal, and provides his unknown comrades with a reference for himself; he talks about breaking into unbreakable Miller safes, when in fact his burglaries went no further than stealing clothes from a wash line at a suburban cottage.

The women he has lived with are extraordinary beauties, virtual millionairesses.

There is something more important and, in essence, dangerous in all this fibbing, these mendacious memoirs, quite apart from a certain aesthetic enjoyment of the process of storytelling—a pleasure for both storyteller and listener.

The fact is that these prison hyperboles are the criminal world's propaganda and agitation material, and the material is quite significant. These stories are a gangster's university, a faculty of their terrible science. Young thieves listen to their elders and reaffirm their faith. Reverence for heroes of nonexistent exploits is instilled into young minds, and they themselves dream of achieving the same. This is the neophyte's initiation taking place. The young criminal remembers these teachings for the rest of his life.

Perhaps the gangster storyteller actually wants, like Gogol's Khlestakov,[59] to believe in his inspired lies. They make him feel stronger and better.

Finally, when a gangster's acquaintance with his new friends is sealed, when the oral questionnaires of the new arrivals have been filled in, when the waves of bragging die down and some episodes of the memoirs, the most spicy, have been repeated twice and committed to memory so that any one of the listeners will in different surroundings present someone else's adventures as his own, all the same the prison day seems never-ending. Then suddenly someone has a good idea: "How about printing a novel?"

Some tattooed figure then climbs out into the yellow light of the electric bulb, a light of so little candlepower that it is difficult to settle down to reading: the figure then begins with his gabbled "debut," which resembles the usual opening gambit of a chess game: "In the city of Odessa, before the revolution, there lived a famous prince and his beautiful wife . . ."

"Printing," or literally "churning out," means "retelling" in gangster language, and the origin of this colorful slang term is easily guessed. A retold novel is a sort of oral offprint of a narrative.

The novel in this case does not need to be a novel, a tale, or a story in accepted literary forms. It can also be any memoir, movie, or historical monograph. The criminal's novel is always someone else's anonymous work, expounded orally. Nobody ever names or knows the author.

It is essential for the story to be long: after all, one of its purposes is to pass the time.

Such a novel is always half improvised, since it was heard somewhere else and partly forgotten, partly embroidered with new details, the color depending on the storyteller's abilities.

There are several particularly widespread and popular novels, as well as some scenario outlines that even the Semperante improvisation theater[60] would have envied.

These favorites are, of course, detective stories.

It's a curious fact that modern Soviet detective stories are completely rejected by the thieves. Not because they lack ingenuity or talent: the things the thieves do listen to are even more primitive and mediocre. In any case it is up to the storyteller to make up for what Adamov's[61] or Sheinin's stories lack.

No, the thieves are simply not interested in modernity. "We know our own lives better," they say, and rightly so.

The most popular novels are *Prince Viazemsky*, *The Jack of Hearts Club*, the immortal *Rocambole*—the remains of the amazing Russian and foreign pap that Russians read in the nineteenth century, when not only was Ponson du Terrail considered a classic but so was Xavier de Montépin and his multivolume novels *The Detective Murderer* and *An Innocent Man Executed*, etc.[62]

Among the plots taken from good-quality literary works, *The Count of Monte Cristo* used to have a solid place; on the other hand, *The Three Musketeers* was a total failure and was treated as a comic novel. So the idea of a French director to film *The Three Musketeers* as a merry operetta must have had a sound basis.

No mysticism, no fantasies, no psychology: strong plots and naturalism with a sexual bent—that was the slogan for gangsters' oral literature.

One of these novels, if you listened closely, showed that it was derived from Maupassant's *Bel Ami*.[63] Of course, the title and the heroes' names were quite different, and the plot itself was subjected to considerable changes. But the basic structure, the career of a pimp, remained.

Anna Karenina was reworked by the gangster novelists in exactly the same way as it was when it was staged by the Moscow Art Theater. The whole Levin-Kitty plot was swept aside. Without its scenery and with the heroes renamed, the novel made a strange impression. Passionate love, arising instantly. A count squeezing (in the literal sense of the word) the heroine at the entrance to the railway carriage. The errant mother visiting her son. The count and his mistress on a spree abroad. The count's jealousy and the heroine's suicide. It was only the wheels of the train, Tolstoy's rhyme for the railway carriage, that told you what was going on.

Les Misérables was a story that people were happy to tell and to listen to. The author's mistakes and naïvety in portraying French criminals was condescendingly corrected by Russian gangsters.

Even the biography of the poet Nekrasov (apparently using one of Kornei Chukovsky's books)[64] was used to concoct an absolutely amazing detective story with Panov (Nekrasov's pseudonym) as the main hero.

These novels were narrated by the thieves who liked them, but mostly in a monotonous and boring voice: it was uncommon to find a gangster storyteller who was the sort of artist, or born poet, or actor capable of bringing any plot to life with a thousand surprises. If such an expert was found, all the gangsters who happened to be in the prison cell at the time would gather around to listen. Nobody would go to sleep until morning, and the expert's underworld fame would reach a long way. The fame of such a novelist would be not less but rather greater than that of any Kaminka or Andronikov.[65]

In fact, every storyteller was called a novelist. This was a concept with a definite meaning, a term in the criminal vocabulary: "novel" and "novelist."

The novelist or storyteller was, of course, not necessarily a criminal. In fact a noncriminal, *freier* novelist was even more highly valued, for the stories he could tell were stories that criminals could give only in a limited range, just a few popular plots, nothing else. It was always possible that a new man, an outsider, might have memorized some interesting story. If he was able to tell this story, then he would be rewarded by the old crooks' patronizing attention, for art wasn't enough to save your clothes or your parcel from home. The Orpheus legend was just a legend, after all. But if there was no real cause to fight over, then a novelist would get a place on a bunk next to the gangsters and an extra bowl of soup at dinner.

But it would be wrong to assume that novels existed only to while away prison time. No, their significance was greater, deeper, more serious, more important.

The novel was virtually the only way in which gangsters came into contact with art. The novel responded to the gangster's monstrous but powerful aesthetic needs: he didn't read books, magazines, or newspapers; he "scoffed his culture" (a special expression) in this oral form.

Listening to novels is a sort of cultural tradition highly respected by gangsters. Novels have been recited since time immemorial; they are sanctified by the entire history of the criminal world. That is why it is considered a sign of good manners to listen to novels, to love and patronize this sort of art. The gangster is a traditional Maecenas to novelists; he's brought up to like them, and nobody will refuse to listen to a novelist, even if they are bored to tears. It's clear, of course, that robberies, thieves' discussions, and the obligatory passionate interest in cards, with its unbridled recklessness, are all rather more important than novels.

Any minute of leisure puts people in the mood for novels. Card games are forbidden in prison, and although a pack of cards can be manufactured with incredible speed using a piece of newspaper, a stub of an indelible pencil, and a bit of chewed bread—this shows the thousand years of experience of generations of thieves—it's still not always possible to play cards in prison.

No criminal will ever admit he doesn't like novels. Novels are, as it were, a sacrosanct part of the thieves' confession; they are included in his code of conduct and his spiritual needs.

Criminals don't like books or reading. Very seldom does one come across any who have been taught from childhood to love books. Such "monsters" read virtually in secret, hiding from their comrades, for they are afraid of biting, coarse sarcasm, as if they were doing the devil's work, something unworthy of a gangster. Gangsters hate intellectuals because they envy them: they feel any unnecessary education to be something foreign, alien. And yet it is *Bel Ami* or *The Count of Monte Cristo*, as they appear in their novel version, which arouse general interest.

Of course, a reading gangster could explain to a listening gangster what it was all about, but . . . traditions are very powerful.

No literary historian, no writer of memoirs, has even touched on this variety of oral literature, which has existed from time immemorial to our own times.

Using the old crooks' terminology, "novels" are not only novels, and what matters is not just the way they stress the word, as *róman* instead of *román*. Even a literate chambermaid, carried away by Anton Krechet,[66] or Nastia in Gorky's story, spending her time reading *Fateful Love*, got the stress wrong.

"Printing novels" is the most ancient of thieves' customs, with all its religious obligations, which are part of the gangster's credo, along with playing cards, drunkenness, debauchery, robbery, escape attempts, and courts of honor. This vital element of the criminal way of life is their equivalent of fiction.

The concept of a novel is fairly broad. It includes various prose genres: the novel, the tale, and any short story, authentic ethnographical essays, theater plays, radio plays, and a retelling of a movie someone has seen, the language rendered from screenplay into libretto version.

The outline of the plot is interwoven with the storyteller's improvisations: strictly speaking, a "novel" is a momentary creation, like a theater performance. It happens just once and becomes even more ephemeral and fluid than an actor's art on the stage, for the actor is still keeping to a fixed text that the playwright gave him. In the well-known "theater of improvisation" there was far less improvisation than in any prison or camp "novel."

The older novels, like *The Jack of Hearts Club* or *Prince Viazemsky*, have long vanished from the Russian reader's market. Historians of literature will sink no lower than *Rocambole* or Sherlock Holmes.

Nineteenth-century Russian pulp fiction still survives in the gangsters' underground. These are the old novels that criminal novelists tell (or "churn out"). They are criminal classics, as it were.

A *freier* storyteller, in the overwhelming majority of cases, can retell a work that he read on the "outside." To his own great amazement, it is in prison that he first finds out about *Prince Viazemsky*, after he has heard it from a criminal novelist.

"It happened in Moscow, on Razguliai; Count Pototsky often came to a high-society 'hideout.' He was a healthy young man."

"Slow down, slow down," the listeners say.

The novelist slows down the tempo. He usually goes on telling the story until he is completely exhausted: until at least one listener has fallen asleep it is considered indecent to break off the story. Decapitated heads, packets of dollars, jewels found in the stomach or intestines of some high-society "Marianne" come one after the other in the story.

Finally, the novel is over, and the exhausted novelist clambers back to his place, while the satisfied listeners unfold their colorful quilted blankets—essential possessions in the life of any self-respecting gangster.

That's what a novel is like in prison. It's different in the camps.

Prison and labor camp are different things, quite unlike each other in their psychological content, despite seeming to have much in common. Prison is far closer to ordinary life than camp life.

The almost invariably innocent, amateur literary aura that being a novelist has for a *freier* in prison suddenly takes on a tragic and ominous nuance.

You might think that nothing has changed. The same gangsters who ask for the stories, the same evening hours for telling them, the same subjects for novels. But now novels are recited for a crust of bread, for a gulp of soup poured into your tin mug from an empty tin can.

Here there are more novelists than anyone needs. Dozens of hungry men have a claim to that crust of bread or gulp of soup; there were cases when a half-dead novelist collapsed, unconscious from hunger, in the middle of the story. To prevent such cases, the custom arose to let the next novelist have a sip of soup before he "churned." That sensible custom became fixed.

In the crowded camp's solitary cells, like a prison within a prison, the gangsters were usually in charge of distributing food. The administration hadn't the strength to do battle with that way of doing things. After the gangsters had their fill, the rest of the barracks would then get to eat.

An enormous earthen-floor barracks was illuminated by a smoking kerosene lamp.

Everyone except the thieves had done a full day's work, spending many hours in the icy cold. The novelist wanted to get warm, to sleep, to lie down, to sit down, but even more than sleep, warmth, and peace, he wanted food, any food. By an unbelievable, fabulous effort of will, he mobilizes his brain for a two-hour novel to give the gangsters pleasure. And as soon as he finishes his detective story, the novelist sips his "gulp of soup," which is now cold and covered with a crust of ice, and then laps up and licks the homemade tin mug until it is dry. He doesn't need a spoon: his fingers and tongue will be more use to him than any spoon.

In total exhaustion, in constant vain efforts to fill, if only for a minute, his shrunken stomach, which is now devouring itself, a former university lecturer offers himself as a novelist. He knows that if he is successful and his customers approve, he will be fed and protected from beatings. The professional criminals believe in his storytelling abilities, no matter how emaciated and exhausted he is. In the camps people don't judge others by their clothes, and any "scruff" (a colorful term for a bedraggled individual dressed in torn rags, with the cotton-wool padding sticking out from all over his pea coat) may turn out to be a great novelist.

Having earned his soup and, if lucky, a crust of bread, the novelist shyly chomps it in a dark corner of the barracks, arousing his comrades' envy, for they don't know how to churn out novels.

If he is even more successful, the novelist will be treated to some tobacco, too. That is the height of bliss! Dozens of eyes will watch his trembling fingers rubbing the tobacco and rolling a cigarette. Should the novelist clumsily spill a few precious flakes of tobacco on the ground, he may burst into real tears. How many hands will be stretched out in the darkness toward him, so as to light up his cigarette with a coal from the burning stove and, as they light it up, at least get a breath of tobacco smoke. And quite a few pleading voices behind his back will utter the tried and tested formula, "Let's have a smoke," or use the mysterious synonym of this formula, "forty..."[67]

That's what the novel and the novelist are like in the camps.

From the day the novelist enjoys success, nobody will be allowed to upset him, or to beat him: he'll even be given bits and pieces to eat. He can now boldly ask gangsters for a smoke, and they will leave him their stubs: he will now have won a position at court, and will wear a gentleman-in-waiting's uniform.

Every day he has to be ready with a new novel—there's a lot of competition—and it will be a relief for him one evening when his masters are not in the mood for cultural nourishment, not in the mood to "scoff culture," and he can sleep the sleep of the dead. But his sleep may, however, be roughly interrupted if the criminals have a sudden whim and decide to cancel their game of cards (something that happens very seldom, for a game of bezique or blackjack is far more precious than any novel).

Among the hungry novelists you meet ones with ideas, especially when they have had several days of being fed. They then try to tell their listeners something a bit more serious than *The Jack of Hearts Club*. This sort of novelist imagines he is a cultural worker to the thieves' throne. Such people include former writers, proud of their fidelity to their true profession, which now finds an outlet in such unlikely circumstances. There are some who imagine they are snake charmers, flautists playing music to a swirling cluster of poisonous reptiles...

Carthage is to be destroyed!

   The criminal world is to be exterminated!

1959

BOOK FIVE

The Resurrection of the Larch

My book The Resurrection of the Larch *is dedicated to Irina Pavlovna Sirotinskaya.*

    Without her this book would not exist.

THE PATH

I HAD A wonderful path in the taiga. I made it myself one summer when I was collecting a supply of firewood for the winter. There was a lot of dead wood around the cabin: conical larches, gray as if made of papier-mâché, were stuck like stakes into the marsh. The cabin stood on a hillock and was surrounded by bushes of dwarf pine with their green clusters of needles, and as autumn came, the cones were swollen with seeds and the branches bent earthward. It was through this undergrowth of dwarf pines that the path led to the marsh, which had not always been a marsh: a forest had grown there, but water had rotted the tree roots and the trees had died, but that was a long, long time ago. The living forest had receded along the foothill toward the stream. The road for trucks and people was on the other side of the hillock, some way up the mountain slope.

At first I felt bad trampling on the thick red lilies of the valley; the irises looked like enormous mauve butterflies because of both their petals and their patterns, and the enormous thick blue snowdrops made an unpleasant crunching sound when I trod on them. The flowers were like all the flowers in the Far North: they had no scent. Initially, I found I was moving like an automaton, picking a bunch of flowers and lifting it to my nostrils. But I learned not to do that. Every morning I would look at what had happened on my path overnight: a lily of the valley that my boots had stepped on might have straightened up, a bit crooked but revived nonetheless. But another lily of the valley might be irrevocably crushed and lie there like a telegraph pole with its porcelain insulators, the torn cobwebs hanging like broken overhead wires.

Later, however, the path was well trodden, and I no longer noticed branches of dwarf pine blocking my way; I broke off any branches that lashed my face and stopped taking notice of the broken stumps. On either side of the path there were young larches about a century old: I watched them turn green; I watched them drop their fine needles onto the path. Every day the path became darker until, finally, it was an ordinary dark gray mountain path. I was the only person who used it. Blue squirrels used to leap over it, and I often saw partridge footprints, looking like Egyptian cuneiform; occasionally I saw a hare's footprints, but there were more birds and animals than you could count.

I walked this personal path for almost three years. It was good for writing poetry. Sometimes you'd come back from a trip, take a walk on the path, and, as you walked, you would be certain to compose a verse or two. I was used to the path; I began using it as a forest study. I remember the cold and ice taking hold of the mud on the path even before winter had come: the mud seemed to be covered in sugar crystals, like jam. For two autumns, before the first snow, I would go to the path to leave deep footprints that I could then see frozen solid for the whole winter. In spring, once the snow had thawed, I would see the marks I had left the previous year, I would walk in my old footprints, and it was easy to write poetry again. In winter, of course, this study of mine was deserted: subzero temperatures inhibit thinking; writing can only be done in the warmth. But in summer I knew everything by heart; everything on that magical path was much more colorful than in winter: the dwarf pine, the larches, and the briar bushes never failed to make me recall a poem, and if I couldn't remember poems by other poets that suited my mood, then I would mumble my own, which I wrote down when I got back to the cabin.

But in my third summer someone else used my path. I wasn't home at the time. I don't know if he was a wandering geologist or a mountain postman doing his rounds on foot or a hunter, but he had left heavy boot prints. After that it was impossible to write poetry on that path. The stranger's tracks were left in the spring, and I didn't compose a single line on that path all the following summer. By winter I'd been transferred somewhere else: not that I was sorry, for the path had been irrevocably spoiled.

This is the path I've tried many times since to write a poem about, but I've never managed to do so.

1967

GRAPHITE

WHAT DO they use to sign death sentences? Indelible ink, India ink, ballpoint ink, or mordant red diluted with pure blood?

One thing you can be certain of: no death sentence is ever signed in ordinary pencil.

We didn't need ink in the taiga. Rain, tears, blood dissolve any ink or indelible pencil. Indelible pencils are banned from parcels and confiscated in searches. There are two reasons for doing so: first, a prisoner may forge any document; second, these pencils provide printer's ink for thieves to make playing cards, "rip-offs," so . . .

Only black pencils, ordinary graphite, are allowed. Graphite has an extraordinary and special part to play in Kolyma.

Mapmakers will have a chat with the heavens, relying on a star-studded sky, looking hard at the sun to fix their bearings on our earth. Then they erect a tripod, made of wooden beams on a marble tablet, over this bearing, which is set in stone on top of a mountain. This tripod indicates a precise place on a map, and an invisible path stretches from it, from the mountain and the tripod, over the glens and hollows, through clearings, the scrub, and thin forest of the marshes, creating an invisible network of meridians and parallels. Clearings are felled in the thick taiga; every ax mark, every notch, is caught in the intersecting hairlines of the leveler and theodolite. The earth is measured, the taiga is measured, and as we walk, on every fresh notch we see the mapmaker's, the topographer's, and the land surveyor's marks made in simple black pencil.

The Kolyma taiga is crisscrossed with topographers' clearings. But these clearings are not to be found everywhere: only in forests around settlements or "production." Scrubs, clearings, thin forest, forested tundra, and bare moors are crisscrossed only by imaginary aerial lines. There is not a single tree there to mark with a tag; there are no reliable reference points. Reference points can be put on rocks, on riverbeds, on top of bare mountains. These reliable, biblical bearings are the basis for measuring the taiga, Kolyma, or a prison. Markers on trees create a network of clearings, which enables the taiga to be seen and assessed through a theodolite telescope and intersecting hairlines.

In fact, only black pencil works for tree markers: indelible pencil doesn't. Indelible pencil marks are blurred and dissolved by tree sap, washed off by rain, dew, fog, and snow. Indelible pencil, being artificial, is no good for recording anything eternal and immortal. But graphite is carbon, compressed under high pressure over millions of years and transformed not into coal or diamond but into what is even more precious, a pencil, into graphite, which can record everything you've known and seen ... It is a greater miracle than diamonds, even though the chemical nature of graphite and diamonds is the same.

The topographers' instructions forbid them to use indelible pencils, and not just for markers and notches. Any written instructions, or draft instructions, for theodolite surveys require graphite for permanence. The instructions demand graphite for immortality. Graphite is nature; graphite takes part in the earth's revolution, sometimes resisting time better than stone does. Rain, heavy wind, river waves destroy limestone mountains, but a young larch tree—it's only two hundred years old and it is to live longer—keeps in its notch the numbered mark of the biblical link with contemporary times.

A number, a symbolic mark, is made on a fresh notch, on a fresh wound in the tree oozing sap or pitch, as if they were tears.

Graphite is the only way of writing in the taiga. Topographers always have stubs and broken pieces of graphite pencils in the pockets of their quilted jackets, their pea jackets, their body warmers, trousers, and fur jackets.

Paper, a notebook, a plotting board, an exercise book, and a notched tree.

Paper is one of the pupal stages, one of the metamorphoses of wood into diamond and graphite. Graphite is eternity: the highest form of solidity that turns into the highest form of softness. The trace left by a graphite pencil in the taiga is eternal.

Notches are cut out very carefully. At waist level two saw cuts are made in a larch trunk, and still-living wood is broken out with the corner of an ax head, so as to leave a place for writing. A roof, a little house, a clean board, sloping to keep the rain off, is made, and this will preserve the writing forever—in practical terms, to the end of the larch's six-hundred-year life.

The larch's wounded body is like a newly revealed icon, the Chukotka Mother of God, if you like, or the Virgin Mary of Kolyma, expecting a miracle and declaring a miracle.

And you breathe in the slight, subtle scent of pitch, the smell of larch sap, of blood, curdled by a human being's ax, as if it were the distant smell of childhood, of incense dew.

The number is set down, and the wounded larch, burned by the wind and the sun, keeps this "tag," which leads from the depths of the taiga to the wide world, through a clearing to the nearest tripod, a mapmaker's tripod on top of a peak, where a pit under the tripod has been filled with stones, concealing a marble tablet on which the true longitude and latitude are engraved. We then return to our world along a thousand threads, which stretch from that tripod, over thousands of lines from notch to notch, so that we can remember life for all eternity. Mapmakers are in the service of life.

But in Kolyma the mapmaker is not the only person obliged to use graphite pencils.

As well as the service of life, we also have here the service of death, which likewise forbids the use of indelible pencils. The instructions for Archive No. 3, the name of the department that keeps count of prisoner deaths in the camps, are to attach a tag, a plywood tag with the number of the case file, to the left shin of the corpse. The case file number must be written with an ordinary graphite, not indelible, pencil. Artificial pencils even in this case are at odds with immortality.

You might wonder what the idea behind this is: Possible exhumation? Or resurrection? Reburial? There are plenty of common graves in Kolyma where corpses were thrown in untagged. But instructions are instructions. Theoretically, all the guests of the permafrost are immortal and ready to return to us, so that we can remove the tags from their left shins and work out whom we knew and whom we are related to.

The crucial thing is to put the number on the tag in ordinary black pencil. Neither rain nor groundwater will wash away the case file number, nor will spring floods touch the ice of the permafrost, which sometimes gives way to the heat of summer and thus reveals its subterranean secrets, or at least a part of them.

The case file is a formula that stands in for the prisoner's passport, with the addition of photographs, full face and profile, all ten fingerprints, and a description of any special features. The recordkeepers employed by Archive No. 3 are obliged to compile five copies of a death certificate for each prisoner, with all the fingerprints and an indication whether any gold teeth have been pulled out. Gold teeth require a special certificate. This has been the camp practice since time immemorial, and when news came of teeth being pulled out in Germany, nobody in Kolyma was at all surprised.

No state wants to lose the gold in its corpses. Certificates of pulled gold teeth have been drawn up since time immemorial in prison and camp administrations. In 1937 a lot of people with gold teeth were brought into pretrial prisons and camps. The only gold contributed to the state by those who died at the pit faces of Kolyma—and they died very soon after they arrived—was the gold in the teeth that were pulled out after they died. The weight of the gold in these people's false teeth was greater than that of the gold they had dug, scraped, and pickaxed over their short lives at the Kolyma gold-mine pit faces. Statistics is a science with many applications, but this is an aspect it is unlikely to have examined.

The corpse's fingers had to be dipped in printer's ink, and every recordkeeper had a supply of this ink, which was used in great quantities.

The reason that fugitives who'd been killed had their hands cut off with an ax was to obviate the need to transport the body for identification: two human hands in a soldier's knapsack were far more convenient to carry than bodies or corpses.

The leg tag was a sign of civilization. Andrei Bogoliubsky didn't have a tag and had to be recognized by his bones, if we recall Bertillon's calculations.[1]

We believe in fingerprinting: it's a trick that's never let us down, however much criminals have tried to mutilate their fingertips by burning them, spilling acid on them, or slashing them with a knife. Fingerprinting hasn't let us down—there are ten fingers, after all—and none of the professional criminals has gone so far as to burn the ends off all ten.

We don't trust Bertillon, the head of French criminal investigation, the father of the anthropological principle in criminology, who suggested that remains could be authenticated by a series of measurements and the correlation of body parts. Bertillon's discoveries may be of use to artists and portrait painters, but to the rest of us the distance from the end of the nose to the earlobe reveals nothing.

We do believe in fingerprinting. Everyone knows how to "play the piano," to take fingerprints. In 1937, when everybody was being swept up, those whose prints had been taken before automatically put their accustomed fingers in the prison warders' accustomed hands.

These prints are kept forever in the case file. The tag with the number of the case file preserves not only the place of death but its secret too. That tag number is written in graphite.

The mapmaker, the trailblazer on earth, laying down new paths for humanity, and the gravedigger, seeing that the burial is done correctly, according to the laws for the dead, are both compelled to use the same thing: a black graphite pencil.

1967

HELL'S DOCK

THE HEAVY doors to the hold over our heads were opened, and one by one we slowly came up the narrow iron staircase onto the deck. The escort guards were standing shoulder to shoulder along the railings at the steamship's stern, their rifles pointed at us. But nobody paid any attention to them. Someone was yelling, "Hurry up, hurry up," the crowd jostled: it was like any dockside passenger boarding. Only the first men were shown where to go—along the line of rifles to a wide gangway, then onto a barge and from the barge down another gangway to the land. Our sea trip was over. Our ship had brought twelve thousand men, and there was time to take a look around while we were being disembarked.

After the autumnal warmth of the days in Vladivostok, after the strikingly pure colors of the Far East sky at sunset, after those immaculate, bright colors with no halftones and no mottling, colors we would remember for the rest of our lives ... a cold drizzle was falling from the whitish and murky monochrome sky. We were faced by bare, treeless, green rocky moors, and in the clearings between them and at the bottom of these foothills shaggy, dirty gray tufts of cloud were snaking. This gloomy mountainous district seemed to be covered by clumps of stuffing from an enormous quilt. I remember well that I was completely calm, ready for anything, but that I couldn't stop my heart racing and sinking. When I averted my eyes, I was struck by the idea that we'd been brought here to die.

My jacket was being slowly drenched. I was sitting on my suitcase, which I had grabbed from home in the inevitable bustling of people that accompanies any arrest. Absolutely everybody had baggage: suitcases, rucksacks, blanket bundles ... It was much later that I realized that the ideal equipment for a prisoner is a small linen food bag with a wooden spoon in it. Anything else, whether a pencil stub or a blanket, only gets in the way. If there was anything that had been instilled in us, it was contempt for personal property.

I was looking at the steamship, which was pressed against the pier: it was so small, rocked by the dark gray waves.

Through the gray grid of rain you could see the dark silhouettes of the rocks surrounding Nagayevo Bay; only where the ship had come from could you see the infinitely curved ocean, like an enormous beast lying on the shore, sighing heavily, as the wind ruffled its fur, which was flattened by the waves that shone even in the rain and looked like fish scales.

It was cold and frightening. The hot autumnal brightness of sunny Vladivostok was somewhere far behind, in the other, real world. This was a hostile and gloomy world.

There were no houses to be seen nearby. The only road circled the moor and then disappeared somewhere higher up.

At last the disembarkation was finished, and now that it was twilight the party of prisoners slowly moved into the hills. Nobody asked any questions. A crowd of soaked men crawled along the road, stopping frequently to rest. Their suitcases had become too heavy; their clothing was drenched.

Two turns in the road, and next to us, but above us, on an overhanging part of the moor, we saw rows of barbed wire. People on the other side were pressing against it. They were shouting something, and suddenly loaves of bread were flung at us. The bread was thrown over the wire, and we caught it, broke it into pieces and shared it. We had already endured months of prison, forty-five days being transported by train and five by sea. Everyone was hungry. Nobody was given travel money. We ate the bread greedily. Anyone lucky enough to catch a loaf shared with all who wanted a share: a generosity that took three weeks for us to abandon forever.

We were being led farther and farther, higher and higher. The halts became more frequent. And now there were wooden gates, barbed wire, and inside, rows of tarpaulin tents darkened by the rain: they were white and bright green, and enormous. We were counted and put into separate groups, filling one tent after another. The tents contained two-story wooden bunks, as in railway sleeping carriages, but each bunk was meant for eight men. We each found our place. The tarpaulin leaked; there were puddles on the floor and on the bunks, but I was so exhausted (and everyone was just as tired as I was, thanks to the rain, the air, the long trek, the wet clothes, and the suitcases) that I curled up as best I could and, without thinking about how or even where to dry my clothes, I lay down and went to sleep. It was dark and cold ...

1967

SILENCE

WE WERE amazed, suspicious, wary, and afraid. All of us, the whole brigade, took our seats around the dirty, sticky tables in the camp refectory where we had eaten during our entire life here. Why should the tables be sticky? No soup had been spilled here, there was "no slip between cup and lip" here, not that there were any spoons, and any spilled soup would have been swept up to one's mouth with a finger and just licked.

It was the night shift's dinnertime. Our brigade had been tucked away on the night shift, away from anyone's sight, as if there were anyone looking! Our brigade was made up of the weakest, the most inept, the hungriest. We were human refuse, but we still had to be fed, and not on refuse or even leftovers. We were assigned a certain amount of fats, cooked food, and, above all, bread, of completely identical quality to the bread that the best brigades ate, the brigades that had not yet lost their strength and were still fulfilling the plan for basic production, getting out the gold, gold, gold.

Provided we were still being fed, it didn't matter that we came last in the line, at night or in daytime.

This night too we were also served last.

We all came from the same barracks, the same section. I knew one or two of these living corpses from my stay in prison and in the transit camps. Every day I moved along with these lumps of torn pea jackets, the rough hats with earflaps that people never took off between one visit to the bathhouse and the next, cloth boots made from torn trousers and singed by bonfires: it was only my memory that helped me to recognize the Tatar Mutalov, the only inhabitant of Chimkent who had owned a two-story house with a tin roof, and Yefimov, who used to be first secretary of the Chimkent Party Town Committee, and who had in 1930 liquidated Muralov[69] for class reasons.

Oksman, the former chief of the political section of a division, was here: he had been chased out of the division for being Jewish by Marshal Timoshenko, who was at the time not yet a marshal.

Lupilov was also here: he had been the deputy supreme prosecutor of the USSR, Vyshinsky's deputy, and a train driver at the Saviolovo depot. We also had the former head of the NKVD from Gorky, who had started a quarrel with one of his "protégés" at a transit camp: "So they hit you? So what? You signed, so you're an enemy, you're misleading Soviet authority, you interfere with our work. It's reptiles like you that got me fifteen years."

I intervened: "When I listen to you I don't know whether to laugh or to spit at your ugly face."

There were all sorts of people in this brigade of "drifters." There were sectarians from the "God knows" sect (or perhaps it had another name; it was just that this was the only answer the sectarians gave to any question from the authorities).[3]

Naturally, I can still remember the sectarian's surname, Dmitriev, although he himself never answered to it. It was Dmitriev's comrades and foreman who moved him about, lined him up, and led him around.

The escort guards often changed, and almost every one of them tried to divine the secret behind this refusal to answer, by yelling threateningly "Respond!" when the sectarian came out to do his so-called labor.

The foreman would briefly explain the circumstances, and the guard, much relieved, would go on with the roll call.

Everyone in the barracks was fed up with the sectarian. We couldn't sleep at night for hunger, and we kept trying to get warm by the iron stove, embracing it, trying to catch the sinking warmth in the cooling iron, moving our faces close to the metal.

Naturally, we were blocking the other inhabitants of the barracks from this pathetic source of warmth. They were lying in the far corners of the barracks, covered in hoarfrost and, like us, unable to sleep because of hunger. It was from there, those distant dark corners covered in hoarfrost, that someone would leap out, someone who had a right to shout, or even a right to hit out, and chase the hungry workers away from the stove with curses and kicks.

You could stand by the stove and make bread into rusks, but who had bread to dry out? And how many hours would it take to turn a piece of bread into a rusk?

We hated our bosses, we hated each other, but more than anybody, we hated the sectarian for his songs, his hymns, and his psalms.

We were all silent as we hugged the stove. The sectarian sang and sang in his hoarse chilled voice. He sang quietly, but he was singing hymns, psalms, verses. There was no end to these songs.

I was the sectarian's work partner. The others in the section had a break, while they were working, from the hymns and psalms; they had a break from the sectarian, while I had no relief.

"Shut up!"

"I'd have died a long time ago if it weren't for the songs. I'd have walked away into the freezing cold. But I haven't got the strength. If only I had a little more strength. I don't ask God for strength: He sees everything anyway."

There were other people in the brigade, too, wrapped in rags, all equally dirty and hungry, with the same shining eyes. Who were they? Generals? Heroes from the Spanish Civil War? Russian writers? Collective farmers from Volokolamsk?

We were sitting in the refectory, puzzled because we were not being fed: What were they waiting for? What new announcement would there be? Any news could only be good for us. There is a line after which anything that happens to a man is for the better. The news could only be good. We all understood that with our bodies, if not with our brains.

The door of the food hatch was opened from the other side, and they began to serve us bowls of soup—and it was hot! Then there was porridge—warm! And the third course, blancmange, was almost cold! Each man was given a spoon, and the foreman warned us that the spoons had to be given back. Of course we'd hand them back. What did we want a spoon for? To swap for tobacco in another barracks? Of course we'd hand them back. What did we need them for? We'd long been used to slurping our food straight from the bowl. Why should we want a spoon? Anything left on the bottom you could push to the rim with a finger and get it out.

There was no need for further thought: we had food, nourishment, in front of us. We were given handfuls of bread, two hundred grams each.

"Just eat your ration of bread," the foreman solemnly declared. "The rest is to fill your belly."

So we filled our bellies. All soups were divided into two parts: the solids and the broth. We were given the broth to fill our bellies. But the second course of porridge was the real thing. The third course was lukewarm water with a slight aftertaste of starch and a barely detectable trace of dissolved sugar: that was the blancmange.

Prisoners' stomachs are not at all coarsened: their ability to distinguish taste is not in the least dimmed by hunger and the rough food. On the contrary, a hungry prisoner's stomach has an extraordinary sensitivity to taste. The reaction to quality in a prisoner's stomach is just as subtle as that of any physical laboratory in any country in the second half of the twentieth century.

No free man's stomach would have detected the presence of sugar in the blancmange we were eating, or rather, drinking, that Kolyma night at the Partisan mine.

We, however, found the blancmange to be sweet, wonderfully sweet, a miracle; each man was reminded that sugar still existed in this world and can even get into the prisoners' cooking pots. Who was the magician?

The magician was not far away. We had a good look at him after the first course of our second dinner.

"Just eat your ration of bread," said the foreman. "The rest is to fill your belly." And then he looked at the magician.

"Yes, yes," said the magician.

He was a tidy-looking, dark, well-scrubbed little man with a face that hadn't yet suffered frostbite.

Our bosses, our warders, foremen, clerks of work, camp chiefs, escort guards had all had plenty of experience of Kolyma, and on absolutely every face Kolyma had inscribed its words and left its trace, carving out extra wrinkles, leaving a permanent stain from frostbite, an indelible mark, a branding that can't be removed.

The tidy-looking dark man didn't have a single stain; he had no branding on his pink face.

He was the new senior instructor in our camp and had just arrived from the mainland. This senior instructor was carrying out an experiment.

The instructor had an agreement with the camp chief and insisted on ignoring a Kolyma custom, according to which the leftovers of soup and porridge, the "good stuff at the bottom," was taken away every day, following a tradition that may have been hundreds, if not thousands of years old: they were taken from the kitchen to be given to the thieves' barracks and the barracks of the best brigades, so as to give sustenance to the least hungry rather than the most hungry brigades, so as to make everything work for the plan, turning everything into gold—the souls and bodies of all the bosses, guards, and prisoners.

These brigades, including the thieves, were now accustomed to getting these leftovers. Along with the inevitable moral damage.

But the new instructor disagreed with this custom and insisted on distributing the leftovers of food to the weakest and the hungriest: he said that their consciences would then be awoken.

"They don't get consciences; they get horns on their heads," a foreman said, trying to intervene, but the instructor stood firm and was authorized to carry out the experiment.

The hungriest brigade, our brigade, was chosen to test it out.

"You'll see, a man gets something to eat and is so grateful to the state that he'll work better. You can't expect these goners to work, can you? Goners is the word for them, isn't it? Goners was the first word of criminal slang that I learned in Kolyma. Am I right?"

"You're right," said the local chief, a free man and an old Kolyma hand who had sent many thousands of men at this mine to their graves "under the moors." He'd come to watch this wonderful experiment.

"You can try feeding these loafers and malingerers meat and chocolate for a month with full rest breaks: even then they're not going to do any work. Something's changed permanently in their thick skulls.

They're slag, refuse. It'd be more valuable for production to feed the men who are still working, not these loafers!"

They were arguing and shouting by the kitchen hatch. The instructor was saying something and the argument was heated. The local chief listened with a scowl; when he heard the name Makarenko[4] mentioned, he dismissed everyone with a wave of the arm and stepped aside.

Every day we prayed to our god, while the sectarian prayed to his. We prayed that the hatch would stay open, that the instructor would have his way. The collective willpower of two dozen prisoners was harnessed, and the instructor had his way.

We went on eating, reluctant to part from this miracle.

The local chief took out his watch, but the camp siren had already sounded, and its piercing shriek was calling us to work.

"Well, you workmen," the new instructor said, pronouncing with some diffidence this word that was so superfluous here, "I've done as much as I can. I've got something for you. It's up to you to respond with your labor, nothing else."

"We'll work, sir," a former assistant supreme prosecutor of the USSR solemnly pronounced as he tied his pea jacket with a dirty piece of toweling and breathed into his gauntlets to get some warm air into them.

The door opened and let white mist in; we crawled out into the freezing cold, to remember for the rest of our lives this piece of good luck: some of us would live. The temperature seemed a little higher, a little more bearable. But this did not last for long. The cold was too extreme for anyone to defeat it.

We arrived at the pit face, sat in a circle, waiting for our foreman; we sat down where we used to have a bonfire and warm ourselves, breathing into the golden flames and singeing our gauntlets, hats, trousers, pea jackets, cloth boots in our vain attempts to get warm and save ourselves from the subzero temperatures. Our guard sat down, rearranged the burning coals in his fire, and fanned the flames. There was the smell of his sheepskin jacket as he sat on a beam and stacked his rifle.

The pit face was enveloped in white haze, and the only light was from the guard's fire. The sectarian sitting next to me got up, walked past the guard into the mist, toward the sky.

"Stop! Stop!"

The guard was not a bad fellow, but he knew what his rifle was for.

"Stop!"

Then a shot rang out, the dry click of a rifle bolt: the sectarian hadn't yet disappeared in the haze, and there was a second shot.

"Well then, there's a dummy for you," the local chief told the senior instructor, using the criminal slang word. They had both arrived at the pit face. But the instructor didn't dare show any astonishment at the killing, while the local chief was incapable of being astonished by such things.

"So much for your experiment. Those bastards are working even worse. Too much dinner gives them too much strength to fight the cold. The cold is the only thing, you dummy, that will squeeze any work out of them. Not your dinner and not my soft touch, only the cold. They wave their hands around to get warm, and we put pickaxes and spades into those hands—does it matter what they wave about?—then we provide a wheelbarrow, an ore box, shovels, and the mine fulfills the plan. It gets the gold out. Now those men have had plenty to eat, so they won't work at all. Feeding them is pointless. You really showed what a fool you were when you did that dinner. I'll forgive you since it's the first time. We were all dummies to begin with."

"I didn't know they were such reptiles," said the instructor.

"Next time you'll believe your seniors. One man's been shot today. A loafer. He's been eating state rations for six months and done nothing. Repeat, 'He's a loafer.'"

"He's a loafer," repeated the instructor.

I was standing there, but that didn't bother the bosses. I had a legitimate reason for waiting: the foreman had to bring me a new work partner.

The foreman brought me Lupilov, the former assistant supreme prosecutor of the USSR. And we began shoveling dynamited rock into the ore boxes, doing the work I and the sectarian had been doing.

We went back by the usual route, as always, never fulfilling the norm and not bothered about it. But we seemed to be less frozen than usual.

We did try to work, but our life was too remote from whatever can be expressed in figures, in barrow loads or percentages of the plan. Figures were a wicked mockery. But for an hour or so, a moment or so, we had found some strength, moral and physical, and we were fortified by that nighttime dinner.

The realization chilled me, but I realized that this nocturnal dinner had given the sectarian the strength to commit suicide. What my partner had lacked in order to decide to die was an extra serving of porridge: sometimes a man has to make haste or he'll lose the will to die.

As always, we surrounded the stove. Only today there was nobody to sing hymns. And, to be honest, I was even glad that now we had silence.

1966

TWO ENCOUNTERS

MY FIRST foreman was Kotur, a Serb who ended up in Kolyma after the Moscow International Club[5] was broken up. Kotur didn't take his responsibilities as foreman seriously: he understood that his fate, like everyone else's, was being decided not at the gold-mine pit faces but in quite a different place. All the same, every day Kotur set us to work, joined the warder in measuring the results and shaking his head reproachfully. The results were deplorable.

"Take you, for example. You know the camp. Show how to wield a spade," Kotur told me.

I took a spade and broke up the light subsoil before rolling a wheelbarrow up. Everybody laughed.

"Only idlers work like that."

"Let's talk about it in twenty years."

But we weren't fated to have a talk twenty years later. A new boss, Leonid Mikhailovich Anisimov, came to the mine. On his first tour of inspection of the pit faces he removed Kotur. And Kotur disappeared.

Our foreman was sitting in a wheelbarrow, and he failed to get up when the boss approached. It goes without saying that the wheelbarrow is well designed for work. But its body is even better designed for rest. It's hard to get up and lift yourself out of its deep, deep armchair—you need to exert your will and your strength. Kotur was sitting in the wheelbarrow and failed to get up when the new boss approached him; he didn't have time to get up. Execution by shooting.

Once the new boss had come—he had at first been the deputy chief of the mine—people were taken from the barracks and driven away every day and every night. None of them ever came back to the mine. Aleksandrov, Klivansky—the names have been erased from my memory.

The men who came to replace them had no names at all. In the winter of 1938 the authorities decided to send a party of prisoners on foot from Magadan to the mines in the north. Of a column of five hundred men, over the five hundred kilometers to Yagodnoye, only thirty or forty managed the journey. The rest were stranded on the way, frostbitten, hungry, and shot dead. None of those who made it were addressed by their surnames: they were people from other groups, and they were indistinguishable from one another by voice, frostbite patches on their cheeks, and frostbite blisters on their fingers.

There were now fewer brigades: trucks were driving day and night on the road to the "Serpentine," where the Northern Administration's execution teams were, and they came back empty.

Brigades were merged: there weren't enough men, but the government demanded the plan be fulfilled and promised to provide a workforce. Every mine boss knew that he wouldn't be held accountable for what he did to his men: of course not, his men, his management, were the most valuable asset. Every boss had learned that in his political propaganda sessions, and he had a practical demonstration at the pit faces of his gold mine.

By now the boss of the Partisan mine of the Northern Mining Administration was Leonid Mikhailovich Anisimov, who would eventually be the top boss of Kolyma, a man who devoted his entire life to Far East Construction, who was the boss of the Western Administration and of Chukotka Construction.

But Anisimov began his camp career at the Partisan mine, my mine.

It was under his management that the mine was flooded with escort guards, zones and NKVD officers' administrations were marked out, and whole brigades as well as individuals were taken off and shot. At roll calls before and after work, readings were held of endless execution orders. These orders were signed by Colonel Garanin, but the surnames of men from the Partisan mine—and there were a lot of them—were provided to Garanin by Anisimov. The Partisan mine was small: in 1938 it had no more than two thousand men on its lists. The neighboring mines V. At-Uriakh and Storm each had twelve thousand.

Anisimov was a hardworking boss. I remember very well two personal conversations I had with Mr. Anisimov. The first was in January 1938, when Mr. Anisimov deigned to attend the roll call before work; he stood on one side watching his assistant run around faster than was normal under the boss's gaze. But not fast enough for Anisimov.

Our brigade was lining up, and Sotnikov, the clerk of works, pointed his finger at me, extracted me from the ranks, and put me before Anisimov.

"Here's a loafer. He won't work."

"Who are you?"

"I'm a journalist, a writer."

"All you'll write here are labels on cans of food. I'm asking you who you are."

"A pit-face getter, in Firsov's brigade, prisoner such-and-such, sentence: five years."

"Why don't you work, why are you wrecking the government?"

"I'm ill, sir."

"What's wrong with you, you look pretty healthy."

"I've got a bad heart."

"Heart. You've got a bad heart. I have a bad heart myself. The doctors have ruled out the Far North. But I'm here."

"It's different for you, sir."

"Watch out, all those words a minute. You have to shut up and work. Think before it's too late. You and I will have accounts to settle."

"Yes, sir."

My second conversation with Anisimov was in the summer, when it was raining, on the fourth section where we were being held up, drenched to the skin. We were boring test shafts. Because of the downpour, a brigade of criminals had been sent back to the barracks long before us, but we were politicals, convicted under article 58, so we stood up to our knees in our shallow pits. The escort guards had an umbrella-like shelter to hide in.

While this rain was pouring down, we were visited by Anisimov and the mine's manager of explosive works. The boss had come to check whether we were capable of work, and whether his order about article 58 men was being carried out, an article that required no certification and that was meant to be a preparation for paradise, paradise, paradise.

Anisimov was wearing a long raincoat with a special hood. The boss waved his leather gloves as he came.

I knew that Anisimov was in the habit of hitting prisoners in the face with his gloves. I knew those gloves, which he swapped in winter for fur gauntlets that went up to his elbow; I knew he liked hitting people's faces with his gloves. I'd seen those gloves in action dozens of times. There was a lot of talk in the prisoners' barracks at Partisan about this peculiarity of Anisimov. I witnessed heated discussions, arguments that almost led to bloodshed in the barracks, about whether the boss hit you with his fists, his gloves, or a stick, or a riding crop, or a horse whip, or whether he used his "hand revolver." Human beings are complex creatures. These arguments used to end in something like a brawl, yet the participants in these arguments were former professors, party men, collective farmers, army officers.

On the whole, Anisimov was praised: he hit you, but then, everyone did. On the other hand, Anisimov's gloves left no bruises, and even if he made someone's nose bleed with his gauntlet, then that was due to "pathological changes in a person's capillary system as a result of prolonged imprisonment," as explained by one doctor, who wasn't allowed to work as a doctor under Anisimov's rule but was forced to do physical labor like everybody else.

I'd long promised myself that if anyone hit me, that would be the end of my life. I would hit the boss and I would be shot. Alas, I was a naïve boy. Once I became weak, so did my willpower and my reason. I found it easy to persuade myself to put up with it and I couldn't find the moral strength in myself to hit back, to commit suicide, to protest. I was the most ordinary goner and I was living according to goners' psychology. All that came much later, but when Mr. Anisimov and I met again, I still had my strength, by firmness, my faith, and my decision.

Anisimov's leather gloves were getting closer, I got my pickax ready.

But Anisimov didn't hit me. His handsome dark brown eyes caught my gaze, and he averted his eyes.

"They're all like him," the mine boss said to his companion. "All of them. No good will come of them."

1967

GRISHKA LOGUN'S THERMOMETER

WE WERE so tired that we sat down in the snow by the roadside before going home.

Instead of yesterday's minus forty, it was only minus twenty-five, and the day seemed like summer.

Grishka Logun, the clerk of works on the neighboring section, walked past us, his fur jacket unbuttoned over his bare chest. He was carrying a new pickax handle. Grishka was young, with an amazingly red face, and he was hot-tempered. He had been a foreman, a junior foreman in fact, and often he couldn't refrain from using his shoulder to push a truck that was stuck in the snow, or to help lift a heavy beam, or to move a box full of soil that had frozen to the ground—actions that were definitely demeaning for a clerk of works. He kept forgetting that he was a clerk of works.

Vinogradov's brigade was coming toward him: they were nothing special as workmen, no more than we were. They were made up of the same sort of people as our brigade: former secretaries of provincial and town committees, professors and lecturers, middle-ranking military men.

The men had timidly clustered by the snow-covered side of the road: they were coming back from work and making way for Grishka Logun. But it was he who halted: the brigade was working on his section. Vinogradov stepped forward from the ranks: he was a talkative man, and had been the manager of a motor-tractor station in Ukraine.

Logun had by now moved away from where we were sitting, and we couldn't hear their voices, but we didn't need to in order to understand. Vinogradov was waving his arms about as he explained something to Logun. Then Logun poked his pickax handle in Vinogradov's chest, and Vinogradov fell onto his back. He didn't get up. Logun jumped onto him and trampled him, while waving his stick about. Not a single man of Vinogradov's brigade of twenty made a move to defend their foreman. Logun picked up his hat, which had fallen off, waving a menacing fist. Vinogradov then got up and walked on as if nothing had happened. The other men—the brigade was walking past us—expressed no sympathy and no indignation. When we caught up with him, Vinogradov twisted his smashed, bleeding lips into a grimace.

"That Logun thermometer is some thermometer," he said, meaning "pickax handle."

"'Trampling' is the gangster version of dancing," Pavlov said quietly. "Or the song 'Oh my lobby, my lobby…'"[6]

"Well," I said to Vavilov, my friend with whom I had come to the mine all the way from Butyrki prison, "what have you got to say? We need to come to a decision. Yesterday we hadn't been beaten yet. Tomorrow we may be. What would you do if Logun did the same to you as he did to Vinogradov? Eh?"

"I'd probably put up with it, I expect," Vavilov replied quietly. And I realized that he had thought about the inevitability of it long ago.

Later I grasped that the whole point was physical superiority, as far as foremen, orderlies, or warders, all of them unarmed, were concerned. As long as I was the stronger one, they wouldn't hit me. Once I weakened, everybody would hit me. The orderly would, and so would the bathhouse attendant, the barber, the cook, the foremen, both the free man and the fellow prisoner, as would any gangster, even the feeblest. The physical superiority of the escort guard was in his rifle.

The strength of a boss who might hit me was the law, the courts, the tribunal, the guards, and the troops. It would not be hard for him to be stronger than me. The gangsters' strength was in their numbers, their "collective," the fact they could cut my throat before I said another word (and how many times I'd seen that). But I was still strong. A boss, a guard, or a gangster could hit me. The orderly, the foreman, and the barber couldn't hit me for the time being.

Once Poliansky, who had been a professional physical trainer in the past, and who received a lot of parcels and never shared a single piece of food with anyone, told me reproachfully that he just could not understand how people could let themselves sink so low as to accept being hit. He was outraged by my objections. But less than a year later, when I met Poliansky, he was a goner, a living skeleton, scrounging cigarette ends, longing to tickle the heels of some criminal bosses in exchange for soup.

Poliansky was a decent man. He was tormented by secret pangs, such strong and acute and permanent pangs that they were able to penetrate the ice, death, indifference, and beatings, the starvation, sleeplessness, and fear.

Once we had a day off: on such days we were kept under lock and key—that was called holiday isolation. It was during those "isolations" that people met each other, got to know each other, trusted each other. However terrible and degrading this isolation was, for the article 58 prisoners it was easier than work. Isolation was, after all, rest, if only for minutes, and who could have then worked out how long we needed— a minute, twenty-four hours, a year, or a century—to get back to our former bodies? We no longer counted on getting back to our former souls. And, of course, we didn't get back. Nobody did. So, Poliansky was a decent man, my neighbor on the bunks on an isolation day.

"There's something I've been meaning to ask you for a long time."

"What is it?"

"When I was looking at you a few months ago, the way you walked, when you couldn't walk over a tree trunk on the road but had to go around it, even though a dog could get over it, when you were scraping your feet on the stones and the slightest unevenness, a tiny bump on the road seemed like an insuperable barrier to you, causing you palpitations, breathlessness, and making you take long breaks, I looked at you and thought: that's an idler, a loafer, a cunning bastard, a malingerer."

"Well? And then you realized?"

"Then I realized. I did. When I myself lost my strength. When everyone started pushing me around, hitting me; yet there's no better feeling for a man than to sense that someone else is even weaker, even worse off."

"Why are the shock workers invited to discussions, why is physical strength a moral criterion? Does being physically stronger mean that a man is better, more moral than me? Of course it does: he can lift up a rock that weighs a hundred and sixty kilos and I am bent double by a thirty-kilo stone."

"I realized all that and that's what I want to tell you."

"Thanks for that much."

Poliansky died shortly afterward: he fell down somewhere at the pit face. The foreman punched him in the face. The foreman wasn't Grishka Logun but one of our own, Firsov, a military man, also convicted under article 58.

I well remember when I was hit for the first time. The first of a hundred thousand slaps that happened every day, every night.

It's impossible to remember all the slaps, but I well remember the first blow: I was even prepared for it by Grishka Logun's behavior and by Vavilov's submissiveness.

In the midst of the hunger, the cold, the fourteen-hour workday, and the freezing white haze of the stony gold-mine pit face, there was a glimpse of something different, of some happiness, some alms foisted on you, not in the form of bread, medicine, but in the form of time, unscheduled rest.

The mining inspector in charge of our sector was Zuyev, a free man, but a former political prisoner who knew what it was like to be in the camps.

There was something in Zuyev's dark eyes, an expression of sympathy, perhaps, for a woeful human fate.

Power depraves. The wild beast hidden in the human soul, once let off its chain, seeks to satisfy the greed of its inextinguishable human essence by beatings and killings.

I don't know if there is any satisfaction to be had from signing a death warrant. Probably that too gives some grim enjoyment for an imagination that doesn't look for excuses.

I had seen people, and a lot of them, who had ordered someone to be shot; now they themselves were being murdered. All you saw and heard was cowardice, a shout: "There must be some mistake, I'm not the one that should be killed for the good of the state, I can do the killing myself!"

I don't know the people who issued execution orders. I have only seen them from a distance. But I think that the order to execute people is based on the same inner force, the same inner core, as the actual execution, the killing done personally.

Power depraves.

The intoxication that comes from having power over people, from impunity, from humiliating and from encouraging: that is the moral measure of a boss's career.

But Zuyev beat people less than the others did: we were lucky.

We had only just come to work, and the brigade was huddling in the stillness, hiding from the piercing power of the wind behind an outcrop of rock. Covering his face with his gauntlets, Zuyev, the inspector, came up to us. He assigned us our jobs at the pit face, but I was left with nothing to do.

"I have a request," said Zuyev, gasping at his own boldness. "A request. Not an order. Write a petition to Kalinin for me: to annul my conviction. I'll tell you what it's all about."

In the inspector's little hut, where a stove was burning, people like me were never admitted (any workmen who dared to open the door, just to get a breath of this hot air of life, were chased out with kicks and slaps).

Some animal instinct led us to this fatal door. We would invent requests: "Tell me the time?" and questions: "Is the pit face turning right or left?" "Are we allowed to smoke?" "Is Zuyev or Dobriakov here by any chance?"

But nobody in the hut was taken in by these requests. Those who came were kicked back through the open door into the freezing cold. But it was still a moment of warmth.

I wasn't being chased away now. I was sitting right by the stove.

"Who's he? A lawyer?" someone hissed scornfully.

"Yes, he was recommended to me, Pavel Ivanovich."

"Fancy that." This was the senior inspector, who took a patronizing view of his subordinate's predicament.

Zuyev had finished his sentence the previous year; his case was the most ordinary rural case, which began with payments in support of his parents, the reason why Zuyev ended up in prison. He hadn't long left to serve, but the authorities still managed to transfer him to Kolyma.

Colonizing the region demands a firm line to create every possible obstacle for anyone trying to leave, to provide state assistance and constant attention to ensure that people come or are transported to Kolyma. A trainload of prisoners is the simplest way to bring life to a new and difficult land.

Zuyev wanted to settle his accounts with Far East Construction, so he asked for his conviction to be annulled and for permission at least to go to the mainland.

I found it difficult to write, and not only because my hands had become so rough that the fingers could bend only around a spade or a pickax handle, and unbending them was unbelievably hard. All I could do was wrap the pencil and pen with the thickest rag I could find, so as to make it feel like a spade or a pickax handle.

Once I had found the way to do this, I was ready to trace out the letters.

It was hard to write because my brain had become as rough as my hands and was bleeding as badly as they were. I had to bring the words back to life, to resurrect words that had left my life, as I believed, forever.

As I wrote this document, I sweated and rejoiced. It was hot in the cabin, and the lice immediately started moving and crawling all over my body. I was afraid to scratch, lest I be chased out into the freezing cold; I feared giving my savior cause for revulsion.

By evening I had written a petition to Kalinin. Zuyev thanked me and put a bread ration in my hand. I had to eat it straightaway, like anything else that could be eaten straightaway; there was no point saving it for tomorrow, that was something I had learned.

The day was now ending, to judge by the inspector's clock, since the white haze remained the same whether it was midnight or midday: we were led home.

When I slept I had the usual repeated Kolyma dream: loaves of bread floating through the air, filling all the houses, the streets, the whole world.

In the morning I waited to see Zuyev: perhaps he'd give me a cigarette.

Zuyev did come. Not holding anything back from the brigade or the escort guards, he roared at me and dragged me from my shelter into the wind: "You've deceived me, you son of a bitch!"

He'd read the petition the previous night. He didn't like it. His neighbors, also inspectors, also read it and disapproved. It was too dry. Not enough tears. It was pointless submitting a petition like that. Rubbish like that wouldn't arouse Kalinin's pity.

I was utterly unable to squeeze a single extra word out of my brain, desiccated as it was by the camps. I couldn't suppress my hatred. The reason I hadn't managed to do the job was not because there was too big a gap between freedom and Kolyma, nor because my brain was too tired, too exhausted, but because the repository where I used to keep grandiose adjectives now had nothing in it except hatred. Just think about poor Dostoyevsky, writing miserable, tearful, humiliating but touching letters to his seniors for all of the ten years he spent as a soldier after the "House of the Dead." Dostoyevsky even wrote poems to the empress. There was no Kolyma in the "House of the Dead." If there had been, Dostoyevsky would have been struck dumb, just as I was when I was unable to write Zuyev's petition.

"You deceived me, you son of a bitch!" yelled Zuyev. "I'll show you what happens when people deceive me!"

"I didn't deceive you ..."

"You spent a day in a warm hut. You reptile, I have to answer for you with an extra sentence, thanks to your idleness! I thought you were a decent person!"

"I am a decent person," I whispered, my blue, frostbitten lips moving uncertainly.

"I'll show you right now what sort of person you are!"

Zuyev flung his arm out and I felt a light, almost weightless touch, not stronger than a gust of the wind that had several times blown me off my feet at that same pit face.

I fell over and, covering my face with my hands, used my tongue to lick something sweet and sticky that was oozing on the edge of my lips.

Zuyev's felt boot kicked me several times in the side, but it didn't hurt.

1966

A ROUNDUP

A WILLYS jeep carrying four soldiers turned sharply off the main highway and accelerated, bumping over the hillocks on the hospital territory, over the shifting, treacherous road that was covered with white limestone. The jeep made its way to the hospital, and Krist's heart sank at the anxiety that was usual when encountering bosses, escort guards, fate.

The jeep jerked forward and got stuck in the bog. It was about five hundred meters from the highway to the hospital. This section of road was built by the head doctor in the most economical way, using the state method of working Saturdays, which in Kolyma were called "shock-work days." This was the same method as was used for all construction sites in the Five-Year Plan. Convalescent patients were herded out onto this road to carry stone, two stones at a time, stretcher-loads of rubble. Male nurses who had been patients—no nursing staff was allotted to the little hospital for prisoners—took part on these shock Saturdays without any objections: otherwise they could expect to go back to the mine, to the gold-mine pit face. Nobody who worked in the surgical department was sent to work on these Saturdays: grazed, injured fingers would have made surgical department workers unfit for work for a long time. But an instruction from Moscow was needed in order to convince the camp bosses of this fact. Other prisoners were morbidly, madly envious of this privilege of not working on shock-work Saturdays. What, you might wonder, was there to envy? You only had to fulfill two or three hours of shock work, like everyone else. But no, the point was that your comrades were being let off, and you weren't. And that was hurtful beyond measure, something you remembered all your life.

Patients, doctors, male nurses all picked up a stone, sometimes even two, and went to the edge of the bog to throw the stones into the marshy ground.

That was how roads were built; it was how Genghis Khan drained seas, only Genghis Khan had more men than the chief doctor of this Central District Hospital for prisoners, as it was so pompously called.

Genghis Khan had more men, and he was drying out seas, not a bottomless permafrost that thawed during the short Kolyma summer.

A road in summer was not nearly as good as a winter road: it couldn't compete with the snow and ice. The more the bog thawed, the more bottomless it became and the more stone was needed, so that gangs of patients even over three summers could not lay a reliable road. Only toward autumn, when the earth was already in the grip of frost and the permafrost stopped thawing, was it possible to get anywhere with this Genghis Khan type of project. The hopelessness of the undertaking had been obvious for ages to the chief doctor and the sick workers, but everyone had long been used to the futility of their labor.

Every summer the convalescent patients, doctors, paramedics, and male nurses carried stone for this damned road. The marsh would slurp, open up, and suck, suck in stone without end. The road, surfaced with white limestone, was very unreliably paved.

This was a bog meadow, a quagmire, an impassable marsh, and the road surfaced with weak white limestone only indicated the route and suggested a direction. A prisoner, a boss, or a guard could walk these five hundred meters by stepping from slab to slab, from stone to stone, stepping, jumping, and walking from one to the other. The hospital stood on a small hill: it had a dozen single-story barracks, open on all sides to the wind. There was no barbed-wire zone around the hospital. Anyone who was discharged was fetched by an escort guard from the administration six kilometers from the hospital.

The jeep accelerated, bounced, and got stuck permanently. The soldiers leapt out of the jeep; then Krist saw something unusual. There were new epaulets on the soldiers' old greatcoats, while a man who got out of the jeep had silver epaulets on his shoulder. This was the first time Krist had seen epaulets. He had only seen them when films were being shot, as well as on the cinema screen and in magazines like *The*

Sun of Russia. And once, after the revolution, in the twilight of the provincial town where Krist was born, he saw epaulets being ripped off the shoulders of an officer taken prisoner in the street and standing at attention in front of…Who was this officer standing in front of? Krist couldn't remember. The late childhood and youth that followed his early childhood were such that each year had enough impressions that left such a deep trace and were of such vital importance that you could have fit dozens of lives into each year. Krist thought that no officers or soldiers had crossed his path. Now there was an officer and soldiers dragging a jeep out of the marsh. But there was no sign of a cinema cameraman, or a director having come to Kolyma to stage some modern play. Any plays here were invariably staged with Krist's involvement, and he wasn't interested in any other plays. Clearly, the jeep that had arrived, the soldiers, and the officer were acting out something, a scene that involved Krist. The man with the epaulets was an ensign. No, here that's called a lieutenant.

The jeep leapt over the most dangerous place, and the car sped up to the hospital, to the bakery, where the one-legged baker, blessing fate for making him an invalid, for taking away a leg, jumped up to give the officer, who was getting out of the jeep, a soldier's salute. The fine silver stars, two nice new stars, sparkled on the officer's shoulder. The officer had gotten out of the jeep, and the one-legged night watchman had made a quick movement, limping as he leapt up and aside. But the officer boldly and casually held the one-legged man back by his pea jacket.

"No need for that."

"Sir, permission to—"

"No need for that, I said. Go back to the bakery. We'll deal with everything."

The lieutenant waved his arms, pointing right and left, and three soldiers ran off to encircle and take by surprise the big deserted, silent settlement. The driver got out of the jeep. The lieutenant and a fourth soldier rushed to the porch of the surgical department.

The chief doctor, a woman, came down the hill, clicking her heels, but the night watchman was too late to warn her.

The twenty-year-old chief of the separate camp quarters, a former frontline officer who had been relieved of frontline duties because of a hernia, or perhaps that was just talk and, more probably, because he had influence, someone higher up who could transfer a lieutenant and get him promoted, after dealing with Guderian's tanks,[7] one rank higher with a move to Kolyma.

The mines were desperate for men, men. The predatory efforts to exploit gold, which had previously been forbidden, were now encouraged by the government. Lieutenant Soloviov had been sent to prove his ability, his understanding, his knowledge, and his entitlement.

It's not the job of camp institutions to dispatch parties of prisoners personally; they don't involve themselves in patients' medical histories, they don't look gift horses or people in the mouth, they don't feel their slaves' muscles.

All that is done in the camps by the doctors.

The number of prisoners listed—the workforce of the mines—was shrinking with every summer day, and every Kolyma night the number going out to work was getting smaller and smaller. Men from the gold-mine pit faces were either "under the moor," that is, buried, or in the hospital.

The district administration had long ago squeezed out everything it could, cut down on everything possible, except of course its personal batmen, or orderlies, as they called them in Kolyma, and apart from the top bosses' orderlies, the prisoners who were personal cooks, personal servants. Everything everywhere had been cleaned out.

There was only one part subject to the young boss that hadn't made the required contribution: the hospital. That was where the reserves were hidden. Criminal doctors were sheltering malingerers.

We, the reserves, knew why the boss had come, why his jeep had driven up to the hospital gates. Actually, the hospital had neither gates nor fences. The district hospital was surrounded by taiga marsh and stood on a small hill: two steps to either side, and you had lingonberries, chipmunks, squirrels. The hospital was called Squirrel, although there hadn't been a single squirrel there for some time. An ice-cold rivulet, hidden by scarlet moss, ran down a mountain ravine. The hospital stood where the rivulet joined a stream. Neither the rivulet nor the stream had names.

Lieutenant Soloviov knew the local topography when he planned his operation. Even a squad of soldiers wouldn't have been enough to surround a hospital like this in a taiga marsh. His dispositions were different. The lieutenant's military knowledge gave him no peace; he was seeking a solution in his deadly but perfectly risk-free game: a battle with a prisoners' world that had no rights.

This hunt was a game that stirred Soloviov's blood: he was hunting people, hunting slaves. The lieutenant wasn't looking for literary comparisons; this was a military game, an operation that he'd planned well in advance: D-Day.

Guards were bringing Soloviov's booty, people, out of the hospital. Everyone who was dressed, everyone whom the boss found on their feet, not in bed, as well as people taken out of their beds whose lack of pallor aroused Soloviov's suspicions: they were all taken to the supply stores where the jeep was standing. The driver took out his pistol.

"Who are you?"

"A doctor."

"To the stores! We'll sort you out there."

"Who are you?"

"A paramedic."

"To the stores!"

"Who are you?"

"A night nurse."

"To the stores!"

Lieutenant Soloviov was personally running this operation to recruit more workmen for the gold mines.

The boss himself inspected all the cupboards, all the attics, where, in his opinion, people might be concealed, trying to hide from the metal, from "metal No. 1."[8]

The one-legged night watchman was also told to stand by the stores: that was where they'd sort him out.

Four women, medical nurses, were taken to the stores. That was where they'd be sorted out.

Eighty-three people were standing packed together around the stores.

The lieutenant made a short speech: "I'll show you how to put together a party of prisoners. We're going to smash your little nest. Papers!"

The driver took out several sheets of paper from his boss's map case. "Doctors, step forward."

Three doctors stepped forward: they were all the hospital had.

A pair of paramedics stepped forward: the other four stayed with the ranks. Soloviov was holding the hospital's staff list.

"Women, step forward; the rest of you, wait!"

Soloviov made a telephone call from the hospital office. Two trucks he had ordered the day before drove out to the hospital.

Soloviov picked up an indelible pencil and a piece of paper.

"Come and sign up. Leave out your article of conviction and your sentence. Just your surname, we'll sort you out when we get there. Right!"

"Surname?"

"I'm sick."

"What's wrong with him?"

"Polyarthritis," said the chief doctor.

"I don't know what words like that mean. He looks in good shape. For the mines." The chief doctor decided not to argue.

Krist was standing in the crowd, and a familiar anger pounded in his temples. Krist knew by now what he had to do.

Krist stood there, thinking calmly: People distrust you so much, boss, that you have to search the hospital attics personally and use your own blue eyes to look under every hospital bed. After all, you could have just given the orders and sent everybody off without putting on this show. If you are a boss, in charge of the camp services at the mines, you write the lists personally, you catch people personally. So I'll show you how to make a run for it. "I just need a minute to get my things . . ."

"Five minutes to get your things. Hurry!"

Those were the words Krist was waiting for. After entering the barracks where he lived, Krist didn't pick up his things: he took only his quilted jacket, hat with earflaps, a piece of bread, matches, tobacco, and a newspaper, stuffed everything he had squirreled away into an inner pocket, and then put an empty food can into the outer pocket. Then he went out, not to the supply stores but to the barracks and into the taiga, easily avoiding the sentry, who believed the operation and the hunt were now over.

For a whole hour Krist climbed up along the rivulet, until he could choose a safe place, lie down on the moss, and wait.

What was he relying on? He was relying on the following: if it was an ordinary roundup, anyone they grabbed in the street would be shoved into a truck and driven to the mine, and they wouldn't hold up a truck until nighttime. But if it was a proper hunt, then they would send out a search party for Krist that evening, they wouldn't even let him into the hospital, and they would do their utmost to deliver Krist, even if it meant digging him out of the ground and sending him on separately.

They wouldn't give him an extra sentence for absenting himself like this. If a bullet didn't get him while he was leaving—and nobody was shooting at Krist—then he would be a hospital nurse again. And if it was Krist who had to be sent away, that would be done by the chief doctor, without Lieutenant Soloviov's involvement.

Krist took a palmful of water and drank his fill, then smoked, letting the smoke go up his sleeve, lay for a while, and when the sun began to set, he went downhill along the ravine to the hospital.

On the pavement Krist was met by the chief doctor. She smiled, and Krist realized that he was going to stay alive.

The dead, deserted hospital was coming back to life. New patients were putting on old gowns and being admitted by the male nurses, thus beginning, perhaps, their path to salvation. Doctors and paramedics issued medicines, and took the temperatures and the pulses of the seriously ill.

1965

BRAVE EYES

The barracks world was hemmed in by a mountain ravine. It was bounded by sky and stone. Here, the past was the other side of a wall, a door, a window; inside, nobody remembered anything. Inside was the world of the present, of everyday trivia, a day that you couldn't even call futile, for this world depended on some stranger's will, not ours.

The first time I left that world it was along a bear track.

We were at an exploration base, and every summer, and the summers were brief, we managed to make short excursions into the taiga, five-day expeditions along streambeds, along the sources of unnamed rivers.

Those who stayed at the base worked on ditches, trial digs, trial shafts; those who were on the march collected samples. The stronger men stayed at the base; the weaker went on the excursions. That included Kalmayev, a seeker of justice, a conscientious objector, a man who never stopped arguing.

The exploration team was building barracks, and the job of assembling eight-meter larch trunks that had been sawed down was for horses. But there were no horses, and all those trunks were dragged back by people harnessed to leather straps and ropes, like the Volga bargemen: one, two, pick it up. Kalmayev didn't like this work.

"I can see you need a tractor," he told the foreman Bystrov when work was over. "So why don't you sentence a tractor to the camps and skid and haul the trees. I'm not a horse."

The second man was Pikulev, who was fifty years old, a Siberian and a carpenter. We didn't have anyone quieter than Pikulev. But Bystrov, whose eye was trained by his experience of the camps, detected a special quality in Pikulev.

"What sort of carpenter are you," Bystrov asked Pikulev, "if your behind is always looking for somewhere to sit down? The moment you finish work, you won't stand for a minute, you won't take a step: you instantly sit on a tree trunk."

The old man found it hard, but Bystrov's words were persuasive.

I was the third man, an old enemy of Bystrov. In winter, the previous winter, when I was taken out to work for the first time and I went up to the foreman, Bystrov said, repeating his favorite joke, into which he put his entire soul, all his deepest scorn, hostility, and hatred of people like me, "What work would you like me to give you: clerical or manual?"

"I don't mind."

"We haven't got any clerical. So let's go and dig a foundation pit."

Although I was very familiar with this saying, and although I could do anything—I could do any work as well as anybody else and could even show others how to do it—Bystrov took a dislike to me. Naturally, I never asked, I never "sucked up"; I didn't give or promise bribes: I could have given Bystrov rubbing alcohol. Sometimes we had rubbing alcohol to use as a bribe. But, in a nutshell, when a third person was needed for an expedition, Bystrov put forward my name.

The fourth man was a contract worker, a free geologist called Makhmutov.

The geologist was young and a know-it-all. When we were on a trip he would suck sugar or chocolate; he ate separately from the rest of us, and would take a newspaper and canned food out of his bag. He did promise to shoot a partridge or a grouse for us; true, twice when we were walking, a capercaillie, not a grouse, flapped its spotted wings, but the geologist was nervous when he fired and he missed. He couldn't hit a bird in the air. Our hopes of having a bird shot for us were dashed. We boiled up canned meat for the geologist in a separate cooking pot, but that wasn't considered to be a breach of custom. In prisoners' barracks nobody ever demanded a share of others' food, and this was a very particular situation where different worlds clashed. All the same, the three of us, Pikulev, Kalmayev, and I, would wake up at night to the sound of Makhmutov crunching bones, chomping and belching. But we weren't all that irritated.

Our hopes for game meat were dashed on the very first day. We set up a tent in the twilight on the banks of a stream that stretched out by our feet like a silver thread; there was thick grass, about three hundred meters of it, on the opposite bank, followed by the next stretch of rocky shore on our right. This grass grew on the streambed: in spring everything around was flooded; it was like a mountain reservoir, and now it was at its greenest.

Suddenly everyone was on the alert. Twilight was just beginning. Some animal—a bear, a wolverine, or a lynx—was moving through the grass and making it wave. Everyone could see the movement through the sea of grass: Pikulev and Kalmayev picked up axes, while Makhmutov, thinking he was a Jack London hero, took his small-caliber rifle off his shoulders and pointed it, loading it with a homemade bullet, a lump of lead, meant for an encounter with a bear.

But out of the bushes we saw the puppy Genrikh, the son of our murdered bitch Tamara, crawling toward us on his belly, his tail wagging.

The puppy had managed to cover twenty kilometers of taiga to catch up with us. After discussing the matter, we chased the puppy back. It took it some time to understand why we were giving it such a cruel reception, but it did understand and crawled off again through the grass, which again was set in motion, this time in the opposite direction.

The twilight thickened, and the next day began with sun and a fresh wind. We were climbing up the tributaries of countless, endless streams, looking for landslips on the slopes that would lead us to exposed seams where the geologist Makhmutov could detect signs of coal. But the land was silent, and we followed a bear track uphill. There was no other path in this area of downed timber, chaos, trees hurled down into the ravine by storms. Kalmayev and Pikulev dragged the tent up the stream, while the geologist and I went into the taiga, found a bear path, and, hacking our way through the fallen trees, climbed the path.

The larches were covered with green needles, the coniferous scent broke through the subtle smell of rotting tree trunks, even the mold had something of spring, of greenery about it, and the dead trunks exuded the smell of life. The green mold on a trunk seemed alive, a symbol, a sign of spring. In actual fact it was the color of decrepitude, the color of decomposition. But Kolyma raised more difficult questions for us, and the similarities between life and death did not bother us.

The path was not treacherous; it was an old path, tested by bears. Now people were using it for the first time since the world was created: a geologist with a small-caliber rifle, holding a geologist's hammer, while I followed behind with an ax.

It was spring: all the flowers were in bloom at the same time, the birds were singing their songs all at the same time, and the animals were in a hurry to catch up with the trees in a crazed propagation of their race.

The bear path was blocked by a sloping dead larch trunk, an enormous stump, a tree whose crown had been broken off by the storm, knocked off...When? A year or two hundred years ago? I don't know how centuries are marked, or even if there are any marks. I don't know how long big trees stay upright in Kolyma or what traces time leaves on the stump year after year. Living trees count time by rings: a ring for every year. How the change of seasons is marked on stumps, dead trees, I don't know. How long a dead larch smashed by a boulder or a storm-felled forest can be used as a den or shelter is something the animals know. I don't. What makes a bear choose another den? What makes an animal use one and the same hole twice or thrice?

A storm had bent the broken larch to one side but had been unable to tear it out of the ground: the storm didn't have the strength. The broken trunk hung over the bear path, and the path bent to swerve around the leaning trunk before straightening out again. It was easy to calculate the height of the quadruped.

Makhmutov struck the trunk with his geological hammer, and the tree responded with the dead sound of a hollow trunk, of emptiness. The empty space was a natural hole in a tree, lined with bark, a sign of life. A tiny animal, a weasel, tumbled out straight onto the path. It didn't vanish in the grass, the taiga, or the forest. The weasel lifted its eyes, full of despair and fearlessness, to see the people. The weasel was heavily pregnant: its birth pangs began on the path before our very eyes. Before I had time to do anything, shout, make sense of or stop anything, the geologist had fired his rifle point-blank at the weasel, firing a homemade lead bullet meant for a bear. Makhmutov was a bad shot, even when the game was on the ground.

The wounded weasel crawled down the bear path straight toward

Makhmutov, and he backed away, retreating from its gaze. The pregnant weasel's back paw had been shot away, and the weasel was dragging a bloody gore of unborn little animals, its children that would have been born an hour later when Makhmutov and I would have been well past the broken larch; they would have been born and would have emerged into the hard, serious animal world of the taiga.

I saw the weasel crawling toward Makhmutov, saw the courage, anger, vindictiveness, and despair in its eyes. I saw that there was no fear in those eyes.

"The bloody animal's going to bite through my boots," said the geologist as he backed away, protecting his nice new marsh boots. Then, grabbing his rifle by the barrel, the geologist placed the butt against the face of the dying weasel.

But the weasel's eyes had dimmed, and the anger in those eyes vanished. Pikulev arrived, bent over the dead animal, and said, "It had brave eyes."

Had he understood anything? Or not? I don't know. The bear path led us out to the banks of the stream, to our tent, our meeting point. Tomorrow we would begin the walk home, but by some other path, not this one.

1966

MARCEL PROUST

THE BOOK had vanished. A big, heavy, large-format book that had been lying on a bench had vanished before the eyes of dozens of patients. Whoever saw the theft wasn't going to say anything. There are no crimes in the world without witnesses, animate or inanimate. But suppose there are such crimes? Stealing a novel by Marcel Proust is not the sort of secret one is too afraid to forget. In any case, people are silent if they receive a casual, anonymous threat, which still has an unerring effect even though the threat is casual. Anyone who saw it would stay silent out of fear. The beneficial effects of such a silence are confirmed by everything in camp life, and not only camp life but all experience of civic life. Any *freier* could have stolen the book on the instructions of a professional thief, to prove his boldness, his desire to belong to the criminal world, the real masters of camp life. Any *freier* could have stolen the book, just like that, because it was asking to be stolen. The book really was asking to be stolen: it was on the far end of the bench in an enormous yard of a three-story stone hospital building. Nina Bogatyriova and I were sitting on the bench. I had experienced the bare moors of Kolyma and ten years wandering over those mountain settlements; Nina had experienced the front. We had finished our conversation, sad and nervous, some time ago.

On sunny days patients were taken out for exercise. The women were taken out separately, and Nina, as a nursing assistant, watched over the patients.

I saw her to the corner, and when I came back the bench was still deserted: ambulatory patients were afraid of sitting on this bench; they thought that it was for the paramedics, the supervisors, the escort guards.

The book had vanished. Who was going to read that strange prose, so weightless that it seemed about to fly off into space, a world whose scales were displaced and switched around, so that there was nothing big and nothing small. Everyone is equal in the face of memory, as of death, and the author has the right to remember the servant's dress and to forget the mistress's valuables. The horizons of a writer are expanded extraordinarily by that novel. As a Kolyma man, a political prisoner, I was carried off into a world that I had lost long ago, to other habits I had forgotten and no longer needed. I had plenty of time for reading. I was a paramedic on night duty. I was crushed by *Guermantes*. My acquaintance with Proust began with *Guermantes*, the fourth [sic] volume. The book had been sent to a paramedic I knew, Kalitinsky, who was by then parading himself around the ward in his velvet golf breeches, a pipe between his teeth, wafting the unbelievable scent of Capstan tobacco. The Capstan and the golf breeches came in a parcel that also contained Proust's *Guermantes*. Oh, you wives, you dear, naïve friends! Instead of cheap Russian tobacco, you send Capstan; instead of tough leather trousers, you send velvet golf breeches; instead of a broad, two-meter-long camel-wool scarf, you send something ethereal, more like a bow or a bow tie—a luxurious silk scarf that, wound around one's neck, is about as thick as a pencil.

Those same velvet breeches and silk scarf were sent in 1937 to Fritz David, a Dutch communist—perhaps he had another surname—he was my neighbor in the "intensive regime squad." Fritz David couldn't work: he was too emaciated, but the velvet breeches and luxurious silk tie or scarf couldn't be exchanged even for bread at the mine. So Fritz David died: he fell on the barracks floor and died. It was, however, so tightly packed that we all slept standing up, so it took time for the corpse to reach the floor. My neighbor Fritz David died first, then he fell.

All that was ten years earlier: what had *In Search of Lost Time* to do with that? Kalitinsky and I both recalled our world, our own lost time. I had no golf breeches in my time, but I did have Proust, and I was happy to read *Guermantes*. I didn't go back to the hostel to sleep. Proust was more precious than sleep. Anyway, Kalitinsky was hurrying me.

The book had vanished. Kalitinsky was furious, he was out of his mind with rage. We didn't know each other well, and he was sure that I had stolen the book to sell it for as much as I could. Casual thieving was a Kolyma tradition, a tradition inspired by hunger. Scarves, foot wrappings, towels, pieces of bread, tobacco. Leftovers from anything distributed or stolen vanished without a trace. In Kalitinsky's opinion, there was nothing in Kolyma that couldn't be stolen. I thought the same way. The book had been stolen. You could wait until the evening for some volunteer, some hero, to tip you off and say where the book was and who the thief was. But one evening, ten evenings, passed, and *Guermantes* had vanished without trace.

If it wasn't sold to a booklover—but what booklover was there among the camp bosses? You might meet admirers of Jack London in that world, but Proust? It could only be used to make playing cards: it was a heavyweight large-format book. That was one reason why I didn't keep the book on my lap but put it on the bench. It was a thick volume. It went to make cards, cards ... It would be cut up and that was it.

Nina Bogatyriova was a beauty, a Russian beauty; she'd only recently been brought over from the mainland and placed in our hospital. She had betrayed the motherland. Article 58, paragraph 1a or 1b.

"From occupied territory?"

"No, we weren't in occupied territory. It was near the front line. Twenty-five years plus five years with no civil rights has nothing to do with the Germans. It's down to the major. I was arrested because the major wanted me to sleep with him. I wouldn't. So I got this sentence. Kolyma. I'm sitting on this bench. It's all true. And it's all lies. I wouldn't sleep with him. I'd rather go off with my own kind. You, for example ..."

"I'm spoken for, Nina."

"I'd heard."

"It's going to be hard for you, Nina, because you're beautiful."

"I wish I wasn't: to hell with my looks."

"What are the bosses promising you?"

"To let me stay in the hospital as a nursing assistant. I can train to be a proper nurse."

"Women aren't allowed to stay on here, Nina. Not so far."

"But they've promised to let me. I have someone who'll help me."

"Who's that?"

"It's a secret."

"Be careful: this is an official government hospital. Nobody here has that much authority. None of the prisoners. It doesn't matter if it's a doctor or a paramedic. This isn't a mine hospital."

"I don't care. I'm happy. I'll make lampshades. And then I'll take the courses, as you did."

Nina stayed on in the hospital, making paper lampshades. And when she'd made enough, she was sent back to a party of prisoners.

"Is that your bit of skirt traveling with this party?"

"It is."

I looked around. Volodia, an old taiga wolf, a paramedic with no medical training, was standing behind me. He used to be a propaganda activist or the secretary of a town council.

Volodia was well over forty and he'd known Kolyma for a long time. And Kolyma had known Volodia for a long time. Volodia had been sent here to take the courses, to get some knowledge to back him up in his job. Volodia had a surname—Raguzin, I think—but everyone called him Volodia. Was he Nina's protector? That was too frightening a thought. Volodia's calm voice was behind me, saying, "When I ran the women's camp on the mainland I had everything under control. The moment there were rumors that someone was sleeping with a woman, wham! She was off to join a party of prisoners. And I'd bring in a new one. To make lampshades. And then everything would be under control again."

Nina left. Her sister Tonia stayed behind in the hospital. She was sleeping with the bread distributor—a profitable friendship—Zolotnitsky, a swarthy, good-looking, healthy man, a nonpolitical convict. Zolotnitsky had to pay a big bribe to get the job of hospital bread distributor, a job that promised and provided millions in profit; he was said to have bribed the hospital chief personally. That was fine, but Zolotnitsky turned out to be a syphilitic and had to have further treatment. The bread distributor was removed from his post and sent to the male venereal zone, a camp for men with venereal diseases. Zolotnitsky spent several months in the hospital, but managed to infect only one woman, Tonia Bogatyriova. Tonia too was carted off to a venereal zone.

The hospital was in turmoil. All the medical staff were sent to have an analysis, a Wasserman test. Volodia Raguzin the paramedic scored four crosses: syphilitic Volodia vanished from the hospital.

A few months later, the escort guards brought in some sick women, including Nina Bogatyriova. But then Nina was taken off farther: she had only a rest in the hospital. She was taken to the women's venereal zone.

I went out to meet the party of prisoners.

All that was left of Nina's former features were her deeply set large brown eyes.

"See, I'm off to the venereal zone . . ."

"Why there?"

"You're a paramedic: surely you know why people are sent to the venereal zone. It's Volodia's lampshades. I had twins. They were sickly. They died."

"Your babies died? Lucky for you, Nina."

"Yes. Now I'm as free as a bird. I'll get some treatment. Did you find that book?"

"No, I didn't."

"It was me that took it. Volodia asked me for something to read."

1966

THE FADED PHOTOGRAPH

ONE OF the predominant feelings in the camps is that of unlimited humiliation, with the consolation that there is always, in any situation, someone worse off than yourself. This relativity takes many forms. The consolation is what saves you, and it may well be a man's most important secret. This feeling...This feeling is what saves you, like a white flag, and at the same time it means accepting the unacceptable.

Krist had only just been saved from death, saved at least for today but no longer than that: a prisoner's tomorrow is a mystery that cannot be divined. Krist was a slave, a worm, certainly a worm, for in the entire living world the worm is the only creature that has no heart.

Krist had been admitted to the hospital, his dry skin flaking off with pellagra: the wrinkles had inscribed his last sentence on Krist's face. He was trying, at the bottom of his soul, in the last surviving cells of his skeletal body, to find enough strength, physical and spiritual, to survive until the next day. And so Krist puts on the male nurse's dirty overalls and sweeps the wards, makes the beds, washes patients, and takes their temperature.

Krist is now a god, and the new hungry men, the new patients, look at him as they would at their fate, a divinity that may help them, save them, but the patient doesn't know from what. All the patient knows is that he is facing a nurse who is himself a patient, who can put in a word to the doctor, so that the patient can stay an extra day in the hospital. Or Krist, when he is discharged, might even hand on his job, his bowl of soup, his nurse's overalls to the patient. And if that doesn't come to pass, it doesn't matter: there are always plenty of disappointments in life.

Krist put on his overalls and became a divinity.

"I'll wash your shirt for you. Your shirt. In the bathroom at night. And I'll dry it over the stove."

"There's no running water here: we get it brought in."

"Well, keep back a gallon or so."

Krist had long wanted to wash his tunic. He would have done so himself, but he was so tired that he could barely stand. The tunic was from the mines and completely soaked with salty sweat, so it was more a bundle of rags than a tunic. Very likely, the first wash would turn that tunic into dust, ashes, and compost. One pocket had torn off, but the other pocket was still usable, and that was where Krist kept everything that he considered for some reason to be important and necessary.

All the same, it had to be washed. It was just that this was a hospital, Krist was an assistant, and the garment was dirty. Krist recalled being taken on a few years earlier to copy out cards in the accounts office: the cards gave ten days of food rations, issued according to the percentage of production. He also recalled all those who lived in the same barracks hating him for those sleepless nights that gave him an extra dinner voucher. Krist recalled being immediately "sold down the river" by someone who complained to a staff accountant, a nonpolitical convict, and pointed to Krist's shirt, out of which a louse, as hungry as Krist, was crawling. He recalled somebody's iron hand dragging him that very instant from the office and throwing him out of the building.

Yes, it would be best to wash the tunic.

"You can sleep while I do the washing. A piece of bread will do, but if you haven't got any, never mind."

Krist didn't have any bread. But somebody at the bottom of his soul was shouting that even if he had to go hungry, the shirt still had to be washed. And Krist stopped resisting this alien, frightening willpower of a hungry man.

Krist slept as always, not a sleep but an oblivion.

A month earlier, when Krist hadn't yet been admitted to the hospital but was staggering about in an enormous crowd of goners from refectory to clinic, from clinic to barracks, in the white mist of the camp zone, a disaster had befallen him. Krist's tobacco pouch was stolen. It was empty, of course. That wasn't the first year he'd had no tobacco in his tobacco pouch. But he kept things—why?—in the pouch:

photographs and letters from his wife, a lot of letters. A lot of photographs. And although Krist never reread these letters and never looked at the photographs—that was too harrowing—he kept the package for what he hoped would be better times. It would have been hard to explain why during all his travels as a prisoner he carried about these letters, written in a large child's hand. A pile of letters had accumulated in his tobacco pouch. And now it had been stolen. The thief must have thought there was money in it, that a paper-thin ruble note had been slipped in between the photos. There was no ruble. Krist never found the letters. There were well-known rules about theft, observed by gangsters and would-be gangsters outside prison: papers had to be thrown into garbage cans, photographs had to be posted back or thrown in the trash. But Krist knew that these relics of humanity were completely eradicated in the Kolyma world. The letters were bound to have been burned on some campfire, or in the camp stove to get a little more light from feeding the fire: of course the letters were never going to be returned or just dropped where they could be found. But why the photos, the photos?

"You'll never find them," a neighbor told Krist. "The criminals have taken them."

"But what do they want them for?"

"Think about it! Photographs of a woman?"

"Well, yes."

"For jerking off."

Krist stopped asking questions.

He had kept old letters in his tobacco pouch. But a new letter and a photograph—a new passport photograph—were kept in the left pocket, the only remaining pocket, of his tunic.

As always, Krist slept not a sleep but an oblivion. And he woke up with a feeling: something good was definitely going to happen today. It didn't take Krist long to remember. A clean shirt! He flung his heavy legs off the trestle bed and went to the kitchen. Yesterday's patient came up to Krist.

"I'm drying it, drying it. It's over the stove."

Suddenly Krist broke out into a cold sweat. "The letter?"

"What letter?"

"In the pocket."

"I didn't unbutton the pocket. I couldn't allow myself to unbutton your pockets, could I?"

Krist stretched out a hand for his shirt. The letter—though soggy—was intact. The tunic was nearly dry, but the letter was wet, streaming water or tears. The photograph was washed out, faded, distorted, and only the general features recalled a face familiar to Krist.

The writing on the letter was also faded and washed out, but Krist knew the letter by heart and could read every phrase.

It was the last letter Krist had received from his wife. He hadn't been carrying it for long. The words of this letter had quickly burned out, dissolved, and Krist's memory began to be unsure of the text as a whole. Both photograph and letter had been irrevocably faded, rotted, annihilated after an especially thorough disinfection at the paramedic courses in Magadan, which had turned Krist into a true, not an imaginary, Kolyma divinity.

No price was too great, no loss seemed too exorbitant for those courses.

So Krist had been punished by fate. After mature reflection, many years later, Krist conceded that fate was right: he hadn't yet earned the right to have his shirt washed by someone else.

1966

THE BOSS OF THE POLITICAL ADMINISTRATION

THE SIREN kept on howling, howling, howling... It summoned the head of the hospital; it sounded the alarm. The visitors were already coming up the steps of the staircase. They had white gowns stretched over them, and the shoulders of the gowns were being ripped by the epaulets because the hospital uniform was too tight for these military guests.

Striding two steps ahead of everybody else up the staircase was a tall, gray-haired man, whose name was familiar to everybody in the hospital but whose face nobody had ever seen.

It was Sunday, Sunday for the free hired workers. The hospital chief was playing billiards with the doctors, cleaning them all out: everyone made sure to lose when they played the boss.

The hospital chief immediately guessed why the siren was howling, and he wiped the chalk off his sweaty fingers. He sent a messenger to say that he was on his way and would be there very soon.

But the visitors were not going to wait.

"We'll begin with the surgical department."

There were about two hundred men, two eighty-bed wards, one for clean surgery, the other for infected surgery. Everyone in the "clean" ward had closed fractures or dislocations. There were also small post-operative wards. And there was a ward for the dying who'd come from the infected section: sepsis, gangrene.

"Where's the surgeon?"

"He's gone to the settlement. To see his son. His son goes to school there."

"How about the duty surgeon?"

"He'll be here any minute."

But Utrobin, the duty surgeon, whom everybody in the hospital teased by calling him "Out Robbing," was drunk and failed to answer the call from the top bosses.

The top bosses were accompanied by the senior paramedic, a prisoner, as they toured the surgical department.

"No, we don't need your explanations or your medical notes. We know how they are written," a top boss told the paramedic as they entered the big ward, closing the door behind them. "And don't let the head of the hospital come in here for the time being."

A major, one of the adjutants, took up a position by the door to the ward.

"Listen," said the gray-haired boss as he went into the middle of the ward, waving his arm to include the two rows of beds along the walls. "Listen to me. I'm the new head of the political administration of Far East Construction. If anyone has fractures or other injuries inflicted at the pit face or in the barracks by foremen, free or convict, in other words, because of beatings, say so now. We've come to investigate the trauma rate. The trauma rate is appalling. But we are going to put an end to this. Everyone who has suffered these traumas must tell my adjutant. Major, take a record!"

The major opened his pad and took out a fountain pen.

"Well?"

"How about frostbite injuries, sir?"

"We don't want frostbite. Only beatings."

I was a paramedic on that ward. Seventy of the eighty patients were there because of traumas of that kind, and all that was in their notes. But not a single patient responded to the boss's invitation. Nobody trusted the gray-haired chief. You only had to complain for them to deal with you, before you even vacated your hospital bed. But if you left things as they were, you would be allowed to stay in the hospital for an extra day, to thank you for your meek nature and common sense. Staying quiet was much more to your advantage.

"Take me, for example, my arm was broken by a soldier."

"By a soldier? Our soldiers don't hit prisoners, do they? I expect it wasn't a soldier doing guard duty, but some foreman?"

"Yes, it must have been a foreman."

"Well, see what a bad memory you have. And something like this visit of mine doesn't happen often. I'm the top inspector. We won't let anyone hit anyone. An end has to be put altogether to any roughness, senseless violence, and foul language. I've already made a speech at a meeting of the administrative management. I said that if the head of Far East Construction is rude when he talks to the head of the administration, if the head of the mine administration allows himself to use offensive language or obscenities when reprimanding the heads of the mines, then how is the head of the mine going to talk to the heads of the sections? It will be nothing but a torrent of obscenities. And that will only be using mainland language. The head of the section then tells off the clerks of works, the foremen, and the craftsmen in pure Kolyma obscenities. What can the craftsman or foreman do then? Take a stick and flog the workmen. Am I right, or not?"

"Right, sir," said the major.

"Nikishov made a speech at the same conference. He said, 'You're new people, you don't know Kolyma; here conditions are different, and so are the moral principles.' But I told him, 'We've come here to work, and we will do so, but we won't work the way Nikishov says, but as Comrade Stalin tells us to.'"

"Quite right, sir," said the major. Once the patients heard Stalin's name they became completely mute.

The department managers were jostling outside the ward: they'd been called out from the quarters, and the head of the hospital was waiting for the top boss's speech to finish.

"Are they dismissing Nikishov, then?" asked Baikov, the manager of the second therapeutic department, but he fell silent after being hissed at.

The head of the political administration came out of the ward and shook each doctor's hand.

"Come and have a bite to eat," said the head of the hospital. "Dinner is served."

"No, no." The head of the political administration looked at his watch. "I have to be off so as to reach Zapadnoe and Susuman by nightfall. We have a meeting tomorrow. All the same ... But not a full dinner. I know what. Give me my briefcase." The gray-haired boss took a heavy briefcase from the major's hands. "Can you give me a glucose injection?"

"Glucose?" said the puzzled head of the hospital.

"You know, glucose. I need an intravenous injection. I haven't touched alcohol since I was a child . . . I don't smoke. But every other day I take glucose. Twenty cc's of glucose intravenously. When I was still in Moscow, my doctor advised me to. What do you think? It's the best tonic. Better than all those ginsengs, all those testosterones. I always carry glucose on me. But I don't carry needles: I can get injections in any hospital. So give me one."

"I don't know how to," said the head of the hospital. "I'll just hold the tourniquet. Here's the duty surgeon, it's up his alley."

"No," said the duty surgeon. "I don't know how to either. Sir, not every doctor can do that sort of injection."

"Well, a paramedic, then."

"We don't have any paramedics who aren't convicts."

"How about this one?"

"He's a former political prisoner."

"Odd. Never mind. Can you do it?"

"I can," I said.

"Boil the syringe."

I boiled the syringe and cooled it. The gray-haired boss took a box of glucose out of his briefcase, and the head of the hospital poured alcohol over his hands and, along with the party organizer, broke the top off the vial and sucked the glucose into the syringe. The head of the hospital put the needle on the syringe and handed it to me, then, taking a rubber tourniquet, restricted the top boss's upper arm. I injected the glucose and pressed cotton wool on the injection site.

"I've got a docker's veins," the boss kindly joked to me.

I said nothing.

"Well, I've had my rest: it's time I was off." The gray-haired boss stood up.

"Won't you look at the therapeutic wards?" asked the head of the hospital, afraid that if his visitors had to come back to inspect the therapeutic patients, then he was bound to receive a reprimand for not reminding them in good time.

"There's no need for us to see the therapeutic patients," said the boss of the political administration. "This visit is for a specific purpose."

"How about dinner?"

"No dinners. Work comes first."

The siren roared, and the boss's car vanished in the freezing haze.

1967

RIABOKON

THE MAN in the hospital bed next to Riabokon—a trestle bed with
a mattress stuffed with chopped dwarf-pine needles—was Peters, a
Latvian who had fought, like all Latvians, on every front in the Civil
War. Kolyma was Peters's last front. The Latvian's enormous body was
like that of a drowned man—it was bluish white and swollen from
starvation. It was a young body with all the folds smoothed out, all the
wrinkles gone: everything was understood, narrated, and explained.
Peters was silent for days on end; he was afraid to make the slightest
movement—his bedsores now smelled, stank, in fact. Only his whitish
eyes followed the doctor, Dr. Yampolsky, when he entered the ward.
Dr. Yampolsky, the head of the health service, wasn't a doctor. He
wasn't even a paramedic. Dr. Yampolsky was simply an arrogant guy
who had made his career by denouncing people. But Peters didn't know
that and forced his eyes to show some hope.

Riabokon did know Yampolsky: whatever else, Riabokon had once
been a free man. But Riabokon hated both Peters and Yampolsky in
equal measure, and kept a malicious silence.

Riabokon was not like the drowned man. He was enormous and
bony, and his veins had shriveled. The mattress was too short for him,
and the blanket went up only to his shoulders, but Riabokon didn't
care. His Gulliver-size feet overhung the bunk, and Riabokon's yellow,
bony heels, looking like billiard balls, banged on the floor, which was
made from rough-sawn planks, whenever he moved to bend and poke
his head through the window: it was impossible to push his bony
shoulders through to the outside, to the sky, to freedom.

Dr. Yampolsky was expecting the Latvian to die in the next few hours: dystrophics like Peters were supposed to die very quickly. But the Latvian was prolonging his life and increasing the bed-occupancy rate. Riabokon was also waiting for the Latvian to die. Peters had the only long trestle bed in the hospital, and Yampolsky had promised Riabokon he could have this bed when Peters died. Riabokon was breathing by the window, unafraid of the cold, intoxicating spring air; he was filling his lungs and thinking about getting into Peters's bed after Peters died, and being able to stretch out his legs for at least a few days and nights. All he had to do was lie down and stretch out, and certain special muscles would rest, and Riabokon would then live.

The doctor's round was over. There was no medicine: potassium permanganate and iodine worked miracles even in Yampolsky's hands. So, there being no medicine, Yampolsky hung on, acquiring experience and seniority. He wasn't blamed for deaths. Anyway, who was ever blamed for deaths?

"Today we'll give you a bath, a warm bath. All right?"

Anger flared up in Peters's whitish eyes, but he didn't say or even whisper a word.

Four patients acting as male nurses, along with Dr. Yampolsky, crammed Peters's enormous body into a wooden barrel, which had contained solidol truck grease but had been steam-cleaned and scrubbed.

Dr. Yampolsky made a note of the time, checking his wristwatch, a gift to the beloved doctor from the criminals at the mine where Yampolsky used to work, before he came to this stone mousetrap.

Fifteen minutes later the Latvian started making croaking noises. The nurses and the doctor dragged their patient out of the barrel and onto the trestle bed. The Latvian managed to pronounce clearly: "Sheets! Sheets!"

"What sheets?" asked Dr. Yampolsky. "We don't have any."

"He's asking for a shroud," Riabokon guessed.

Looking closely at Peters's trembling chin, his eyes that were now closing, and the swollen blue fingers groping all over his body, Riabokon thought that Peters's death was his, Riabokon's, good fortune, not only because of the long bunk but also because Peters and he were old enemies: they had clashed in battles somewhere near Shepetovka.

Riabokon had been a fighter for the Greens under Makhno. Now his dream had come true: he lay down on Peters's bunk. And I lay down on Riabokon's bunk, and am writing this story.

Riabokon was in a hurry to talk, in a hurry to tell me his story, and I was in a hurry to remember. We were both experts on life and death.

We knew the memoir writer's law, the basic constitutional law: whoever writes last is right. He outswims the current of witnesses and pronounces sentences with the look of someone in possession of the absolute truth.

Suetonius's history of the twelve Caesars is based on something as subtle as crude flattery of his contemporaries and curses of all the dead, curses none of the living respond to.

"Do you think Makhno was anti-Semitic? That's all nonsense. His advisers were Jews. Iuda Grossman-Roshchin, Baron. I was just an ordinary soldier with a machine-gun carriage. I was one of the two thousand that Makhno led off to Romania. I didn't have any luck in Romania. A year later I crossed the border. I was given three years' exile, then I came back, was on a collective farm, and was swept up in 1937…"

"Preventative imprisonment? The usual 'five years in distant camps.'"

Riabokon had an enormous round rib cage, and the ribs stood out like hoops on a barrel. It seemed that if Riabokon had died before Peters, you could turn the Makhno fighter's rib cage into hoops for a barrel, the Latvian's last bath, as prescribed by Dr. Yampolsky.

With his skin stretched over his skeleton, Riabokon seemed to be nothing but a teaching aid for topographical anatomy, a pliable living carcass in place of some waxwork. He didn't say much, but he could still summon the strength to preserve himself from bedsores by getting up and walking around. His dry skin was flaking off all over his body, and the blue patches that precede bedsores could be seen on his hips and loins.

"Well, I came. There were three of us. Makhno was on the porch. 'Can you shoot?'—'Yes, sir.'—'Well, tell me, if you're attacked by three men, what do you do?'—'I'll think of something, sir.'—'That's the right thing to say. If you said, "I'll kill the lot of you," I wouldn't take you into the squad. Cunning is the only way, cunning.' Anyway, what's the point of going on about Makhno? A Cossack leader. We're all going to die. I heard he died, too."

"Yes. In Paris."

"God rest his soul. It's time we went to sleep."

Riabokon pulled a decrepit blanket over his head, exposing his legs beneath the knees, and then began to snore.

"Listen . . ."

"What?"

"Tell us about Maruska and her gang."

Riabokon pushed the blanket off his face. "What's there to tell? A gang's a gang. Sometimes on our side, sometimes on yours. She was an anarchist, that Maruska. She spent twenty years doing a heavy-labor sentence. She escaped from Novinskaya prison in Moscow. She was executed by Slashchov in the Crimea. 'Long live anarchism,' she yelled when she died. Do you know who she was? Her surname was Nikiforova. She was a real hermaphrodite. Had you heard that? Well, let's go to sleep."

When the natural Makhnovite's five-year sentence was over, he was released but not allowed to leave Kolyma. Riabokon had to work as a loader at the stores where he had labored for five years as a prisoner. This was unbearably insulting, like having his ears boxed or his face slapped: not many could have borne it. Apart from the specialists,[9] of course. But a prisoner's main hope is that things will change, change completely when he is released. Departure, transfer, a change of place can also calm him, save him.

The salary was small. Could he steal from the stores, as he used to? No, Riabokon's plans were different.

Along with three other former prisoners, Riabokon went "on the ice," that is, he ran off deep into the taiga. He and some others formed a group of bandits: they were all *freiers*; none of them had anything to do with the criminal world, but they had breathed the same air as the criminals for several years.

Such an escape was attempted in Kolyma only by free men, free citizens not prisoners, for prisoners are guarded and counted at roll calls four times a day. This gang included the mine's chief accountant, a former prisoner, like Riabokon. He too had been a prisoner. Of course, there were no contract workers in the gang—contract workers come to Kolyma for the ruble bonuses; they were all former prisoners. These men had no bonuses: the only source of a bonus for them was a holdup.

The four murderers robbed people up and down the central main road, a thousand-kilometer highway, for a whole year. For a year they roamed freely, robbing cars and trucks and settlement apartments. They would hijack a truck and dump it down a mountain ravine.

Riabokon and his friends didn't hesitate to kill anyone. They weren't afraid of getting new sentences.

A month, a year, ten years, twenty years were all identical sentences, to judge by the Kolyma example and the northern morality.

This venture ended as they all do. A brawl, a quarrel, an unequal distribution of the spoils. The accountant, who was the gang leader, lost his authority. He had given false information and had blundered. A trial. Twenty-five years and five years' deprivation of civic rights. At the time murder didn't incur the death penalty.

Not a single recidivist criminal belonged to this group. They were ordinary *freiers*. Even Riabokon. The moral ease with which he'd killed people in Guliai-Pole[10] during the Civil War he had acquired for life.

1966

THE LIFE OF ENGINEER KIPREYEV

FOR MANY years I thought that death was a form of life and, reassured by my untested judgment, I tried to work out the formula for actively protecting one's existence on this woebegone earth.

I thought that a man can consider himself human only when he feels at any moment with his entire body that he is prepared to commit suicide, prepared to intervene in his own life. Being aware of this choice is what gives someone the will to live.

I tested myself many times and, as I felt I had the strength to die, I remained alive.

Much later I realized that I had merely built myself a refuge, that I had backed away from the question, for at the decisive moment I wouldn't be the person I am now, when life and death are a game of willpower. I would have weakened, changed; I would not be true to myself. I didn't start thinking about death, but I sensed that my former decision needed an adjustment, that making oneself promises and swearing youthful vows was too naïve and too dependent on the circumstances.

What convinced me of this was the story of engineer Kipreyev.[11]

I have never betrayed or sold out anyone in my life. But I don't know how I would have held up if I had been beaten. I went through all my interrogations in the luckiest way: without any beatings, without method No. 3. My interrogators never laid a finger on me. That was sheer luck, nothing else. It was just that I was interrogated at an early point in the first half of 1937, when torture was not yet in use.

But engineer Kipreyev was arrested in 1938, and he knew all about the dreaded prospect of beatings under interrogation. He endured it by hurling himself on his interrogator and was put, thoroughly battered, in solitary confinement. But the interrogators had no trouble getting the signature they required from Kipreyev: he was intimidated by the threat of his wife being arrested, so he signed.

Kipreyev had to endure this terrible moral trauma for the rest of his life. There are plenty of humiliations and degradations in a prisoner's life. In the diaries of those who were in Russia's liberation movement there is one terrible trauma: the plea for mercy. Before the revolution this was considered a disgrace, an indelible disgrace. Even after the revolution so-called petitioners, those who had for any reason at any time asked the tsar for release or for mitigation of their punishment, were categorically barred from joining the Society of Political Convicts and Forced Exiles.

In the 1930s everyone was forgiven everything, not only the "petitioners" but also people who had knowingly signed deliberate lies, sometimes deadly ones, denouncing themselves or others.

The living examples long ago became elderly or perished in the camps, in exile, while those who were in prison and underwent interrogation were without exception "petitioners." For that reason nobody even knew what moral tortures Kipreyev doomed himself to endure when he left for the Sea of Okhotsk to Vladivostok and Magadan.

Kipreyev was a physicist and engineer from the Kharkov Physics Institute, which came close to producing a nuclear reaction before any other research institute in the Soviet Union. Kurchatov[12] worked there, too. The institute did not escape the purges. One of the first victims in our atomic science program was engineer Kipreyev.

Kipreyev knew his worth. But his bosses didn't. In any case, it became obvious that moral steadfastness has little connection to talent, scientific experience, or even a passion for science. Those are different things. Knowing about beatings by the interrogators, Kipreyev prepared himself very simply: he was going to defend himself like a wild animal, to respond blow for blow, not distinguishing between those who operated within the system and those who created the system, namely method No. 3. Kipreyev was badly beaten and thrown into solitary confinement. Everything began again from the beginning. The physical forces were changing, and this was followed by a change in morals. Kipreyev signed. He had been threatened with his wife's arrest. Kipreyev was very ashamed of his weakness, of the fact that he, an intellectual, had yielded when he'd encountered crude force. It was then that Kipreyev, in prison, swore a lifelong oath never to repeat his shameful action. In fact, Kipreyev was the only person who thought his action was shameful. His neighbors on the bunks had also signed and slandered. They lay there without dying. Shame has no bounds, or rather, its boundaries are always personal, and anyone under interrogation will make different demands of themselves.

Kipreyev arrived in Kolyma with a five-year sentence. He was sure he would find a way to be released early, to make a breakthrough that would lead to freedom and the mainland. Of course, an engineer would be appreciated. And an engineer could earn working-day credits, freedom, a reduced term. Kipreyev despised manual camp labor; he quickly realized that nothing but death lay at the end of that path. If he worked where he could apply at least a semblance of the special knowledge he had, he would emerge a free man. And at least he wouldn't lose his qualifications.

The experience of working at the mine resulted in broken fingers caught in a scraper and physical weakness to the point of frailty: Kipreyev ended up in the hospital, and after the hospital, a transit camp.

There was more trouble: the engineer couldn't stop inventing, looking for scientific and technical solutions to the chaos of camp life.

The camp and the camp authorities, however, saw Kipreyev as nothing more than a slave. Kipreyev had cursed his own energy a thousand times, but it was looking for an outlet.

The stake in this gamble had to be worthy of an engineer, a scientist. That stake was freedom.

A nine-month winter is not the only thing that makes Kolyma a "wondrous planet." During the war, an apple cost a hundred rubles in Kolyma; an error in the distribution of fresh tomatoes, imported from the mainland, led to bloody dramas. All those things—apples and tomatoes—were naturally for the free man, the world of free contract workers, to which the prisoner Kipreyev did not belong. Kolyma is a wondrous planet not only because "the law of the taiga" applies there. Just because Kolyma was Stalin's special camp for extermination, or because there were shortages of tobacco or tea to make chifir,[13] the hard currency of Kolyma, its real gold that can buy anything, didn't make it a "wondrous planet."

There was a scarcity of glass: glass objects, laboratory glassware, instruments. The below-zero temperatures made glass more brittle, but the allowances for breakages were not increased. A simple medical thermometer cost about three hundred rubles. But there was no black market for thermometers. A doctor had to apply to the local NKVD officer about any application to replace one—for hiding a medical thermometer was harder than hiding a stolen *Mona Lisa*—but he never did. He simply paid the three hundred rubles and brought a thermometer from home to take the temperatures of seriously ill patients.

You could write a poem about empty food cans in Kolyma. A tin food can was a measure, always convenient and available. It was a measure for water, pearl barley, blancmange, soup, tea. It was a mug for chifir, which was brewed to its notable strength easily enough. It was a sterile container, cleansed by fire. Tea and soup were warmed up in cans placed on the stove or over a campfire flame.

A three-liter can was the classic cooking pot for goners: it had a wire handle that could easily be fixed to your belt. And who wasn't or wouldn't eventually be a goner in Kolyma?

A glass jar could become a light when framed in a wooden lattice. Bits of broken glass were used in cellular frames. A glass jar was a convenient transparent container for drugs in a laboratory. A half-liter jar held the dessert course in the camp refectory.

But the scarcest items in Kolyma were neither thermometers, nor laboratory equipment, nor empty cans, but electric lamps.

Kolyma has hundreds of mines, ore plants; thousands of sectors, trial seams; tens of thousands of gold, uranium, lead, and wolfram pit faces; thousands of camp expeditions, free workers' settlements, camp zones, and barracks for the guard squads, and all of them need light, light, and more light. For nine months Kolyma does without sunlight, without any light. The intrusive sun that never sets gives no salvation or anything else.

The light and energy come from tractors and locomotives coupled to generators.

Industrial drills, sizing trommels, pit faces demand light. Pit faces lit by projector lamps prolong the night shift and make labor more productive.

Electric lamps are needed everywhere. They are brought in from the mainland, three-hundred, five-hundred, and one-thousand candlepower, fit to light up the barracks and the pit face. The uneven current from small engines dooms the lamps to wear out early.

Electric lamps are a state problem in Kolyma.

It's not only the pit face that has to be lit: so too must the zone and the barbed wire running from the guard towers to a flag the Far North raises and never lowers.

A guard squad has to be guaranteed lighting. Just certifying that the prisoners are there (as they do at a mine pit face) is not enough, for here we're dealing with people who may try to escape, and although it is clear that there is nowhere to escape to in a Kolyma winter and that nobody has ever run away anywhere in a Kolyma winter, the law is still the law and, if there is no light and no lamps, burning flares are carried around the zone and left in the snow until dawn. The flare is made of a rag soaked in heating oil or kerosene.

Electric lamps soon burn out, and they can't be repaired.

Kipreyev wrote a report that amazed the director of Far East Construction. The director could already feel a medal on his tunic (a proper tunic, of course, not a soft-collared army tunic and not a civilian jacket).

Lamps could be repaired as long as the glass was intact.

Now ominous orders flew across Kolyma. All burned-out lightbulbs were to be delivered to Magadan. At an industrial site, at kilometer 47, a special factory was built. A factory for renovating electric lights.

Engineer Kipreyev was appointed the head of the factory floor. All the other personnel, the staff section that grew up around the repair of lightbulbs, was free contract labor. Success was entrusted to reliable, freely hired hands. But Kipreyev paid no attention to this. Those who built the factory, however, were compelled to pay attention to him.

The results were outstanding. Of course, the bulbs didn't work for long after they were repaired. But Kipreyev had saved Kolyma a certain number of golden hours and days. These days amounted to a great deal. The state benefited enormously, as did the military and the gold mines.

The director of Far East Construction was rewarded by a Lenin medal. All the bosses who had any connection to the repair of lightbulbs received medals.

But neither Moscow nor Magadan even thought of singling out prisoner Kipreyev. For them, he was a slave, a clever slave and nothing more.

All the same the director of Far East Construction didn't consider it possible to completely forget his correspondent from the taiga.

There was a great Kolyma holiday, celebrated by Moscow, in a small circle, at a formal evening in honor of whom?—in honor of the director of Far East Construction and every person who had received a medal and a letter of thanks. Apart from the government decree, the director of Far East Construction had issued his own decree about letters of thanks, awards, and incentives, sent to all who had taken part in the repair of lightbulbs, including all the managers of the factory that had a workshop for renovating lamps. There were, apart from medals and letters of thanks, also American wartime parcels. These parcels, which were part of the lend-lease supplies,[14] consisted of a suit, a tie, a shirt, and a pair of shoes. The suit seemed to have gone missing in transit, while the shoes, red leather American shoes with thick soles, were every boss's fantasy.

The director of Far East Construction consulted his assistant and they decided that the imprisoned engineer couldn't dream of a greater fortune or present.

As for reducing the engineer's term of imprisonment or releasing him unconditionally, the director of Far East Construction wouldn't even think of asking Moscow at such a tense time. The slave should be satisfied with his boss's old shoes and a suit the boss had only recently been wearing.

All Magadan and all Kolyma were talking about these gifts. The bosses here got more than enough medals and letters of thanks. But an American suit and thick-soled shoes were something like a journey to the moon, a flight to another world.

The formal evening came, the shiny cardboard boxes with the suits were piled up on a table covered with red cloth.

The director of Far East Construction read his decree, in which, of course, Kipreyev's name was not mentioned and couldn't be mentioned.

The head of the political administration read out the list for the gifts. The last name called out was Kipreyev's. The engineer came up to the table, which was brightly lit with lamps, his lamps, and took a box from the hands of the director of Far East Construction.

Kipreyev said loudly and clearly, "I'm not going to wear American hand-me-downs," and put the box on the table.

He was arrested there and then and given eight more years on his sentence, under an article that I don't know and that doesn't have any significance in Kolyma and doesn't interest anyone.

In any case, what article applies to refusing American gifts? But it wasn't just that, no, not that. The interrogator's conclusion on Kipreyev's new "case" stated, "He said that Kolyma was Auschwitz without the gas ovens."

Kipreyev accepted his second sentence calmly. He knew what he was risking by refusing American gifts. But Kipreyev did take some measures to ensure his own safety: he asked a friend to write a letter to his wife on the mainland to say that he, Kipreyev, had died. And he stopped writing letters himself.

The engineer was removed from the factory and sent to a mine to do manual labor. Soon the war was over and the camp system became even more complicated: Kipreyev, as a double recidivist, could expect the dreaded "numbered" camp that had no name.

The engineer fell ill and ended up in the central hospital for prisoners. Here Kipreyev's work was badly needed: an X-ray machine had to be assembled and restored to working order; it had to be assembled from old materials, from discarded and broken parts. Dr. Doctor, the head of the hospital, promised his release, a reduced sentence. Engineer Kipreyev had little faith in such promises: he was "listed" as a patient, and working days were credited only to hospital workers. But he wanted to believe the boss's promise: an X-ray room was not a mine or a gold-mine pit face.

At this point Hiroshima happened.

"That's the bomb, what we were working on in Kharkov."

"Forrestal's suicide.[15] The flood of sarcastic telegrams."

"Do you know what the real point is? For a Western intellectual it is very complicated, very difficult to make the decision to drop an atomic bomb. Depression, madness, suicide: this is the price a Western intellectual pays for such decisions. A Russian Forrestal would not have gone mad. How many good people have you met in life? Really good people whom you'd want to imitate and serve?"

"I can name you some right now: the engineer-wrecker[16] Miller and about five others."

"That's a very big number."

"The General Assembly has signed the Agreement on Genocide."

"Genocide? What's that when it's served for dinner?"

"We signed the agreement. Of course, 1937 wasn't genocide. It was the extermination of enemies of the people. Doesn't stop you signing the agreement."

"The regime is tightening the screws on everything. We mustn't keep quiet. Remember your alphabet book? 'We're not slaves. Slaves aren't us.'[17] We have to do something, prove something to ourselves."

"The only thing you can prove to yourself is your own stupidity. Living and surviving is the task. And not to fail ... Life is more serious than you think."

Mirrors don't preserve memories. But what is tucked away in my suitcase can hardly be called a mirror: a fragment of glass, as if the water's been clouded, and the river has remained turbid and dirty forever, after committing to memory something important, infinitely more important than the crystal current of a transparent river, so clear that the riverbed is visible. The mirror has become clouded and no longer reflects anything. But once the mirror was a mirror, it was a selfless gift I carried through two decades of camps, through freedom indistinguishable from camp life, and through everything that came after the Twentieth Party Congress. The mirror that was given to me was not a deal made by engineer Kipreyev; it was an experiment, a scientific experiment, the trace of that experiment in the darkness of the X-ray room. I had a wooden frame made for that piece of glass. I didn't make it, I ordered it. The frame is still intact, it was made by a carpenter, a

Latvian, a convalescent patient, in exchange for a bread ration. By then I was able to exchange a bread ration for such a personal and frivolous item.

I look at that frame: it was crude, painted with the oil paint used for floors—the hospital was being refurbished and the carpenter scrounged a little bit of paint. Then he lacquered the frame: the lacquer wore off a long time ago. You can't see anything in the mirror, but at one time I used it to shave with in Oymiakon, and all the free workers envied me. They envied me until 1953, when some wise free man sent a parcel of mirrors, cheap ones, to the settlement. Even those tiny, ten-cent mirrors, round or small, could be sold at prices reminiscent of the price of lightbulbs. But everyone took money from their savings books and bought them. The mirrors were all sold within a day, within an hour.

After that my homemade mirror didn't arouse envy in any of my visitors.

I still have the mirror. It's not an amulet. I don't know if it brings me any luck. Perhaps it attracts rays of evil, or reflects them and stops me from merging in the flow of humanity where nobody apart from me knows Kolyma or engineer Kipreyev.

Kipreyev didn't care. A criminal, almost a gangster, a recidivist more literate than most, a literate gangster was invited by the boss to be trained, a man who could understand the secret of the X-ray room, a secret that consisted of switching handles on and off; a criminal who went by the name of Rogov learned X-ray technology from Kipreyev.

The authorities had major plans; the last thing they were thinking of was Rogov the gangster. All the same, Rogov was installed with Kipreyev in the X-ray room, without doubt in order to keep an eye on him, to follow him, to denounce him, to take part in work of state importance as a friend of the people. He kept the authorities constantly informed and gave advance notice of all conversations and visits. And if he didn't interfere, he would denounce and supervise.

That was the authorities' main aim. In addition, Kipreyev was preparing some nonpolitical prisoner as his own replacement.

As soon as Rogov learned his trade, which was a profession for life, Kipreyev would be sent to Berlag, a numbered camp for recidivists.

Kipreyev understood all this and had no intention of contradicting fate. He taught Rogov and didn't think about himself.

Kipreyev was lucky in that Rogov was a bad student. Like every nonpolitical criminal who understood the main thing, that the authorities would not abandon a nonpolitical convict under any circumstances, Rogov was not an attentive student. But the hour came when Rogov said he could work, and Kipreyev was sent to the numbered camp. Then something broke in the X-ray machine and, thanks to the doctors' intervention, Kipreyev was sent back to the hospital. The X-ray room started working.

This is when Kipreyev experimented with the lens hood, the *blenda*.

A 1964 dictionary of foreign words defines *blenda* as "(4) a diaphragm (a shade with an adjustable opening), used in photography, microscopy, and X-ray machines."

Twenty years ago, *blenda* didn't exist in the dictionary of foreign words. This was a wartime innovation, an accidental invention originating from electron microscopy.

A page torn from a technical magazine fell into Kipreyev's hands, and the lens hood was used in the hospital X-ray room for prisoners on the left bank of the Kolyma River.

The lens hood was the pride and hope of engineer Kipreyev: a weak hope, however. There was a report on the lens hood for a medical conference, and a paper was sent to Magadan and to Moscow. There was no answer.

"And can you make a mirror?"

"Of course."

"A big one. Like a wall mirror."

"Any. Provided I have silver."

"Would silver spoons do?"

"They would."

Thick glass for the desks in bosses' offices was ordered from the stores and transported to the X-ray room.

The first experiment was unsuccessful, and Kipreyev in his fury smashed the mirror with a hammer.

One of the fragments is my mirror, a Kipreyev gift.

The next time everything went well and the boss got his dream from Kipreyev, a wall mirror.

The boss didn't even think of thanking Kipreyev with anything. Why should he? A sensible slave ought to be grateful in any case for being kept in a hospital with a bunk to lie on. If the lens hood had attracted the authorities' attention, he might have had a letter of thanks, but no more. The wall mirror was reality, the lens hood was a myth, it wasn't solid ... Kipreyev agreed fully with the authorities.

But at night, as he fell asleep on his trestle bed in a corner of the X-ray room, after waiting for his assistant and informer's latest woman to leave, Kipreyev had no confidence in Kolyma or even in himself. After all, the lens hood was no joke. It was a technical marvel. No, neither Moscow nor Magadan cared at all about engineer Kipreyev's lens hood.

In the camps nobody answers letters and nobody likes to be reminded. You just have to wait. Wait for an unexpected opportunity or the chance to meet someone important.

All that was bad for the nerves: Balzac's wild ass's skin[18] may still have been intact, but it was torn and crumpled.

For prisoners, hope is a form of shackling. Hope is always an absence of freedom. A man who has hopes of something changes his behavior, is more likely to go against his conscience than a man who has no hope. As long as the engineer was waiting for a decision about the accursed lens hood, he would bite his tongue, ignore all the jokes, called-for or uncalled-for, that his immediate superiors amused themselves with, not to mention his assistant who was waiting for the hour and day when he would be in charge. Rogov had learned by now how to make mirrors and assure himself profits and extras.

Everyone knew about the lens hood. Everyone teased Kipreyev, including the pharmacist Krugliak, the secretary of the party organization in the hospital. This ugly pharmacist was not a bad guy, but he was hot-tempered and, above all, he had been taught that prisoners were the lowest form of life. As for that Kipreyev...The pharmacist had only recently joined the hospital and hadn't heard at all about the renovation of lightbulbs. He would never have thought it worthwhile assembling an X-ray room in the depths of the Far North taiga.

Krugliak considered the lens hood to be a cunning fiction of Kipreyev's, a desire to "pass off a fake," to "palm off trash"—phrases the pharmacist had already learned.

In the surgical department treatment room Krugliak swore at Kipreyev. The engineer grabbed a stool and swung it at the secretary of the party organization. The stool was immediately ripped out of Kipreyev's hands and he was led away into the ward.

Kipreyev was liable to be shot, or sent to a punishment mine, which was worse than execution. Kipreyev had a lot of friends in the hospital, and not just because of his mirrors. The story of the lightbulbs was widely known and still fresh. He got support. But this was a question of article 58, paragraph 8: terrorism.

The head of the hospital was approached. This was done by the women doctors. The hospital chief, Vinokurov, didn't like Krugliak. Vinokurov valued the engineer and was expecting something to come of the inquiry about the lens hood. Above all, he wasn't a spiteful person; as a boss, he didn't use his authority to do evil. He looked after his own interests and was a careerist, so he didn't do people any good, but he had no malice toward anyone either.

"All right, I won't pass on the matter to the NKVD to start a case against Kipreyev," said Vinokurov, "provided that Krugliak, who is the victim, doesn't report it. If he does report it, a case will be opened. Punishment mine is the minimum."

"Thank you."

The men, his friends, had a talk with Krugliak.

"You must understand that the man will be shot. He's defenseless, after all. It's not like me or you."

"But he tried to hit me."

"He didn't hit you, nobody saw that. But if I quarreled with you, then I'd smash your face in before you said another word, because you're always poking your nose in and going for everybody."

Krugliak, basically a good-natured fellow, utterly unfit to be a Kolyma boss, yielded to persuasion. He didn't report the matter.

Kipreyev stayed in the hospital. Another month passed, and Major

General Derevianko, the deputy director of Far East Construction in charge of camps, the highest authority for prisoners, visited the hospital.

The bosses liked to stop over in the hospital. It was somewhere for a big northern boss to stay, where he could get a drink and a bite to eat, and have a rest.

Major General Derevianko put on a white gown and went from department to department, to stretch his legs before dinner. The major general's mood was cheerful, so Vinokurov decided to take a chance.

"I have a prisoner here who's done work of importance for the state."

"What sort of work?"

The hospital chief explained as best he could to the major general what the lens hood was.

"I want to recommend this prisoner for early release."

The major general asked about the details in the prisoner's file and, when he was told, he growled.

"I'll tell you this, chief," he said, "the lens hood is all very well, but you'd better send that engineer . . . that Korneyev—"

"Kipreyev, sir."

"Yes, yes, Kipreyev. Send him where he's supposed to be, with those details in his file."

"Yes, sir."

A week later, Kipreyev was sent away, and a week later the X-ray machine broke down, and Kipreyev was called back to the hospital.

Things now were serious: Vinokurov was afraid of the major general's wrath.

The chief of the administration was not going to believe that the X-ray machine had broken down. Kipreyev was supposed to go off with a party of prisoners but fell ill and stayed behind.

There could no longer be any question of his working in the X-ray room. Kipreyev was well aware of that.

Kipreyev had mastoiditis from a chill in the head, after sleeping on a camp bunk at the mine, and an operation was essential for his survival. But nobody would believe his temperature or the doctors' reports. Vinokurov raged as he demanded an immediate operation.

The hospital's best surgeons were ready to operate on Kipreyev's mastoiditis. The surgeon Braude was virtually a specialist in it. There are more chills than there should be in Kolyma, and Braude was very experienced and had performed hundreds of such operations. But he could only assist. The operation had to be done by Dr. Novikova, a major ear, nose, and throat surgeon, a pupil of Voyachek, who had worked for many years in Far East Construction. Novikova had never been a prisoner, but she had worked in the northern districts for many years, not because of the bonuses but because she could get away with a lot in the Far North. She was an alcoholic. After the death of her husband, this talented ear specialist, a beautiful woman, spent years roaming the Far North. She would begin brilliantly, but then go to pieces for weeks on end.

Novikova was getting on toward fifty. There was nobody with better qualifications. At the moment this ear specialist was on a drinking binge, but the binge was coming to an end, and the hospital chief authorized Kipreyev to be kept back for a few days.

Over those next few days Novikova got back on her feet. Her hands stopped trembling, and she operated brilliantly on Kipreyev, giving this X-ray technician a farewell gift, a completely medical one. She was assisted by Braude, and Kipreyev was given a bed in the hospital.

Kipreyev realized that he couldn't hope for more, that he wouldn't be kept in the hospital for an hour longer than was necessary.

He had the numbered camp waiting for him, and there, men went to work in lines of five, elbow to elbow, with thirty dogs surrounding the column of men as they were chased along.

Even in this utterly hopeless situation, Kipreyev remained true to himself. When the department head ordered a special diet for him—improved nutrition for this patient who had been operated on for mastoiditis, a serious operation—Kipreyev refused, declaring that in a department with three hundred patients there were those worse off than him with more rights to a special order.

So Kipreyev was driven away.

I spent fifteen years looking for engineer Kipreyev. I dedicated a play to his memory: that was an effective means for a man to interfere with the world beyond the grave.

Writing a play about Kipreyev and dedicating it to his memory was not enough. As fate had it, a female friend, whom I had known for a long time and who lived in a communal apartment in central Moscow, had a new neighbor, because of an advertisement and an apartment exchange.

The new neighbor, when she got to know the other tenants, came in and saw on the table the play dedicated to Kipreyev: she picked it up and turned a page or two.

"The initials are the same as a friend of mine's. Except that he's not in Kolyma but somewhere completely different."

My woman friend rang me. I refused to carry on with the conversation. It was a mistake. In any case, the hero of the play was a doctor, and Kipreyev had been a physicist and engineer.

"That's it, a physicist and engineer."

I put on a coat and went to see the new tenant in the communal apartment.

Fate weaves very cunning patterns. But why? Because it needs so many coincidences for its will to reveal itself so persuasively? We don't expend a lot of effort looking for one another, so fate takes our lives in its hands.

Engineer Kipreyev was still alive and in the north. He had been released as long as ten years ago. He'd been taken to Moscow, where he worked in closed camps. After his release, he returned to the north. He wanted to work in the north until he got his pension.

I went to see engineer Kipreyev.

"I'm not going to be a scientist now. Just an ordinary engineer will do. To come back with no rights, and out of touch, when my former colleagues and fellow students all have prizes and awards—"

"What nonsense!"

"No, it's not nonsense. I find it easier to breathe in the north. It will be easier to breathe until I get my pension."

1967

PAIN

THIS IS a strange story, so strange that anyone who hasn't been in a camp, who doesn't know the dark depths of the criminal world, the realm of gangsters, cannot even understand it. The camps are the very bottom of life. The criminal world isn't the bottom of the bottom. It's an utterly, utterly different and inhuman world.

There is a banal saying that history repeats itself twice: the first time as a tragedy, the second time as a farce.

No. There is also a third reflection of the same events, the same plot, a reflection in the underworld's distorting mirror. The plot is unimaginable but nevertheless real: it genuinely exists and is there alongside us.

The utterly real gallows "courts" and "courts of honor" that the criminals hold at the mines are reflected in the distorting mirror of feelings and actions. Here war games are played, scenes of war are re-enacted, and real blood is shed.

There is a world of higher forces, a world of Homeric gods who come down to our world to reveal themselves and to improve the human race by their example. True, the gods tend to be late. Homer praised the Achaeans, but we are enthused by Hector: the moral climate has changed a little. Sometimes the gods would invite human beings to heaven to observe their "lofty spectacles." All this is a mystery that the poet solved a long time ago. There is a world and an underground hell from which people sometimes return, where they do not disappear forever. Why do they return? These people have hearts filled with an undying anxiety, an eternal horror of the dark world, and that is not the world beyond the grave.

This world is more real than Homer's heavens.

*

Shelgunov "got stuck" in the Vladivostok transit camp: he was a ragged, dirty, hungry, badly but not yet fatally beaten objector to work. People had an urge to live, but the ships and their prisoners, one party after the other, were constantly being transported across the sea, on ship after ship, like the train cars feeding the Auschwitz gas ovens. On the other side of a sea from which nobody ever returned, Shelgunov had been in the valley of death on which the hospital stood, and he was lucky enough to be sent back to the mainland: Shelgunov's bones were not good enough for the gold mines.

At this moment danger was again coming close; the lack of certainty that affected all of a prisoner's life was becoming more and more palpable to Shelgunov. And there was no escape from that uncertainty, from the fragility of hope.

The transit camp was an enormous settlement, divided in various directions into zones, which were precise squares, and entangled with barbed wire; it lay in the line of fire of a hundred or so guard towers, and it was lit, flooded with light by a thousand searchlights that blinded the prisoners' weak eyes.

The bunks at this enormous transit camp were the gates to Kolyma: they could suddenly empty and then fill up again with exhausted dirty people, new parties of prisoners from the outside world.

The steamships came back, the transit camp belched out a new portion of men, was emptied and then filled again.

In the zone, the largest in the transit camp, where Shelgunov was staying, all the barracks had been cleaned out, except for the ninth. The ninth was where the gangsters lived. That was where the King, the godfather, held sway. Wardens didn't show their faces there; the camp staff would go every day to the porch and collect the bodies of those who'd pushed their luck too far with the King.

The cooks carted off to this barracks the kitchen's best dishes and best items—the clothes brought by all the parties of prisoners always ended up as stakes in the gambling games of the ninth barracks, the King's.

Shelgunov, a direct descendant of the Shelgunovs of the People's

Will,[19] had a father who was an academician and a mother who was a professor in civilian life; since childhood, he had lived on books and for books; a bibliophile and a bookworm, he sucked in Russian culture with his mother's milk. Shelgunov was shaped by the nineteenth century, the golden age of humanity.

Share your knowledge! Trust people, love people! That was what Russian literature taught, and Shelgunov had some time ago felt enough strength to give back to society what he had inherited. Self-sacrifice was for everyone. To rise up against lies, however petty, especially if they were close by.

Prison and exile were the state's first response to Shelgunov's attempts to live as books had taught him to live, as the nineteenth century had taught him.

Shelgunov was struck by the vileness of the people surrounding him. There were no heroes in the camps. Shelgunov refused to believe that the nineteenth century had deceived him. A deep disillusionment in people, acquired during his interrogations, during his journey as a prisoner and in the transit camp, was suddenly replaced by his old cheerfulness, his old exaltation. Shelgunov found what he wanted, what he had been seeking and dreaming of: living examples. He met a force about which he had read a great deal, and which inspired a belief that was absorbed by his blood. This was the world of gangsters and criminals.

The bosses trampled down and despised Shelgunov's neighbors and friends, as well as Shelgunov himself, but they feared and revered the professional criminals.

Here was a world that boldly set itself against the state, a world that could help Shelgunov in his blind, romantic thirst for good and for vengeance.

"You wouldn't have a novelist here, would you?"

Someone had put a foot on the bunk to change his footwear. Judging by the necktie and the socks, in a world where only foot wrappings had existed for many years, Shelgunov quite rightly classified the man as someone from the ninth barracks.

"We have one. Hey, writer!"

"You've got a writer here!"

Shelgunov twisted himself around into the light.

"Let's go and see the King. You can 'print' us something."

"I'm not coming."

"What do you mean, you're not coming? You'll be dead before nightfall, you stupid fool."

The fiction he'd read was a good preparation for Shelgunov when he met the criminal world. Shelgunov crossed the threshold of the ninth barracks in a spirit of reverence. All his nerves, all his gravitation toward the good were tensed, as resonant as taut strings. Shelgunov had to have success, had to gain attention, trust, love from his noble listener, the barracks boss, the King. And Shelgunov did have success. All his miseries stopped the moment that the King's dry lips parted in a smile.

God knows what Shelgunov "printed"! Shelgunov absolutely refused to begin by playing an ace, *The Count of Monte Cristo*. No. He resurrected before the King's very eyes Stendhal's chronicles, Cellini's autobiography, the bloodthirsty legends of medieval Italy.

"Great stuff, great stuff!" rasped the King. "Those cultures really knew how to fill their bellies."

After that evening there was no question whatsoever of Shelgunov doing any work in the camp. He was brought a dinner and tobacco, and the next day he was moved to live permanently in the ninth barracks, officially, if that could be done officially in a camp.

Shelgunov became the court novelist.

"What's making you so miserable, novelist?"

"I'm thinking about home, about my wife . . ."

"Well . . ."

"You know, the interrogations, the train journey, the transit camp. I'm not allowed to write until I'm taken to the gold mines."

"You really are dumb. What are we here for? Write to your little beauty, and we'll send the letters . . . We don't use the post, we have our own railway. Okay, novelist?"

So once a week Shelgunov sent letters to Moscow.

Shelgunov's wife was a performer, a Muscovite performer and the daughter of a general.

Some time ago, at the time of his arrest, they had embraced.

"I don't mind if I don't get any letters for a year or two. I'll wait, I'll always be with you."

"The letters will come before that." Shelgunov confidently calmed his wife as husbands do. "I'll find my own channels. And you'll get my letters through those channels."

"Yes! Yes! Yes!"

"Shall I get the novelist? Or are you bored with him?" Karzubyi, concerned, asked his boss, the King. "Shouldn't I bring you a nancy from the new party? You can have one of our lot, or one of the politicals, the article fifty-eighters."

"Nancy" was the criminal's word for a homosexual.

"No, call the novelist. Mind you, we've stuffed ourselves enough on that literature. It's nothing but novels and theory. There's another game we can play with that *freier*. We've got all the time in the world."

"My dream, novelist," said the King, when all the ceremonies of going to sleep had been observed: he'd had his heels tickled, a cross hung around his neck, and prison "hot cupping"—tweaks with the fingernail—on his back. "My dream, novelist, is for a woman like yours to write to me from the outside. She's a looker!" The King turned in his hands a crumpled, faded photograph of Shelgunov's wife, Marina, which he'd managed to hang on to despite thousands of searches, disinfections, and thefts. "A real looker! Just right for a séance. A general's daughter! A performer! You *freiers* really are lucky, all our lot get are the poxy ones. And we don't even notice the clap. All right, time for bed. I'm already dreaming."

The next evening the novelist printed no novels.

"There's something I like about you, *freier*. You may be a dummy, but there's a drop of crook's blood in you. Write a letter to the wife of my pal, a real man, to put it in a nutshell. You're a writer. Make it really tender and clever: you know all those novels. I'll bet no woman can resist a letter from you. What are we? Just ignorant. Write. The man will copy it and send it. You even have the same name: Aleksandr. That's a laugh. Mind you, he's only Aleksandr for the job he's in here for. But he's still Aleksandr, Shura for short, or Shurochka."

"I've never written that sort of letter," said Shelgunov. "But I can have a go."

For each letter the King told him the overall gist, and Shelgunov-Cyrano[20] turned the King's ideas into reality.

Shelgunov wrote fifty of those letters.

One said, "I've confessed to everything; I'm asking Soviet power to forgive me."

"Do convicts, I mean gangsters," asked Shelgunov, unable to go on with the letter, "really ask for forgiveness?"

"Of course they do," said the King. "This bit of writing is a dummy, a hoax, a spoof. Military tactics."

Shelgunov asked no more questions; he just meekly wrote whatever the King dictated.

Shelgunov would read his letters out loud, polish the style, proud of his still-flamboyant brain. The King gave his approval, his lips barely parting in his royal smile.

Everything comes to an end. So did writing letters for the King. But there may have been an important reason: there was a rumor through the camp grapevine that the King was eventually going to be sent with a party of prisoners to Kolyma, where he had sent, by murder and deceit, so many others. He was going to be grabbed while he was asleep, it was said, his arms and legs bound, and then put on board the steamship. It was time to stop the correspondence; after all, Shelgunov had been speaking words of love to Roxane in Christian's voice for nearly a year now. But the game had to end the criminal way, with real live bloodshed...

Blood was congealing on the temple of a corpse lying before the King's eyes.

Shelgunov tried to cover the corpse's face, the reproachful look in its eyes.

"You see who it is? It's the man with your name, Aleksandr, Shura, the man you wrote the letters for. The special action squad finished him off today, cut his head off with an ax. He seems to have been walking around with his face covered by a scarf. Write: 'It's a friend of your Shura writing! Shura was executed today, and I am writing as fast as I can to let you know his last words...' Have you written that?" asked the King. "We'll copy it, and then we're quits. No need to write any more letters. I could have written that letter on my own." The King smiled. "We value education, writer. We're an ignorant lot."

Shelgunov wrote the funereal letter.

The King must have been clairvoyant: he was seized that night and sent overseas.

Shelgunov couldn't get in touch with home, and despaired. He struggled on, all alone, for a year, for two, for three, moving from hospital to work, outraged with his wife for having turned out to be a bitch or a coward, not using the "safe channels" to get in touch, forgetting him, Shelgunov, and trampling on every memory she had of him.

But it so happened that the hell of the camps ended and Shelgunov was released. He came back to Moscow.

His mother told him that she knew nothing about Marina. His father had died. Shelgunov found the address of a girlfriend of Marina's who worked in the same theater and he went to her apartment.

The girlfriend cried out.

"What's happened?" asked Shelgunov.

"Didn't you die, Shura?"

"What do you mean, die? I'm standing here, aren't I?"

"You'll live forever." A man emerged from the next room. "That's the belief."

"Marina is dead. After you were executed, she threw herself under a train. Not where Anna Karenina did it but in Rastorguyevo. She put her head under the wheels. The head was cut off clean and even. After all, you'd confessed to everything, but Marina refused to hear of it, she believed in you."

"I confessed?"

"You wrote so yourself. But a friend of yours wrote about your being executed. Look, that's her chest."

The chest contained all fifty letters that Shelgunov had written to Marina through his Vladivostok channels. The channels had worked perfectly, but not for *freiers*.

Shelgunov burned his letters. But where were Marina's letters with her photograph, that she had sent to Vladivostok? Shelgunov imagined the King reading his love letters. He imagined the King using the photograph "for a session." And Shelgunov burst into tears. After that, he wept every day for the rest of his life.

Shelgunov rushed to see his mother, to find at least something, at least a line in Marina's hand. It didn't have to be to him. There were such letters, two faded letters, and Shelgunov learned them by heart.

The general's daughter, the performer, was writing letters to a gangster. Gangster slang has a word "blagging," meaning "bragging." The word, *khlestat'sia* in Russian, came into gangster jargon from the boastful hero of a major literary work, Gogol's *Government Inspector*'s Khlestakov. The King certainly had something to "blag" about: that *freier* of a novelist. Good for a laugh. That nice Shura. But the proper way to write letters is "You disgusting bitch, you can't put two words together…" The King was reading phrases from his own affair with the prostitute Zoya Talitova.

"I haven't had an education."

"There's no such thing. You sluts should learn how to live."

Shelgunov, standing under a dark Moscow arch, could see all that easily. It was the scene with Cyrano, Christian, and Roxane, but acted in the ninth circle of hell, almost on the ice of the Far North. Shelgunov had trusted gangsters, and they had made him kill his wife with his own bare hands.

The two letters had become moldy, but the ink hadn't faded and the paper had not turned to dust.

Shelgunov read these letters every day. How could he keep them forever? What glue would repair the crevices, the cracks in these dark sheets of writing paper that once were white. Certainly not liquid glass: that would burn and annihilate them.

All the same, letters can be restored so that they last forever. Every archivist knows how to do this, especially one who works in a literary museum. All you have to do is make the letters speak.

The lovely woman's face was fixed to the glass next to a twelfth-century Russian icon, just above an icon of the Three-Handed Virgin. A female face, Marina's photograph was perfectly apt here: it was superior to the icon… In what way was Marina less of a Virgin, a saint? In what way? Why are there so many women who are saints, apostolic martyrs, while Marina was only an actress, an actress who put her head under a train? Or does the Orthodox religion not accept suicides as angels? The photograph was tucked away among the icons and was itself an icon.

Sometimes Shelgunov would wake up in the night and, without turning on the lamp, search the table with his hands for Marina's photograph. His fingers, frostbitten in the camp, could not distinguish an icon from a photograph, or wood from cardboard.

But perhaps Shelgunov was merely drunk. He drank every day. Of course vodka is bad for you, alcohol is hell, while disulfiram, the cure for alcoholism, is good. But what can you do if Marina's icon is on the table?

"Do you remember that *freier*, that novelist, the writer, Genka? Eh? Or did you forget him ages ago?" asked the King, when the time came to get to sleep after all the ceremonies had been carried out.

"Why should I forget him? I remember him. He was that jerk, that ass!" And Genka waved his stretched-out fingers over his raised ear.

1967

THE NAMELESS CAT

BEFORE the cat could jump out of the building, Misha the driver caught it in the entrance. He took an old industrial drill bit, like a short steel crowbar, and broke the cat's spine and ribs. Grabbing the cat by the tail, the driver opened the door with his foot and threw it out into the snow, the night, and the minus-fifty-degree frost. The cat belonged to Krugliak, the secretary of the hospital's party organization. Krugliak had an apartment to himself in a two-story house in the free settlement, and he kept a piglet in the room above Misha's. The plaster on Misha's ceiling was getting damp, swelling, and turning dark; yesterday it had collapsed, and pig manure had dripped from the ceiling onto the driver's head. Misha went to have it out with his neighbor, but Krugliak chased him out. Misha wasn't a spiteful man, but his feelings had been badly hurt, so when the cat fell into his clutches ...

Upstairs, in Krugliak's apartment, there was silence: nobody had come out when the cat shrieked, groaned, and howled for help. Was the cat calling for help, anyway? The cat didn't believe that people—whether Krugliak or the driver, it didn't matter—would come to its aid.

Coming to in the snow, the cat crawled out of a snowdrift onto an icy path that shone in the moonlight. I was passing by and took the cat with me to the hospital, a hospital for prisoners. We were not allowed to keep cats in the ward, although there were countless rats and no amount of strychnine or arsenic, let alone rattraps or snares, were of any use. The strychnine and arsenic were kept locked up and were not for use against rats. I begged the paramedic in the neurological and psychiatric department to take this cat for his psychos. The cat came to life and regained its strength there. Its frostbitten tail fell off, leaving a stump; it had a broken paw and broken ribs. But its heart was undamaged, and its bones mended. In two months the cat was doing battle with the rats and cleared the hospital's neurological and psychiatric department of them.

The cat's protector was Lionechka, a malingerer whom nobody could be bothered to expose: a nonentity who was saved for the duration of the war at the doctor's unaccountable whim. The doctor was a protector of the gangsters, and he trembled at every encounter with a recidivist, not because he was afraid but because he was overcome by delight, respect, and reverence for them. "A big thief," the respected doctor would say of his patients, who were blatant malingerers. It wasn't that the doctor had mercenary reasons—bribes or extortions. No. The doctor just lacked the energy for any selfless good action, and so he was pushed around by the thieves. Patients who were really ill were unable to get admitted to the hospital; they couldn't even get seen by the doctor. Besides, where is the boundary between a real or an imaginary illness, especially in the camps? A malingerer, an exaggerator, and a genuinely suffering patient are not so different from one another. A genuine patient needed to be a malingerer if he wanted to get a hospital bed.

But the whim of those psychos saved the cat's life. Soon the cat went on a spree and had kittens. That's life.

After that, gangsters came to the department, killed the cat and two kittens, and cooked them in a pot; they gave my friend the duty paramedic a pot of meat soup in exchange for his silence and as a mark of friendship. The paramedic saved one kitten for me, a little gray kitten whose name I don't know: I was afraid to give it a name, to baptize it, lest I bring misfortune to it.

I was then leaving for my sector in the taiga and under my shirt I took the kitten, the daughter of the nameless crippled cat eaten by the criminals. In my outpatient clinic I fed the kitten, made it a ball to play with, and left it a can of water. The problem was that my work involved constant excursions.

There was no question of locking the cat up for days at a time in the clinic. The cat had to be given to someone whose job in the camp might allow him to feed another being, human or animal, it didn't matter. The foreman hated animals. The guards? The guards' barracks kept only dogs, German shepherds. Why doom a kitten to endless torments, to daily outrages, to persecutions and kickings?

I handed the kitten to the camp cook Volodia Buyanov. Volodia was the man who distributed food in the hospital where I worked. In the big can, the pot in which the patients' soup was boiled, Volodia discovered a mouse, a mouse that had been boiled to pieces. Volodia made a fuss, although it wasn't a big fuss or a useful one, since there wasn't a single patient who would have refused an extra portion of this mouse soup. The story ended with Volodia being accused of doing it deliberately, etc. The woman kitchen manager was a free contract worker: Volodia was dismissed and sent to the forest to chop and saw firewood. That was where I was working as a paramedic. The kitchen manager's vengeance caught up with Volodia even in the forest. A cook's job is one that everyone wants. People volunteered to write denunciations of Volodia and to watch him day and night. Each of these volunteers knew that they wouldn't end up getting Volodia's job, but they still denounced, watched, and exposed him. Finally, Volodia was dismissed and he brought the kitten back to me.

I gave the kitten to the ferryman.

The little Duskania river, what they called in Kolyma the "spring," along whose banks we were lumberjacking, was, like all Kolyma rivers, streams, and rivulets, of variable, unstable width, depending on the water flow, and the water flow depended on the rain, the snow, and the sun. Even though this spring seemed to dry up in summer, a boat was necessary to get people from one bank to the other.

There was a hut by the stream where the ferryman lived; he was also a fisherman.

Hospital jobs acquired through good "connections" are not always easy ones. Usually these people were doing three jobs instead of one, while patients who had been assigned to a hospital bed on the basis of their medical notes found things were even more complicated and more subtle.

The ferryman was chosen in order to catch fish for the bosses. Fresh fish for the hospital chief's table. There were fish in the Duskania spring, but not many. This ferryman put great personal effort into catching fish for the hospital chief. Every evening the hospital driver and wood carrier would get from the fisherman a dark, wet sack filled with fish and wet grass: they flung the sack into the cab and drove the truck to the hospital. In the morning the driver brought the fisherman an empty sack.

If there were a lot of fish, the boss would pick out the best for himself, then call in the chief doctor and other lower-ranking men.

The bosses never gave the fisherman even tobacco: they considered that the fisherman's job should be valued by anyone who had "notes," that is, medical notes in the hospital.

Trusted men—foremen, office staff—willingly kept an eye on the fisherman, in case he sold fish behind the boss's back. And again, everyone wrote reports, exposing him, denouncing him.

The fisherman was an old camp hand, he was well aware that the very first time he failed at his job he would be packed off to the mine. But there were no failures.

Grayling, Manchurian trout, and Arctic cisco moved about in the shade under rocks, along the bright middle of the stream, following the current, the fast current, taking refuge in the darker, deeper, quieter, and safer places.

But this was where the fisherman's boat was moored, with fishing rods hanging from the prow, teasing the grayling. The cat, too, sat there, as stony as the fisherman, looking at the floats.

It seemed as if it were the cat that had cast the rods and the bait over the river. The cat quickly got used to the fisherman.

When it was thrown off the boat, the cat easily, if unwillingly, swam back to the bank and home. It didn't need to be taught to swim. But the cat never learned to swim of its own accord toward the fisherman when his boat was moored on two poles across the current and the fisherman was angling. The cat patiently waited for its master to return to the bank.

On the other side of the stream, and also along the bank, in pits, crossing the hollows and washed-out riverbed, the fisherman stretched out fishing weirs, a line with hooks and small live bait. That was how larger fish were caught. Later the fisherman would fence off a branch of the stream with stones, leaving four outlets, and he would then block those outlets with fish traps that he had plaited from willow. The traps were set well in advance, so that when the fish's autumn migration began, he wouldn't miss his chance.

Autumn was still a long way off, but the fisherman realized that the fish's autumn migration was his last job as a fisherman in the hospital. He would then be sent to the mine. True, for some time the fisherman could gather berries and mushrooms. If he lasted just an extra week, that would be good. But the cat didn't know how to gather berries and mushrooms.

Still, autumn wasn't coming any day soon. Meanwhile, the cat caught fish with its paws in the shallows, digging its hind legs firmly in the gravel on the bank. This was not very successful fishing, but the fisherman did give the cat all the fish leftovers.

After each haul, each day's fishing, the fisherman sorted through his catch: the bigger fish were for the hospital chief, and put in a special keep, a willow cage in the water. Middling fish were for middling bosses, since everyone wanted fresh fish. The smallest fish were for himself and the cat.

The soldiers working at our "outpost" were moving to a new place, and they left the fisherman with a puppy about three months old, which they would take back later. The soldiers wanted to sell the puppy to one of the bosses, but they didn't have any customers lined up, or they couldn't agree on a price: whatever the reason, nobody came to fetch the puppy until well into the autumn.

The puppy easily fit in with the fishing family and made friends with the cat, which was older, not just in years but in its knowledge of life. The cat wasn't in the least afraid of the puppy, and responded to the puppy's first lighthearted attack with its claws, silently scratching the puppy's nose. Then they made peace and became friends.

The cat taught the puppy to hunt. It had all the qualifications. Two months or so previously, when the cat was still living with the cook, a bear had been killed and skinned: the cat hurled itself at the bear, triumphantly digging its claws into the red, raw corpse of the bear. The puppy, however, howled and hid under a bunk in the barracks.

This cat had never hunted with its mother. Nobody had taught it these skills. I had raised the kitten on milk when it survived its mother's death. And now it was a fighting cat that knew everything a cat is supposed to know.

Even when it was still with the cook, the tiny kitten caught a mouse, its first mouse. Mice in Kolyma are bigger, not much smaller than a kitten. The kitten strangled its enemy. Who taught it to be so vicious, so murderous? It was a well-fed kitten living in a kitchen.

The cat would sit for hours outside a mouse's hole, while the puppy would freeze, just like the cat, imitating its every movement, waiting for the outcome of the hunt, for the pounce.

The cat shared its catch with the puppy, as it would have with a kitten; it threw the mouse it had caught, and the puppy growled as it learned to catch mice.

The cat itself had never been taught anything. It knew everything from birth. I saw so many times this hunting instinct show itself, not just an instinct but knowledge and skill.

When the cat was ambushing a bird, the puppy would be extremely excited and freeze as it waited for the pounce, the strike.

There were a lot of mice and birds. And the cat didn't slack.

The cat and the puppy were close friends. Together, they devised a game the fisherman told me a lot about, but I also saw the game for myself three or four times.

There was a big clearing in front of the fisherman's hut, and a thick larch stump, about three meters high, in the middle of the clearing. The game began with the puppy and the cat rushing around the taiga and chasing striped chipmunks—ground squirrels, small, big-eyed animals—one after the other into the clearing. The puppy ran in circles, trying to catch a chipmunk, while the chipmunk tried to escape by climbing up the stump and waiting for the puppy to get bored, after which it would jump down and vanish in the taiga. The puppy ran in circles, to see the clearing, the stump, and the chipmunk on top of the stump.

The cat would run across the grass to the stump and climb after the chipmunk. The chipmunk would jump and fall into the puppy's mouth.

The cat would leap off the stump and the puppy would release its prey. The cat would inspect the dead little animal and use its paw to move the chipmunk toward the puppy.

At that time I often traveled down that road, and I'd make myself chifir, very strong tea, in the hut and eat and sleep before my long walk along the taiga path: I had to walk twenty kilometers to get home to my clinic.

I would watch the cat, the puppy, the fisherman, and their merriment as they played with each other; each time I thought about the inexorability of autumn, about the frailty of this little period of happiness, about the right everyone has to this frailty, whether beast, man, or bird. Autumn would part them, I thought. But the parting happened before autumn. The fisherman was driven to the camp to fetch food, and when he got back, the cat wasn't there. The fisherman spent two nights looking for it, climbing high upstream, inspecting all his snares, all his traps, shouting, calling it by a name it didn't have and didn't know.

The puppy was at home but unable to say what had happened. The puppy howled, calling for the cat.

But the cat did not come.

1967

SOMEONE ELSE'S BREAD

IT WAS someone else's bread, my comrade's. I was the only person he trusted: he'd gone to work the day shift, and I kept his bread in a small Russian wooden box. These boxes aren't made anymore, but in the 1920s they were a fashion accessory for Moscow girls: they were sporty little suitcases covered in "crocodile" vinyl. The bread, a bread ration, was in this box. If you shook the box with your hand, the bread would roll about in it. I kept the box under my head. I couldn't sleep for a long time. Hungry men sleep badly. But the reason I couldn't sleep was because I had bread, someone else's bread, my comrade's bread. I sat up on the bunk. I felt that everyone was looking at me, that they all knew what I was about to do. The orderly, however, was by the window sewing a patch on something; someone else, whose name I didn't know, working, like me, on the night shift, was now lying on someone else's place in the middle of the barracks, with his feet pointing to the warm iron stove. I was too far away to feel the warmth. This man was lying on his back, his face upward. I went up to him: his eyes were closed. I looked at the upper bunks: there, in the corner of the barracks, some-one was asleep, or just lying there, covered in a pile of rags. Making a firm decision to go to sleep, I lay down again in my place. I counted to a thousand and got up again. I opened the box and took out the bread. It was a three-hundred-gram ration, as cold as a lump of wood. I lifted it to my nose, and my nostrils furtively caught the barely perceptible smell of bread. I put the piece back in the box and then took it out again. I turned it over and let a few crumbs fall on the palm of my hand. I licked them up with my tongue, and my mouth immediately filled with saliva as the crumbs melted away. I stopped hesitating. I pinched off three little pieces of bread, the size of my pinkie, put the bread back in the box and lay down. I pinched off and sucked the crumbs. And I went to sleep, proud that I hadn't stolen my comrade's bread.

1967

A THEFT

It was snowing, and the sky was gray, and the earth was gray, and the chain of men, making their way from one hill of snow to the next, stretched over the entire horizon. Then a long wait had to be endured while the foreman lined up his brigade, as if there were a general or somebody hiding behind the hill of snow.

The brigade lined up in twos and turned off the path, the shortest route home to the barracks, to another path, one meant for horses. Not long ago a tractor had passed through here, and the snow hadn't yet covered its tracks, which were like the paw prints of some prehistoric beast. Walking here was far harder than on the first path: everyone was in a hurry, every minute someone lost their footing and, lagging behind, hastily tugged off their quilted cloth boots, now full of snow, and then ran to catch up with their fellow workers. Suddenly, after the brigade came around the side of a big snowdrift, the black figure of a man wearing an enormous white sheepskin coat came into view. Only when I got closer did I see that the snowdrift was in fact a low stack of sacks of flour. A truck must have gotten stuck here, been unloaded, and towed away empty by the tractor.

The brigade was heading straight toward the night watchman, passing the stack at a quick march. Then the brigade relaxed its pace, and its ranks broke up. Stumbling in the darkness, the workers finally reached the light of the big electric lamp hanging over the camp gates.

The brigade hurriedly formed ragged ranks in front of the gates; they were complaining of cold and tiredness. A warder came out, unlocked the gates, and let the men into the zone. Even inside the camp, people went on walking in ranks right up to the barracks: I still didn't understand a thing.

Only just before daybreak, when flour from the sacks was handed out in a black cooking pot for want of any ladle, I realized that for the first time in my life I was taking part in a theft.

This didn't cause me much excitement. I had no time to think about it, I needed to boil my share any way I could or any way that was available to us then: making dumplings, dough flakes, the famous "Russian macaroni," or just rye-flour muffins, pancakes big or small.

1967

THE TOWN ON THE HILL

I WAS BROUGHT for the second time in my life to that town on the hill in the summer of 1945. I had been taken from that town for trial by tribunal two years earlier and was given ten years, and I had roamed about on vitamin-gathering expeditions, which were fraught with death, prospecting trips where I had to strip dwarf pines; I was in the hospital and then worked at outposts, and I ran away from the Diamond Spring sector, where conditions were unbearable: I was caught and sent for interrogation. My new sentence was only just beginning, and the interrogator reasoned that the state would not benefit much from a new investigation, a new sentence, a new start to my sentence, and a new count of my time as a prisoner. His memorandum was about a punishment mine, a special zone, where I was to stay from then on, forever and ever. But I refused to say amen.

There is a rule in the camps not to send or "dispatch" prisoners who have been retried back to the mines where they were previously working. This rule makes a lot of practical sense. The state ensures the lives of its informers, its snitches, its oath-breakers and false witnesses. That is their minimal right by law.

But I was dealt with differently, and not just because my interrogator was lazy. No, the heroes of the confrontations, the witnesses of my previous case had already been taken away from the special zone: Nesterenko the foreman, his deputy Krivitsky, the journalist Zaslavsky, and a Shailevich, all of whom I didn't know were no longer at Jelgala. They had been taken from the special zone as men who had reformed and who had proved their loyalty. Evidently, the state paid snitches and false witnesses a decent rate for their work. The price, their pay, was my blood, my new sentence.

I was no longer being summoned for interrogation, and I quite enjoyed sitting in a tightly packed pretrial cell of the Northern Administration. I didn't know what they would do with me: whether my escape attempt would be considered absence without leave, an immeasurably less serious infringement than attempted escape.

About three weeks later I was called out and taken to a transit cell where there was a man in a raincoat wearing good boots and a strong, almost new quilted jacket. He "gave me the once-over," as gangsters say, and immediately saw that I was the most ordinary goner with whom he had nothing in common. And I gave him the once-over too: whatever I looked like, I was not just a *freier* but a beaten *freier*. I was facing one of the gangsters who, I worked out, would be taken somewhere with me.

We were going to be driven to a special zone at Jelgala, which I knew well.

An hour later our cell doors were opened.

"Who's Ivan the Greek?"

"Me."

"There's a parcel for you." The soldier handed Ivan a package that he put without any haste on the bunks.

"Soon, is it?"

"The truck's coming."

A few hours later, engine roaring and gasping, the truck managed to crawl to the Jelgala guardhouse.

The camp elder stepped forward and examined my documents and Ivan the Greek's.

This was the same zone where they sent men out to work "minus the last one," where I'd witnessed Alsatian dogs chasing everybody out, both the sick and the well, to the guardhouse; the roll call before work was done behind the guardhouse, by the zone gates, from where a steep road went downhill, a downhill run through the taiga. The camp was on a hill, and the work was carried out at the bottom, which showed that there were no limits to human cruelty. Two warders would stand on the square in front of the guardhouse, pick up anyone who had refused to work by the hands and feet, swing them to and fro, and then throw them downhill. The prisoner would fall and tumble for about three hundred meters, and at the bottom he would be met by a soldier. If the objector wouldn't get up and pokes and blows couldn't make him walk, then they tied him to a sled and he would be dragged by horses to work: it was at least a kilometer to the pit faces. I saw this scene every day until I was sent away from Jelgala. Now I was back there.

Not that throwing people down the hill was the worst thing: that was how special zones were meant to be. It wasn't that a horse dragged a workman to his place of work. The terrible thing was the end of the day, for after exhausting work in freezing temperatures, after a whole working day, you had to crawl uphill, grabbing hold of twigs, branches, stumps. You crawled and you also dragged wood up for the guards. You had to drag the wood right into the camp, as the camp bosses put it, "for your own selves."

Jelgala was a serious enterprise. Of course, there were Stakhanovite shock brigades, like Magarian's; there were brigades like ours that were not so good; and there were gangsters. As at all the mines in First Category Special Camp Areas, there was a guardhouse with the sign: "Labor is a cause for glory, a cause for valor and heroism."

It goes without saying that there were denunciations, lice, criminal investigations, and interrogations here.

The Jelgala clinic no longer had Dr. Mokhnach, who had seen me every day for several months at outpatient surgery, and who had in my presence written as the interrogator demanded: "Prisoner, name so-and-so, is healthy and has never complained to Jelgala clinic."

The interrogator Fiodorov guffawed as he told me: "Give me the names of any ten prisoners in the camp, any of your choice. I'll process them in my office and they will all give evidence against you." That was genuinely true, and I knew it as well as Fiodorov did.

Fiodorov wasn't at Jelgala now: he'd been transferred somewhere else. Nor was Mokhnach there.

Then who was running the Jelgala clinic? Dr. Yampolsky, a former prisoner, but now a free contract worker.

Dr. Yampolsky hadn't even been a paramedic. At the Spokoinoye mine, where we first met, he treated the sick with just potassium permanganate and iodine, and no professor would have given a prescription different from that of Dr. Yampolsky... The top bosses knew there were no drugs, so they were not very demanding. The battle against lice was hopeless and futile; the formal conclusions in the documents signed by the clinic's representatives were always to "keep under observation": that was all that was asked of Yampolsky by the top bosses. The paradox was that, while not being answerable for anything and not giving anyone any treatment, Yampolsky was gradually accumulating experience and was valued as highly as any doctor in Kolyma.

I had a special kind of clash with him. The chief doctor of the hospital I had been admitted to sent a letter to Yampolsky, asking him to help me get admitted to the hospital. The best Yampolsky could think of was to hand this letter to the chief of the camp; in other words, to denounce me. But Yemelianov misunderstood Yampolsky's real intention and, when he met me, said, "We'll send you, we will." And they did. Now Yampolsky and I met again. At my very first visit, Yampolsky declared that he would not let me off work, that he would expose me and show me up for what I was.

Two years ago I was driven in here in a black military prisoner truck. I was on a list compiled by Mr. Kariakin, the section chief of the Arkagala mine. This sacrificial party was put together from lists given by all the administrations, all the mines; the prisoners were moved to the new Kolyma Auschwitz, the Kolyma special zones, the extermination camps, as in 1938, when the whole of Kolyma was one big extermination camp.

Two years earlier, they had walked me out of here to be tried—over eighteen kilometers of taiga, nothing for the soldiers who were in a hurry to get to the cinema but a serious business for a man who had spent a month in a windowless dark solitary cell on a mug of water and three hundred grams of bread a day.

I found the solitary-confinement cell, too, or at least a trace of it, for the camp had long had a new solitary block: demand was rising. I remembered the warder in charge of solitary, an armed guard, was afraid to let me do the washing up in the sun—in water running not from a stream but from a sizing trommel down a wooden pipe—it didn't matter that it was just summer, sun, and water. The warder running the solitary block was afraid to let me do the washing up; he was not just too lazy to do it himself but thought such work was disgraceful for a warder in charge of solitary. It was not his job. But there was only one prisoner not allowed to leave his cell, me. Other prisoners under confinement were allowed out: their washing up had to be done. I was happy to do the washing up because I got air, sun, a bowl of soup. Who knows: but for that daily outing, I might not have been able to get to my trial or survive all the beatings that were my fate.

The old solitary block was dismantled, and only the traces of its wall, the burned-out pits where the stove had stood, remained; I sat down on the grass and remembered my court appearance, my "trial."

There was a pile of old iron rods, a bundle that fell apart easily; stepping over the iron rods I suddenly saw my little short-bladed knife, which a hospital paramedic once gave me for the journey. I didn't have much use for the knife in the camp: I managed without one. But every camp prisoner is proud to have such a possession. The blade had a cross marked by a file on both sides. This knife was confiscated when I was arrested two years ago. And now I was holding it again. I put it back in the pile of rusting rods.

Two years earlier I was driven in here with Varpakhovsky: a long time ago he had been in Magadan, with Zaslavsky, and had been some time ago in Susuman. As for me, this was my second time in a special zone.

Ivan the Greek was led away.

"Wait a bit."

I knew what it was all about. The half belt at the back of my quilted jacket, and its folding collar, the knitted cotton scarf, broad and a meter-and-a-half long, which I took care to hide, had attracted the practiced eye of the camp elder.

"Undo your jacket!"

I did so.

"We'll swap that." The elder pointed to the scarf.

"No."

"Look, we'll give you something good."

"No."

"Later will be too late."

"No."

A full-scale hunt for my scarf began, but I guarded it carefully, tying it around me at bath time, never taking it off. Soon it was infested with lice, but I was ready to endure even this agony as long as I could keep the scarf. Sometimes at night I took off the scarf so as to have a break from the louse bites, and in the light I saw the scarf twitching and moving. There were that many lice in it. One night it somehow became unbearable, the stove had been stoked up and it was hotter than usual, so I took off the scarf and laid it next to me on the bunk. That was when the scarf vanished, and vanished forever. A week later, when I came out for roll call and was expecting to end up in the warders' hands and to be flung down the hill, I saw the elder standing by the mine gates. The elder's neck was wrapped up in my scarf. Naturally, the scarf had been laundered in boiling water and disinfected. The elder didn't even look at me. And I only looked once at my scarf. Two weeks had been enough for me, two weeks of prolonged vigilance and battle. I expect the elder had paid the thief less bread than he would have given me on the day I arrived. Who knows? I wasn't thinking about that. I even felt relieved, and the louse bites on my neck began to heal, and I began to sleep better.

Nevertheless, I shall never forget that scarf, which I possessed for so short a time.

In my camp life there were almost no anonymous hands to support me in a blizzard or a storm, no anonymous comrades to save my life. But I remember all the pieces of bread I ate that came from strangers, not officials, all the rough-tobacco cigarettes. I ended up in the hospital many times, for nine years my life alternated between the hospital and the pit face; I did not hope for anything, but I never spurned anyone's alms. Many times, I would leave the hospital only to be stripped of my clothes by gangsters or by the camp authorities at the first transit camp.

The special zone had expanded: the guardhouse, the solitary block, all in the line of fire of guard towers, were new. So were the towers, but the refectory was just the same as in my time, two years ago, when the former minister Krivitsky and the former journalist Zaslavsky amused themselves in front of all the brigades with a terrible camp pastime. They would throw away bread, a three-hundred-gram ration, and leave it unguarded on the table, as if it didn't belong to anybody, a ration "abandoned" by an idiot; then one of the goners, half crazed with hunger, would fling himself on this ration, snatch it from the table, and carry it off to a dark corner and try with his scurvy-ridden teeth, which left spots of blood on the bread, to swallow it. But the former minister, who had also been a former doctor, knew that a starving man could not swallow the bread instantly, because he hadn't got the teeth: he let the show develop, so that there was no going back, and the proof would be all the more convincing.

A crowd of infuriated workmen would hurl themselves at the thief caught in flagrante. Each man considered it his duty to punish this crime with a blow, and although a blow from a goner couldn't break any bones, it still knocked the spirit out of you.

This was an utterly human form of heartlessness. A feature that shows how far human beings have grown apart from wild animals.

Badly beaten, covered in blood, the failed thief would huddle in a corner of the barracks, while the former minister, now the deputy foreman, would deliver deafening speeches to the brigade about how bad theft was and how sacred the prison bread ration was.

All that was part of the life I witnessed and, looking at the goners at dinner, licking their bowls clean with a classic, deft tongue movement, I, too, licked my bowl clean just as deftly, thinking, "Soon the bread bait, the 'live bait' will appear on the table. The former minister is here too, probably, as well as the former journalist, framers of cases, provocateurs, and false witnesses." The live-bait game was a very popular spectacle in the special zone in my time there.

In a way, this heartlessness reminded me of gangsters' affairs with hungry prostitutes (if they were prostitutes), when the "fee" was a bread ration or, more likely, by mutual agreement, as much of the bread ration as the woman could eat while they were lying down together. Anything she didn't manage to eat was repossessed and taken away by the gangster when he left.

"I'll freeze that bread ration in the snow first and then shove it in her mouth: she won't be able to gnaw off much when it's frozen. When I get back I'll still have all the bread."

The heartlessness of gangster love has nothing human about it. No human being could devise such entertainments for himself, except for the gangster.

As each day passed, I came nearer to death, and I had no expectations.

All the same I tried to crawl out through the zone gates and go to work. Anything, except refusing to work. Three refusals and you were executed. That was how it was in 1938. Now it was the autumn of 1945. The laws were the same, especially for the special zones.

I hadn't yet been thrown down the hill by the warders. I waited for the escort guard to wave his arm and then I rushed to the edge of the icy hill and rolled down, using branches, overhanging rocks, and icicles to slow my descent. I managed to join the lineup and march off to the curses of the whole brigade, because I marched badly, only a little worse, however, and a bit more tentatively than the others. But it was this insignificant difference in strength that made me the object of everyone's anger and hatred. My comrades seemed to hate me more than they hated the guards.

My cloth boots shuffling in the snow, I made my way to the workplace, while a horse dragged today's victim of hunger and beatings past us behind a sled. We yielded way to the horse and crawled in its wake toward the start of the working day. Nobody thought about the end of the working day: that would come anyway, and it didn't seem important whether a new evening, a new night, and a new day would come or not.

Work became harder with each day, and I could feel that special measures were called for.

"Gusev, Gusev! Gusev will help."

Since the previous day Gusev had been my working partner in cleaning up a new barracks: burning trash, burying the rest in the earth, in the permafrost under the floor.

I knew Gusev. We had met at a mine about two years ago. It was Gusev who helped me find a parcel that had been stolen from me, and showed me whom I had to hit: the man was beaten by the whole barracks, and my parcel was found. Then I gave Gusev a lump of sugar and a handful of stewed fruit: I couldn't give him the entire parcel for locating it and denouncing the thief. But I could trust Gusev.

I found a way out: I would break my arm. I hit my left arm with a short crowbar, but all I got were bruises. Either I didn't have the strength to break a human arm, or there was some watchman inside me who wouldn't let me swing my right arm properly. So Gusev could swing his.

Gusev refused.

"I could denounce you. The law says you have to denounce self-mutilators, and you'd get another three years on your sentence. But I won't do that. I remember the stewed fruit. But don't ask me to pick up a crowbar, I won't do that."

"Why not?"

"Because when they start beating you at the NKVD office, you'll say I did it."

"I won't."

"End of conversation."

I had to find some really easy work, so I asked Dr. Yampolsky to take me on as a hospital building worker. Yampolsky hated me, but he knew I'd previously worked as a male nurse.

I turned out to be the wrong sort of person to be a building worker.

"What's wrong with you," said Yampolsky, scratching his Assyrian beard, "that you don't want to work?"

"I can't."

"You're telling me, a doctor, that you can't?"

"After all, you're not a doctor," I wanted to say, for I knew who Yampolsky was. But, as the saying went, "If you don't believe me, take it as a fairy tale." Everyone in the camp, whether prisoner or free man, workman or boss, was whoever he claimed to be. That was both a formal principle and a real one.

Of course Dr. Yampolsky was head of the health service and I was a laborer, a punishment prisoner, a special zone prisoner.

"I've got the hang of you now," said the doctor angrily. "I'll teach you how to live."

I said nothing. So many people in my life had tried to teach me how to live.

"Tomorrow I'll show you. You'll find out from me tomorrow…" But tomorrow never came.

That night, forcing a way up along the stream, two heavy trucks got to our town on the hill. Roaring as they revved their engines, they crawled up to the zone gates and started unloading.

The trucks were carrying men dressed in handsome foreign uniforms.

They were repatriated Soviet citizens. From Italy, labor squads from Italy. From Vlasov's army? No. Actually, the phrase "Vlasov's men"[21] sounded to us old Kolyma hands, who were cut off from the world, too vague, whereas for new Kolyma prisoners the phrase was too familiar and alive. A defensive reflex told them to keep quiet. We, on the other hand, were forbidden by Kolyma ethics to ask.

At Jelgala mine in the special zone there had long been talk that repatriated citizens would be brought here. With indeterminate sentences. Their sentences were lagging behind them somewhere and would come later. But these people were alive, more alive than the Kolyma goners.

For the repatriated this was the end of a journey that had begun at meetings in Italy. "The motherland is calling for you. The motherland forgives you." At the Russian border armed guards were put in their carriages. The repatriated traveled directly to Kolyma, so as to separate Dr. Yampolsky and myself and save me from the special zone.

The repatriated had nothing left but their silk underwear and nice new military uniforms. As they traveled, the repatriated had swapped their gold watches and civilian suits and shirts for bread. The same had happened to me: it was a long journey, and I knew it. To move a party of prisoners from Moscow to Vladivostok takes forty-five days; then it takes five days and nights for the steamship to get from Vladivostok to Magadan, after that come endless days and nights in transit camps, and finally Jelgala.

The trucks that had brought the repatriated citizens took away fifty special prisoners bound for the administration, or for an unknown destination. I wasn't on the list, but Dr. Yampolsky was, and I never saw him again in my life.

The camp elder was driven away, so I saw my scarf around his neck for the last time, a scarf that had caused me such agony and anxiety. The lice had, of course, been steamed out and exterminated.

So it would be the repatriated Soviet citizens who would be swung in the air that winter by the warders and flung downhill to be tied to a sled and hauled to work at the pit face. Just as we had been . . .

It was early September when the Kolyma winter began.

The repatriated were forced to undergo a search that had them all trembling. Practiced camp warders extracted from them everything that had survived dozens of searches in "the free world," from Italy onward: a small piece of paper, a document, a Vlasov manifesto! But this event made not the slightest impression. We'd never heard of Vlasov or the Russian Liberation Army, so what was a manifesto to us?

"What will they get for that?" asked one of the men drying bread around the stove.

"Nothing at all."

I don't know how many of them had been officers. Vlasov officers were executed; possibly, these men were just lower ranks, if we remember certain peculiarities of Russian psychology and nature.

About two years after all this, I happened to be working as a paramedic in the Japanese zone. Any job there—orderly, foreman, male nurse—had to be allotted to an officer, and that was considered sensible without further ado, although in the hospital officers who were prisoners of the war zone didn't wear any special uniforms.

But in our camp the repatriated citizens were unmasked and exposed along lines that had long been familiar.

"Do you work in the health clinic?"

"Yes."

"Malinovsky has been appointed as a male nurse. Allow me to inform you that Malinovsky collaborated with the Germans and worked in their chancellery in Bologna. I saw him myself."

"That's none of my business."

"Then whose is it? Who should I go and see?"

"I don't know."

"That's odd. Does anyone want a silk shirt?"

"I don't know."

A very happy orderly came up: he was leaving, leaving, leaving the special zone.

"What, dear fellow, you've been caught, have you? Wearing Italian uniforms and off to the permafrost. You've got what was coming to you. You shouldn't work for the Germans."

The newcomer would then say quietly, "At least we saw Italy. How about you?"

The orderly then turned grim and fell silent. Kolyma hadn't frightened the repatriated.

"On the whole, we like everything here. You can live. The only thing I don't understand is why none of you eats the bread in the refectory—those two or three hundred grams, depending on your work record. You get percentage bonuses here, don't you?"

"Yes, we do here."

"A man eats his soup and porridge without the bread, which he for some reason takes away to the barracks."

The repatriated soldier had accidentally touched on the main question of life in Kolyma.

But I had no desire to respond: "After two weeks every one of you will do the same."

1967

THE EXAMINATION

I SURVIVED; I survived the hell of Kolyma only because I became a medic, because I finished my paramedic classes in the camp and passed the state examination. But before that, ten months before, I had another examination, an entry examination, more important in a special sense both for me and for my fate. I had survived the stress test. A bowl of camp cabbage soup may have been something like ambrosia: at secondary school I wasn't taught about the food of the gods, for the same reason that I didn't know the chemical formula for plaster of paris.

The world where gods and people live is the same. There are events that are equally dreadful for people and for gods. Homer's formulas are very true. But in Homer's time there was no underground criminal world, no world of concentration camps. Pluto's underworld seems a paradise, heaven compared with that world. But even our world is only one story below Pluto's: people can rise from it to the heavens, and gods sometimes come down the stairway to a place lower than hell.

The state ordered that only nonpolitical criminals should be accepted into these classes. Of those convicted under article 58, only those with paragraph 10, "agitation," could be accepted, none of the others.

I happened to have article 58, paragraph 10: I'd been condemned during the war for declaring that Ivan Bunin was a Russian classic. But I had been condemned a second and third time under articles that would have barred me from being a valid student. It was worth a try, however: the camp records were in such a mess after the purges of 1937 and after the war, too, that it was worth staking your life.

Fate is a bureaucrat, a pedant. It has been remarked that it is as hard to stop the executioner's sword once it is swung over the condemned man's head as it is to stop the hand of a prison warder unlocking the door to freedom. A run of luck, roulette, Monte Carlo, which was poeticized by Dostoyevsky as a symbol of blind chance, suddenly turned out to be a scientifically verifiable scheme, a subject for proper science. A passionate determination to grasp the "system" in a casino made that passion scientific, and a subject for study.

Is a faith in luck, in success, in the limits of that success, something a human being can comprehend? And isn't intuition, the blind animal will to make a choice, based on something greater than the fortuitous? "While you're still lucky, you have to agree to anything," the camp cook used to tell me. Was it a matter of being lucky? Misfortune is unstoppable. But so is good fortune, or at least what prisoners call good fortune, a prisoner's good luck.

Was one to trust to fate, given a favorable wind at one's back, and to repeat for the millionth time the voyage of the *Kon-Tiki* across the seas of humanity?

Or else was one to wedge oneself into a crack in the cage—there's no cage without a crack—and slither back into the darkness? Or squeeze into a crate that is being taken to the sea, although there isn't any room in the crate, but before you can be found out, the bureaucratic pedantry will have saved you?

All that was just a thousandth of the thoughts that might have occurred to me then, but didn't.

The sentence was shattering. My body weight had already been reduced to the level necessary for death. My period of investigation passed in an underground windowless, unlit solitary cell. A month on just a daily mug of water and three hundred grams of bread.

I had, though, been in rather worse solitary cells. The roadwork outpost at Kadykchan is on the territory of a punishment zone. Punishment zones, special zones, the Kolyma Auschwitzes and Kolyma gold mines change their locations; they are permanently in dreadful motion, leaving common graves and solitary-confinement blocks behind them. At the Kadykchan roadwork outpost, the solitary block had been carved into a rock in the permafrost. You only had to spend one night there to die, to get fatal hypothermia. Eight kilos of firewood would not save you in a solitary cell like that. The road maintenance people used this cell: they had their own administration, their own laws, and, in the absence of guards, their own way of doing things. After the road men, the solitary block was taken over by the Arkagala camp, and the chief of the Kadykchan sector, the engineer Kiseliov, was also given the right to imprison "until morning." His first experiment was unsuccessful: two men, two pneumonias, two deaths.

I was the third. "Remove all outer clothing and into solitary until morning." But I had more experience than the previous two. The stove was an odd thing to stoke, for the icy walls thawed and then froze again; there was ice overhead and underfoot. The rough-planed timber floor had long ago been burned up. I spent all night pacing about, my head tucked into my pea jacket, and I got away with losing only two toes to frostbite.

My whitened skin burned brown in the June sun in two or three hours. I was tried in June: a tiny room in the settlement of Yagodnoye, where everyone sat pressed together—the tribunal members and the guards, the accused and the witnesses—where it was hard to work out who was on trial and who was trying him.

It turned out that the sentence brought me life, not death. My crime was being punished under a less severe article than the article that had brought me to Kolyma.

My bones ached, my ulcers and sores refused to close up. Above all, I didn't know whether I would be able to study. It may be that the scars in my brain, caused by starvation, beatings, and kickings, were permanent, and that until the day I died I was doomed only to growl like a wild animal over my camp bowl and to think only about camp matters. But it was worth the risk: the necessary number of cells had survived in my brain to make that decision. My wild animal's decision was to take a wild animal's leap to reach the realm of the human being.

If I was going to be beaten up and thrown out of the classes—back to the pit face, to the hated spade, to the pickax—so what? I would simply remain a wild animal, that was it.

All this was my secret, a secret it was so simple to keep: all I had to do was not think about it. That is what I did.

The truck had long ago left the graded central highway and was bouncing over the potholes and pits, potholes and pits, throwing me against the side. Where was it taking me? I didn't care where: it couldn't be worse than what I had turned my back on during those nine years of wandering the camps from pit face to hospital and back. The wheel of the camp truck was pulling me back to life, and I desperately wanted to believe that this wheel would never stop.

Yes, I was being admitted to the camp department, led into the zone. The duty officer opened the packet of papers and did not yell at me to move aside. Wait! There was a bathhouse where I could leave my underwear—a gift from the doctor—I hadn't always had underwear in my wanderings from mine to mine. A gift for the journey. Here, in a hospital camp, there were different arrangements: here underwear was "depersonalized" in the old camp fashion. Instead of strong calico underwear, I was given patched rags. That didn't matter. Rags were fine. Depersonalized underwear was fine. But I didn't have all that long to be pleased by the underwear. If it was "yes," then I would have time to wash myself at the next bath time; if it was "no," then it wasn't worth washing. We were being taken to barracks with two-story bunks on the railway carriage system. That meant, yes, yes, yes . . . But all this would come later. Everything was drowning in a sea of rumors. If it was article 58, paragraph 6, you wouldn't be accepted. After that announcement, one of us, Luniov, was driven away, and he disappeared forever from my life.

Article 58, paragraph 1—ah!—is not accepted. Counterrevolutionary Trotskyist Activity—under no circumstances. That was worse than any kind of treason to the motherland.

How about Counterrevolutionary Agitation? CRA was no worse than article 58, paragraph 10: you were accepted.

How about Anti-Soviet Agitation? Who has ASA? "I do," said a man with a pale, dirty, prison face, a man with whom I had been shaken about in that truck.

ASA was just the same as CRA. How about Counterrevolutionary Activity? CRA with Activity was, of course, not as bad as CRTA with the Trotskyism, but it was worse than CRA with just Agitation. Counterrevolutionary Activity was not acceptable.

The best thing was just article 58, paragraph 10, with no extra letters.

Article 58, paragraph 7: sabotage. Not acceptable. Article 58, paragraph 8: terror. Not acceptable.

I had article 58. Paragraph 10. I stayed in the barracks.

The admissions committee for paramedical classes at the central hospital admitted me to the tests. Tests? Yes, examinations. The entry examination. What else would you expect? The classes were a serious initiative, which resulted in documented qualifications. The classes had to know whom they were dealing with.

But no need to be scared. An examination on each subject—Russian language, written; mathematics, written; and chemistry, oral. Three subjects, three sets of marks. Before the examination all future students would be interviewed by hospital doctors who taught the classes. A dictation. My hand hadn't unbent for nine years; it had been permanently bent to fit a spade handle, and when I tried to unbend it, it crackled and hurt and could only be straightened in the bathhouse when it was steamed by hot water.

I unbent my fingers with my left hand and inserted the pen, dipping it into the non-spill inkwell with a shaking hand, in a cold sweat, and I wrote that damned dictation. My God!

Twenty years earlier, in 1926, when I entered Moscow University, was the last time I had taken a Russian-language examination. I had gotten 200 percent on a "free" topic and was exempted from oral tests. Here there were no oral tests. All the more, then! All the more caution: Turgenev or Babayevsky? I really didn't care. An easy text ... I checked the commas and full stops. A semicolon after the word "mastodon." Obviously, Turgenev. Babayevsky couldn't possibly have any mastodons; or semicolons, for that matter.

"I wanted to set a Dostoyevsky or Tolstoy text, but I was frightened I'd be accused of counterrevolutionary propaganda," the examiner, the paramedic Brodsky, told me later. All the professors and teachers agreed to refuse to hold Russian-language tests: they were too unsure of their knowledge. The results came the next day. An A. My only A; the dictation marks were deplorable.

The mathematics interviews frightened me. The problems that had to be solved were solved by revelation, by serendipity, which gave me a terrible headache. All the same, they were solved.

These preliminary interviews calmed me down, after having frightened me. And I eagerly awaited the last examination, or rather the last interview, on chemistry. I didn't know any chemistry, but I thought that my fellow students would tell me. But nobody shared their studying; each one tried to remember his own learning. In the camps no one helped anyone else, so I wasn't offended; I just waited for my fate, relying on an interview with the teacher. In the classes, chemistry was taught by the academician Boichenko of the Ukrainian Academy of Sciences: Boichenko had been sentenced to twenty-five years, plus five years deprivation of civic rights; he was the examiner.

At the end of the day, when the chemistry examinations were announced, we were told that Boichenko would not hold any preliminary interviews. He didn't consider it necessary. He would sort everything out during the examination.

That was a catastrophe for me. I had never studied chemistry. During the Civil War our secondary-school chemistry teacher, Sokolov, had been executed. That night I lay there for a long time in the student barracks, trying to remember Vologda during the Civil War. On the bunk above me was Suvorov, who had come to the examination from a mine administration as remote as mine, and who suffered from urine incontinence. I couldn't be bothered to swear at him. I was afraid that he might offer to change places, and then he would complain about the man lying above him. I merely turned my face away from the evil-smelling drips.

I was born in Vologda and spent my childhood there. That northern town is unusual. There, during the course of the centuries, a strata had formed of tsarist exile protestants, rebels, and various critics who over many generations had created a special moral climate of a higher level than in any other Russian town. There, moral demands and cultural demands were far higher. There, young people felt the urge earlier to become living examples of self-sacrifice and devotion.

And I was always amazed at the thought that Vologda was the only town in Russia where there had never been any rebellion against Soviet power. Such rebellions had shaken the whole of the north: Murmansk, Arkhangelsk, Yaroslavl, Kotlas. The northern districts burned with rebellions, as far as Chukotka, Ola, not to mention the south, where every town underwent several changes of power.

It was only Vologda, snowy Vologda, Vologda of the exiles, that stayed silent. I knew why... There was an explanation.

In 1918 Vologda was visited by the chief of the northern front, M. S. Kedrov. His first measure to strengthen the front and the rear was to shoot hostages. Two hundred persons were shot in Vologda, a town of sixteen thousand. Kotlas, Arkhangelsk had their own toll.

Kedrov was a living Shigalov,[22] as predicted by Dostoyevsky.

This execution was so unusual even for those bloodthirsty times that Moscow demanded an explanation from Kedrov. Kedrov didn't even blink. He put on the table a personal note from Lenin, neither more nor less. It was published in the *Military Historical Journal* in the early 1960s, or perhaps a little earlier. This is roughly what it said: "Dear Mikhail Stepanovich, You are appointed to a post of importance to the republic. I ask you not to show any weakness. Lenin."

After that, Kedrov worked for a number of years in the Cheka and the Ministry of the Interior, constantly unmasking people, denouncing, tracking, checking, destroying enemies of the revolution. Kedrov thought that Yezhov[23] was the greatest of Lenin's commissars, Stalin's commissar. But Beria,[24] who replaced Yezhov, was disliked by Kedrov. Kedrov organized a tracking of Beria... Then he decided to entrust the results of his observations to Stalin. By then, Kedrov's son Igor had grown up and was working in the Ministry of the Interior. They agreed that the son would report on his bosses and that if he was arrested, then his father would tell Stalin that Beria was an enemy of the people. Kedrov had very reliable channels to secure this link.

The son made an official report, was arrested and then shot. His father wrote to Stalin, was arrested and subjected to an interrogation conducted personally by Beria. Beria broke Kedrov's back with an iron bar.

Stalin had merely shown Kedrov's letter to Beria.

Kedrov wrote a second letter to Stalin about his broken back and the interrogations that Beria conducted.

After that Beria shot Kedrov in his cell. Stalin had shown the second letter, too, to Beria. The two letters were found in Stalin's personal safe after his death.

Khrushchev told the Twentieth Party Congress about these letters, their content, and the background to this correspondence. All this was repeated by Kedrov's biographer in his book.

I don't know if Kedrov recalled, before he died, the Vologda hostages whom he had shot.

Sokolov, our chemistry teacher, was one of the murdered hostages. That is why I never studied chemistry. I didn't know Mr. Boichenko's subject, and he never had time for a consultation.

That meant going back to the pit face and not regaining my human form. My old anger gradually built up inside me, pounding at my temples: I was no longer afraid. Something had to happen. A run of good luck was just as irrevocable as a run of bad luck: every gambler who plays cards—bezique, poker, or blackjack—knows this.

Should I ask my fellow students for a textbook? There weren't any. Should I ask them to tell me something about chemistry? But did I have the right to take up my fellow students' time? Curses were the only answers I could expect.

I just had to get ready, to tense myself and wait.

How often events of the highest order had come into my life as powerful imperatives, dictating, salvaging, repelling, wounding, but undeserved and unexpected . . . A major recurrent feature of my life was linked with that examination, with that execution a quarter of a century earlier.

I was one of the first to be examined. A smiling Boichenko was extremely well disposed toward me. True, the man facing him might not be an academician of the Ukrainian Academy of Sciences, nor a doctor of chemistry, but he appeared to be a literate man, a journalist, with two As. Admittedly, he was badly dressed, and an emaciated idler, probably a malingerer. Boichenko had not yet ventured any farther than the twenty-third kilometer from Magadan, at sea level. This was his first Kolyma winter. Whatever oaf he was faced with, he still had to help the man.

The record book of questions and answers was open in front of Boichenko.

"Well, I hope that we won't take much time dealing with you. Write down the formula for plaster of paris."

"I don't know it."

Boichenko was stunned. This was some brazen idler who didn't want to study.

"And the formula for lime?"

"I don't know that either."

We were both raging. Boichenko was the first to contain himself. There must have been some secrets behind this response that Boichenko wouldn't or couldn't understand, but possibly these secrets had to be treated with respect. Moreover, he'd been warned in advance that this was a very suitable student, and he was not to find fault with him.

"The rules say that I have to ask you three questions and record the answers," Boichenko was now talking to me in a familiar tone. "I've asked two; here's the third: Mendeleyev's periodic table."

I was silent as I summoned to my brain, to my throat, tongue, and lips everything that I might know about the periodic table of elements. Of course, I knew that the poet Blok was married to Mendeleyev's daughter, and could have told him all the details of that strange affair. But that was not what a doctor of chemistry wanted. Somehow I mumbled something very distant from the periodic table of elements, while the examiner watched me scornfully.

Boichenko gave me a C, and I survived; I walked out of hell.

I finished the classes, ended my sentence, outlived Stalin, and then returned to Moscow.

Boichenko and I never got to know each other or have a conversation. During my studies, he loathed me and considered my answers at the examination a personal insult to a man of science.

Boichenko never found out about the fate of my chemistry teacher, the executed Vologda hostage.

This was followed by eight months of happiness, uninterrupted happiness, greedily devouring, sucking in knowledge, studying, where a recorded grade meant staying alive for each student; all the teachers, except Boichenko, knew this and gave everything they knew and could offer to the mixed and ungrateful crowd of prisoners, and they did it at least as thoroughly as Boichenko.

The examination for life had been taken, the state examination had been passed. We all received the right to give treatment, to live, to hope. I was sent as a paramedic to the surgical department of the big hospital for prisoners, where I treated people and worked, lived, and was transformed, very slowly, into a human being.

About a year passed.

Suddenly I was summoned to the head of the hospital, Dr. Doctor. He was a former political department official who devoted his entire life in Kolyma to sniffing out and exposing people; to vigilance, investigations, denunciations, and persecutions of prisoners convicted under political articles.

"Paramedic prisoner so-and-so, here at your summons."

Dr. Doctor was fair-haired and reddish; he had sideburns like Pushkin's. He was sitting at his desk, leafing through my personal file.

"Tell me, how did you get into those classes?"

"How does a prisoner get into classes, sir? He's told to, his case file is taken, it's handed to the escort guard, he's put in a truck, driven to Magadan. How else, sir?"

"Get out of here," said Dr. Doctor, turning white with rage.

1966

FETCHING A LETTER

A HALF-DRUNK radio operator flung my doors wide open.

"There's a message from the administration for you; come and see me in my quarters." Then he vanished in the snow and haze.

I moved the hare bodies, which I had brought back from a trip, away from the stove: it was a good season for hares; you hardly had time to set the snares, and half of the barracks roof was covered with carcasses, frozen carcasses... There was no way you could sell them to the workmen, so that a gift of ten hare carcasses was not so expensive that it needed to be repaid, or paid for. But first of all the hares had to be thawed out. At the moment I had other things to do.

The message from the administration was a telegram, a radiogram, or telephonogram addressed to me: my first in fifteen years. It was overwhelming, alarming, as it would be in this country where any telegram is tragic, associated with death. Was it a summons for my release? No, there was no hurry to release anybody, and I had been released long ago. I went to see the radio operator in his fortified castle, a station with embrasures and a triple stockade, triple gates with bolts and locks, which the radio operator's wife opened for me; I squeezed through the doors to get to the operator's residence. I passed the last door and strode into a loud flurry of wings and the stench of chicken droppings as I fought my way past chickens that were flapping their wings, and past singing cockerels; I bent down to protect my face and crossed one more threshold, but the operator wasn't there. There were just pigs, scrubbed and well-fed, three small boars and a big sow. That was the last barrier.

The operator was sitting surrounded by boxes of gherkin seedlings and spring onions. The radio operator was well on his way to being a millionaire. That was how people got rich in Kolyma. Ruble bonuses, high salaries, Polar Circle rations, percentage points were one way. Trading in tobacco and tea was another. Breeding chickens and pigs was the third way.

With all his fauna and flora filling the space right to the edge of his desk, the radio operator handed me a pile of papers—they were all identical—like a parrot that was supposed to tell my fortune.

I dug about in the telegrams, but couldn't make head or tail of them; I didn't find the one for me, so the operator kindly picked out my telegram with his fingertips.

"Come letter," in other words, I had to come and collect a letter: the postal service saved money on the sense, but the addressee would of course understand what it was about.

I went to see the district chief and showed him the telegram.

"How many kilometers?"

"Five hundred."

"All right then."

"I'll turn it around in five days."

"Good, and get a move on. No need to wait for a truck. Tomorrow the Yakuts will take you by dog sled and drop you off at Baragon. There you can get a reindeer team if you're not too stingy. The main thing for you is to reach the central highway."

"All right. Thanks."

I left the chief's office, realizing that I'd never reach that damned highway, or even Baragon, because I didn't have a fur parka. I was a Kolyma man with no fur jacket. It was my own fault. A year ago, when I was released from the camp, the foreman Sergei Ivanovich Korotkov gave me an almost new white fur parka. He gave me a big cushion as well. But I was trying to get away from the hospitals and leave for the mainland, so I sold both the fur parka and the cushion, simply to avoid having any unnecessary possessions, which would end up the same way, being stolen or taken off me by gangsters. I failed to depart: the personnel department and the Magadan Ministry of the Interior combined to refuse me permission to leave, and when my money ran out, I was forced to go back and work for Far East Construction. I joined them and left for the place where the radio operator and his flying chickens lived, but I didn't manage to buy a fur parka. If I asked someone to lend me one for five days, I'd be laughed at: in Kolyma such requests were laughable. I could only buy a fur parka in the settlement.

In fact, I found both a fur parka and a seller. Only the fur parka, black, with a luxurious sheepskin collar, was more like a quilted jacket: it had no pockets, it had no bottom half; it had just a collar and wide sleeves.

"What have you done? Cut off the bottom?" I asked the seller, Ivanov, a camp warder. Ivanov was a bachelor and a gloomy man. He'd cut off the hem to make gauntlets, and each pair of gauntlets cost as much as a whole fur parka. What was left could not, naturally, be called a fur parka.

"Why should you care? I'm selling a fur parka. For five hundred rubles. You're the buyer. There's no need to ask if I've cut off the bottom or not."

True, there was no need to ask, and I was in a hurry to pay Ivanov and bring my fur parka home, to try it on and start to wait.

The dog team, the quick gaze of the Yakut's black eyes, my unfeeling fingers clutching the dog sled, and the sudden turns: some stream, ice, bushes that hurt when they struck your face. But I had everything tied up and fixed down. Ten minutes flying along, and then the post settlement, where—

"Maria Antonovna, will they drop me off?"

"They will."

Only last year, in summer, a small Yakut five-year-old boy got lost, and Maria Antonovna and I tried to find out where he'd come from. His mother was no help. She was smoking her pipe and wouldn't stop for some time, and then she fixed her black eyes on Maria Antonovna and me.

"No need to look for him. He'll turn up by himself. He won't get lost. This is his land."

Now came the reindeer: bells, sleds, the musher's stick. A reindeer musher's stick is called a *khorei*, whereas a dogsled driver's stick is an *ostol*.

Maria Antonovna was so bored that she would accompany every passing traveler for a considerable distance, to the outskirts—or what is called the outskirts—of the taiga.

"Goodbye, Maria Antonovna."

I was running alongside the sled, but mostly I rode it, trying to sit down, grabbing hold of the sled, then falling off and running again. By evening we could see the lights of the main highway and hear the noise of trucks as they sped, roaring their engines, through the haze.

I settled up with the Yakuts and went to warm myself up at the roadside stop. There was no firewood, so the stove was out. But at least there was a roof and walls. By now there was a line for a truck to the center, to Magadan. The line wasn't long—just one man. A truck honks, the man runs into the haze. A truck honks. The man has left. Now it's my turn to run out into the freezing cold.

The five-tonner shudders, barely stopping to pick me up. There's a spare seat in the cab. You can't ride in the back for such a distance in such freezing cold.

"Where to?"

"The Left Bank."

"I can't take you. I'm taking coal to Magadan, and it isn't worth getting on just for the Left Bank."

"I'll pay you for the whole trip to Magadan."

"That's different. Get in. You know the tariff?"

"Yes. A ruble a kilometer."

"Money in advance."

I took out the money and paid.

The truck was enveloped in white haze and slowed down. We could go no farther in the fog.

"Shall we get some sleep, eh? At Yevrashka."

What did *yevrashka* mean? It was the local word for groundhog. A groundhog station. We curled up in the cabin and kept the engine running. We lay there until daybreak, and the white haze didn't seem so terrible as in the evening.

"I'll just brew up some chifir and then we'll be off."

The driver brewed a whole packet of tea in a mug made from an old can, cooled it in the snow, and drank it. He brewed a top-up, drank that, and put away his mug.

"Let's go! Where are you from?"

I told him.

"I've been there. I even used to work as a driver in your district. There's a real bastard in your camp: Ivanov, a warder. He stole a sheep-skin jacket from me. He asked me to lend it him for a journey—it was cold last year—and that was the last I saw of it. Not a trace. He just wouldn't give it back. I sent him a message; he said he hadn't taken it, and that was it. I keep meaning to go there and take it back. It was a black one, nice and thick. What would he want a sheepskin jacket for? He'd only cut it up for gauntlets and sell it off. That's the latest fashion. I could have made gauntlets like that myself, but now I haven't got gauntlets, or a sheepskin jacket, or Ivanov."

I turned around, fingering the collar of my fur jacket.

"It was black, just like yours. The bastard. Right, we've had some sleep, we'll have to step on the gas."

The truck sped up, hooting and roaring at the bends: the driver was restored after his chifir.

Kilometer after kilometer, bridge after bridge, mine after mine. It was now light. Trucks were overtaking each other, coming in both directions. Suddenly everything crashed and collapsed, and the truck stopped, parked on the shoulder of the road.

"It's all gone to hell!" shouted the driver, dancing about. "The coal's gone! The cab's gone! The back of the truck's gone! Five tons of coal's gone!"

He didn't even have a scratch on him, and I couldn't understand what had happened.

Our truck had been hit by an oncoming Czechoslovak Tatra truck. There wasn't even a scratch on its steel side. Drivers braked and got out.

"Quickly," shouted the driver of the Tatra, "add up what your dam-age is worth, the coal, the new sides. We'll pay. But no paperwork, you've got it?"

"All right," said my driver. "It'll be . . ."

"That's fine."

"How about me?"

"I'll get you on some truck going the same way. It's only forty kilometers, they'll get you there. Do me a favor. Forty kilometers will only take an hour."

I agreed, got in the back of a truck, and waved to Ivanov's friend.

Before I was completely frozen, the truck began braking: a bridge. The Left Bank. I got off.

I had to find somewhere to spend the night. I couldn't spend the night where the letter was.

I went into the hospital where I used to work. But outsiders aren't allowed to warm themselves in a camp hospital, and I had dropped in only to stand in the warmth for a minute. A free paramedic whom I knew passed by, and I asked him if I could spend the night.

The next day I knocked at an apartment, entered, and was handed a letter, written in a hand I knew well—an urgent, fast-moving, but at the same time precise and readable hand.

It was a letter from Pasternak.

1966

THE GOLD MEDAL

IN THE beginning there were explosions. But before the explosions, before Aptekarsky Island, where Stolypin's dacha flew into the air,[25] there was the Riazan girls' school, and a gold medal for excellent achievement and conduct.

I'm looking for a side street. Leningrad, a museum city, preserves the features of Petersburg. I shall find Stolypin's dacha on Aptekarsky Island. Fonarnyi Lane, Morskaya Street, Zagorodny Boulevard. I turn into the Trubetskoi bastion of Petropavlovsk fortress, where the trial and the sentencing took place: I know the details by heart and I recently held in my hands a copy of the sentence with the lead seal of the Moscow Notary Office.

> In August 1906, while being a member of a criminal organization calling itself the combat organization of Maximalist revolutionary socialists which deliberately made the aim of its activity the violent change of the basic method of government established by law...amounts to immediate complicity in an attempt on the life of the minister of internal affairs by an explosion of the dacha he resides at on Aptekarsky Island for the purpose of carrying out his official duties...

The judges didn't care about grammar. The literary failings of these sentences are noticeable fifty years later, not earlier.

The gentlewoman Natalia Sergeyevna Klimova, twenty-one years old, and the merchant's daughter Nadezhda Andreyevna

Terentieva, twenty-five years old ... to undergo capital punishment by hanging with consequences indicated under article 28.

Whatever the court meant by "hanging with consequences" is known
only to lawyers and jurists.

Klimova and Terentieva were not hanged.

The chairman of the district court received, during the investigation,
a petition from Klimova's father, a Riazan lawyer. The petition has a
very strange tone, it was unlike a request or a complaint; it was something like a diary, a conversation with himself: "You must judge me
right in thinking that in this case you are dealing with a frivolous girl,
carried away by today's revolutionary era."

Over her life she has been a good, gentle, and kind girl, but she
has always been easily carried away. It was only eighteen months
ago at most that she was carried away by Tolstoy's teachings, the
preaching of "thou shalt not kill" as the most important commandment. For two years she led the life of a vegetarian and
acted like a simple working girl, not allowing the servants to
help her do her laundry or tidy her room or wash the floors, and
now she has become a participant in a terrible murder whose
motive appears to be the fact that Mr. Stolypin's policies do not
suit contemporary conditions.

I make so bold as to assure you that my daughter has absolutely
no understanding of politics; she was obviously a puppet in the
hands of stronger people, to whom the policies of Mr. Stolypin,
it may well be, seem extremely harmful.

I have tried to instill correct views into my children, but at
such chaotic, I must admit, times, a parent's influence has no
effect at all. Our young people are causing the greatest misfortunes
and sufferings to all who surround them, including their parents ...

The argument is original. The comments in passing are strange. The
tone of the letter is in itself amazing.

This letter saved Klimova. It would be more accurate to say that it wasn't the letter but the sudden death of Klimov senior just after he had written and sent this letter.

His death gave the petition such moral weight and shifted the whole legal process to such moral heights that not a single general in the gendarmerie would have dared to confirm the death sentence on Natalia Klimova. No, thank you!

On the original sentence the following confirmation is written:

I confirm the sentence of the court, but with a substitution for both of the accused of the death sentence by exile with hard labor for life, with all the consequences of this punishment, January 29, 1907. Assistant Chief Commander, Infantry General Gazenkampf. Certified as a true copy: Court Secretary State Counselor Menchukov. With the seal of the St. Petersburg District Court.

In the court session dealing with the Klimova and Terentieva case there is an extremely curious scene, something unique and unprecedented in Russia's political trials, or in any country's. This scene is recorded in the summary of the trial by a laconic bureaucratic formula.

The accused were given the last word.

The court trial in the Trubetskoi bastion of Petropavlovsk fortress was very short, no more than two hours or so.

The accused decided not to object to the prosecution's speech. Admitting the fact of their involvement in the assassination attempt on Stolypin, they did not admit their guilt. The accused decided not to appeal.

And now in her last word—before her death, before her execution this "easily carried away girl" Klimova suddenly yielded to her nature, her raging blood, and said and did something for which the court chairman interrupted her last word and removed her from the courtroom "for indecent behavior."

Memory breathes easily in Petersburg. It is harder in Moscow, where Khamovniki has been chopped up by avenues, where Presnia has been crushed,[26] and the links between side streets and between different times have been broken ...

Merzliakovsky. I was often on Merzliakovsky Street in the 1920s, when I was a university student. There was a women's student hostel on Merzliakovsky Street: the same rooms where twenty years earlier, at the start of the century, lived a student of Moscow's pedagogical institute, the future schoolteacher Nadia Terentieva. But she never became a teacher.

Povarskaya Street, house No. 6, where the concierge records show that Natalia Klimova and Nadezhda Terentieva lived together: damning evidence for the investigation.

This is the house to which Natalia Klimova dragged three fifteen-kilo dynamite bombs: 49 Morskaya Street, apartment 4.

Was it not at 6 Povarskaya Street that Mikhail Sokolov, "the Bear," met Klimova, so as to transport her to death and glory, because there are no vain victims, no nameless exploits. Nothing is ever lost in history; only the scales become distorted. And if time wants to lose the name of Klimova, we shall do battle with time.

Where is this house?

I am searching the side streets. That is a pastime for young people: climbing staircases already marked by history but not yet turned into museums. I try to imagine and repeat the movements of people who used to climb these stairs, who stood at the same crossroads, so as to accelerate the pace of events and hurry up the course of time.

And time moved on.

Children are brought to the altar of victory. That is an ancient tradition. Klimova was twenty-one when she was condemned to death.

The Passions of the Lord, a mystery that revolutionaries performed in the theater of daggers and swords, disguising themselves, hiding in the entrances to buildings, changing from horse tram to fast sled: knowing how to lose a detective was one of the entry examinations in that Russian university. Anyone who completed the course in full ended up on the gallows.

A lot, a great deal, too much, has been written about this.

But what I need are not books but people, not street plans but the quiet side streets.

First came the cause. Initially, there were explosions, a sentence passed on Stolypin, forty-five kilos of dynamite placed in three black-leather briefcases; what the outer casings were made of and what the bombs looked like, I won't say. "The bombs were brought by me, but I shan't say when, where from, or even in what." What makes a person taller? Time. The turn of the century was the century's flowering, when Russian literature, philosophy, science, and moral thinking had risen to unprecedented heights. Everything morally important and powerful that the great nineteenth century had accumulated was all turned into a living cause, into a living life, a living example, and thrown into a final battle against autocracy. Self-sacrifice, renunciation to the point of anonymity: how many terrorists perished without anyone knowing their names. The sacrificial nature of a century that had found its highest freedom and highest strength in combining word with deed. They began with "thou shalt not kill," with "God is love," with vegetarianism and serving one's neighbor. Their moral demands and selflessness were so great that the best of the best, disillusioned by nonresistance to evil, moved from "thou shalt not kill" to "executions," taking up revolvers, bombs, and dynamite. They had no time to become disillusioned by bombs: all the terrorists died young.

Natalia Klimova was born in Riazan. Nadezhda Terentieva was born at the Beloretsk factory in the Urals. Mikhail Sokolov was born in Saratov.

Terrorists were born in the provinces. They died in Petersburg. There is logic in this fact. Classical literature, nineteenth-century poetry, and their moral demands were most deeply rooted in the provinces, and it was there that literature generated a need to find an answer to the question "What is the meaning of life?"

They sought the meaning of life passionately, selflessly. Klimova found the sense of life by preparing to repeat and supersede Perovskaya's exploit.[27] It turned out that Klimova had the moral strength: it was significant that she had spent her childhood in an extremely remarkable family—her mother was Russia's first female doctor.

All that was missing was some personal encounter, a personal example so that all her moral, spiritual, and physical strength could be brought to the greatest tension, and for Natalia Klimova's rich inner resources to give her a reason for putting her straight into the canon of Russia's most prominent women.

Such an impulse, a personal acquaintance was Natalia Klimova's meeting with Mikhail Sokolov, the Bear.

This friendship took Natalia Klimova's fate to the highest peaks of Russian revolutionary heroism, an ordeal by self-renunciation and self-sacrifice.

The "cause," inspired by the Maximalist Sokolov, was the battle against autocracy. An organizer to the marrow of his bones, Sokolov was also a prominent party theoretician. Agrarian terror and factory terror were the Bear's contributions to the program of the Socialist Revolutionary "oppositions."

As chief battle commander at Presnia during the December uprising—it was thanks to Sokolov that Presnia held out so long—Sokolov didn't get on with the party and left it after the Moscow uprising, creating his own "fighting organization of socialist-revolutionary Maximalists."

Natalia Klimova was his assistant and his wife.

Wife?

The chaste world of the revolutionary underground has a special response to this simple question.

"She lived using a passport naming her as Vera Shaposhnikova, with a husband Semion Shaposhnikov."

"I wish to add that I didn't know that Semion Shaposhnikov and Mikhail Sokolov were one and the same person."

Using a passport? But on Morskaya Street, Natalia Klimova lived using a passport naming her as Yelena Morozova, with a husband Mikhail Morozov, the man who was blown up by his own bomb in Stolypin's reception room.

An underworld of forged passports and genuine feelings. It was considered that everything personal had to be suppressed, subordinated to the great goal of a struggle in which there was no difference between life and death.

Here is an excerpt from the police textbook *The History of the Socialist Revolutionary Party*, written by the gendarmerie general Spiridovich:

On December 1st, Sokolov himself was picked up in the street and on the 2nd he was executed by sentence of the court.

On the 3rd, Klimova's secret apartment was discovered; here, among various things, twenty-two kilos of dynamite, 7,600 rubles in banknotes, and seven seals of various government institutions were found. Klimova herself was arrested, as well as other prominent Maximalists.

Why did Klimova live in Petersburg for all of three months after the explosion on Aptekarsky Island? They were waiting for the Bear: the Maximalists had a congress in Finland, and only at the end of November did the Bear and other maximalists return to Petersburg.

During her brief investigation, Natalia learned of Sokolov's death. There was nothing surprising about his execution, yet Natalia was alive, and the Bear was missing. In "Letter Before Execution," the death of close friends is mentioned calmly. But Natalia never forgot Sokolov.

In the barracks of the Petersburg House of Preliminary Detention, Natalia Klimova wrote her famous "Letter Before Execution," which instantly became known all around the world.

This is a philosophical letter written by a girl of twenty. It is not a farewell to life but a glorification of the joy of life.

It is colored in tones of unity with nature—a motif Klimova was faithful to all her life. This letter is unusual in the freshness of its feelings, in its sincerity. There isn't even a shadow of fanaticism or didacticism. It is a letter about a higher form of freedom, about the happiness of uniting word and deed. This letter is not a question but an answer. It was printed in the magazine *Education* along with Marcel Proust's novel.

I have read this letter, riddled with a series of "outtakes" by censorship and by very significant rows of dots. Fifty years later, the letter was reprinted in New York, but the cuts were the same, as were the inaccuracies and misprints. The censorship of the time made its own cuts in the New York version: the text lost its fire, it was faded, but the words kept all their strength and remained true to their lofty sense. Klimova's letter excited the whole of Russia.

Even now, in 1966, however broken the link between times,

Klimova's name finds an echo in the hearts and memory of Russian intellectuals.

"Ah, Klimova! That's the 'Letter Before Execution'... Yes. Yes. Yes."

There is more than prison bars, more than gallows, more than the echo of the explosion in this letter. No. In her letter Klimova was expressing something particularly meaningful for humanity, something particularly important.

In the major metropolitan newspaper *The Word*, the philosopher Frank[28] devoted a lengthy article, "Overcoming Tragedies," to Klimova's letter.

Frank saw this letter as a manifestation of religious awareness and wrote that "the moral value of these six pages will outweigh all the many volumes of the contemporary philosophy and poetry of tragicism."

Struck by the depth of feeling and thinking in Klimova—and she was only twenty-one years old—Frank compares her letter to Oscar Wilde's *De Profundis*. This is a liberation letter, an exit letter, an answer letter.

So why are we not in Petersburg? Because both the attempt on Stolypin's life and "Letter Before Execution" were not, it turns out, sufficient for this big and important life, which, most significant, had found itself in time.

"Letter Before Execution" was printed in the autumn of 1908. The waves of light, sound, and magnetism that were caused by this letter covered the whole world, and a year later they still had not abated or died down, when suddenly a new amazing piece of news struck every corner of the globe. Thirteen women sentenced to hard labor in Siberia had escaped, along with Tarasova, a prison warder from Moscow's Novinskaya women's prison.

Here it is: "The List of Persons Who Escaped on the Night of June 30 and July 1, 1909 from Moscow Province Women's Prison":

No. 6: Klimova, Natalia Sergeyevna, sentenced by Petersburg Military District Court on January 29, 1907, to capital punishment by hanging, capital punishment being commuted to indefinite hard labor by the assistant commander of Petersburg

Military District. Twenty-two years old, fuller figure, dark hair, blue eyes, pink face, Russian type.

This escape, which hung by such a slender thread that a thirty-minute delay would have been the same as death, was a brilliant achievement.

German Lopatin, a man who was an expert on escapes, called the convicts who escaped from the Novinskaya prison "Amazons." In Lopatin's mouth that word was not just friendly praise, slightly ironic and approving. Lopatin felt the reality behind the myth.

Lopatin understood better than anyone what a successful escape from a prison cell was, when the cell was a fortuitous mix of recently assembled convicts with very different "causes," interests, and fates. Lopatin realized that the willpower of an organizer was essential for transforming this varied collective into a battle squad, bonded by the underground's discipline, a discipline even greater than the military's. Natalia Sergeyevna Klimova was such an organizer.

With very different "causes." This escape involved the anarchist Maria Nikiforova, or Marusya, the future Cossack female ataman under Makhno in the Civil War. General Slashchov would execute the ataman Marusya: she was early on transformed into a cinematic image of the beautiful woman bandit, but in reality Maria Nikiforova was a genuine hermaphrodite and nearly ruined the escape attempt.

There were ordinary criminals, two women with their children, in the same cell (number eight!).

It was for this escape that members of Mayakovsky's family made clothes for the fugitives: Mayakovsky himself was in prison (being interrogated by the police about this case) because of this escape.

The women convicts learned the script of their upcoming performance by heart; they studied their encrypted parts until they knew them cold.

There were lengthy preparations for the escape. A foreign representative of the Central Committee of the Socialist Revolutionary Party, the "general," as the escape organizers Koridze and Kalashnikov called him, came to liberate Klimova. The general's plans were rejected. The Moscow Socialist Revolutionaries were already carrying out "detailing." This was a liberation from within, using the forces of the women convicts themselves. The prison warder Tarasova was to free the convicts and flee abroad with them.

Before midnight on June 30, the women convicts disarmed the warders and emerged onto Moscow's streets.

A lot was written in magazines and books about the escape of the thirteen, about "the liberation of the thirteen." This escape is another item in the anthology of the Russian revolution.

It should be remembered that the key put into the keyhole of the exit door was not turned by Tarasova's hands, although she was the first one out. She stood there helpless. It was the firm fingers of the prisoner Gelme that took the key from Tarasova's hands, put it in the keyhole, turned it, and opened the door to freedom.

It should be remembered that the convicts were emerging from the prison when the telephone on the desk of the duty warder rang. Klimova picked up the receiver and responded in the voice of the duty warder. The police chief said, "We have information that an escape is being prepared in Novinskaya prison. Take measures."

"Your order will be carried out, your excellency. Measures will be taken." And Klimova put the receiver back and hung up.

Klimova's mischievous letter should be remembered—here it is, I'm holding it now, two sheets of writing paper, crumpled but still alive. The letter was written on May 22 to children, her younger brothers and sisters, whom her aunt Olga Nikiforovna Klimova had several times taken, although they were tiny infants, to see Natalia in Moscow. Natalia herself initiated the children's visit to the prison. She considered that such impressions and encounters could only do a child's soul good. And so Klimova writes on May 22 a mischievous letter, ending with words that were not to be found in any other letter from a woman sentenced to indefinite hard labor: "Goodbye! We'll meet soon!" The letter was written on May 22, and on June 30, Klimova escaped from prison. In May the escape was not only decided but all the parts had been learned, and Klimova couldn't resist a joke. Not that they did meet soon: the brothers and sisters never met their elder sister again. War, revolution, and Natalia's death.

The freed convicts were met by friends and vanished into the hot, black Moscow night of July 1. Natalia Klimova was the major figure in this escape; saving her and helping her escape presented particular difficulties. The party organizations were at the time full of provocateurs; Kalashnikov[29] guessed what the police were thinking and solved the chess problem. Kalashnikov undertook personally to get Klimova away and that same night handed her to a man who had no party connections at all: this was no more than a private acquaintance; the man was a railway engineer, sympathetic to revolution. Klimova spent a month in Moscow in the engineer's house. Both Kalashnikov and Koridze[30] were very soon arrested, and all Riazan was turned upside down by searches and roundups.

A month later the engineer took Natalia, as his wife, on a journey on the Great Siberian Railway. Klimova crossed the Gobi desert on a camel and reached Tokyo. From Japan she took a ship to Italy, and then went to Paris.

Ten of the women convicts reached Paris. Three were caught on the day they escaped: Kartashova, Ivanova, and Shishkariova. They were tried and given additional sentences; their lawyer at the new trial was Nikolai Konstantinovich Muraviov, the future chairman of the Provisional Government commission that interrogated the tsar's ministers, and the future lawyer for Ramzin.

So the surnames of people from the most varied rungs of the social ladder are interlinked in Klimova's life, but in all cases they were the best of the best, the most able of the able.

Klimova was a "ninth wave" person.[31] Before she had time to recover from two years of hard labor and a round-the-world journey of escape, she was looking for work involving fighting. In 1910 the Socialist Revolutionary Party's Central Committee entrusted Savinkov[32] with recruiting a new fighting group. Choosing such a group is not an easy task. On Savinkov's instructions, Cherniavsky, a member of the group, travels all over Russia, goes to Chita. Former fighting members refuse to revert to bombs. Cherniavsky returns empty-handed. This is his report, published in *Hard Labor and Exile*:

My journey (to Russia, to Chita to see A.V. Yakimova and V. Smirnova) did not result in any recruitment to the group. Both possible candidates refused to join. On the return journey I was anticipating how much this failure would depress the comrades' mood, which was already very poor. My apprehensions turned out to be wrong. The failure I reported was made up for by a fortunate event that happened in my absence. I was introduced to a new member of the group, Natalia Klimova, a well-known Maximalist who had recently escaped from a Moscow hard-labor prison with a group of women political convicts. One of the Central Committee members always knew where our group was at any given moment, so we made contacts. Through this member, Natalia told Savinkov about her wish to join the group and, of course, she was accepted with enthusiasm. We all understood perfectly how much Natalia's entry strengthened the group. I have already mentioned that, in my opinion, M. A. Prokofieva was the strongest person in the group. Now we had two powerful persons, and I couldn't help comparing and juxtaposing them. I remembered Turgenev's well-known prose poem "The Threshold." A Russian girl crosses a fateful threshold, despite a warning voice predicting for her all sorts of misfortune beyond the threshold: "Cold, hunger, hatred, mockery, scorn, insults, prison, disease, death" up to and including disillusionment in what she now believes. Klimova and Prokofieva crossed that threshold a long time ago and have experienced a fair measure of the misfortunes predicted by the warning voice, but their enthusiasm is not in the least weakened by the ordeals they have undergone, while the willpower has in fact been tempered and strengthened. As far as devotion to the revolution and readiness for any sacrifices are concerned, one could without hesitation put an equal sign between these two women: they are equal in strength and in value. But one had only to take a closer look at them over a few days to be convinced how unlike each other they are, and in some respects diametrically opposite. Above all, one is struck by the contrast in the state of their health. Klimova, who has managed to recover after a hard-labor prison, showed herself to be in her prime, a healthy, strong woman; Prokofieva suffered from tuberculosis and the process has gone so far and is so obviously reflected in her physical appearance, that one cannot help thinking that we are faced with a candle that is about to go out.

Their tastes, their attitude to life around them, their entire inner natures were just as different.

Prokofieva had grown up in a family of Old Believers, which had inherited generations-old sectarian and ascetic habits and preferences. School and her subsequent enthusiasm for the liberation movement completely purged her outlook of religious views, but her character preserved a barely noticeable trace of something that resembled scorn for or condescension toward any of the joys of existence, a trace of a vague urge for higher things, for detachment from the earth and from earthly vanities. This aspect of her character may, in part, have been supported and emphasized by her illness. Klimova was the complete opposite. She accepted all the joys of existence, whatever they were, because she accepted all of life with all the woes and joys that were organically bound to one another and inseparable from one another. This was not a philosophical view; it was the immediate reaction of a rich and powerful nature. She regarded heroic exploits and sacrifices as the greatest and most desirable joys of existence.

When she came to us, she was full of joy and laughter; she brought considerable animation into the group. We felt we had no need to wait any longer. Why not move into action with the forces we had available? But Savinkov pointed out that there was a question mark hanging over the group. He told me that while I was away, Kiriukhin, who had arrived from Russia, had lived with the group and had in a very short time aroused Savinkov's doubts.

"He talks a lot of rubbish," explained Savinkov. "Once I had to give him a whole formal warning on the need to take a stricter attitude to his chatter. It may be that he just has a loose tongue. He's back in Russia now; he's had a daughter. He should be here any day now. We'll have to take a closer look at him."

Shortly after I arrived in Guernsey, another black spot appeared on our horizon. "Ma" (M.A. Prokofieva) was obviously fading away; every day she was weaker. Naturally, we began to fear that our flickering candle would soon go out. We all felt how precious and much needed her quiet, pure light was in our dark underground world, and we were all anxious. A local doctor advised us to put the patient in a special sanatorium, preferably in Davos. Savinkov had to use a lot of energy to convince M. A. to set off for Davos. After a prolonged struggle, an agreement was reached between them. The conditions were, apparently, as follows: Savinkov undertook to visit her when the group was ready to be sent to Russia, and she was allowed the right to be guided by her own view of her health and to decide for herself whether to go on with the treatment or to leave the sanatorium and rejoin the group.

By this time Savinkov received information that a fighting member, F. A. Nazarov, whom he knew, had finished his hard labor sentence and had become a deported settler. Nazarov had killed the provocateur Tatarov, but was convicted on other charges and sentenced to a short term of hard labor. At the same time that he sent M. A. to Davos, Savinkov sent a young man from Paris to Siberia to propose to Nazarov that he should join the group. When the group was being formed, Nazarov had offered to be a member, but he was rejected. Now he was promised admission into the group if he was successful in carrying out a mission.

The group moved from Guernsey to the Continent, settling in a small French village five or six kilometers from Dieppe. Kiriukhin had arrived. Now there were seven of us. Savinkov and his wife, Klimova, Fabrikant, Moiseyenko, Kiriukhin, and Cherniavsky. Kiriukhin's behavior was unchanged: simple and calm. No idle talk as far as anyone could see. We had a dreary life. A flat, mournful seashore. Mournful autumn weather. In the daytime we gathered driftwood cast ashore for firewood. We'd given up cards since our time spent waiting in New York; chess was also abandoned. There was not a trace of our former conversations about life. We would occasionally exchange curt phrases, but mostly we stayed silent. Each of us watched the patterns in the fire in the stove, interweaving our grim thoughts with them. It seemed that experience had taught us that the most exhausting work was to sit twiddling our thumbs, not knowing how long the waiting period would last.

Once someone made a suggestion: "Let's bake potatoes in the stove. That way, we'll kill two birds with one stone: (1) we'll have something interesting to do in the evenings and, (2) we'll save money on supper."

The suggestion was taken, but all the intellectuals turned out to be very bad bakers; only the sailor (Kiriukhin) showed great talent in this area. I apologize for devoting so much attention to such trivia, but I cannot pass over the baked potatoes.

About a month passed: it must have been December 1910. We were all bored, but Kiriukhin was more bored than anyone else. He began making occasional trips to Dieppe and once he came home tipsy. That evening he sat by the stove where he usually sat and got down to his usual task. Sitting by the fire, he went to pieces: the potatoes got out of hand, and even his own hands wouldn't do as they were told. Natasha (Natalia) Klimova began teasing him.

"Yakov, you must have lost your touch somewhere in Dieppe … I can see that you're not going to have any luck today…"

A verbal duel began. Kiriukhin used his most meaningful phrase: "We know all about you."

"You don't know anything. Well, tell me what you know."

Kiriukhin lost his temper completely. "Tell you? Well, do you remember you Maximalists having a council meeting in a private room at Palkin's restaurant, under the guise of an orgy? When the vice director of the police department was in the main room of the restaurant? Do you remember? And do you remember where you went after the meeting—and you weren't alone!" he finished triumphantly.

Natasha's eyes nearly popped out of her head, they were about to burst out of their sockets, she was so astonished. She called in Savinkov and told him: it was all true; they did have a meeting in a private room under the guise of an orgy. They were informed that the vice director of the police department was in the main room. But they held the meeting in full and went home without any trouble. Natasha left to spend the night with her husband in a hotel on the islands.

The next morning Kiriukhin was asked how he came to know so much. He replied that he'd been told by Feit. So Savinkov went to Paris and summoned Kiriukhin there, then quickly returned home alone. Apparently, Feit knew nothing and couldn't have told this story, since he had no knowledge of the facts in question. Kiriukhin was asked again the source of the facts he had cited. This time he replied that his wife had told him, and she had found out from some gendarmes she knew. Kiriukhin was expelled.

When he returned to the group, Savinkov put to a vote the question of whether we had the right to declare Kiriukhin a provocateur. The answer was unanimously positive. A decision was taken to address the Central Committee and ask them to print an announcement in the party organ that Kiriukhin was a provocateur. After our wait in New York, when we became convinced that Rotmistr was a provocateur, we nevertheless decided not to declare him as such, since we felt that we had insufficient data for such a step. So we limited ourselves to informing the Central Committee that we had expelled him from the group on suspicion of being a provocateur. We knew that he had settled in Meudon (I think that's the name of the little town near Paris), well away from other émigrés.

The unexpected incident with Kiriukhin showed us how ridiculous and absurd we were to play hide-and-seek in various secluded corners of Western Europe when the police department could know all it needed to about us if it took any interest: it could even find out which of us liked baked potatoes the most. That was why we left the village and moved to Paris. That was the first conclusion we drew from the incident. The second conclusion was a decision to reexamine the Rotmistr case. Since our perspicacity had proved to be disgracefully bad with respect to Kiriukhin, doubts naturally arose whether we had made the same mistake, but in the reverse direction, with respect to Rotmistr; in other words, by casting suspicion on an innocent man. Once Kiriukhin was exposed in such a way that there could be no doubts about him, we naturally had to pose the question "How about Rotmistr? Does that mean he was not a provocateur?" Savinkov decided to meet Rotmistr and have it out with him in all sincerity. For the time being he suggested that Moiseyenko and I should go to Davos and inform Prokofieva of the important events in our group.

We spent, I think, about two weeks in Davos. We visited "Ma" every day in her sanatorium. Her health had improved significantly. She was gradually putting on weight, the doctors were relaxing her strict regimen, allowing her to go on walks, and so on. We wanted to extend our stay in Davos as long as we could, when we suddenly received a telegram from Savinkov: "Come. Rotmistr is dead."

When we saw Savinkov, I was struck by his extremely depressed appearance. He passed me a sheet of paper and grimly uttered the words, "Read it. We drove him to it." It was Rotmistr's deathbed letter. It was short, probably no more than ten lines, written simply and not at all like the pompous letter he sent to us in New York. I shan't try to recall it. I'll just summarize the essence: "Yes, so that's what it was, I was suspected of being a provocateur, whereas I thought that all the trouble came from my quarreling with B.V. Thank you, comrades!"

This is how it happened. Savinkov sent Rotmistr a request to come to Paris for talks. Rotmistr came. Savinkov told him about Kiriukhin's fall from grace; Savinkov admitted that he had expelled Rotmistr because of suspicions that he was a provocateur. He urged Rotmistr to be frank, to explain why he had lied about the train and the bath. Rotmistr admitted that both were lies, but he gave no explanations; he kept a sullen silence. Unfortunately, it was not possible to bring the conversation to any conclusion, since visitors came to the flat where they were meeting, and this made it impossible to carry on with the discussion. Savinkov asked him to come the following day, but he didn't: he was found in his room, with a suicide note. He had shot himself.

Before we had time to digest this "self-denunciation" by a "man with a clean conscience," we were faced with a corpse. Everything in our heads was turned upside down. We all adopted Savinkov's formula: "We drove him to it."

Some time after that we were forced to admit V. O. Fabrikant into a sanatorium for the mentally ill. We were all downcast, but we still tried to make the best of it, thinking, "Nazarov will come and then we'll immediately set off for Russia." I don't remember how long we had to wait. Finally, the young man sent to Siberia came back. He told us that Nazarov had agreed to join the group; they had both gotten as far as the border, but when they were crossing it, Nazarov got lost. Near the border they had been hiding in a shed. The young man was forced for some reason to part from Nazarov for a short while, but when he came back, Nazarov was no longer in the shed. Very likely, he had been arrested: that was what the young man thought, and so did we. This misfortune was the last straw for the group. It was disbanded.

After the group was dissolved, I heard my name called out in a Paris street. It was Misha. I knew that after he had been expelled from the group, he had, at Savinkov's request, been found a job in Paris as a driver for an automobile company. Now he was standing by his car, waiting for a customer. We talked about the past and the present. He made a proposal: "I'd like to take you for a ride. Get in." I refused. We went on talking, but I soon noticed tears welling up in Misha's eyes, and I hurriedly took my leave.

"Still the same unbalanced character," it occurred to me.

I left for Italy. After a few months I received news that Misha had shot himself, and that in his suicide note he had asked to be buried next to Rotmistr...

That was how close death got to these people and their daily life. How easily decisions were made about their own deaths. The right to die was employed widely and easily.

Savinkov's group, Guernsey–Dieppe–Paris, the last fighting routes of Natalia Klimova. She was unlikely to be crushed by failure. She had the wrong sort of character. Klimova was used to major deaths; she had trained herself for them, and human vileness was unlikely to be unheard-of in the revolutionary underground. Azef had been exposed a long time ago, and Tatarov had been killed.[33] The group's failures could not convince Natalia Sergeyevna of the autocracy's omnipotence or of the hopelessness of her efforts. All the same, this was the end of Klimova's active service. This trauma left, of course, some traces in Natalia Sergeyevna's psyche . . .

In 1911 Natalia Sergeyevna made the acquaintance of a Socialist Revolutionary fighter who had escaped from hard labor in Chita. He was a man from the same province as Mikhail Sokolov, the Bear.

It wasn't hard to fall in love with Natalia. She was well aware of this fact herself. Her visitor was going to the "Amazon" colony with a letter for Natalia and he had been sent with a joking warning: "Don't fall in love with Klimova!" The front door was opened by Aleksandra Vasilyevna Tarasova, the woman who had freed the "Amazons" from Novinskaya prison: the visitor took Tarasova to be the owner of the house and was amazed at the baselessness of other people's judgment. But then Natalia came out, and the visitor, who meant to leave for home, got off the train at the first station and returned to the house.

Natalia's hasty affair and hasty marriage.

All this passionate self-assertion suddenly switches to maternity. A first child. A second. A third. The difficult life of an émigré.

Klimova was a "ninth wave" person. In the thirty-three years she had lived, fate had flung Natalia onto the highest, most dangerous crests of the waves of the revolutionary storm that was shaking Russian society, and Natalia had managed to cope with this storm.

The doldrums ruined her. Doldrums that Natalia adopted just as passionately and selflessly as she had the storm. Motherhood—a first, second, and third child—was as sacrificial, as full as her life as a dynamiter and terrorist.

The doldrums ruined her. A failed marriage, the trap of family life, trivia, scurrying around like a mouse, bound her hand and foot. As a woman, she accepted even this as her lot—she listened to nature, which she had been taught to submit to ever since childhood.

A failed marriage: Natalia never forgot the Bear, and it really didn't matter whether he had been her husband or not. Her husband came from the same province as Sokolov; he had done hard labor and was in the revolutionary underground, a worthy man of the highest degree, and the affair had developed with all the enthusiasm and recklessness typical of Klimova. But Klimova's husband was an ordinary man, while the Bear had been a man of the ninth wave, the first and only love of the university student Lokhvitskaya-Skalon.

Instead of bombs with dynamite, she had to carry diapers, loads of children's diapers, launder and iron them, do the cleaning and scrubbing herself.

Klimova's friends? Her closest friends had perished on the gallows in 1906. Nadezhda Terentieva, who had been her cellmate on Aptekarsky Island, was not a close friend of Natasha's. Terentieva was a comrade in the revolutionary cause, and no more. Mutual respect, sympathy, no more. There was no exchange of letters, no meetings, no desire to know more of each other's fate. Terentieva was doing hard labor in the Maltsevo mine in the Urals, where the Akatuy women's prison was, and she was released when the revolution came.

From the Novinskaya prison, where there was a very mixed group of women doing hard labor, Natalia took just one friendship, that of the warder Tarasova. This friendship lasted forever.

After Guernsey, more people entered Klimova's life: Fabrikant, who had married Tarasova, and Moiseyenko became her close friends. Natalia didn't keep up close relations with the Savinkov family and made no efforts to build on that acquaintance.

Just like Terentieva, Savinkov was for Klimova no more than a comrade in the cause.

Klimova was no theoretician or fanatic, no agitator or propagandist. All her urges and her actions were a tribute to her own temperament, "sentiments with philosophy."

Klimova was good for anything, except ordinary life. It turned out that there were things that she found harder than waiting and starving for months on end, baking potatoes for supper. The everyday hassle to earn money, to get financial support, to care for and make decisions for two small children.

After the revolution, her husband left for Russia in advance of his family, and their relationship was broken off for several years. Natalia was desperate to go to Russia. Pregnant with her third child, she moved from Switzerland to Paris, so as to reach Russia via London. The children and Natalia fell ill and missed the special children's boat.

Oh how many times Natalia used to send letters from the Petersburg House of Preliminary Detention, giving advice to her younger sisters, whom her stepmother, Auntie Olga Nikiforovna, had promised to bring from Riazan to Moscow to see Natalia in prison.

Thousands of bits of advice. Don't catch cold. Don't stand under the skylight. Or the journey will be called off. And the children listened to the advice of their elder sister and arrived, well cared for, for a prison visit in Petersburg.

In 1917 Natalia herself had no such adviser. Her children caught chills, the ship left without them. In September her third child was born, a girl who did not live long. In 1918 Natalia made her last attempt to leave for Russia. Tickets were bought for the boat. But both of her little girls, Natasha and Katia, caught the flu. Klimova herself fell ill caring for them. The 1918 flu was a global plague, the Spanish flu. Klimova died, and the children were brought up by her friends. Their father, who was in Russia, did not meet his children until 1923.

Time passes more quickly than people think.

There was no family happiness.

War. Natalia Sergeyevna, an active and passionate supporter of defensive war, took Russia's military defeat very badly, while she had a very morbid reaction to the revolution with its turbid currents.

You might think that Natalia would undoubtedly have found herself in Russia. But did Savinkov find himself? No. Did Nadezhda Terentieva find herself? No.

Here Natalia Klimova's fate overlaps with the great tragedy of the Russian intelligentsia, the revolutionary intelligentsia.

The best people of the Russian Revolution made the greatest sacrifices; they perished young, nameless; and as they shook the throne to its foundations, they made such sacrifices that by the time revolution came, their party no longer had the strength or the people to carry Russia with it.

The crack that marks the split in the times—not just in Russia but in the world, where on one side we have all of nineteenth-century humanism, its self-sacrificing nature, its moral climate, its literature and art, and on the other side Hiroshima, bloody wars and concentration camps, medieval tortures, and the debauching of souls—is betrayal, in terms of moral worth, a frightening mark of totalitarian states.

Klimova's life and fate are inscribed into human memory because this life and fate are the crack that marks the split in the times.

An ordinary life leaves fewer traces than the life of an underground revolutionary who deliberately hides and conceals himself with aliases and disguises.

Somewhere this chronicle is being written, occasionally surfacing, like "Letter Before Execution," as a memoir, as a record of something very important.

Such are the tales of Klimova. There are quite a few of them. Natalia Klimova left enough traces. It's just that these records have not been brought together into a single monumental collection.

A story is a palimpsest that keeps all its secrets. A story is a pretext for magic, an object of sorcery, a living thing that has not yet died, that has seen its hero. Perhaps this thing is in a museum: a relic; or in the street: a house, a square; or in an apartment: a picture, a photograph, a letter...

Writing a story is a search, and the smell of a lock of hair, of a scarf, or of a handkerchief lost by the hero or heroine has to enter the brain's confused mind.

A story is a *palaios*, an ancient tale, not paleography. There is no such thing as a story. Things tell stories. Even in a book or a magazine the material elements of the text—the paper, the font, the articles before and after—have to be unusual.

I held Natalia Klimova's letter from prison in my hands, as well as the letters of her last years from Italy, Switzerland, France. The letters are in themselves a story, a *palaios* with a rounded, strict, and alert plot.

I held in my hands Natalia Klimova's letters after the bloody iron broom of the 1930s, when both the name of a human being and his or her memory had been hounded out and exterminated: there were not many letters left in the world in Natalia Klimova's hand. But these letters exist and provide us with features more brightly colored than anything. These are the letters from Petersburg, from Novinskaya prison, from abroad, after her escape, to her stepmother and aunt, to her younger brothers and sisters. It is just as well that at the beginning of the twentieth century writing paper was made from rag: the paper has not turned yellow and the ink has not faded.

The death of Natalia Klimova's father, which came at the most vulnerable moment in her life, while she was being investigated over the explosion at Aptekarsky Island, was a death that saved Klimova's life, for no judge would risk condemning to death a daughter whose father had himself died while submitting a petition.

The tragedy at home in Riazan brought Natasha closer to her stepmother, it welded them to each other in blood: Natasha's letters become unusually warmhearted.

Her attention to domestic cares becomes stronger.

The children get stories about red flowers growing on the tops of the highest mountains. She wrote a story, "The Red Flower," for the children. There was enough of Klimova to go around for everyone. In her letters from prison to the children there is a whole program for the upbringing of a child's soul, without pedantry or pedagogy.

Molding the human being was one of Natalia Klimova's favorite topics.

There are rather more colorful lines in her letters than in her "Letter Before Execution." An enormous vital strength is what decides a question, not doubts about whether one has taken the right path.

Three dots in a row was Natalia Klimova's favorite punctuation mark. There were more of them than is usual in normal literary Russian. Her dots conceal not just hints or secret meanings. They are a manner of speaking. Klimova knows how to use dots in an extremely expressive way and does so often. Dots of hopes and criticism. Dots of arguments and disputes. Three dots in a row are a way of describing things that are jocular or dreadful.

In the letters of her last years there are no lines of dots.

Her handwriting becomes less confident. Full stops and commas are, as before, in their proper places, but the lines of dots have vanished.

Calculating the exchange rate for the franc does not require lines of dots.

Her letters to children are full of descriptions of nature, and you feel that this is no bookish insight into the philosophy of the sense of things, but a child's communication with the wind, a mountain, or a river.

There is a splendid letter about gymnastics and dance.

The letters to children take into account, of course, a child's understanding of a question, and the prison censorship, too.

Klimova knew how to describe solitary punishment: she was often put in solitary, and the reason, as in all prisons, was that she spoke out for prisoners' rights. I. Kakhovskaya came across Klimova in Petersburg and in Moscow—in prison cells, of course—and has a lot to say about this.

I. Kakhovskaya writes that in the next solitary cell of the Petersburg transit prison, "Natasha Klimova used to dance the weirdest dances to the rhythmic sound of her shackles," and describes her tapping Balmont's verses on the wall:

> He who wants the shadows
> To vanish and disappear,
> Who does not want repeated
> The boundlessness of grief,
> Must help themselves—
> Must with a mighty hand
> Throw uselessness aside—

"These are the verses from Balmont that N. Klimova, sentenced to life imprisonment, tapped on the wall for me in response to my lamentations about it. Six months earlier she had endured the execution of the people closest to her, Petropavlovsk prison, and a death sentence."

Balmont was Natalia Klimova's favorite poet. He was a "modernist," and Natalia sensed what "art with modernism" was, even though she would not have put it like that.

A whole letter about Balmont was written to the children from prison. Natalia Klimova's nature needed immediately to justify her feelings logically. Her brother Misha used to call this aspect of her character "sentimentalism with modernism."

Balmont means that Natalia's literary taste, like her whole life, also followed the leading poetic avant-garde of her times. And if Balmont justified Klimova's hopes, then Klimova's life was enough to justify both the existence and the work of Balmont. Klimova in her letters was very concerned about his verse, and she tried to have his collection *Let Us Be Like the Sun* with her at all times.

If there was any motif or tune in Balmont's poetry that made the strings of an instrument like Klimova's soul resonate, then Balmont is justified. One would have thought that Gorky and his storm petrel would have been simpler and more in tune, or Nekrasov... No, Klimova's favorite poet was Balmont.

Blok's motif of a destitute, wind-torn Russia was also very strong in Klimova, especially in her years abroad, when she was like an orphan.

Natalia Klimova could not imagine being away from Russia, without Russia and not for Russia. Her longing for Russian nature, Russian people, her home in Riazan—pure nostalgia—was expressed very sharply in her letters from abroad and, as always, passionately and logically.

And there is one other letter that is frightening. Natalia experienced separation with all her passionate nature and constantly thought about her homeland, repeating what sounded like magic spells, suddenly becoming pensive and saying words that were quite unbecoming of a rationalist, a freethinker, someone who inherited the lack of faith of the nineteenth century. She writes in a state of alarm, overwhelmed by premonitions that she will never see Russia again.

What is left of this passionate life? Only a gold medal from school in the pocket of a prison-camp quilted jacket, worn by Natalia's eldest daughter.

I'm not the only one trying to follow Klimova's traces. Her eldest daughter is there, too, and when we find the house we are looking for, the woman goes inside, to the apartment, while I stay in the street or, following after her, hide somewhere by a wall or merge with the window blind.

I saw her when she was just born; I recalled her mother's strong, firm hands hauling without difficulty fifteen-kilo dynamite bombs, meant to kill Stolypin, and embracing with eager tenderness the little body of her first child. The child would be called Natasha, given her mother's name so as to doom her daughter to heroic exploits, to upholding her mother's cause, so that this voice of blood, this call of fate would sound for all her life, so that, given her mother's name, she would spend her whole life responding to her mother's voice as it called out her name.

She was six when her mother died.

In 1934 we visited Nadezhda Terentieva, a Maximalist who was involved in the same plot as Natalia Klimova, in the first notorious case, that of the Aptekarsky Island.

"She's not like her mother, not like her," Terentieva shouted at this new Natasha, an auburn-haired daughter, unlike her dark-haired mother.

Terentieva couldn't detect the mother's strength; she failed to divine or feel the enormous vital power that Klimova's daughter would need for ordeals greater than those ordeals by fire and storm that her mother was fated to undergo.

We also visited Nikitina, who took part in the escape by the thirteen, and we read her two short books about that escape.

We went to the Museum of the Revolution: there were two photographs on the 1900s stand. Natalia Klimova and Mikhail Sokolov. "Send me the photographs where I'm wearing a white jacket and have an overcoat over my shoulders: a lot of people are asking me for one, but if there aren't any (Misha used to say that they'd been lost), then send me a school photograph. A lot of people are asking me for one."

These cordial lines come from Natalia's first letter after she escaped.

It is now 1947, and once again we're standing at Sivtsev Vrazhek.[34]

The quilted jacket still has not lost the barely detectable scent, like the trace of expensive perfume, of the Kazakhstan prison-camp stables.

This was a sort of proto-scent, from which all the scents of the earth have evolved, the smell of humiliation and of dandyism, the smell of paupery and of luxury.

In the camp in the Kazakhstan steppes, the woman grew to love horses for their freedom, the lack of inhibitions in a herd of horses that for some reason never tried to trample down, destroy, crush, or eradicate anything from the face of the earth. The woman wearing the quilted camp jacket, Klimova's daughter, understood late in life that she had an amazing gift for winning animals' and birds' trust. Although a town dweller, she had known the devotion of dogs, cats, geese, and pigeons. The last look of an Alsatian dog in Kazakhstan, when they were separated from each other, was also a sort of boundary, a bridge burned in her life: the woman used to go into a stable at night, listening to the horses' lives, which were free, unlike human beings', and surrounding her with their curiosity, their language, their life. Later, at the Moscow hippodrome, the woman would try to meet horses again. She was to be disillusioned. Racehorses in harnesses, covered in ribbons, hats, carried away by being wildly spurred on, were more like people than like horses. The woman never met horses again.

But all that was later; now the quilted jacket still had not lost the barely detectable scent of the Kazakhstan prison-camp stables.

What had happened? The salmon had returned to their native stream to scrape their flanks against the riverbank rocks. "I very much loved dancing: that was my only sin in the grim Moscow of 1937." She had come back to live in the land where her mother had lived, to reach Russia on the same boat Natalia Klimova had missed. Salmon don't listen to warnings; their inner voice is stronger and more commanding.

The ominous life of the 1930s: close friends' treachery, mistrust, suspicions, spite, and envy. The woman then understood for the rest of her life that there was no sin worse than the sin of distrust, and she swore . . . But before she could swear an oath, she was arrested.

Her father was arrested and vanished in the prison-camp cellars, where the floors were slippery with blood: he had "no rights to correspondence." Her father had cancer of the throat, and he could not have lived long after his arrest. But when an attempt was made to inquire, the answer came that he had died in 1942. That fabulous anticancer, anticarcinogenic quality of the prison camp where her father had lived and died has not attracted the attention of the world's medical science. It was a grim joke, of which there were many at the time. For years, two women would search for just a shadow of a trace of a father and a husband, but find nothing.

Ten years of the camps, endless manual labor, frostbitten hands and feet—until the day she died, cold water would hurt her hands. Deadly blizzards when you could die at any minute. Nameless hands that hold you up in the blizzard, bring you to the barracks, rub you down, warm you up, and bring you back to life. Who are these nameless people, as nameless as the terrorists in Natalia Klimova's youth?

Herds of horses, of Kazakhstan prison-camp horses, freer than human beings, with their own particular life: a city woman had the strange gift of inspiring trust in animals and birds. Animals, after all, are better at sensing people than people are at sensing one another, and they distinguish human qualities better than people do. Animals and birds treated Natasha Klimova with trust, the very feeling that people lacked so badly.

In 1947, when the interrogation and ten years in the camps were over, the ordeals were only beginning. The mechanism that ground you down, killed you, seemed to be everlasting. Those who held out, who survived to the end of their sentences, were doomed to more peregrinations, to new endless torments. This hopeless lack of rights, this doom was the bloodred dawn of yet another day.

She had thick, heavy, golden hair. What next? No rights, years and years of moving around the country, registrations, finding work. After she was freed, after the camps, her first job was as a servant for some camp boss—a piglet that had to be washed and looked after—or back to the saw and lumberjacking. Then salvation: work as a cash collector. More trouble getting residence permits, "restricted rights" towns and districts, a stigma stamp in your passport, an insult of a passport.

How many boundaries had to be crossed, how many bridges had to be burned . . .

Now it was 1947, and the young woman understood and sensed for the first time that she had not come to earth to glorify her mother's name, that her fate was not an epilogue, not an afterword to someone else's life, however closely related or great it might be.

She understood that she had her own fate. And the path to assert that personal fate had only just begun. That she was representative of her age and her times, exactly as her mother had been.

That to keep her faith in humanity, despite her personal experience and her life, was an exploit as great as her mother's cause.

I have often wondered why the all-powerful, omnipotent camp mechanism failed to crush the soul of Klimova's daughter, and failed to grind down her conscience. The answer I found was that for disintegration in the camps, for annihilation there, for humanity to be trampled underfoot, some considerable groundwork is needed.

The degeneration was a process, and a prolonged process over many years. The camp was the finale, the finishing touch, the epilogue.

Émigré life preserved Klimova's daughter. But even émigrés were no better at "holding out" under interrogation in 1937 than the "locals" were. It was the family traditions that saved her. And that enormous vital power that can withstand an ordeal by domestic piglets only teaches you never to weep again.

Not only would she preserve her faith in people but she would make the restoration of that faith constant, unremitting proof of her faith in people, her rule for living: "to consider before anything else that every human being is good. Only the opposite needs proof."

Amid the evil, the mistrust, envy, and spite, her pure voice would be very noticeable.

"The operation was very difficult: liver stones. It was 1952, the hardest and worst year of my life. And, lying on the operating table, I was thinking...These operations, for liver stones, are not done under general anesthesia. General anesthesia in such operations has a 100 percent mortality rate. I was operated under local anesthetic, and I thought about only one thing. I had to stop suffering, stop living, and it was so easy: I had only to relax my willpower a little, and the threshold would be crossed, and the door to nonexistence would open... Why live? Why resurrect and relive 1937? 1938, 1939, 1940, '41, '42, '43, '44, '45, '46, '47, '48, '49, 1950, 1951, all my awful life?

"The operation was underway, and although I could hear every word, I tried to think my own thoughts, and somewhere very deep down, deep inside me, a little stream of willpower and life began to bubble up. That little stream became more and more powerful, and suddenly I breathed easily. The operation was over.

"In 1953 Stalin died, and my new life began with new hopes, a real life with living hopes.

"What resurrected me was a tryst with March 1953. Coming back to life on the operating table, I knew that I had to live. So I was resurrected."

We wait for an answer at Sivtsev Vrazhek. The woman of the house comes out, her heels tapping; her white overall is buttoned up, her white cap is pulled tightly onto tidily arranged gray hair. She takes her time examining, with her large, handsome, dark and farseeing eyes, the woman visiting her.

I was standing there, merged with the window curtain and the blind with its thick layer of dust. I knew the past and foresaw the future. I had been in a concentration camp, I myself was a camp "wolf" and was able to appreciate the grip of a wolf's jaws. I understood something of wolves' behavior.

I felt growing anxiety: not fear but anxiety. I saw the coming days of this short, auburn-haired woman, Natasha Klimova's daughter. I saw her coming days and my heart sank.

"Yes, I've heard of that escape. A romantic time. And I've read 'Letter Before Execution.' Lord! All educated Russia . . . I remember, I remember it all. But romantic times are one thing, and life is—forgive me—different. How many years were you in the camps?"

"Ten."

"You see, then. I can help you, for your mother's sake. But we don't live on another planet. I live on earth. Perhaps your relatives have something in gold: a ring, with or without a stone . . ."

"All I have is a medal, Mama's school medal. I don't have a ring."

"It's a pity you haven't got a ring. A medal can be melted down for gold crowns. I'm a dentist, after all, and I make false teeth. I go through a lot of gold in my work."

"You need to leave," I whispered.

"I need to live," said Natasha Klimova's daughter firmly. "Here you are." And she pulled something wrapped in rags from her quilted camp jacket.

1966

BY THE STIRRUP

THE MAN was old, he had long arms, and he was strong. When he was young, he had undergone a moral trauma: he'd been convicted as a wrecker, sentenced to ten years, and taken to a construction site, the Vishera paper plant in the northern Urals. Here the country turned out to be in need of his engineering knowledge, and he was sent to supervise the construction, instead of digging the earth. He was in charge of one of the three sections of the construction, along with other imprisoned engineers, Mordukhai-Boltovsky and Budzko. Piotr Petrovich Budzko was no wrecker. He was a drunk, convicted under article 109. The authorities found a man with a nonpolitical conviction more convenient, even though Budzko seemed to his comrades to be a deepdyed political, article 58, paragraph 7. The engineer wanted to get to Kolyma. Berzin, the director of Vishera Chemical Plant, had closed his files and gone off looking for gold and recruiting men to join him. People expected Kolyma to be a candy-rock mountain with an almost immediate early release. The engineer Pokrovsky applied to go and couldn't understand why Budzko was accepted but he wasn't; tormented by the uncertainty, he decided to get an interview with Berzin in person.

Thirty-five years later I wrote down Pokrovsky's story.

Pokrovsky stuck to this story and to the same tone all his life as a great Russian engineer.

"Our boss was a great democrat."

"A democrat?"

"Yes. Do you know how hard it is to get to see a big boss? A director of a trust, a provincial committee secretary? Register your interest with the secretary. Why? What's the reason? What are you aiming at? Who are you? And now, here you are, a man with no rights, a prisoner, and suddenly it's so simple to see a boss who is so high-ranking, and what's more, a military man. And with a life story like his: the Lockhart affair,[35] working with Dzerzhinsky. It's a miracle."

"Like seeing a governor-general?"

"Precisely. I can tell you quite honestly and unashamedly, I've done a few things for Russia myself. And professionally I'm world renowned. I specialize in water supply. The name's Pokrovsky. Heard of it?"

"No, I haven't."

"Well, what can I do but laugh? It's a Chekhov story, or as they say now, a model. A Chekhov model from the story 'The First-Class Passenger.'[36] Well, let's forget who I am and who you are. My engineering career began when I was arrested: prison, criminal charges, and a sentence of ten years in the camps for wrecking." Pokrovsky continued:

I was living through the second wave of trials for wrecking: we were still denouncing and condemning the first lot, the Don basin miners.[37] Now, in 1930, we had the next lot. I ended up in the camps in the spring of 1931. The miners were small fry: not worth talking about. Just refining the benchmarks, getting the population and their managers ready for a few innovations, which became clearer in 1937. But at the time, in 1930, ten years was a shockingly heavy sentence. A sentence for what? The lack of rights was shocking. So I was now at Vishera, building something, erecting something. And I had access to the very top boss.

Berzin didn't have any special days for meeting people. Every day his horse was brought to his office, usually a riding horse, sometimes a carriage. And while the boss was getting into the saddle, he would receive any prisoner who wanted to see him. Ten men per day, no bureaucracy, and it didn't matter whether it was a gangster, or a sectarian, or a Russian intellectual. Though gangsters and sectarians never came to Berzin with any requests. A constantly changing queue. The first day I came, I was too late:

I was the eleventh man and after he'd seen off ten men Berzin put his heels to his horse and galloped off to the construction site.

I meant to go up to him at work, but my comrades persuaded me not to, in case I ruined things. Rules are rules. Ten men per day, while the boss is getting into the saddle. The next day I came a bit earlier and waited to be seen. I asked him to take me to Kolyma.

I remember every word of our talk.

"Who are you?" Berzin moved the horse's head aside with his hand, so as to hear me better.

"Engineer Pokrovsky, sir. I'm in charge of the section at Vishera Chemical Plant. I'm building the main block, sir."

"And what do you want?"

"Take me with you to Kolyma, sir."

"What's your sentence?"

"Ten years, sir."

"Ten? I won't take you. If you had three, or even five, that would be different. But ten? That means there's something going on. Something or other."

"I swear, sir..."

"Well, all right. I'll put your name in the book. What's your surname? Pokrovsky. I'll write it down. You'll get an answer."

Berzin's horse moved off. I wasn't taken to Kolyma. I was given an early release at this construction site and was free to travel the wide world. There was work everywhere. But I never enjoyed work as much as I did at Vishera under Berzin. It was the only site where everything was done on time, and if it wasn't, Berzin would issue orders and things would appear out of nowhere. The engineers (and all of them prisoners, would you believe it?) were given the right to detain people at work so as to exceed the norm. We all got bonuses and were recommended for early release. There were no credits for working days then.

And the bosses used to tell us: put your heart into your work, because anyone who works badly will be sent away. To the north.

And they used to point their hands up the Vishera River. So what the north is like, I don't know.

I knew Berzin. At Vishera. At Kolyma, where Berzin died, I never saw him: I was taken to Kolyma too late.

General Groves was utterly contemptuous of the scientists' Manhattan Project. And he wasn't shy about expressing his contempt. The dossier on Robert Oppenheimer was enough in itself. In his memoirs, Groves explains his desire to be promoted to general before he was appointed chief of the Manhattan Project: "I have often had occasion to observe that symbols of power and rank have a stronger effect on scientists than they do on the military."

Berzin was utterly contemptuous of engineers. All those wreckers —Mordukhai-Boltovsky, Pokrovsky, Budzko. Imprisoned engineers, who were building the Vishera plant. Let's get it done in time! Lightning speed! The plan! These people aroused only contempt from the boss. Berzin simply didn't have time to be amazed, to be philosophically amazed at the bottomless, boundless humiliation of human beings, at the decay of the human being. The powers that made him the boss had seen people better than he was.

The heroes of the first trials of wreckers—the engineers Boyarshinov, Inozemtsev, Dolgov, Miller, and Findikaki—worked cheerfully for their rations, in the vague hope of being recommended for early release.

There were then no working credits, but it was already clear that some sort of scale for the stomach was needed to make it easier to manage human consciences.

Berzin undertook to build the Vishera plant in 1928. He left Vishera for Kolyma at the end of 1931.

I was at Vishera from April 1929 to October 1931, so I coincided with and saw only Berzin's work.

Berzin's personal pilot (by hydroplane) was a prisoner, Volodia Gintse, a Moscow pilot convicted of aviation wrecking and sentenced to three years. Being close to the boss gave Gintse hope of early release, and Berzin, for all his contempt for people, understood this very well.

When he was traveling, Berzin always slept wherever he happened to be—in the chief's office, of course—and didn't bother to provide himself with bodyguards. His experience had told him that when Russian people were involved, any conspiracy would be betrayed, sold; that in any case, voluntary informers would pass on even a shadow of a rumor of conspiracy. These informers were usually former communists, wreckers, or intellectuals from good families, or hereditary gangsters. Don't worry, it will be reported. You can sleep soundly, sir. Berzin understood this aspect of prison-camp life well; he slept soundly, he traveled overland and by air without any worries, and when the time came, he was killed by his own bosses.

The same north that was used to scare Pokrovsky existed, and how! The north was just gathering strength and getting up to speed. The north had its administration in Ust-Ulsa, where the Ulsa River joins the Vishera, and diamonds had been found there. Berzin was looking for diamonds, too, but never found them. Timber was being exploited in the north, the heaviest work for a prisoner at Vishera. The Kolyma open shafts, the pickax of the Kolyma stone quarries, work at minus sixty degrees, all that lay ahead. Vishera achieved quite a lot to help Kolyma come into being. Vishera was the 1920s, the end of the 1920s.

In the north, in the forest sections of Pel and Myk, Vaya and Vetri-anka, when prisoners were moved (prisoners don't go by themselves, they are "moved," that's the official term), they demanded that their hands be tied behind their backs so that the escort guard had no excuse to kill them "for attempting to escape." "Tie my hands, then I'll go. Draw up a statement." Anyone who didn't have the foresight to beg the bosses to tie his hands was in mortal danger. There were a lot of people "killed while attempting to escape."

In one of the sections of the camps, gangsters were taking every parcel sent to the *freiers*. This was too much for the camp chief: he shot three gangsters. And he exhibited the corpses in their coffins in the guardhouse. The corpses were there for three days and three nights. The thefts stopped; the chief was removed from his post and transferred somewhere else.

The camp seethed with arrests, provocations, internal interrogations and investigations. A third section, enormous in its numbers, was formed of convicted secret policemen who had committed crimes and had come under special escort to work for Berzin: they immediately were employed as interrogators. Without exception, every former secret policeman was given a job that fit his qualifications. Colonel Ushakov, the chief of criminal investigation at Far East Construction, who survived Berzin's fall safe and sound, had been sentenced to three years for overstepping his authority, article 110. He stayed on to work for Berzin and went off with Berzin to set up Kolyma. Quite a lot of people were serving sentences "because of Ushakov," and were in preliminary detention. True, Ushakov was not a political policeman. His job was investigation, investigating fugitives. Ushakov was also in charge of the regime departments[38] in Kolyma, and it was he who actually signed "The Rights of Detainees," or, to be precise, the rules for keeping detainees, which consisted of two parts: (1) obligations: that which a prisoner must do or may not do; (2) the right to complain, the right to write letters, the right to a little sleep, the right to a little food.

In his youth Ushakov had been a detective working for Moscow's Criminal Investigation Department, but he made a mistake, was given a three-year sentence, and left for Vishera.

Zhigalov, Uspensky, and Pesniakevich were in charge of a major case against the chief of the third section (Beriozniki). This case concerned bribes and false accounting, but came to nothing because of the firm stand taken by several prisoners who spent four months in solitary confinement in the camp prisons being interrogated and threatened.

Extra sentences were quite common at Vishera. Lazarenko and Glukhariov received them.

At the time no extra sentence was given for attempting to escape: the rule was three months in a solitary-confinement cell with an iron floor, which in winter, for men who were stripped to their underwear, was fatal.

I was arrested by the local organs twice, and twice I was sent under special escort from Beriozniki to Vizhaikha; twice I went through investigation and interrogation.

This solitary confinement was terrifying for experienced men. Fugitives and gangsters used to beg Nesterov, the commandant of the first section, not to put them into solitary. They would never ever run away again. And Nesterov, showing them his hairy fist, used to say, "Right, choose: a slapping, or solitary!"

"A slapping!" the fugitive would reply plaintively.

Nesterov would swing his arm and the fugitive would fall to the ground, covered in blood.

In April 1929, in our party of prisoners, every night the guards would get Zoya Vasilyevna, a dentist, drunk and gang-rape her. Zoya Vasilyevna had been convicted under article 58 in the *Quiet Flows the Don* case.[39] The sectarian Zayats was in this same party. He refused to line up for roll call. At every roll call he was badly kicked by a guard. I stepped out of line, protested, and that same night I was taken out into the freezing cold, stripped naked, and forced to stand in the snow until the guard was satisfied. That was in April 1929.

In the summer of 1930, at the Beriozniki camp, there was an accumulation of about three hundred prisoners who were certified under article 458 to be released because of illness. These were people unique to the north: they had black-and-blue skin blotches; they had contractions due to scurvy; they had hands and feet without fingers or toes because of frostbite. Self-mutilators were not released under article 458: they stayed in the camps until they either finished their sentence or happened to die.

Stukov, the chief of the camp section, meant to make arrangements for the sick to be taken out for exercise as treatment, but all the transit prisoners refused, in case they then recovered and ended up in the north again.

Yes, they had good reason to threaten Pokrovsky with the north. In the summer of 1929 I saw for the first time a party of prisoners from the north: a big snaking dust column, sliding down the hill, visible from far away. First, through the dust, you could see the flash of bayonets, and then their eyes. Their teeth did not gleam: they'd all fallen out because of scurvy. Their dry, cracked mouths, their gray Solovetsky Islands hats, their cloth earflaps, their cloth pea jackets, their cloth trousers. I remembered that party for the rest of my life.

Didn't all that happen when Berzin was in charge? Berzin, by whose stirrup engineer Pokrovsky trembled?

There is a terrible feature of the Russian character: degrading servility, reverence, toward every camp chief. Engineer Pokrovsky was only one of thousands who were prepared to pray to a top boss and lick his hand.

The engineer was an educated man, but that didn't make him bow down any less.

"What did you like so much at Vizhaikha?"

"Why ask? We were allowed to wash our clothes in the river. After prison, after being in a convoy of prisoners, that really means something. It means we were trusted, too. Amazing trust. We did our washing right in the river, on the bank, and the soldiers guarding us saw us and didn't shoot. They saw and they didn't shoot!"

"The river where you bathed was inside the guarded zone, ringed by guard towers spaced over the taiga. What risk was Berzin taking by letting you wash your clothes? And outside the ring of towers was a ring of taiga secrets—patrols, special search groups. And the flying inspection patrols check up on each other."

"Ye-e-es..."

"And do you know the last word our Vishera said to me when he was seeing me off, when I was released in the autumn of 1931? You were washing your clothes in the river at the time."

"What was it?"

"Goodbye. You've had your stay at a little outpost; next time you'll be at a big one."

The legend of Berzin is due to a beginning that seems exotic to an ordinary person—the Lockhart affair, Lenin and Dzerzhinsky—and to his end, shot by Yezhov and Stalin in 1938. And that legend is blown out of proportion by lush and colorful exaggeration.

In the Lockhart affair everyone in Russia had to make a choice, to toss a coin: heads or tails. Berzin decided to surrender Lockhart, to sell him. Such actions are often dictated by chance: you haven't slept well, or the band in the park was playing too loud. Or there was something in Lockhart's emissary's face that repelled you. Or did a tsarist officer see his action as a testimony to his devotion to a power that had not yet been born?

Berzin was the most run-of-the-mill camp boss, a diligent agent of the will of whoever sent him there. Berzin stayed near him, working for him in Kolyma, all those members of the Leningrad OGPU who were involved in the Kirov affair. These people were simply transferred to Kolyma as part of their service: they kept their seniority, bonuses, and so on. Filip Medved, the chief of the Leningrad department of OGPU, was a chief in Kolyma of the Southern Mining Administration, and he was shot along with Berzin, who was summoned to Moscow and removed from a train near Aleksandrov.

Neither Medved, nor Berzin, nor Yezhov, nor Berman, nor Prokofiev were in any way capable or remarkable.

Berzin also committed murder when ordered to by his superiors in 1936. The newspaper *Soviet Kolyma* was full of notifications and articles about trials, full of calls for vigilance, full of speeches of repentance, of calls for cruelty and mercilessness.

In the course of 1936 and 1937 Berzin himself made such speeches—constantly, carefully, afraid to leave anything out, to miss anything. Executions of enemies of the people were taking place in Kolyma as early as 1936.

One of the main principles behind the killings in Stalin's time was the elimination by one cohort of party activists by another cohort. And the new cohort would in turn perish at the hands of new men, from the third cohort of killers.

I don't know who benefited and whose behavior showed confidence or any logic. Not that this is very important.

Berzin was arrested in December 1937. When he died, he was still killing for the same Stalin who killed him.

It is easy to debunk the Berzin legend: one has only to look at the Kolyma newspapers of the time—1936! 1936! And as for 1937, of course, the Serpentinnaya, the pretrial prison of the Northern Mining Administration, where there were mass executions under Colonel Garanin in 1938, was an outpost set up in Berzin's time.

Something else is harder to understand. Why does talent not find enough inner strength, enough moral fiber to treat itself with respect and not to revere uniform and rank?

Why does an able sculptor make a statue of some Gulag boss with enthusiasm and self-abandon and reverence? Where is the compelling attraction for an artist in a Gulag boss? True, even Ovid was the boss of a state labor camp, but that is not what Ovid is famous for.

Well, let's say that an artist, a sculptor, a poet, or a composer may be inspired by an illusion, that he may be caught up in and carried away by a burst of emotion and then create some symphony, interested as he is only by the current of colors, the current of sounds. But why, all the same, should this current be generated by the figure of a Gulag boss?

Why does a scientist draw formulas on a blackboard for the same Gulag boss and feel inspired by this figure in his engineering searches for materials? Why does a scientist feel such reverence for some boss of Separate Camp Point? Only because he is the boss.

Scientists, engineers, and writers, intellectuals who have ended up in chains, are ready to be sycophants for any semiliterate fool.

"Don't ruin my life, sir," an arrested accountant of a camp department said in my presence to the local OGPU officer. The accountant's surname was Osipenko. Before 1917 Osipenko was the secretary to the metropolitan bishop Pitirim, and took part in Rasputin's orgies.

Never mind Osipenko! All these Ramzins, Ochkins, Boyarshinovs behaved in the same way...[40]

There was Maisuradze, a cinema technician before he was arrested, who made his career under Berzin and ended up as the boss of the Accounting and Distribution Section. Maisuradze understood what "standing by the stirrup" meant.

"Yes, we're in hell," Maisuradze used to say. "We are in the next world. Before prison we were the lowest. But here we will be the highest people. And all the Ivan Ivanoviches will have to take us into consideration." (Ivan Ivanovich was what an intellectual was called in professional criminal jargon.)

I have thought for many years that all this "Mother Russia" was just the unthinkable depths of the Russian soul.

But reading Groves's memoirs about the atomic bomb, I saw that this servility in communicating with a general is characteristic of the world of scientists—the world of science, no less.

What is art? Science? Does it ennoble man? No, no, and no. It is not from art nor from science that man gets his minute positive qualities. Something else gives men moral strength, but it is not their profession or their talent.

All my life I have been observing the slavish self-abasement and self-degradation of the intellectuals, not to mention the other strata of society.

In my early youth I would tell any scoundrel to his face that he was a scoundrel. In my mature years I saw the same things. Nothing changed after my curses. Only I myself changed: I became more cautious, more cowardly. I know what is concealed by the secret of people who stand "by the stirrup." It is one of the secrets I shall take with me to the grave. I shan't reveal it. I know and I won't say.

I had a good friend in Kolyma, Moisei Moiseyevich Kuznetsov. Not really a friend, there was no friendship there, but just a human being whom I respected. He was the camp blacksmith. I worked with him as a hammerer. He told me a Belarusian parable about three men of the gentry—this was in the times of Tsar Nicolas I, of course—who spent three days and three nights without a break flogging a wretched Belarusian peasant. The peasant wept and yelled, "How can you? I haven't eaten."

What's the point of this parable? There isn't one. It's just a parable.

1967

KHAN-GIREI

ALEKSANDR Aleksandrovich Tamarin-Meretsky was neither a Tamarin nor a Meretsky. He was the Tatar prince Khan-Girei,[41] a general from Tsar Nicolas II's suite. When General Kornilov was attacking Petrograd in the summer of 1917, Khan-Girei was the chief of staff of the Savage Division, army units especially loyal to the tsar. Kornilov never reached Petrograd, and Khan-Girei was out of a job. Later, when the call—a well-known test of an officer's conscience—came from General Brusilov, Khan-Girei joined the Red Army and turned his weapons against his former friends. At this point Khan-Girei disappeared, and Tamarin the cavalry commander appeared, a commander of a cavalry corps, with three stars, using the relative scale of military ranks of the time. With this rank, Tamarin took part in the Civil War, and as that came to an end he was independently in command of operations against the Turkestan rebels, the Basmachi, and against Enver Pasha. The Basmachi were crushed and routed, but Enver Pasha slipped away in the sands of Central Asia and escaped the clutches of the Soviet cavalry, vanishing somewhere in Bukhara and then reappearing on the Soviet border, only to be killed in an unplanned exchange of fire with patrols. That was the end of the life of Enver Pasha, a talented military leader and politician who at one point declared Holy War against Soviet Russia.

Tamarin was in command of the operation to destroy the Basmachi, and when it turned out that Enver Pasha had escaped, an investigation of the Tamarin case was started. Tamarin argued that he was not at fault and explained why the capture of Enver Pasha had failed. But Enver was too prominent a figure. Tamarin was demobilized, and the prince found himself with no future and no present, either. His wife had died, but his old mother was alive and well; so was his sister. Tamarin, who had trusted Brusilov, felt a responsibility for his family.

Tamarin's consistent interest in literature, even in contemporary poetry, was an interest and taste that gave the former general an opportunity to earn a living in literary work. Tamarin published several articles in *Komsomol Pravda*, signing them A. A. Meretsky.

The high waters break into the riverbanks. But somewhere forms are being rustled, packets are being opened, and, while not yet stapled into a criminal dossier, a document is presented for reporting.

Tamarin was arrested. The new investigation is now conducted in full officially. Three years of concentration camp for nonrepentance. A confession would have mitigated his guilt.

In 1928 Russia had only one concentration camp, USLON—the administration of Special Purpose Solovetsky Island Camps. A fourth department of the Solovetsky Special Purpose Camps was later opened in the upper Vishera, a hundred kilometers from Solikamsk, near the village of Vizhaikha. Tamarin traveled in a party of prisoners to the Urals in a Stolypin prisoners' carriage,[42] thinking over a plan, a very important plan he had worked out in great detail. The carriage in which he was being taken to the north was one of the latest Stolypin carriages. The enormous pressure on the carriage depots, the poor quality of repairs, all led to the Stolypins wearing out and falling to pieces. A Stolypin would jump off the rails and become accommodations for railway repair workers; it would become decrepit, be written off, and then disappear. It was not at all in the interest of the new government to renovate their stock of Stolypin carriages.

There were other things named after Stolypin: the Stolypin necktie was the gallows; peasants had Stolypin ranches. Stolypin's land reform is now history. But people in their simpleminded way talk about Stolypin carriages as prison carriages with bars, special carriages for transporting prisoners.

In fact, the latest Stolypin carriages, devised in 1905, were used up by the state during the Civil War. There haven't been any Stolypin carriages for a long time. Now any carriage with bars is called a Stolypin.

The actual 1905 model of the Stolypin carriages was a heated train car with a small gap in the middle of a wall that was covered with a dense iron grid, a thick door, and a narrow corridor for the escort guards down three sides of the carriage. But what was a Stolypin carriage to Tamarin?

Tamarin was not just a cavalry general; he was a horticulturist who grew flowers. Yes, Tamarin had a dream: he would grow roses, as had Horace and General Suvorov. A gray-haired general with pruning shears in his hand, cutting for his guests a fragrant bouquet of "Tamarin's stars," a special variety of rose that won first prize at an international exhibition in The Hague. Or another variety, "Tamarin's hybrid," the Northern Beauty, the Petersburg Venus.

Tamarin had been obsessed by this dream since he was a child: growing roses is the classic dream of all military men of pensionable age, all presidents, all the ministers in world history.

In cadet school, before bedtime, Khan-Girei saw himself as a Suvorov crossing the Devil's Bridge,[43] or as a Suvorov with pruning shears in the middle of his garden in Konchanskoe village. Actually, no: Konchanskoe was where Suvorov was banished to. But Khan-Girei, worn out by his exploits glorifying Mars, grows roses merely because the time has come; his term is over. After the roses there will be no Mars.

This meek dream kept expanding, until it became a passion. When it became a passion, Tamarin realized that to grow roses he needed to know about the soil, not just Virgil's verses. The grower of flowers imperceptibly became a vegetable grower and a horticulturist. Khan-Girei devoured this knowledge quickly; learning was a joke for him. Tamarin never grudged the time for any experiment in growing flowers. He didn't grudge the time to read yet another textbook on growing plants or on kitchen gardens.

Yes, flowers and poetry! The silvery Latin language lured him to verse by modern poets. But Virgil and roses had priority. But perhaps it was Horace, rather than Virgil. For some reason Dante chose Virgil to be his guide to hell. Was that a good or a bad symbol? Is a poet of country delights a reliable guide to hell?

Tamarin lived long enough to get an answer to that question.

Before growing roses came the revolution, the February 1917 one. The Savage Division, the Civil War, a concentration camp in the northern Urals. Tamarin decided to place a new bet in his life game.

The flowers Tamarin grew in the concentration camp, in the Vishera state farm, were taken to exhibitions at Sverdlovsk and were very successful. Tamarin understood that flowers in the north were a path to his freedom. From then on, a clean-shaven old man in a patched cossack tunic would every day place a fresh rose on the desk of the director of Vishera Chemical Plant, the boss of the Vishera camps, Eduard Petrovich Berzin.

Berzin, too, had heard a few things about Horace and growing roses. He got this knowledge from his classical secondary school. Above all, Berzin trusted Tamarin's good taste. The old tsarist general, putting a fresh rose on the desk of a young secret policeman every day. That wasn't bad. And it demanded gratitude.

Berzin had himself been a tsarist officer, and once, when he was twenty-four years old, he had staked his life on Soviet power, in the Lockhart affair. Berzin understood Tamarin. It wasn't pity but a communality of fate that bound them for a long time. Berzin understood that it was only by chance that he was in the office of the director of Far East Construction, while Tamarin worked with a spade in the camp's kitchen garden. They were people who shared the same upbringing and the same catastrophe. No wonder that computers have calculated the average age of traitors in world history from Hamilton to Wallenrode. That age is twenty-four. So here, too, Berzin must have been a man of his times ... A regimental adjutant, Second Lieutenant Berzin. An amateur artist, expert on the Barbizon school. An aesthete, like all the secret policemen of the time. Actually, he was not yet a secret policeman then. The Lockhart affair was the price for that career, Berzin's entry fee on joining the party.

I arrived in April and in the summer I went to see Tamarin, crossing the river once I had a special pass. Tamarin was living by a conservatory. He had a room with a glass greenhouse roof; there was a heavy, languid smell of flowers, a smell of damp soil; there were greenhouse gherkins and countless boxes of seedlings. Tamarin was longing for someone to talk to. None of his neighbors in the barracks bunk, none of his assistants or bosses could distinguish an Acmeist from an Imaginist.

Soon an epidemic of "reforging" began. Corrective institutions were handed over to OGPU, and the new bosses applying the new laws scattered in every direction, opening more and more camp sections. The country was covered with a dense network of concentration camps, which were by now renamed "corrective-labor" camps.

I remember a big meeting of prisoners in the summer of 1929, in Vishera's Administration of Special Purpose Camps: Teplov, a secret policeman undergoing punishment, talked of the Soviet power's new plans, of new borders in the camp business. Piotr Peshin, a party lecturer from Sverdlovsk, asked, "Tell me, sir, what is the difference between corrective-labor camps and concentration camps?"

Teplov repeated the question loud and clear, and with pleasure. "Is that what you were asking?"

"Yes, that is it," said Peshin.

"There is no difference," Teplov pronounced loud and clear.

"You haven't understood me, sir."

"I have." Teplov then averted his eyes, looking over or under Peshin, and not responding to his signals: a request to be allowed another question.

The wave of reforging was what transferred me to Beriozniki, to Usolskaya station, as it was then called.

But before then, on the night before I departed, Tamarin came to the camp, to the fourth squad, where I lived, to say goodbye. It turned out that I wasn't the one being taken away: Tamarin was being taken under special guard to Moscow.

"Congratulations, Aleksandr. That means a reexamination, release."

Tamarin was unshaven. His facial hair grew so fast that when he was at the tsar's court he had to shave twice a day. But in the camp he only shaved once a day.

"No, it's not for release or reexamination. I've got a year left of my three-year sentence. Do you really think anyone reexamines cases? Some supervisory prosecutor, or some other organization? I have never sent any applications. I'm old. I want to live here, in the north. I like it here. Earlier, when I was young, I didn't know the north. My mother likes it here; so does my sister. I wanted to die here."

And now he had the special escort.

"They're sending me with a party of prisoners tomorrow to set up

Berzin's outpost, to dig the first spadeful for the main construction site of the second Five-Year Plan. Can't we go together?"

"No, I have a special escort."

We said our farewells, and the next day we were loaded onto a wooden motor launch that went downriver to Dediukhin, to the Lionva River, where an old warehouse became the quarters for the first party of prisoners who had erected the main building of the Beriozniki Chemical Construction on their backs, with their blood.

In Berzin's time there was a great deal of scurvy, and not just in the dreaded north, from where dusty columns of prisoners who'd finished work kept snaking down. The north was used as a threat in the administration and in Beriozniki. The north then meant Ust-Ul and Kutim, where there are diamonds now. Diamonds had been looked for before, but Berzin's emissaries had no luck. In any case, the camp, with its scurvy, its beatings, its soldiers beating prisoners with their rifle butts all the time, with extrajudicial murders, inspired no trust in the local population. It was only later that the fate of the exiled families of dispossessed rich peasants from Kuban during collectivization suggested to everyone that the country was preparing for major bloodletting.

The transit camp on the Lionva was in the same barracks where we were housed, or rather in the upper story of the barracks.

A guard had just brought in a man with two suitcases, in a worn cossack tunic. His back was very familiar.

"Aleksandr Tamarin?"

We embraced. Tamarin was dirty but cheerful, far more cheerful than he had been at Vizhaikha when we last met. And I immediately realized why.

"Reexamination?"

"Reexamination. I had three years, now I've got ten, death penalty commuted to ten years, so I'm going back! To Vishera!"

"Why are you so happy about it?"

"Can't you see? About staying on to live, that's the main thing in my philosophy. I'm sixty-five. I'm still not going to live to the end of my new sentence. But at least all the uncertainty has gone. I asked Berzin to let me die on the state farm, in my bright room with a ceiling of hothouse frames. After my new sentence I could have asked to go anywhere, but I spent a lot of effort asking to be allowed to go back, to go back. The sentence doesn't mean anything at all. A big outpost or a small one, that's what makes the difference. So I'll get some rest, spend the night here and tomorrow go off to Vishera."

Reasons, reasons . . . Of course, there are reasons. There are explanations.

Enver's memoirs saw the light of day abroad. The memoirs don't say a word about Tamarin, but Enver's former adjutant wrote the foreword. The adjutant wrote that Enver escaped only thanks to Tamarin's cooperation, and that Enver, in the adjutant's words, knew Tamarin as a friend and had been in correspondence with him when Khan-Girei was at the tsar's court. This correspondence had gone on in later times. The investigation naturally found that if Enver hadn't been killed at the frontier, Tamarin, a secret Muslim, would have taken over command of the Holy War and laid Moscow and Petersburg at Enver's feet. That whole style of investigation blossomed in its luscious bloody color in the 1930s. It was a "school," and the handwriting never changed.

But Berzin was familiar with provocateurs' handwriting and didn't believe a word of the new investigation into the Tamarin case. Berzin read Lockhart's memoirs, and Lockhart's articles about his own Berzin case. Nineteen eighteen. In those memoirs the Latvian was portrayed as an ally of Lockhart's, not as a Soviet spy. Tamarin kept his permanent place in the village farm. A boss's promises are something fragile, but even so a bit stronger than eternity, as the times were proving.

Tamarin began preparing for work that was very different from what he wanted to do in the first days after his case had been "reexamined." And although the old agronomist in a tunic still put a fresh Vishera rose or orchid on Berzin's desk every day, he was thinking about other things as well as roses.

Tamarin's first three-year sentence was over, but he didn't think about that. Fate requires blood sacrifice, and that sacrifice has to be made. Tamarin's mother, an enormous, cheerful Caucasian old lady, died. She loved the north so much and she tried to cheer up her son, to believe in his enthusiasm, his plan, his path in life, his fragile path. When it turned out that his new sentence was ten years, the old lady died. She died quickly, within a week. She loved the north so much, but her heart could not withstand the north. Tamarin's sister was still there. She was younger than Aleksandr, but she too was a gray-haired old lady. She worked as a seamstress in the Vishera Chemical Plant office, still believing in her brother, his good fortune, his fate.

In 1931 Berzin took on his new, major post in Kolyma as the director of Far East Construction. This was a posting where Berzin was not just the supreme power of this border region, one-eighth of the Soviet Union, he was the supreme party, Soviet, military, trade union, and other power, too.

Geological prospecting—Bilibin and Tsaregradsky's expedition[44]— gave excellent results. The gold reserves were rich, the problems were trivial: getting this gold out in temperatures of minus sixty.

The fact that there was gold in Kolyma had been known for three hundred years. But none of the tsars decided to extract this gold using forced labor, prisoner labor, slave labor: only Stalin did. After the first year—the White Sea canal, after Vishera—it was decided that you could do anything with a human being, that there were no limits to his degradation or his physical strength. It turned out that one could devise a scale for the second course of dinner, the scale being productivity, shock and Stakhanovite workers, as they started in 1937 calling the highest ration of camp inmates, or Kolyma army men, as the newspapers then called them. For this gold-mining enterprise, for the business of colonizing the country, and then for the physical extermination of enemies of the people, they needed to find a man. And they couldn't find anyone better than Berzin. Berzin had utter contempt for people— not hatred, just contempt.

As the first Kolyma boss with rights rather greater than the governor-general of Siberia, Ivan Pestel (the father of Pestel the Decembrist rebel), Berzin took Tamarin with him for the agricultural side, to experiment, prove, and glorify. Village farms were set up on the Vishera model, at first around Vladivostok and then near Elgen.

The stronghold for agriculture at Elgen, in the center of Kolyma, was an obstinate whim of both Berzin's and Tamarin's.

Berzin considered that the future center of Kolyma was not the coastal town of Magadan but the Taskansk valley. Magadan was just a port.

The Taskansk valley had soil just a tiny bit deeper than the bare rocks of the whole of the Kolyma district.

A state farm was set up there, and millions were wasted to prove the unprovable. Potatoes would not ripen, so they grew potatoes in hotbeds, then planted them like cabbages in endless shock-working days and camp-style Saturdays, making the prisoners work there, planting seedlings "for themselves." For themselves? I worked quite a lot on those Saturdays.

After a year the Kolyma camps produced their first gold, and in 1935 Berzin was awarded a Lenin medal. Tamarin was given rehabilitation and his convictions were annulled. By then his sister had died, but Tamarin still clung on. He wrote articles for magazines, this time not about young Komsomol poetry but about his agricultural experiments. Tamarin had bred a new variety of cabbage: "Tamarin's hybrid" was a special northern variety, a Michurin-type variety,[45] producing thirty-two tons a hectare. A cabbage, not a rose! The photograph shows a cabbage that looks like a rose: a big, tightly packed flower bud. "Tamarin's pumpkin-melon" weighing forty kilos! Tamarin's selected potatoes!

Tamarin was in charge of the Kolyma department of plant-growing in the Far East Academy of Sciences.

He gave lectures at the Academy of Agriculture, he traveled to Moscow, he was in a hurry.

The alarms of 1935, the blood of 1935, the torrents of prisoners, including many of Berzin's friends and acquaintances, frightened and alarmed Tamarin. Berzin made speeches denouncing and unmasking people; he judged various wreckers and spies among his subordinates, as "people who have oozed their way into the ranks," until the day came when he himself became a "wrecker and spy."

Commission after commission studied Berzin's empire, interrogated and summoned.

Tamarin sensed how shaky and fragile his position was. After all, it was only in 1935 that his convictions had been annulled and he had been "restored to all his rights."

Tamarin won the right to come to Kolyma as a freely hired worker in the agriculture of the north, as a Far East Michurin, as a magician working for Far East Construction. The contract was signed in Moscow in 1935.

The successful vegetable harvests in camps near Vladivostok were impressive. The unpaid prisoner workforce, which was unlimited in the Far East Construction transit camp, performed miracles. Agronomists, chosen from the prisoner parties, inspired by a promise of early release and credits for days worked, did not spare themselves, trying any experiments. For the time being people were not prosecuted for failure. Success was feverishly sought after. But that was still the mainland, Russia proper, the Far East, not the Far North. But even in the Far North, experiments were beginning in the Taskansk valley, at Elgen, in Seimchan, on the coast near Magadan.

But there was none of the freedom, prepared so carefully, with such infinite degradation, ingenuity, and caution. Echelons of prisoners came from the mainland to Kolyma. A world, created for Tamarin by Berzin, was shattering into little pieces. Many of those who were active in Kirov's time and before had found work under Berzin as a sort of reserve. Thus, Filip Medved, the boss of the Leningrad OGPU when Kirov was assassinated, was Berzin's chief of the southern OGPU. Earlier, GP had stood for "State Political," but now it only stood for "Mining Industry": the linguistic games of those who worked for the "organs."

Then 1936 came, with executions, unmaskings, and repentance. After 1936 came 1937.

There were a lot of trials in Kolyma, but those local sacrifices were not enough for Stalin. A rather bigger victim had to be thrown down Moloch's maw.

In November 1937 Berzin was summoned to Moscow with the prospect of a year's leave. Pavlov was appointed the director of Far East Construction. Berzin introduced the new boss to the party activists at Far East Construction. There was no time to travel with Pavlov to the mines for a handover of the industry: Moscow was in a hurry.

Before he left, Berzin helped Tamarin to get leave to go to the mainland. As a Far North man with two years behind him, Tamarin hadn't yet earned leave. This leave was the last act of kindness that the director of Far East Construction did for General Khan-Girei.

They traveled in the same carriage. Berzin was, as usual, surly. When they were near Moscow, at Aleksandrov, Berzin went onto the platform, into an icy blizzard of a December night. He never came back. The train arrived in Moscow without Berzin. Tamarin, after a few days of real freedom, his first for twenty years, tried to find out about the fate of the man who had been his chief and patron for so many years. During one of his visits to the office of Far East Construction, Tamarin found out that he too had been dismissed "from the system," dismissed in his absence and forever.

Tamarin decided to try his luck once more. Any application, complaint, request in those years meant drawing attention to the plaintiff, and it was a lethal risk. But Tamarin was old. He didn't want to wait. Actually, it wasn't that he had become an old man: he just wouldn't and couldn't wait. Tamarin wrote an application to the administration of Far East Construction, asking to be sent back to Kolyma to work. He received a refusal: Kolyma after Berzin no longer needed such specialists.

It was March 1938 when all the transit camps in the country were packed full of echelons of prisoners. The sense of the reply was: if you are taken back, it will be under armed guard only.

That was the last trace of Khan-Girei, gardener and general of our land.

The fates of Berzin and Tamarin are very similar. They both served force and obeyed it. They believed in force. And force let them down.

Berzin was never forgiven for the Lockhart affair, which was never forgotten. In the West, people writing memoirs considered Berzin to be a true participant in an English conspiracy. Neither Lenin nor Dzerzhinsky, who knew the details of the Lockhart affair, were still alive. And when the time came, Stalin killed Berzin. Even for people as cold-blooded as Berzin, the proximity of state secrets is too hot.

1967

EVENING PRAYER

IT WAS in 1930 that the fashion for selling engineers began. The camp had a substantial income from selling on the side those who had technical knowledge. The camp got the full salary, minus the cost of feeding the prisoner, his clothes, his escort guards, the investigation system, even the Gulag. But still after all these communal charges were deducted, a decent sum of money was left. This money certainly was not put in the hands of the prisoner or into his current account. No. The money went into the state's income, and the prisoner got wholly arbitrary bonus money, which was sometimes enough to buy a packet of Cannon cigarettes,[46] sometimes even several packets. If the camp bosses were a little cleverer, they tried to get Moscow to authorize them to pay a certain, albeit small, percentage of the earnings and to let the prisoner have this money. But Moscow did not authorize such payments, and the engineers received arbitrary sums. As, incidentally, did the diggers and the carpenters. For some reason, the government was afraid of even an illusory salary and turned it into an award—a bonus, as it was called.

One of the first imprisoned engineers from our camp department to be sold for construction work was Viktor Petrovich Findikaki, my neighbor in the barracks.

Findikaki was sentenced to five years under article 58, paragraphs 7 and 11; he was the first Russian engineer—this was in the Ukraine— to set up machinery for rolling nonferrous metals. His work is well known in the field of Russian technology. When Findikaki was asked by his new boss at the Beriozniki Chemical Plant to edit a textbook on the subject, he undertook the job with enthusiasm but soon became downcast. I had trouble getting out of Findikaki the reasons for his disappointment.

Without a shadow of a smile, he explained that the word "harm" occurred in the textbook he was editing, and that he had crossed it out and replaced it with the word "hinder." The results were now with the bosses.

Findikaki's editing aroused no objections from the bosses: he continued working as an engineer.

This is, of course, trivial. But for Findikaki it was a serious business, a matter of principle: now I'll explain why.

Findikaki was a man who had "cracked," to use the gangster's and camp boss's expression. At his trial he had helped the investigation: in one-on-one confrontations, he was intimidated, completely confused, and trampled underfoot. And, apparently, not just in the figurative sense. Findikaki went through several "conveyor belts," a term for the nonstop interrogations that became universal four or five years later.

Pavel Petrovich Miller, the chief of the production camp, knew Findikaki from prison. And although Miller himself had withstood the conveyor belts and the slappings and had gotten ten years, he somehow was not particularly bothered by Findikaki's actions. Findikaki himself suffered horrible torment because of his betrayal. All these sabotage cases had involved executions. Only a few, it's true, but the executions were already happening. Boyarshinov, who had been convicted in the miners' case, came to the camp and seemed, likewise, to talk to Findikaki in a hostile way.

The awareness of a lapse, of an abysmal moral failure, stayed with Findikaki for a long time. Findikaki (his bunk was next to mine in the barracks) refused to take any privileged job that could be had only by bribery or pulling strings, such as a foreman, a warder, or being an assistant to Pavel Petrovich Miller.

Findikaki was physically strong, not tall but broad-shouldered. I remember him slightly astounding Miller when he asked to be sent to join a brigade of loaders at the soda plant. This brigade had no freedom of movement and could be called out of the barracks at any time of the day or night to load or unload railway wagons. Speedy work was an advantage that the administration, for fear of penalties from the railways, valued very highly. Miller advised the engineer to talk to the loaders' foreman. Yudin, the foreman, lived in the same barracks and burst out laughing when he heard Findikaki's request. A hard man by nature, Yudin did not like white-collar workers, engineers, or anyone with higher education. But he gave way to Miller's wishes and took Findikaki into his brigade.

After that Findikaki and I seldom met, even though we slept next to each other.

After some time, Chemical Construction needed a clever slave, an expert slave. They needed an engineer's brain. There was work for Findikaki. But he refused: "No, I don't want to go back to a world where I hate every word spoken, where every technical term seems to be in the language of informers, in the vocabulary of traitors." Miller shrugged, and Findikaki went on working as a loader.

But soon his ardor cooled, and the trauma he had suffered at his trial began to heal a little. Other engineers, who had also cracked, arrived in the camp. Findikaki took a look at them. They were living with, not dying from, their personal shame or from the scorn of those around them. And there was no boycott: they were treated as normal human beings. So Findikaki began to have regrets about his whim, his childishness.

There was another engineering job on the construction site, and Miller, through whom the boss's request went, refused it to several newly arrived engineers. Findikaki was asked again and agreed. But this appointment led to a sharp, wild protest by the loaders' foreman. "My best loader is being taken away for some office job. No, Pavel Petrovich. No string pulling here. I'll take it as far as Berzin, and I'll unmask the lot of you."

A genuine investigation into Miller's wrecking activity began, but fortunately someone from the previous authorities reprimanded the loaders' foreman. And Findikaki went back to engineering.

We began again to fall asleep at the same time, our trestle beds next to each other. Again I heard Findikaki whispering what seemed to be a prayer before he slept: "Life is shit. A lump of shit." For five years.

The tone and the text of Findikaki's magic formula never changed.

1967

BORIS YUZHANIN

ONE AUTUMN day in 1930 a party of prisoners arrived: heated-goods car No. 40 of a train heading north, north, north. All the tracks were at full capacity. The railway could barely cope with the transportation of dispossessed kulaks—prosperous peasants: the kulaks and their wives and children were being herded to the north, so as to deposit in the dense Urals taiga men from Kuban who had never seen a forest in their lives. Commissions had to be sent a year later around the timber sites of Cherdyn, since the deportees were dropping dead and the plan for timber production was under threat. But all that came later: for now, the "deprivees" were still drying themselves on brightly colored Ukrainian embroidered towels, washing, not knowing whether to be glad of the rest when they were delayed or not. The train was delayed; it was giving way to—who else but—trainloads of prisoners. The latter knew their fate: they would be brought and put under rifle guard, and then each one would have to use his cunning to fight for his fate, to "break" it. But the peasants from Kuban knew nothing: what death they would die, where or when. All the Kuban peasants were sent off in heated-goods cars. The prisoner trains, rather greater in number, also started off as heated-goods cars, real Stolypin carriages, but there weren't enough heated vans so ordinary, former second-class carriages were refitted and ordered from the factories. These prisoner carriages were called what they were for the same reason that central Russia was in Kolyma called the mainland, although Kolyma is not an island but a province on the Chukotsk peninsula. But the Sakhalin vocabulary, where any dispatch can be only by ship on a sea journey of many days, all creates the illusion of an island. Psychologically, there is no illusion: Kolyma is an island. People come back from it to the mainland, to the "big land." Mainland and big land are everyday items of vocabulary, used in magazines, newspapers, and books.

For the very same reason the name Stolypin was attached to a prisoners' carriage, even though the prisoners' carriage of 1907 was completely different.

So, there were thirty-six prisoners on the list for heated-goods car No. 40. The norm! The party was traveling without overcrowding. There was a column on the guard's handwritten list for "special qualifications," and a clerk's sharp eye had noted an entry: "blue-blouse" worker! What sort of specialty was that? Not a metalworker, not an accountant, not a culture worker, but a "blue-blouse man." Obviously, the prisoner wanted to assert something he considered important by adding this qualification to a camp form. Or to attract someone's attention.

This was the description on the list: Gurevich, Boris Semionovich (Yuzhanin); article s.e. (suspicion of espionage); sentence, three years— unthinkably short for such an article, even for those times—born 1900 (the same age as the century); special qualifications: "blue-blouse man."

Gurevich was brought into the camp office. A swarthy man with a shaved head and dirty skin, he had a smashed pince-nez with no lenses fixed to his nose. It was still attached by a piece of string to his neck. He had no shirt, no underwear, no linen. All he had were tight blue cotton trousers with no buttons, obviously someone else's, obviously given in exchange for his own. The gangsters had clearly taken everything. They used the things of ordinary people, especially *freiers*, to gamble with. A pair of dirty naked feet with overgrown toenails, and a pathetic, trusting smile affixed to a face with big brown eyes, which I knew very well. This was Boris Yuzhanin, the famous director of the Blue Blouse, whose fifth anniversary was celebrated in the Bolshoi Theater, when Yuzhanin sat not far from me, surrounded by the pillars of the Blue Blouse movement: Tretiakov, Mayakovsky, Foregger, Yutkevich, Tenin, Kirsanov, authors and employees of the magazine *The Blue Blouse*, all of whom stared at Boris Yuzhanin, ideologist and leader of the movement, and hung on his every word.

There was something to hang on to: Yuzhanin was always talking, persuading, or leading on.

The Blue Blouse is now forgotten. At the beginning of the 1920s, people had high hopes for it. It was not only a new form of theater, brought to the world by the October Revolution, it was becoming world famous.

The Blue Blouse men considered even Meyerhold to be insufficiently left-wing, and they offered a new form not only of theatrical action, "the living newspaper" as Yuzhanin called the Blue Blouse, but of a philosophy of life as well.

The Blue Blouse, as seen by the leader of the movement, was a sort of chivalrous order. Aesthetics in the service of the revolution would lead to ethical victories.

In the first issues of the new literary magazine *The Blue Blouse* (there were a lot of issues over five or six years), authors were anonymous, no matter how famous they were (Mayakovsky, Tretiakov, Yutkevich).

The only signature was that of the editor, Boris Yuzhanin. Authors' fees went to the Blue Blouse fund, to develop the movement further. The Blue Blouse, Yuzhanin considered, had to remain amateur. Every institution, every factory and plant had to have their collectives. Self-governing collectives.

The Blue Blouse texts were meant to be set to simple, familiar tunes. No trained voices were needed. But if there was a voice, talent, so much the better. The Blue Blouse man was then moved on to an "exemplary" collective. These consisted of professionals, for the time being.

Yuzhanin denounced the old theatrical art. He was diametrically opposed to the Art Theater and the Maly Theater, to their working principles.

It took a long time for theaters to adjust to the new Soviet power. Yuzhanin spoke in its name, promising new art.

Central to this new art was a theater of reason, a theater of slogans, a political theater.

The Blue Blouse came out in sharp opposition to the theater of experience. Yuzhanin revealed and promoted what was called "Brechtian theater." The point here being that Yuzhanin, having empirically found a whole series of new artistic devices, was unable to generalize, develop, or bring them to the international stage. That had been done already by Brecht: honor and praise to him!

The first Blue Blouse performed at a club, a Communist Youth stage in 1921. Five years later there were four hundred collectives in Russia. As its key base, with round-the-clock stagings, the Blue Blouse was given the Chat Noir cinema on Strastnaya Square, a building that was demolished in 1967.

The anarchists' black flag was still hanging over the next building, the anarchist club on Tverskaya Street, where not so long ago Mamont Dalsky, Iuda Grossman-Roshchin, Dmitri Furmanov, and other apostles of anarchism had performed. A capable journalist, Yaroslav Gamza, took part in polemics about the direction and fate of the new Soviet theater, of new theatrical forms.

There were eight central collectives: the Exemplary, the Model, the Shock, and the Basic were their names. Yuzhanin preserved their equality.

In 1923, Foregger's theater joined the Blue Blouse, but kept its separate identity.

Yet, for all this growth, this expansion in breadth and depth, the Blue Blouse lacked something.

The addition of Foregger's theater was the Blue Blouse's last victory.

Suddenly it turned out that the Blue Blouse had nothing to say, that the theatrical "left" gravitated more to Meyerhold's theater, to the theater of the revolution, to the Chamber Theater. These theaters had kept their energy, their inventiveness, and their professional core staff— far better qualified than Yuzhanin's "exemplary" collectives. Boris Tenin and Klavdiya Korneyeva, who later moved to the Theater for Children, are the only famous names who had their start with the Blue Blouse. Yutkevich began to gravitate toward the cinema. Even the Blue Blouse composer Konstantin Listov was unfaithful to the "living newspaper."

It also became clear that the academic theaters had recovered from their concussions and were in agreement, even close agreement, about serving the new power.

Spectators drifted back to auditoriums with stage curtains that featured a seagull; young people were breaking down the doors of the old theater schools.

There was no place for the Blue Blouse. And somehow it became clear that it had all been bluff and mirage. That art had its reliable paths.

But that was at the end; in the beginning there was nothing but triumph. Actors came onstage wearing blue blouses: shows began with an entry parade. These entry parades were all the same, like a sporting march before a broadcast game of football:

> We are the Blue Blouses,
> We are trade unionists,
> We're not nightingale singers.
> We're just the bolts
> Of a big construction
> Of one laboring family.

The "left" follower S. M. Tretiakov was an expert on these "bolts" and "constructions." The editor of *The Blue Blouse* also wrote a few oratorios, sketches, and scenes.

After the parade a few scenes were acted. The actors wore no makeup, they were in "prose clothes," as they later put it; they had no costumes, only symbolic pieces of colored paper. The parade finished with:

> Everything we knew
> We have sung to you,
> We have sung you all we could,
> And definitely we've succeeded
> If we've done you good.

This scanty world of newspaper editorials, retold in theatrical jargon, was extraordinarily well received. It was the new art of the proletariat.

The Blue Blouse went to Germany. Two collectives headed by Yuzhanin himself. In 1924, I think. To the working men's clubs of the Weimar Republic. Here Yuzhanin met Brecht and overwhelmed him with the originality of his ideas. "Overwhelmed" was the word Yuzhanin used. He met Brecht as often as was possible in those times of suspicion and mutual surveillance.

The first trip abroad by shock workers, a round-the-world cruise, dates back to 1933. Then there was one political commissar for each shock worker.

Quite a few political commissars accompanied Yuzhanin, too. These trips were organized by Maria Fiodorovna Andreyeva.[47]

After Germany the Blue Blouse moved on to Switzerland and, exhausted by its triumphs, returned to the homeland.

A year later Yuzhanin took to Germany two more Blue Blouse collectives, who had missed out on the first journey.

The same triumph. More meetings with Brecht. A return to Moscow. The collectives prepared to travel to America and Japan.

Yuzhanin had one feature that hindered him as the leader of a movement: he was a poor speaker. He didn't know how to prepare a speech, or how to crush opponents in a debate or a lecture. At the time, however, debates were very popular: there was meeting after meeting, dispute after dispute. Yuzhanin was a very modest, even timid man. All the same, he didn't want to play a secondary part, or to stand in the wings.

Battles in the wings demand a lot of ingenuity, and a lot of energy. Those were qualities that Yuzhanin lacked. He was a poet, not a politician. A dogmatic poet, a fanatical poet as far as his Blue Blouse cause was concerned.

I was faced by a filthy man in rags. He didn't know where to put his dirty bare feet: Boris Yuzhanin was shifting from one leg to the other.

"The gangsters?" I asked, nodding my head at his bare shoulders.

"Yes, the gangsters. It's better for me like this, easier. I got a suntan in the carriage."

Arrangements and orders were already being prepared in the highest circles to deal with the Blue Blouse people: their finances were to be cut, and they were to be deprived of subsidies. There were already people wanting to claim the Chat Noir cinema. The theoretical side of the Blue Blouse manifestos was getting more and more pallid.

Yuzhanin failed to bring, and couldn't have brought, his theater to the world revolution. In any case, the prospect of doing so had faded by the middle of the 1920s.

Love of the Blue Blouse ideals! That turned out to be insufficient. Love means responsibility, it means arguments at the Moscow City Council department, it means memoranda, a storm in a teacup, talks with actors who are losing their salaries. The fundamental question: Who is the Blue Blouse? Are they professionals or amateurs?

The ideologist and director of the Blue Blouse cut this Gordian knot with one blow of his sword.

Boris Yuzhanin fled abroad.

Like a child's escape, his failed. He handed all his money to a sailor in Batumi who then led him off to OGPU: Yuzhanin spent a long time in prison.

The Moscow investigation gave the hero of new theatrical forms the initials "s.e."—suspicion of espionage—and three years in a concentration camp.

"What I saw abroad was so unlike what was being written in our newspapers. I didn't want to be a living newspaper. I wanted to have a real life."

I made friends with Yuzhanin. I managed to do him a few favors, having to do with linen and the bathhouse, but very soon he was summoned to the administration in Vizhaikha, where the center of the Special Camps was, for work that suited his profession.

The ideologist and creator of the Blue Blouse movement became the manager of the Blue Blouse in the Vishera concentration camps; he became a prisoner's living newspaper. A spectacular end!

I too wrote, in collaboration with Boris Yuzhanin, a few sketches, oratorios, and couplets for this camp Blue Blouse.

Yuzhanin became the editor of the magazine *New Vishera*. Copies of that magazine can be found in the Lenin Library.

Yuzhanin's name has been preserved for posterity. It is Gutenberg's great achievement, even if the printing press has been replaced by the copier.

One of the principles of the Blue Blouse was using any text, any plot.

If it was beneficial, both the words and the music could be by any author. There was no literary theft involved. Here plagiarism was a matter of principle.

In 1931 Yuzhanin was taken away to Moscow. For his case to be reexamined? Who knows?

For some years Yuzhanin lived in Aleksandrov,[48] so his case couldn't have been reexamined very much.

In 1957 I chanced to hear that Yuzhanin was still alive: Moscow of the 1920s could not fail to know and remember him.

I wrote him a letter, offering to tell Muscovites of the late 1950s about the Blue Blouse. My offer of an article aroused a sharp protest from the magazine's chief editor: he had never heard of the Blue Blouse. I didn't have an opportunity to push my suggestion through, and I cursed myself for being too hasty. Later I fell ill, and the 1957 letter to Yuzhanin is still on my desk.

1967

MR. POPP'S VISIT

MR. POPP was the vice president of the American firm Nitrogen, which was the initial installer of gasholders for Beriozniki Chemical Construction.

It was a big order, work was going well, and the vice president deemed it necessary to be present in person when the work was handed over.

Various firms of the "Capitalist International," as the construction chief M. Granovsky called it, were involved in construction. The Germans were installing Hanomag boilers. The steam engines were installed by the English firm Brown and Boveri, the boilers by Babcock and Wilcox, the gasholders by the Americans.

The German work was behind schedule—later, that was declared to be wrecking. The English electrical plant was behind schedule. Later that too was declared to be wrecking.

At the time I was working at the electrical plant, a thermal power station, and I remember well the arrival of the chief engineer of Babcock and Wilcox, a Mr. Holmes. He was very young, about thirty. Holmes was met at the station by Granovsky, the head of Chemical Construction, but Holmes didn't go to the hotel: he went straight to the boilers and the installation work. One of the English installers took Holmes's coat and dressed him in special overalls, and Holmes spent three hours inside a boiler, listening to the installer's explanations. There was a meeting in the evening. Mr. Holmes was the youngest of the engineers. Mr. Holmes replied to all the reports and comments with one short word, which the interpreter translated as, "Mr. Holmes is not worried by that." All the same, Holmes spent two weeks at the plant; the boiler was put into service and gave 80 percent of its planned output. Granovsky signed the certificate, and Mr. Holmes flew back to London.

A few months later the boiler's output fell, and one of our own experts, Leonid Konstantinovich Ramzin, was called in as a consultant. The hero of a sensational trial, Ramzin, in accordance with the agreement, had not yet been released, or rewarded with a Lenin medal, or given a Stalin prize. All that would come later, and Ramzin knew it: he behaved very self-confidently at the power plant. He did not arrive alone but in the company of a very expressive-looking fellow traveler, with whom he also departed. Unlike Mr. Holmes, Ramzin didn't climb into the boiler; he sat in the office of Kapeller, the station's technical manager, another exile, sentenced for wrecking at the mines in Kizel.

The nominal director of the power plant was a certain Rachiov, a former Red director, not a bad fellow, a man who didn't deal with any questions about things he knew nothing about. I was working at the power plant, in the Office for Economics and Labor. Much later, I was the bearer of a complaint by the stokers addressed to Rachiov. This document, in which the stokers complained of their numerous deprivations, included a very typical and very simple decision by Rachiov: "To the Manager of the Office for Economics and Labor: Please investigate and, if possible, refuse."

Ramzin gave a few pieces of practical advice, but had a very low opinion of Mr. Holmes's work.

Mr. Holmes used to turn up at the power station, not in the company of Granovsky, the head of construction, but in that of his deputy, the chief engineer Chistiakov. There is nothing in life more dogmatic than diplomatic etiquette, in which form and content are identical. This is a dogma that poisons life and makes businesslike people waste their time working out rules of mutual politeness, of ranking, of seniority, something that is historically immortal—not in an amusing sense but in essence. For example, Granovsky had as much spare time as he wanted, but did not consider it right for him to accompany a firm's chief engineer around the construction site. Now if the boss of the firm came, that would be a different matter.

Mr. Holmes was accompanied around the site by the chief engineer Chistiakov, a massive, burly man, the sort that novels describe as "looking like a country squire." Chistiakov had an enormous office in the plant, opposite Granovsky's office, where he spent quite a few hours behind locked doors with the office's young messenger girl.

I was young then and didn't understand the physiological law that answers the question: Why do top bosses sleep not only with their wives but with their messenger girls, typists, and secretaries? I often had dealings with Chistiakov, and I frequently used to curse loudly outside that locked door.

I was living in the same hotel next to the soda factory where Konstantin Paustovsky wrote his novella *Kara-Bugaz*.[49] Judging by what Paustovsky said about those times—1930, 1931—he had completely failed to see the main thing that then tainted the whole country, the entire history of our society.

Here, before Paustovsky's very eyes, a great experiment was carried out to deprave human souls, an experiment that was extended to the entire country and that developed into the bloodshed of 1937. It was here that the first test of the new camp system was conducted—self-guarding, reforging, distribution of food according to the results of labor—a system that reached its full flowering on the White Sea canal and foundered on the Moscow–Volga canal, where to this day human bones are found in mass graves.

The experiment at Beriozniki was carried out by Berzin. Not personally, of course. Berzin was always a loyal implementer of other people's ideas, with or without bloodshed, he didn't mind. But Berzin was the director of Vishera Chemical Plant, also a construction of the first Five-Year Plan. He had Filippov as a subordinate for the camp: the Vishera camp, which included Beriozniki and Solikamsk with its potassium mines, was enormous. At Beriozniki alone there were three thousand to four thousand men working at the Beriozniki Chemical Plant site. The workmen of the first Five-Year Plan.

It was here and nowhere else that the question was decided whether camps should exist or not, after trying to do the job with rubles and salaried workers. After the Vishera experiment, which the authorities considered successful, camps covered the whole of the Soviet Union, and there wasn't a province without a camp, and not a single construction site without prisoners working in it. It was after Vishera that the number of prisoners in the country reached twelve million. It was

Vishera that inaugurated the beginning of a new path for places of imprisonment. Houses of correction were handed over to the NKVD, and the latter set about their work, lauded by poets, playwrights, and film directors.

That is what Paustovsky failed to see, when he was so carried away by his *Kara-Bugaz*.

At the end of 1931 I shared my hotel room with Levin, a young engineer. He was working as a German-language interpreter at the Beriozniki Chemical Plant site and was attached to one of the foreign engineers. When I asked Levin why he, a chemical engineer by training, was working as an ordinary interpreter for three hundred rubles a month, he said, "Yes, I see what you mean, but this is better. No responsibility at all. For example, the start-up has been postponed ten times, and a hundred men will be imprisoned, but not me. I'm an interpreter. And what's more, I don't have much work to do; I have all the free time I want. I spend it profitably." He smiled.

I smiled too.

"You didn't understand, did you?"

"No."

"Haven't you noticed that I get back just before dawn?"

"No, I haven't."

"You're not very observant. I do work that brings me a sufficient income."

"What is that, then?"

"I play cards."

"Cards?"

"Yes. Poker."

"With foreigners?"

"No, why would I do that? Apart from a criminal charge, what would I earn by playing with foreigners?"

"With our people?"

"Of course. There are masses of bachelors here. And the stakes are high. And I've got the money. I thank my dad for my life: he taught me how to play poker. Wouldn't you like to try? I'll teach you in no time."

"No, but thanks."

It's purely by chance I've put Levin into a narrative about Mr. Popp, a story I can find no way of beginning.

The installation by the Nitrogen firm was going very well, the order was a big one, and the vice president had come to Russia in person. M. Granovsky, the head of Beriozniki Chemical Construction, had been reminded in good time, and a thousand times, about Mr. Popp's arrival. Reasoning on the basis of diplomatic protocol that he, Granovsky, an old party member and the head of construction on a major site of the first Five-Year Plan, was superior to the boss of an American firm, he decided not to personally meet Mr. Popp at the Usolie station (later that station would be called Beriozniki). That would not be dignified. He would meet him in his office, in his own room.

M. Granovsky was aware that the American guest was traveling on a special train, a locomotive and a visitor's carriage, and the head of construction knew seventy-two hours in advance by telegram from Moscow about the train's time of arrival.

The ritual for the meeting had been worked out in advance: the guest would be given the head of construction's personal automobile, and the chauffeur would take him to the hotel for foreigners, where Tsyplakov, a specially promoted party member, as commandant of the hotel had for the past seventy-two hours been saving for his overseas visitor the best room in the hotel for foreigners. After freshening up and having breakfast, Mr. Popp had to be delivered to the office, and then the business part of the visit, scheduled by the minute, would begin.

The special train with the overseas guest was due at nine a.m.; the evening before, Granovsky's chauffeur was summoned, given his instructions, and sworn at several times over.

"Perhaps, sir, I should drive the car to the station the evening before? Then I'd spend the night there," suggested the worried chauffeur.

"Certainly not. We have to show that everything we do is scheduled by the minute. The train sounds its whistle, slows down, and you drive up to the station. That's the only way."

"Very good, sir."

Worn out by repeated rehearsals, the car traveling empty to the station ten times, the chauffeur calculated the speed and worked out the time, and the night before Mr. Popp arrived, the chauffeur fell asleep and dreamed he was on trial—or perhaps people didn't yet dream of being on trial in 1931.

The duty man at the garage—the head of construction had not had any confidential discussions with him—woke the chauffeur after a telephone call from the station, and quickly starting up the automobile, the chauffeur sped off to meet Mr. Popp.

Granovsky was a businesslike man. That day he arrived at his office at six a.m., conducted two meetings, and gave three "carpetings." When he heard a slight noise downstairs, he pulled the blinds back and looked through the window at the road. There was no overseas guest.

At half past nine the duty controller at the station rang, asking for the head of construction. Granovsky took the receiver and heard a muffled and strongly accented foreign voice. The voice expressed amazement that Mr. Popp was getting such a poor reception. There was no automobile. Mr. Popp was asking for one to be sent.

Granovsky was out of his mind with fury. Running down the stairs two at a time, breathing heavily, he got to the garage.

"Your chauffeur left at half past eight, sir."

"What do you mean, half past eight?"

A car horn was then heard. The chauffeur, smiling drunkenly, strode across the garage threshold.

"What are you up to, you effing effer?"

The chauffeur explained. At half past eight the Moscow passenger train arrived. Grozovsky, the chief of the financial section of the site, had returned from leave with his family, as he had always done. The chauffeur tried to explain about Mr. Popp. But Grozovsky declared it was all a mistake—he knew nothing—and ordered the chauffeur to go to the station. The chauffeur did so. He thought the foreigner had been canceled, and anyway, Grozovsky or Granovsky, he didn't know which one to obey, and his head was spinning. Then they went four kilometers to Churtan, the new settlement, where Grozovsky's new apartment was, and the chauffeur helped to carry the luggage, after which the Grozovskys treated him to one for the road ...

"You and I will be having a talk about who's the most important, Grozovsky or Granovsky. For now, just get to the station as fast as you can."

306 · SKETCHES OF THE CRIMINAL WORLD

The chauffeur dashed to the station: it was not yet ten. Mr. Popp was not in a good mood.

Uncertain of the route, the chauffeur rushed Mr. Popp to the hotel for foreigners. Mr. Popp settled into his room, washed, changed his clothes, and calmed down.

It was now Tsyplakov, the commandant of the hotel for foreigners, who was worried. He was not called director or manager, but commandant: whether it was because that title made him cheaper than, for instance, "director of the water tank," I don't know, but that was what the job was called then.

Mr. Popp's secretary appeared at the door of the hotel room.

"Mr. Popp would like breakfast."

The hotel commandant took from the buffet two big unwrapped sweets, two jam sandwiches, and two sausage sandwiches, arranged all this on a tray and, adding two glasses of tea, very weak tea, took it to Mr. Popp's room.

The secretary immediately brought the tray back and put it on a small table by the entrance to the room.

"Mr. Popp is not going to eat this breakfast."

Tysplakov rushed off to report to the chief of construction. But Granovsky already knew everything, he'd been informed by telephone.

"What do you think you're doing, you old son of a bitch," yelled Granovsky. "It's not just me you're disgracing, it's the state. Resign! Get working. In the sand quarry! Pick up a spade! Wreckers! Snakes! I'll see you rot in the camps!"

Tsyplakov, a man with gray hair, was waiting for the boss to exhaust his repertoire of swear words. He thought, "He really will see me rot."

It was time to move to the business part of the visit, and here Granovsky became a little calmer. The firm was doing good work on the site. Gasholders were being installed in Solikamsk and in Beriozniki. Mr. Popp was bound to visit Solikamsk, too. That's the reason for his visit, and he had no desire to say that he was annoyed. And, in fact, he wasn't. He was amazed, actually. None of this was important.

Granovsky went in person with Mr. Popp to the construction site, after abandoning his diplomatic considerations and postponing all conferences and meetings.

Granovsky went in person with Mr. Popp to Solikamsk and came back with him.

The documentation was signed, and a satisfied Mr. Popp was about to go home to America.

"I have some time," Mr. Popp told Granovsky. "I saved two weeks or so thanks to the good work of our—" the visitor fell silent for a while, "your craftsmen. The Kama is a beautiful river. I want to go by boat down the Kama to Perm, or even to Nizhni Novgorod. Is that possible?"

"Of course," said Granovsky.

"Can I lease a ship?"

"No. You know, our system is different, Mr. Popp."

"Buy one, then?"

"You can't buy one, either."

"Well, if you can't buy a passenger ship, I understand. It would disrupt the movement on a major water artery. How about a tugboat then, huh? Something like that *Seagull* out there," said Mr. Popp, pointing to a steam tugboat passing the windows of the office of the head of construction.

"No, you can't buy a tugboat either. I ask for your understanding..."

"Of course, I've heard a lot of things...Buying would be the simplest way. I'll leave it in Perm. As a gift to you."

"No, Mr. Popp, we can't accept gifts like that."

"Well, what's to be done? This is absurd, you know. Summer, lovely weather. One of the best rivers in the world—it's the real Volga, so I've read. And, lastly, time. I've got time. But I can't just go? Ask Moscow."

"What's Moscow got to do with it? Moscow's a long way away," Granovsky recited as if it were a habitual quotation.

"Well, you decide. I'm your guest. Whatever you say, so be it."

Granovsky asked for half an hour of thinking time, summoned Mironov, the head of shipping, and Ozols, the head of the secret police, to his office. He told them about Mr. Popp's wishes.

Only two ships passed Beriozniki then: *Red Urals* and *Red Tatary*. The routes were Cherdyn to Perm. Mironov informed Granovsky that *Red Urals* was downstream near Perm and could not possibly arrive soon. *Red Tatary* was approaching upstream in the direction of Cherdyn. If it was quickly turned back—which your fine men can help with,

Ozols!—and accelerated with no stops, then tomorrow in the daytime *Red Tatary* would arrive at Beriozniki port. Mr. Popp could travel.

"Get on your closed telephone circuit," Granovsky told Ozols, "and put some pressure on your men. Have one of your men board the ship and come, and don't let them waste time by stopping. Tell him it's a mission of state importance."

Ozols got in touch with Annov, the port for Cherdyn. *Red Tatary* had left Cherdyn.

"Put some pressure on them."

"We are putting pressure."

The head of construction visited Mr. Popp in his hotel room—the commandant had already been replaced—and informed him that a passenger ship would have the honor the next day at two p.m. to take their valued guest on board.

"No," said Mr. Popp. "Tell me the exact time, so we don't have to hang around on shore."

"Then at five o'clock. At four I'll send a car for your luggage."

At five, Granovsky, Mr. Popp, and his secretary arrived at the landing stage. There was no ship.

Granovsky apologized, took his leave, and rushed to the OGPU closed telephone.

"It hasn't even passed Icher yet."

Granovsky groaned. At least two hours.

"Perhaps we should go back to the hotel, and when the ship comes, we'll turn up. We can have something to eat," Granovsky suggested.

"We'll have bre-e-akfast, you mean," Mr. Popp pronounced meaningfully. "No, thank you. It's a fine day. Sun. Sky. We'll wait on the shore."

Granovsky stayed on the landing stage with his visitors, smiling, saying something, looking at the bend in the river upstream, around which the ship was bound to come at any moment.

Meanwhile Ozols's colleagues and their district boss were hanging on all the telephone connections, putting on pressure, pressure, pressure.

At eight in the evening *Red Tatary* appeared after rounding the bend and slowly began to approach the landing stage. Granovsky was smiling, thanking, saying goodbye. Mr. Popp thanked him, but without smiling.

The ship approached. And then an unexpected problem arose, a delay that nearly sent Granovsky, a man with a bad heart, to his grave, and a problem that was overcome only thanks to the experience and organizational skills of Ozols, the head of the OGPU district section.

The ship turned out to be full, packed with people. The ships ran at long intervals, an impossible number of people traveled on them, and all the decks, all the cabins, and even the engine room were crowded. There was no room on *Red Tatary* for Mr. Popp. Not only were all the tickets sold and all the cabins booked and occupied, but each cabin had a district committee secretary, or a factory manager, or the director of an enterprise of all-Soviet importance traveling on leave to Perm.

Granovsky sensed that he was losing consciousness. But Ozols had far more experience with such problems.

Ozols climbed up to the top deck of *Red Tatary* with four of his fine young men, with weapons and in uniform.

"Everyone out! Take your things with you!"

"But we've got tickets. Tickets all the way to Perm!"

"To hell with you and your tickets. Get off this deck, into the hold. I give you three minutes to think about it. An armed escort will accompany you to Perm. I'll explain on the way."

Five minutes later, the upper deck was cleared, and Mr. Popp, the vice president of Nitrogen, climbed onto the deck of *Red Tatary*.

1967

THE SQUIRREL

THE TOWN was surrounded by forest, a forest that extended into the town. You only had to move to the next tree and you were in the town, on the boulevard, not in the forest.

Pines and firs, maples and poplars, elms and birches—they were all the same, whether in the forest clearing or on the Square of Struggle with Speculation, as the town's market square had just been renamed.

When the squirrel looked at the town from afar, it thought that the town had been sliced in two by a green knife, a green beam, that the boulevard was a green river that you could sail along until you got to an eternal forest just as green as the one in which the squirrel lived. That the stone would soon finish.

And the squirrel plucked up its courage.

The squirrel was moving from poplar to poplar, from birch to birch, in a businesslike, calm way. But there was no end to the poplars and birches, which led it into dark ravines, onto stony clearings, surrounded by low-growing shrubs and isolated trees. The birch branches were more flexible than the poplar branches, but the squirrel had always known that.

Soon the squirrel realized that it had chosen the wrong route, that the forest was getting thinner, not thicker. But it was too late to turn back.

It had to run across that dead, gray square and then into the forest that followed. But dogs were now yapping, and passersby were sticking their necks out.

The coniferous forest was safe: a thick shield of pines, silky fir trees. The rustling poplar leaves were treacherous. A birch branch supported the squirrel better and for longer, and the animal's nimble body, swinging as it balanced, could work out for itself the limits to the branch's tension: the squirrel spread its paws out and flew through the air, half bird, half animal. The trees had taught it about the sky and about flying. Letting go of the branches, spreading the claws on all four paws, the squirrel flew, trying to find a support that was stronger and more reliable than the air.

The squirrel really was like a bird; it was a little like a yellow hawk, hovering over the forest. How the squirrel envied the hawk's unearthly flight. But the squirrel was not a bird. The call of the earth, the weight of the earth, its tonnage, was something the squirrel felt every minute, when the tree's muscles began to relax and the branch began to bend under the squirrel's weight. It had to summon all its strength, to call up new strength from deep inside its body, so as to leap up again onto a branch, or fall to the ground and never get back to the green treetops.

Screwing up its narrow eyes, the squirrel leapt, clutching at branches, swinging from side to side, taking aim, and not seeing that people were chasing it.

A crowd was now gathering on the town's streets.

The town was quiet and provincial: it rose with the sun, at the call of the cockerels. The town's river was so quiet that sometimes the flow stopped altogether, and the water even flowed backward. The town had two amusements. The first was fires, the alarm balloons on the firemen's water tower, the rumbling of the fire engines, racing down the cobbled roads, the teams of firemen: bay horses, dappled horses, black horses—each fire station had its own color. Taking part in extinguishing fires was for the brave; just watching was for everyone else. It was an education in courage for everybody: whoever could walk took their children, leaving only the paralyzed and the blind at home, and went "to the fire."

The other popular spectacle was hunting squirrels—the townspeople's classic pastime.

Squirrels passed through the town and did so often, but only at night, when the town was asleep.

The town's third pastime was revolution: the bourgeoisie in the town were killed, hostages were shot, ditches were dug, rifles were distributed, young soldiers were trained and sent off to die. But no revolution in the world could drown out the attraction of a traditional popular sport.

Everyone in the crowd was burning with the desire to be the first to hit a squirrel with a stone and kill it. To have the best aim, to be the best at using a catapult—the biblical sling, which Goliath used against David's soft body. The Goliaths chased after the squirrel, whistling and hooting at it, jostling one another in their murderous thirst. Here you could find a peasant who had brought half a sack of rye to market, aiming to exchange it for a grand piano or mirrors—in the year of mass death, mirrors were cheap—or the chairman of the town's Railway Workshops Revolutionary Committee, who had come to the market to catch the small traders; or the Soviet Consumers Union bookkeeper; or the vegetable gardener Zuyev, famous since tsarist times; or a Red commander with pink-striped riding breeches—the front was only a hundred kilometers away.

The women of the town stood by the fences, or the garden gates, or looked out of the windows, spurring the men on, holding out their children to see the hunt and learn how to hunt...

Boys who weren't allowed to persecute a squirrel on their own—there were enough grown-ups—brought up stones and sticks, to ensure that the animal didn't get away.

"Here you are, uncle: hit it."

And uncle would try to hit it, the crowd would roar, and the chase went on.

Everyone rushed down the town boulevards after the red animal: sweaty, red-faced householders of the town, carried away by a passionate desire to kill.

The squirrel had no time to lose: it had long guessed what this roar and this passion meant.

It had to get to the ground, then clamber up, choosing branches big and small, calculating its flight, swinging and balancing, flying...

The older men, veterans of provincial battles, amusements, hunts, and clashes, didn't even dream of catching up with the young. Following the mob at a distance, these experienced killers gave sensible advice, businesslike advice, important advice to those who were able to dash, catch, and kill. The older men could no longer dash about or catch a squirrel. They were hindered by lack of breath, fat, excess weight. But they had great experience, and they gave advice: which direction to run so as to intercept the squirrel.

The crowd kept getting bigger: now the old men divided the crowd into squads, into armies. Half went off to ambush and intercept.

Before the people saw it, the squirrel saw people running out from a side street and understood everything. It had to get to the ground, run twenty yards, and then there were more trees on the boulevard, and the squirrel could show these dogs, these heroes, what it could do.

The squirrel leapt to the earth, then rushed straight into the crowd, even though it was met by a volley of sticks and stones. And it jumped through these sticks and through the people yelling, "Hit it, hit it, don't let it get away." Then the squirrel looked around. The town was catching up with it. A stone hit its flank, the squirrel fell, but immediately jumped up and dashed forward. The squirrel ran to a tree, to salvation, and clambered up the trunk, then ran onto a branch, a pine branch.

"Can't kill it, the bastard!"

"Now we have to surround it by the river, by the shallows!"

But there was no need to encircle it. The squirrel could hardly move along the branch, and people immediately noticed and snarled at it.

The squirrel swung on the branch, harnessed all its strength for the last time, and fell straight into the howling, rasping mob.

A movement started in the crowd, as if in a boiling cauldron, then, as if the cauldron were taken off the fire, the movement died down, and people began retreating from the place in the grass where the squirrel lay.

The crowd quickly thinned: everyone had to get to work; everyone had business in town, in life. But not one of them went home without taking a look at the dead squirrel, so as to see with their own eyes and be sure that the hunt had been successful, that duty had been done.

I forced my way through the thinning crowd to get as near as I could: I too had hooted and had killed. I had the right, as had everybody, the whole town, all classes and parties.

I looked at the squirrel's little yellow body, at the blood clotted on its lips, its nose; I looked at its eyes that calmly surveyed the blue sky of our quiet town.

1966

THE WATERFALL

IN JULY, when the temperature by day reaches forty degrees centigrade—the thermal balance of continental Kolyma—submitting to the heavy force of sudden rains, enormous slippery jacks appear in the forest clearings. These mushrooms scare people: they have slippery skins and bright spots just like snakes, red, blue, and yellow…The sudden downpours bring only a momentary relief to the taiga, the forest, the stones, the mosses, the lichens. Nature never anticipated this fertile, life-giving, beneficial rain. Rain releases all of nature's hidden strength, and the caps of the slippery jacks grow heavy and big—up to half a meter in diameter. These are frightening, monstrous fungi. The rain gives only momentary relief—the winter's permanent ice still lies in the deep ravines. The mushrooms and their young fungal strength are not meant for ice. No amount of rain, no torrents of water can frighten these smooth, aluminum ice patches. Ice covers the stony streambeds, it becomes like the cement of an airfield runway. The water, which has accumulated on the mountain strata after days of nonstop rain, flies down this riverbed, this runway, getting faster and faster; it joins up with the melting snow, which the water has turned to water and called up to go to the sky, to fly…

The stormy water runs and flies down the gullies from the mountaintops, then reaches the riverbed, where the duel between sun and ice is now over, and the ice has thawed. The ice hasn't yet thawed in the stream. But three meters of ice is no hindrance to the stream. The water heads straight to the river over this frozen runway. Against the blue sky the stream seems to be made of aluminum, opaque but bright and light aluminum. The stream runs freely over the smooth, shiny ice. It runs freely and leaps into the air. Long ago, at the start of the run, the stream considered itself to be an airplane in the rocky peaks, and its only desire was to soar over the river.

A freely running, cigar-shaped aluminum stream flies up into the air, leaping from a cliff into the air. You are the serf Nikitka[50] who invented birdlike wings. You are the *Letatlin*, made by Tatlin,[51] who entrusted wood with the secrets of a bird's wing. You are Lilienthal...[52]

The freely running stream leaps: it can't help leaping; the oncoming waves push the ones that are nearest to the cliff.

It leaps into the air and smashes against the air. The air turns out to have the strength of stone, the resistance of stone: it is only at first sight from afar that the air seems to be a "medium," what the textbooks call a free medium where it is possible to breathe, move, live, and fly.

The water can clearly be seen to hit a blue wall of air, a solid wall, a wall of air. It strikes and is shattered to smithereens, to spray, to drops, falling helplessly from a height of ten meters into the ravine.

It turns out that there is enough of this gigantic quantity of water accumulating in the ravine, strong enough in its momentum to bring the rocky banks crashing down, to uproot trees and hurl them into the torrent, to loosen and break up rocks, to sweep away everything in its path by the laws of floodwater and torrent: but this strength is not enough to cope with the obtuseness of the air, the air that is so easy to breathe, the air that is transparent and yielding, yielding to the point of being invisible, and that seems to be a symbol of such freedom. This air turns out to have hidden strength that no rock, no water can rival.

The spray, the drops instantly reunite and fall again, again smash themselves and, shrieking and roaring, reach the riverbed of enormous stone boulders polished by the centuries, by the millennia.

The stream crawls toward the river down a thousand paths between the boulders, stones, gravel that the drops, the rivulets, and the threads of tamed water are afraid even to move. Once smashed and tamed, the stream calmly and soundlessly crawls into the river, describing a bright semicircle in the dark water running past the river. The river is not concerned with this stream of *Letatlin*, this stream of Lilienthal's. The river has no time to wait. But the river does step back a little, yielding to the bright water of the smashed stream, and the mountain graylings can be seen rising up from the depths toward this bright semicircle, glancing at the stream. The graylings stand in the dark river near the bright semicircle of water, where the stream disgorges into the river. Fishing is always good here.

1966

TAMING THE FIRE

I HAVE been in a fire, and several times, too. As a boy, I used to run down the street of our wooden town when it was burning, and I shall never forget the bright daytime streets, lit up as if the town could not get enough sun and it had itself asked for fire. The windless alarm of the hot bright-blue blazing sky. Force was building up in the fire itself, in the ever-growing flames. There was no wind at all, but the house growled and shook from head to toe, flinging burning boards onto the roofs of houses on the other side of the street.

Inside was simply dry, warm, and bright, and as a boy I had no trouble and felt no fear going through streets that allowed me to pass alive and that there and then burned down to cinders. Everything on the other side of the river burned down; only the river saved the main part of the town.

I have also experienced this feeling of calm at the height of a fire when I was an adult. I have seen quite a few forest fires. I have walked over burning, blue, luxurious meter-thick moss, when it was burned right through, as if it were a cloth. I have made my way through a larch forest felled by fire. Larches were uprooted and felled by fire, not wind.

Fire was like a storm, and it created storms itself, felling trees, leaving a permanent black trace in the taiga. And I have fallen exhausted by the banks of a stream.

A bright yellow flame ran across the dry grass. The grass swayed, moved, as if a snake had run through it. But there are no snakes in Kolyma.

The yellow flame climbed up a tree, up a larch trunk, and, gathering strength, the fire roared and shook the trunk.

These convulsions of the trees, deathbed convulsions, were the same everywhere. I have several times seen a tree's Hippocratic face.

For three whole days rain poured down over the hospital, which is why I thought about a fire and remembered fire. Rain would have saved the town, the geologists' store, the burning taiga. Water is stronger than fire.

The convalescent patients were on the other side of the river, gathering berries and mushrooms: there were masses of bog blueberry, lingonberry, outcrops of monstrous, slimy, many-colored slippery jacks with slippery cold caps. The fungi seemed cold, like cold-blooded living creatures, like snakes, or anything except fungi. The fungi here didn't fit the usual classifications of naturalists: they looked as if they were creatures from some neighboring class of amphibians or snakes.

Fungi appear late, after the rains; they don't appear every year, but once they do they surround all the tents and fill the whole forest, each patch of scrub.

We spent every day gathering this wild harvest.

Today was cold, a cold wind was blowing, but the rain had stopped, and through the ragged clouds one could see a pale autumn sky: it was clear that there would be no rain today.

We could, and we had to, go and gather fungi. After the rain came the harvest. The three of us crossed the river in a small boat, as we did every morning. The water level had risen only slightly and the river ran a little faster than usual. The waves were darker than they usually were.

Safonov pointed to the water, against the current, and all three of us understood what he meant.

"We've got plenty of time. There are lots of fungi," said Verigin.

"We're not turning back," I said.

"I know what," said Safonov. "By four o'clock the sun will be opposite that mountain over there, and we should come back to the riverbank then. We'll tie the boat up a little upstream..."

We went off in different directions: we all had our favorite mushroom places.

But as soon as I started walking through the forest I saw that there was no need to hurry, that there was a wealth of fungi under our feet.

The caps of the honey fungus were the size of a hat or your hand, and it didn't take long to fill two baskets.

I brought my baskets out by the tractor track in the clearing, so as to find it straightaway, and then went ahead empty-handed, if only to take a brief look and see what fungi had appeared there in my best patches, patches I had noted some time ago.

I entered the forest, and my fungus-collector's soul was shocked: everywhere there were enormous boletus mushrooms, growing apart from one another, higher than the grass, higher than the bog bilberry, firm, resilient, fresh, and extraordinary.

Lashed by rainwater, the fungi had grown into monsters, with caps half a meter wide; wherever you looked, there they were, and they were all in such good shape, so fresh, so strong, that there was only one decision to be made: to go back and throw out onto the grass everything collected earlier and to return to the hospital with this fungal miracle in my hands.

That is what I did.

All this required time, but I had calculated that it would take me half an hour to stride back along the path.

I climbed down the hill, parted the bushes: cold water had flooded the path for several meters. The path had vanished under the water while I was gathering mushrooms.

The forest was rustling, the cold water was rising higher and higher. The roar was louder and louder. I climbed up the hill and kept going along the hill slope, keeping right toward our meeting point. I didn't abandon the mushrooms: two heavy baskets, tied together with a towel, hung from my shoulders.

At the top I came to a copse where the boat should have been. The copse was flooded, and the water was still rising.

I made my way onto the bank, onto a rise.

The river was raging, tearing out trees and throwing them into the current. There was not even a bush left of the forest where we had landed the boat in the morning: the trees had been washed away, ripped out and swept off by the muscular water's terrible force in a river that was like a wrestler. The opposite bank was rocky, and the river took its revenge on the right bank, where I was, the bank with the greenery.

The little river we had been crossing in the morning had long ago been transformed into a monster.

It was getting dark, and I realized that I had to retreat into the mountains in the darkness and wait for dawn there, as far as possible from the raging icy water.

Soaked through to the bone, my feet taking on water every minute, leaping in the darkness from one mound to another, I hauled the baskets to the foot of a mountain.

The autumn night was black, starless, cold; the muffled growling of the river made it impossible to listen for voices. And where could I have heard anyone's voice?

Light suddenly flared up in a small side valley, and it took me awhile to realize that this was not the evening star but a fire. Was it a geologist's campfire? Or a fisherman's? Or was it lit by men making hay? I walked toward the fire, leaving the two baskets by a big tree until morning and taking a small basket with me.

In the taiga distances are deceptive: a hut, a rock, a forest, a river, the sea can be unexpectedly close or unexpectedly far.

It was easy to make a decision. If it was a fire, then I had to head for it without further ado. Fire was an important new force in this night of mine. A salutary force.

I prepared myself to meander tirelessly, if necessary feeling my way: after all, this was a fire at night, which meant there were people, there was life, there was salvation. I followed the ravine, never losing sight of the fire, and half an hour later, as I came around an enormous rock, I suddenly saw a fire right in front of me, above me, on a small stone clearing. It had been lit in front of a tent as low as the rock. People were sitting around the fire. They paid no attention to me at all. I didn't ask what they were doing here, I went straight up to the fire and began warming myself.

Unwinding a dirty rag, the senior haymaker silently offered me a lump of salt, and soon the water in the cooking pot screeched and bubbled as it turned white with foam and heat.

I ate my tasteless miracle fungus, washed it down with the boiling hot water, and felt a little warmer. I dozed off by the fire, and slowly, without a sound, dawn began to break and day came; I went to the riverbank, without thanking the haymakers for taking me in. My baskets under the tree could be seen a kilometer away.

The water level was now falling.

I walked through the forest, grabbing hold of the broken branches of trees that had survived, albeit stripped of their bark.

I was walking over stones, sometimes stepping on drifts of mountain sand.

The grass, which would grow even more after the storm, was hidden deep under the sand and stones, clinging to the tree bark.

I went up to the riverbank. Yes, it was the riverbank, a new one, not the unstable margin of the floodwater.

The river, still heavy with rainwater, was racing, but it was clear that the water was receding.

A long way away, on the other bank, as though on the other shore of life, I could see figures of people waving their arms. I could see the boat. I started waving my arms, they understood and recognized me. They used poles to raise the boat along the riverbank, two kilometers or so upstream from where I was standing. Safonov and Verigin landed the boat much lower, near me. Safonov proffered me my bread ration for the day, six hundred grams, but I didn't feel like eating.

I dragged out my baskets of miracle fungi.

It had been raining, and I had dragged the fungi through the forest, catching the baskets on the trees in the night: all the baskets now held were fragments, fragments of fungi.

"Should I throw them out?"

"No, why should you?"

"We threw ours away last night. It was all we could do to move the boat to safety. You know what we thought about you," Safonov said firmly. "We'll be more answerable for the boat than for you."

"Nobody has to answer for me much," I said.

"Quite right. We don't have to answer for you, nor does the chief, but as for the boat . . . I did the right thing, didn't I?"

"You did," I said.

"Get in," said Safonov, "and bring those damned baskets."

We shoved the boat off the riverbank and started rowing: a fragile boat on a stormy river that was still thundering.

At the hospital I was received without any cursing and without any joy. Safonov was right when he made the boat his chief concern.

I had lunch, dinner, breakfast, and lunch and dinner again: I ate all my rations for two days, and I began to feel sleepy. I warmed myself up.

I put a pot of water on the fire. Tamed water on a tamed fire. And soon the pot started bubbling and boiled. But I was asleep by then . . .

1966

THE RESURRECTION OF THE LARCH

WE ARE superstitious. We demand a miracle. We invent symbols for ourselves and live by those symbols.

In the Far North man looks for an outlet for his sensitivity, when it hasn't been destroyed or poisoned by decades of living in Kolyma. A man sends an airmail parcel: not books, not photographs, not poetry, but a larch branch, a dead branch from living nature.

This strange gift, withered and windblown by the airplane's airflow, crumpled and broken in the post wagon, this bright brown, hard, bony northern branch of a northern tree is put in water.

It's put in an empty food can, filled with nasty chlorinated, disinfected Moscow tap water, which could probably desiccate with pleasure every living thing: Moscow's dead tap water.

Larches are more serious than flowers. There are a lot of flowers, colorful flowers in this room. Bouquets of bird cherry, of lilac are put in hot water, and the branches are crushed and dipped in boiling water.

The larch stands in cold water, just warmed up a little. The larch used to live closer to the Chornaya River than all these flowers and all these branches of bird cherry and lilac.

The woman of the house understands this. So does the larch.

Submitting to a human being's passionate will, the branch summons all its strength, physical and spiritual, because physical strength, that of Moscow's warmth, chlorinated water, and an indifferent glass jar, is not enough to resurrect the branch. Other, secret forces are awoken in the branch.

Three days and three nights pass, and the woman of the house is woken up by the strange, vague smell of turpentine, a faint, subtle, new smell. New, young, living bright-green fresh conifer needles have opened and become visible in the hard wooden skin.

The larch is alive, the larch is immortal, this miracle of resurrection is inevitable: after all, the larch has been put into a jar of water on the anniversary of the death in Kolyma of the husband of the lady of the house: he was a poet.

Even this memory of a dead man is also part of the reanimation, the resurrection of the larch.

This tender smell, this dazzling green are important elements of life. Weak but alive, resurrected by some secret spiritual force, these elements in the larch have now come to light.

The smell of the larch was weak but clear, and no force in the world could have drowned out this smell or extinguished this green light and color.

For how many years, distorted by winds, frosts, turning to follow the sun, has the larch stretched out every spring its young green needles to the sky?

How many years? A hundred. Two hundred. Six hundred. A dahurian larch is mature at three hundred years.

Three hundred years! A larch, whose branch, whose twig is on a table in Moscow, is the same age as Natalia Sheremeteva Dolgorukova[53] and can remind us of her lamentable fate: about the vicissitudes of life, about fidelity and firmness, about inner staunchness, about physical and moral torments, which in no way differ from the torments of 1937, with the raging nature of the north, which hates humanity, the mortal danger of spring floodwaters and winter blizzards, with denunciations, the coarse arbitrary bosses, deaths, quarterings, husbands broken on the wheel, brothers, sons, fathers, all denouncing each other and betraying each other.

Isn't that an utterly eternal Russian story?

After the rhetoric of that moralist Tolstoy and Dostoyevsky's rabid preaching came wars, revolutions, Hiroshima and concentration camps, denunciations, and executions by shooting.

The larch tree displaced all scales of time and shamed human memory by reminding it of the unforgettable.

The larch tree that witnessed the death of Natalia Dolgorukova and saw millions of corpses, immortal in the Kolyma's permafrost, which saw the death of a Russian poet, is living somewhere in the north, so that it can see and shout out that nothing has changed in Russia, neither men's fates, nor human spite, nor indifference. Natalia Sheremeteva told the whole story, she recorded everything with her melancholy strength and faith. The larch, whose branch came to life on a Moscow table, was living when Sheremeteva was traveling on her sorrowful journey to Beriozovo, so very like the journey to Magadan, across the Sea of Okhotsk.

The larch tree exuded—exuded is the right word—its smell, like sap. The smell merged with the color, and there was no boundary between them.

In the Moscow apartment the larch breathed in order to remind people of their human duty, so that people did not forget the millions of corpses, of people who perished in Kolyma.

The persistent faint smell was the voice of the dead.

In the name of these corpses, the larch plucked up the courage to breathe, speak, and live.

Strength and faith are needed for resurrection, and that is by no means all. I also used to put a larch branch in a jar of water: the branch withered and became lifeless, delicate, and brittle—life had left it. The branch passed into oblivion, it vanished, it did not resurrect. But the larch in the poet's apartment came to life in a jar of water.

Yes, there are branches of lilac and bird cherry, there are love songs that tug at your heartstrings; the larch is not an object, not a theme for love songs.

The larch is a very serious tree. It is the tree of the knowledge of good and evil; it is not an apple tree or a birch. It is a tree that stood in the garden of paradise before the expulsion of Adam and Eve.

The larch is the tree of Kolyma, the tree of concentration camps.

No birds sing in Kolyma. Kolyma's flowers are garish, hasty, coarse, and they have no scent. The short summer—in the cold, lifeless air—is one of dry heat and chilling night cold.

The only scent in Kolyma comes from the mountain briar with its ruby flowers. The pink lily of the valley, which looks so crudely molded, doesn't smell, nor do the enormous, fist-size violets, nor the sickly junipers, nor the evergreen dwarf pine.

Only the larch fills the forests with its vague smell of turpentine. At first it seems that this is the smell of rotting, the smell of corpses. But on closer inspection, when you take a really deep breath of this smell, you will understand that this is the smell of life, the smell of resistance to the north, the smell of victory.

In any case, corpses don't smell in Kolyma: they are too emaciated and exsanguinated, and they're preserved in permafrost.

No, the larch is a tree that is unfit for love songs; you can't sing about this branch, you can't compose a love song. Here you need words of a different depth, you need another layer of human feelings.

A man sends a branch of Kolyma by airmail: he wants to remind people of something other than himself. Not a memory of him but a memory of the millions who were killed and tortured to death, who are laid in common graves to the north of Magadan.

To help others to remember, to take this heavy burden off one's soul: to see something like this, to find the courage not just to tell it to somebody but to fix it in one's own memory. It's the same as a man and his wife adopting a little girl, a child prisoner whose mother had died in the hospital—taking upon themselves an obligation, to carry out a personal duty, at least in their own personal sense.

Helping one's comrades, those who have come out alive from the concentration camps of the Far North.

To send this hard, pliant branch to Moscow.

By sending the branch, the man didn't understand, didn't know or think that the branch would be brought back to life in Moscow, nor that, once resurrected, it would give out the smell of Kolyma, would blossom in a Moscow street, that the larch would show its strength, its immortality. Six hundred years of a larch's life is practically immortality for man, so that people in Moscow would touch this shaggy, unfussy hard branch, look at its dazzling green needles, its rebirth, its resurrection, would breathe in its smell—not as a memory of the past but as real life.

1966

BOOK SIX
The Glove, or, Kolyma Stories II

for Irina Pavlovna Sirotinskaya

THE GLOVE

SOMEWHERE in the ice my knight's gloves are preserved. More close-fitting than kid leather or Ilse Koch's finest chamois,[1] they kept my fingers safe for all of thirty-six years.

These gloves live in museum ice as a testimony, a document, an exhibit of the fantastic realism of my reality then; they are biding their time, like newts or coelacanths, to become some other member of the *Latimeria* genus.

I trust the official record; I myself am a fact recorder, a fact hunter by profession, but what can one do if there are no such records? No personal files, no archives, no patient notes.

The documentation of our past has been destroyed, the guard towers have been sawn down, the barracks razed to the ground, the rusty barbed wire has been rolled up and taken away somewhere else. The rosebay willow herb—the flower of fires, of oblivion, the enemy of archives and human memory—has flowered over the ruins of the Serpantinka.

Did we exist?

I reply "We did" with all the expressiveness of an official statement, with the responsibility, the precision of a document.

This is a story about my Kolyma glove, an exhibit in the museum of health or of local history, perhaps.

Where are you now, my challenge to time, my knightly glove, dropped on the snow, onto the face of the Kolyma ice of 1943?

I was a goner, a staff invalid of fate on the hospital grounds, I was even snatched by the doctors from the clutches of death. But I see no good, for myself or for the state, in my immortality. Our concepts have changed the scales, have overstepped the boundaries of good and evil. Salvation may be a good thing, or perhaps it isn't: I still can't decide this question for myself.

Can it be possible to hold a pen in a glove like that, which ought to be preserved in the formalin of a museum exhibit but is lying on the nameless ice?

A glove, which over thirty-six years became part of my body and a symbol of my soul.

Everything ended trivially, and my skin grew back. Muscles grew on my skeleton, only my bones had suffered somewhat, crippled as they were by osteomyelitis after frostbite. Even my soul grew around these damaged bones, so it would seem. Even my fingerprints on that dead glove and on my present live hand, now holding a pencil, are the same. Here is a real miracle of criminological science. Those twin gloves. One day I'll write a detective story about them and make a contribution to that literary genre. But at the moment I can't be bothered with a detective story. My gloves are two human beings, twins with the same fingerprint pattern, a miracle of science. A worthy subject for all the world's criminologists, philosophers, historians, and doctors to contemplate.

I'm not the only one to know the secret of my hands. The paramedic Lesniak and Dr. Savoyeva held this glove in their hands.

Is it possible that newly grown skin, new skin and muscles grown on bone are entitled to write? And if they are, then are they the same words that could be traced out by my Kolyma glove—a workman's glove, a callused hand, rubbed by the crowbar until it bled, with fingers bent to fit a spade handle? Certainly that glove would never have written this story. Those fingers couldn't unbend in order to pick up a pen and write about themselves.

The fire of new skin, the pink flame of a ten-candle pair of frost-bitten hands, is surely a miracle, isn't it?

Could there be written, in a glove attached to a patient's notes, the story not only of my body and my fate and soul but the history of a state, of time, of the world?

History could be written in that glove.

But now, although the fingerprint pattern is the same, I am looking at the thin, pink skin in the light, not at my dirty, bloodstained hands. At the moment I am further from death than I was in 1943 or 1938, when my fingers were those of a corpse. Like a snake, I have shed my old skin in the snow. But even now my new hand reacts to cold water. The blows of frostbite are irreversible, eternal. Yet all the same, my hand is not the hand of a Kolyma goner. The goner's skin was ripped off my flesh, it slaked off my muscles like a glove, and it was attached to my patient notes.

The fingerprint pattern is the same on both gloves: it is a drawing of my genes, the genes of sacrifice and of resistance. Just like my blood type. The red blood cells of a victim, not of a conqueror. The first glove was left in the Magadan museum, the museum of the health administration, whereas the second glove was taken to the mainland, the world of human beings, so as to leave anything not human on the other side of the ocean, beyond the Yablonovy Mountains.

When fugitives were caught in Kolyma, their hands were hacked off, to avoid the trouble of dealing with a body or a corpse. The amputated hands could be taken away in a briefcase or a field knapsack, since a man's passport in Kolyma, whether he was a free man or a prisoner, was his fingerprint pattern. Everything needed for identification could be brought in a briefcase, in a field knapsack, but not on a truck, or a pickup, or a Willys jeep.

But where is my glove? Where is it being kept? After all, my hand wasn't hacked off.

Well into the autumn of 1943, shortly after I was given a new ten-year sentence, when I had neither the strength to live nor any hope of living, when I had too few muscles on my bones to preserve in them a long-forgotten and discarded feeling such as hope, which human beings didn't need, I was a goner who was chased away from all the outpatient clinics in Kolyma, and who landed in the lucky wave of an officially sanctioned struggle against dystrophy. I, a man with chronic diarrhea, now obtained impressive proof of my need to be hospitalized. I was proud of the fact that I could present my backside to any doctor and, above all, to any non-doctor, and that backside would excrete a small lump of salutary mucus, show the world its greenish-gray emerald with blood-filled capillaries: the jewel of dysentery.

That was my pass to paradise, where I had never been before in all the thirty-eight years of my life.

I was marked out for the hospital: included in the endless lists by some hole punched in a card, included, inserted into a salutary, life-saving wheel. In fact, salvation was the last thing I thought about, and I had no idea what a hospital was. I merely gave in to the age-old law of a prisoner's automatic responses: reveille, breakfast, lunch, work, dinner, sleep, or a summons to the NKVD officer.

I was resurrected many times, only to drift back again, as I wandered from the hospital to the pit face for many years, not days, not months, but years, Kolyma years. I had medical treatment until I started giving medical treatment myself and, by the same mechanical wheel of life, was cast ashore on the mainland.

As a goner, I was waiting for a party of prisoners, but I was not going to end up at the gold mine where I had just been given a ten-year addition to my sentence. I was too emaciated for the gold mine. It was my fate now to be sent on "vitamin" expeditions.

I was waiting at the commandant's Special Camp Point in Yagod-noye for a party of prisoners to be assembled. Everyone knew the way transits were organized: all the goners would be herded out to work by armed guards with dogs. As long as there were guards, there would be goners. None of their work was ever recorded anywhere; they were forced to go, if only to make pits by hammering the frozen ground with crowbars, or to drag beams for firewood back to the camp, or at least to saw up stumps in the wood stacks, walking ten kilometers from the settlement to do so, and working until lunchtime.

If you refused? Solitary confinement on three hundred grams of bread and a bowl of water. And a record of the offense. In 1938 three refusals in a row meant you were shot at the Serpantinka, the north's pretrial prison. I was well aware of this procedure, so I didn't even think of avoiding or refusing work, wherever they might take us.

On one of these journeys we were taken to a sewing factory. There were barracks behind a fence where old trousers were made into gauntlets and shoe soles were made from the quilted padding.

New canvas gauntlets with leather edging could hold out when you were using a crowbar to drill the ground—and I had done a lot of manual crowbar drilling. They held out for about half an hour. Quilted gauntlets lasted about five minutes. The difference was not enough to give you hope that special work clothes would be imported from the mainland.

About sixty men were making gauntlets in the Yagodnoye sewing factory. The factory had stoves and a fence for a windbreak, so I was very anxious to be sent to work there. Unfortunately my pit-face worker's fingers, bent by the spade handle and the pickax handle, couldn't hold a needle properly, and people stronger than me were chosen even to repair gauntlets. The craftsman who had watched me trying to cope with a needle rejected me with a wave of his hand. I had failed my tailoring examination, and I prepared myself for a long journey. Not that I cared in the least whether the journey would be long or short. The additional sentence I had just been given didn't bother me at all. There was no sense in planning your life more than one day ahead. And in our fantastic world the very concept of "sense" was probably inadmissible. It wasn't my brain but some prisoner's animal feeling, a feeling of the muscles, which concluded that one day was all you could plan on: an axiom had been found that could not be doubted.

You might think that the longest journeys had been made, the darkest and most remote roads traveled, the deepest crannies of the brain had been lit up, the extremes of humiliation, the beatings and the slappings had been endured: jostlings, daily beatings. I had endured all that very well. My body had taught me everything I needed to know about how to cope.

The first blow from a guard, a foreman, a clerk of works, a gangster, or a boss had knocked me to the ground, and I hadn't been pretending. As if I would! Many times Kolyma had tested my vestibular system, not just my Ménière's syndrome[2] but my entire balance in the absolute—that is, incarcerated—sense.

In the icy centrifuges of Kolyma I had passed my examination, as a cosmonaut passes his in order to fly into the heavens.

My mind could sense, however fuzzily, that I'd been struck, knocked off my feet, trampled on, that my lips were smashed and blood was flowing from my scurvy-ridden teeth. I had to writhe, lie down, flatten myself on the ground, on mother earth. But the ground was snow and ice; in summer it was stone, not mother earth. I was beaten many times. For anything. For being a Trotskyist, for being a "four-eyed" intellectual. My body had to answer for all the sins of the world: I had become an object for officially sanctioned vengeance. And yet, for some reason, the last blow and the final pain hadn't happened.

At the time I wasn't thinking about a hospital. "Pain" and "hospital" are, especially in Kolyma, completely unrelated concepts.

What was the real surprise was to be hit by Dr. Mokhnach, the chief of the medical center at Jelgala special zone, where I had been put on trial just a few months earlier. I went to Dr. Vladimir Osipovich Mokhnach's outpatient surgery every day, trying to get released from work, if only for a day.

When I was arrested in May 1943, I demanded medical certification and a record that I had been treated as an outpatient.

The interrogator made a note of my request, and that night the doors of my solitary cell, where I was lying on a dirt floor (there was no bunk or any other furniture in the cell) with no light, with a mug of water and a three-hundred-gram daily bread ration for a whole week, were flung open and a man in a white gown appeared on the threshold. This was Dr. Mokhnach. He didn't approach but just looked at me, once I had been taken, or rather pushed, out of the cell. He used a flashlight to inspect my face and then, without hesitation or delay, sat at his desk to write something on a piece of paper. Then he left. I saw that piece of paper on June 23, 1943, at my Revolutionary Tribunal trial. It was cited as documentary evidence. I remember the text by heart. It read: "Certificate. Prisoner Shalamov never came to outpatient clinic No. 1 at Jelgala special zone. Head of the medical center, Dr. Mokhnach."

This document was read aloud at my trial, to the greater glory of the NKVD officer Fiodorov who was in charge of my case. Everything in my trial was a lie: the indictment, the witnesses, and the expert evidence. The only authentic aspect was human depravity.

That June 1943 I never even managed to take pleasure from the fact that the ten-year sentence was my birthday present. "It was a present," said all those who were familiar with such situations. "After all, you weren't shot. You weren't given your sentence by weight, seven grams of lead."

None of that seemed of any importance, compared with the reality of the needle that I wasn't able to hold as a tailor would.

But that, too, was unimportant.

Somewhere—whether above or below, I never found out at any point in my life—propellers were in motion, propelling the ship of fate, a pendulum that swung from life to death, rhetorically speaking.

Somewhere circulars were composed, special-access telephones crackled. Somewhere, somebody was responsible for something. And as a trivial outcome of the most official medical resistance to death at the hands of the punitive sword of the state, the highest authority gave birth to instructions, orders, and formal responses. A paper sea's waves lapped at the shores of fate, which was anything but paper. Kolyma's goners and dystrophics had no right to medical help or hospitalization for their real illnesses. Even in the morgue the truth was rigorously distorted by the pathologist, who lied postmortem by giving a different diagnosis. The real diagnosis of alimentary dystrophy appeared in the camp medical documentation only after the Leningrad blockade: during the war, starvation could be called starvation, but for now the goners were laid on their deathbeds with a diagnosis of polyavitaminosis, influenza-virus pneumonia, or, very occasionally, SPE, "severe physical emaciation."

Even scurvy had statistical limits, beyond which doctors were not encouraged to exceed bed days in groups B and C. Too many bed days meant objections from the top bosses and the doctor losing his job.

Dysentery was the diagnosis by which it was authorized to hospitalize prisoners. The flow of dysentery patients swept away all the official obstacles. A goner had a fine intuition for the weak points: the way, and by what gates, he could be allowed to rest, to get his breath back, if only for an hour or a day. A prisoner's body or stomach is not a barometer: it can't give prior warning. But the instinct for self-preservation leads the goner to look at the door to the outpatient clinic as a door that may lead to death or may lead to life.

"A patient with a thousand ailments" is a designation that all patients and medical authorities laugh at, but it is profound, just, exact, and serious.

The goner snatches from fate as little as a day off, in order to find a way back to his paths on earth, which are so similar to the paths of heaven.

The main thing is the target number, the plan. To become part of the plan is a difficult task, however great the flood of diarrhea patients might be, for strait is the door to the hospital.

The vitamin plant where I lived was assigned just two dysentery places in the district hospital, two precious entitlements, and even these were obtained only with a struggle for the "vitamin people," because dysentery at a gold or lead-ore mine or on road construction was far more expensive than dysentery at a vitamin factory.

What was called the vitamin factory was just a shed where dwarf pine was boiled down in cauldrons to make an extract: poisonous, vile, very bitter, chestnut colored, a thick mixture that resulted after many days of boiling it down. This mixture was made from conifer needles, "nipped" by prisoners all over Kolyma, by goners who had lost their strength at the gold-mine pit face. They were taken out of the gold seams and made to die as they created a vitamin product, a pine-needle extract. The most bitter irony was the actual name of the factory. The authorities' idea and the age-old experience of the world's northern travelers taught them that pine needles were the only local treatment for scurvy, the disease of polar explorers and of prisons.

This extract was adopted as an official weapon in all northern medicine in the camps: it was considered to be the only means of salvation, and if dwarf-pine needles didn't do any good, then nothing could.

We were given the nauseating mixture three times a day, and we were not allowed food in the refectory unless we took the mixture. However intently the prisoner's stomach awaits any soup with dumplings made from flour, to celebrate any food at all, this grave moment that comes three times a day was irredeemably ruined by the administration that forced one to take a preliminary gulp of conifer extract. The very bitter mixture made you retch, and your stomach was convulsed for several minutes, while your appetite was irrevocably ruined. There was a punitive element, something vindictive, in this dwarf-pine extract.

The narrow passage to the refectory was guarded by bayonets: there was a table where the camp "quack," a medical assistant, sat with a bucket and a tiny ladle made from a food can—he poured a salutary dose of poison into each prisoner's mouth.

Over the years, one feature of this torture by dwarf-pine extract, this punishment by ladle, something practiced all over the Soviet Union, was that the extract, boiled down in seven cauldrons, contained no vitamin C, which might have saved people from scurvy. Vitamin C is extremely volatile and is destroyed after fifteen minutes of boiling.

But medical statistics were kept, fully reliable ones, proving beyond doubt "with the figures to hand" that the mines produced more gold and bed days were reduced. It was also proven that the only reason people, or, rather, goners, died of scurvy was that they had spat out this lifesaving mixture. Charge sheets were actually drawn up against those who had spat it out, and they were put into solitary confinement, or sent to Intensive Regime Squads. Quite a few tabular graphs of such people were compiled.

The whole struggle against scurvy was a bloody, tragic farce, quite befitting the fantastic realism of our life at the time.

After the war, when this blood-soaked subject was gone into at the very highest level, dwarf pine was absolutely and universally banned.

After the war, rose hips, which really did contain vitamin C, began to be imported to the north in great quantities.

There are unlimited supplies of briar roses in Kolyma: a low-growing highland rose with hips that have a violet-colored flesh. But when we were there, we were forbidden to go near the briar roses during work, and anyone who tried to eat the fruit, the hips, although utterly ignorant of their healing properties, was shot at and killed. The guards were protecting the briar roses from the prisoners.

The briars would rot, wither, vanish under the snow, but reappear in the spring, looking sweetly and tenderly alluring from under the ice, tempting the tongue with just their taste, with a mysterious faith, not knowledge, not the science to be found in circulars where only dwarf pine was recommended, the extract from the vitamin factory.

The goner, bewitched by the briar rose, would step outside the zone, the magic circle outlined by the guard towers, and he would get a bullet in the back of the neck.

In order to acquire hospital admission for dysentery, you had to present a "stool," a lump of mucus slime from the anus. A prisoner who is a goner, on a normal camp diet, has a stool no more frequently than once in five days. Yet another medical miracle. Every crumb was sucked in by any cell in the body, not only, apparently, by the gut and the stomach. The skin, too, was willing and ready to absorb food. The gut would surrender, reject something that made no sense: it was hard even to explain what it was throwing out.

A prisoner could not always make his rectum excrete into a doctor's hand the verifiable and lifesaving lump of mucus. We are, of course, not talking about embarrassment or shame. Shame is a concept that is too human.

But a chance of salvation appears, and the gut refuses to work: it fails to excrete that lump of mucus.

The doctor is there, waiting patiently. No lump, no hospital. Someone else will make use of the warrant, and there are plenty of others. You happen to be the lucky one, but your behind, your rectum, can't make the spurt, the gob that gives you a head start into immortality.

In the end, something falls out, squeezed from your gut's labyrinths, from those twelve meters of pipes whose peristalsis has just failed.

I was sitting by a fence, squeezing my belly with all my strength, begging my rectum to squeeze out and produce the sacred quantity of mucus.

The doctor was sitting there patiently, smoking his cigarette of homegrown tobacco. The wind was shifting the precious warrant, held down by the "Kolyma" kerosene lamp, on his desk. Only a doctor was supposed to sign such warrants, and then he was taking personal responsibility for the diagnosis.

I called on all my anger to help me. And my gut did its job. My rectum threw out a sort of gob, a spray. If the word "spray" can have a singular sense, then it was a lump of gray-green mucus with a precious red thread, a layer that was extremely valuable.

The quantity of excrement was put in the middle of an alder leaf; at first I thought there was no blood at all in my mucus.

But the doctor had more experience than I did. He lifted my rectum's gob to his eyes, sniffed the mucus, threw off the alder leaf, and, without washing his hands, signed the warrant.

That same white northern night I was driven to the Belichya (or Squirrel) district hospital. This hospital had the title of Central District Hospital for the Northern Mining Administration—a combination of words that was used in conversation, in everyday life, and in official correspondence. What came first, I don't know: did everyday life legitimate the bureaucratic pattern, or did the formula merely express the bureaucratic soul? "If you don't believe it, take it as a fairy tale," goes the gangster proverb. In actual fact, however, Belichya served the northern district, just as similar hospitals served the western, southwestern, and southern districts. The central hospital for prisoners, however, was the enormous one near Magadan, towering over kilometer 23 of the main Magadan–Susuman–Nera highway: it had a thousand beds; later it was moved to the left bank of the Kolyma River.

This gigantic thousand-bed hospital with its subsidiary enterprises, including fishing and a state farm, had a thousand deaths a day at the peak months for Kolyma's goners. It was here, at kilometer 23, that documentation took place: the last stage before the sea and a journey either to freedom or to death at some camp for invalids near Komsomolsk. It was at kilometer 23 that the dragon's teeth were unclenched for the last time to "release" people, those, of course, who had chanced to survive in the struggles of Kolyma, the subzero temperatures.

Belichya was at kilometer 501 of the highway, not far from Yagodnoye, just six kilometers from the northern center that had some time ago now turned into a town; but in 1937 I forded the river to get there, and our armed guard shot a big grouse outright, not bothering to make his party of prisoners stand aside or sit on the ground.

Yagodnoye was where I had been tried a few months earlier.

Belichya was a hospital with about a hundred beds for prisoners and with a modest service staff: four doctors, four paramedics, and four male nurses, all prisoners themselves. The chief doctor was the sole contract worker, a party member, Nina Vladimirovna Savoyeva. She was an Ossete and was known as Black Mama.

Apart from this staff, the hospital was able to keep people on all sorts of "convalescent teams" and "convalescent points"; after all, it was no longer 1938, the time of Colonel Garanin and mass executions, when the hospital at Partisan had no such things as convalescent points.

The downside, the loss of people at that time, was easily made up by new arrivals from the mainland, so ever more new parties of prisoners were sent into this deadly carousel. In 1938, parties of prisoners were even led on foot to Yagodnoye. Of a column of three hundred men only eight got to Yagodnoye: the rest were stranded on the journey, their feet frostbitten, dying. There were no "convalescent teams" for enemies of the people.

It was different during the war. Moscow was unable to supply replacement men. The camp bosses were ordered to preserve the contingents on their lists, those who were already abandoned there and fixed there permanently. That was when medicine was given a few rights. It was then that I came across an amazing figure at the Spokoinoye mine. Of a listed contingent of three thousand men there were only ninety-eight working on the first shift. The others were either inpatients or semi-inpatients in the hospital, or released to attend outpatient clinics.

So Belichya then had the right to keep patients as convalescent teams or even to have a convalescent point.

There was then a large unpaid prisoner workforce concentrated around the hospitals: people who would move whole mountains of any ore, as long as it wasn't the stony subsoil of a gold-mine pit face, in exchange for a bread ration, or for one more day spent in the hospital.

At Belichya convalescents were physically and mentally able to move mountains of gold: they had actually done so, and the traces of their labor were the gold seams in the mines of the north; but they couldn't cope with the chief doctor Black Mama's wild dream of draining Belichya. They couldn't fill in the marsh that surrounded the hospital. Belichya stood on a small hill a kilometer off the central highway from Magadan to Susuman. This kilometer posed no problems in winter for men on foot or on horseback, or coming by automobile. The "winter surface" was the best thing about the Kolyma roads. But in summer the marsh would loudly gulp and slurp as you passed, and the guard would lead the patients one by one, making them hop from tussock to tussock, from stone to stone, from path to path, even though in winter there was a path hacked out and perfectly marked through the permafrost by the experienced hand of an engineer who was also a patient.

But in summer the permafrost begins to retreat and nobody knows the limits, the last frontiers to which the permafrost has retreated. By a meter? By a thousand meters? Nobody knows. Not a single hydrographer arriving from Moscow on his DC aircraft, not a single Yakut, whose fathers and forefathers were born in this marshy land.

Ditches were filled with stones. Mountains of limestone were broken up right here; there were life-threatening underground shocks, rock falls, landslides, all under a dazzling bright sky: in Kolyma there was no rain. Rain and mist occurred only near the sea.

Soil improvement was the job of the sun that never set.

Forty thousand working days and millions of hours of convalescents' labor were invested in this marshy road, just one kilometer from Belichya to the highway. Each man had to throw a rock into the impassable depths of the marsh. The hospital staff threw rocks into the marsh every summer day. The marsh chomped and swallowed the gifts.

The Kolyma marshes are graves more significant than Slav grave barrows or the isthmus strewn with the remains of Xerxes's army.

Every patient, when being discharged from Belichya, was obliged to throw a rock into the hospital's marsh: a slab of limestone, cut by other patients or by the hospital staff during one of their shock working days. Thousands of men had thrown rocks into the marsh. The marsh chomped and swallowed the slabs.

Three years of energetic work produced no results whatsoever. Once more a frozen winter road was needed, and the inglorious struggle with nature died down until spring. In spring it all began again. But three summers of work did not succeed in making a road that would enable a truck to get to the hospital. As before, discharged patients had to be led out, jumping from tussock to tussock, just like the patients brought in for treatment.

After the uninterrupted general efforts of three summers, all that was achieved was a set of way markers, some sort of unreliable zigzagging route from the highway to Belichya, a route that could not be walked, run, or driven: it could only be passed by leaping from slab to slab, just as people had leapt from tussock to tussock for the last thousand years.

This inglorious duel with nature had embittered the chief doctor, Black Mama.

The marsh had triumphed.

I used to make my way to the hospital in a series of jumps. The driver, an experienced lad, stayed with his truck on the highway, to keep any passersby from taking the truck or stripping the engine. On a white night like this, robbers could appear from anywhere, and drivers never left their trucks even for an hour. Such was life there.

The guard made me jump from one white slab to another until we reached the hospital; there he left me sitting on the ground by the porch while he took my packet to the hut.

Just beyond the two wooden barracks were rows of enormous tarpaulin tents, as gray as the taiga. A causeway of laths was laid between the tents, a footpath of willow wands, raised to a considerable height over the rock. Belichya was built at the confluence of a stream, and it was vulnerable to floods, downpours, and thunderstorms, Kolyma high water.

The tarpaulin tents not only reminded one of the frailty of this world but emphasized in the grimmest of tones that you, the goner, were an undesirable, even if you were meant to be here. Your life would count for little here. At Belichya there was no sense of refuge, only of "all hands on deck."

The tarpaulin sky of Belichya's tents was exactly like the tarpaulin sky of the tents at the Partisan mine in 1937: they were torn, open to all the winds. They were no different, either, from the vitamin factory's two-bunk dugouts, reinforced and insulated with peat, which protected you from the wind but not from the subzero cold. But for a goner, even protection from the wind is of major importance.

The stars, however, which you could see through the holes in the tarpaulin ceiling, were the same wherever you were: an outline of the Far North's squinting sky.

There was no difference in the stars or one's hopes, but then, one had no use for stars or hopes, either.

At Belichya the wind was free to rove through all the tents, which bore the names of departments of the Central District Hospital, opening doors for a patient, slamming the doors of the treatment rooms.

None of this bothered me much. I simply never had a chance to appreciate the comfort of a wooden wall and compare it with a tarpaulin one. My walls were tarpaulin, so was my sky. When I recalled occasional nights spent under wood in transit camps, they didn't seem like luck, or hope, or an opportunity that might be taken advantage of.

The Arkagala mine was where there was the most wood. But there was also a lot of torment, and Arkagala was the place I had left to get my sentence in Jelgala. In Arkagala I had been marked out as a victim; I was on the lists and in the skilled hands of provocateurs from the special zone.

The hospital's tarpaulin was a disappointment for my body, not for my soul. My body shivered every time the wind blew; I writhed, unable to stop my skin, from my toes to the back of my neck, from shivering.

There wasn't even a stove in the dark tent. Somewhere in the middle of an enormous number of freshly hewn trestle beds was my place for today and tomorrow: a trestle bed with a wooden headboard, without a mattress or a pillow. Just a trestle bed, a headboard, and a decrepit faded blanket like a Roman toga or a Sadducee cloak to wrap up in. You could see Roman stars through the faded blanket. But Kolyma's stars were not Roman. The map of the Far North's starry sky was different from that of the Gospel regions.

I wrapped my head tight in the blanket, as if it were the sky, warming myself in the only possible way, one I was very familiar with.

Someone took me by the shoulders and led me somewhere along a dirt path. I was barefoot and stumbled as I tripped over some object. My toes were rotting from the frostbites of 1938, which had still not healed.

Before I could lie down on my trestle bed, I had to be washed. The man who was going to wash me was Aleksandr Ivanovich, wearing two gowns over his quilted jacket. He was a prisoner, and what's more, one with a "letter" to his crime, which meant he was an article 58 convict.

He worked as a male nurse at the hospital, but on the basis of his "patient notes," not as a member of the staff, since only a nonpolitical convict could be on the staff.

A large wooden tub, a barrel of water, a ladle, a linen cupboard were all fitted into one corner of the barracks where Aleksandr Ivanovich's trestle bed was placed.

He poured me a tub full of water from the barrel. Over many years I had gotten used to symbolic bathhouses, to the extra-scrupulous dispensation of water, which was taken from dried-up streams in summer and from heated snow in winter. I was able to wash with any quantity of water, from a teaspoonful to a cistern. If it was just a teaspoon, I would wash my eyes and nothing else. But here I had a whole tub.

I didn't have to be shaved: I'd received a decent shave from an electric shaver in the hands of the former colonel of the general staff, Rudenko, who was now a barber.

The water, symbolic hospital water, was, of course, cold. But it wasn't icy, as was all water in Kolyma, whether in winter or summer. Not that this was of any importance. Even boiling water would not have warmed my body. And if a ladle of hell's pitch had been splashed onto my skin, hell's heat would not have warmed up my insides. I didn't think about being burned even in hell when I pressed my bare belly to a hot boiler pipe in the gold seam of the Partisan mine. That was in the winter of 1938, a thousand years ago. After Partisan I was resistant to hell's pitch. But hell's pitch was not in use at Belichya. The sight, or rather the feel, of a tub of cold water, in the opinion of Aleksandr Ivanovich's finger, could not be hot or warm. It wasn't icy: and that, in Aleksandr Ivanovich's opinion, was sufficient. I didn't care in the least about any of that, in the opinion of my own body, and a body is more to be reckoned with, more demanding than a human soul, for a body has more moral qualities, rights, and obligations.

Before washing me Aleksandr Ivanovich shaved my pubic region with a dangerous razor, had a go at the area around my armpits, then took me to the doctor's surgery, after dressing me in much-darned but clean old hospital linen. The doctor's surgery was partitioned off by the same tarpaulin walls as the rest of the tent.

The tarpaulin flap was thrown back, and an angel in a white coat appeared on the threshold. The angel was wearing a quilted jacket under the white coat. It wore quilted trousers and had an old fur jacket, well into its second life, but still solid enough, over its gown.

June nights are no joke for free men or for prisoners, let alone idiots or hard workers. None of this applies to goners. Goners have simply crossed the boundaries of good and evil, warmth and cold.

This angel was the duty doctor, Dr. Lebedev. He was not a doctor and had no medical degree; he wasn't even a paramedic; he was just a secondary-school history teacher, a specialization everyone knows is highly inflammable.

After being a patient, he began to work as a paramedic intern. Being addressed as "doctor" had long ago ceased to embarrass him. He wasn't, in fact, a bad person; he denounced people in moderation, and perhaps he never denounced anyone at all. At the very least, Dr. Lebedev took no part in the plotting that tore every hospital institution apart, and Belichya was no exception. Lebedev understood that if he let himself get carried away it could cost him not only his medical career but his life.

He received me without enthusiasm and filled in my patient notes without any sign of interest. But I was struck: my surname was being written down in fine handwriting on a real "patient notes" form, which may not have been printed at a printshop but had been drawn up by someone who was used to handling a ruler.

The form was more reliable than the phantasmal, fantastic nature of the Kolyma white night, the tarpaulin tent for two hundred prisoners' trestle beds. A tent through whose tarpaulin walls I could hear that so familiar sound of the Kolyma prisoners' barracks.

A man in a white gown, furiously banging a schoolchild's pen in a non-spill inkwell, was writing things down, and not calling for any assistance from the handsome writing set in the middle of the desk in front of him. The writing set was handmade by a prisoner in the hospital. It was made from a branch that could have been three years old or three thousand, the same age as a Ramses or Assargadon—I couldn't work out the age or count the annual rings in the branch. This crafts-man's skillful hand had cleverly chosen a rare, unique natural bend in the wood, which had been twisted by doing battle with the Far North's subzero frosts. The bend had been caught, the branch had been stopped, cut off by a master hand, and the essence of the bend and of the wood had been exposed. Once the bark had been removed, a standard of standards had appeared: a perfectly marketable item, the head of Mephistopheles bending over a barrel from which a fountain of wine is about to gush. Wine, not water. The miracle at Cana or the miracle in Faust's cellar failed to become a miracle because in Kolyma only human blood could gush: alcohol could not (there was no wine in Kolyma), nor could any hot-water underground geyser, the Yakut spa of Talaya healing source.[3]

Here was the danger: pull the cork and what would flow would be not water but blood. Whether it was holding back the miracle-worker Mephistopheles or Christ didn't matter.

The duty doctor Lebedev was also afraid of the unexpected, so he preferred to use the non-spill inkwell. The warrant for vitamin collection was neatly glued to a new form. Instead of glue, Lebedev used the extract of willow, of which a whole barrel stood by his desk. The willow mercilessly stuck to the poor piece of paper.

Aleksandr Ivanovich took me to my place, explaining something by gestures: apparently, it was officially still night, even though it was as bright as day, and one was supposed to speak only when instructions called for speech, or to follow medical tradition and whisper, although sleeping goners in Kolyma couldn't be woken even by a cannon fired over the patient's ear, for every one of my two hundred new neighbors was considered to be a future corpse and nothing more.

Aleksandr Ivanovich's gesticulations amounted to just a few pieces of advice: if I wanted to relieve myself, then God forbid that I should run off somewhere to the toilet, a hole cut in the boards in a corner of the tent. First I had to register and check in with Aleksandr Ivanovich, so as to present the results of my session in the toilet in his presence.

Aleksandr Ivanovich then had to use his own hand or a stick to push the results into the lapping stinking sea of human excrement of a dysentery hospital, a sea that was never absorbed, unlike the white limestone slabs, by any Kolyma permafrost, but had to wait to be transported to other places in the hospital.

Aleksandr Ivanovich did not use chlorine or carbolic acid or the great and ubiquitous potassium permanganate: there was nothing like that at hand. But what did I care about these all too human problems? Our fate didn't even need disinfection.

I ran several times to produce a stool, and Aleksandr Ivanovich would record the results of my gut's work; my gut was working just as unpredictably and willfully as it had by the fence at the vitamin factory. Aleksandr Ivanovich bent down close to my excrement and made some mysterious marks on a plywood board he was holding.

Aleksandr Ivanovich was a very important person in the department. The dysentery department's plywood board gave an extremely accurate, daily, hourly picture of the progress of every single patient suffering from diarrhea.

Aleksandr Ivanovich treasured his board: he would tuck it under his mattress for the few hours when he was exhausted by the vigilance of his round-the-clock duties. He would fall into oblivion, the usual sleep of a Kolyma prisoner, not removing his quilted jacket nor his two gray gowns, but just collapsing against the tarpaulin wall of his existence, momentarily losing consciousness, only to get up again after an hour, or at most two hours, and crawl out to his table, where he would light up his "bat" kerosene lamp.

Once upon a time Aleksandr Ivanovich was the secretary of a provincial committee of one of Georgia's autonomous republics; he came to Kolyma with a conviction under article 58 and an astronomical sentence.

He had no medical education; he wasn't even a recordkeeper, even if he was an "accountant" in the terminology of Dr. Kalembet. Aleksandr Ivanovich had been through the pit face, had "drifted" and fallen on the usual road that takes a goner to the hospital. He was a career man, a faithful soul for any boss.

He was kept by hook or by crook working on patients' notes, but not because he was a fine expert in surgery or soil science: he was a peasant turned careerist. He faithfully served any authority and would move mountains at the orders of the top bosses. It wasn't he but Dr. Kalembet, the head of the department, who had thought up the plywood board. That board had to be in reliable hands, and Dr. Kalembet found Aleksandr Ivanovich to be those reliable hands. Their service was mutually beneficial. Kalembet kept Aleksandr Ivanovich doing patients' notes, and the latter provided the department with exact records, and up-to-the-minute, too.

Aleksandr Ivanovich couldn't be a staff male nurse: I realized that right away. A staff nurse was a god and had to be a nonpolitical convict, dreaded by anyone condemned under article 58: he had to be the ever-vigilant eye of the district NKVD section. A staff nurse has many voluntary assistants who work just for a bowl of soup. If a staff nurse, a nonpolitical, goes to get his food in the kitchen, then he does so in the company of a dozen slaves with varying access to this demigod, the man who distributes food, the master of the goner's life or death. I have always been struck by the deep-rooted Russian habit of being unable to do without a slave to serve oneself. So that nonpolitical orderlies are more gods than orderlies: they can hire someone, an article 58er, to do their work in exchange for a cigarette, some tobacco, or a piece of bread. But even an article 58 worker doesn't stay idle: by some means or other he can become a clerk of works, and thus inevitably find his own slaves. A worker will crumble half the tobacco into his own pocket, will divide his bread or soup into two portions and recruit his own comrades, pit-face getters at the gold mine, to tidy up for the nonpoliticals. These getters would be staggering from exhaustion and starvation after a fourteen-hour workday at the mine. I myself was one of those workers, a slave of slaves, and I know what all this costs.

That is how I immediately understood why Aleksandr Ivanovich was determined to do everything himself: washing, laundering, issuing dinner, taking temperatures.

His universality was bound to make Aleksandr Ivanovich a valuable man for Dr. Kalembet, or for any department chief who was himself a prisoner. The main thing, however, was not only the information on the form but the original sin. The very first nonpolitical doctor did not depend as heavily on Aleksandr Ivanovich as Kalembet did and discharged Aleksandr Ivanovich to the mines, where he died, for the Twentieth Party Congress of 1956 was still a long way off. He almost certainly died the death of a just man.

Being sent to the mines by your boss was, in fact, the main danger for many dying goners: Aleksandr Ivanovich was incorruptible because he depended on his own patients' notes. From the very first day, as invariably happened everywhere, he staked his future on the bosses, on his efficiency, on the honesty with which he performed his main job: the pursuit of the human excrement from two hundred dysentery patients.

Aleksandr Ivanovich was the mainstay of the treatment in the dysentery department. Everyone understood that.

The plywood board for tracking progress had cells corresponding to the number of diarrhea patients who needed regular inspection. No gangster who got to the hospital by riding the fashionable wave of dysentery could bribe Aleksandr Ivanovich. He would have immediately reported the gangster to the authorities. He would have ignored the inner voice of fear. After working at the pit face in the mines, he had his own accounts to settle with gangsters. But the gangsters used to bribe the doctors, not the male nurses. They would threaten the doctors, not the nurses, least of all nurses who had been patients and were employed on the basis of their patients' notes.

Aleksandr Ivanovich tried to live up to the trust placed in him by the doctors and the state. His vigilance was not applied to political matters. He punctiliously carried out everything to do with inspecting human excrement.

Given the torrent of malingerers (were they malingerers?) pretending to have dysentery, it was extremely important to inspect the patient's daily stool. What else could you measure? Boundless exhaustion? Acute emaciation? All that lay outside the remit of the vigilance not just of the nurse but of the head of the department. Only a doctor was obliged to inspect a patient's stool. In Kolyma any record "based on what was said" was dubious. And since the center of centers of a patient with dysentery was his gut, it was extremely important to know the truth, and if the truth wasn't personally witnessed, then it had to be through someone trustworthy, a personal representative in the fantastic world of the Kolyma prisoners' underworld, in the distorted light of windows made from bottle glass: the truth had to be ascertained if only in a rough, approximate shape.

The scales of concepts and evaluations in Kolyma were unbalanced and sometimes turned upside down.

Aleksandr Ivanovich's vocation was to inspect not the recovery but the deceit, the theft of bed days from the beneficent state. He considered it a privilege to keep the record of the excretions of the dysentery barracks, while Dr. Kalembet, an acting but not a qualified doctor, just like the symbolic Dr. Lebedev, would have considered it a privilege to be counting shit instead of pushing a wheelbarrow, just as any intellectual, any "four-eyes," any "number cruncher" would, without exception.

Piotr Semionovich Kalembet may have been a doctor by profession, even a professor of the Military Medical Academy, but in 1943 he considered it a privilege to be recording stools in the patients' notes, instead of excreting his own stool on the toilet to be calculated and analyzed.

The wonderful plywood board was the main document in diagnosis and clinical treatment for the dysentery department of Belichya: it comprised a list of all the patients with diarrhea, a list that was constantly changing.

There was a rule: you could relieve yourself in the daytime only if a paramedic was watching. Not exactly a paramedic but someone acting as one, surprisingly, the angelic Dr. Lebedev. This occurred when Aleksandr Ivanovich slept, only to wake up suddenly in combat readiness for his night battle with diarrhea patients.

Such was the good that a simple piece of plywood could do in the virtuous hands of Aleksandr Ivanovich, on a truly state level.

It was a pity he didn't live to see the Twentieth Party Congress; nor did Piotr Semionovich Kalembet. After serving his ten years and being released, he took the job of chief of the health section of some department; then he sensed that nothing in his fate had changed, except for his job title: the former prisoner's lack of rights was only too obvious. Like all decent Kolyma hands, Kalembet harbored no hopes. The situation didn't change even after the war was over. Kalembet committed suicide in 1948 at Elgen, where he was head of the health section. He injected a vein with morphine solution and left a note with a strange but utterly Kalembetian explanation: "The fools won't let me live."

So Aleksandr Ivanovich died a goner's death before he finished serving his twenty-five-year sentence.

The plywood board was divided vertically into columns for number and surname. What was missing were the apocalyptic columns for the article of conviction and the sentence, which rather astonished me when I first touched this precious piece of plywood, sanded by a knife and carved with a shard of broken glass. The column that came after the surname was titled "color," but this wasn't about the coloring of chickens or dogs.

The column after that had no heading, although one existed: "consistency." It might have seemed too difficult for Aleksandr Ivanovich, being a long-forgotten or even wholly unknown term from the dubious realm of Latin cuisine, and Aleksandr Ivanovich's lips were unable to repeat the word correctly in order to engrave it on a new piece of plywood. He simply omitted it, keeping it "in his mind," but understanding perfectly the sense of the response he had to record in this column.

A stool could be liquid, solid, semiliquid, semisolid, formed, formless, or mushy... These were the few responses that Aleksandr Ivanovich kept in his mind.

More important still was the last column, which was headed "frequency." Compilers of frequency dictionaries should remember that Aleksandr Ivanovich and Dr. Kalembet were the first of their kind.

It was "frequency" that defined this plywood board: a frequency dictionary of the behind.

In this last column Aleksandr Ivanovich would use the stub of an indelible pencil to make a tick, just like a cybernetic machine marking a unit of excretion.

Dr. Kalembet was very proud of his cunning invention that allowed biology and physiology to be quantified, that exposed the gut's processes with mathematics.

He even argued for and advocated the benefits of his method, asserting his priority in the field at some conference; possibly this was entertainment of some kind, the professor of the Military Medical Academy gloating over his own fate. Or possibly this was a perfectly serious northern displacement, a trauma that affected the psychology even of people who weren't goners.

Aleksandr Ivanovich led me to my trestle bed, and I fell asleep. I slept obliviously; for the first time in Kolyma I was not in a workers' barracks, nor in solitary confinement, nor in an Intensive Regime Squad.

Almost immediately—though many hours, years, centuries might well have passed—I woke up to the light of the "bat," a lantern shining right in my eyes, although it was a white night and everything could easily be seen without it.

Someone in a white gown and fur jacket—Kolyma is the same for everybody—was shining a light in my face. The angelic Dr. Lebedev was towering right over me, and the jacket was no longer over his shoulders.

Someone's voice rang out with a questioning tone: "Accountant?"

"Accountant, Piotr Semionovich," the angelic Dr. Lebedev, who had been recording my "data" in the patient notes, confirmed.

The head of the department used the term "accountant" for all the educated men who ended up in the extermination storm of Kolyma in 1937.

Kalembet himself was an accountant.

So was Lesniak, the paramedic in the surgical department, who had been a first-year student in the medical faculty of the first Moscow State University, a fellow Muscovite and a fellow student in tertiary education, a man who played a major role in my fate in Kolyma. He worked as a male nurse under Traut in the surgical department in the neighboring surgical tent.

He hadn't yet intervened in my fate, and we didn't yet know each other.

Another accountant was Andrei Maksimovich Pantiukhov, who sent me to the paramedic classes for prisoners, which decided my fate in 1946. Completing those classes and earning a diploma that gave me the right to treat patients was an instant answer to my problems at the time. But 1946 was still a long way off, all of three years, which by Kolyma reckoning was an eternity.

Valentin Nikolaevich Traut was an accountant too. This surgeon from Saratov was of German origin and so was treated worse than others: even the end of his sentence didn't solve his problems. Only the Twentieth Congress soothed Traut's anxieties, bringing his talented surgeon's hands confidence and peace of mind.

In Kolyma, Traut's personality was completely crushed: he was afraid of any authority, and he would slander whomever the authorities pointed out to him; he never defended anyone persecuted by the authorities. But he preserved his surgeon's soul and hands.

And of course there was the accountant Nina Vladimirovna Savoyeva, the Ossete contract worker. A young woman of about thirty, she was a party member and the chief doctor of Belichya.

Nina Vladimirovna had no time at all for lofty questions. But what she understood, she understood profoundly, and she tried to prove that she was right, or simply that she was strong. The strength of acquaintance, protection, influence, and lies can be used for good causes, too.

As an extremely egotistical person who could not stand any objections, Nina Vladimirovna found united against her all the vile privileges of all the bosses in the Kolyma upper class of the time, and she declared war on this vileness, using the same means.

Nina Vladimirovna was an exceedingly capable administrator. She needed only one thing: to be able to cast an eye over everything she was responsible for, to be able to yell directly at any of the workers.

Promoting her to chief of the district's health section was unsuccessful. She didn't know how to command and manage by memos.

There were a series of conflicts with the top bosses, and Savoyeva was blacklisted.

In Kolyma all the bosses feather their nests. Nina Vladimirovna was no exception. But at least she didn't write denunciations of other bosses, and she suffered for that reason.

Others started writing denunciations of her: she was summoned, interrogated, counseled in the closed party circle of the administration.

When her fellow countryman and protector, Colonel Gagkayev, left, albeit for a post in Moscow, Nina Vladimirovna began to suffer persecution.

Her cohabitation with Lesniak the paramedic ended by Savoyeva being expelled from the party. That was when I got to know the famous Black Mama. She is still in Magadan. So are Boris Lesniak and their children. After Boris Lesniak was freed, Nina Vladimirovna immediately married him, but this did not alter her fate.

Nina Vladimirovna always belonged to some group or was the head of that group; she made superhuman exertions to get some scoundrel dismissed from his job. Equally superhuman exertions were made to overcome any "radiant personality."

Boris Lesniak introduced different goals, moral ones; he brought into her life the elevated culture in which he himself had been brought up. Boris was a hereditary "accountant": his mother had been in prison and in exile. She was Jewish, and his father had worked as a customs officer on the Chinese-Eastern Railway.

Boris found the energy to act in accord with personal decency; he made vows and kept them.

Nina Vladimirovna followed him, living by his values, and she treated all her free contract worker colleagues with hatred.

During what was the hardest time for me I owe everything to Lesniak and Savoyeva.

I cannot forget Lesniak bringing bread or a handful of tobacco to my barracks for me every evening, literally every evening: these were precious things in my semi-existence then as an advanced Kolyma goner.

Every evening I waited for this hour, that piece of bread, that pinch of tobacco, and I was afraid that Lesniak would not come, that I had imagined all this, that it was a dream, a hungry Kolyma mirage.

But Lesniak did come, filling the doorway.

At the time I had no idea that Nina Vladimirovna, the chief doctor, had a friendship of sorts with my benefactor. I took these gifts to be a miracle. All the good things that Lesniak could do for me, he did: work, food, rest. He knew Kolyma well. But he could only do this thanks to the hands of Nina Vladimirovna, the chief doctor; she was a strong person who had known conflict, intrigue, and ambush since childhood. Lesniak had shown her a different world.

It turned out that I didn't have dysentery at all.

What I was suffering from was called pellagra, alimentary dystrophy, scurvy, extreme polyavitaminosis; but it wasn't dysentery.

After something like two weeks of treatment and two weeks of illicit rest, I was discharged from the hospital, and I was already putting on my rags, albeit with utter indifference, at the exit to the tarpaulin tent although not yet outside it. At the very last moment I was summoned to Dr. Kalembet's office, the same screened-off area with a Mephistopheles where Lebedev had admitted me.

Whether Kalembet himself had initiated this conversation or whether Lesniak had advised him to is unclear. Kalembet was not a friend of Lesniak's or of Savoyeva's.

I don't know if Kalembet had detected in my hungry eyes some particular shine that inspired him with hope. But while I was hospitalized, my bunk was moved closer several times to various neighbors, the hungriest, most hopeless of the accountants. That was how my trestle bed came to be next to that of Roman Krivitsky, the editorial secretary of *Izvestiya*, a man who had the same surname as the well-known but unrelated deputy minister of the armed forces who had been shot by Rukhimov.

Roman Krivitsky was pleased to have me next to him; he told me a few things about himself, but his chubby, swollen skin alarmed Kalembet. Roman Krivitsky died while he was next to me. He was interested, of course, entirely in food, as we all were. But as a more longstanding goner, Roman was exchanging soup for porridge, porridge for bread, and bread for tobacco, all measured in grains, pinches, grams. Nevertheless, his losses were lethal: Roman died of dystrophy. My neighbor's bed was freed. It wasn't the usual trestle bed made of laths. Krivitsky's bed had springs, a real metal lattice with round, painted sides—a proper hospital bed among the two hundred trestle beds. This was another whim of a patient with extreme dystrophy, and Kalembet had indulged it.

Now, however, Kalembet said, "Listen, Shalamov, you don't have dysentery, but you are emaciated. You can stay on for two weeks working as a ward assistant; you'll take temperatures, show the patients about, wash the floor. In short, you'll do everything that Makeyev, the present ward assistant, does. He's spent long enough lounging about and eating: he's being discharged today. So decide. Don't be afraid of taking away somebody's place. I'm not promising you much, but I'll keep you on for two weeks on the basis of your patient notes."

I agreed, and Makeyev, the protégé of a free contract paramedic called Mikhno, was discharged instead of me.

A struggle, a full-scale war for influence was going on: the free contract paramedic Mikhno, a member of the Communist Youth, was gathering a group of colleagues in order to do battle with Kalembet. Kalembet's record was, in essence, more than just vulnerable: a whole squad of informers, headed by Mikhno, was preparing to muzzle the head of the department. But Kalembet struck his blow and discharged Mikhno's trusted man, the nonpolitical Makeyev, to the mines.

I realized all of this later. At the time I set to my ward work with enthusiasm. However I lacked not just Makeyev's strength but any strength at all. I wasn't versatile enough, nor respectful enough to my seniors. In short, I was shoved out the day after Kalembet was transferred somewhere. But during the interval, an entire month, I had managed to get to know Lesniak. It was Lesniak who gave me a whole series of important tips. He said, "Try to get a travel warrant. If you have that, you won't be sent back and won't be refused admission to the hospital." Boris, for all his good advice, didn't understand that I had been a goner for a long time, that no form of work, even the most symbolic, such as copying, or the most healthy, such as gathering berries and mushrooms, or bringing in firewood or catching fish, with no norms, in the fresh air, was now going to be of any help to me.

Nevertheless, Boris was doing all this along with Nina Vladimirovna, and they were puzzled by how little my strength was recovering. I didn't have anything as specific as tuberculosis or nephritis, and trying to push your way into a hospital with just emaciation or alimentary dystrophy was too risky: you could misjudge your step and end up in the morgue instead. It had cost me great effort to get back into the hospital that second time, but I did succeed. The paramedic at the vitamin center, I forget his name, used to beat me, and he let the guard beat me every day at the roll call after work for being a loafer, a shirker, a speculator, an objector; he refused outright to have me hospitalized. I managed to deceive the paramedic: one night my surname was attached to somebody else's dispatch order—the paramedic was loathed by the whole Special Camp Point, and people were happy to show me some support in Kolyma style, so that I crawled away to Belichya. I literally crawled for six kilometers, but I reached the admissions room. The dysentery tents were empty, and I was put in the main building where Dr. Pantiukhov was in charge. All four of us new patients piled the

mattresses and blankets on top of us and lay down together, our teeth
chattering until morning: not every tent had a stove. The next day I
was transferred to a tent that did have a stove, and I stood there by it
until I was summoned for injections or examinations. I had difficulty
understanding what was being done to me: all I could feel was hunger,
hunger, hunger.

My disease was called pellagra.

It was during this second hospitalization that I got to know Lesniak
and the chief doctor Nina Vladimirovna Savoyeva, Traut, and Pantiukhov—all the doctors in Belichya.

My condition was so bad that it was no longer possible to do me
any good. I didn't care whether I was being done good or evil. Even
putting a drop of goodness into my pellagrous Kolyma goner's body
was a pointless thing to do. Warmth was more important than kindness. But they tried to treat me with hot injections: the gangsters had
bought a vitamin B3 injection in exchange for a bread ration, and
pellagra sufferers would exchange the hot injection for bread, the lunch
ration of three hundred grams, so that some professional criminal
would go to the surgery to get his infusion instead of the goner. And
he would get it. I didn't sell my B3 to anyone and got it in my own vein,
instead of *per os*, "by mouth," as bread.

It's not for me to judge who was right and who was wrong. I don't
condemn anyone, neither those who sold their goner's hot injections
nor the gangsters who bought them.

Nothing had changed. No desire to live was aroused. Everything I
ate, any food I swallowed, was eaten as if mechanically, with no appetite.

During this second hospitalization I felt my skin flaking uncontrollably; the skin all over my body itched, throbbed, and fell off in flakes,
even whole layers. I was suffering from the classic diagnostic form of
pellagra; I was a knight of the three Ds: dementia, dysentery, dystrophy.

I don't remember much of this second hospitalization in Belichya.
There were some new acquaintances, faces, licked spoons, an icy stream,
a walk to gather mushrooms where, because of the river flooding, I
wandered all night over the mountains, retreating from the river. I saw
mushrooms, gigantic honey fungus and orange-cap boletus, visibly
growing, turning into a fifteen-kilo fungus that wouldn't fit into the

bucket. This was not a sign of dementia but an utterly real spectacle, a miracle of the same kind as hydroponics: mushrooms turn into Gullivers right before your eyes. The berries I gathered in the Kolyma way, by beating the bush: I swept the bucket over the bilberry bushes . . . But all that came after the skin flaking.

For the time being the skin was falling off me in sheets. As well as having scurvy ulcers, my fingers and toes were rotting because of osteomyelitis following frostbite. I had loose scurvy teeth, pyodermic ulcers, which have left traces that are still visible on my legs. I remember the passionate, constant desire to eat, and the crowning symptom: my skin coming off in layers.

I didn't have dysentery after all, but I did have pellagra: the lump of mucus that had brought me to these remote paths on earth was a lump excreted from the gut of a pellagra sufferer. My excrement was pellagrous.

That was even more ominous, but at the time I didn't care. I was not the only pellagra sufferer in Belichya, but I was the worst and the most obvious.

I was composing verse by now: "The dream of a polyavitaminosis sufferer"—I was reluctant to call myself a pellagra sufferer even in verse. In any case, I wasn't really sure what pellagra was. I merely felt that my fingers were writing, both in rhyme and without, that my fingers had not yet said their last word.

That was when I sensed a glove separating itself and falling from my hand. It was interesting, not frightening, to see one's own skin fall off in layers from one's body, seeing sheets fall from one's shoulders, belly, and arms.

I was such a distinct pellagra sufferer, such a classic example, that gloves could have been taken whole from both hands and socks from both feet.

Now I was being shown to passing medical chiefs, but none of them were amazed by these gloves.

The day came when my skin was completely renewed, but my soul was not.

It was explained to me that the pellagrous gloves had to be removed from my hands and the pellagrous socks from my feet.

Lesniak and Savoyeva, Pantiukhov and Traut took off these gloves and socks, and attached them to my patient notes. They were then sent to Magadan along with my notes, as a living exhibit for the museum of local history, or at least of local medical history.

Lesniak didn't send all my detritus with the notes. He sent only the socks and one glove but kept the second glove and the rather diffident prose and the hesitant verse I had written at the time.

A dead glove was no use for writing good prose or verse. The glove itself was prose, an indictment, a document, a statement.

But the glove perished in Kolyma, which is why this story is being written. The author guarantees that the fingerprint pattern on both gloves is identical.

I ought to have written a long time ago about Boris Lesniak and Nina Vladimirovna Savoyeva. It is to them and to Pantiukhov that I am indebted for real help during my hardest Kolyma days and nights. I owe them my life. If life is to be considered a good thing, which I doubt, then I am indebted to them, three real people in 1943, not for sympathy or condolence but for real help. It should be recorded that they came into my life after I had spent eight years roaming from a gold-mine pit face to a pretrial institution and a Kolyma execution prison, into the life of a goner at the gold-mine pit face in 1937 and 1938, a goner who had revised his opinion about life as a good thing. By then the only people I envied were those who had found the courage to commit suicide when a new party of prisoners was being assembled for Kolyma in July 1937 in the deportation wing of Butyrki prison. Those were the people I really envied: they never saw what I saw in the seventeen years that followed.

My view of life as a good thing, as happiness, changed. Kolyma taught me something utterly different.

The principle of my age, my personal existence, all my life, the conclusion I have reached from my personal experience, the rule I have arrived at after this experience, can be expressed in just a few words. The first thing to be returned are the slappings; gifts are the second thing to be returned. One should remember evil before one remembers good. Remembering everything good takes a hundred years; everything bad takes two hundred. That is the difference between me and all the Russian humanists of the nineteenth and twentieth centuries.

1972

GALINA PAVLOVNA ZYBALOVA

IN THE first year of the war, the smoky wick of the lamp of vigilance was turned down a little. The barbed wire was removed from the barracks where politicals convicted under article 58 were housed, and the enemies of the people were allowed to carry out important functions such as stoking boilers or being orderlies or night watchmen—jobs that the camp constitution allowed only nonpolitical and, in the worst case, recidivist criminals to take.

Dr. Lunin, the head of our health section for prisoners, a realist and pragmatist, rightly considered that the moment had to be seized and the iron struck while it was still hot. The orderly at the chemistry laboratory of Arkagala coal district was caught stealing government glycerin (honey! fifty rubles a jar!), and the new watchman who replaced the orderly stole twice as much on his very first night—things were getting hot. During all my wanderings from camp to camp, I observed that the first thing each prisoner does on arriving at a new job is to look around and see: what can I steal here? That applies to everyone, from orderlies to chiefs of administration. There is a mystical element in a Russian's yearning to steal, under camp conditions, northern conditions, Kolyma conditions, in any case.

As situations arise and have to be resolved, regular opportunities are seized by the enemies of the people. When the second nonpolitical orderly's career collapsed right after the first one's, Lunin recommended me as an orderly at the chemistry laboratory; I was someone, he said, who wouldn't steal chemical treasures but would keep the barrel stove lit and would use coal to do so. Every article 58 prisoner during that time in Kolyma was mentally and physically more capable than any stoker at keeping a stove burning. After 1939 at Magadan transit camp,

I knew very well how to wash floors in the sailor fashion, with a rag tied to a stick. In the end, as a famous Magadan floor-mopper, I had this job all through the spring of 1939, and for the rest of my life never forgot what I had learned.

I was working then in a mine, fulfilling my "percentage": coal was nothing like a gold mine, but, naturally, I didn't even dream of getting work as an orderly in a chemistry laboratory.

I acquired an opportunity to rest, to wash my face and hands: my mucus-filled throat, saturated with coal dust, would become as clean as a whistle only after many months, or even years, of working as an orderly. I didn't even get to thinking about the color of what I was coughing up.

The laboratory, which took up a whole barracks in the settlement and had a big staff—two chemical engineers, two technicians, three laboratory workers—was run by a young Communist Youth woman from the capital, Galina Pavlovna Zybalova. She was a contract worker, like her husband, Piotr Yakovlevich Podosionov, an automobile engineer who ran the garage of the Arkagala coal district.

Prisoners watch the lives of the free workers as they would watch a film: it might be a drama, or a comedy, or a picture film, as the classical prerevolutionary separation of genre defined films for distribution. The heroes of films (before the revolution the word "film" was feminine) rarely stepped down from the screen into the stalls of the electrotheater (as the early cinema theaters used to be called). The pleasure gotten from them was special. No decisions needed to be made. You were not to interfere with their lives. This coexistence of two worlds produced no actual problems for prisoners. It was just another world.

This was where I stoked the stoves. You have to know how to treat coal, but it's not a complicated science. I washed floors. Above all, I was treating my toes: the osteomyelitis I got in 1938 healed only when I got back to the mainland, almost by the time of the Twentieth Party Congress. And it may not have healed even then.

Wrapping my legs in clean rags, changing the bandages on the toes of both feet that were oozing pus, I stiffened in bliss by the well-stoked stove, as I felt the subtle pain, the aching of those toes, injured by the mines, crippled by gold. Full bliss demands a drop of pain: the history of society and literature tells us this, too.

Now my head was throbbing and aching—I'd forgotten about my toes; the feeling had been superseded by something else, more dominant and of more vital importance.

I still hadn't remembered anything or decided anything or found anything, but my entire brain, with all its withered cells, was tense with anxiety. Memory, which no Kolyma man needs—in fact, what would a camp prisoner want with something so unreliable and so fragile and so clinging and so all-powerful as memory—was meant to suggest a decision for me. Alas, what a memory I used to have—four years ago! My memory had been like a shot: if I couldn't remember something right away, I would fall ill and become immobilized until I'd recalled what I needed to. There were very few cases of such delayed delivery in my life; I could count the number of occasions. The memory itself of such delays somehow stimulated and accelerated my memory, which in any case moved at full speed.

But my brain now at Arkagala, exhausted by Kolyma in 1938, exhausted by four years of alternating between the hospital and the pit face, was holding back a secret and refusing to obey any order, request, plea, prayer, complaint.

I implored my brain, as one implores a higher being, to reply, to reveal some partition, to light up some dark crack where what I needed was hidden.

And my brain took pity on me, carried out my request, and indulged my plea.

What was I asking for?

I was repeating endlessly the surname of the woman who managed the laboratory: Galina Pavlovna Zybalova! Zybalova! Pavlovna! Zybalova!

I had heard that surname somewhere. I used to know someone called Zybalov—not Ivanov, Petrov, or Smirnov. This was a metropolitan surname. And suddenly, sweating with tension, I recalled it. Not Moscow, not Leningrad, not Kiev, where a man with a metropolitan surname was close to me.

In 1929, when I received my first sentence, I was working in the northern Urals at Beriozniki; there I met the head of the planning section at the Beriozniki soda plant, an exile by the name, I believe, of Pavel Pavlovich Zybalov. He had been a member of the Menshevik Central Committee, and he was pointed out to other exiles at a distance, from the doorway of the room in the soda plant office where he worked. Soon Beriozniki was flooded by a torrent of prisoners of various kinds—exiles and camp prisoners, deported collective farmers—after the heavily publicized trials began. The name of Zybalov was somewhat overshadowed by the new heroes. He stopped being one of the sights of Beriozniki.

As for the soda factory, once called Salve, it became part of the Beriozniki Chemical Plant and was merged with one of the gigantic construction projects of the first Five-Year Plan, Beriozniki Chemical Construction, which sucked in hundreds of thousands of workmen, engineers, and technicians, both Soviet and foreign. There was a settlement that housed foreigners, ordinary exiles, special deportees, and camp prisoners at Beriozniki. One shift of camp prisoners alone could comprise up to ten thousand men. The flow in construction work was unbelievable: three thousand free workers were taken on in a month by contract and by recruitment, while four thousand ran away without being paid off. This construction project has yet to be described. The hopes invested in Konstantin Paustovsky were not realized. Paustovsky stayed there to write *Kara-Bugaz*, hiding from the stormy, seething mob in Beriozniki's hotel, never showing his face outdoors.

The economist Zybalov moved from working at the soda factory to Beriozniki Chemical Construction, where there was more money and more scope, while the ration system played an important part.

At the Beriozniki Chemical Plant he organized a group on economics for voluntary students. It was free of charge and open to anyone who wanted to attend. The group was Zybalov's contribution to society, and he worked in the main office of Beriozniki Chemical Construction. Through this group I attended several of Zybalov's practical classes.

Zybalov was a professor from the metropolis and an exile: he taught the classes willingly and easily. He had missed his lecturing and teaching work. I don't know if he had given eleven thousand lectures over his lifetime, as another acquaintance of mine in the camps had, but there was no doubt that the number was in the thousands.

When Zybalov was an exile at Beriozniki his wife died: he was left with a daughter of about ten, who sometimes visited her father while we were studying.

I was well known at Beriozniki. I had refused to accompany Berzin to Kolyma to start up Far East Construction, and I tried to settle at Beriozniki.

But in what role? As a lawyer? I had an unfinished education in law. But it was Zybalov himself who advised me to accept the post of manager of the office of labor economics at the Beriozniki thermoelectric power station. The acronyms for the office and the power plant (BET and TET) were the famous linguistic innovations of the time: they arose when we were working on the first Five-Year Plan at our site. The director of the power station was a wrecker, the engineer Kapeller, a person who had been through trials, perhaps the mine trials or some other list. The power station was not construction but management of a working plant: the commissioning period was shamelessly prolonged. Such shamelessness had become the rule. Kapeller could find no way of attuning himself, a man sentenced to ten or even fifteen years, to the tone of all this rowdy construction, when workers and technicians were changed on a daily basis, where bosses were arrested and shot, and where whole trainloads of exiles, because of collectivization, were unloaded. In his hometown of Kizel, Kapeller had been convicted of far more minor misdemeanors than the chaos in production that was increasing here like a mighty avalanche. Hammers were still banging next to his office, and special repair workers had been summoned from overseas by Moscow telegrams for the boiler that was being installed by the Hanomag firm.

Kapeller took me on, and did so without caring at all who I was: he was interested in technical questions, technical tragedies, which were as plentiful as the economic and everyday ones.

To help Kapeller, the party organization had recommended as an assistant director on consultations about production a Timofei Ivanovich Rachiov, a semiliterate but energetic person who made it a principle "not to let people yell at you." The office of labor economics was subordinated to Rachiov, and I kept a piece of paper with his orders for some time. The stokers handed in an enormous, well-argued complaint about nonpayments and double billing: they kept coming to see Rachiov about it for a long time. Rachiov wrote, without reading their complaint: "To the Manager of the Office for Economics and Labor: Please investigate and, if possible, refuse."

This was the work that I, a lawyer who had not completed his degree, found myself doing, on Zybalov's advice.

"Act boldly. Get down to it and make a start. Even if you're thrown out after two weeks—the collective agreement won't let that happen earlier—you will acquire some sort of experience over those two weeks. Then apply again. After being fired five times like that, you will be a fully fledged economist. Don't be afraid. If anything complicated turns up, come and see me. I'll help. After all, I'm not going anywhere. The laws of labor flow don't apply to me."

I accepted this well-paid job.

At this time Zybalov was organizing an evening technical college. Pavel Pavlovich (I think that was his patronymic) was the head teacher of this college. A place was made ready for me, too, as a teacher of "hygiene and the physiology of labor."

I had already applied to join this new technical college and was thinking about a plan for my first lesson, when I suddenly received a letter from Moscow. My parents were alive, my comrades from the university were alive, too, and staying on at Beriozniki seemed to be like death. So I left without waiting to be paid by the power station, while Zybalov remained at Beriozniki.

I remembered all this at Arkagala, in the chemistry laboratory of the Arkagala coal district, at the threshold of solving the mystery of humic acids.

Chance plays a major part in life, and although the general world order punishes any exploitation of chance for personal gain, it does sometimes happen that there is no punishment. That Zybalov question had to be followed through to the end. Or perhaps it hadn't. I no longer needed a piece of bread then. A coal mine is not a gold mine; coal is not gold. Perhaps it wasn't worth constructing this house of cards: the wind would collapse the building and blow it away to the four corners of the world.

The arrest in the "lawyers' case" three years earlier did at least teach me one important camp law: never go around asking things from people you used to know when you were free—it's a small world, and such encounters happen. Such requests in Kolyma are almost always unpleasant, sometimes impossible, and can lead to the death of whoever is asking.

Such a danger existed in Kolyma—and in any camp. I had a meeting with Chekanov, my cellmate in Butyrki prison. Chekanov not only recognized me in the crowd of workmen, when as a foreman he took on our sector, but he would drag me out every day by the hand from the ranks, beat me, and send me to do the heaviest work, where I had no hope, naturally, of making the percentage. Every day Chekanov would report my behavior to the head of the sector and assure him that he would exterminate this plague of a man, that he didn't deny knowing me personally but would prove his devotion and justify the trust put in him. Chekanov was convicted of the same crime as I was. In the end, Chekanov chucked me out into a punishment center, and I survived.

I also knew Colonel Ushakov, the head of Kolyma's Criminal Investigation and, later, River sectors: I knew Ushakov when he was just an agent of Moscow CID, condemned for some crime in his employment.

I never tried to remind Colonel Ushakov of my existence. I would have been killed as soon as it could be arranged.

Finally, I knew all the top bosses of Kolyma, from Berzin onward: Vaskov, Maisuradze, Filippov, Yegorov, Tsvirko.

Knowing the camp tradition, I never stepped out of the prisoners' ranks to make any request of any boss I knew personally, or to attract attention.

In the "lawyers' case" it was only by chance that I escaped a bullet at the end of 1938 at the Partisan mine, when the Kolyma executions were in full flow. In the lawyers' case all the provocations were directed against the chairman of the Far East District Court, Vinogradov. He was accused of giving bread and a job to Dmitri Sergeyevich Parfentiev, his former colleague at the faculty of Soviet law and once the prosecutor for Cheliabinsk and for Karelia.

When he visited the Partisan mine, Vinogradov, the chairman of the Far East District Court, didn't think it necessary to conceal his acquaintance with a pit-face getter, Professor Parfentiev, and asked the head of the mine, L. M. Anisimov, to give Parfentiev an easier job.

The order was immediately carried out, and Parfentiev was made a pile driver, the easiest job at the mine: at least there was no wind under an open sky in temperatures of minus sixty, no crowbar, no spade, no pickax. True, it meant a blacksmith's forge with a flapping, half-open door and open windows, but at least there was the fire of the kiln and you could take refuge from the wind, if not the cold. Parfentiev the Trotskyist, enemy of the people, had one lung operated on for tuberculosis.

The head of the Partisan mine, Leonid Mikhailovich Anisimov, carried out Vinogradov's wish, but immediately denounced him by reporting him to all the necessary and possible offices. The foundations of the lawyers' case were laid. Captain Stolbov, the head of the Magadan NKVD's Secret Political Section, arrested all the lawyers in Kolyma, checking their links, snaring them with a noose of provocation he flung over them and tightened.

At Partisan both Parfentiev and I were arrested, driven to Magadan, and put in Magadan prison.

But twenty-four hours later Captain Stolbov was arrested, and all those who had been arrested on warrants signed by him were released.

I gave all the details about this in my story "The Lawyers' Conspiracy,"[4] where every letter is documented.

I was released not into freedom, since freedom in Kolyma is understood as being kept in a camp, but to a general barracks with the usual minimal rights. There is no freedom in Kolyma.

I was released along with Parfentiev into a transit camp, a camp for thirty thousand men; I was released with a special violet-colored brand on my personal file: "Arrived from Magadan prison." This brand doomed me to an infinite quantity of years spent under the lantern of vigilance, to the attention of the authorities until the violet-colored brand on my old personal file was exchanged for the clean cover of a new personal file, a new punitive sentence to be served. I was lucky that this new sentence was not given "by weight," a seven-gram bullet. Or perhaps I wasn't lucky: a sentence issued by weight would have saved me from many more years of torments, which were of benefit to nobody, not even to me for supplementing my inner or moral experience and physical resilience.

In any case, by recalling all my peregrinations after my arrest in the lawyers' case at Partisan mine, I made it a rule for myself to never use my initiative to turn to anyone I knew, and to never summon to Kolyma a shade from the mainland.

But where Zybalova was concerned, it somehow seemed to me that I wouldn't do any harm to the woman who had this surname. She was a good person, and if she distinguished the free from the prisoners, she didn't do so from the standpoint of an active enemy of prisoners—which is what all the contract workers were taught to do in all the political departments of Far East Construction from the moment they signed contracts. A prisoner can always sense a nuance in a free man. Is there something in those contracts other than government instructions or not? There are many such nuances—as many as there are people. But there is a boundary, a transition, a dividing line between good and evil, a moral limit that can immediately be sensed.

Like her husband, Piotr Yakovlevich, Galina Pavlovna Zybalova did not take the extreme standpoint of being an active enemy of any prisoner just because the latter was a prisoner, although Galina Pavlovna was the secretary of the Communist Youth organization of the Arkagala coal sector. Piotr Yakovlevich was not a party member.

In the evenings, Galina Pavlovna often stayed late in the laboratory—the family barracks where they lived was probably no more comfortable than the offices of the chemical laboratory.

I asked Galina Pavlovna whether she had lived in Beriozniki in the Urals at the end of the 1920s and the beginning of the 1930s.

"I did!"

"And was your father Pavel Pavlovich Zybalov?"

"Pavel Osipovich."

"Quite right. Pavel Osipovich. And you were a girl of about ten then?"

"Fourteen."

"And you wore a maroon-colored overcoat."

"A cherry-colored fur coat."

"All right, a fur coat. And you used to bring Pavel Osipovich breakfast."

"I did. My mother died there, at Churtan. Piotr Yakovlevich was in prison here. Listen Petia, Varlam Tikhonovich used to know Daddy."

"I used to study in his group."

"And Petia was born in Beriozniki. He was a local. His parents had a house in Veretye."

Piotr Yakovlevich Podosionov named a number of surnames, well known in Beriozniki, Usolie, Solikamsk, Veretye, Churtan, and Dediukhino, such as the Sobianikovs, the Kichins, but for autobiographical reasons I never had an opportunity to remember and know the local people.

To me all these names sounded like "Choctaws and Comanche,"[5] like poetry in a foreign language, but Piotr Yakovlevich, getting more and more inspired, recited them like prayers.

"All that's buried under sand now," said Podosionov. "The chemical plant."

"And Daddy's in the Don basin now," said Galina Pavlovna: I understood that her father was serving yet another term of exile.

That was how it ended. I was experiencing real pleasure, a moment of bliss because my poor brain had worked so well. A purely academic pleasure.

About two months, no more, passed; Galina Pavlovna came to work and summoned me to her office.

"I've had a letter from Daddy. Here it is."

I read the legible lines in a large hand that I didn't recognize at all: "I don't know Shalamov and I can't remember him. After all, I led those groups for some twenty years in exile, wherever I happened to be. I'm still taking them. That's not the point. What is this letter you've written to me? What sort of checks are you making? And on whom? On Shalamov? On yourself? On me? As for me," Pavel Osipovich Zybalov wrote in his large hand, "this is my answer. Treat Shalamov as you would treat me if you came across me in Kolyma. But to know my answer you didn't have to write a letter."

"So you see the result," Galina Pavlovna said sadly. "You don't know Daddy. He'll never ever forgive my blunder."

"I didn't tell you anything in particular."

"And I didn't write anything in particular to Daddy. But you can see how Daddy looks at these things. Now you can't work as an orderly anymore," Galina Pavlovna sadly reflected. "We have to look for a new orderly again. But I can get you classified as a technician: we have a job opening in the free-worker staff. As soon as the chief of the coal sector Svishchev leaves, he'll be replaced by chief engineer Yuri Ivanovich Kochura. I can get him to classify you."

Nobody was dismissed from the laboratory, I didn't have to go anywhere to "live," and, guided and helped by the engineers Sokolov and Oleg Borisovich Maksimov, who is now flourishing as a member of the Far East Academy of Sciences, I began my career as a laboratory assistant and technician.

At the request of Piotr Yakovlevich Podosionov, Galina Pavlovna's husband, I wrote a substantial work of literary research: I compiled by memory a dictionary of gangster vocabulary, its origin, its changes, its meanings. There were about six hundred words in the dictionary: this was not like the specialist literature that criminal investigation produces for its employees: it was more broad-based and more hard-hitting. The dictionary I presented to Podosionov was the sole work of prose that I wrote in Kolyma.

My unclouded happiness was not darkened by the fact that Galina left her husband: the film romance remained a film romance. I was just a spectator: even a large-scale plan of somebody else's life, somebody else's drama and tragedy, didn't provide a spectator with the illusion of life.

And it wasn't Kolyma, a country that made all aspects of family and women's problems extremely acute, acute to the point of monstrous, to the point of displacing all scales of every kind, which was the cause for the breakdown of this family.

Galina was a clever women, a beauty of a slightly Mongolian type, a chemical engineer, a representative of what was then a fashionable and innovative profession; she was the only daughter of a Russian political exile.

Piotr Yakovlevich was a shy man from Perm in the Urals: he did everything he could to let his wife have her own way—in her development, interests, and demands. It was quite obvious that these spouses were not a match, and although there are no laws for family happiness, in this case the family seemed doomed to fall apart, as, by the way, every family is.

Kolyma accelerated, catalyzed the process of disintegration.

Galina had an affair with the chief engineer of the coal sector, Yuri Ivanovich Kochura: it was more second love than a mere affair. But Kochura had children and a family. I was also shown to Kochura before I was initiated as a technician.

"This is the man, Yuri."

"Good," said Yuri, not looking at me or Galina but down at the floor in front of him. "Write a report about his recruitment."

But everything in this drama was yet to come. Kochura's wife complained to the political administration of Far East Construction, commissions began coming out, witnesses were questioned, signatures were collected. All the apparatus of state power came to the defense of the first family for which a contract had been signed in Moscow with Far East Construction.

The highest authorities in Magadan took Moscow's advice that separation was certain to kill this love and send Yuri Ivanovich back to his spouse, so they dismissed Galina Pavlovna from her post and transferred her elsewhere.

Naturally, nothing came, or could ever have come, of these transfers. Nevertheless, separation from his beloved was the sole method approved by the state for putting the situation right. There were no means other than the ones indicated in *Romeo and Juliet*. This is a tradition of primitive society, and civilization has not contributed anything new to solving the problem.

After her father's reply, my relations with Galina became more confidential.

"Look, Varlam, what happened to that Postnikov, the one who collected hands?"

Naturally, I couldn't resist taking a look at Postnikov, the one who collected hands.

Some months earlier, when I was still doing the donkey work at Kadykchan, and a transfer to Arkagala—even to a coal mine, not to a laboratory—seemed an impossible miracle, one night a fugitive emerged in our barracks, or rather a tarpaulin tent, insulated against a temperature of minus sixty degrees by a layer of either roofing felt or rubberoid (I don't remember) and a twenty-centimeter air gap (the air layer specified by Magadan and Moscow instructions).

The shortest overland route from the mainland lay along the Arkagala River, through the Arkagala taiga with its streams, bare moors, and side valleys—via Yakutia, Aldan, the Kolyma and Indigirka Rivers. This was the migratory route of fugitives, who kept a mysterious map in their breasts, and people traveled along it, instinctively guessing the direction. That direction was as predictable as the migration of geese or cranes. Chukotka is, after all, not an island but a peninsula, and the mainland is called so by a thousand analogies: a long journey across the sea, dispatch in ports, passing the island of Sakhalin, places of hard labor in tsarist times.

The authorities are well aware of this. That is why in the summer there are checkpoints, flying squads, NKVD squads in civilian clothes and in military uniform.

A few months earlier, Second Lieutenant Postnikov detained a fugitive; he didn't want to take him the ten or fifteen kilometers to Kadykchan, so the second lieutenant shot him on the spot.

What do you have to produce in the record office of a CID in almost any country in the world? How do you identify a man? There is one identity document, a very precise one: the prints of ten fingers. These fingerprints are kept in the personal file of every prisoner—in Moscow in the central card index, and in Magadan in the local administration.

Not bothering to deliver the detained prisoner to Arkagala, young Lieutenant Postnikov took an ax and cut off the fugitive's hands, put them in a bag, and drove off with his report on the capture of a prisoner.

But the fugitive got up and came to our barracks one night, pale, having lost a lot of blood, unable to speak: he merely stretched out his arms. Our foreman ran to get a guard, and the fugitive was led off into the taiga.

Either they delivered the fugitive to Arkagala, or else they just took him into the bushes and finished him off, which would have been the simplest solution both for the fugitive and for the guard, not to mention for Second Lieutenant Postnikov.

Postnikov never had to answer for what he had done. And nobody expected him to have to. But there was a lot of talk about Postnikov, even in the hungry enslaved world in which I then lived: the incident was totally new.

That was why I grabbed a piece of coal to get the stove going again, and went into the office of the woman director.

Postnikov had been a fair-haired man, but not an albino, more of a northern, blue-eyed, maritime type, slightly taller than average, a very ordinary man.

I remember taking a close and eager look, trying to detect the slightest sign of any Lavater or Lombroso feature[6] on Second Lieutenant Postnikov's face . . .[7]

One evening we were sitting by the stove, and Galina said, "I want to ask your advice."

"About what?"

"About my life."

"Galina, ever since I became an adult, I've been living according to an important commandment: 'Don't give your neighbor advice.' Like a Gospel commandment. Each person's fate is unique. All recipes are wrong."

"But I thought that you writers—"

"The trouble with Russian literature, Galina, is that it pokes its nose into other people's affairs, tries to direct other people's fate, gives an opinion on questions it understands nothing about, when it has no right at all to intervene in moral problems, to condemn, when it doesn't know anything and doesn't want to know."

"Fine. Then I'll tell you a fairy tale, and you can evaluate it as a work of literature. I take all responsibility for any artificiality or realism—which seem to me to be the same thing."

"Excellent. Let's hear the fairy tale."

Galina quickly sketched the most ordinary diagram, a triangle, and I advised her not to leave her husband.

"For a thousand reasons. First, habits: knowing a man, however little that may be, is unique, whereas elsewhere you get surprises, a boxful of the unexpected. Of course, you can leave him, too."

The second reason was that Piotr Yakovlevich was obviously a good person. I had been to his homeland, I had written, with real sympathy, a work about gangsters for him. But I didn't know Kochura at all.

Finally, the third and most important reason: I don't like any changes. I come home to sleep, to the house I live in, I don't even like anything new in the furnishings; I have trouble getting used to new furniture.

Violent changes in my life have always occurred against my will, because of someone else's spiteful will, for I have never sought change and never thought that there was anything better than the good.

There was another reason to absolve the adviser of his mortal sin. When one's own heart is concerned, advice is only taken when it doesn't contradict the inner will of the person: everything else is rejected or annulled by changing the concepts.

Like any oracle, I wasn't risking much. I wasn't even risking my good name.

I warned Galina that my advice was purely literary and did not conceal any moral obligations.

But before Galina made a decision, superior forces intervened, in complete accord with the traditions of nature, which was in a hurry to help Arkagala.

Piotr Yakovlevich Podosionov, Galina's husband, was killed. It was a plot that Aeschylus could have devised. With a well-studied plot situation. Podosionov was knocked down by a passing truck in the winter darkness, and he died in the hospital. There were a lot of fatal vehicle accidents in Kolyma; nobody said anything about a possible suicide. And he wouldn't have killed himself. He was something of a fatalist: if it wasn't fated to happen, it wouldn't. There was no need at all to kill Podosionov. Do people get killed because they are good-natured? Of course, goodness is a sin in Kolyma, but so is evil. This death solved nothing, it untied no knots, it cut nothing free: everything stayed the same. All that one could see was that superior forces had taken an interest in this little, trivial Kolyma tragedy and had taken an interest in the fate of one woman.

A new chemist arrived to take Galina's place. His very first action was to dismiss me, which I expected. As far as prisoners—and, it seems, free workers, too—were concerned, the Kolyma bosses didn't need to formulate reasons, and in any case I didn't expect any explanations. That would have been too literary, too much in the style of Russian classics. Instead at morning roll call for work a camp clerk of works yelled out my name from a list of prisoners to be sent to the mine, and I joined the ranks, straightened my gauntlets, and the guards counted us, gave the order, and went down a familiar road.

I never in my life saw Galina Pavlovna again.

1970–1971

LIOSHA CHEKANOV, OR, A FELLOW-ACCUSED IN KOLYMA

LIOSHA Chekanov, a hereditary Ukrainian farmer, a technical builder by education, was my neighbor in the bunks of cell No. 69 of Butyrki prison in the spring and summer of 1937.

As the cell elder, I gave Liosha Chekanov initial help, as I did for many others: I gave him his first injection, an injection of the elixir of good cheer, hope, sangfroid, anger, and self-respect—a complex medicinal mixture that a man needs in prison, especially if he is new to it. Gangsters express the same feeling—and one cannot deny their age-old experience—in the familiar three commandments: "Don't believe, don't be afraid, and don't ask."

Liosha Chekanov's spirit was fortified, and he set off in June for the distant Kolyma lands. He was condemned on the same day as me, under the same article of the Criminal Code, and to the same period of imprisonment. We were taken to Kolyma in the same railway carriage.

We underestimated the deviousness of the authorities: by the time we arrived, Kolyma was to change from paradise on earth to hell on earth.

We were taken to Kolyma to die, and beginning in December 1937 we were plunged into the Garanin shootings, beatings, starvation. The list of those to be shot was read out day and night.

All those who perished at Serpantinnaya—a pretrial prison of the mining administration where in 1938 tens of thousands were shot, the noise drowned out by the roar of tractor engines—were executed according to lists, which were read to the sound of a band playing a flourish twice a day at roll call, once for the day shift, once for the night shift.

After surviving these gory events by luck, I didn't escape my own fate, which had been marked out for me in Moscow: in 1943 I got a new ten-year sentence.

I was "drifting off" again and again, alternating between the pit face and the hospital, and by December 1943 I found myself at an outpost on a tiny team that was building a new mine, Spokoiny.

The guards—or as they were called in Kolyma, warders—were too high-ranking for me: they had a special mission, a special fate, whose trajectories could not intersect with mine.

Our warder was transferred somewhere. Every prisoner has a fate that is intertwined with the battles of some higher forces. An imprisoned human being, or a human prisoner, without being aware of it, becomes a tool in a battle that has nothing to do with him and perishes knowing the immediate reason but not the ultimate one. Or he knows the ultimate reason but not the immediate one.

It was according to the laws of this mysterious fate that our warder had been removed and transferred somewhere. I don't know and I had no need to know either the warder's surname or his new post.

A new warder was appointed to our brigade, which consisted of just ten goners.

Kolyma, and not just Kolyma, is distinct in that everyone there is a boss, everyone. Even a little brigade of two persons has a senior and a junior man; given the universality of the dual system, people are not always divided into equal parts; even two people aren't divided into equal parts. For every five men a permanent foreman is singled out, not that he is exempted from labor, of course: he is just as much a workman. When the brigade consists of fifty men, the foreman is always exempted, so that he is a foreman with a stick.

After all, you are living without hope, and the wheel of fate is inscrutable.

A tool of state politics, a means for physically annihilating the state's political enemies—this is the main role of a foreman in production, and even more so when the production is serving an extermination camp.

In such cases the foreman cannot protect anyone; he himself is doomed, but he will clamber upward, clutching at every straw that the bosses throw him, and he destroys other people for the sake of this illusory salvation.

For the authorities, choosing a foreman is a priority task.

The foreman seems to be the man who gives his brigade food and drink, but does so only within the limits set for him from above. He himself is strictly controlled, and there is little scope at the mines: the surveyor when he next measures out the pit face will unmask any false, overestimated cubic meters, and then that's the end of the foreman.

So the foreman proceeds along a well-trodden and reliable path: to get those cubic meters banged out of the workmen and goners, to bang them out in the literal, physical sense, hitting men's backs with a pickax, and when there is nothing left to bang out, the foreman, it would seem, has to become a workman himself and share the fate of the people he has killed.

But sometimes things are different. A foreman is transferred to a new brigade, to make sure his experience isn't wasted. He deals with the new brigade. The foreman stays alive, his brigade is buried in the ground.

Apart from the foreman, there is also his official deputy, the orderly, the murderer's assistant, who guards the foreman's sleep from any attacks.

When foremen were being hunted down during the war at Spokoiny, it was necessary to blow up a whole corner of the barracks, where the foreman was sleeping, with ammonite. That was a sure way of doing things. Both the foreman and the orderly died, as well as their close friends who slept next to the foreman so that an avenger's knife hand couldn't reach the foreman himself.

The crimes committed by foremen in Kolyma are beyond count: after all, they were the physical executives for Moscow's policies in the Stalin years.

But the foreman was himself subject to control. In everyday life he was watched by inspectors of the Special Camp Centers during the few hours when a prisoner is taken off work and sleeps in semi-oblivion.

The foreman was also watched by the head of the Special Camp Centers, and by the NKVD interrogator.

Everyone in Kolyma was keeping track of everyone else and denouncing them daily to the appropriate authority.

Informers and snitches experienced few scruples: they had to report everything so the bosses could then sort out what was true and what was not. Truth and lies were categories that did not concern an informer.

But this was all observation within the zone, within the camp soul. The bosses—guards were called, as in Sakhalin, so in Kolyma, warders—in charge of production also kept a very thorough and completely official watch on the foreman's work. The warder was watched by the senior warder, and the senior warder was watched by the sector's clerk of works, who was watched by the head of the sector, who was watched by the chief engineer and head of the mine. I don't want to go higher in that hierarchy, for it has too many bifurcations and is too varied, and it gives free range for the fantasies of any dogmatic or poetic inspiration.

What must be emphasized is that the foreman is the point where heaven and earth make contact in camp life.

The best foremen, ones who have proved their murderous enthusiasm, are recruited as warders, and warders have a rank far higher than the foremen. A warder has already traveled the foreman's bloodstained path. The warder's power over the workman is unlimited.

In the flickering light of a Kolyma kerosene lamp—an empty can with four holes for burning rag wicks and the only light for Kolyma workmen and goners except for the stoves and the sun—I made out something familiar in the figure of the new warder, the new master of our lives and deaths.

A joyful hope warmed my muscles. There was something familiar in the new warder's face. Something from the distant past, but real, eternally alive, like human memory.

It is very difficult to rake through one's memory in a withered, hungry brain: the effort of recalling is accompanied by a sharp pain, a purely physical pain.

The nooks and crannies of memory have already swept themselves clean of all unnecessary dirt, such as poetry. Some thought, more important, more everlasting than art, had tensed itself, rung out, yet was utterly unable to burst into my vocabulary at the time, into the few cerebral parts that the goner's brain still uses. Someone's iron fingers were pressing on the memory, like a tube of hardened glue, trying to squeeze out, to force out a drop, just a tiny drop that still had human properties.

This process of recall, which required one's whole body to take part—cold sweat breaking out on one's withered skin, except that there wasn't even sweat to help me speed up the process—ended with victory... A surname surfaced in my brain: Chekanov!

Yes, it was him, Liosha Chekanov, my neighbor in Butyrki prison, the man I had saved from fear of the interrogator. This salvation had appeared in my cold, hungry barracks: eight years, eight centuries, had passed, the twelfth century had come, Scythians were saddling their horses on Kolyma's rocks, Scythians were burying their kings in mausoleums, and millions of nameless workmen were piling into the common graves of Kolyma.

Yes, it was him, Liosha Chekanov, the companion of my bright youth, the bright illusions of the first half of 1937, which did not yet know the fate allotted to them.

Salvation had appeared in my cold, hungry barracks in the form of Liosha Chekanov, a technical builder by profession, our new warder.

That really was good news! This was a miraculous event, worth waiting eight years for!

"Drifting down"—I allow myself to claim priority for this neologism or, at least, for using it in the imperfect tense. A goner, a man who has "drifted down," doesn't do this in one day. Losses have to accumulate: first physical, then moral ones—the remains of the nerves, vessels, and tissue are no longer enough to retain old feelings.

In their place come new, ersatz feelings, ersatz hopes.

There is a limit in the process of drifting down when the last supports crumble; this is a boundary after which everything is beyond good and evil, and the process of drifting down accelerates like an avalanche. A chain reaction, to use modern terms.

At the time we didn't know about the atom bomb, about Hiroshima and Enrico Fermi.[8] But the uncontrollable and irreversible nature of drifting down was something we knew very well.

The gangster's slang has a brilliant insight into this chain reaction: it is a term that has found its way into the dictionary—"flying down the slope," an absolutely exact term, created without Fermi's equations.

384 · SKETCHES OF THE CRIMINAL WORLD

Some statistical sets and many memoirs have noted the precise, historically devised formula: "A man can drift down in two weeks." Two weeks was the norm for a strong man if he was required to do heavy labor in the minus sixty Kolyma cold, and beaten, fed only camp rations, and prevented from sleeping.

That was why Medvedev's children still can't understand why their father died so quickly—a healthy man of about forty, especially as he sent his first letter from the ship at Magadan, and the second from the hospital at Seimchan, the hospital letter being the last. That was why General Gorbatov, when he ended up at the Maldiak mine, became a complete invalid in two weeks, and only his luck in being sent to the fishing port of Ola saved his life. That was why Orlov, Kirov's consultant, by the time he was executed at Partisan in the winter of 1938, was already a goner who would never, in any case, have found his place on earth.

Two weeks is the time needed to turn a healthy man into a goner.

I knew all that, I understood that there was no salvation in work, and I alternated between the hospital and the pit face for eight years. Finally, salvation had come. At the moment when it was most needed, the hand of providence had brought Liosha Chekanov to our barracks.

I calmly went to sleep and slept a deep, happy slumber with a vague feeling of some joyful event that was about to happen any minute.

At roll call the next day—roll call was what the procedure for taking people off for work at Kolyma was called, and it happens for warders and for millions of men at the same hour of the day, when the iron rail is struck, just like the call of the muezzin, or the ringing of the bell on Ivan the Great's bell tower (the Terrible and the Great are synonyms in Russian)—I was convinced that I was miraculously right, that I was right to have a miraculous hope.

The new warder really was Liosha Chekanov.

But just recognizing someone else in this situation is not enough: you have to be recognized in this two-sided mutual radiation process.

It was only too clear from Liosha Chekanov's face that he had recognized me and, of course, would help me. Liosha Chekanov smiled warmly.

There and then he asked the foreman about my work conduct. The reference he got was negative.

"Well, you son of a whore," Liosha said loudly, looking me in the eye, "do you think that you don't need to work, just because we were in the same prison? I don't help shirkers. Earn it by working. By honest work."

From then on I was persecuted more energetically than ever. A few days later Liosha Chekanov declared at roll call: "I don't want to hit you for your bad work, I'm just sending you to the sector, to the zone. That's the place for you sons of whores. You'll go to Polupan's brigade. He'll teach you what life's all about. Or else you might think you've got a friend! From the outside! A pal! It's sons of bitches like you who've destroyed us. All these eight years I've been suffering because of reptiles like you, booklovers!"

That evening the foreman took me and a packet of documents off to the sector. At the central sector of the administration of Spokoiny mine I was put in a barracks where Polupan's brigade lived.

I met the warder himself the next morning at roll call.

Sergei Polupan, the warder, was a young man of about twenty-five, with an open face and a fair forelock, like a gangster's. But he wasn't a gangster. He was a former peasant boy. Polupan had been swept up by the iron broom in 1937 and given a sentence under article 58: he told the bosses he would redeem his guilt by making honest men out of the enemies of the people.

The offer was accepted and Polupan's brigade was turned into something like a punishment squad with a sliding, ever-changing list of names. A punishment center in the punishment center itself, a prison within a prison in the worst punishment mine, which did not yet exist. We were building a zone and a settlement for it.

A barracks made of green larch beams, unseasoned beams of a tree that, like the people of the Far North, struggles to stay alive and is therefore full of contortions and gnarls, with a twisted trunk. These unseasoned barracks could not be warmed by any stove. There was never enough firewood to dry these three-hundred-year-old bodies that had grown up in a marsh. The barracks were dried by human beings, by the bodies of the builders.

This is where one of my passions began.

Every day, in front of the whole brigade, Sergei Polupan beat me:

with his feet, his fists, with a log, a pickax handle, a spade. He was beating the literacy out of me.

The beatings were repeated every day. Warder Polupan was wearing a warm jacket, a pink calfskin jacket that someone had given him, or bribed him with to be relieved of his fists, to get a longed-for break, if only for a day.

I know a lot of situations like that. I didn't have a jacket myself, and if I had, I wouldn't have given it to Polupan—probably the gangsters would have pulled it off my arms or ripped it off my shoulders.

When he got worked up, Polupan would take off his jacket and wear just his quilted jacket, so that he could swing his crowbar and pickax more freely.

Polupan knocked several of my teeth out and broke a rib.

All that was done in front of the whole brigade. Polupan's brigade had twenty men in it. It had a sliding, changing composition; it was an apprentice brigade.

The morning beatings went on as long as I was at that Spokoiny mine.

After a report from warder Polupan, confirmed by the head of the mine and the bosses of the Special Camp Center, I was sent to the Central Northern Administration, to the settlement of Yagodny, as a malicious shirker, for a new criminal case and a new sentence.

I was under investigation in solitary confinement at Yagodny; a case was started, and interrogations were in progress. Liosha Chekanov's initiative was pretty clearly marked.

This was the spring of 1941, a bright Kolyma wartime spring.

In solitary, those under investigation are still made to go to work, in an attempt to extract at least one working hour from the transit day, and none of the prisoners under investigation liked this deep-rooted camp and transit prison tradition.

But the reason I went to work was not, of course, to try to dig the norm in a stone pit but simply to get a breath of air, to ask for an extra bowl of soup, if there was any.

In a town, a camp town such as Yagodny, things were better than in solitary, where every wooden beam smelled of the sweat of death.

For going out to work we were given soup and bread, or soup and porridge, or soup and a herring. I will still find time to write a hymn to Kolyma herring, the prisoner's only protein—for the protein balance in Kolyma is not maintained by meat. It was herring that chucked the last logs to stoke a goner's energy. And if the goner managed to stay alive, it was because he was eating herring, salted of course, and drinking: water didn't count in that lethal balanced diet.

Above all, when you were outside you could indulge in tobacco, have a smoke, a sniff when a fellow prisoner was smoking if you didn't get a smoke yourself. Not a single prisoner believed in the harmfulness of nicotine or the carcinogenic nature of tobacco. In any case, it could be explained by the nicotine, a drop of which can kill a horse.

"Taking a puff," just one draw, certainly gave you not much poison but a lot of dreamy satisfaction.

Tobacco was the prisoner's greatest pleasure; it meant a continuation of life. I repeat that I don't know whether life is a blessing or not.

Trusting only my animal instinct, I moved down the streets of Yagodny. I worked, I crowbarred pits, scraped with my spade so as to scrape up something for the pillars of the settlement I knew so well. I had been tried there only a year earlier and given ten years, and classified as an "enemy of the people." This ten-year sentence, a new one, which had begun so recently, prevented, of course, my having a new case started against me for refusing to work. A sentence could be extended for refusals and for shirking, but when the new sentence had only just started it was difficult.

We were taken out to work under heavy guard: all the same we were men under investigation, if we were still human . . .

I took my place in the stone pit and tried to have a good look at people passing by: we happened to be working on the road, and in winter no new paths are made in Kolyma, not in Magadan or on the Indigirka.

The chain of pits stretched along the street. Our guards, however many of them there were, were spaced out outside the boundary set according to instructions.

Along our pits, a large brigade, or rather a group of people not yet split into brigades, was coming toward us. To make brigades, people had to be divided into groups of no fewer than three men and given guards armed with rifles. These people had only just been unloaded from a truck, which was still standing there.

A soldier from the escort guards that had brought the people to our Special Camp Center at Yagodny asked our guard something.

Suddenly I heard a voice, a heartrending, joyful yell: "Shalamov! Shalamov!"

It was Rodionov from Polupan's brigade, a hard worker and a goner, like me, from the punishment center of Spokoiny.

"Shalamov! I've killed Polupan. I took an ax to him in the refectory. I'm being taken in for interrogation for it. To my death!" Rodionov was dancing in ecstasy. "In the refectory with an ax."

That joyful news genuinely gave me a warm feeling.

The guards pulled us apart.

My investigation petered out and I wasn't charged with a new sentence. Someone high up decided that the state would not gain much by giving me yet another new sentence.

I was released from the pretrial prison and sent on one of the vitamin expeditions.

I don't know how the investigation of Polupan's murder ended. At the time quite a few foremen had their heads staved in with an ax, while in our vitamin team gangsters took a two-handed cross-saw and sawed the head off a much-hated foreman.

I never again met Liosha Chekanov, my acquaintance from Butyrki prison.

1970–1971

THIRD-CLASS TRIANGULATION

IN THE summer of 1939, washed ashore by storm waves onto the marshy banks of Black Lake, assigned to a coal prospecting team as an invalid unfit for work after spending 1938 at the pit face of the Partisan gold mine, and subject to execution by shooting but not actually shot, I did not think at night about what had happened to me and how it had happened. "What for?" was a question that didn't arise where man and the state were concerned.

But, weak willed as I was, I wanted somebody to tell me the secret of my own life.

The spring and summer of 1939 saw me in the taiga, and I was still unable to understand who I was; I couldn't understand that my life was continuing. I seemed to have died at the gold-mine pit faces of Partisan in 1938.

First of all, I had to find out whether 1938 had actually existed. Or was that year delirium, it doesn't matter whose—mine or yours, or history's.

My neighbors, the five men who had arrived with me from Magadan a few months earlier, couldn't tell me anything: their lips were sealed forever, their tongues tied forever. I didn't expect anything else of them. They were Vasilenko the boss, Frizorger the hard worker, Nagibin the skeptic. They even included the snitch Gordeyev. Altogether, they constituted Russia.

It wasn't from them that I expected a confirmation of my suspicions, a check on my feelings and thoughts. And it wasn't from the bosses, of course.

The head prospector Paramonov, when he was getting "people" in Magadan for his district, confidently chose invalids. This former head of Maldiak was well aware of how they died and how they clung to life. And how quickly they forgot.

After a period—perhaps many months, or maybe immediately— Paramonov felt there'd been enough rest, and that we invalids were no longer invalids. But Filippovsky was a locomotive driver, Frizorger was a carpenter, Nagibin was a stove maker, and Vasilenko was a mining foreman. Only I, a Russian writer, turned out to be suitable for manual labor.

I was already being taken out for this manual labor. The warder Bystrov gave a contemptuous look at my filthy, louse-ridden body, my ulcerating leg wounds, the marks left after scratching louse bites, the hungry shine in my eyes, and he pronounced with enjoyment his favorite joke: "What sort of work do you want? Nonmanual? Or manual? We don't have nonmanual work. We only have manual work."

At the time I was a boilermaker. But the bathhouse had been built some time ago, and the water was boiled there: I had to be sent somewhere.

A tall man in a cheap new blue suit, a free man's clothes, was standing on a stump outside the tent.

Bystrov was a construction warder, a free man, a former prisoner who had come to Black Lake to earn money so as to get back to the mainland. "You'll go to the mainland wearing a top hat," joked his boss, Paramonov. Bystrov loathed me. Bystrov saw literate people as the main evil in life. He saw me as the incarnation of all his troubles. His hatred and vindictiveness were blind and vicious.

Bystrov spent 1938 at the gold mine as a warder. He dreamed of raking in as much as he used to rake in. But his dreams were destroyed by the wave that swept away everyone and everything: the wave of 1937.

Now he was living without a penny to his name in that accursed Kolyma where enemies of the people were refusing to work.

He would have liked to beat me, but he didn't have the authority. I had passed through the same hell, only from below, from the pit face, the wheelbarrow, and the pickax, and Bystrov knew about it because he had seen it: our history was written for all to see on our faces, on our bodies.

The question of manual and nonmanual work—his only witticism

—was put to me a second time by Bystrov, although I had already given him my answer in the spring. But Bystrov had forgotten. Perhaps he hadn't forgotten and repeated it on purpose, enjoying the opportunity to put the question to me. Whom had he asked before, and where?

Perhaps I had imagined all this, and Bystrov didn't care in the least what he asked me and what answer he got.

Perhaps the whole of Bystrov is just my inflamed brain that refuses to forgive anything.

In a word, I got a new job as a topographer's assistant, or, to be precise, a rod man.

A free topographer had arrived at Black Lake coal sector. He was a member of the Communist Youth, a journalist on the Ishim newspaper, Ivan Nikolayevich Bosykh. He was my age and had been convicted under article 58, paragraph 10, and sentenced to three years, not five as I was. He had been convicted considerably earlier than I had, in 1936, and immediately brought to Kolyma. Just like me, he spent 1938 at the pit face and in the hospital; he had been drifting down but, to his own amazement, survived and even got papers allowing him to leave. He was here now for a job of short duration, making a topographical "tie-in" for Magadan of the Black Lake district.

So I was going to be his workman, carrying the rod, the theodolite. If two rod men were needed, we would take on another workman. But everything that could be done by two men, we would do together.

Because of my weakness, I couldn't carry the theodolite on my shoulders, but Ivan Nikolayevich Bosykh carried it himself. I carried just the rod, but even that was too heavy for me, until I got used to it.

At that time, acute hunger, the hunger of the gold mine, had passed, but my greed was still the same, and as before, I ate everything I could see and grab hold of.

The first time we went out to work and sat down to rest in the taiga, Ivan Nikolayevich unwrapped a parcel of food—for me. I didn't need it, but I wasn't shy, and I picked at the biscuits, butter, and bread. Ivan Nikolayevich was astounded by my modesty, but I explained my reasons.

A native Siberian, a man with a classic Russian surname, Ivan Nikolayevich Bosykh tried to get me to give him an answer to insoluble questions.

It was obvious that the topographer was no snitch. Snitches weren't needed in 1938; everything was done regardless of the snitches' intentions, following higher laws of human society.

"Did you go and see the doctors when you fell ill?"

"No, I was afraid of Legkodukh, the paramedic at the Partisan mine. He didn't try to save the drifters."

"When I was at Utina, Dr. Beridze was the man who decided my fate."

Kolyma doctors can commit two sorts of crimes: crimes of action, when the doctor sends you to a punishment zone for a bullet. After all, by law, no certification of a refusal to work can be signed without doctors sanctioning it. That's one type of crime in Kolyma. The other sort of medical crimes are crimes of inaction. Beridze was a case of crime by inaction. "He did nothing to help me, he didn't care about my complaints. I had turned into a goner, but I hadn't yet managed to die. Why have you and I survived?" asked Ivan Nikolayevich. "Because we're journalists. That explanation makes sense. We know how to cling to life to the very end."

"I think that's more like animals than journalists."

"Not at all. Animals are weaker than humans in the struggle for life."

I didn't argue. I knew all that myself. That a horse dies in the north, unable to stand a season at the gold-mine pit face; that a dog dies if fed human rations.

Another time, Ivan Nikolayevich talked about family problems.

"I'm a bachelor. My father died in the Civil War. My mother died when I was in prison. I have nobody to hand down my hatred, or my love, or my knowledge to. But I do have a brother, a younger one. He believes in me as if I were a god. So I live in order to get to the mainland, to the city of Ishim, into our apartment on Vorontsov Street, number two, to look my brother in the eye and tell him the whole truth. Get it?"

"Yes," I said. "That's a goal worth pursuing."

Every day, and there were a lot of them, for more than a month, Ivan Nikolayevich would bring me his food—it was no different from our Polar Circle rations and I, so as not to offend the topographer, shared his bread and butter.

Bosykh even brought me his alcohol: free workers were given alcohol.

"I don't drink."

I did drink. This spirit was such low proof after going through several warehouses and several bosses, that Bosykh was not risking anything. It was almost water.

In 1937 Bosykh had spent several days at Partisan, in the days when Berzin was still in charge, and was present when the famous Gerasimov brigade was arrested. That was a mysterious case few people know about. When I was brought to Partisan on August 14, 1937, and put in a tarpaulin tent, there was a low wooden-log barracks, half a dugout, opposite our tent; the doors hung on just one hinge. Door hinges in Kolyma are not made of iron but of a piece of truck tire. The old hands explained to me that Gerasimov's brigade had lived in that barracks: seventy-five men, Trotskyists who did no work at all.

In 1936 the brigade had gone on a hunger strike several times and forced Moscow to concede them permission not to work; they got a "production" ration, not a punishment one. Food then came in four "categories"—the camp used philosopher's terms like "category" in the most inappropriate contexts: "Stakhanov" rations, when the norm was achieved by 130 percent or more, was a kilo of bread; "shock worker's," from 110 to 130 percent, was 800 grams; "production," from 90 to 100 percent, was 600 grams; and "punishment" was 300 grams. During my time there, those who refused to work were put on punishment rations, just bread and water. But it didn't stay that way.

In 1935 and 1936 there was a struggle, and thanks to a series of hunger strikes the Trotskyists at the Partisan mine got their legitimate 600 grams.

They were deprived of access to the shop, of orders for paid extras, but they weren't forced to work. The main essential was heating, since winter lasts ten months in Kolyma. They were allowed to travel to fetch firewood for themselves and the rest of the camp. Those were the conditions under which Gerasimov's brigade existed at Partisan mine.

If anyone at any time of the day or night expressed a desire to move to a "normal" brigade, he was immediately transferred. On the other hand, anyone who refused to work could be taken straight from roll call not just to an Intensive Regime Squad or a Punishment Squad or to solitary confinement but to Gerasimov's brigade. In the spring of 1937 there were seventy-five men living in that barracks. One night that spring they were all driven away to Serpantinnaya, which was then the pretrial prison of the Northern Mining Administration.

Nobody ever saw any of them again. Ivan Nikolayevich Bosykh had seen these people, but all I saw was their barracks door open to the wind.

Ivan Nikolayevich explained to me the tricks of the topographer's trade: starting from the tripod we would set out a number of pegs in the ravine, put the theodolite on the tripod, and catch them in the "crosshairs."

"Topography's a nice piece of work. Better than medicine."

We cut clearings, wrote numbers on the notches we hacked, notches that oozed yellow pitch. We used an ordinary black pencil to write the numbers, only black graphite, the brother of diamonds, was reliable: any chemical colors, blue or green, were no use for measuring the earth.

The area we were exploring was gradually surrounded by an easily imagined line through clearings in which the theodolite's eye could detect a number on the next pillar.

The streams and rivulets were already freezing under a white coating of ice. Small autumn leaves covered our paths, and Ivan Nikolayevich began to hurry.

"I need to get back to Magadan and hand my work over to the administration as fast as I can, get my pay, and leave. The ships are still sailing. I'm being well paid, but I've got to hurry. There are two reasons for my being in a hurry. First, I want to get to the mainland: three years in Kolyma are enough to learn about life. Although they say that the mainland is still foggy for travelers like you and me. But I have to be bold for a second reason."

"What is the second reason?"

"The second reason is that I'm not a topographer. I'm a journalist, a newspaper man. I learned topography here in Kolyma at the Razvedchik mine, where I was rod man to a topographer. I learned all the tricks of the trade, since I couldn't rely on Dr. Beridze. It was my boss who advised me to take this work, tying in Black Lake to the places it needed to be tied in to. But I've got some things wrong and left some things out. And I haven't got time to start this tie-in all over again."

"So that's it..."

"The work you and I have been doing is rough topography. It's called third-class triangulation. But there are superior sorts—second class and first class. I can't think about them, and I'm not likely ever to have anything to do with them."

We said goodbye, and Ivan Nikolayevich left for Magadan.

The next year, the summer of 1940, although I had been working with prospectors using my pickax and spade, I had another stroke of luck: a new topographer from Magadan began a second tie-in. I was assigned to him as an experienced rod man, but of course I never said a word about Ivan Nikolayevich's doubts. All the same, I asked the new topographer about what had happened to Ivan Bosykh.

"The bastard's been on the mainland for ages. Now we're putting his work right," the new topographer uttered gloomily.

1973

WHEELBARROW I

THE GOLDEN season is short. There's a lot of gold, but how do you get it out? The gold fever at Klondike, the overseas neighbor of Chukotka, was able to revive the dead, and in a very short time. But was it possible to rein in that gold fever, to calm the feverish pulse of the prospector and the gold miner, to slow it down so that it was barely detectable, so that life became just a smoldering ember in dying people? The answer was more striking than Klondike. It was a result that the person who picks up the sifting tray or the barrow, the actual miner, wouldn't know about. The person who mines the gold is just a miner, just a digger, just a stonemason. He's not interested in the gold in his barrow. And not even because he's not supposed to be but because of hunger, cold, physical and spiritual emaciation.

It is difficult, but it is possible to ship a million people to Kolyma and give them work for a summer. But what are these people to do in the winter? Get drunk in Dawson? Or in Magadan? How do you occupy a hundred thousand or a million men in winter? Kolyma's climate is severely continental; the temperature drops to minus sixty in winter, and if it's only minus fifty-five, then it's a working day.

All through the winter of 1938 the temperature was documented, and prisoners stayed in their barracks only if the temperature was minus fifty-six or lower, Celsius, of course, not Fahrenheit.

In 1940 this minimum temperature was changed to minus fifty-two!

How can you colonize the region?

In 1936 a solution was found.

Removal and preparation of the subsoil by explosive and pickax and loading that subsoil were inseparably linked. The engineers worked out the optimal movement of the wheelbarrow, the time it took to bring it back, the time it took to fill it using spades and pickaxes and sometimes crowbars to take apart a gold-bearing rock.

Nobody actually wheeled a barrow for their own benefit: that was done only by prospectors working on their own. The state organized work differently for prisoners.

While the barrow man was pushing the wheelbarrow, his comrades or comrade had to get another wheelbarrow filled.

So this was a calculation of the number of men needed for loading and barrowing. Were two men enough to form a chain, or were three needed?

In this gold-mine pit face the barrows always came in twos. It was a peculiar sort of conveyor to allow nonstop work.

If work had to be done by horse-drawn carts, this was done on the "covering," when peat was removed in summer.

The phrase needs explaining: in gold mining the "peat" is the layer that is not gold-bearing, whereas "sand" is the gold-bearing layer.

All the summer work with a horse-drawn cart was to remove the peat and expose the sand. Once exposed, it was carted away by other brigades, not by us. But we didn't care.

The horse-drawn carts also came in pairs. We uncoupled the pit-pony man's empty cart and replaced it with a loaded one we had already prepared. The Kolyma conveyor belt was operational.

The gold-mining season is short. From the second half of May to the middle of September: three months in all.

That was why, in order to meet the plan's deadlines, all sorts of technical and supertechnical solutions were thought up.

A pit-face conveyor belt would have been too elementary a solution, even though the two-barrow system took away all our strength, threatened to finish us off, turned us into goners.

There was no mechanization, except for a cable route operated on a loop winch. The pit-face conveyor was Berzin's contribution to the system. As soon as it became clear that every mine would have an assured supply of slave workers at any cost and in any quantity—even if Far East Construction had to bring in a hundred ships a day—people were no longer spared. And the plan began to be literally deadlined. This was with full approval, understanding, and support from above, from Moscow.

But what about the gold? It had been known for three hundred years that there was gold in Kolyma. When Far East Construction became active in Kolyma, there were a lot of organizations—useless, lacking authority, afraid of overstepping some line with the workers they had recruited. There were offices of precious metals and gold and cultural centers, all working with free men recruited in Vladivostok.

Berzin brought prisoners.

Berzin didn't bother to look for paths: he began to build a road, a Kolyma highway that stretched from the sea across the marshes and mountains...

date unknown

WHEELBARROW II

THE WHEELBARROW is a symbol of the era; its emblem is the prisoner's wheelbarrow.

> The Special Tribunal is a machine
> With two handles and just one wheel.

The Special Tribunal involved a minister, a People's Commissar, and OGPU (the secret police); its signature, without any trial, was enough to dispatch millions of men to their death in the Far North. Every personal file, a cardboard folder, slim and new, had two documents in it: one was an extract from the Special Tribunal's decision, and the other was a special instruction that prisoner X was to be used only for heavy manual labor and that X was to be deprived of any opportunity to use the post or the telegraph, that he had no right to correspondence. Additionally, the camp authorities were to inform Moscow of prisoner X's conduct at least once every six months. A similar memorandum or report was to be sent to the local administration once a month. "To serve his sentence in Kolyma" was a death sentence, a synonym for a killing, slow or fast, depending on the inclination of the local chief of the gold or ore mine, or of the Special Camp Center.

This nice new slim folder was to acquire a whole pile of information: it would swell with documentation about refusals to work, copies of denunciations of the prisoner by his comrades, memorandums from the investigative organs about all and every kind of "data." Sometimes the folder didn't last long enough to swell: quite a few people perished during their first summer of intercourse with the "Special Tribunal machine" and its two handles and one wheel.

I was one of those whose file became swollen and so heavy that the paper seemed to be saturated with blood. And the writing never fades, for human blood is a good fixative.

In Kolyma a wheelbarrow is called "minor mechanization." I was a highly qualified barrow man. I pushed my wheelbarrow in the open pit faces of the Partisan mine in gold-bearing Far East Construction Kolyma all of the autumn of 1937. In winter, when the gold season and the panning season are over, boxes of subsoil were carted in Kolyma: four men took each box, moving mountains of spoil, taking off the peat shirt and exposing the sand, the gold-bearing layer, for summer. In the early spring of 1938, I took up the handles of the Special Tribunal machine again and dropped them only in December 1938, when I was arrested at the mine and driven off to Magadan as an accused in the Kolyma lawyers' case.

A barrow man chained to his wheelbarrow is the emblem of tsarist penal servitude on the island of Sakhalin. But Sakhalin was no Kolyma. Sakhalin was surrounded by the warm Kuroshio Current. It is even warmer in Sakhalin than in Magadan, on the coast, where it is only minus thirty to minus forty degrees, and there is snow in winter and rain in summer. But the gold is not in Magadan. The Yablonovy Pass, at a thousand meters above sea level, is the boundary of the gold-mining climate. At a thousand meters above sea level, it is the first serious pass on the road to gold. A hundred kilometers from Magadan and farther along the highway things get higher and higher, colder and colder.

Sakhalin's penal servitude was not the example we followed. Being chained to a wheelbarrow was more of a moral torment. Just as shackles were. In tsarist times, shackles didn't weigh much, and they were easy to remove from your legs. Parties of prisoners walked thousands of kilometers in those shackles. They were a means of humiliating people.

In Kolyma people weren't chained to their wheelbarrows. For a few days in the spring of 1938, I had working with me as a partner Derfel, a French communist from Cayenne, who'd been in the prisoners' stone quarries there. Derfel spent two years doing French penal servitude. It was nothing like ours. It was easier there, it was warm, and there were no politicals. There was no hunger, no cold, no frostbitten hands and feet.

Derfel died at the pit face: his heart stopped. But the Cayenne experience was still helpful to him: he held out at the pit face a month longer than his fellow workers. Was that good or bad? It was an extra month of suffering.

Alternating with Derfel, I pushed a wheelbarrow for the very first time.

You can't love a wheelbarrow. You can only hate it. Like any physical work, the work of a barrow man is infinitely degrading because of its enslaved, Kolyma nature. But, like any physical work, working with a wheelbarrow requires a few habits to be learned, some attention, and some self-sacrifice.

When your body understands these few things, pushing the barrow becomes easier than swinging a pickax, hitting with a crowbar, scraping with a shovel.

The difficulty lies entirely in balancing, in keeping the wheel on the gangway, which is a narrow board.

An article 58 prisoner gets only a pickax, a long-handled spade, a set of crowbars for making holes, an iron spoon to scrape the subsoil out of the drill holes. And a barrow. There is no other work. There is no place for an article 58er by the panning equipment, where you have to "scrub," scraping the soil with a wooden scraper, moving it up and down to push around and break up the subsoil. Work at the scrubber is for nonpolitical prisoners. The work is rather easier and you get closer to the gold. It is forbidden for an article 58er to work over the scrubbing pan. He is allowed to work with a horse: pit-pony men are recruited from article 58ers. But a horse is a delicate creature, subject to all sorts of illnesses. The grooms, the grooms' bosses, and the pit-pony men steal the horse's northern rations. The horse grows weak and dies in temperatures of minus sixty before a human being does. There are so many additional problems that a wheelbarrow seems simpler and better than the horse-drawn cart, and you feel less dishonest, because you are closer to death.

The state plan goes as far as the mine, the sector, the pit face, the brigade, the pair of workers. A brigade consists of pairs or trios, and each pair or trio gets wheelbarrows. A pair or a trio as necessary, but never just one barrow.

This is a big production secret, the Kolyma hard-labor secret.

There is another job in the brigade, a permanent one that every workman dreams of every morning: this is the tool-carrier's job.

Pickaxes quickly get blunt when they hit stone. Crowbars blunt quickly. Slaves have the right to demand good tools, and the bosses try hard to do everything to keep tools sharp, spades easy to handle, barrow wheels well greased.

Every productive gold sector has its own smithy, where a blacksmith and a hammer man can flatten a pickax and sharpen a crowbar. The blacksmith has a lot of work, and the only moment when a prisoner can rest is when he has no tool because it's been taken to the blacksmith. Of course, he doesn't sit around: he sweeps up the pit face, he fills the barrow. But all the same . . .

So this is the work, carrying tools, which every man would like to get, if only for a day, or just until lunchtime.

The authorities have studied the blacksmith question thoroughly. There were many suggestions about how to improve the use and supply of tools, to change ways of doing things that hindered the fulfillment of the plan, so as to make the hand of the authorities weigh even more heavily on the prisoners' shoulders.

Isn't there some analogy with the engineers working to find a technical solution to the scientific problem of creating an atom bomb? Herein lies the advantage of physics, as Fermi and Einstein used to say.

What do I care about the human being, the slave? I'm an engineer and I am responsible for technical questions.

Indeed, during a consultation in Kolyma on how best to organize labor at a gold-mine pit face, that is, on the best and quickest way to kill people, an engineer spoke up, saying that he could transform Kolyma if he was given portable furnaces, portable blacksmith's furnaces. With such furnaces, all the problems would be solved. Tools would no longer have to be carried off. The tool carriers would have to pick up wheelbarrow handles and move around the pit face, not be hanging around at the smithy, not holding everyone and everything up.

The tool carrier in our brigade was a boy, a sixteen-year-old schoolboy from Erevan, accused of attempting to assassinate Khandjian, the first secretary of the Erevan District Committee. The boy had been sentenced to twenty years in prison, and he died very soon: he couldn't withstand the severity of a Kolyma winter. It turned out that Beria personally shot Khandjian in his office. By some chance I have never forgotten the whole case, and the boy's death at a Kolyma pit face.

I very much wanted to be a tool carrier, if only for a day, but I understood that the boy, a schoolboy with his frostbitten fingers wrapped in filthy mitts, with a hungry gleam in his eyes, was a better candidate than I was.

So I was left with just the wheelbarrow. I had to know how to use a pickax and cope with a spade, as well as drill with a crowbar: all very well, but in that stone pit for an open gold seam I preferred the wheelbarrow.

The gold-mining season is short—from the middle of May to the middle of September. But even when the daytime heat reaches forty degrees in July, there is icy water under a prisoner's feet. We worked in rubber boots. But, as with the tools, there was a shortage of rubber boots at the pit face.

The bottom of the open seam, an irregular-shaped stone pit, was paved with thick boards, not just laid but packed close in a special engineering way, a central gangway. The width of this gangway was half a meter, no more. The gangway was reinforced so that it didn't move, so that the boards didn't overhang, and the wheels didn't wander, and the barrow man could push his barrow at a run.

The gangway was about three hundred meters long. There was one in each open seam; it was part of the seam, its soul, the soul of hard labor with the application of minor mechanization.

Side paths led off the gangway: there were a lot of them branching to every pit face, to each corner of the seam. Boards led to each brigade; these were not so well fixed as the central gangway, but they were reliable enough.

The larch slabs of the central gangway, worn down by the barrow's frantically spinning wheel—for the gold-mining season is short—were constantly replaced with new ones. Just as the men were.

You had to use skill to wheel onto the central gangway: you pushed the barrow out from your own gangway, turned it around without getting the wheel into the main rut that had been worn into the middle of the board and that stretched out like a ribbon or a snake—not that there are any snakes in Kolyma—from the pit face to the trestlework, from the beginning to the very end, the bunker. It was important, once you pushed the barrow onto the central gangway, to turn it, keeping it balanced with your own muscles and, seizing the right moment, shift into a frantic run onto the central gangway, where you wouldn't be overtaken or left behind, for there was no room for overtaking, and you had to push your barrow up at a gallop, up and up along the central gangway that slowly rose on its supports, relentlessly upward, at a gallop, so that you weren't knocked off the boards by people who were well-fed or who were new to the job.

You couldn't hang around, and you had to watch out in case others knocked you off, until you got your barrow onto the trestlework, which was three meters high. That was the limit, since the bunker was wooden and lined with beams, and you then had to tip your barrow over into the bunker, which was the end of your responsibility. An iron wagon passed under the trestlework, and this wagon was taken off to the gold-washing equipment, the scrubber, not you. The wagon went along rails to the scrubber for the soil to be washed. But that was none of your business.

You then had to tip the barrow handles up, empty it all over the bunker—the best bit!—and then grab the empty barrow and quickly move aside to look around, catch your breath, and give way to anyone who was still being fed well.

There was a secondary gangway, made of worn-out old boards from the central gangway, but still solid and properly nailed down, leading back from the trestlework to the pit face. You had to give way to anyone running toward you, let them pass, and take your barrow off the gangway—you would hear the warning shout—if you didn't want to be pushed off. You had to get a rest somehow—cleaning the barrow or letting others pass, for you had to remember: when you get back along the spare gangway to your pit face, you won't get a minute's rest, a new barrow will be waiting for you on the work gangway, which your fellow workers will have filled for you while you were pushing the first barrow to the trestlework.

That's why you had to remember: the art of pushing a barrow consists of wheeling the empty barrow back down the spare gangway in quite a different way from the way you pushed the loaded barrow up. An empty barrow has to be turned up, so that the wheel is in front, and your fingers are on the now upright handles of the barrow. This is your rest, economizing your strength, letting the blood flow back from your arms. The barrow man comes back with his arms raised. The blood flows back. The barrow man preserves his strength.

When you've wheeled your barrow back to the pit face, you just abandon it. There's another barrow ready for you on the working gangway, and nobody can stand idle at the pit face, motionless, not shifting, at least nobody with article 58. Under the harsh gaze of the foreman, the warder, the guard, the head of the Special Camp Center, the head of the mine, you grab the other barrow by the handles and move onto the central gangway: that's what is called a conveyor, a replacement barrow. One of the most terrible laws of production, which is always closely watched over.

It's good if your own fellow workers are merciful—you can't expect that from the foreman but you can from the senior man in your pair or trio—after all, there are seniors and juniors everywhere, and everybody has an opportunity to become the senior, even if they are article 58ers. If your fellow workers are merciful and let you just get your breath back. There's no chance of a break for a smoke. Smoking in 1938 was a political crime, sabotage, to be punished under article 58, paragraph 14.

No. Your fellow workers keep an eye out to make sure you don't cheat the state and don't rest when you're not supposed to. They need you to earn your ration. Your comrades don't want to have to do your work for you, or to compensate for your hatred, your anger, your hunger and cold. And if your comrades don't care one way or another—and there were few such in 1938 in Kolyma—then the foreman will care for them, and if the foreman's gone off somewhere to get warm, he will have left an official observer to take his place, a workman who is the assistant foreman. That was how Dr. Krivitsky, the former deputy of the People's Commissariat for Industry,[9] drank my blood for days on end in the Kolyma special zone.

And if the foreman doesn't see you, then the guard or warder will, or the clerk of works, or the head of the sector, or the head of the mine. An armed guard will see you and teach you with the butt of his rifle not to take liberties. You'll be seen by whoever's been put on duty at the mine by the local party organization; you'll be seen by the district NKVD officer and a network of his informers. You'll be seen by the representative of the Western, Northern, and Southwestern Administrations of Far East Construction or of Magadan itself, or by a Moscow representative of the Gulag. Everyone watches your every movement: all the literature and all the journalism, whether you took time off for a crap—it's hard to unbutton your trousers, because your hands won't bend. They unbend to fit the pickax handle and the wheelbarrow handle. They suffer from virtual contractions. But the guard shouts: "Where's your shit? Where's your shit, huh?"

And he waves his rifle butt at you. The guard doesn't need to know about pellagra, scurvy, or dysentery.

That's why the barrow man rests as he moves.

Our tale about wheelbarrows is now interrupted by a document: an extensive quotation from an article, "The Problem of the Wheelbarrow," published in the newspaper *Soviet Kolyma* in November 1936:

> For a period we are forced to link the problem of removing soil, turf, and sand closely to the problem of the wheelbarrow. It is hard to say how long this period will last, during which we will be carrying out soil removal manually by wheelbarrow, but we can with reasonable precision say that the pace of productivity and the cost of production are to an enormous degree dependent on the construction of the wheelbarrow. The fact is that these wheelbarrows turn out to have a volume of only 0.075 cubic meters, whereas we need a minimum volume of 0.12 cubic meters ... Our mines in the next few years require several tens of thousands of wheelbarrows. If these barrows don't meet all the requirements that the workers and the pace of productivity themselves demand, then, first, we shall be slowing down produc-

tion, second, we will be using the muscular strength of the workers unproductively, and third, we will be pointlessly wasting enormous financial resources.

That is all true. There is only one inaccurate statement: in and after 1937, it wasn't several tens of thousands but several millions of the bigger, tenth-of-a-cubic-meter barrows that were needed, barrows that "corresponded to the demands of the workers themselves."

Many, many years after this article, about thirty years later, a good friend of mine was given an apartment, and we gathered at his house-warming party. Everyone gave him whatever present they could, and a very useful one was a lampshade with wires. In the 1960s you could already buy such lampshades in Moscow.

Men were utterly unable to cope with wiring up this gift. It was then that I came in, and a woman I knew yelled, "Take your coat off and show these useless jerks that a Kolyma man can do anything, has learned every trade."

"No," I said. "In Kolyma, all I was taught was to push a wheelbarrow. And to pickax stone."

In fact, when I came back from Kolyma I had not acquired any knowledge or skill.

But my whole body knows, and I can physically and mentally still repeat, the wheeling and the pushing of a barrow.

When you take hold of a wheelbarrow—the much-hated big one (ten barrows to the cubic meter) or the "much-loved" little one—the barrow man's first task is to straighten up. To straighten your whole body, by standing upright and holding your hands behind your back before lifting the barrow. The fingers of both hands must solidly grip the handles of the loaded barrow.

The first push to make it move comes from the whole body, your back, legs, and the shoulder muscles, so that the shoulder area gives the force. Once the barrow has started moving, and the wheel is turning, you can move your arms forward a little, and relax your shoulder muscles just a bit.

The barrow man can't see the wheel, he can only feel it, and all the turns are done blind, from the beginning to the end of the journey.

The shoulder muscles and the forearm are what you need to turn, to transfer and push the barrow up on the steep ramp to the trestlework. In actually moving the barrow along the gangway, these muscles are not the most important.

Unity of wheel and body, direction, balance are supported and restrained by the whole body, by the neck and back as much as by the biceps.

Until this movement becomes an automatic reflex, there isn't the strength to drive the barrow forward; there isn't a barrow man to go with the barrow's wheel.

Once these habits have been learned, the body remembers them for life, forever.

There were three sorts of wheelbarrows in Kolyma: the first was the ordinary "prospector's" barrow with 0.03 cubic meter capacity, thirty barrows to a cubic meter of ore. How much does such a barrow weigh?

Prospector's barrows were banned from Kolyma's gold-mine pit faces by the mining season of 1937: they were considered almost criminally underweight.

The Gulag or Berzin barrows for the 1937 and 1938 seasons had a capacity of 0.1 to 0.12 cubic meters and were called big wheelbarrows. Ten barrows per cubic meter. Hundreds of thousands of these barrows were manufactured for Kolyma and brought over from the mainland as a load more important than vitamins.

There were also metal wheelbarrows at the mines, also manufactured on the mainland, riveted steel ones. These barrows had a capacity of 0.075 cubic meters, twice as much as a prospector's barrow, but naturally the bosses didn't like them. The Gulag was gathering strength.

These last barrows were of no use for Kolyma pit faces. About twice in my life I found myself working with such a barrow. There was a mistake in their construction: the barrow man couldn't straighten up when he pushed the barrow, he couldn't get a unity of body and metal. The human can come to terms with wooden construction and easily connect with it.

This barrow could be pushed ahead only if you coiled up your whole body, and the wheel kept coming off the gangway. Nobody could get the barrow onto the gangway on his own. You needed help.

You couldn't hold back metal barrows by the handles, even if you straightened up and were pushing the barrow ahead, and it was impossible to alter the construction, the length of the handle, the angle of the barrow. So these barrows were taken out of action, after tormenting men worse than the bigger barrows.

I happen to have seen Kolyma reports on "basic production," on "first metal (gold)"—one has to remember that statistics is a false science, and the exact figures are never published. But even if you recognize the figure communicated as official, the reader and onlooker can easily work out the Kolyma secrets. You can take these Kolyma figures to be true, and they consisted of the following:

(1) Removing sand from open seams by manual barrowing up to 80 meters, etc.

(2) Removing peat (i.e., winter work, taking away stone and ore) by manual barrowing up to 80 meters.

Eighty meters is a significant amount to barrow away. This average figure means that the best brigades—nonpolitical convicts, gangsters, any "leaders of production" who still received more than goners' rations, and still got a Stakhanov or shock-worker ration, and still managed to work the norm, were given the closest and most advantageous pit faces, where they only had to barrow for five or six meters from the bunker and the trestlework.

This was a production argument, a political argument, and one of inhumanity and murder.

Over eighteen months of working at the Partisan mine, from August 1937 to December 1938, I don't ever remember our brigade working a single day or hour at a close, advantageous pit face, the only one a goner could possibly cope with.

But we weren't providing the "percentage," and that was why our brigade (there was always a brigade like this, and I always worked in these goners' brigades) was put on long-distance barrowing. Three hundred or two hundred fifty meters of barrowing is murder, planned murder, for any brigade, even the best ones.

So we were barrowing up those three hundred meters to the sound of yelping dogs, but even those three hundred meters, when the average distance was eighty, were hiding yet another secret. The article 58ers, who had no rights, were constantly being cheated by having their work attributed to those very gangsters or nonpoliticals who were barrowing just ten meters away from the trestlework.

I well remember a summer night when I was wheeling a barrow that my fellow workers had loaded onto the gangway. In our pit face we were not allowed to use small wheelbarrows. The barrow was loaded with quicksand—in Kolyma that was the gold-bearing layer, which might be shingle, or quicksand, or rocks and river sand.

My muscles were trembling with weakness and shook every minute in my emaciated, exhausted body, which ached from the beatings, and in the scurvy ulcers, which were the result of untreated frostbite. I had to push the barrow from our corner onto the central gangway, to move it from the board that led from our pit face onto the central gangway. Several brigades were barrowing, with noisy rumbling, along the central gangway. Nobody was going to wait for you there. The bosses were patrolling the gangway, chasing you with sticks and curses, praising those who barrowed at a run and cursing the hungry snails like myself.

I still had to barrow through the beatings, the curses, the roars, and I shoved the barrow onto the central gangway, turned it to the right, and turned myself, keeping up with the movement of the barrow so I could correct it if the wheel veered to the side.

You can barrow well only if your body is attuned to the barrow: only then can you control it. The physical feeling is like riding a bicycle. But a bicycle used to be a sort of victory, whereas the wheelbarrow was a defeat, an insult that aroused self-hatred and self-contempt.

I dragged the barrow onto the gangway, and it rolled up toward the trestlework, while I ran behind it, following the barrow along the gangway, placing my feet to either side of it, swaying from side to side, desperately trying to keep the barrow on the board.

A few dozen meters, and then another brigade's berth would join the central gangway, so that from that board, that point on, the barrow could only be wheeled at a run.

I was immediately shoved off the gangway, roughly shoved, and it was all I could do to keep the barrow balanced: after all it was quicksand and whatever was spilled on the way had to be shoveled up and carried farther. I was even glad to have been shoved, so that I could get a short break.

You couldn't rest even for a minute at the pit face. You would be beaten for doing so by the foremen, the warders, the guards—I knew that well, so I "alternated" by just switching the muscles: instead of my shoulder muscles, some other muscles kept me going.

The brigade with big wheelbarrows went past me, and I could wheel my barrow back onto the central gangway.

You didn't think whether you would be given anything to eat that day: you didn't think about anything; there was nothing left in your brain except for the curses, the anger—and the helplessness.

At least half an hour passed before I got my barrow to the trestle-work. The trestlework wasn't high, just a meter, paved with thick boards. There was a pit—the bunker, and down that bunker, a fenced-in funnel, where you had to tip your soil.

Iron wagons pass under the trestlework, and they are towed by a cable to the scrubber, where the washing machinery is, and the soil is washed by a stream of water so that the gold settles on the bottom of the pan. At the top of the scrubbing pan, which is twenty meters long, people work, shoveling in the soil, scrubbing it. The barrow men don't scrub, and 58ers aren't allowed near the gold. For some reason, scrubbing work—which is easier, of course, than pit-face work—was considered permissible only for "friends of the people." I chose a time when there were no other brigade's barrows on the trestlework.

The trestlework wasn't high. I had worked on higher ones, needing a climb of about ten meters. At the entrance to the trestlework a special man stands who helps the barrower to get his load to the top, to the bunker. That is a more serious job. That night, the trestlework was a small one, but even so I didn't have the strength to push the barrow up it.

I felt I was taking too long, and by harnessing my last drop of strength I pushed the barrow to the start of the climb. But I didn't have the strength to push this barrow up, even though it wasn't full. I had been walking the mine's earth for a long time now, shuffling my feet, forcing one leg to follow the other, without letting the soles of my feet leave the ground, too weak to do anything else, either to lift my leg or move faster. I had been walking around the camp and the pit face like that for a long time, jostled by the foremen, the guards, the warders, the clerks of work, the orderlies, and the supervisors.

I felt a jolt in my back, not a strong one, and sensed that I was falling down the trestlework along with my barrow, the handles of which I was still holding on to, as if I had to go farther, to anywhere other than hell.

I had simply been pushed aside: the big barrows of the article 58ers were heading for the bunker. It was my fellow workers, a brigade that worked in the next section. But both the brigade and its foreman Fursov merely wanted to show that he and his brigade and his big barrow had nothing in common with starving fascists such as I.

Piotr Brazhnikov, a free man, the clerk of works for our sector, was standing by the bunker; so was the head of the mine, Leonid Mikhailovich Anisimov.

So I set to shoveling up the quicksand: it was a slippery, stony mush, like mercury in its weight, and just as much an elusive and slippery stony dough. It had to be cut into pieces by the spade and then hooked up in order to throw it into the barrow: it was impossible; I didn't have the strength, so I used my hands to tear off pieces of this heavy, slippery precious quicksand.

Anisimov and Brazhnikov were standing by, waiting for me to collect the last pebble and put it in the barrow. I dragged the barrow toward the gangway and began the climb, again pushing the barrow uphill. The bosses were worried only about my blocking the path for other brigades. I got the barrow onto the gangway and tried to force it onto the trestlework.

Once again I was knocked off. This time I expected to be struck, and I managed to drag the barrow aside on the rise itself. Other brigades came and left, and again I began my climb. I wheeled it all the way and tipped it: the load wasn't that big, and I scraped the sides of my barrow clean of the remains of the valuable quicksand with a spade; then I wheeled the barrow onto the parallel gangway, the second one leading back for empty barrows returning to the gold-mine pit face.

Brazhnikov and Anisimov waited for me to finish the task and stood around me, while I gave way to other brigades' empty barrows.

"And where's the hook man?" asked the chief of the mine in a tenor voice.

"There's not supposed to be one here," said Brazhnikov. The head of the mine was an NKVD man and took charge of mining questions in the evenings. "Well, the foreman won't let us have a man; he says they can take the goners in the brigade. Venka Byk refuses. Hooking, he says, isn't my job for that trestlework. Who can't push a wheelbarrow up two meters along a ramp? An enemy of the people, a criminal."

"Yes," said Anisimov. "Yes!"

"After all, he's deliberately falling down in front of us. We don't need a hook man here."

The hook man, or height compensator, was an extra worker who would on a slope hook the front of the barrow to the bunker with a special hook and help tip out the precious load onto the trestlework. These hooks were made of pile-drilling bits a meter long; the tip was flattened and bent into a hook by the blacksmith.

Our foreman refused to give up a man who might help other brigades.

I could go back to the pit face.

The barrow man has to feel his barrow, its center of gravity, its wheel, its axle, the wheel's direction. After all, the barrow man can't see the wheel, either when moving with a load or when going back. He has to feel the wheel. There are two types of wheels on a barrow: one has a thinner disk with a broader diameter; the other has a thicker disk. In accordance with the laws of physics, the first is easier on the move, but the second is more stable.

The wheel has a linchpin and it is greased with tar, then with solidol, a wheel grease, and is inserted to fit tightly in the bottom of the barrow. The barrow has to be greased carefully.

Usually, there are barrels of this grease in the toolsheds.

How many thousands of wheelbarrows get broken in the Kolyma gold-mining season? The figure of tens of thousands comes from just one small area.

In the road administration, where there is no gold mining, the same barrows are used, both big and small. Stone is the same everywhere. So is a cubic meter. So is hunger.

The actual highway is a peculiar gangway for the central trans-Kolyma gold district. Side roads branch out from the highway: stone two-lane offshoots. The central highway has eight lanes for the trucks that link the mines and the ore deposits to the highway.

The highway runs straight to Nera over twelve hundred kilometers, and with the road in the Deliankir–Tenkinsk district direction it amounts to two thousand kilometers.

But during the war bulldozers came to the highway. And before that, mechanical excavators.

In 1938 there were no mechanical excavators.

Six hundred kilometers of the highway had been constructed beyond Yagodny, and the roads to the Southern and Northern Administrations had already been built. Kolyma was now producing gold, and the bosses were getting medals.

All those billions of cubic meters of dynamited rocks, all those roads, approaches, paths, the gold-panning equipment, the building of settlements and cemeteries was done by hand, with wheelbarrows and pickaxes.

1972

WATER HEMLOCK

THE AGREEMENT was this: if they were to be dispatched to the special Berlag camp, all three would commit suicide. They would not go to that world, the world of the numbered camps.

It was the usual camp mistake. Each camp prisoner clings to the day he has just lived through, thinking that somewhere outside his world there is a place that is even worse than where he spent the last night. And he's right. There are worse places, and the danger of being transferred to one is always hanging over the prisoner's head: no camp prisoner has any urge to go away anywhere. Even the winds of spring don't bring any desire for a change of place. Changes are always dangerous. That is one of the important lessons a man learns in a camp.

People who haven't been in a camp believe in changes. A camp prisoner is against all forms of change. However bad it is here, around the corner it could be even worse.

So a decision was made to die at the crucial moment.

The modernist artist Anti, an Estonian, an admirer of Čiurlionis,[10] spoke Estonian and Russian. The unqualified doctor Draudvilas, a Lithuanian, a fifth-year student, a lover of Mickiewicz, spoke Lithuanian and Russian. Garleis, a second-year student, spoke Latvian and Russian.

All three Balts agreed in Russian to commit suicide.

Anti, the Estonian, was the brain and the will behind this Baltic hecatomb.

But how?

Should they leave letters? Wills? No. Anti was against letters, as was Garleis. Draudvilas was for them, but the others convinced him that if their attempt failed, letters would be an indictment, a complication that demanded explanations under interrogation.

They decided not to leave any letters.

All three had gotten onto the lists some time ago, and all of them knew that they were meant for a numbered camp, a special camp. All three decided not to tempt fate any more. Since Draudvilas was a doctor, the special camp was no threat to him. But the Lithuanian recalled how hard it had been for him to get employed as a medic in an ordinary camp. It took a miracle. Garleis was of the same opinion; Anti, the artist, understood that his art was even worse than an actor's or singer's and would certainly be unwanted in any camp, just as it had been unwanted so far.

The most obvious way to commit suicide was to throw yourself in the way of a guard's bullet. But that would mean a wound and being beaten. Whom did they ever shoot outright? The camp sharpshooters were like the soldiers of King George in Bernard Shaw's play *The Devil's Disciple*: they could miss. The guards were not to be relied on, so that method was rejected.

Drowning in the river? The Kolyma River was nearby, but it was winter now, and where would you find a hole in the ice big enough to squeeze a body through? The three-meter-thick ice froze up any holes while you watched, almost instantly. Finding a rope was easy. And reliable. But where could a suicide hang himself—at work, in the barracks? There was no suitable place. You'd be cut down and disgraced forever.

Shooting yourself? Prisoners don't have guns. Attacking a guard was even worse than running away from him: agony, not death.

Opening your veins like Petronius was quite impossible. You needed warm water, a bath, or you would just come out of it an invalid with a crooked arm, an invalid, if you trusted to nature, to your own body.

Only poison—a cup of water hemlock—was a reliable method.

But what would serve as water hemlock? You couldn't get hold of potassium cyanide, after all. But the hospital, the pharmacy, were poison stores. Poisons worked for diseases; they destroyed the sick part and made room for life.

No, only poison would do. Only a cup of water hemlock: Socrates's lethal chalice.

The water hemlock was found, and Draudvilas and Garleis guaranteed that it was certain to work.

It was phenol. Carbolic acid solution. The most powerful antiseptic, with a permanent supply kept in the little cupboard of the surgical department where Draudvilas and Garleis worked.

Draudvilas showed the fatal bottle to Anti, the Estonian.

"Just like brandy," said Anti.

"Similar."

"I'll make a label: 'Three Stars.'"

Once every three months the special camp would gather its victims. Raids were arranged, for even in an institution like the central hospital, there were places where you could "tuck" yourself away and wait for the storm to pass. But if you weren't able to "tuck" yourself away, you had to put your jacket on, gather your things, pay off your debts, sit on a bench, and patiently wait to see if the ceiling would collapse on the heads of the people who had come or, the alternative, on your own head. You had to wait meekly to see if the head of the hospital would keep you on, ask the buyers to let him keep the goods, say that the boss needed you, and it made no difference to the buyer.

The hour or day had come, and it became clear that nobody was able to save you or stand up for you, and you were still on the lists for the "party."

That was the time for the water hemlock.

Anti took the bottle from Draudvilas's hands and stuck a brandy label to it and, as Anti was forced to be a realistic artist, he hid his modernist tastes at the bottom of his soul.

The last work by this admirer of Čiurlionis was a "Three Star" brandy label, a purely realistic image. Anti thus yielded to realism at the very last moment. Realism turned out to be more precious.

"But why three stars?"

"Three stars are us, an allegory, a symbol."

"Why have you portrayed this allegory so naturalistically?" joked Draudvilas.

"Well, if someone comes in and snatches it, we can explain: we're having a farewell drink of brandy, a canful each."

"Clever."

In fact, people did come in, but they didn't snatch it. Anti managed to shove the bottle back in the medicine cupboard; as soon as the guard left, he took it out again.

Anti poured out three canfuls of phenol.

"Well, here's to your health!"

Anti drank it; so did Draudvilas. Garleis just took a sip but didn't swallow it; he spat it out, and stepped over the bodies of the fallen to get to the water pipe, where he rinsed his burned mouth with water. Draudvilas and Anti were writhing and rasping. Garleis tried to work out what he would have to say at the investigation.

Garleis spent two months in the hospital; his burned throat mended. Many years later, Garleis was passing through Moscow and visited me. He swore to me that the suicide was a tragic mistake, that the "Three Star" brandy was real, that Anti had confused the bottle of brandy in the medicine cupboard with a similar bottle of phenol, of death, that he had taken out.

The investigation was drawn out, but Garleis was not condemned: he was acquitted. The bottle of brandy was never found. It is hard to judge who won it as a prize, if it ever existed. The interrogator had nothing against Garleis's version: what was the point of going through the agony of getting an admission, a confession, and so on. Garleis offered the investigation a reasonable and logical conclusion. Draudvilas and Anti, the organizers of the Baltic hecatomb, never found out if they were talked about too much or too little. And they were talked about a lot.

Meanwhile Garleis changed his medical specialization: he narrowed it down. He turned out to have become a dental technician, and he mastered that profitable craft.

Garleis had come to see me for some legal advice. He had been refused registration in Moscow. He was allowed to live only in Riga, where his wife had been born. Garleis's wife, a Muscovite, was also a doctor. The trouble was that when Garleis applied for rehabilitation, he asked one of his Kolyma friends for advice, and told him in detail about what he had done in his Latvian youth, such as being a Boy Scout and something else.

"I asked for advice; I asked if I should write all that down. And my best friend said, 'Write the whole truth. Everything exactly how it was.' So I did and didn't get rehabilitated. All I got was permission to reside in Riga. He really let me down, my best friend..."

"Garleis, he didn't let you down. You wanted advice on something that nobody could advise you about. If he'd given you any other answer, what would you have done? Your friend may have thought you were a spy, a snitch. And if you weren't a snitch, then why should he take risks? You got the only advice he could give in response to your question. Someone else's secret is much harder to keep than your own."

1973

DR. YAMPOLSKY

In my wartime memories the surname of Dr. Yampolsky recurs frequently. During the war, fate brought us together several times in Kolyma's punishment sectors. After the war I myself worked as a paramedic, once I had finished medical classes in Magadan in 1946, and I no longer encountered Dr. Yampolsky as a practicing doctor and the head of the mine's health department.

Dr. Yampolsky had no doctorate and was not a medical doctor. He was a Muscovite convicted of some nonpolitical crime, and once in prison, he quickly worked out the safety and solidity of a medical education. But Yampolsky didn't have time to get a doctor's or even a paramedic's education.

Initially he was a patient himself. By taking patients' temperatures, being a ward assistant, cleaning the wards, and looking after the seriously ill, he managed to carry out the functions of a paramedic intern. That wasn't forbidden in the free world, and in the camps it opened up wide prospects. A paramedic's experience is easily obtained, and given the permanent shortage of medical staff in the camps, this proved to be a reliable way of earning his bread.

Yampolsky did have a secondary-school education, so that he was able to make sense of some of the doctors' explanations.

Practical experience under the supervision of not just one doctor but several—for Yampolsky's medical bosses were constantly changing—increased his knowledge and, above all, his self-confidence. This was not entirely a paramedic's self-confidence: it is well known that paramedics think they know that patients don't have a pulse, but all the same they take the patient's hand, count it, check it against the clock—a self-confidence that has long been a joke.

Yampolsky was cleverer. He had by now been working for several years as a paramedic, and he knew that a stethoscope would not reveal any secrets when he used it if he didn't have medical knowledge.

The life of an imprisoned paramedic gave Yampolsky the opportunity to serve his term without worries and to see it through to the end, safe and sound. It was here, at an important junction in life, that Yampolsky marked out a completely safe and legally justifiable plan for his life.

Yampolsky decided to stay on as a medic after his imprisonment. But he didn't do this to get a medical education; he did it to get onto the lists of medical staff, not of accountants or agronomists.

As a former prisoner, Yampolsky was not supposed to get bonuses, but he wasn't even thinking about the special high salaries.

He was already sure of getting a special high salary, thanks to his position as a doctor.

But if a paramedic intern can work as a paramedic only under a doctor's supervision, then who would supervise his medical practice as a doctor?

In the camps, both in Kolyma and the rest of the country, there was the administrative job of head of the health department. Since 90 percent of medical work consisted of paperwork, then one might think that this job would leave time free for specialists. It was an administrative, economy, office job. It was good if a doctor took it on, but a nondoctor was no problem, as long as the person was energetic and knew what he was doing when organizing his work.

All these heads of hospitals and of health departments were doctors working in health administration, or else nothing but heads of hospitals. Their salaries were rather higher than those of specialist doctors.

This was the sort of post that Yampolsky's thoughts were focused on.

He wasn't able, physically or mentally, to treat people. He lacked the courage. He undertook a series of medical posts, but on every occasion he backed off, citing his position as head of the health administration, as an administrator. That was a job where no inspection could catch him out.

Mortality was high. So what? A specialist was needed, and there wasn't one. So Dr. Yampolsky would have to remain in the job.

Moving gradually from one post to the next, Yampolsky relentlessly acquired medical experience and, above all, learned how to be silent at the right time, and when to denounce and inform.

None of that would have been bad, were it not that it was accompanied by Yampolsky's growing hatred for all goners and for intellectual goners in particular. Like all the rest of the camp bosses in Kolyma, Yampolsky saw every goner as a shirker and an enemy of the people.

Unable to understand a human being, and refusing to trust one, Yampolsky was taking on the major responsibility of sending people on their last legs to the Kolyma camp ovens—that is, to temperatures of minus sixty—where they would die in those ovens. Yampolsky did not hesitate to take it upon himself to sign death certificates filled in by the bosses, and he even wrote them out personally.

I first encountered Dr. Yampolsky at the Spokoiny mine. After questioning the patients, a doctor in a white gown, with a stethoscope over his shoulder, selected me for the job of ward assistant: taking temperatures, cleaning the wards, looking after the seriously ill.

My experience at Belichya at the beginning of my difficult medical path had taught me how to do all that. After I became a goner, I was admitted with pellagra to the northern district hospital and unexpectedly recovered, got out of bed, and stayed on to work in the ward; then I was thrown out by the top bosses to that same Spokoiny mine, where I fell ill. I had a temperature, and Dr. Yampolsky, after studying my Kolyma dossier, which I gave him orally, limited himself to the medical side of the case, because he understood that I hadn't tried to deceive the hospital doctors and hadn't confused their names and patronymics: so he himself suggested I work as a ward assistant.

But at the time my condition was such that I was unable even to work as a ward assistant. Yet the limits of human endurance are unknowable: I began taking temperatures, once I laid my hands on a treasured item, a real thermometer, and I started filling in temperature records.

However modest my hospital experience, I clearly understood that only the dying had hospital beds.

When a swollen giant from the camps, puffed up by edemas and utterly unable to get warm, was pushed into a warm bath, even in the bath the dystrophy patient couldn't get warm.

Patient notes were kept for all these patients; various procedures, which nobody ever carried out, were recorded. There was nothing in the health administration pharmacy except for potassium permanganate. Permanganate was administered, either internally in weak dilutions, or as a compress for scurvy and pellagra ulcers.

Possibly this was not actually the worst treatment, but it had a depressing effect on me.

There were six or seven men in the ward.

These men, today's or tomorrow's corpses, had a daily visit from the head of the health department of the mine, the free worker Dr. Yampolsky, in his snow-white shirt, his well-ironed gown and gray civilian suit, a present from the gangsters for sending them to the central hospital on the Left Bank, even though they were perfectly healthy, while Yampolsky kept the corpses for himself.

That's where I met the Makhno anarchist Riabokon.

The doctor in his shiny starched gown would walk past eight trestle beds with mattresses stuffed with branches of dwarf pine, conifer needles ground down to a powder, a green powder, and branches that bent like living or at least like dead human hands, just as thin and just as black.

Lying on these mattresses, covered with blankets that had outlived their lifespan ten times over, unable to retain even a drop of warmth, neither I nor my dying neighbors, a Latvian and the Makhno, man could get warm.

Dr. Yampolsky declared to me that his boss had ordered him to build his hospital on an economic basis, and so we—he and I—would the very next day start this construction. "For the time being you'll be here on the basis of your patients' notes."

I wasn't overjoyed by the offer. All I wanted was death, but I hadn't the will to commit suicide, and so I kept putting things off day after day.

When he saw that I was utterly incapable of helping him with his building plans—I couldn't move thin sticks, let alone joists, and I just sat there (I meant to write "on the ground," but people don't sit on the ground in Kolyma because of the permafrost; it isn't done, for it can have a lethal outcome) on some beam or other, on a piece of fallen timber, looking at my boss and his feeble attempts to remove the bark from a tree trunk, now cleared of branches—Yampolsky decided not to keep me on at the hospital and immediately took on another ward assistant, and the mine's site manager sent me off to help the charcoal burner.

I worked for several days with the charcoal burner, then I left to do another job, and after that my meeting with Liosha Chekanov turned my life in a deadly direction.

During a case at Yagodnoye having to do with refusal to work, a case that was dropped, I was lucky enough to get in touch with Lesniak, my guardian angel in Kolyma. Lesniak wasn't the only guardian angel in the destiny meted out to me: Lesniak and his wife, Nina Vladimirovna Savoyeva, couldn't have had the strength to do that on their own, as we all three understood. But all the same it was worth a try: you could put a spanner in the works of that machinery of death.

But being a "strike first" man, as the gangsters put it, I prefer to deal with my enemies before I repay my debt to my friends.

The sinners have the first turn, and the just come afterward. So Lesniak and Savoyeva yielded way to the scoundrel Yampolsky.

That, apparently, is as it should be. I wouldn't lift a finger to extol a just man until I've named the scoundrel. After this lyrical but indispensible digression, I return to my story about Yampolsky.

When I came back to Spokoiny from pretrial solitary imprisonment, all doors to the health department were, of course, closed to me: I had completely exhausted the limits of attention, and when he met me in the zone, Dr. Yampolsky averted his face, as if he had never seen me.

But before we met in the zone, Dr. Yampolsky had received a letter from a free contract doctor, the head of the district hospital, Nina Savoyeva, asking him to give me assistance (Lesniak had told her about my situation) by simply sending me as a patient to the district hospital. I was in fact ill.

This letter was brought to Spokoiny by some doctor or other.

Dr. Yampolsky didn't call for me or tell me anything: he merely handed Savoyeva's letter to Yemelianov, the head of the Special Camp Center, In other words, he denounced Savoyeva.

I was also informed about this letter, and I blocked Yampolsky's path in the camp and, using, of course, the most respectful expressions, as my experience of the camps had taught me, I inquired about what had happened to that letter. Yampolsky said that he had given it, entrusted it, to the head of the Special Camp Center, and I should apply there, not to him in the health administration.

I wasted no time: I applied to see Yemelianov. The head of the Special Camp Center knew me slightly, and personally—we had gone together through a snowstorm to open this mine, in a single day's journey, when the wind made it impossible to stand up, whether free men or prisoners, bosses or workmen. Of course, he couldn't remember me, but he treated the head doctor's letter as a perfectly normal request.

"We'll send you, we'll send you."

A few days later I found myself at Belichya thanks to being sent on the forestry team of the Yagodnoye Special Camp Center, where the paramedic was a certain Efa, also an unqualified apprentice, like nearly all the Kolyma paramedics. Efa agreed to tell Lesniak that I had arrived. Belichya was six kilometers from Yagodnoye, and this was the third and final time that I had ended up in the northern district hospital, the hospital where a year earlier they'd skinned the gloves off my hands as part of my patient notes.

Here I was working as the culture organizer quite officially, if there was anything official in Kolyma. Until the end of the war in the spring of 1945 I read the newspapers to the patients. In the spring of 1945 the head doctor Savoyeva was transferred to another post, and the hospital was taken over by a chief doctor with one artificial eye, I can't remember whether the left or the right—so they called her Flatfish.

This Flatfish, a woman doctor, immediately dismissed me and sent me under armed guard that same evening to the commandant's office at the Special Camp Center in Yagodnoye, where that same night I was sent off to make pylons for the high-voltage line to Diamond Spring. I have described what happened there in my story "Diamond Spring."

Although there was no armed guard there, the conditions were inhuman, exceptionally so, even for Kolyma.

Those who failed to deliver the daily norm were simply refused bread. Lists were displayed of the persons who would get no bread tomorrow because of their work today.

I had seen a lot of arbitrariness, but I had never ever seen such things anywhere. When I ended up on those lists, I wasted no time: I ran away and made my way to Yagodnoye on foot. My escape was successful. It could have been called absence without leave, after all, I hadn't left "for the ice" but reported to the commandant's office. I was imprisoned once again and a new investigation was started. And again the state considered that my new sentence was at too early a stage for yet another one to be imposed.

This time I wasn't sent to a transit camp but got transferred to the Jelgala special zone, the same place where I had been tried a year earlier. Usually you are not returned after a trial to the place where you had been brought to trial. Now it was different, perhaps owing to a mistake.

I walked through the same gates, climbed the same mountain to the mine where I had been before and received ten years.

Neither Krivitsky nor Zaslavsky were at Jelgala anymore, and I realized that the bosses dealt with their collaborators fairly, not just limiting them to cigarette ends and a bowl of gruel.

Suddenly it became clear that I had a very powerful enemy among the free contract workers at Jelgala. But who? The new head of the health administration at the mine, Dr. Yampolsky, who had only just been transferred to work there. Yampolsky was shouting to everyone that he knew me well, that I was a snitch, that he was informed that a personal letter had been written about my destiny by the free contract doctor Savoyeva, that I was an idler, a shirker, a professional camp informer who had nearly been the death of the unfortunate Krivitsky and Zaslavsky.

Savoyeva's letter! A proven snitch! But he, Yampolsky, had been instructed by the top bosses to make my life easier, and he had carried out the order and preserved this scoundrel's life. But now we were here in a special zone, and Yampolsky would show me no mercy.

There was no question of any medical work, and yet one more time I prepared myself for death.

This was in the autumn of 1945. Suddenly Jelgala was closed. The special zone with its carefully devised geography and topography was needed, and needed urgently.

A whole "contingent" was being rushed to the west, to the Western

Administration near Susuman, and until they had found somewhere for a special zone, this contingent would be housed in Susuman prison.

Jelgala was the destination for the repatriated—the first foreign harvest, straight from Italy. They were Russian soldiers who had been serving in the Italian army. The very same repatriates who obeyed the summons after the war to return to the motherland.

At the border their trains were surrounded by armed guards, and they all took the express Rome–Magadan–Jelgala.

They were still wearing Italian uniforms, although they hadn't kept their linen nor their gold objects, which they had exchanged for bread on the journey. They were still cheerful. They were fed the same food the same way as we were. After the first lunch in the camp refectory, one of the more curious Italians asked me, "Why do your men eat the soup and porridge in the refectory but save the bread, the bread ration, to bring it with them?"

"In a week you'll understand why," I said.

I was taken off along with the special zone party of prisoners to Susuman, a lesser zone. There I was hospitalized and, with the help of Dr. Andrei Maksimovich Pantiukhov, I got into the paramedic classes for prisoners in Magadan, or to be precise, at kilometer 23 of the highway.

It was thanks to those classes, which I completed successfully, that my Kolyma life was divided into two: from 1937 to 1946, ten years alternating between hospital and pit face, with an extra ten-year sentence in 1943; and from 1946 to 1953, when I worked as a paramedic, being freed in 1951 because of working days credited.

After 1946 I realized that I had actually survived and that I would survive to the end of my sentence and beyond, that the problem would be—as a basic premise—to go on living as I had been living for all those fourteen years.

I didn't make many rules for myself, but the ones I made I kept and am still keeping.

1970–1971

LIEUTENANT COLONEL FRAGIN

Lieutenant Colonel Fragin, head of the Special Department,[11] was a police general who had been demoted. A major general in the Moscow police who had waged a successful battle against Trotskyism throughout his valorous career, he was a trusted worker for SMERSH[12] during the war. Marshal Timoshenko, who hated Jews, demoted Fragin to lieutenant colonel and suggested that he be demobilized. Big rations, high ranks, and wide prospects were to be had, despite his demotion, in camp work: that was the only place where war heroes kept their rank, position, and rations. After the war the police general became a camp lieutenant colonel. Fragin had a big family, and he had to find work in the Far North where family needs could be satisfied: nursery, kindergarten, school, and cinema.

So Fragin ended up at the Left Bank in the prisoners' hospital: he wasn't one of the management, as he and the bosses would have liked, but he was head of the Culture and Education Section. He was assured that he could cope with educating prisoners. The assurances were well-founded. On the understanding that all these Culture and Education Sections were a waste of time, a sinecure, Fragin's appointment was accepted with approval, or at best with indifference. In actual fact, this elegant lieutenant colonel, with curly gray locks and a shirt collar that was always clean and perfumed with some cheap, but not thrice-distilled, eau de cologne, was far more likable than his predecessor, Second Lieutenant Zhivkov.

Zhivkov had taken no interest in concerts, or cinema, or meetings: he concentrated all his activity on finding happy solutions to the question of marriage. Zhivkov was a bachelor, a fit and handsome man, who was living with two women prisoners at the same time. They both worked in the hospital. The hospital was like a village in the depths of Tver Province: it had no secrets, and everybody knew everything. One of his girlfriends was a bold beauty from Tbilisi. Several times the gangsters had tried to make Tamara see reason, but it was always in vain. Tamara replied to all the "godfathers," when they ordered her to appear to fulfill her classic duties, with curses and laughter instead of the usual timid silence.

Zhivkov's other girlfriend was an Estonian nurse, convicted under article 58, a blond beauty in a distinctly German style, the complete opposite of the swarthy Tamara. The two women were outwardly very different. Yet they both received the second lieutenant's wooing very graciously. Zhivkov was a generous man. At the time there were difficulties with the rations. The free contract workers were issued groceries on certain days, and Zhivkov would always bring to the hospital two identical parcels, one for Tamara and one for the Estonian woman. It was widely known that Zhivkov's amorous visits occurred on a particular day, almost to the hour.

This Zhivkov, a good fellow, whacked one of the prisoners over the neck in front of everybody, but since the bosses belonged to another world, a higher one, such blows were not punishable. Yet it was he who was replaced by the handsome gray-haired Fragin. Fragin had been looking for a job as head of the third section, the Information and Investigation Section, work that fit his qualifications, but there was no such job to be had. So the senior staff specialist was forced to take up the cultural education of the prisoners. The salary for both jobs was identical, so Fragin hadn't lost anything. The gray-haired lieutenant colonel did not have affairs with women prisoners. For the first time we listened to newspapers being read to us and, what was more important, we heard personal stories about the war from someone who had taken part in it.

Until then we had been told about the war by the Vlasov men, the men who had worked as policemen for the Germans, marauders, and other collaborators. We understood the difference in their information, and we wanted to listen to a victorious hero. The lieutenant colonel was such a man, and at his first meeting for the prisoners he gave a lecture about the war, telling us about the leading commanders. Naturally,

Rokossovsky aroused particular interest. We had heard about him a long time ago. Fragin, however, happened to be someone who had worked in Rokossovsky's SMERSH. Fragin praised Rokossovsky as a commander who was on the lookout for a fight, but when the main question was raised—whether Rokossovsky had been in prison, and whether it was true that he had gangsters in his units—Fragin refused to answer. This was the first time since the day I was arrested in January 1937 that I had heard about the war from the horse's mouth. I remember that I hung on every word. This was in the summer of 1949 at a big forestry outpost. Among the lumberjacks was Andrusenko, a fair-haired tank commander who had taken part in the Battle of Berlin, and who was a Hero of the Soviet Union, but had been convicted of looting, of robberies committed in Germany. We were well aware of the legal boundary that splits a man's life into events before and events after the date a law is passed; one and the same man, behaving the same way, is a hero today and a criminal tomorrow, and he himself doesn't know whether he is a criminal or not.

Andrusenko had been sentenced to ten years for looting. The law had only just been passed. Lieutenant Andrusenko was struck down by it and swept off from a Soviet military prison in Berlin to Kolyma. The farther he was taken, the harder it was to argue that he was a real Hero of the Soviet Union who had the title and the medals. The number of false heroes was still increasing. Arrests and exposures of con men and retribution were continuing at the same rate just a few months later. In 1949 we had a chief doctor, a Hero of the Soviet Union from the frontline staff, who turned out to be neither a doctor nor a hero. Andrusenko's complaints went unanswered. Unlike other prisoners, who had come to Kolyma from the war, Andrusenko had kept a cutting with his photograph from the frontline newspaper of 1945. Fragin, as the head of the local Culture and Education Section, was able to appreciate Andrusenko's sincerity and helped to get him released.

I have lived all my life with a very emphatic feeling for justice, and I am unable to differentiate between events of different scales. And it was in this hospital, with these resonant names—Andrusenko, Fragin—that I most remember a chess tournament organized by Fragin, on an enormous chessboard that hung in the hospital vestibule. It was this board on which the tournament took place, a tournament that, Fragin calculated, Andrusenko would win: a prize, some gift, had already been bought. The prize was a pocket chess set, an object that looked like a leather cigarette case. The chief had already given it to Andrusenko before the contest was over, but it was I who won the tournament. And I didn't get a prize.

Portugalov, who had tried to influence the bosses, suffered complete defeat, and Fragin, when he went out to see the prisoners in the corridor, declared that the Culture and Education Section had no money for a prize. His response to me was a flat no.

The war and victory passed, Stalin was dethroned, the Twentieth Congress was held, and the direction of my life changed sharply. I had been in Moscow for many years, but I remember the first postwar years for that injury to my pride, Fragin's reply. One remembers such trivia just as well as starvation and executions. In fact, Fragin was capable of more than trivia.

I moved into the hospital admissions room and, because of my job, Fragin and I met more often. By then he had left the Culture and Education Section for the Accounting Section, in charge of prisoners' cases, and he showed enthusiasm and vigilance. I had a male nurse, Grinkevich, a good young man, who had obviously been sent to the camps for no good reason, also straight from the war, in the turbid torrent of false generals and disguised gangsters. Grinkevich's relatives wrote a lot of applications and complaints, and finally there was a review of the case and his sentence was annulled. Lieutenant Colonel Fragin failed to summon Grinkevich to his Accounting Section, and instead turned up in my admissions room and in a loud voice read out to Grinkevich the text of a document he had received.

"So you see, citizen Shalamov," said Fragin, "the people who should be released are released. All mistakes are put right, but people who shouldn't be, are not released. Have you got that, citizen Shalamov?"

"Completely, sir."

When in October 1951 I was released, on the basis of working days credited to me, Fragin objected in the most outright manner against my working as a free contract worker in the hospital until spring, when the shipping season started again. But the matter was settled by the intervention of the then head of the hospital, N. Vinokurov. Vinokurov promised to send me off with a party in the spring but not to include me on the staff; until spring he would hire me as a worker for the admissions room. This was legally possible, and the status did exist.

Men released from a camp had the right to government-paid group travel to the mainland. It was too expensive to travel as a contract worker: a ticket from the Left Bank of the Kolyma River to Moscow cost more than three thousand rubles, not including the cost of food. The main misfortune, the worst inconvenience in a man's life, was the need to eat three or four times a day. In a government-funded group, food was provided on the journey; there were refectories and cooking pots in the prisonlike transit camps. Sometimes you were in the same barracks: when traveling in one direction, the barracks is called a staging post; when traveling in the other direction, it is a quarantine post. But these were the same barracks, and there were no distinguishing signs outside the barbed-wire barriers.

In short, I spent the winter of 1951–1952 as an admissions room paramedic in the hospital, with the status of "in transit." In the spring I wasn't sent anywhere, and the chief of the hospital gave me his word to dispatch me in the fall. But in the fall I wasn't sent anywhere.

"Anyway," said the new young psychiatrist Dr. Shafran, hanging around in the admissions room: he was a liberal and a windbag who lived in the apartment next to Fragin's, "would you like me to tell you why you're still in the hospital and not with a group of returnees?"

"Tell me, Arkadi Davydovich."

"You were on the lists last autumn, and they had a truck ready for you. And you would have left, if it weren't for Lieutenant Colonel Fragin. He had a look at your papers and realized who you were. 'A card-carrying Trotskyist and an enemy of the people.' That's what it said in your papers. True, that was a Kolyma memorandum, not a Moscow one. But memoranda are compiled out of thin air. Fragin was trained in the capital, he immediately realized that he had to show vigilance in this case, and the outcome would only be for the best."

"Thank you for telling me, Dr. Shafran. I'll make a note of the lieutenant colonel in my list of people to pray for."

"It's the way people are trained to serve," Shafran roared merrily.

"If only the lists had been compiled by some second lieutenant, but Fragin is a general, after all. He has a general's vigilance."

"Or a general's cowardice."

"But vigilance and cowardice are almost the same thing these days. And not only these days, in fact," said the young doctor, who had been educated as a psychiatrist.

I made a written application to be paid off, but got a typical Vinokurov decision: "To be dismissed on the basis of the Labor Law Code." That meant I was deprived of the rights of someone "in transit" to have free travel. I hadn't earned a penny, but, of course, I wasn't even thinking of changing my decision. I had my ID papers in my hands, although it had no residence permit: residence in Kolyma is registered differently from the mainland—all the stamps are put in your papers retroactively, when you are released. I hoped to receive a permit in Magadan to leave with a group, such as the one I had missed the year before. I demanded papers, I ordered my first and only employment-record book, which I still have, I packed my bags, sold everything I didn't need—my fur parka, my pillow; I burned my verses in the disinfection chamber of the reception room and started looking for a lift to Magadan. It didn't take long to get a lift.

That night I was woken up by Lieutenant Colonel Fragin and two armed guards; they took away my ID papers, sealed them in a packet along with some document, and handed it to the guard, pointing a hand into the air.

"You can hand him over there."

"Him" was me.

Over many years, I had gotten used to treating the figure of "a man with a gun" with sufficient respect, and millions of times I had seen arbitrary behavior that was a million times worse: Fragin was merely an unadventurous pupil of his many high-ranking teachers. So I said nothing and submitted to this insultingly illegal and unexpected stab in the back. True, they didn't handcuff me, but they showed me my place sufficiently clearly as that of a former prisoner in our serious world. Once more I traveled the five hundred kilometers to Magadan under armed guard, a journey that I had made so often. They wouldn't receive me in the district NKVD office in Magadan, and the guard stayed outside, not knowing whom to hand me over to. I advised him to hand me over to the personnel department where I ought to have been sent, given that I was being released. The head of the personnel department—I don't remember his surname—expressed the greatest astonishment at the way a free contract worker was being tossed about. But he gave the armed guard a receipt, handed me my ID papers, and I came out into the street to the gray Magadan rain.

1973

PERMAFROST

THE FIRST time I began working on my own as a paramedic, I was put in charge of the paramedic sector at Adygalakh, in the Highways Administration, where there were only visiting doctors. This was the first time I wasn't working under a doctor, as I had always had some supervision previously at the central hospital on the Left Bank.

I was the senior person in the medical service at Adygalakh. I had to service a total of three hundred prisoners in three different locations. After doing the rounds and giving every one of those in my care a medical examination, I sketched out an action plan for myself for my next steps in Kolyma.

I had six surnames on my list.

Number one was Tkachuk. He was the head of the Special Labor Center where I was now going to work. Tkachuk was due to hear from me that I had found lice on all the prisoners in my care, but as a new paramedic I had a plan to make sure all louse infections were liquidated quickly. I would take responsibility by personally disinfecting everything using heat, and I invited anyone to watch. Lice had long been the scourge of the camps. All Kolyma's disinfection chambers, except for the Magadan transit camp, were merely a torment for the prisoners; they didn't kill the lice. But I knew of an effective way; I had learned it from a bathhouse attendant at a forestry outpost on the Left Bank: roasting clothes with hot steam in empty jerry cans resulted in the extermination of all lice and nits. But you couldn't put more than five sets of clothes in each container. I had done this eighteen months ago at Debin, and I demonstrated it at Baragon.

Number two was Zaitsev. Zaitsev was a prisoner-cook whom I had gotten to know at kilometer 23, at the central hospital. He was now working as a cook under my supervision. He had to be persuaded, by appealing to his cook's conscience, that the rations allowance, as we both knew, could be stretched to provide four times as many dishes as we were now issuing. The loss was simply due to Zaitsev's idleness; the problem was not that supervisors and others were stealing. Tkachuk was a strict man and gave thieves no leeway, but the cook's mere whims were making the prisoners' diet worse. I succeeded in convincing and shaming Zaitsev. Tkachuk had made him a few promises, and Zaitsev began producing far more from the same supplies; he even started delivering hot soup and porridge in jerry cans to the workplaces, an unheard-of thing for Kiubiuma and Baragon.

Number three was Izmailov. He was a free contract bath attendant who washed the prisoners' linen and did so badly. It was impossible to get rid of anyone who was extremely physically healthy and send them either to the pit face or to a prospecting job. A prisoner bath attendant is paid a pittance. But Izmailov clung on to his job and refused to listen to any advice: the only thing to do was to dismiss him. There was no great secret about his behavior. Izmailov was careless about the prisoners' washing, but he did excellent work washing for all the nonprisoner bosses, including the NKVD officer, and received generous gifts in return—money and groceries. But Izmailov was a free contract worker and I hoped I could succeed in insisting that a prisoner got this job.

Number four was Likhonosov. He was a prisoner who went missing during a medical inspection at Baragon and, as I had to go away, I decided not to put off my departure just for the sake of one man, and to confirm the formulas in his personal file. But Likhonosov's file was missing from the Accounts and Records Section: since Likhonosov was working as an orderly, I was supposed to revisit this delicate topic. Somehow, when I was passing through the sector, I found Likhonosov and had a chat with him. He was a strong, well-fed, pink-cheeked man who looked about forty, with shiny teeth, a head of thick gray hair, and an impressive gray beard. Age? That was the aspect of Likhonosov's file that interested me.

"Sixty-five."

Likhonosov was old enough to be considered unfit for work, and for that reason was working as an orderly in the office. This was a clear falsification. I was looking at a well-grown healthy man who was perfectly capable of manual labor. Likhonosov had a fifteen-year sentence; his article was not 58 but 59, but then again, that was just his account.

Number five was Nishikov. Nishikov was my male nurse in the outpatient clinic, a former patient. Such male nurses were to be found in all the camp outpatient clinics. But Nishikov was too young, about twenty-five, and too rosy cheeked. I had to give him some thought.

When I wrote down number six, there was a knock at the door and Leonov, number six on my list, crossed the threshold of my room in the free men's barracks. I put a question mark by Leonov's name and turned to speak to him.

"Leonov, how is it they let you through the guardhouse at this time?"

"They know me, I used to wash the floors for the previous paramedic. He was very fussy about cleanliness."

"Well, I'm not so fussy. They don't need washing today. Go back to the camp."

"How about the other free men?"

"They don't need it, either. They can wash their own floors."

"I wanted to ask you, sir, to let me keep my job."

"You don't have a job."

"Well, they've got me down for some job or other. I'll wash the floors, it will be nice and tidy; I'm a sick man, I've got a pain inside me."

"You're not sick, you're just trying to pull the wool over the doctors' eyes."

"Sir, I'm afraid of the pit face, I'm afraid of the brigade, I'm afraid of manual labor."

"Well, everyone is. You are a completely healthy man."

"But you're not a doctor."

"True, I'm not. But either you go tomorrow to do manual labor, or I send you to the administration. The doctors can examine you there."

"I warn you, sir, I won't survive if I'm taken off this job. I'll complain."

"That's enough of your babbling: go. Tomorrow you're in the brigade. You can stop muddying the water."

"I'm not muddying the water."

Leonov closed the door without making a noise. His footsteps crunched past the window, and I went to bed.

Leonov didn't turn up to roll call and, Tkachuk guessed, he had probably gotten a lift on a passing truck and had some time ago arrived at Adygalakh to make a complaint.

About noon on an Indian summer day, which in Kolyma is marked by the dazzling rays of a cold sun in a bright blue sky, and in the cold windless air, I was summoned to Tkachuk's office.

"Let's go and draw up a statement. Prisoner Leonov has committed suicide."

"Where?"

"He's hanging in the old stables. I've ordered them not to cut the body down. I've sent for the NKVD officer. Well, you're a medic, so you can give a death certificate."

It was not easy to hang yourself in the stables: they were too small. Leonov's body took up a two-horse stall; the only place high enough for him to raise himself and kick away the support, a bathhouse basin. He'd been hanging there for some time: there was a marked scar around his neck. The NKVD officer, the man whose laundry Izmailov the free contract bath attendant had been doing, wrote: "A strangulation furrow passes..."

Tkachuk said, "Topographers have the word triangulation. Has that anything to do with strangulation?"

"Nothing at all," said the NKVD man.

We all signed the statement. Prisoner Leonov had left no note. His corpse was taken away, to have a tag with the number of his file attached to the left leg, and to be buried in the stones of the permafrost, where the late Leonov would wait until Judgment Day or some other resurrection from the dead. And I suddenly realized that it was too late for me to learn about both medicine and life.

1970

IVAN BOGDANOV

IVAN BOGDANOV had the same surname as the head of the district at Black Lake; he was a handsome fair-haired, gray-eyed man with an athlete's build. Bogdanov had been convicted under article 109, a crime committed in the course of employment, and sentenced to ten years. But he understood the situation well, and realized what was what when Stalin's scythe was sending heads rolling. Bogdanov understood that only sheer chance had saved him from the lethal brand of article 58.

We were prospecting for coal, and Bogdanov worked as an accountant with us. A prisoner was deliberately chosen as bookkeeper, because he could be shouted at, he could be ordered to patch up and tinker with a badly presented account of siphoned-off money used to feed the family of Paramonov, the top boss of the district, as well as his immediate circle, who were exposed to the "gold rain" and all the concentrates and Polar Circle rations, etc., that came with it.

Bogdanov's remit was the same as that of another Bogdanov, the head of the district, who had been an interrogator in 1937—I wrote exhaustively about him in my story "Bogdanov": the remit was not to uncover abuses but, on the contrary, to cover up all the sins and to make everything look reasonably respectable.

There were only five prisoners in the district in 1939, when prospecting began. (They included myself, an invalid after the storm that swept through the gold-mine pit faces in 1938.) So it was impossible, of course, to squeeze anything out of prisoner labor at the time.

Custom says—and this is an age-old camp tradition ever since the times of Ovid who was, as everyone knows, a Gulag chief in ancient Rome—that any breaches can be patched up by unpaid forced labor, by prisoners who receive no pay, labor that, according to Marx's theory of labor value, constitutes the main value of production. In this case slave labor could not be used, for there were too few of us for any serious economic prospects.

It was possible to use the labor of semi-slaves, free men who were former prisoners, and there were more than forty of them. Paramonov promised them that in a year's time they would go to the mainland "wearing top hats." Paramonov, the former head of the Maldiak mine, where General Gorbatov spent his two or three Kolyma weeks before he drifted down and became a goner, had a lot of experience in "opening" polar enterprises, and he knew what was what. Consequently, Paramonov avoided being put on trial for arbitrary acts at Maldiak, since there had been no arbitrary acts: it had been the hand of fate waving the lethal scythe and annihilating free people and, more important, prisoners with a conviction for Counterrevolutionary Trotskyist Activity.

Paramonov was acquitted; Maldiak, where thirty men a day died in 1938, was by no means the worst place in Kolyma.

Paramonov and Khokhlushkin, his deputy for economic matters, understood well that they had to act quickly while there was no checking and no responsible or qualified accounts department in the district.

This was theft, and things like food concentrates, canned food, tea, wine, sugar, can make any boss a millionaire once he touches the realm of the modern Kolyma Midas. All that was perfectly clear to Paramonov.

He also understood that he was surrounded by informers, that his every step was being carefully watched. But arrogance is another form of luck, as the gangster saying goes, and Paramonov knew gangster slang.

In short, after his administration, which was very humane and seemed to restore the balance after the arbitrary rule of the previous year—that is, 1938, when Paramonov was at Maldiak—there turned out to be an enormous amount of the most Midasian valuables missing.

Paramonov found a way of buying himself off, by showering his investigators with gifts. He wasn't arrested but merely removed from his post. The two Bogdanovs, the boss and the accountant, came to restore order. Order was restored, but because of all the money squandered by the bosses, they were forced to pay those forty or so free workers who had, like us, received nothing, ten times less than the proper amount. By falsifying documents, the two Bogdanovs managed to patch up the gaping hole that Magadan had seen.

This was the problem facing Ivan Bogdanov. His education, secondary school and some bookkeeping courses, was cut short when he was imprisoned.

Bogdanov came from the same village as the poet Aleksandr Tvardovsky and would tell people quite a few details of Tvardovsky's real biography, but at the time we were not much interested in Tvardovsky's fate: we had rather more serious problems ...

Ivan Bogdanov and I became friends, and although the instructions told nonpolitical prisoners to keep away from camp prisoners like me, Bogdanov acted completely differently in our tiny outpost.

Ivan Bogdanov loved a good joke, to listen to a "novel," and to tell stories himself: the classic story of the bridegroom's trousers came into my life in his version. The story was told in the first person, and the essence was that Ivan's bride ordered him trousers before the wedding. The groom was rather poorer, and the bride's family a bit richer, so that was an action in keeping with the spirit of the age.

For my first marriage, too, on the bride's insistence, all the money in her savings book was taken out and the best quality black trousers were ordered from the best tailor in Moscow. True, my trousers didn't undergo the same transformations as Ivan Bogdanov's. But there was psychological truth and documental plausibility in Bogdanov's trouser episode.

The plot of the Bogdanov trouser story is that just before the wedding, the bride ordered him a suit. And the suit was made twenty-four hours before the wedding, but the trousers were about ten centimeters too long. They decided to take the trousers to the tailor the next morning. The tailor lived a few dozen kilometers away, and the wedding day had been booked, the guests invited, the cakes baked. The wedding was about to be canceled because of these trousers. Bogdanov had agreed to come to his wedding in his old clothes, but his bride refused to hear of it. Because of the arguments and reproaches, the bride and groom went back to their respective homes.

Then something happened overnight. The wife decided to put the tailor's mistake right herself; she cut ten centimeters off her future husband's trousers and went to bed thoroughly pleased, sleeping the sound sleep of a faithful wife.

It was then that the groom's mother-in-law woke up: she had the same solution to the problem. She got up and, with the aid of a ruler and chalk, cut off another ten centimeters, ironed the creases and cuffs properly and slept the sound sleep of a faithful mother-in-law.

The disaster was discovered by the groom himself: his trousers had been shortened by twenty centimeters and irrevocably ruined. The wedding had to be celebrated in his old clothes, which was what the groom had suggested anyway.

Later I read all this in a story by someone like Zoshchenko or Averchenko, or in some Muscovite *Decameron*. But the first time this story came into my life was in the barracks at Black Lake in a coal prospecting post of Far East Coal.

We had a vacancy for a night watchman: a very important problem, for it gave someone the opportunity for a blissful existence over a long period.

The night watchman had been a free contract worker, and now it was a job everyone wanted.

"Why haven't you put in a request for the job?" Ivan asked me soon after this major event.

"I wouldn't be given a job like that," I said, remembering 1937 and 1938, when I went to see the free worker Sharov, the boss of the Culture and Education Section at Partisan, with a request to let me earn my living doing clerical work.

"We won't even let you write labels for food cans!" the head of the Culture and Education Section exclaimed joyfully, which vividly brought back to me a conversation I had with Comrade Yozhkin in the Vologda district People's Education Section in 1924.

Sharov, the head of the Culture and Education Section, was arrested and shot in connection with the Berzin case two months after this conversation, but I don't see myself as a ghost from *A Thousand and One Nights*, although everything I had seen goes far beyond the imagination of the Persian or any other nation.

"I won't be given that sort of job."

"Why not?"

"I have Counterrevolutionary Trotskyist Activity."

"Dozens of people I know in Magadan have the same Trotskyist Activity, but still got jobs like that."

"In that case, the problem is my being deprived of the right to correspondence."

"What's that?"

I explained to Ivan that every personal file sent to Kolyma has a printed insert with a blank space for surname and other basic directives: (1) to deprive of the right to correspondence; (2) to use exclusively for heavy manual labor. The second point was the main one; compared with this directive, the right to correspondence was trivial, hot air. There were other directives: not to allow the prisoner to use any means of communication—a clear tautology, if we're talking about the right to correspondence for those being kept in special regime conditions.

The last point was that every head of a camp subsection had to be informed of the conduct of X no less often than once every three months.

"It's just that I've never seen this insert. I have looked at your file after all, because I now happen to be also the deputy in charge of the Accounts and Records Section."

A day passed, no more. I was working at the pit face, in a hillside pit over a stream, at Black Lake. I'd lit a bonfire to keep the mosquitoes away and I wasn't particularly concerned about fulfilling the norm.

The bushes parted and Ivan Bogdanov came up to my open pit; he sat down, lit a cigarette, and dug about in his pockets.

"Would this be it?"

What he was holding was one of two copies of the notorious deprivation of the "right to correspondence," which had been ripped out of my file.

"Of course," Ivan Bogdanov said pensively, "there are two copies of a prisoner's file: one is kept in the central card catalogue of the Accounting and Registration Section, and the other travels around all the Special Camp Centers and their outposts, along with the prisoner. But all the same, no local boss will ever ask Magadan if there is a piece of paper in your file that deprives you of the right to correspondence."

Bogdanov showed me the piece of paper again and then burned it in the flames of my little bonfire.

"And now apply for the night watchman's job."

But I still wasn't taken on as a night watchman: they gave the job to Gourde, an Esperanto enthusiast who had been given twenty years under article 58, but who was an informer.

Shortly after this, Bogdanov—the head of the district, not the bookkeeper—was dismissed for drunkenness, and his place was taken by the engineer Viktor Plutalov, who was the first man to organize work at our coal prospecting post in a businesslike engineering and construction way.

If Paramonov's administration was marked by depredations, and Bogdanov's by persecution of enemies of the people and hopeless drunkenness, Plutalov was the first to show people that the labor front was not denunciations but a real labor front, a quantity of cubic meters that each man could dig out even if he was working in abnormal Kolyma circumstances. But what we knew was only the degradation of work with no prospects of rest, senseless work for many hours a day.

In fact, we were probably mistaken. In our enslaved forced labor from sunrise to sunset—and those who know the habits of the polar sun know what that means—some higher sense was hidden: there was a state sense in the senselessness of labor.

Plutalov tried to show us another side to our own work. He was a new man, who had only just arrived from the mainland.

His favorite saying was: "I'm not an NKVD worker, after all."

Unfortunately, our prospecting team didn't find any coal, and our district was shut down. Some of the men were dispatched to Kheta (where Anatoli Gidash[13] was working as an orderly). Kheta was seven kilometers away. Others were sent to Arkagala, to the district coal mines. I went to Arkagala too; within a year, I was ill with the flu in the barracks, afraid to ask Sergei Mikhailovich Lunin for release, since Lunin favored only gangsters and others in the authorities' good books: so I forced myself to get up, went to the mine, and endured the flu on my feet.

It was in the flu-inspired delirium at the Arkagala barracks that I had a passionate desire for an onion, which I hadn't tasted since Moscow, and although I had never been an admirer of the onion diet, for some unknown reasons I had a dream in which I passionately longed to bite an onion. A frivolous dream for anyone in Kolyma, or so I thought when I woke up. But I woke up not to the sound of the iron rail being struck but, as I often did, an hour before roll call.

My mouth was full of saliva, anticipating the onion. I thought that if a miracle were to happen and an onion appeared, I would recover.

I got up. The length of the whole barracks, as everywhere else, was taken up by a long table with a bench on either side.

A man in a pea jacket and fur jacket was sitting with his back to me: he turned to face me. It was Ivan Bogdanov.

We greeted each other.

"Well, let's celebrate with a cup of tea; we've each got our own bread," I said, going off to fetch a mug. Ivan got out his mug and his bread. We began drinking tea.

"Black Lake's been closed down, there's not even a night watchman. That's it, they've left. As the bookkeeper I was in the last group to come here. I thought you'd be better off with food supplies. I did hope I might get some cans of food. All I've got in my sack is a dozen or so onions: I had nowhere to put them, so I put them in the sack."

I turned pale. "Onions?"

"Yes, onions. Why are you acting so crazy?"

"Give us them!"

Ivan Bogdanov emptied his sack. Five onions thumped to the floor. "I had more, but I gave them away on the journey."

"It doesn't matter how many. Onions! Onions!"

"What's wrong with you here? Is it scurvy?"

"It's not scurvy, and I'll tell you later. After tea."

I told my story to Bogdanov.

Afterward, Ivan Bogdanov had a job to match his qualifications in the camp accounts office; it was at Arkagala that he met the war. Arkagala was the district administrative headquarters: any meetings between a nonpolitical and a political with a crime denoted in acronyms had to be stopped. But we saw each other occasionally, and told each other things.

In 1941, when I was threatened by the first bolt from the blue—an attempt to get me on a falsified charge having to do with a mining accident—the attempt failed because of the unexpected stubbornness of my work partner, a Black Sea sailor, a nonpolitical called Chudakov. After Chudakov had spent three months in solitary confinement and was freed, that is, back in the zone, we met. Chudakov told me the details of his interrogation. I told Bogdanov all this: I wasn't really asking for advice—nobody in Kolyma ever wants advice; in fact they have no right to ask for advice, which might weigh heavily on the psyche of the person asked and cause a sudden explosion as a result of the wish to do the opposite, or at the very least will result in no answer, no attention, and no help.

Bogdanov was interested in my problem.

"I'll find out. I'll find out from them!" he said, pointing expressively to the horizon, to the horse stables where the NKVD officer's little house stood. "I'll find out. I've worked for them, after all. I'm an informer. They won't hide anything from me."

But Ivan didn't manage to carry out his promise. I had already been sent to the special zone at Jelgala.

1970–1971

YAKOV OVSEYEVICH ZAVODNIK

YAKOV Ovseyevich Zavodnik was a little older than me—he was twenty or twenty-five when the revolution happened. He came from an enormous family, but not one that was the pride of the yeshiva. Although he struck one as typically Jewish in appearance—a black beard, black eyes, a big nose—Zavodnik knew no Yiddish: he made short, inflammatory speeches in Russian, speeches that were slogans or commands, and I could easily imagine Zavodnik as a military commissar in the Civil War, rousing Red Army men to come out and attack Admiral Kolchak's trenches, leading them into battle by his personal example. In fact, Zavodnik was a commissar, a military commissar of the front against Kolchak, and had two Fighting Red Banner medals. He was a loudmouthed bawler, a brawler, and he liked his drink: "he got his fist in first," to use the gangster term. Zavodnik dedicated his best years, his passion, the reason for his life to raids, battles, attacks. Zavodnik was an excellent cavalryman. After the Civil War, he worked in Minsk, in Belarus, working for the Soviets along with Zelensky, with whom he had made friends during the Civil War. When Zelensky went to Moscow, he took Zavodnik with him to the People's Commissariat for Trade.

Involved in the "Zelensky case," Zavodnik was arrested in 1937; but he wasn't shot—he got fifteen years in the camps, which was a heavy sentence for early 1937. Like me, he was sentenced in Moscow to serve his term in Kolyma.

Zavodnik's wild temperament, the blind rage that came over him at important moments in his life, which had made him gallop to meet Kolchak's bullets, didn't change even under interrogation. In Lefortovo prison he threw himself and the bench he was sitting on at

447

the interrogator and tried to hit him in response to an invitation to expose Zelensky as an enemy of the people. Zavodnik had his hip broken in Lefortovo and was put away in the hospital for a long time. When his hip bone healed, he was sent off to Kolyma. Permanently lame after Lefortovo, Zavodnik survived at the mines and in the punishment zones.

Zavodnik was not shot; he was given fifteen years, plus five "on top," that is, deprivation of civic rights. Zelensky, with whom he had been tried, had long been sent to the next world. In Lefortovo, Zavodnik signed everything that could save his life. Zelensky had been shot; Zavodnik's leg had been broken.

"Yes, I signed everything they asked me to. After they broke my hip and the bone healed, I was discharged from Butyrki hospital and sent back to Lefortovo for the interrogation to continue. I signed everything without reading a single statement. By then Zelensky had already been shot."

When Zavodnik was asked in the camp why he was lame, he would reply, "Ever since the Civil War." But in fact, the lameness originated in Lefortovo prison.

Zavodnik's wild temperament and his explosions of fury quickly led to a whole series of conflicts in Kolyma. When he first started at the mines, Zavodnik was beaten several times by the guards and the warders for the loud and stormy arguments he started over trivial issues. Zavodnik got into a fight, a real battle, with the punishment-zone warders for refusing to shave his beard and cut his hair. Everyone has their hair cut by clippers in the camps: keeping their hair and their hairstyle was a sort of privilege, an encouragement that prisoners never fail to take advantage of—for example, imprisoned medical workers were allowed to have long hair, which always aroused general envy. Zavodnik was neither a doctor nor a paramedic, but he had a long, thick black beard. His hair was more like a bonfire of black flames. Defending his beard against the clippers, Zavodnik hurled himself at a warder and got a month in solitary as punishment, but he still wouldn't give up his beard and was forcibly shaved by the warders. "Eight men held me down," Zavodnik would proudly boast; the beard grew again, and Zavodnik once more sported it defiantly.

The battle for this beard was the way a former commissar at the front asserted his identity; it was his moral victory after so many moral defeats. After many more adventures, Zavodnik ended up as a long-stay patient in the hospital.

It was clear he would never get his case reexamined. He could now only wait and live.

Someone suggested to the authorities that they should use this Civil War hero's temperament and nature, his loudness, his drive, his personal honesty and inexhaustible energy, in the capacity of a camp foreman. But there was no question of any legitimate staff work for enemies of the people, Trotskyists. So Zavodnik would take on the status of a member of a team of convalescents at the notorious CC (Convalescent Center) or CT (Convalescent Team), following the satirical couplet:

First Convalescent Centers, then the Teams,
A tag on your ankle, and now sweet dreams.

But Zavodnik didn't have a tag tied to his left ankle, as camp prisoners have when they are buried. Zavodnik started chopping firewood for the hospital.

On a planet where winter lasts ten months, firewood is a very serious problem. The central hospital for prisoners kept a hundred men on this job all year round. A larch matures in three to five hundred years. The logging areas assigned to the hospital were, of course, sheer destructiveness. Nobody bothered even to think about replacing Kolyma's forest resources, and if they did think about it, then it was only as a bureaucratic formality or a romantic dream. Those two concepts have a lot in common, a fact that historians, literary critics, and philosophers will realize one day.

In Kolyma, forests are to be found in the ravines and side valleys, and along riverbeds. So Zavodnik took a horse and rode around all the larger streams and springs nearby, and presented the head of the hospital with his report. The head of the hospital at the time was Vinokurov, a man who feathered his own nest but who was not a complete villain, not one of the malevolent bosses. A forestry outpost was set up, and timber was brought out. Of course, as in all the hospitals, it was not the patients who did the work but the healthy people, or at least the Convalescent Centers or Convalescent Teams should have been sent back to the mines long ago, but they were now irreplaceable. Vinokurov was considered to be a good manager. The difficulty lay in the quantity of fuel (a very big one) that had to be stored, quite apart from what was on the books, in the reserves that the NKVD men, the local production managers, and the head of the hospital himself were accustomed to draw on without any checks or forethought, completely without charge and without limit. For such benefits as firewood, the middle layer of the free contract workers in the hospital had to pay, while the top bosses got everything free of charge, and that was quite a tidy sum.

And Yakov Zavodnik had been put in charge of this complicated business of extracting and storing firewood. Not being an idealist, he was happy to be in charge of both production and storage, reporting only to the head of the hospital. Together with the head of the hospital, he had no scruples about robbing the state every day and every hour. The hospital head had guests from all over Kolyma; he kept a cook and received guests, while Zavodnik, as the head of the fuel supplies, stood with his cooking pot by the lunch cauldron when lunch was brought. Zavodnik was one of the camp foremen, former party members, who always ate with their brigade, doing so openly, refusing the slightest privilege in the form of clothing or food, except, of course, for keeping his black beard.

That was how I acted, too, when I was working as a paramedic. I was forced to leave the hospital after the major, acute conflict that affected even Magadan in the spring of 1949. I was then sent as a paramedic to Zavodnik's forestry outpost, about fifty kilometers from the hospital, at the Duskania spring.

"That's the third paramedic Zavodnik's dismissed: the son of a bitch doesn't like any of them."

That was how my fellow workers greeted me.

"Who do I take the medical duties over from?"

"From Grisha Barkan."

I knew Grisha Barkan, not personally but by reputation. Barkan had been a military paramedic and had been repatriated from Western

Europe and given a job in the hospital a year ago, working in the tuberculosis department. His comrades didn't have much to say in Grisha's
favor, but I had learned not to pay much attention to talk about informers and snitches. I was too helpless to fight the higher power of nature.
But once we happened to be producing a wall newspaper[14] for some
anniversary occasion, and one member of the editorial committee was
the wife of our new NKVD man, Baklanov. I was waiting to see her
outside her husband's office to get my text back after she had censored
it; when I knocked, I heard a voice say "Come in!" and I did so.

The NKVD man's wife was sitting on the sofa; Baklanov was con-
ducting an interrogation.

"Barkan, you've written in your statement that Saveliev the paramedic" (he too had been summoned there) "was cursing Soviet power
and praising the fascists. Where did this happen? In a hospital bed.
And what was Saveliev's temperature at the time? Perhaps he was rav-
ing. Take your statement back."

That's how I knew Barkan was a snitch. As for Baklanov, he was
the only NKVD man I came across in all my time in the camps who
didn't strike me as a proper interrogator: he wasn't a professional secret
policeman, of course. He had come straight from the front to Kolyma
and had never worked in the camps. And he hadn't learned how to.
Working in Kolyma didn't appeal to either Baklanov or his wife. After
serving their term there, they both returned to the mainland and lived
for many years in Kiev. Baklanov himself came from Lvov.

The paramedic lived in a separate hut, half of which was an outpatient clinic. The hut was attached to the bathhouse. For more than ten
years I hadn't spent a single night or day alone, and my entire being
now relished this joy, one that was also imbued with the subtle scent
of green larches and countless, rapidly blooming herbs. A stoat ran
across the last of the snow, bears emerged from their dens and passed
by, making the trees shake... Here I began to write poetry. Those
notebooks of coarse yellow paper have survived... Some of the notebooks were made of better-quality white wrapping paper. It was the
snitch, Grisha Barkan, who gave me two or three rolls of that paper,
the finest in the world. The whole of his outpatient clinic was packed
with those rolls: where he got them from, or took them to, I don't

know. He didn't work in the hospital for long; he was transferred to a nearby mine, but he often turned up in the hospital, when he was off on one of his trips.

A handsome man, and a dandy, Barkan thought he would travel standing on top of the barrels on the back of a truck, so as not to stain his patent-leather shoes and blue civilian trousers with gas. The cab of the truck was full. The driver let him get into the back for this ten-kilometer journey, but when the truck was climbing a hill, it shook badly, and Barkan flew out onto the highway and split his skull open on a stone. I saw his body in the morgue. Barkan's death was the one time, apparently, that fate didn't intervene on a snitch's side.

I very soon guessed why Barkan couldn't get along with Zavodnik. He was probably giving "tip-offs" about something as subtle as timber supplies, and failed to ask himself what the origin of the deceit was and who was benefiting from it. As soon as I got to know Zavodnik, I told him I wouldn't interfere in his business, but that I would ask him not to interfere in mine. None of my exemptions from work were to be questioned. And I wasn't going to let him instruct me to let anyone off work. My attitude toward the gangsters was widely known, and Zavodnik needn't have any worries about pressure or unpleasant surprises on their part.

Like Zavodnik, I shared the common cooking pot. The lumberjacks lived at three places in a radius of about a hundred kilometers from the main sector. And I would move from one group to another, spending two or three nights at each sector. Duskania was the base. At Duskania I found out something that was very important for any medic to know: I learned from the bathhouse attendant (a Tatar who'd come there from the war) how to disinfect clothes without a disinfection chamber. It was a major problem for the Kolyma camps, where lice were a workman's inseparable companions. I had a 100 percent success rate disinfecting clothes in steel barrels.

Later, my knowledge produced a sensation in the Highways Administration: lice bite guards and the military as well as convicts. I carried out a lot of disinfections, invariably successful, but I learned the technique when I was at Duskania under Zavodnik. When he saw that I deliberately abstained from any complicated fiddling with tree stumps, wood stacks, cubic meters of wood, Zavodnik warmed up to me; when he found that I had no favorites, he thawed completely. That was when he told me about Lefortovo and his battle to keep his beard. He gave me a book of Ehrenburg's poetry. Zavodnik had no sympathy for any sort of literature. He disliked novels and similar things, and would yawn over the very first lines. Newspapers and political news were quite different: they always aroused a response. Zavodnik liked real interaction with real people. Above all, he was bored, he languished when he didn't know what to do with his own powers; he tried to fill his whole day, from waking up to going to sleep, with the concerns of this day and the next. He even slept as close as he could to work: near the workmen, the river, the log rafts, in a tent or on a trestle bed in a barracks, with no mattress or pillow, just his quilted jacket under his head.

In 1950 I needed to get to Bakhaiga, about forty kilometers up the Kolyma River, where we had a sector with prisoners living by the riverbank: I had to go there as part of my next rounds. The Kolyma River has a strong current: it would take a launch ten hours to go those forty kilometers. You could get back on a log raft in one hour, or even less. The launch boatman was a free worker, he even had a contract; he was a mechanic, a profession of which there was a shortage. Like any mechanic in Kolyma who could handle motors, he was very drunk when his launch set off, but he was drunk in a reasonable, Kolyma way: he could still stand and he talked sense, even though his breath was heavy with alcoholic fumes. The launch man helped move the lumberjacks from place to place. The launch should have set off the previous day, but it sailed only at dawn in the Kolyma white night. The launch man knew, of course, that I was making the trip, but some boss, or boss's friend, or just a passenger who paid well, had gotten into the launch and, turning his face away, was waiting for the launch man to stop talking to me and to refuse to take me.

"There's no room. I said, no. You can go next time."

"But yesterday you said—"

"I might have said anything yesterday... But today I've changed my mind. Get away from the landing."

All that was spiced with well-chosen swear words, the Kolyma camp cursing.

Zavodnik was staying nearby, in a tent on the hill; he slept in his clothes. He realized at once what was going on and somehow pulled on his rubber boots, leapt out onto the riverbank, in just his shirt, without a hat. The launch man was standing in the water by the launch in his rubber wading boots, pushing the launch into the water. Zavodnik went to the water's edge.

"What's this? Are you refusing to take the paramedic?"

The launch man straightened up and turned to face Zavodnik. "Yes! I won't take him. I told him so, and that's it."

Zavodnik punched the launch man in the face; he fell down and disappeared under the water. Thinking that we had a tragedy on our hands, I moved toward the water, but the launch man emerged, water flowing off his canvas suit. He got to the launch, clambered to his place without saying a word, and started the engine. I took my medical bag and sat on the edge, stretching out my legs. The launch moved off. It was still light when we tied up at the mouth of the Bakhaiga.

All Zavodnik's energy and mental strength were focused on carrying out the wishes of Vinokurov, the head of the hospital. This was a silent agreement between master and slave. The master took on full responsibility for concealing an enemy of the people, a Trotskyist who was otherwise destined to live in special zones, while the grateful slave, not expecting any credit for his working days, nor any concessions, created prosperity for the master in the form of firewood, fresh fish, game, berries, and other gifts of nature. Zavodnik ruled his woodcutters with a firm hand; he wore only official clothes and ate from the same cooking pot as they did. The slave understood that his master had no authority to make any appeals for his early release, but the master was allowing the slave to stay alive, in the most literal and elementary sense of the word. Zavodnik was released when his sentence was served, to the very month, week, and day: there was no credit for days worked for anyone convicted under his article of the legal code. Zavodnik was released in 1952, on the fifteenth anniversary of the day he was sentenced in Lefortovo prison in Moscow. He had long understood that it was pointless writing appeals to have his case reexamined. He didn't get a single reply to any of his complaints, written in the first naïve Kolyma years. Zavodnik spent all his time on projects such as an "ice store" for timber; he designed and built a wagon for the lumberjacks that ran not so much on wheels as on caterpillar tracks. The brigade could move about when it looked for timber. The Kolyma forests are sparse: this is the forested tundra belt and there are no thick trees. To save the trouble of putting up tents or making log cabins, Zavodnik planned a permanent wagon on runners with two stories of bunks. It could easily take a brigade of twenty lumberjacks and their tools. But it was summer at the time, and summer in Kolyma is very hot: only the days are hot, while the nights are cold. The wagon was fine, but much inferior to a simple tarpaulin tent. In winter the wagon's walls were too cold and thin. The Kolyma cold will test any rubberoid, roofing felt, or plywood by making it crumble and break. The wagon was uninhabitable in winter, and the lumberjacks went back to the cabins that had been tried and tested for a thousand years. The wagon was abandoned in the forest. I advised Zavodnik to hand it over to the Magadan regional museum, but I don't know if he took my advice.

Zavodnik and Vinokurov's other pastime was the aerosled, a propeller-driven snowmobile that flies over the snow. Aerosleds, to be obtained somewhere in the mainland, were strongly recommended in textbooks about the exploitation of the north. But aerosleds demand limitless white spaces, while Kolyma's soil is 100 percent hummocks and pits, with a sparse covering of snow that is blown out of every cranny during gales or storms. Kolyma has very low snowfall, and aerosleds broke at the very first test flights. But Vinokurov, of course, when he wrote his reports, laid great emphasis on these wagons and aerosleds.

Zavodnik's patronymic was Ovseyevich: not Yevseyevich but Ovseyevich, which he insistently and loudly proclaimed at all roll calls and checks, something that always upset the registration workers. Zavodnik was perfectly literate and had beautiful handwriting. I don't know Zuyev-Insarov's[15] opinion about the characteristics of Zavodnik's handwriting, but he had an amazing signature, which was invariably unhurried and very complicated. He didn't write his initials, Y. Z., or a careless squiggle: he carefully and slowly made a complicated pattern, something you could only learn and remember in early youth or in a late term of imprisonment. Zavodnik spent a least a minute drawing his surname. It contained, in the most subtle yet striking form, his first-name initial Y and his patronymic initial O, a very round special O, and the surname Zavodnik was written out in big, clear letters, while an energetic flourish, which covered only the surname, and some subsequent especially complicated, especially ethereal ornaments seemed to mark the artist's farewell to a work he had carried out for love. I checked it many times in all sorts of circumstances, in the saddle or on the drawing board: Commissar Zavodnik's signature was always unhurried, confident, and clear.

We were on more than just good terms, we were on excellent terms. At the time, the summer of 1950, I was invited to return to the hospital as the manager of the admissions room. Admissions in an enormous thousand-bed camp hospital is a complicated business, and for years it had been impossible to organize it properly. On the advice of all the organizations involved, I was invited to do so. I came to an agreement with Amosov, the new head doctor, about a few principles to base the work of the admissions room on, and he agreed. Zavodnik came running up to me.

"I'll get it all canceled: all this bribery and corruption will be stopped."

"No, Yakov," I said. "We both know the camps. Your fate is Vinokurov, your boss. He's about to go on leave. A week after he leaves, you'll be discharged from the hospital. Vinokurov is not that important as far as my work is concerned. I want to sleep in the warmth, once it is possible, and I want to work on a certain problem and do some good."

I realized that I wouldn't succeed in writing poetry in the admissions room, or if I did, it would be very seldom. I used up all of Barkan's paper for my notes; every free minute there I wrote. A poem whose last line was "Frosts happen in paradise" was written at the frozen outlet of the Duskania spring, scrawled on a prescription notepad. Only fifteen years later was it printed in *The Literary Newspaper*.

Zavodnik had no idea that I wrote poetry, and he wouldn't have understood anything, anyway. The territory of Kolyma was too dangerous a place for prose: all you could risk was verse, not putting anything down in prose. That was the main reason why I wrote only verse in Kolyma. True, I did have another example: Thomas Hardy, the English writer, who spent the last ten years of his life writing only verse, and when asked by reporters why, used to reply that he was worried by the fate of Galileo. If Galileo had written only in verse, he wouldn't have had that unpleasantness with the church. I refused to take the Galileo risk, although not, of course, because of any literary or historical tradition but simply because my prisoner's intuition told me what was good and what was bad, where it was warm, where it was cold, whenever I played hide-and-seek with fate.

And in fact, I could have been looking at a crystal ball: Vinokurov left, and one month later Zavodnik was sent off to a mine somewhere: there he stayed until his sentence ended. But no crystal ball was needed. All that was very simple, elementary in the art or science that is called life. This was elementary.

When a man like Zavodnik is released, his prisoner's personal account should have zero point zero in it. That was what he got. Naturally, he wasn't allowed back to the mainland, and he found himself a job as a controller at a vehicle depot in Susuman. Although as a former prisoner he didn't get the northern bonuses, the pay was enough to live on.

In the winter of 1951 a letter was delivered to me. A woman doctor called Mamuchashvili had brought me a letter from Pasternak. So I took some leave (I was working as a paramedic in the Highways Administration) and set off, getting lifts from passing trucks. The temperature was already subzero, and these lifts cost a ruble a kilometer. I was then working not far from Oymiakon, the "Cold Pole," and from there I got to Susuman. On a street in Susuman I came across Zavodnik, the vehicle depot controller. What could be better? At five in the morning, Zavodnik got me into the cabin of an enormous Tatra truck that was pulling a trailer. I dropped my suitcase in the back. I could have traveled in the back, but the driver wanted to do as his boss had asked and gave me a seat in the cab. I had to take the risk of letting my suitcase out of my sight.

The Tatra sped along.

The truck was empty and braked at every settlement, picking up hitchhikers. Some would get off, others would climb in. At one small settlement an army man stopped the Tatra and loaded it with ten soldiers from the mainland, young people who had come here to do their military service. None of them had yet been touched by the sharp northern sun; they hadn't been burned by the Kolyma rays. After about forty kilometers they were met by a military truck, which turned aside. The soldiers loaded their luggage into it and moved off. I asked our driver to stop and I looked in the back. My suitcase had gone.

"That's the soldiers," said the driver. "But we'll catch up with them, they're not going anywhere."

The Tatra roared and grumbled into action and rushed ahead down the highway. In fact, within half an hour, it caught up with the soldiers' truck and overtook their ZIS. Our driver blocked the road with his Tatra. We explained what it was all about, and I found my suitcase with Pasternak's letter.

"I just took that suitcase thinking it was ours, I didn't mean anything by it," the warrant officer explained.

"Well, if you didn't mean to, you didn't mean to: all's well that ends well."

We reached Adygalakh, and I got out to stop a truck going to Oymiakon or Baragon.

By 1957 I was living in Moscow, where I found out that Zavodnik had returned to work in the Ministry of Trade, in the same job that he had twenty years earlier. I was told this by Yarotsky, a Leningrad economist who had done a lot for Zavodnik in Vinokurov's time. I thanked him, got Zavodnik's address from him, and wrote. I received an invitation to meet him, at his workplace where there would be a pass waiting for me, and so on. The letter was signed with the calligraphic flourish I knew so well. It was exactly the same, without a single extra squiggle. I found out from the letter that Zavodnik was "killing time" until his pension, that he just needed a few months to meet the conditions. I was indignant that Yarotsky had not succeeded in returning to Leningrad, even though he had parted from Kolyma far earlier than I or Zavodnik had, and that Yarotsky was now forced to live in Chisinau.

Yarotsky's case, one involving a Leningrad Young Communist who had voted for the opposition, was very familiar to me. There were no reasons whatsoever why he should not live in a capital city, but Zavodnik suddenly said, "The government has its reasons. You and I may be clear-cut cases, but Yarotsky's is probably quite different."

After that I never visited Yakov Ovseyevich Zavodnik again, even though I am still his friend.

1970–1971

DR. KUZMENKO'S CHESS

DR. KUZMENKO tipped the chess pieces onto the table.

"Lovely things," I said, as I set the pieces out on the plywood board. The chess pieces were a very fine set, a work of art. They were inspired by the topic "The Time of Troubles in Russia": Polish soldiers and Cossacks surrounded the tall figure of the first pretender, the white king. The white queen had the sculpted, energetic features of Marina Mniszek. German Sapega and Radziwill were on the board as the pretender's officers. The black pieces were dressed in monastic clothes and headed by Metropolitan Filaret. Peresvet and Osliabia wore armor over their monks' robes and had drawn their swords. On squares a8 and h8 were the towers of the Trinity Sergei Monastery.[16]

"They are indeed lovely. I can't take my eyes off them ..."

"Only," I said, "there is one historical error: the first pretender never laid siege to the monastery."

"Yes, yes," said the doctor. "You're right. But don't you find it strange that even today history doesn't know who the first pretender, Grishka Otrepiev, was?"

"That's just one of many theories, and it's not even a very plausible one. It's Pushkin's, though. And Boris Godunov, too, was not as Pushkin portrays him. There you have the poet's, playwright's, novelist's, composer's, and sculptor's job. The interpretation of an event is up to them. That's the nineteenth century with its eagerness to explain the inexplicable. Midway into the twentieth century, a document would supersede everything else, and people would trust only the document."

"There is a letter by the pretender."

"Yes, Prince Dmitri proved that he was a man of culture, a literate ruler, as worthy as the best tsars on the Russian throne."

"But who was he, then? Nobody knows who the ruler of Russia was. There's a Polish secret for you. The helpless state of historians. Something shameful. If this were Germany, documents would turn up somewhere. The Germans like documents. But the pretender's high-ranking masters knew very well how to keep a secret. How many people who got near that secret were murdered!"

"You're exaggerating, Dr. Kuzmenko, if you're denying our ability to keep a secret."

"I don't deny it at all. Isn't the death of Osip Mandelstam a secret? Where did he die, and when? There are a hundred witnesses to his death from beatings, starvation, and cold—there is no dispute about the circumstances of his death, but each of a hundred witnesses makes up his own story, his own legend. How about the death of the son of German Lopatin, murdered only because he was the son of German Lopatin?[17] People have been looking for a trace of him for the last thirty years. The relatives of former party leaders like Bukharin and Rykov received death certificates that were spaced out over many years from 1937 to 1945. But nobody ever came across these people anywhere after 1937 or 1938. All those certificates were to console the relatives. The dates of death were random. The safest conjecture is that they were all shot in Moscow dungeons no later than 1938."

"I think—"

"Do you remember Kulagin?"

"The sculptor?"

"Yes! He vanished without trace, at a time when many people did. When he vanished, he had someone else's surname, which was changed in the camp to a number. And the number was changed yet again to a third surname."

"I've heard about those tricks," I said.

"Well, he was the man who made this chess set. He made them out of bread in Butyrki prison in 1937. All the prisoners in Kulagin's cell chewed bread for hours. The important thing was to get the right moment when saliva and chewed bread make a unique combination: that was what the sculptor himself worked out, and that was his success. You took the dough out of your mouth when it was ready to take on any shape that Kulagin's fingers molded it into, and then it hardened permanently, like the cement in the Egyptian pyramids.

"Kulagin made two sets like that. The other one is 'Cortez's Conquest of Mexico.' The Mexican 'time of troubles.' Kulagin sold or gave away his Spaniards and Mexicans to one of the prison bosses, but he took the Russian 'Time of Troubles' with him when he was sent off with a party of prisoners. He used a match and his fingernail to make it: you weren't allowed to have anything metallic in prison."

"There are two pieces missing," I said. "The black queen and the white castle."

"I know," said Kuzmenko. "There are no castles at all, and the black queen, which is missing its head, is locked in my desk. So I still don't know which of the black defenders of the monastery in the Time of Troubles was the queen.

"Alimentary dystrophy was a terrible thing. Only after the Leningrad blockade was this disease called by its real name in the camps. Otherwise the diagnosis was 'polyavitaminosis, pellagra, emaciation due to dysentery.' And so on. Another way of ensuring secrecy. The secrecy of prisoners' deaths. Doctors were forbidden to speak or write about starvation in official documents, in patient notes, at conferences, in classes for postgraduates."

"I know."

"Kulagin was a tall, well-built man. When he was brought to the hospital, he weighed just forty kilos—he was nothing but skin and bones. That was the irreversible phase of alimentary dystrophy. All starving patients have an especially bad moment when their mind goes, when their logic goes awry, when they become demented: one of the Ds of the notorious Kolyma triad: dementia, diarrhea, dystrophy... You know what dementia is, do you?"

"Madness?"

"Yes, yes, madness, acquired madness, acquired idiocy. When Kulagin was admitted, as a doctor I immediately realized that the new patient had shown signs of dementia some time ago... Kulagin never regained his right mind before he died. He had with him a bag full of chess pieces that had withstood everything: disinfection and the gangsters' greed. Kulagin ate, sucked at, and swallowed the white castle, then he bit off, crumbled up, and swallowed the black queen's head. And he only bellowed when the ward assistants tried to take the bag out of his hands. I think he meant to swallow his entire work, just to destroy it, to eradicate every trace of himself from the earth.

"He should have begun swallowing the chess pieces a few months earlier. They would have saved Kulagin."

"But did he want to be saved?"

"I gave orders that the castle was not to be removed from his stomach. That could have been done during the autopsy. And the black queen's head, too...That's why this set is missing two pieces. Your move, maestro."

"No," I said. "Somehow I've lost the urge."

1967

THE MAN OFF THE SHIP

"KEEP writing, Krist, keep writing," the tired, elderly doctor was saying.

It was past two in the morning, the pile of cigarette butts on the desk in the treatment room was getting higher and higher. A thick, rough layer of ice was stuck to the windowpanes. A lilac-colored fog of tobacco smoke filled the room, but there was no time to open a skylight and ventilate the room. We'd begun working at eight in the evening, and there was no end in sight. The doctor was chain-smoking, quickly rolling himself "navy" cigarettes, tearing up pieces of newspaper to do so. Or, if he wanted to relax a little, he would roll himself what was called a "goat's foot," a funnel-shaped cigarette. His fingers, which were stained like a peasant's by tobacco smoke, flickered before my eyes, and the non-spill inkwell was tapping away like a sewing machine. The doctor's strength was coming to an end: his eyelids were drooping, and neither the goat's feet nor the navy cigarettes could overcome his tiredness.

"How about some chifir? Shall I brew up chifir?" asked Krist.

"Where are you going to get the chifir from?"

Chifir was especially strong tea: the gangster's and long-distance truck driver's joy—fifty grams per glass, a particularly reliable way to fight off sleep. It was the Kolyma hard currency, a long-distance hard currency, for when you had go on trips that took many days.

"I don't like it," said the doctor. "Actually, I don't see that chifir has any deleterious effect on health. I've seen quite a few addicts. And it's a time-honored drug. It wasn't the gangsters or the truck drivers who invented it. Jacques Paganel[18] used to brew chifir in Australia and treated Captain Grant's children to it. Half a pound of tea to a liter of water, to be boiled for three hours: that was Paganel's recipe ... And you say it was 'truckers,' gangsters! There's nothing new under the sun."

"Go to bed."

"No. Later. You need to learn how to ask the preliminary questions and do the first examination. Although it's forbidden by medical law, I do have to sleep at some point. Patients come in around the clock. It wouldn't be a disaster if you were to do the first examination: you're a man in a white gown. Who knows whether you're a male nurse, a paramedic, a doctor, an academician: you might be mentioned in memoirs as the sector, mine, or administration doctor."

"You think there'll be memoirs?"

"Certainly. If anything important happens, wake me up. Right," said the doctor, "let's make a start. Next."

A dirty, naked patient was sitting on the stool facing us. He didn't look like a training dummy; he looked like a skeleton.

"It's good training for paramedics, isn't it?" said the doctor. "And for doctors, too. Actually, a medic needs to see and know something quite different. Everything we're presented with today is a question for a very narrow, specific qualification. And if our islands—do you understand what I'm saying?—were to be swallowed up by the earth ... Keep writing, Krist, keep writing."

"Year of birth: 1893. Sex: male. I want you to pay attention to this important question. Sex: male. That is a question for the surgeon, the pathologist, the morgue statistician, the metropolitan demographer. But it is of no interest at all to the patient, he's not bothered about his sex ..."

My non-spill inkwell started banging away.

"No, the patient needn't stand up: bring him a drink of hot water. Melted snow from a can. Then he'll warm up and we can start analyzing his vita; the data about his parents' illnesses," the doctor tapped the printed patient-notes form, "you needn't collect them, don't waste time on trivialities. Ah, yes: previous illnesses: alimentary dystrophy, scurvy, dysentery, pellagra, avitaminoses A, B, C, D, E, F, G, H, I, J, K, L, M, N, O, P, Q, R, S, T, U, V, W, X, Y, Z ... You can stop the count at any point. He denies having venereal disease, he denies any intercourse with enemies of the people. Keep writing ... He has made complaints about frostbite on both feet, the result of prolonged tissue contact with cold. Got that down? Tissue contact . . . Cover yourself with this blanket." The doctor snatched a thin blanket, covered with ink stains, off the duty doctor's bunk and threw it over the patient's shoulders. "When are they going to bring that damned boiling water? We really need some sweet tea, but there's no provision for tea or sugar in the admissions room. Let's continue. Height: average. What exactly? We don't have a height ruler. Hair: gray. Nutritional state?" The doctor took a look at ribs over which a pale, dry, withered skin was stretched. "When you see a nutritional state like that, you have to write 'below average.'"

The doctor pulled at the patient's skin with two fingers.

"Skin turgor weak. Do you know what turgor is?"

"No."

"Elasticity. Has this anything to do with therapy? No, this is a patient for surgery, isn't he? Let's leave a blank in the patient notes for Leonid Markovich: tomorrow, or more probably this morning, he'll take a look and write something. Write in Cyrillic letters 'status localis.' Put a colon. Next!"

1962

ALEKSANDR GHOGHOBERIDZE

IT'S LIKE this: only fifteen years have passed, and I've forgotten the camp paramedic Aleksandr Ghoghoberidze's patronymic. Sclerosis! I thought that name would be carved in my brain cells forever; Ghoghoberidze was one of those people who make one proud to be alive, and I've forgotten his patronymic. He was not just a paramedic in the southern section of the central hospital for prisoners in Kolyma; he was my pharmacology professor, a lecturer on the paramedic courses. Oh, how hard it was to find a pharmacology teacher for the twenty lucky prisoners who were guaranteed life and salvation by taking paramedic classes. The Brussels professor Umansky agreed to teach Latin. Umansky was a polyglot, a brilliant expert on Oriental languages, and he knew the morphology of words even better than he did pathological anatomy, which he lectured on at the paramedic courses. Actually, the pathology course had some omissions. Knowing a little about the camps (Umansky was serving his third or fourth sentence, like everyone who had been convicted in the Stalin cases of the 1930s), the Brussels professor refused outright to lecture to his Kolyma students about the chapter on sexual organs, male and female. In short, students were invited to study that chapter on their own. There were a lot of people who wanted to study pharmacology, but it so happened that the person who was supposed to teach that subject had left "for the periphery" or "to the taiga" or "to the highway," as the expression went in those years. So the courses were started late, and here Ghoghoberidze, formerly the director of a major pharmacological scientific research institute in Georgia, seeing that the classes were threatened with cancellation, suddenly gave his consent. The classes started.

Ghoghoberidze understood how significant these classes were, both for the twenty "students" and for Kolyma. The classes taught people something good; they sowed the seeds of reason. A camp paramedic has great power, and he can do very significant good (or harm).

I discussed that with him later, when I became a fully qualified camp "quack" and used to visit him in his "hut" at the hospital's dermatological department. Hospital barracks were constructed to a standard plan, unlike the buildings that were farther away from Magadan, where hospitals and outpatient clinics were more like taiga dugouts. In that case, the mortality rates were such that the dugouts had to be abandoned and living-quarter barracks had to be reassigned as medical sites. The notorious "group B," men temporarily exempted from work, whose numbers kept increasing uncontrollably, also needed accommodation. Death is death, however you explain it. The explanations may be a bunch of lies, forcing doctors to invent the most fanciful diagnoses, a whole scale of words ending in -osis and -itis, and, if there was any chance of blaming something secondary, you concealed the obvious cause. But even when it was impossible to conceal the obvious, doctors in a hurry were helped by "polyavitaminosis," "pellagra," "dysentery," "scurvy." Nobody dared pronounce the word "starvation." Only after the Leningrad blockade did the term "alimentary dystrophy" appear in pathologists' and, less often, clinical diagnoses in the patient notes. This immediately simplified things by superseding all the polyavitaminosis cases. It was then that the lines of Vera Inber's poem "The Pulkovo Meridian" became very popular:

> The burning of a guttered candle,
> All the signs and laconic checklists
> Of what the learned doctors call
> Alimentary dystrophy.
> And what anyone who is not a Latinist
> Or philologist calls in Russian "starvation."

Alas, Professor Umansky as a pathologist was also a philologist and a Latinist. Year after year he would fill in the records with many a wise -osis and -itis.

Aleksandr Ghoghoberidze was taciturn and unhurried: the camps had taught him to be restrained and patient; he had learned to accept people not according to their clothes—a pea jacket and a Baikal-Amur railway hat with earflaps—but according to a whole set of inexplicable but reliable signs. Sympathy always depends on such elusive signs. People haven't exchanged two words before they feel a mutual inner disposition to each other, or hostility, or indifference, or caution. In the "free world" this process takes more time. Here, however, these subconscious sympathies or antipathies arise in a more assured, rapid, and unerring way. The camp prisoner's enormous experience of life, his tensed nerves and the greater simplicity of human relationships, the greater simplicity in knowing people—all these things are the reason for the accuracy of such judgments.

In the hospital barracks, a building with two exits and a corridor in between them, there were little rooms, so-called "cabins," which were easily turned into a storeroom, a medicine cupboard, or a hospital "cell" for isolating patients. The prisoner-doctors and paramedics usually lived in one of these "cabins." It made for very essential privileged living conditions.

The cabins were tiny, two meters square, or two by three meters. Such a little room contained a bedstead, a bedside table, sometimes what purported to be a tiny desk. In the middle of the "cabin," a small stove, like the heater used in Kolyma truck cabs, was kept constantly lit, summer and winter. The stove and its firewood, small offcuts, took up quite a lot of the living area. But nevertheless, this was personal accommodation, like a self-contained Moscow apartment. There was a little window with a gauze curtain. The rest of the cabin was filled by Ghoghoberidze. He was gigantic, broad-shouldered, with thickset arms and legs; his head was always shaved, he had big ears, and was very much like an elephant. His white paramedic's gown was too tight for him and only increased the "zoological" impression he made. Only Ghoghoberidze's eyes were not elephantine: they were gray, quick-moving, aquiline eyes.

Ghoghoberidze thought in Georgian and spoke in Russian, choosing his words slowly. He instantly understood whatever was said and grasped the essence: the shine in his eyes proved that.

I think he was well over sixty when we met in 1946, near Magadan. He had an old man's big, puffy, bluish hands. He walked slowly and almost always used a stick. He had spectacles for farsightedness, and his hand was practiced at putting these "old man's" glasses on. We very soon found out that this gigantic body still preserved its flexibility and all of its menace.

Ghoghoberidze's direct superior was Dr. Krol, a doctor who specialized in skin diseases and who had been convicted of a nonpolitical crime, something like speculation or fraud. A vulgar giggling sycophant, in his lectures Krol used to assure students attending his classes that they could "always put butter on their bread" if they studied skin diseases, but he shunned any "politics" like the plague (but who was not afraid of politics in those years?). A bribe-taker and camp speculator, a con man, he was always in league with thieves, who brought him stolen suits and trousers.

Krol had been "hooked" by the thieves long ago, and they could twist him around their little fingers. Ghoghoberidze refused outright to talk to his superior: he did his job—injections, bandaging, organizing treatment—but would not enter into conversation with Krol. Once, however, Ghoghoberidze found out that Krol was demanding patent-leather boots from one of the prisoners who was a *freier*, not a gangster, before he would admit the patient to the right department for treatment, and that the reward had already been handed over: Ghoghoberidze strode through all the hospital departments to Krol's room. Krol was now at home, the room was barred by a heavy bolt, which one of the patients had devised for him. Ghoghoberidze took the door off its hinges and strode into Krol's room. His face was scarlet, his hands were shaking. Ghoghoberidze bellowed, he trumpeted like an elephant. He grabbed the boots and flogged Krol with them in front of the male nurses and patients. Next, he returned the boots to their owner. Ghoghoberidze then started waiting for a visit from the clerk of works or the commandant. When Krol reported this, the commandant would of course put the hooligan into solitary confinement, and perhaps the camp chief would send Ghoghoberidze to do general hard labor: in such "punishment" regimes, old age would not save you from retribution. But Krol didn't report it. It wasn't to his advantage to have any light shed on his dark deeds. The doctor and paramedic went on working together.

At the school desk, side by side with me, there was another student, Barateli. I don't know what article he was convicted under, but I don't think it was article 58. Barateli did tell me once, but the Criminal Code in those years was very elaborate, and I forgot what article it was. Barateli spoke poor Russian and failed the admission tests, but Ghoghoberidze had been working in the hospital for some time; he was respected and people knew that he would be able to get Barateli accepted. Ghoghoberidze tutored him, fed him his own rations for a whole year, bought him tobacco and sugar; Barateli responded warmly and gratefully to the old man. And so he should have!

Eight months of this heroic tutoring passed; I was leaving as a fully qualified paramedic to work at a new hospital five hundred kilometers from Magadan.

So I came to say goodbye to Ghoghoberidze. Then he asked me very, very slowly, "Do you know where Eshba is?"

This question was asked in October 1946. Eshba was one of the prominent activists in Georgia's Communist Party. He had been repressed a long, long time ago, in the Yezhov era.

"Eshba is dead," I said. "He died at Serpantinnaya at the very end of 1937, or he may have survived until 1938." He was with me at the Partisan mine, but at the end of 1937, when "it started" in Kolyma, Eshba was taken, among many, many others on the "lists," to Serpantinnaya, the pretrial prison of the Northern Highways Administration, where executions were taking place almost nonstop throughout 1938.

What a name that was: Serpantinnaya! The road leading to it winds through the mountains, just like a serpentine ribbon, which is why the mapmakers called it that. Mapmakers have extensive rights. Kolyma has a river with a fox-trot name, "Rio-Rita," and a "Lake of Dancing Graylings," and springs called "Leave It," "Wait," and "Well Then!": stylists having fun.

In 1952 I happened to be traveling from pillar to post: on reindeer and dog sleds, in the back of trucks, on foot, and then another truck, an enormous Czechoslovak Tatra, horses, dogs, and reindeer, to a hospital where a year earlier I had been working. It was there that I found out from the hospital doctors that Ghoghoberidze—who had a sentence of fifteen years plus five years' deprivation of civic rights—had survived to the end of his sentence and been given permanent exile in Yakutia. That was even harsher than the usual lifelong restriction to the nearest settlement to the camp—this was the practice there even later, almost until 1955. Ghoghoberidze managed to get the right to remain in a Kolyma settlement and not move to Yakutia. It was obvious that the old man's constitution would not survive such a journey in the Far North. Ghoghoberidze settled in Yagodnoye, at kilometer 543 from Magadan. He worked in the hospital there. When I was coming back to my workplace at Oymiakon, I stopped at Yagodnoye and went to see Ghoghoberidze. He had been admitted to the free workers' hospital as a patient; he wasn't working there as a paramedic or pharmacist. High blood pressure! Very high blood pressure!

I dropped into the ward. Red and yellow blankets, brightly lit up from the side, three empty beds, but on the fourth, covered with a bright yellow blanket to the waist, lay Ghoghoberidze. He immediately recognized me, but he was almost speechless because of his headache.

"How are you?"

"So-so." His gray eyes had the same luster and vivacity. He had more wrinkles.

"Get better, recover."

"I don't know, I don't know." We said goodbye to each other.

That's all I know about Ghoghoberidze. When I was back on the mainland, I was told in letters that Aleksandr Ghoghoberidze had died in Yagodnoye, and had thus not lived to see himself rehabilitated.

That was the fate of Aleksandr Ghoghoberidze, who perished solely because he was the brother of Levan Ghoghoberidze.[19] If you want to know about Levan, read Mikoyan's memoirs.[20]

1970–1971

LESSONS IN LOVE

"You're a good man," our gangway-man told me recently. He was the brigade's carpenter who made and maintained the gangways for barrowing ore and sand to the washing equipment, the trommel. "You never refer to women badly or in a dirty way."

The gangway-man was Isai Rabinovich, who used to be the manager of the USSR State Insurance. At one point he traveled to take receipt of gold from the Norwegians in exchange for the sale of Spitsbergen in the North Sea; in stormy weather he would transfer sacks of gold from one ship to another, so as to keep the deal secret and erase all traces. He spent almost all his life abroad and was a friend of many important wealthy men—Ivar Kreuger, for example. Ivar Kreuger, the "match king," ended by committing suicide, but he was still alive in 1918, and Isai Rabinovich and his daughter were Kreuger's guests on the French Riviera.

The Soviet Union was looking for orders from abroad, and Isai Rabinovich acted as Kreuger's guarantor. In 1937 Isai was arrested and given ten years. He left a wife and daughter in Moscow: they were his only relatives. During the war, his daughter married the US naval attaché, First Rank Captain Tolly. Captain Tolly was given command of a Pacific battleship and left Moscow to take up his new post. Before that, Captain Tolly and Rabinovich's daughter wrote letters to the concentration camp where her father, his future father-in-law, was imprisoned, asking for permission to marry. Tolly's parents sent their blessing. The naval attaché married. When he was about to leave, his wife, Rabinovich's daughter, was not allowed to accompany her husband. The couple immediately divorced, and the ex-wife worked in some minor post at the People's Commissariat of Foreign Affairs. She stopped corresponding with her father. Captain Tolly wrote neither to his ex-wife nor to his ex-father-in-law. Two wartime years passed, and Rabinovich's daughter received a short-term posting to Stockholm. A special aircraft was waiting for her in Stockholm, and Captain Tolly's wife was delivered to her husband.

After this, Rabinovich began receiving letters in camp with American stamps, letters written in English, which the censors found extremely irritating...This story of an escape made after two years of waiting—for Captain Tolly considered his marriage to be anything but a Moscow romance—is one of those stories that were sadly missing from our lives. I had never noticed whether I spoke well or badly of women, and I certainly didn't even dream of any encounters with them. To be a masturbator of the kind one meets in prison, you have first of all to be well-fed. You can't imagine being depraved, whether a masturbator or a homosexual, if you are starving.

There was a handsome young man of about twenty-eight, a foreman at a hospital construction site, Vasia Shvetsov, a prisoner. The hospital was attached to the women's state farm; the warders were inefficient and, in any case, bribed. Vasia Shvetsov had astonishing success.

"I've known a lot of women, a lot. It's all very simple. But would you believe it, I'm nearly thirty and I've still never been in bed with a woman: I never got the chance. It was all very hurried, on boxes, on sacks, a quickie, and that was it...After all, I've been in prison since I was a boy..."

Another example was Liubov, a gangster, or rather a "hustler," "a perverted snitch": and this sort of person produces people whose vicious imagination can go further than the sick imagination of any thief. Liubov, tall, smiling, arrogant, always moving about, would talk about his luck: "I've done well with women, I must admit, well. My previous place in Kolyma was a women's camp, and we were the camp carpenters: I gave the clerk of works a pair of trousers, nearly new gray ones, to be sent there. You had to pay for it there, a bread ration, six hundred grams, and the terms were that she had to eat it while we were in bed together. Whatever she didn't eat I had the right to take back. That was the way they'd been doing business for ages: we didn't start it. Well, I outwitted them. I'd get up in the morning and go outside the barracks and put the bread ration in the snow. I'd then bring it to her all frozen: she could try to gnaw at the frozen stuff, she wouldn't bite off much. So we had the best of it ..."

Could you invent a man like that?

Who could imagine a women's camp barracks at night where there are lesbians, a barracks where any warders and doctors with any humanity would rather not go, and which only sex-crazed warders and sex-crazed doctors like to visit? And the weeping Nadia Gromova, a beautiful lesbian of nineteen, a "man" in lesbian love, with crew-cut hair, wearing men's trousers, making herself comfortable, to the horror of the male nurses, in the sacred armchair, a unique, specially ordered armchair meant for the woman in charge of the admissions room, crying because she wasn't being admitted to the hospital.

"The duty doctor won't admit me because he thinks I ... I swear on my honor, never, never. And look at my hands, you can see how long my nails are—so how could I?"

The outraged old male nurse Rakita spits indignantly. "Ah you nasty bitch, you nasty bitch."

But Nadia Gromova wept and couldn't understand why people refused to understand her: after all, she had grown up in the camps with lesbians.

And the plumber and metalworker Khardzhiev, a young, rosy-cheeked twenty-year-old, who had served in Vlasov's army and been in prison in Paris for thieving: Khardzhiev had been raped by a black man in the Paris prison. The black man had syphilis, the acute form prevalent during World War II, and Khardzhiev had genital warts of the anus, syphilitic growths, the notorious "cabbage." He was sent from the mine to the hospital with a diagnosis of "prolapsus recti," a prolapse of the rectum. People at the hospital had long ago stopped being amazed by such things: an informer who'd been thrown off a moving truck and had multiple fractures of the hip and legs was sent to the hospital by the local paramedic with a diagnosis of "prolapsus ex truck." Khardzhiev was a very good metalworker, and the hospital needed him. It was convenient that he had syphilis, because while they carried out a whole course of treatment, he worked for no pay at all, as a patient occupying a bed, on assembling the steam heating.

In Butyrki pretrial prison, women were almost never discussed. Everyone there did his best to present himself as a good family man, and perhaps they were; some wives, if they weren't party members, would come to visit them, bringing money, and proving that Herzen, in volume one of *My Past and Thoughts*, was right in his estimation of women in Russian society after December 14, 1825.[21]

It's doubtful whether love includes the debauching by a gangster of a bitch dog, with which he lived in full view of the camp, as if it were his wife. The debauched bitch would wag its tail and behave like a prostitute with the man it loved. For some reason, the gangster wasn't put on trial, even though the Criminal Code does have an article dealing with "bestiality." But there were all kinds of people and crimes that didn't come to trial in the camp. Dr. Penelopov, an elderly homosexual, whose "wife" was the paramedic Volodarsky, was not put on trial.

It is doubtful whether our topic is relevant to the fate of a little woman who had never been imprisoned, but who came here with her husband and two children a few years earlier. Her husband was murdered: he was a foreman and he tripped one dark night over a metal scraper being pulled by a winch. The scraper hit the man in the face; he was alive when he was brought to the hospital. The blow had struck his face diagonally. All the bones in his face and skull below the brow had been pushed back, but he was still alive and survived several days. His wife was left with two small children, aged four and six, a boy and a girl. She soon remarried: the second husband was a forester, and she lived with him for three years in the taiga, never showing her face in any of the larger settlements. She had two more children in those three years, a girl and a boy, and gave birth on her own: her husband handed her the scissors, with trembling hands, and she herself bandaged and cut the umbilical cord and anointed the end with iodine. With four children, she spent one more year in the taiga, when her husband caught a chill in the ear, refused to go to the hospital, and the middle ear became infected and inflamed. The inflammation went deeper, his temperature rose, and he arrived at the hospital. He had an urgent operation, but it was too late, and he died. She returned to the forest; she didn't weep—what use were tears?

Is our topic relevant to the horror of Igor Vasilyevich Glebov, who forgot his own wife's first name and patronymic? The temperature was well below zero, the stars were high and bright. At night, the guards are more human; by day, they are afraid of their bosses. At night we were allowed to go and take turns warming ourselves by the boiler, where the water was heated by steam. Pipes carrying hot water led from the boiler to the pit faces, where the drillers used steam to drill openings in the ore, holes in which the men would put explosives to blow up the subsoil. The boiler was in a shed made of boards, and the shed was warm when the boiler was stoked. The boiler man had the most enviable job in the mine: everybody dreamed of it. Even people convicted under article 58 could be chosen for this job. In 1938, at all the mines the boiler men were engineers, for the authorities didn't like to entrust such "technical" things to gangsters—they were afraid of card games or something else.

But Igor Vasilyevich Glebov was no boiler man. He was a getter at the pit face in our brigade: before 1937 he had been a professor of philosophy at Leningrad University. It was the freezing cold and starvation that made him forget his wife's name. When the temperature is far below zero, you can't think. You can't think about anything: the subzero temperature clears your head of thoughts. That is why camps are set up in the north.

Igor Glebov was standing by the boiler, his quilted jacket sleeves rolled up, his shirt lifted, warming his naked frozen belly against the boiler. As he warmed it, he wept, and the tears didn't freeze on his eyelashes or cheeks, as they did with every one of us, because the boiler was hot. Two weeks later Glebov, all radiant, woke me up in the barracks. He'd remembered: his wife was called Anna Vasilyevna. I didn't swear at him; I just tried to get back to sleep. Glebov died in the spring of 1938: he was too heavily built a man to survive on the camp rations.

Only in the zoo did bears seem real to me. In the Kolyma taiga and, before that, in the northern Urals taiga I came across bears several times. Each time it was in the daytime, and each time they seemed to me to be toy bears. And bears appeared in that particular spring when last year's grass still lay everywhere and not a single bright green blade of grass had yet put its head out, and only the dwarf pine was bright green, not to mention the brown larches with their emerald claws, and there was a smell of conifer—in Kolyma only the young larches and the flowering briar rose have any smell.

A bear ran past the hut where our guards, armed soldiers, lived—Izmailov, Kochetov, and a third man, whose surname I can't remember. The previous year this third man had often come to the barracks where the prisoners lived and taken a hat and quilted jacket from our foreman—he would be traveling to the highway to sell bilberries by the glassful or "lock, stock, and barrel," and it would have been embarrassing to wear his uniform cap. These guards were well behaved; they realized that in the forest they had to behave differently than they did in the settlement. They were never rude and they didn't force anyone to work. Izmailov was in charge. When he had to go away, he hid his heavy rifle under the floor, using an ax to gouge up and shift the heavy larch blocks. The second guard, Kochetov, was afraid to hide his rifle under the floor: he took it with him everywhere. That day, only Izmailov was at home. When he heard from the cook that a bear was passing, Izmailov put on his boots, grabbed his rifle, and ran outside in his underwear. But the bear had already disappeared into the taiga. Izmailov and the cook ran after it, but there was no sign of the bear, the marsh was too sticky, and they returned to the settlement. The settlement stood on the banks of a small mountain spring, but the opposite bank was an almost vertical slope, sparsely covered with low larches and bushes of dwarf pine.

The whole hillside was visible, from top to bottom, right down to the water, and it seemed very near. Two bears were in a small clearing, one bigger, one, the female, smaller. They were fighting, breaking the larches, hurling stones at each other; they were in no hurry and hadn't noticed the human beings below them, nor the log cabins of our settlement, which were altogether no more than five in number, including the stables.

Izmailov, still in his underwear, carrying his rifle, followed by the settlement's inhabitants, each one carrying an ax or a piece of metal, the cook holding an enormous kitchen knife, creeping up in the leeward toward the playing bears. They seemed to have gotten quite close when the cook shook his enormous knife over the head of Izmailov the guard and rasped, "Fire! Fire!"

Izmailov laid the rifle on a rotten fallen larch; the bears heard something, or had a prey's premonition of a hunter, a premonition that undoubtedly exists, which warned the bears of danger.

The female bear rushed up the slope, running faster than a hare, while the old male didn't run. Instead, he moved at a leisurely pace along the contours of the hillside, gradually speeding up, taking on himself all the danger that the animal, naturally, had sensed. A rifle shot rang out, and at that very moment the female bear vanished over the crest of the hill. The male bear ran faster, over the storm-felled timber, over the green mossy rocks, but Izmailov skillfully aimed and fired his rifle a second time, and the bear rolled down the hill like a beam, like an enormous rock, straight into the ravine onto a thick layer of ice over the stream, a stream that doesn't begin to thaw until August. The bear lay motionless on the dazzling ice: it was like an enormous child's toy. It had died the death of a wild animal, of a gentleman.

Many years earlier, when I was part of a prospecting group, ax in hand, I was walking down a bear track. The geologist Makhmutov was following me; he had a small-caliber rifle over his shoulder. The path bent around a half-rotten tree, full of holes; as I passed, I banged the ax handle against the tree, and a weasel fell out of a hole onto the grass. The weasel was giving birth and could hardly move on the path: it didn't try to run away. Makhmutov took his small-caliber rifle off his shoulder and fired point-blank at the weasel. He failed to kill it: he only shot off its leg, and the tiny, blood-covered animal, a dying pregnant mother, crawled silently toward Makhmutov, biting at his fabric boots. Its shiny eyes were fearless and angry. The geologist took fright and ran along the path away from the weasel. I thought he could pray to his god for me not to kill him with my ax on that bear track. There was something in my eyes that stopped Makhmutov from taking me with him on his next geological exploration...

What do we know of others' grief? Nothing. About others' happiness? Even less. We try to forget even about our own grief, and our memory for grief and misfortune is conscientiously weak. To know how to live is to know how to forget, and nobody knows that so well as the people of Kolyma, the prisoners.

What was Auschwitz? Literature, or... But in Stefa's case, Auschwitz gave her the rare joy of liberation and then, among tens of thousands of others, she landed, as a victim of spy mania, in something worse than Auschwitz: she ended up in Kolyma. Of course, Kolyma didn't have death chambers; here they preferred to freeze people to death, to "drive them into the ground"—that was the most satisfactory result.

Stefa was a ward assistant in the women's tuberculosis department of the hospital for prisoners: all the ward assistants were also patients. For decades the lie had been that the mountains of the Far North were a sort of Switzerland, so that "Grandfather's Bald Patch" was supposed to look something like Davos. In the first annual medical reports from Kolyma, the word "tuberculosis" was mentioned not at all, or very seldom.

But the marshes, the damp, and the starvation did their work, and laboratory analyses showed that tuberculosis was increasing and confirmed the mortality rate. There was no possibility of blaming it (as they would in the future) on the Germans like, say, syphilis in the camps, imported from Germany.

They started to admit tuberculosis patients to the hospital and to exempt them from work: tuberculosis won its "civic rights." But what was the price? Working in the north was more terrible than any disease: healthy people fearlessly went into tuberculosis departments by deceiving the doctors. They would take mucus, a "gob," from those known to have tuberculosis, from dying patients, carefully wrap up the mucus in a rag, hide it, like a charm, and when analyses were being collected for the laboratory, they would put the mucus with what they considered "benign bacteria" into their mouths and cough into the vessel the laboratory assistant offered them. The laboratory assistant was experienced and reliable, which was more important than having a medical education, as the authorities then considered, and he made the patient cough up the mucus in his presence. No attempts to educate people about this had any effect: life in the camp and work in the freezing cold were more frightening than death. Healthy men quickly became sick and then had a legitimate right to use the notorious bed day.

Stefa was a ward assistant: she did the laundry, and the mountains of dirty cotton laundry and the acrid smell of soap, lye, human sweat, and stinking warm steam enveloped her "workplace."

1963

ATHENIAN NIGHTS

WHEN I finished my paramedic classes and started work in a hospital, the main camp question, to live or not to live, was removed from the agenda, and it was clear that only a shot, or a blow from an ax, or the universe collapsing over my head would stop me from living to whatever limit heaven prescribed.

I felt all this with all my camp body, without any participation by thought. To be precise, thought did make an appearance, but without any logical preparation, as an illumination that crowned purely physical processes that were beginning to penetrate my emaciated and exhausted scurvy wounds: in my camp body, in human tissue tested to the point of tearing, yet still retaining, to my own amazement, a colossal reserve of strength, these wounds had not closed even after ten years.

I saw that Thomas More's formula had acquired new content. In his *Utopia* Thomas More defined man's four basic feelings that, when satisfied, provide the highest form of bliss, in his opinion. More put hunger and the satisfaction derived from eating food first; second in its intensity came sex; the third was urination; and the fourth was defecation.

It was those four main satisfactions that we were deprived of in the camps. The bosses felt that love was a feeling that could be expelled, fettered, distorted ... "You'll never see another live cunt in your life" was the camp bosses' standard joke.

The camp bosses fought lovingly to obey the circulars and see that the law was observed. Alimentary dystrophy was their unfailing ally, a powerful one in the fight against the human libido. But the three other feelings also underwent the same changes, distortions, and mutations under the blows of fate, in other words, the camp bosses.

The hunger was insatiable, and nothing can compare with the feeling of hunger, a hunger that gnaws at you—the constant condition for a camp prisoner if he is there under article 58 and happens to be a goner. Nobody has celebrated the hunger of a goner. Collecting bowls in the refectory, licking other people's dishes, crumbs of bread tipped into their palms and then licked up: all this arouses only a qualitative reaction when it gets to the stomach. It is no simple matter to quench such hunger; in fact it is unquenchable. Many years will pass before the prisoner unlearns his constant readiness to eat. However much he eats, he wants to do so again in half an hour or an hour.

Urination? Urine incontinence is endemic in a camp where people are starving or are goners. Where is the satisfaction in urinating, when somebody else's urine is falling onto your face from the bunk above, and you have to put up with it? You happen to be on the lower bunk, but you could have lain on an upper bunk and urinated on the man below you. That's why you curse him only half-heartedly, and just wipe the urine off your face and go back to your heavy sleep, dreaming of just one thing: loaves of bread flying like angels in the heavens, soaring up.

Defecation. But a goner has a lot of trouble defecating. Buttoning up his trousers when it is minus fifty degrees is beyond him, and in any case a goner defecates only once in five days, thus refuting the textbooks on physiology, even on pathophysiology. Excreting dry balls of excrement means that your organism has already squeezed out everything that could keep you alive.

No goner ever gets any satisfaction or pleasant feeling from defecation. Just as in urinating, the body works regardless of its owner's will, and the goner has to pull down his trousers in a hurry. The cunning, half-bestial prisoner uses defecation as a rest break, to get his breath back on the calvary of the gold-mine pit face. It is the prisoner's only trick in struggling against the power of the state—a million-strong army of soldiers and guards, social organizations and state institutions. The goner uses the instinct of his own behind to resist this great force.

A goner places no hopes on the future—in all the memoirs and novels, a goner is mocked as a shirker who is an obstacle to his comrades, who lets down the brigade, the pit face, and the mine's gold-production plan. Some mercenary writer comes along and represents the goner as a comic figure. Such writers have attempted to do this before, considering that they are entitled to have a laugh at the camp's expense. There's a time for everything, they tell themselves. The path to the camp is not closed for a joke.

To me, at least, words like these are blasphemous. I consider that composing them and dancing an "Auschwitz" rumba or playing the "Serpantinnaya blues" is something only someone vulgar or mercenary (which is often the same thing) would do.

The camps cannot be a topic for comedy. Our fate is not a subject for humorous writing. And it will never be a subject for humor—tomorrow, or a thousand years later.

It will never be possible to approach the ovens of Dachau or the ravines of Serpantinnaya with a smile.

Attempts to take a break, by unbuttoning one's trousers and squatting down for a second, for a moment less than a second, to distract oneself from the agony of work, merit respect. It is only the novices who make these attempts—later, it becomes even more difficult and painful to straighten one's back afterward. But a novice will sometimes use this illicit way of resting, to steal a few of the government's minutes from the working day.

It is then that a guard, rifle in hand, intervenes to unmask this dangerous criminal and malingerer. In 1938 I myself witnessed a guard at the Partisan gold-mine pit face waving his rifle about, ordering my comrade: "Show us your shit! That's the third time you've squatted. Where's the shit?" He accused the half-dead goner of malingering.

They couldn't find any shit.

I saw the goner, Seriozha Klivansky, my university comrade, a second violinist at the Stanislavsky Theater, being accused of sabotage for taking an illicit break while defecating when the temperature was minus sixty degrees: he was accused of delaying the work of his pair, of the brigade, of the sector, of the mine, of the region, of the state. It was like the famous song about the horseshoe that was missing a nail.[22] It was not only the guards and warders who accused Seriozha, it was his fellow workers, all engaged in this salutary labor that redeemed all sins.

In fact, there was no shit in Seriozha's gut, but there was the need "to go." But you had to be a medic, and not just a Kolyma one, you had to be a metropolitan, mainland, prerevolutionary medic to understand all that and explain it to others. Here, however, Seriozha could expect to be shot simply because he turned out to have no shit in his gut.

But Seriozha wasn't shot.

He was shot later, a little bit later, at Serpantinnaya during the mass executions under Garanin.

My discussion with Thomas More has gone on longer than expected, but it is now ending. These four feelings that were trampled on, smashed, and crumpled—destroying them was not yet the end of life—were resurrected again. After the resurrection, although it was distorted and monstrous in all four cases, the camp prisoner would squat over the latrine hole, interested in his sensation of something soft creeping down his ulcerated gut, painlessly, gently, warmly, as if the excrement were reluctant to part with the gut. The excrement would fall into the pit with splashes and spurts. In a latrine pit the excrement floats on the surface for a long time before it finds its place: this is the miraculous beginning. You can now even urinate in limited amounts, interrupting the urination whenever you wish. That too is a small miracle.

Now you meet women's eyes with a certain vague, unearthly interest—not excitement, no, because you don't know what you have left in you for them, and whether your impotence (or might it be more correct to say castration) is reversible. Impotence for men, amenorrhea for women—those are the standard consequences of alimentary dystrophy, or to put it simply, starvation. This is the knife with which fate stabs all prisoners in the back. Castration is the result not of prolonged abstinence in prison and camp but of other causes, more direct and more certain. The camp rations hold the secret, whatever Thomas More's formulations might be.

It's more important to overcome hunger. And all your organs are desperately trying not to consume too much. You are hungry for many years to come. You find it hard to split the day up into breakfast, lunch, and dinner. Nothing else has existed in your brain or your life for years on end. You are unable to have a good lunch, a filling one, a solid one—you want to eat all the time.

But the hour and the day come when you can make an effort of willpower to reject all thoughts of eating, of nutrition, of whether you will get buckwheat for dinner or whether it will be kept over until breakfast the next morning. There are no potatoes in Kolyma. So potatoes are not included in the menu of my gastronomic dreams, and for very good reasons, since otherwise dreams would cease to be dreams; they would become too unreal. The Kolyma prisoners' gastronomic dreams were about bread, not pastries; about porridge from wheat, oats, pearl barley, fox, or ordinary millet, but not about potatoes.

For fifteen years I never had any potato in my mouth; when I was released, back in the mainland, at Turkmen in Kalinin Province, I tried it, and it seemed to me to be a poison, an unfamiliar, dangerous dish: I reacted like a cat to something life-threatening forced into its mouth. It took at least a year before I got used to potatoes again. But I only got used to them; even now I'm incapable of relishing a side dish of potatoes. Once more I was convinced that the advice of camp medicine, "the table of substitutes" and "nutritional norms," were based on thoroughly scientific considerations.

Potatoes, indeed! Long live pre-Columbian times! The human body can do without potatoes.

There is a new feeling, a new need, which is more acute than the thought of food; it was totally forgotten by Thomas More in his crude classification of four feelings.

The fifth feeling is a need for poetry.

Every literate paramedic, a fellow employee in hell, turns out to have a notebook where he writes down, in ink of any color he can get, other people's poetry, not quotations from Hegel or the Gospels but poetry. So this then is the need that lies behind hunger, sexual feelings, defecation, and urination.

A need to listen to poetry, something that Thomas More did not take into account.

And all of them have poetry.

Dobrovolsky would pull a dirty, thick notebook from under his shirt and divine sounds would come from it. A former screenwriter, Dobrovolsky worked in the hospital as a paramedic.

Portugalov, who directed the hospital's Culture Brigade, struck one with his samples of an actor's memory in splendid working order, once it was lubricated by a tiny bit of grease from working with culture. Portugalov never read anything from a piece of paper: it was all done from memory.

I racked my brain, which once gave up so much time to poetry, and to my own amazement, I saw that, without making any effort of will, words that I had long forgotten appeared in my throat. I could recall not my own poetry but the poetry of my favorite poets—Tiutchev, Baratynsky, Pushkin, Annensky—all in my throat.

There were three of us in the bandaging section of the surgical department where I worked as a duty paramedic. Dobrovolsky was the duty paramedic in the eye department, Portugalov was an actor from the cultural staff. Our meeting place was my room, and the responsibility for the evening was also mine. But nobody thought about responsibility: everything was improvised. Faithful to my old, in fact invariable, habit of acting first and asking for permission afterward, I began these readings in the bandaging room of the infectious surgical department.

It was an hour of poetry reading. An hour when we returned to a magical world. We were all worked up. I even dictated to Dobrovolsky Bunin's "Cain": the poem had stuck in my memory by chance—Bunin was not a great poet, but in an oral anthology compiled in Kolyma, it was very, very resonant.

These poetic evenings began at nine, after the last checks in the hospital, and ended at eleven or midnight. Dobrovolsky and I were on duty, but Portugalov was entitled to be late. We held several of these poetry evenings, which in the hospital were later called Athenian Nights.

It immediately became clear that we were all admirers of Russian lyrical poetry from the beginning of the twentieth century.

My contribution was Blok, Pasternak, Annensky, Khlebnikov, Severianin, Kamensky, Bely, Yesenin, Tikhonov, Khodasevich, and Bunin. And from the classics I contributed Tiutchev, Baratynsky, Pushkin, Lermontov, Nekrasov, and Aleksei Tolstoy.

Portugalov's contribution was Gumiliov, Mandelstam, Akhmatova, Tsvetayeva, Tikhonov, Selvinsky, and, from the classics, Lermontov and Grigoriev, whom Dobrovolsky and I knew more by repute than directly, and the full extent of whose astonishing verse we experienced only in Kolyma.

Dobrovolsky's share was Marshak and his translations of Burns and Shakespeare, Mayakovsky, Akhmatova, Pasternak—right up to the latest works in what was then called samizdat, self-publishing. It was Dobrovolsky who recited Mayakovsky's "Lilichka! (instead of a letter)," and it was then that we also learned Pasternak's "Winter Is Approaching." The first Tashkent version of Akhmatova's *Poem Without a Hero* was also recited by Dobrovolsky. Pyryev and Ladynina[23] had sent this to him, as the former scriptwriter for *The Tractor Drivers*.

We all understood that poetry was poetry, and doggerel was doggerel, and that fame was not the deciding factor in poetry. We each of us had our own accounts with poetry, and I would have called it a "Hamburg Account,"[24] if that term were not such a cliché. We were all agreed that in our poetry evenings we shouldn't waste time by including such names as Bagritsky, Lugovskoi, or Svetlov in our oral poetry anthology, although Portugalov had belonged to the same literary group as one of them. Our list had been established well in advance. Our voting system was a well-kept secret: we had voted for the same names many years previously, each independently of the others, in Kolyma. Our choices coincided in names, poems, stanzas, and even lines that each of us had singled out. The poetic heritage of the nineteenth century was not enough for us; it seemed insufficient. Each of us would recite whatever he could remember and record in the interval between these poetry evenings. We didn't get around to reciting our own verse; it was clear that all three of us were writing or had been writing verse, but our Athenian Nights were interrupted in an unexpected way.

There were more than two hundred sick prisoners in the surgical department, and the whole hospital had a thousand beds for prisoners. Part of the T-shaped block was set aside for patients who were free contract workers. That was a sensible and useful measure. Doctors who were prisoners—and they included quite a few stars of medicine on a national scale—were officially granted the right to treat free patients, acting as consultants available at any time of the day, the year, the decades...

In the winter when we held our poetry evenings, there was still no department for free contract workers. Only in the surgical department was there a two-bed ward for free workers in case of emergency admissions, traumas such as a traffic accident, for example. At the time there was a girl of twenty-three in the ward; she was one of the Moscow Young Communists recruited for the Far North. She was entirely surrounded by criminals, but that didn't bother her: she had been the secretary of a Young Communist organization at a neighboring mine. The girl didn't even think about the criminals, very likely because she had no idea of the peculiar nature of Kolyma. She was dying of boredom. It turned out that she didn't have the illness for which she was admitted as an emergency. But medicine is medicine, and the girl had to stay in bed for the prescribed quarantine period before she could cross the hospital's threshold and vanish in the subzero abyss. She had some high-up connections in the Magadan administration itself, which was why she had been admitted to a male camp hospital.

The girl asked me if she could listen to a poetry evening. I said she could. As soon as the next recital began, she came into the bandaging room of the infectious surgical department and stayed right to the end of the reading. She attended the next poetic evening, too. These evenings were held when I was on duty, which was for twenty-four hours every three days. Another evening passed, but when the third evening began, the door to the bandaging room was flung open and the head of the hospital himself, Dr. Doctor, strode in.

Dr. Doctor loathed me. I had no doubt that he had received denunciations of our poetry evenings. Kolyma bosses usually act on the basis that they took measures if they got a "signal." The word "signal" had been established as a term for information even before Norbert Wiener[25] was born, and it was always applied in the sense of information in prisons and criminal investigations. But if there was no signal, in other words, no verbal complaint, or formal snitching, or an order from senior bosses who had detected a signal, the principle was that you could hear as well as see better from the top of the mountain. Bosses rarely used their own initiative to start an official inquiry into any new phenomenon in the camp life under their remit.

Dr. Doctor was different. He considered it his vocation, his moral imperative to persecute all "enemies of the people" in any way, on any pretext, in any circumstances, and at every opportunity.

Completely confident that he would catch us at something serious, he flew into the bandaging room, without even bothering to put on a gown, although the duty paramedic of the therapeutic department was rushing after him, holding Doctor's gown in his outstretched hands. This duty paramedic was the red-faced Pomane, a Romanian officer, a favorite of King Michael I of Romania. Dr. Doctor entered the bandaging room wearing a leather jacket, tailored like Stalin's tunic; even his Pushkinian white sideburns—Dr. Doctor was proud of his resemblance to Pushkin—were sticking out with the tension of the hunt.

"A-a-a," drawled the hospital chief, looking at each participant of the reading in turn, and fixing his gaze on me, "you're the man I'm looking for!"

I stood at attention, and reported as I was supposed to.

"And where are you from, girl?" Dr. Doctor pointed his finger at the girl who was sitting in a corner and who had not stood up when the dreaded boss had appeared.

"I'm a patient here," she said without expression, "and I would ask you to speak to me politely."

"What do you mean, a patient?"

The commandant had come in with the chief and explained the girl's status as a patient.

"Fine," said Dr. Doctor in a menacing tone, "I'll sort this out. We'll have another talk!" And he left the bandaging room. Both Portugalov and Dobrovolsky had long since slipped out of the bandaging room.

"What's going to happen now?" asked the girl, but her tone showed no fear, only interest in the legal nature of what would ensue. Interest, but no anxiety or fear for her own or anyone else's fate.

"Nothing," I said, "is going to happen to me, I think. But you might be discharged."

"Well, if he discharges me," the girl said, "I'll see that Dr. Doctor has a wonderful time. If he utters so much as a squeak, I'll introduce him to all the top bosses that can be found in Kolyma."

But Dr. Doctor dropped the matter. She wasn't discharged. The doctor had found out about her powers and decided to let this matter drop. The girl spent the prescribed quarantine time and then left, dissolved in nonexistence.

The hospital chief didn't have me arrested, either; he didn't put me in solitary, he didn't dispatch me to a punishment mine, he didn't make me do heavy manual work. But at the next report to the general assembly of the employees of the hospital, in a packed six-hundred-seat cinema auditorium, the hospital chief gave a detailed account of the disorders that he, as chief, had personally witnessed when on his rounds in the surgical department, when paramedic X was sitting in the operating theater eating bilberries from the same bowl as a woman who had come in there. Here, in the operating theater…

"It wasn't the operating theater, it was the bandaging room in the infectious department."

"Well, that's just the same!"

"It certainly isn't the same!"

Dr. Doctor screwed up his eyes. It was Rubantsev, the new manager of the surgical department, who had spoken: he was a doctor who'd come from the battlefront. Dr. Doctor warded off this impertinent critic with a gesture and went on with his invective. The woman wasn't named. Dr. Doctor, who had unlimited power over our souls, hearts, and bodies, was for some reason concealing the heroine's surname. In similar cases, when there is a report or an order, all details, possible and impossible, are usually set out in full.

"And what happened to this ex-prisoner paramedic for such a flagrant breach of the rules, especially when caught in flagrante by the chief in person?"

"Nothing."

"And her?"

"Nothing, either."

"Who was she?"

"Nobody knows."

Someone had advised Dr. Doctor to repress his administrative zeal just for this occasion.

Six months or a year after these events, when even Dr. Doctor had long vanished from the hospital—he was transferred for his devotion to duty somewhere farther and higher—a paramedic, who'd been on the same course as me, asked me as we were walking down the hospital surgical department corridor, "Is this the bandaging room where your Athenian Nights were held? They say that there was—"

"Yes," I said, "it is."

1973

A JOURNEY TO OLA

IT WAS a sunny day in Magadan, a bright Sunday, and I was watching a match between the local teams, Dinamo-3 and Dinamo-4. The breath of Stalinist unification was responsible for this boring sameness in the names. The finals and the semifinals were all played by teams called Dinamo, which is what you would expect, after all, in the city where we were. I was sitting at some distance, one of the far upper seats, and, I felt, I was a victim of an optical illusion, for the players on both teams seemed to be moving very slowly as they got themselves in the right position to score a goal, and when the ball is sent into the goal, it has such a slow trajectory in the air that the whole act of scoring can be compared to a slow-motion television replay. But there were no slow-motion television replays then, there were no televisions, so that my comparison would be a sin only too familiar in literary studies. Actually, there was slow-motion filming even in my times: it appeared in the world before I did, or at the same time. I could have compared this soccer match with slow-motion filming and only later realized that it wasn't a matter of filming but just that the soccer match was in the Far North, in other longitudes and latitudes, that the players move as slowly as their whole life does. I don't know if the players included any victim of Stalin's famous punishment of soccer players. At the time, Stalin interfered not only in literature and music but in soccer, too. The Army Central Sports Club team, the best in the country, was dissolved in 1952 after losing at the Olympics. And the team was never resurrected. There shouldn't have been any of those players on the Magadan match teams. But the four Starostin brothers, Nikolai, Andrei, Aleksandr, and Piotr, all players on the national team, might have played in Magadan.

In my times, in the times under consideration, as historians put it, all the Starostin brothers were in prison, accused of being Japanese spies.

Mantsev, the chairman of the Supreme Council of Physical Culture, was annihilated: he was executed. Mantsev was one of the Old Bolsheviks, active participants in the October Revolution. That was why he was eliminated. The sinecure that Mantsev held in the last months before he died was, of course, not enough to quench Stalin's thirst for vengeance.

I was told in the Magadan district NKVD section: "We have no objections to your leaving for the mainland, for Russia proper. Find yourself a job, get your release, and leave; there will be no obstacles on our part, and there is absolutely no need to turn to us."

That was an old trick, a game I had been familiar with since childhood. The lack of any way out, the need for three meals a day, forced former prisoners to listen to lectures like that. I had handed in my first free man's papers, scrappy free man's documents, to the personnel department of Far East Construction, my work book with just one entry, a copy of my certificate of completion of paramedic classes, certified by two doctors who taught me, as witnesses. Two days later I applied for the job of paramedic at Ola, an ethnic minority region where state authority was protecting the population from a torrent of prisoners: the torrent of many millions made a detour, heading north along the Kolyma highway. The coast meant Arman, Ola, settlements where Erik the Red, if not Columbus, might have stayed, and that had been known since antiquity on the Okhotsk coast. There was a top-onymical legend in Kolyma that the river and the whole region itself had been named for Columbus, no less, and that the famous explorer of the seas had been there several times during his visits to England and Greenland. The coast was protected by laws. Not all former prisoners were permitted to live there: gangsters, whether former, present, reformed, or still active, were banned from that region, but as a newly hatched free man I had the right to visit these islands of the blessed. There was fishing there, and that meant food. There was hunting there, and that also meant food. There were village farms there, a third source of food. There were herds of reindeer there, a fourth source of food.

Those reindeer herds—and apparently Berzin had also introduced yaks or something similar when Far East Construction started its activities—were quite a problem for the state. They required enormous subsidies. Among the numerous oddities, I well remember Far East Construction's hopeless efforts over many years to teach German shepherds to guard reindeer. The German shepherds, which had the greatest possible success all over the Soviet Union in guarding people, escorting parties of prisoners, searching for escapees in the taiga, refused outright to guard herds of reindeer, and the local population was forced to guard the reindeer herds with its usual huskies. Not many people know this astonishing historical fact. What was the problem here? Was it that the brains of the German shepherds were programmed for people, not reindeer? Can that be true? Group hunting, which wolves, for example, use when hunting reindeer herds, has all the elements of guarding reindeer. But not a single German shepherd could ever learn to guard a herd. Experienced dogs couldn't be retrained, and there was no success in raising puppies as herders instead of hunters. The experiment ended in failure, in nature's total victory.

So I expressed a wish to go to Ola, land of reindeer, fish, and berries. Of course, the salaries were half those in the camps run by Far East Construction, but at least at Ola there was governmental order and shirkers, thieves, drunks were not tolerated but were expelled from the region to Magadan, to Far East Construction territory, where other laws applied. The district committee chairman had the right to carry out these expulsions, without trial or investigation, to send the just man back to the world of sinners. These arrangements did not, of course, apply to the aborigines. The expulsion was not at all complicated: it was a hundred kilometers by sea to Magadan and thirty through the taiga. A policeman took the sinner by the arm and led him to the purgatory of a Magadan transit camp, where there was a transit camp even for free men, a "quarantine point," just like the arrangements for prisoners. All this I found attractive, so I took a warrant for travel to Ola.

But how could I get to Ola? Of course, I would be paid travel and living expenses from the moment I picked up my travel warrant, which was poked out of the window of the tunnel by the fragrant hand of some lieutenant inspector in the personnel department, but winter passed quickly here, and I would have preferred to get to my workplace

—after all, novices aren't allowed to stay long at Ola. Hitching a lift? I entrusted the decision to the institute of public opinion, just like a Gallup poll: I questioned all my neighbors standing like me in the endless line at the personnel department, and 99.9 percent recommended taking the launch. I decided to take the launch that went from Vesiolaya Bay. Then I had a fabulous, amazing piece of luck. In the street I met Boris Lesniak, who, along with his wife, Savoyeva, had given me so much help in one of my starving years, those Pharaoh's lean years.

There's a well-known scientific expression, "a run of luck." Luck can be minor or major. Troubles, they say, don't come singly. Nor does luck. The next day, when I was working out how I could catch the launch, I also met Yarotsky, the hospital's former chief bookkeeper. Yarotsky had a job at Vesiolaya Bay, and his wife allowed me to do my laundry at his apartment, so I spent the whole day happily washing everything that had accumulated when I was traveling in Lieutenant Colonel Fragin's hands. And that was a stroke of luck, too. Yarotsky gave me a note to hand to the boat dispatcher. The launch sailed once a day, I lugged my two suitcases onto it, as cunningly as any gangster, since one suitcase was empty and the other contained my only suit, a cheap blue one, bought at the Left Bank when I was still a prisoner, and my notebooks of verses, slim notebooks, no longer made of Barkan's wrapping paper. Without my intending to, I had gradually filled one notebook with rhyming lines, and it was not meant to arouse any suspicions should it be stolen. But it wasn't stolen. At the appointed time, the launch sailed and delivered me to Ola, to the tuberculosis hospital for aborigines. The barracks-hotel also housed the district health department and its young doctor. The manager was off on a trip, so that I had two or three days to wait. I got to know Ola.

Ola was empty and silent. The dog salmon and humpback salmon were swimming back to the open sea after spawning, leaping the rapids with the same haste and passion as when they had swum upstream. The same hunters lurked in the same ambushes. The entire settlement—men, women, children, bosses, and subordinates—were all standing in the river bringing in this harvest of fish. The fish factories, the smokeries, the salting huts were working around the clock. Only the duty staff were still in the hospital: all the convalescents were also out fishing. From time to time, a wagon would cross the dusty settlement with a silvery sea of dog salmon and humpback salmon thrashing about in an enormous box made of two-meter boards. Someone was yelling out desperately, "Senka. Senka!" Who could shout on a harvest day as mad as this? A shirker? A saboteur? A seriously ill patient?

"Senka, give me a fish!"

Without stopping the wagon, Senka dropped the reins for an instant and threw out an enormous two-meter-long dog salmon, its skin flashing in the sun. A local old man, the night watchman and the duty paramedic, told me, when I hinted that it would be nice to eat something, if my hosts had anything to spare, "What can I give you? We've got yesterday's dog salmon soup, but it's dog salmon, not humpback. It's fine. Have some and warm yourself up. But you're not going to eat it, after all. We don't eat yesterday's food, generally."

After half a cooking pot of yesterday's dog salmon and a rest, I went to the shore to bathe. Bathing in the Sea of Okhotsk was to bathe in a dirty, cold, salty sea, as everyone knows, but I swam for a short while just as a matter of general education.

Ola was a dusty settlement. When the wagon passed it raised mountains of dust. But it had been hot for a long time and I never found out if this dust would turn into clay as hard as stone, as it would, for example, in Kalinin Province. The day I spent in the Ola settlement helped me to see two peculiarities of this northern paradise.

There was an extraordinary number of an Italian breed of chickens, white-winged leghorns: all the householders kept this breed only because of its egg-laying capacity, apparently. One egg at Magadan market cost a hundred rubles at the time. And as all the chickens looked the same, each householder marked the wings of his chickens with a lick of paint. The combinations of colors—seven colors weren't enough—made the chickens look like soccer players dressed for mass spectacles; they reminded you of official parades or geographical maps. In a word, they looked like anything but a flock of chickens.

The second remarkable sight was that every household had identically colored fences: the fences were very close to the houses; their kitchen gardens were tiny, but they were still kitchen gardens. Fences made of boards or barbed wire are a state monopoly, but a Russian garden fence is not much protection for its owner, which is why all the houses in Ola had fences covered with old fishing nets. This made them beautiful and colorful, as if the whole Ola world were laid out on graph paper so that it could be carefully examined: the chickens were protected by fishermen's nets.

I had a travel warrant to the island of Siglan in the Sea of Okhotsk, but the woman in charge of the NKVD district there wouldn't let me come "because of my record" and suggested I return to Magadan. This was no great loss to me: I still had my papers. By some chance I still have those travel warrants of mine. To get to Magadan I had to take the same launch that brought me to Ola. That turned out to be difficult, and not just because I was a tramp with no papers or a former prisoner.

The launch boatman was a resident of Ola, and it was particularly difficult, it turned out, to dislodge him and get him to his work, his launch. After three days of heavy drinking and doing nothing, the boatman was finally physically dragged out of the hut where he lived and delivered, periodically dropped on the ground and picked up again, to the landing where his launch was moored and where a large group of passengers—about ten of them—had gathered. It took at least an hour, possibly two, to get him there. This gigantic carcass approached, crawled into the helmsman's section, and started up the Kawasaki engine. The launch shuddered, but it was a long time before it actually departed. After all sorts of banging about and rubbing of hands by the boatman, the usual position by the helm was occupied. Nine passengers (I was the tenth) rushed to the cockpit and begged the boatman to stop and return home. He'd missed the ebb tide, and there was no chance of getting to Magadan in time. Whatever happened, he would have to go back, or drift about in the open sea. The reply we got from the boatman was yelling: all the passengers on the launch could go fuck themselves, but he, the boatman, wasn't going to miss the high tide. The Kawasaki sped to the open sea, while the boatman's wife went around to all the passengers, holding out a hat for his "tip to sober up": I handed over a five-ruble note. Then I clambered onto the deck to watch the seals and whales frolic as we approached Magadan. There was no sign of Magadan, but there was the shore, a rocky shore that we were heading for but on which we could not land.

"Jump, jump," I suddenly heard a woman advise me: this wasn't the first time she had made the sea trip from Ola to Magadan. "Jump, jump, I'll throw you your cases, you can get your feet on the bottom here."

The woman jumped and stretched her arms high up. The sea came up to her waist. I realized that the tide wouldn't wait for me, so I threw both my suitcases into the sea—which was when I thanked the gangsters for their wise advice—and jumped, feeling the slippery but firm and reliable ocean floor. I retrieved my suitcases from the waves: they had suffered not only from the salty water but from Archimedes' principle, and were following their human fellow travelers to the shore, floating over their heads, chasing the waves of the incoming tide. I landed on the pier of Vesiolaya Bay and waved goodbye to Ola and the boatman forever. When the boatman saw all his passengers safe and sound on the landing, he turned the Kawasaki around and left for Ola, to drink up whatever he had left.

1973

A LIEUTENANT COLONEL IN THE MEDICAL SERVICE

IT WAS fear of old age that brought Lieutenant Colonel Riurikov to Kolyma: he would soon be pensionable, and the northern salaries were twice the Moscow ones. Riurikov, a lieutenant colonel in the medical service, was not a surgeon, nor a general practitioner, nor a venereal disease specialist. In the first years of the revolution he had matriculated from workers' evening classes to the university's medical faculty and graduated as a neurologist. But he had forgotten everything long ago, and he had never, not even for one day, worked as a doctor: he had always been an administrator, a hospital's chief doctor, a manager. So he had arrived here as the chief of a major hospital for prisoners, the thousand-bed central hospital. It wasn't as if the salary of a hospital chief in Moscow was insufficient for him. Lieutenant Colonel Riurikov was well over sixty, and he lived on his own. His children had grown up, and all three were working somewhere or other as doctors, but Riurikov wouldn't hear of living at his children's expense or being helped by them. When he was still a young man he had arrived at a firm conviction that he would never ever depend on anyone and, should this ever happen, he would rather die. There was another side to the matter, something that Lieutenant Colonel Riurikov tried to keep even from himself. The mother of his children had died long ago and before she died demanded that Riurikov make her a strange promise: never to remarry. Riurikov had given his late wife his word and, from the age of thirty-five, had kept it rigorously, never even trying to think of any other solution to the question.

He felt that if he were to take a different view, then he would infringe on something delicate and sacred, that he would commit something worse than sacrilege. Eventually, he got used to things and found it easy. He never told anyone about it, and never asked anyone for advice, neither his children nor the women in his life. The woman he lived with in his last years was a doctor in his hospital; she had children, two schoolgirls, by her first husband, and Riurikov wanted this family to have a slightly better life. That was the second reason why he undertook such a serious journey.

There was a third reason, but it was a childish one. The fact is that Lieutenant Colonel Riurikov had never in his life traveled any farther than the Tuma district in Moscow Province, where he was born, and Moscow, where he grew up, was educated, and worked. Even in his youth, before he married and while he was studying at the university, Riurikov had spent every single day of his leave or holidays with his mother in Tuma district. He thought it was awkward, even improper to holiday at a resort or somewhere similar. He was too frightened of the reproaches his own conscience would make. His mother lived a long life and refused to move to live with her son; Riurikov understood her, for she had spent her whole life in the village where she was born. His mother died just before the war. Riurikov didn't have to go to the front, even though he put on a military uniform; he spent the whole war as the chief of a military hospital in Moscow.

He had never been abroad or to the south, or the east, or the west; he often thought he might die any day without having seen anything in life. He was particularly excited by and interested in pilots who flew to the Arctic, by the whole extraordinary romantic life of the conquerors of the north. His interest in the north was sustained not only by Jack London, whom the lieutenant colonel was especially fond of, but by the flights of Slepniov and Gromov,[26] and the fate of the *Cheliuskin*,[27] which got stuck in Arctic ice.

Surely he wasn't going to live without ever seeing what was dearest to his heart? So when he was offered the chance of going to the north for three years, Riurikov instantly realized that this was the fulfillment of all his desires, a piece of luck, a reward for his many years of toil. He agreed without consulting anyone.

There was just one aspect that worried Riurikov a little. He'd been appointed to a hospital for prisoners. He knew, of course, that there were labor camps in the Far North, just like the Far East, the near south, and the near west. But he would have preferred to work with free contract labor. There were, however, no such vacancies, and all the same, the salaries for free contract doctors working with prisoners were far higher: Riurikov overrode his doubts. In the two interviews the lieutenant colonel had with the authorities, there was no attempt to brush aside or disguise this aspect of the job: in fact, it was emphasized. Lieutenant Colonel Riurikov was asked to pay serious attention to the fact that enemies of the people, enemies of the motherland, were being kept there, that these men were colonizing the Far North, and that there were war criminals who would for their own vile and cunning ends exploit any moment of weakness or indecisiveness on the part of the authorities: he was told that he had to show the highest vigilance as far as that "contingent," as the authorities called them, was concerned. Vigilance and firmness. But Riurikov need have no fears. He could rely on all the free contract workers at the hospital to help him; there was a significant party collective working there in the toughest northern conditions.

In thirty years of administrative work, Riurikov saw his subordinates as something different. He was fed up with their looting of hospital supplies, their intrigues against one another, their heavy drinking. Riurikov was glad when he heard what he was told: he seemed to have been called up to a war against enemies of the state. He would be able to do his duty in his sector. He arrived in the Far North by plane, in armchair class. This was the first time, also, that the lieutenant colonel had flown: for some reason, he had never had the occasion to before, and the feeling was splendid. Riurikov was not airsick, and it was only when the plane landed that his head spun a little. He was sincerely sorry that he hadn't flown before. He was ecstatic about the rocks and the northern sky's pure colors. He became cheerful, he felt almost as if he were twenty years old again, and he refused to stay even for a few days to get to know the town, so anxious was he to get to work.

The head of the health administration gave him his own personal ZIS-110, and the lieutenant colonel arrived at the central hospital, which was five hundred kilometers from the local "capital."

The head of the health administration kindly gave advance notice of the lieutenant colonel's arrival, and not only to the hospital. The previous chief doctor was about to depart for the mainland and had not yet vacated his apartment. Three hundred meters off the highway, next to the hospital, there was the so-called Management House, one of the roadside hotels for the senior bosses, for those of the rank of general.

That was where Riurikov spent the night: he examined with amazement the embroidered velvet curtains, the carpets, the ivory carvings, the massive carved-wood wardrobes installed for handmade clothes.

Riurikov didn't unpack his belongings: in the morning he had tea and then went to the hospital.

The hospital building had been erected not long before the war for a military unit. Nevertheless, the big, T-shaped, three-story building, set among bare rocks, presented too obvious an orientation site for enemy planes (technology had advanced a long way by the time the question of the building was settled and the actual building work was underway), so that the owners no longer required the building and it was handed over to the medical service.

In the short time it took for the regiment to depart, the building was left unsupervised, and the plumbing and sewage system were destroyed, while the coal-fired power station with its two boilers became totally derelict. No coal was delivered, and any usable firewood was entirely consumed, so that all the seats from the auditorium were burned for the army's last party.

The health administration had gradually renovated all this, using the prisoners' and patients' unpaid labor, so that the hospital now presented an imposing appearance.

The lieutenant colonel entered his office and was struck by its size. Even in Moscow he had never had such capacious personal offices. This was more a conference room than an office: it could hold a hundred people, by Moscow standards.

The walls of the neighboring rooms had been demolished to make one room; the windows had linen curtains with wonderful embroidery, and the red autumnal sun picked its way over the picture frames and the leather upholstery of the locally made sofas, then moved across the polished surface of the extraordinarily large desk.

All this met with the lieutenant colonel's approval. He couldn't wait to arrange his office hours, but this was something that had to wait and could only be done two days later. The previous chief was also reluctant to waste any time departing: he had ordered his plane ticket long ago, even before Lieutenant Colonel Riurikov had left Moscow.

Riurikov spent those two days taking a closer look at the hospital and its staff. There was a large therapeutic department in the hospital, managed by Dr. Ivanov, a former military doctor and a former prisoner. The neurological and psychiatric department was run by Piotr Ivanovich Polzunov, who was also a former prisoner, as well as having a PhD. These two men belonged to a category that was especially suspect, as Riurikov had been warned when he was still in Moscow. They were men who, on the one hand, had been schooled by the camps and were thus undoubtedly enemies and, on the other hand, had the right to mix with free men, "contract workers." "After all, they didn't stop hating the state and the motherland on the day they got their release papers," thought the lieutenant colonel. "And yet they have new rights, a new position, which obliges me to trust them." The lieutenant colonel disliked both of these prisoner-managers: he didn't know how to behave in their presence. But Riurikov took a strong liking to the head of the surgical department, the regimental surgeon Gromov: Gromov was a free contract worker, although not a party member; he had fought in the war, and in his department here everything and everyone toed the line. What could be better?

As a medic, Riurikov himself had experienced the army, but only during the war, so that he was more fond of military subordination than he should have been. The organizational contribution it brought to his life was undoubtedly useful, and Riurikov sometimes recalled his prewar working conditions with resentment and annoyance: constantly having to persuade, explain, and suggest to get unreliable promises from his subordinates, instead of giving curt orders and getting back a thoroughly precise report.

That was what he liked about Gromov the surgeon: Gromov had managed to give the hospital's surgical department the atmosphere of a military hospital. Riurikov visited Gromov in the deathly silence of the hospital corridors and the polished brass door handles.

"How do you clean the door handles?"

"With bilberries," reported Gromov. Riurikov was amazed. He himself had gotten hold of a special paste in Moscow to polish his tunic buttons, and here, he now found, there were bilberries to do the job.

Everything was dazzlingly clean in the surgical department. Scrubbed floors, polished aluminum drawers in the medicine dispensary, cupboards full of instruments ...

But behind the ward doors a many-faced monster was breathing, and Riurikov was a little apprehensive about it. All the prisoners looked the same to him: full of anger and hatred ...

Gromov opened the door for his boss to one of the smaller wards. The heavy smell of pus and dirty linen repelled Riurikov: he shut the door and walked on.

This was the day that the former chief and his wife were leaving. It was a pleasing thought that tomorrow he would be a fully independent chief. He was alone in an enormous five-room apartment with a wide veranda-like balcony. The rooms were empty, the former chief's furniture—splendid handmade mirrored wardrobes, a massive carved sideboard—were the dream of the acquisitive former boss. Soft sofas, poufs of various kinds, chairs, all belonged to the former chief. The apartment was bare and empty.

Lieutenant Colonel Riurikov ordered the quartermaster of the surgical department to bring him a bed and bed linen from the hospital; the quartermaster took on the responsibility of also grabbing a bedside table that he put by the wall of the reception room.

Riurikov started sorting out his possessions. He took a towel and a bar of soap from his suitcase and put them in the kitchen.

First of all, he hung his guitar on the wall; it had a faded red border—it was no ordinary guitar. During the Civil War, when the Soviet state had as yet no medals or any other marks of distinction, when in 1918 Podvoisky[28] spoke in favor of introducing medals and he was silenced for his "tsarist belch," the awards for fighting merit at the front, for want of medals, consisted of personalized weapons, or guitars and balalaikas.

So Red Guard Riurikov was given an award for the battle for Tula: a guitar. Riurikov had no ear for music, and only when he was on his own did he cautiously and timidly pluck a string or two. The strings

506 · SKETCHES OF THE CRIMINAL WORLD

hummed and the old man was taken back, if only for a moment, to the world of his youth, so great and precious to him. He had hung on to this treasure for more than thirty years.

He made his bed, put a mirror on the bedside table, undressed, and, putting slippers on his feet, wearing just his underwear, went to the window and looked out: he was surrounded by mountains, which looked like people on their knees, praying. It was as if a crowd of people had come here to see a miracle worker, to pray, to ask for guidance, to be shown the path.

Riurikov sensed that even nature was unable to decide his fate, that nature itself was seeking advice.

He took the guitar off the wall: at night in an empty room, the chords turned out to be especially resonant, especially grave and meaningful. Plucking at the strings calmed him, as it always had. Now his first decisions were taken, playing the guitar at night. He found the willpower to carry them out. He lay on the bed and fell asleep straightaway.

In the morning, even before he began his working day in his new, spacious office, Riurikov summoned Lieutenant Maksimov, his deputy for management, and told him that he would occupy only one room, the largest of the five. The other four rooms could be taken by those colleagues who had nowhere to live. Lieutenant Maksimov was at a loss for words: he tried to explain that this was too casual an approach.

"But I don't have a family," said Riurikov.

"Your predecessor only had a wife," said Maksimov. "But you'll have visitors, lots of important people from the capital, who will be staying here as guests."

"They can stay where I spent my first night. It's only a couple of yards away. So do as you're told."

Maksimov came back to the office several times that day to ask whether Riurikov had changed his mind or not. Only when the new boss began to lose his temper did Maksimov give in.

The first person to be received was the local NKVD man, Koroliov. After introducing himself and giving a brief report, Koroliov said, "I have a request. I'm going to Dolgoye tomorrow."

"What's Dolgoye?"

"It's the district center, eighty kilometers from here ... A proper bus goes there every morning."

"Fine, go," said Riurikov.

"No, you've misunderstood me," Koroliov smiled. "I'm asking for permission to use your personal automobile ..."

"Do I have a personal automobile here?" asked Riurikov.

"Yes."

"And a chauffeur?"

"And a chauffeur ..."

"And did Samokurov" (the name of his predecessor) "ever go anywhere in that personal automobile?"

"Not often," said Koroliov. "I must admit. Not often."

"I'll tell you what," said Riurikov, who had understood everything and made a decision. "You take the bus. Put the car up on jacks for now. And move the chauffeur to the car depot: he can work on the trucks. I don't need an automobile, either. If I need to go anywhere, I'll take either an ambulance or a truck."

The secretary opened the door a few inches.

"Fedotov the repairman wants to see you, he says it's very urgent ..."

The repairman was frightened. Riurikov understood from his incoherent and gabbled account that the ceiling had collapsed on the repairman's first-floor apartment. It had to be repaired, since the plaster had fallen off and water was leaking from above. A repair was needed, but the management was refusing to do the work, while the repairman himself didn't have enough money for the job. And it wasn't fair. The person who should pay was the person responsible for the plaster collapsing, even if he was a party member. After all, the water had come through ...

"Hang on," said Riurikov. "Why is it leaking? There are people living above you, aren't there?"

Riurikov found it hard to take in that there was a piglet living in the apartment above, that manure and urine had accumulated, so that the first-floor plaster had disintegrated, and the pig was urinating on the heads of the tenants in the apartment below.

Riurikov was enraged.

"Anna Petrovna," he yelled to the secretary. "Summon the secretary of the party organization here, and the scoundrel who owns the piglet."

Anna Petrovna gave a wave of her arm and vanished.

About ten minutes later Mostovoi, the secretary of the party organization, came into the office and sat down by the desk. All three men—Riurikov, Mostovoi, and the repairman—were silent. About ten minutes passed.

"Anna Petrovna!"

Anna Petrovna squeezed through the half-open door.

"Where is the owner of the piglet, then?"

Anna Petrovna vanished.

"The owner of the piglet is this man here: comrade Mostovoi," said the repairman.

"Ah, is it now?" Riurikov rose to his feet. "You go home now," he said, showing the repairman to the door.

"How dare you?" he yelled at Mostovoi. "How dare you keep it in your apartment?"

"Don't yell at me," said Mostovoi calmly. "Where else can I keep it? In the street? Just you try to keep a fowl or a boar, and you'll see what happens. I've asked again and again for an apartment on the ground floor. They won't let me have one. It's like that in all the buildings. That repairman talks too much, though. Your predecessor knew how to shut him up. And you go around listening to anyone who talks."

"All the repair costs will be down to you, comrade Mostovoi."

"No, that's not going to happen ..."

But Riurikov had already summoned the bookkeeper by telephone and dictated an order.

The meetings with subordinates had gone very badly. The lieutenant colonel failed to get to know a single one of his deputies, even though he put his signature countless times on countless papers that nimble, practiced hands unfolded for him. Everyone who reported used the enormous paperweight on the chief's desk—a handmade carving of a Kremlin tower with red plastic stars—to dry the ink on the lieutenant colonel's signature.

Things went on like this until dinner, and after dinner the chief went for a tour of the hospital. Dr. Gromov, red in the face and white of teeth, was already waiting for his boss.

"I want to have a look at your work," said the chief. "Show me someone you're discharging today."

A chain of patients shuffled through Gromov's excessively spacious office. For the first time Riurikov saw the men he was supposed to be treating. A chain of skeletons moved in front of him.

"Do you have lice?"

The patient shrugged and looked with fear at Dr. Gromov.

"Come on, these are surgical patients . . . Why are they in this state?"

"That's nothing to do with us," said Dr. Gromov cheerfully.

"And you're discharging them?"

"How long can they be kept in? How about our bed days?"

"And how can you discharge this man?" Riurikov pointed to a patient with dark infected wounds.

"He's going because he stole bread from the men next to him."

Colonel Akimov had driven up: he was the chief of an unspecified military unit—a regiment, a division, a corps, or an army—which was deployed over the enormous territory of the north. This military unit had at one time been constructing the hospital building. Akimov was youthful for his fifty years, with a taut figure, and cheerful. Riurikov cheered up, too. Akimov had brought his sick wife—nobody could do anything for her, it was one of those things, but Riurikov had doctors.

"I'll make the arrangements right now," said Riurikov; he rang and Anna Petrovna appeared in the doorway, with an expression that implied she was fully prepared to carry out any further orders.

"No hurry," said Akimov. "This isn't the first time I've seen a doctor here. Who do you intend to have my wife examined by?"

"Why not Stebeliov?" Stebeliov was the head of the therapeutic department.

"No," said Akimov. "I've got people like Stebeliov at home. I want you to have Dr. Glushakov examine her."

"Fine," said Riurikov. "But Dr. Glushakov is a prisoner. Don't you think—"

"No, I think not," said Akimov firmly; his eyes were not smiling. He was silent for a while. "The fact is," he said, "that my wife needs a doctor, not a ..." The colonel didn't finish his sentence.

Anna Petrovna ran off to order a pass and a summons for Glushakov, while Colonel Akimov introduced his wife to Riurikov.

Glushakov was quickly brought from the camp: he was a gray-haired, wrinkled old man.

"How are you, professor?" said Akimov, getting up to greet Glushakov and shake his hand. "You see, I have a request for you."

Glushakov offered to examine his wife in the camp health department ("There I've got everything I need to hand, but here I don't know anything"), and Riurikov rang his deputy at the camp to give the colonel and his wife a pass.

"Listen, Anna Petrovna," said Riurikov to his secretary once his visitors had gone. "Is it true that Glushakov is such a good specialist?"

"Well, he's more reliable than ours." Anna Petrovna giggled.

Lieutenant Colonel Riurikov sighed. Every day of his life was for Riurikov colored in a special, unique way. There were days of losses, days of failures, days of happiness, days of kindness, days of sympathy, days of mistrust, days of anger ... Everything that had happened that day had an indeterminate nature, and Riurikov was sometimes able to adapt his decisions and his actions to this "background," which seemed not to depend on his will. Today was a day of doubts, a day of disappointments.

Colonel Akimov's remark had touched on something important and fundamental in Riurikov's new life. A window had opened, a window about whose existence Riurikov had been reluctant to think, until Akimov's visit. It was now clear not only that the window existed but that you could see in it things that Riurikov had not seen or noticed before.

Everything that day seemed to be in cahoots with Colonel Akimov. The new, temporary head of the surgical department, Dr. Braude, reported that the ear and throat operations scheduled for today had been postponed because the pride of the hospital, that fine diagnostician, that highly skilled surgeon Adelaida Ivanovna Simbirtseva, an elderly specialist, a pupil of the famous Voyachek, a new arrival at the hospital, had "overdone the drugs," as Braude put it, and was now creating havoc in the treatment room of the surgical department. She was smashing all the glassware she could lay her hands on. What could one do? Could you tie her up, call for a guard, and take her back to her quarters?

Colonel Riurikov made arrangements; Adelaida Ivanovna was not to be tied up, she was to be gagged with a shawl, taken home, and locked up there. Or a sedative—a double dose, definitely a double one, of chloral hydrate—could be poured down her throat and she could be carried away in a somnolent state. But she was to be led or carried away by free workers, not by prisoners.

In the neurological-psychiatric department, a patient had killed the man next to him with an iron pike he had fashioned. Dr. Piotr Ivanovich, the head, reported that the murder was the result of a bloody feud among the criminals, and that both patients, victim and murderer, were thieves.

In Stebeliov's therapeutic department, a prisoner-quartermaster had stolen and sold forty sheets. Lvov, the NKVD man, had now found these sheets hidden under a boat on the riverbank.

The manager of the women's department was demanding that she be given officer's rations, and her case was being decided somewhere in the capital.

But it was Anisimov, the camp deputy, who reported the worst unpleasantness. Anisimov spent a long time sitting on the deep leather sofa in Riurikov's office, waiting for the torrent of visitors to subside. When they were alone, he said, "What are we going to do, Vasili Ivanovich, with Liusia Popovkina?"

"Who is Liusia Popovkina?"

"Surely you must know!"

She turned out to be a ballerina and a prisoner with whom Semion Abramovich Smolokurov, Riurikov's predecessor, had become involved. She had no job: she served only for Smolokurov's amusement. Now ("almost a month later," thought Riurikov) she was still without a job, and no arrangements had been made.

Riurikov felt like washing his hands of it all. "What arrangements? To hell with her, at once."

"A punishment camp?"

"Why does it have to be a punishment camp? It isn't her fault, is it? And I'll give you a reprimand: she hasn't worked for a whole month."

"We've been saving her up," said Anisimov.

"For whom?" Then Riurikov rose to his feet and strode up and down the room. "Send her off immediately, tomorrow."

When Piotr Ivanovich was climbing the narrow wooden staircase to see Antonina Sergeyevna on the second floor, he thought that in the two years they had both worked in this hospital he still hadn't been to the chief doctor's quarters. He gave a laugh: he realized why he had been invited. All right, this invitation was a way of bringing him, a former prisoner, into the local "highest circles." Piotr Ivanovich didn't understand people like Riurikov, and because he couldn't understand them, he despised them. He thought that this was a special career path, the path for the "honest toiler," in big quotation marks, who wants to become no more and no less than head of a health administration. And so he puts on airs, goes through all the motions, trying to present himself as a holy innocent.

Piotr Ivanovich's intuition had not failed him. The smoke-filled room was packed. There was the X-ray doctor, there was Mostovoi, and the chief bookkeeper. Antonina Sergeyevna was personally pouring out warm, weak tea from an aluminum hospital kettle.

"Come in, Piotr Ivanovich," she said, when the neurologist had taken off his canvas raincoat.

"Let's begin," said Antonina Sergeyevna, and Piotr Ivanovich thought, "She's still quite good-looking," and began looking away.

The camp chief said, "I've invited you here, gentlemen" (Mostovoi raised his eyebrows) "to tell you something extremely disagreeable."[29] They all laughed, including Mostovoi, who also thought that this was a literary quotation. Mostovoi had calmed down, normally the bourgeois word "gentlemen" alarmed him, even if it was a witticism or a slip of the tongue.

"What are we going to do?" asked Antonina Sergeyevna. "We'll be destitute in a year. But he's come for three years. He's forbidden all of us to have servants who are prisoners. Why do those wretched girls have to suffer doing heavy manual labor? For whose sake? For his. I won't mention the firewood. Last winter, I didn't put a single ruble in my savings book. After all, I have children."

"We all have children," said the chief bookkeeper. "But what can we possibly do about it?"

"To hell with him: poison him!" roared Mostovoi.

"Try not to say things like that in my presence," said the chief bookkeeper. "Otherwise I shall be obliged to report it in the appropriate place."

"I was joking."

"Kindly refrain from such jokes."

Piotr Ivanovich raised his hand. "We need to summon Churbakov here. And you, Antonina Sergeyevna, need to talk to him."

"Why me?" Antonina Sergeyevna blushed. A major in the medical service, Churbakov was the head of the health administration, and he was famous for his violent debauchery and unbelievable endurance in any drinking orgy. He had children at almost every mine—by women doctors, by women paramedics, nurses, and ward assistants.

"You're just the person. And you can explain to Major Churbakov that Lieutenant Colonel Riurikov is after his job, get it? Tell him that the major has only been a party member since yesterday, while Riurikov—"

"Riurikov has been a member since 1917," Mostovoi said with a sigh. "But why would he want Churbakov's job?"

"Oh, you don't understand a thing. Piotr Ivanovich is quite right."

"Suppose we wrote to Churbakov?"

"Who's going to take the letter? Is anyone ready to have their head roll? Suppose our messenger is intercepted or, even more likely, he takes the letter straight to Riurikov's office? Things like that do happen."

"How about phoning?"

"You can only ask for him to be brought to the phone. You know, don't you, that Smolokurov had the phones tapped."

"Churbakov's phone isn't tapped."

"How do you know? Anyway, caution and energy, energy and caution..."

THE MILITARY COMMISSAR

THE OPERATION was to remove a foreign object from the esophagus: it was registered in the operations list in Valentin Nikolayevich Traut's handwriting; he was one of the three surgeons who would perform the extraction. Traut was not the most important surgeon: the important one in this case was Anna Sergeyevna Novikova, who had studied under Voyachek: she was an ear and throat surgeon from Moscow, a southern beauty who, like her two assistants, Traut and Lunin, had never been imprisoned. It was because Novikova was the chief surgeon that the operation was performed two days later than it could have been. For those forty-eight hours Voyachek's brilliant pupil had buckets of water poured over her, was dosed with salts of ammonia, had her stomach and intestines washed, and was restored with strong tea. After two days, Anna Sergeyevna's fingers stopped trembling and the operation could begin. A binge-drinking alcoholic and a drug addict who, when she was coming out of a bender, poured all the glass containers into one dark chalice and then drank the mixture; she did this to get drunk again and go to sleep. She didn't need much of her concoction to do so. Now Novikova was in her gown and mask, yelling at her assistants and issuing short commands: her mouth had been rinsed and washed, and only occasionally were her assistants able to catch the smell of alcohol fumes. The operating-room nurse's nostrils were twitching as she breathed in these unwanted fumes: she smiled faintly under her mask and hurriedly repressed a smile. The assistants were not smiling or thinking about the fumes. The operation demanded their full attention. Traut had performed similar operations before, though not often, while this was the first time for Lunin. But for Novikova this was a chance to show her special superiority, her master's touch, her unsurpassed qualifications.

The patient didn't understand why the operation had been put off first for twenty-four hours, then for another twenty-four hours, but he kept silent, since this was no place for him to give orders. The patient had been staying with the chief of the hospital, and he'd been told he would be called for at the right time. At first he was informed that Traut would be performing the operation, then another day passed and he was told, "Tomorrow, but Novikova instead of Traut." All that was agonizing for the patient, but he was a military man and had only come back from the front recently, so he controlled himself. The patient was a high-ranking officer; he had a colonel's epaulets, and was one of the eight district military commanders in Kolyma.

By the end of the war Lieutenant Kononov was in command of a regiment; he was reluctant to leave the army, but peacetime demanded different skills. All those who passed a new qualifications test were invited to go on serving in the army with the same rank, but had to do so in the Ministry of the Interior forces, where they would be employed to guard the camps. In 1946 the job of guarding the camps was handed to the professional units, not to the NKVD's guards, and these professional soldiers had ribbons and medals. Everyone kept their old rank and received Polar Circle rations, with salaries, leave, and all the polar privileges of Far East Construction. Kononov, who had a wife and a daughter, quickly found his feet and as soon as he got to Magadan dug his heels in and refused to work in the camps. He sent his wife and daughter back to the mainland, and won himself an appointment to the job of district military commissar. His "territory" stretched for hundreds of kilometers along the highway and ten kilometers to either side of it, where there were people whom the district military commissar had to keep count of. Kononov was quick to understand that summoning anyone to see him was a waste of time for those summoned. It took people a week to get to the settlement where the military commissar lived. And a week to get back. So all the counting and the correspondence were carried out when there was someone traveling to the appropriate destination, while once a month, or more often, Kononov himself would tour his district by car. He coped with his work, but he was waiting not for promotion but for the end of "the north," a transfer, or just demobilization, and he had forgotten about getting a colonel's epaulets. The combination of the north and the lack of facilities had gradually led Kononov to start drinking. That was why he could not explain how a bone, big enough to feel, had gotten into his esophagus, so that it was compressing his windpipe and even forcing him to speak in a difficult whisper.

Kononov and the foreign body in his esophagus could, of course, have gotten to Magadan, where there were doctors at the administration capable of helping him... But Kononov had been working in a military commissariat for about a year, and he knew that the Left Bank, a big hospital for prisoners, was highly praised. Kononov had possession of the military papers of those who worked at the hospital, men and women. When the bone lodged in Kononov's throat and it was clear that no force on earth would remove it without medical help, Kononov got into his car and drove to the prisoners' hospital at the Left Bank.

At the time, the hospital chief was Vinokurov. He had only just taken over the hospital, and was well aware that the hospital's prestige would be assured if the operation was a success. The main hope was Voyachek's pupil, for there were no comparable specialists in Magadan. Unfortunately, Novikova had worked at Magadan only a year earlier. "A transfer to the Left Bank, or dismissal from Far East Construction," she was told. "The Left Bank, then, the Left Bank," Novikova shouted in the personnel department. Before Magadan, Novikova had worked at Aldan, before Aldan in Leningrad. She had been pushed farther north at every point. A hundred promises, a thousand broken solemn promises. She liked being at the Left Bank, and she found her feet there. Every remark she made showed how highly qualified she was. As an ear and throat surgeon she saw both free and imprisoned patients, she looked after the patients, she performed operations, she acted as a consultant, but then she would begin a binge and the patients would be neglected: the free ones would leave, and the prisoners would be left to the care of the paramedics, while Novikova never showed up in the department.

But when Kononov came and it was obvious that an urgent operation was required, an order was given to get Novikova up. The problem, however, was that Kononov would have to stay for a long time in the hospital. Extracting a foreign body is a straightforward operation. Of course, in a big hospital there were two surgical departments, one for infected wounds, the other for clean ones, and they had separate staff, the more competent ones in the clean department, the less competent in the infected department. An eye had to be kept on the way the wound healed, especially an incision in the esophagus. Naturally, a separate ward would be found for the commissar. Kononov was reluctant to go to Magadan. With his colonel's rank, he would have nothing to do in the Kolyma capital. He would be received, of course, but he would get no attention or concern. In Magadan a doctor's time was taken up by generals and their wives. Kononov would have died there. He would have died at the age of forty of some damned bone in his throat. Kononov signed everything he was asked to: he understood that his life was at stake. He was in agony.

"Valentin Nikolayevich, will you be doing it?"

"Yes, I will," said Traut, diffidently.

"So what are we waiting for?"

"We'll just wait a day longer."

Kononov was nonplussed. He was being fed through his nose with liquid, so that he wouldn't starve to death.

"Another doctor will examine you tomorrow."

A woman doctor was brought to Kononov's bed. Her skilled fingers immediately located the bone and touched it, causing him almost no pain.

"Well, Anna Sergeyevna?"

"Tomorrow morning."

This operation had a 30 percent mortality rate. Kononov was the sole occupant of the postoperative ward. The bone turned out to be so enormous that Kononov was ashamed to look at it when he was shown it in a glass a few hours later. Kononov was in the postoperative ward. Sometimes the hospital chief brought him the newspapers.

"Everything's going well."

Kononov was in a tiny ward into which one more bed had been squeezed. The observation period passed, and everything was fine, as good as could be expected: Voyachek's pupil had shown her qualifications. But what a boring observation period it was! A convict, a prisoner can still keep that feeling under control, in a concrete framework: he has an armed guard, prison bars, checks and roll calls, mealtimes, but how can a colonel be given all that? Kononov asked the hospital chief for advice.

"I've been waiting for you to ask that: people are only human. Of course you feel bored. But I can't discharge you for at least a month: the risk is too great, and success is too rare not to be treasured. I can authorize you to move to a prisoners' ward, where there are four men, so you will be the fifth. That's one way of reconciling the hospital's interests with yours."

Kononov immediately agreed. This was a good solution. The colonel wasn't afraid of prisoners. His knowledge of the hospital had assured Kononov that prisoners were like any other human beings: they wouldn't bite him, Colonel Kononov, they wouldn't confuse him with some secret policeman or prosecutor; whatever happened, Kononov was a professional soldier. Colonel Kononov wasn't going to study or observe new people, his new neighbors. He was simply bored being on his own in the hospital, that was all.

Wearing a gray hospital gown, the colonel spent many more weeks roaming the corridors. The gown was official issue for prisoners. I saw the colonel through the open door, wrapped up in his gown, carefully listening to the usual prisoner storyteller.

I was the senior paramedic in the surgical department at the time; later I was transferred to forestry, and Kononov left my life, as did thousands of men, leaving barely noticeable traces in my memory, a barely detectable liking.

On one more occasion, at a medical conference, a lecturer, the new chief doctor at the hospital, a medical Major Koroliov, reminded me of Kononov's surname. Koroliov loved drinking and eating, he was a frontline soldier, and he didn't last long as chief doctor—he couldn't resist small bribes, the minimum being a carafe of government alcohol, and after a major scandal he was demoted and dismissed. He reappeared later as head of the health section of the Northern Administration.

After the war, a whole torrent of con men, frauds, hiding from trial and prison, came to work for Far East Construction in Kolyma, attracted by the extra rubles.

A Major Alekseyev, wearing a Red Star and a major's epaulets, was appointed hospital chief. Once, Alekseyev came on foot to see me; he was interested in the sector, but didn't ask a single question and set off back where he'd come from. The forest medical center was twenty kilometers from the hospital. No sooner had Alekseyev gotten back than he was arrested by men who had come from Magadan. Alekseyev was convicted of murdering his wife. He was neither a doctor nor an officer, but with the help of forged documents he had slipped out of Magadan to hide in the bushes at our Left Bank. The medal and the epaulets were all false.

Before then, the head of the Northern Administration Health Department often came to the Left Bank. This job was later held by a drunken chief doctor. The new arrival was a very well-dressed and perfumed bachelor; he was authorized to improve his qualifications by being present at operations.

"I've decided to retrain as a surgeon," Paltsyn whispered, with a patronizing smile.

Month after month passed, and every operating day, Paltsyn would arrive in his car from the center of the Northern Administration, the settlement of Yagodny, have lunch with the chief, and gently court his daughter. Our Dr. Traut drew our attention to the fact that Paltsyn was unfamiliar with medical terminology. But because of the front and the war, everyone trusted him and was willing to initiate the new boss into the secrets of an operation, especially if it was diuresis. Then suddenly Paltsyn was arrested: again, it was murder committed at the front, and Paltsyn was not a doctor but a former German policeman in hiding.

Everyone expected something similar to happen to Koroliov. But it didn't: the medal, the party card, and his rank were all in order. It was this Koroliov, while chief doctor at the central hospital, who was lecturing at one of the medical conferences. The new chief doctor's lecture was no worse and no better than anyone else's. Of course, Traut was an intellectual, a pupil of Krauze, a government surgeon when the latter worked in Saratov.

But directness, sincerity, and a democratic attitude meet with a response from anybody, as when the chief doctor, the boss of the Left Bank surgeons, at a professional conference that was attended by people from all over Kolyma, began talking with relish about surgical achievements.

"We had a patient who had swallowed a bone, a bone this big," said Koroliov with a gesture. "Would you believe it: the bone was extracted. The doctors are here, and so is the patient."

But the patient wasn't there. Shortly afterward, I fell ill and was transferred to work at a forestry outpost; a year later I returned to the hospital to take charge of the admissions room. Almost two days after I began work there, I came across Colonel Kononov in the admissions room. He was gladder than he could say to see me. All the bosses had been replaced. Kononov couldn't find anyone he knew; mine was the only familiar face, a very familiar one.

I did everything I could: X-rays, a note to the doctors, I rang the chief, I explained that here we had the hero of a famous Left Bank operation. Kononov turned out to have nothing wrong with him, and before he left he dropped into the admissions room to see me.

"I owe you a present."

"I don't accept presents."

"But I brought presents for everybody—the hospital chief, the surgeons, the nurse, even the patients I shared a ward with: I gave each surgeon some cloth for a suit. But I couldn't find you. I want to thank you. With money, after all, you can use money."

"I don't accept presents."

"Well, I'll bring a bottle, then."

"I won't accept brandy, either, so don't bring any."

"What can I do for you?"

"Nothing."

Kononov was taken off to the X-ray room, and the X-ray room free contract nurse said, when she came to fetch Kononov, "He's a military commissar, isn't he?"

"Yes, the district military commissar."

"I can see you know him well, don't you?"

"Yes, I know him: he was here as a patient."

"Ask him, if you really don't want anything for yourself, to put a stamp in my military papers that I've reported to him. I'm a Communist Youth member, and this is my chance: instead of me having to travel three hundred kilometers, God's brought him here."

"All right, I'll tell him."

Kononov came back and I passed on the nurse's request.

"Well, where is she?"

"Standing right here."

"All right, give me your papers, I don't have my stamps with me, but I'll bring it back in a week, I'll be passing then, and I'll bring it." Kononov put her military papers in his pocket. The car was revving at the entrance.

A week passed, and the military commissar didn't come. Two weeks... A month... Three months later the nurse came to have a talk with me.

"Oh, what a mistake that was. I should have... I've been tricked."

"What sort of trick?"

"I don't know, but I'm being expelled from the Communist Youth."

"What are they expelling you for?"

"For links with an enemy of the people, for letting go of my military papers."

"But you handed them to the commissar."

"No, that wasn't how it was. I handed them to you, and you, supposedly, gave them to the commissar... That's what the committee is going to sort out. Who I actually gave them to—you or directly to the commissar. It was you, after all."

"Yes, it was, but you were there when I passed them to the military commissar."

"I don't know anything about that. All I know is that something terrible has happened, and I'm being expelled from the Communist Youth and dismissed from the hospital."

"You need to go to the settlement and the military commissar's office."

"Waste two weeks? That's what I should have done at the start."

"When are you going?"

"Tomorrow."

Two weeks later I met the nurse in the corridor. She looked blacker than thunder.

"Well, what happened?"

"The military commander has left for the mainland, he's already signed off. Now I have real trouble: getting new papers. I'll see to it that you're thrown out of the hospital and packed off to a punishment mine."

"What have I got to do with it?"

"Who else? That was a cunning trick, as they explained to me at the Ministry of the Interior."

I was trying to forget about this business. In the end, nobody accused me of anything else, and I wasn't summoned for interrogation, but my memory of Colonel Kononov was tinged in rather different colors.

Suddenly one night I was summoned to the guardhouse.

"That's him," Colonel Kononov yelled from the other side of the barrier. "Let me through!"

"Pass. Didn't I hear you were off to the mainland?"

"I was about to go on leave, but they wouldn't let me. So I got my pay and resigned. For good. I'm leaving. I've come to say goodbye."

"Just to say goodbye?"

"No. When I was handing over, there was a set of military papers on a corner of the desk—I couldn't remember where I got them from. If they'd been in your name, I'd have remembered. But I never got back to the Left Bank since then. Everything's been done: a stamp, a signature, so take them and give them to the lady."

"No," I said. "You give them to her in person."

"How can I? It's the middle of the night."

"I'll send a messenger to get her here from where she lives. But they have to be handed over in person, Colonel Kononov."

"You know best."

The nurse came rushing up, and Kononov handed her the papers.

"It's too late now, I've already made all the applications, I've been expelled from the Communist Youth. Wait, write a few words on the form."

"I apologize."

And he vanished in the freezing haze.

"Well, congratulations. If it were 1937, you'd have been shot for tricks like that," the nurse said spitefully.

"Yes," I said. "And so would you."

1970–1971

RIVA-ROCCI

STALIN'S death did not arouse any new hopes in prisoners' coarsened breasts, it didn't spur their worn-out engines, exhausted by pushing their curdled blood around their hard, narrowed arteries.

But in the broadcasts on all waves, echoed again and again by the mountains, the sky, one word crept through all the crannies of the prisoner's existence under his bunks: it was an important word, for it promised a solution to all our problems, whether of declaring saints to be sinners, of punishing evildoers, or of finding a way to painlessly replace all the teeth that had been knocked out.

There were the typical, classic rumors arising and spreading: rumors of an amnesty.

Any state's jubilee, whether it is an anniversary or a tercentenary, the coronations of heirs, or a change of authority, even of ministerial cabinets, always descends from the heavens above the clouds into the subterranean world in the form of an amnesty. This is the classic way for the top and the bottom to communicate.

The traditional grapevine that everyone believes in is the most bureaucratic form of prisoners' hopes.

In response to traditional expectations, governments take traditional steps: they declare this amnesty.

Even the government of the post-Stalin era kept to this custom. It believed that carrying out this traditional action, repeating the tsars' gesture, was the same as fulfilling a moral duty to humanity, that the very appearance of amnesty, regardless of what shape it took, had a meaningful and traditional content.

For any new government to carry out its moral duty, there is an old traditional form, and not applying it would mean a dereliction of duty to history and the country.

An amnesty being prepared, and hurriedly, too, to keep to the classic model.

Beria, Malenkov, and Vyshinsky mobilized lawyers, reliable and unreliable, and gave them the idea of an amnesty: the rest was a matter for bureaucratic technology.

The amnesty came to Kolyma after March 5, 1953, for people who had spent the whole war witnessing the pendulum of prisoners' fate swing from blind hope to the depths of disillusionment at each defeat and each success in the war. And there wasn't a farsighted or wise person who could have defined which was better, more advantageous, more salutary for a prisoner: the country's victory or its defeat.

The amnesty came to the Trotskyists and others with convictions defined by letters, not numbers, those who were still alive after the executions organized by Garanin, to prisoners who had lived through the cold and the starvation of the gold-mine pit faces of Kolyma in 1938, Stalin's extermination camps.

All those who hadn't been murdered, shot, beaten to death by the boots and rifle butts of the guards, the foremen, labor organizers, and overseers, all those who had come through, after paying the full price for their life—double, triple additions to the five-year sentence that the prisoner had arrived with in Kolyma from Moscow...

There were no prisoners in Kolyma who had been convicted under article 58 and who had gotten just five years. The five-year prisoners were a tiny proportion of those condemned in 1937, before the secret meeting of Beria, Stalin, and Zhdanov in June 1937, when the five-year terms were abandoned and method No. 3 was authorized for getting evidence.

But not a single person of the tiny number of that short list of men existed by the time war broke out, or during the war, for they had all been given extra makeweight sentences of ten, fifteen, or even twenty-five years.

As for the rare individuals among those five-year prisoners who hadn't been given an extra sentence, nor died, nor ended up in Archive

No. 3, they had long been released and started working as killers—as guards, warders, foremen, or sector chiefs at the same gold mine, so that they themselves began killing their former comrades.

The only people with five-year sentences in Kolyma in 1953 were those who had been convicted at local trials of nonpolitical crimes. They were few in number. The interrogators simply couldn't be bothered to stitch them up with article 58 crimes. Or else the camps' affairs were so assured, so clear about everyday existence, that there was no need to resort to the dreaded old weapon of article 58, a universal article that spared neither sex nor age. A prisoner who had served a sentence under article 58 and who was detained for permanent settlement would use all his cunning to be put away again, only for a crime that everyone—people, God, and the state—respected, theft or embezzlement. In a word, a man who got a sentence for a nonpolitical crime was anything but sad.

Kolyma was a camp for recidivists, not just political ones but ordinary criminal ones.

The height of legal perfection in Stalin's time—even the two schools, two poles of criminal law, Krylenko's and Vyshinsky's, agreed on this—was the "amalgamate," the gluing together of two crimes, a criminal one and a political one. Even Litvinov, in his famous interview where he said that the USSR had no political prisoners but it did have state criminals, was only repeating Vyshinsky.

The essence of the "amalgamate" was to make a purely political person a criminal.

Formally speaking, Kolyma was a special camp, like Dachau, for recidivists, both criminal and political. After all, they were housed together. On instructions from above. On the principal theoretical instruction from above, Garanin could redefine criminals who refused to work as enemies of the people, instead of friends, and try them for sabotage under article 58, paragraph 14.

That was the most profitable solution. In 1938 the major gangsters were shot, and the minor gangsters were given fifteen, twenty, or twenty-five years for refusing to work. They were then housed with the *freiers* who had article 58, which allowed the gangsters to live in comfort.

Garanin was no admirer of the criminal world. Fussing over recidivists was Berzin's obsession. In that respect, Berzin's heritage was revised by Garanin.

Just like slides shown on a projector in a secondary-school program, in the decade including the war, from 1937 to 1947, groups, contingents, categories of prisoners would appear before the eyes of prison directors, the heroes of the camp system, enthusiasts for convict labor, people who had seen everything and gotten used to anything. The groups would succeed and complement one another; as in Bitsch's experiment with merging colors,[30] it depended on how the beam of the legal process illuminated one or another group. Except that it was not a beam but a sword that cut off heads and killed in the most literal way.

In the patch lit up by the slide projector used by the state, prisoners appeared simply, not as "Engineering Technical Workers" but as "Corrective Labor Camps." But the confusion of titles was a confusion of fates, too. Former convicts, former prisoners—a whole social group, an indelible brand depriving them of rights; prisoners of the future, all those whose cases had been started but where due process was not yet completed, and those whose cases had not even started due process.

The inhabitants of penitentiaries had a satirical song in the 1920s, the years of the first labor colonies: the song's composer is anonymous. A bard or a chronicler of recidivist criminality, he used verse to compare the fate of freedom with the fate of the prisoner, giving his preference to the situation of the latter.

> We have freedom to look forward to,
> But what do you have?

This joke was no longer a joke at all in the 1930s and 1940s. The highest spheres were planning to dispatch people from exile to camps, after depriving them of the right to live in one city, they were to be deprived of the right to live in five hundred. Two convictions gave a legal right to use the power of iron bars and zones.

In those years Kolyma had contingents A, B, C, D, and E, each with its own administration and staff.

Contingent E consisted of completely free citizens who were mobilized to work at secret uranium ore mines, and they were guarded in Kolyma far more secretly than any Beideman.[32]

Next to the uranium ore mine, where ordinary prisoners were not allowed, so secret was it, there was the hard labor mine. Here, there were not just prisoners bearing numbers and wearing striped uniforms but gallows and sentences that were carried out quite literally, with all legal forms observed.

Next to the hard labor mine was the Berlag ore mine, also with numbered prisoners, but it wasn't a hard labor convicts' mine where prisoners had a number, a piece of metal, a badge on their backs, and work duty under heavy guard with double the number of dogs.

I set off there myself, but never got that far: selection for Berlag was on the basis of files. A lot of my comrades ended up in those numbered camps.

Things were better, not worse, there than in an ordinary corrective labor camp with a normal regime.

Under a normal regime, the prisoner is the victim of the gangsters and warders, and the foremen chosen from the prisoners. But in numbered camps, the staff were free workers, and free workers were employed in the kitchen and the camp shop. The number on one's back didn't mean much, as long as you weren't robbed of your bread and you weren't forced to work by your own comrades: production by beatings, the only way to fulfill the plan. The state asked "friends of the people" to give physical help in exterminating enemies of the people. Those "friends" were the gangsters, the nonpolitical convicts, and they did this in the literal, physical sense.

There was another mine close by, where the people who worked had been sentenced to prison, but hard labor was more profitable—the sentences were commuted to "clean air" in a labor camp. Those who served their sentence in a prison survived; those who did so in a camp died.

The supply of new prisoners was reduced to zero during the war. On the mainland all kinds of unloading commissions took people out of the prisons and sent them to the front, not to Kolyma, to redeem themselves in punishment squads.

The official number of Kolyma prisoners was also falling catastrophically, even though nobody was transported from Kolyma to serve on the mainland front: not a single prisoner went to the front, although, of course, there were a lot of applications to redeem their guilt from prisoners convicted under every article, except for the gangsters.

People were dying their natural Kolyma deaths, and in the veins of the special camp the blood began to circulate more slowly, every now and again suffering thrombosis or stopping altogether.

An attempt was made to infuse fresh blood with war criminals. In 1945–1946 whole shiploads of novices, repatriated from Europe, came to the camps: they were disembarked from the ship onto the rocky Magadan shore with just a list, with no individual files or other formalities. As always, the formalities lagged behind actual life. They were listed on cigarette paper, crumpled in the guards' filthy hands.

All these people (there were tens of thousands of them) had a perfectly formal legal place in the camp statistics: they were "uncountables."

Here, too, there were various contingents: the range of legal fantasy in those years is still waiting for someone to describe it in particular.

There were very large groups whose "summary" sentences were quite official: "Six years for verification."

The fate of such a prisoner was decided by his behavior over all six years in Kolyma, where even six months was an ominous sentence, a lethal one. But this was six years, not six months, not six days.

The greater part of the six-year men died of overwork, and those who survived were all released on the same day by a decision of the Twentieth Party Congress.

As for the "uncountables," those who had come to Kolyma on a list, the legal staff who had come from the mainland spent days and nights laboring. Interrogations went on for further days and nights in tightly packed dugouts and Kolyma barracks, and Moscow then made decisions: some got fifteen, some got twenty-five, some got the death penalty. I don't remember any acquittals or reprieves, but I wasn't able to know everything. Possibly there were acquittals and complete rehabilitations.

All these men under investigation, and also the six-year men who were in essence under investigation, were made to work, following all the Kolyma laws: three refusals, and you were shot.

They had come to Kolyma to replace the dead Trotskyists, or those who were still alive but were so exhausted that they were unable to extract even a gram of gold from the rock, even to lift a gram of rock.

Traitors to the motherland and looters filled the prisoner barracks and dugouts that had emptied during the war. In the barracks and dugouts doors were repaired, new bars were installed, and new barbed wire was rolled out around the zones; places once seething with life—or rather, seething with death, at least in 1938—were revived.

Apart from article 58, a great number of prisoners had been condemned under a special article, 192. Article 192 passed unnoticed in peacetime, but the first cannon shot, the explosion of bombs, and the first machine-gun fire had made it blossom richly. Like any proper criminal article in those circumstances, article 192 rapidly acquired supplements, footnotes, points, and paragraphs. Article 192a, b, c, d, e instantly appeared, until the whole alphabet was used up. Each letter in that terrible alphabet acquired parts and paragraphs. So there would be article 192, part 1, paragraph 2. Each paragraph acquired footnotes, and article 192, which had once seemed so modest, swelled like a spider, its outlines reminding one of virgin forest.

None of the paragraphs, parts, points, or letters was punishable by less than fifteen years, and none exempted the convict from labor. Labor was the legislators' main concern.

All those condemned under article 192 could expect invariable, ennobling labor in Kolyma: only heavy manual labor with a pickax, spade, and wheelbarrow. And yet this was not the same as article 58.

Article 192 was in wartime the fate of victims of the law from whom it was impossible to extract evidence of agitation, treason, or sabotage.

Or else the interrogator didn't have enough willpower to do his job properly; not being on top of his job, he had failed to stitch the prisoner up with the fashionable label for an old-fashioned crime, either because the individual's physical resistance was such that the interrogator became fed up or because he had been reluctant to give instructions to use method No. 3. The world of interrogation has its ebbs and flows, its fashions, its underground struggle for influence.

A sentence was always the result of a series of active causes, many of them external.

This is a case where the creative psychology has not yet been described, where even the foundations haven't been laid for this major construction project of the times.

It was under this article 192 that a construction engineer from Minsk, Mikhail Ivanovich Novikov, was brought to Kolyma with a fifteen-year sentence.

Novikov had severe high blood pressure, constantly around 240, at the top of the Riva-Rocci scale.[31]

This was hypertonia of a permanent nature. Novikov had been living under the threat of a stroke or apoplexy. That was common knowledge in both Minsk and Magadan. It was forbidden to transport such patients to Kolyma, which was why medical examinations existed. And after 1937 this order was twice confirmed by all the medical institutions for prisons, transit camps, and the camps. But for the sea voyage from Vladivostok to Magadan, for prisoners at special camps, for Counterrevolutionary Trotskyist Activity, and for the contingent as a whole, who were predestined to live and, above all, die in Kolyma, all limits on invalidity and age were removed.

Kolyma was invited to reject its own slag, using the same bureaucratic path of certification, lists, commissions, prisoner parties, and thousands of confirmatory signatures.

A lot of real slag was brought back.

They dispatched to the gold-mine pit faces not just the weak and the legless, not just sixty-year-old men, but also sufferers from tuberculosis and heart disease.

By these criteria a hypertonic was not a sick man but just a healthy red-faced shirker who was refusing to work but eating the state's bread. Putting bread in his mouth and giving nothing back.

In the authorities' eyes engineer Novikov was one of these red-faced shirkers; he was a prisoner at the Baragon sector near Oymiakon's Highways Administration in the Northeast Corrective Labor Camps in the summer of 1953.

Not every medic in Kolyma, unfortunately, knew how to take blood pressure with Riva-Rocci's sphygmomanometer, even though a paramedic, a ward assistant, and a doctor had to know how to take a patient's pulse and feel the artery swelling.

Riva-Rocci's apparatus had been delivered to every medical sector, along with thermometers, bandages, and iodine. But at the center that I had just taken over as a free contract paramedic—my first job as a free man in ten years—there were no thermometers and no bandages. There was only a Riva-Rocci sphygmomanometer; unlike the thermometers, it wasn't broken. Writing off a broken thermometer in Kolyma was problematic, so all the glass fragments were kept until they could be written off and certified, as if they were relicts of Pompeii, fragments of Hittite ceramics.

Kolyma doctors were used to going without thermometers, let alone a Riva-Rocci apparatus. Even in the central hospital, a thermometer was used only for the seriously ill, while other patients had their temperature estimated "by the pulse," as was done in the innumerable camp outpatient clinics.

I knew all that very well. At Baragon I saw that the Riva-Rocci apparatus was in perfect order; it was just that the paramedic I replaced had never used it.

I was taught in my paramedic classes how to use the apparatus. I practiced it a million times during my training; I was entrusted with measuring the blood pressure of everyone in the barracks for invalids. As far as Riva-Rocci was concerned, I was well trained.

I took over the listed patients, about two hundred of them, the drugs, the instruments, and the medicine cupboards. This was no easy matter: I was a free contract paramedic, even though a former prisoner; I was already living outside the zone, not in a separate "cabin" inside the barracks but in a hostel for free men, in a room with four trestle beds, much poorer, colder, and more uncomfortable than my cabin in the camp.

But I had to move on, to look ahead.

I wasn't much bothered by the slight changes in my personal living conditions. I don't drink alcohol, and in every other respect I kept within normal human bounds, which meant prisoners' bounds.

In my first session I had a man of about forty, wearing a prisoner's pea jacket, waiting for me by the door, wanting a face-to-face chat.

In the camps I didn't have face-to-face chats: they always ended with the offer of a bribe, and the bribe, or the promise of one, was always casual, just in case. There were profound reasons for this, and one day I shall examine the question in detail.

Here, at Baragon, there was something in the patient's tone that made me hear him out.

He asked to be examined once more, although he'd already had a general examination about an hour earlier.

"What is the reason for your request?"

"The reason, sir, is this," the man said. "The point is, sir, that I'm ill, but I'm not being exempted from work."

"How can that be?"

"Well, I have a headache and my temples are throbbing."

I recorded in the book: "Novikov, Mikhail Ivanovich."

I took his pulse. The pulse was rumbling, changing speed, and seemed too improbable to count. Puzzled, I lifted my eyes from the hourglass.

"Are you able," Novikov whispered, "to use that apparatus over there?" He pointed to the Riva-Rocci on the corner of the table.

"Of course."

"And can you measure my blood pressure?"

"If you like, I'll do it now."

Novikov quickly took his jacket off, sat at the table, and turned his cuffs up, baring his arms to the shoulder.

I put the phonendoscope to my ears. The pulse came in loud beats; the mercury in the Riva-Rocci apparatus rushed up furiously.

I recorded the Riva-Rocci measurements: 260 over 110.

"Other arm!"

The reading was the same.

I wrote in a firm hand in the book: "To be exempted from work. Diagnosis: high blood pressure 260/110."

"Does that mean I don't have to work tomorrow?"

"Of course you don't." Novikov burst into tears. "But why do you ask? Where's the problem?"

"You see," said Novikov, avoiding the addition of "sir" and thus seeming to remind me that I was a former prisoner, "the paramedic you've replaced didn't know how to use the apparatus and told me that it was out of order. But I was hypertonic even when I was in Minsk, on the mainland, a free man. I was taken to Kolyma without having my blood pressure checked."

"Well then, you'll be given an exemption for the time being, and then you'll be certified and you'll leave, for Magadan, if not for the mainland."

The next day I was summoned to Tkachuk's office: he was the boss of our Special Camp Center, with the rank of warrant officer. The rules stated that the boss of a Special Camp Center had to be a lieutenant: Tkachuk was anxious to keep his job.

"Now you've just exempted Novikov from work. I've checked: he's a malingerer."

"Novikov's not a malingerer, he has high blood pressure."

"I'll phone and get a commission set up. A medical one. Only after that do we exempt him from work."

No," I said, addressing Tkachuk as a free man would, instead of saying "sir" as I would have just a year earlier. "No. First I'll exempt him from work, and then you get a commission from the administration. The commission will either confirm my actions or it will dismiss me. You can report me, but I would ask you not to interfere with my actions when they are purely medical."

That was the end of my conversation with Tkachuk. Novikov stayed in the barracks, and Tkachuk summoned a commission from the administration. There were only two doctors in the commission and they each had a Riva-Rocci apparatus: one was Soviet, just like mine, the other was Japanese with a round manometer, a war trophy. But it was easy to get used to the manometer.

Novikov had his blood pressure checked; the figures coincided with mine. A certificate of invalidity was drawn up for Novikov, and he went back to the barracks and began to wait for a party of prisoners or for a guard who happened to be traveling to Magadan.

As for me, I didn't even get a thank-you from my medical bosses.

My battle with Tkachuk became general knowledge among the prisoners in their barracks.

My liquidation of lice, which I achieved using a method I'd learned in the central hospital, by roasting them in empty gas cans, was a World War II experiment. Liquidating lice in the camp by a portable method, disinfection, reliability, and speed: my delousing system reconciled Tkachuk to my existence.

But Novikov was bored, waiting for a party to go to Magadan.

"I can do something not too strenuous," he once told me at an evening surgery. "If you ask on my behalf."

"I'm not going to ask," I said. The question of Novikov was personal for me, too; it was a question of my reputation as a paramedic.

New stormy events swept aside the drama of high blood pressure and the miracles of delousing.

An amnesty arrived, the amnesty known to history as Beria's amnesty. Its text was printed in Magadan and sent to all the remote corners of Kolyma, so that the grateful humanity in the camps could feel it, rejoice and value it, bow down and give thanks. All prisoners, wherever they were, were eligible for amnesty with full restoration of rights.

All article 58ers were to be freed, all the points, parts, and paragraphs, every single one, with restoration of all rights—but with sentences of up to five years only.

Five years was the sentence under article 58 only at the dawn of the misty youth of 1937. Such people had either died or been freed, or had received additional terms of imprisonment.

The sentences that Garanin had given to gangsters—he tried them for sabotage under article 58, paragraph 14—were annulled: the gangsters were released. A whole series of nonpolitical articles had their terms shortened, so that those convicted under article 192 had their sentences cut.

The amnesty did not apply to prisoners with article 58 who had been convicted more than once, it applied only to recidivist criminals. That was a typical Stalinist volte-face.

Not a single person could leave the camps if he had previously been convicted under article 58. Unless you used the word "person" in gangster terminology. "Person" in gangster language meant gangster, old crook, a member of the criminal world.

That was what Beria's amnesty mainly amounted to. Beria had picked up Stalin's baton.

The only people released were the gangsters, whom Garanin had persecuted so much.

All the criminals who had Beria's amnesty were released with a clean slate, with all rights restored. The government saw them as true friends, a reliable support basis.

The only people not surprised by this blow were the article 58 prisoners: they were used to such surprises.

The blow was a surprise for the Magadan administration. It was extremely surprising for the gangsters themselves: the sky over their heads suddenly cleared. All over Magadan and all Kolyma's settlements, murderers, thieves, rapists wandered, and all of them had to eat four times, or at least three times a day—pearl barley porridge, if not thick cabbage and mutton stew.

So the most reasonable thing for a practical boss to do, the simplest and most reasonable action, was to get vehicles ready to transport this mighty wave farther, to the mainland, to Russia proper. There were two routes: Magadan, then by sea to Vladivostok, the classic route for the inhabitants of Kolyma, which still had all the traditions and terminology of tsarist Sakhalin times, as minted by Tsar Nicolas.

There was a second route: across the taiga to Aldan, and from there to the upper Lena River and by ship down the Lena. That route was less popular, but free men and fugitives managed to get to the mainland by it.

A third route was by air. But flights of northern sea routes, given the fickle Arctic weather, could only be offered as the opportunity arose. In any case, the Douglas cargo plane, which could take fourteen people, was obviously unable to solve the problem of transport.

Everyone wants to be free, so everyone, gangsters and *freiers*, was in a hurry to get the necessary papers and to leave, for, as the gangsters understood, the government might come to its senses and change its decision.

All the trucks in all the Kolyma camps were used to take parties in this turbid wave.

And there was no reason to hope that our Baragon gangsters would be sent away soon.

At the time they were sent in the direction of the Lena River, and then left to find their own way downstream from Yakutsk. The Lena shipping company set aside a ship for the released prisoners and, with a sigh of relief, washed its hands of them.

It turned out that there was not enough food for the journey. Nobody could swap anything with the local inhabitants, for they had no possessions, and there were no inhabitants able to sell anything edible. The gangsters, once they had gotten hold of the ship and the officers (the captain and the helmsman), had a general meeting and decided to use their fellow travelers, the *freiers*, as meat. There were far more gangsters than *freiers*. But even if there had been fewer gangsters, the decision would have been the same.

The *freiers* had their throats cut, and they were boiled in the ship's cauldron one by one, so by the time the ship reached its destination, they had all been slaughtered. Apparently, only the captain or the helmsman survived.

Work at the mines stopped, and it took some time before the usual rhythm was restored.

The gangsters were in a hurry: the mistake might be discovered. The authorities were also in a hurry to get rid of a dangerous contingent. But this was no mistake: it was an utterly deliberate action of Beria and his colleagues' free will.

I'm well acquainted with the details of this story, because Blumshtein, a comrade of Novikov's who'd been convicted with him, left with that party of prisoners. Blumshtein was in a hurry to get out of the wheels of the machine, and he tried to speed up its process and thus perished.

There was an order from Magadan to take all measures to speed up the sorting out and finalization of cases. Special commissions such as exit tribunals were issuing papers in the camps, not in the administration in Magadan, as one way of reducing the dreadful and turbid onrush of these waves. Of waves that could not be called human.

The commission brought the papers, already drawn up, to every locality: some prisoners got a reduction, some a substitution, some got nothing at all, some got complete freedom. The release group, as they were called, were those who had worked well according to the camp records.

Our camp was a highways outpost where there were a lot of non-politicals: it became completely empty. The commission came and in a solemn ceremony, accompanied by the same wind band whose silvery trumpets had played a flourish at the reading of each execution order at the pit faces of 1938, issued a travel warrant to freedom for more than a hundred inhabitants of our camp.

One of those hundred men given release or a reduced sentence (which had to be signed for on a formal printed summary document that had all the imaginable official stamps on it) was the one person in our camp who wouldn't sign for anything and refused to pick up the summary of his case.

That person was Mikhail Ivanovich Novikov, my hypertonic.

The text of the Beria amnesty was posted on all the fences in the zones, and Mikhail Ivanovich Novikov had the time to study and consider it and to make a decision.

Novikov worked out that he should have been released outright, not with some reduced sentence. Outright, like a gangster. But in the documents that were delivered Novikov merely had his sentence altered, so that he still had a few months before he was free. Novikov wouldn't accept the papers and didn't put his signature to any of them.

The commission representatives told Novikov that he ought not to refuse the notification of a new calculation of his sentence. They said that it would be reexamined in the administration and that, if a mistake had been made, the mistake would be corrected. Novikov refused to believe that this was possible. He rejected the papers and made a complaint in response, which was written by a lawyer, Blumshtein, who also came from Minsk. Novikov and Blumshtein had been in Belarus prison and the Kolyma camp together. They had even slept next to each other in the Baragon barracks and, as the gangsters put it, "they dined together." The complaint in response had Novikov's calculation of his own sentence and of what was open to him.

So Novikov remained in the deserted Baragon barracks, labeled as a fool who wouldn't trust the authorities.

Such complaints in response, made by exhausted, tired men at the moment when hope had revived, were extremely rare in Kolyma or in any camps.

Novikov's declaration was sent on to Moscow. Of course it was! Only Moscow was capable of contesting his knowledge of the law and the outcome of this knowledge. And Novikov knew that.

The turbid, murderous torrent swept over the Kolyma land, along the highways, as it made its way to the sea, to Magadan, to the freedom of the mainland. Another turbid torrent was flowing down the Lena River, taking the riverside landings, the airfields, and the railway stations of Yakutia, eastern and western Siberia by storm. It flowed on to Irkutsk, to Novosibirsk, and then farther into the mainland, merging with the turbid and just as murderous waves of the Magadan and Vladivostok torrents. The gangsters had changed the climate of the cities: it was as easy to commit robberies in Moscow as in Magadan. Quite a few years were wasted, quite a few people perished, before this turbid wave was forced back behind bars again.

Thousands of new grapevine rumors crept into the camp barracks, each more dreadful and fantastic than the previous one.

The fast courier post from Moscow via Magadan brought us news that was not on the grapevine—the grapevine rarely used the courier post. It was a document with unconditional release for Novikov.

When Novikov got his papers, he was too late even for the last gasp of the amnesty, and he waited for any truck that might pass, afraid of even thinking of taking the same route as Blumshtein.

Novikov sat every day on my couch-cum-trestle-bed in the outpatient room, waiting, waiting...

Meanwhile Tkachuk had received the first supplement of people, after the amnesty that had devastated the camp. The camp, it turned out, was not being closed: it was being expanded, it was growing. Our Baragon was given new accommodations, a new zone where barracks were being erected and, therefore, a guardhouse and towers, and a solitary-confinement block, and a square for roll calls before work. Now the facade of the arch over the camp gates had the officially adopted slogan nailed to it: "Labor is a matter of honor, a matter of glory, a matter of valor and heroism."

There was all the workforce you could want, the barracks had been built, but the heart of the Special Camp Center was unhappy—there was no flower bed, no lawn with flowers. Everything was at hand: the grass, the flowers, the lawn, the laths for a wooden fence; what was missing was a man who could lay out the flower beds and lawns. Without flower beds and lawns, without camp symmetry, what sort of camp would it be? Third class at best. Baragon was a long way from Magadan, Susuman, or Ust-Nera.

But even third-class camps need flowers and symmetry.

Tkachuk questioned every single camp prisoner; he drove to the neighboring Special Camp Center. Nowhere was there anyone who had an engineer's education, a technician able to lay out a lawn and a flower bed without using a theodolite.

Mikhail Ivanovich Novikov was the man. But because he had been wronged, Novikov would not hear of it. Tkachuk's orders were no longer orders to him.

Given Tkachuk's absolute conviction that prisoners forget everything, he invited Novikov to lay out the camp garden. It turned out that the prisoner's memory was far more retentive than the head of the Special Camp Center had thought.

The "opening" day for the camp was getting nearer. Nobody was capable of laying out the flower bed. Two days before the opening, Tkachuk asked Novikov, repressing his pride by asking, instead of ordering or advising.

Novikov responded to the request by the boss of the Special Camp Center thus: "There is no question of doing anything in the camp at your request. But I will suggest a way you can solve your problem. Tell your paramedic to ask me. Then everything will be ready in a matter of hours."

This entire conversation, with the appropriate swearing at Novikov, was passed on to me by Tkachuk. I realized what the situation was and asked Novikov to lay out the camp garden. It was all done in two hours or so, and the camp was nice and tidy. The flower beds were laid out, the flowers were planted, the Special Camp Center was opened.

Novikov left Baragon with the very last party of prisoners, before the winter of 1953–54.

We met before he left.

"I hope you will leave here and be properly released," I was told by the man who had released himself. "Things are moving that way,

I assure you. I'd give a lot to meet you somewhere in Minsk or in Moscow."

"None of that matters, Mikhail Ivanovich."

"No, it does matter. I'm a prophet. I have a premonition, a premonition that you will be released!"

Three months later I was in Moscow.

1972

NOTES

INTRODUCTION

1   Varlam Shalamov, *Vse ili Nichego: Esse o Poezii i Proze* (St. Petersburg: Limbus Press, 2016), 115–18.

2   Viktor Shklovsky, *Theory of Prose*, trans. Benjamin Sher (London: Dalkey Archive Press, 1990), 6.

3   "Cherry Brandy" appears in the first volume of *Kolyma Stories*.

4   Judith Pallot, "The Gulag as the Crucible of Russia's 21st-Century System of Punishment," *Kritika: Explorations in Russian and Eurasian History* 16, no. 3 (Summer 2015), 681–710.

5   Alexander Etkind describes this process in his rich analysis of the afterlife of the Gulag, *Warped Mourning: Stories of the Undead in the Land of the Unburied* (Stanford: Stanford University Press, 2013).

6   Svetlana Boym, "'Banality of Evil,' Mimicry, and the Soviet Subject: Varlam Shalamov and Hannah Arendt," *Slavic Review* 67, no. 2 (Summer 2008), 342–63.

BOOK FOUR: SKETCHES OF THE CRIMINAL WORLD

1   Jean Valjean, the main hero of Victor Hugo's novel *Les Misérables* (1862), spends nineteen years as a prisoner, convicted of stealing bread; on his release, persuaded by a priest to reform, he begins a respectable life as Monsieur Madeleine, although he is hounded by a vengeful police commissioner.

2   *Freiers* is a term meaning "free people," the ordinary noncriminal. See Shalamov's explanation on page 14.

3   Volga dockers, who loaded the ships that plied the river, were one of the most heavily exploited classes of laborers in tsarist Russia.

4   Akim Akimovich, a model prisoner in Dostoyevsky's *Notes from the House of the Dead*, was an officer convicted of extrajudicially killing a bandit: although a violent man, Akim Akimovich is portrayed as versatile, selfless, and a lover of justice.

5   Petrov, a prisoner in Dostoyevsky's *Notes from the House of the Dead*, was a soldier who stabbed to death a colonel who struck him. The eight-eyed deputy commandant in the same novel is based on the actual commandant of Omsk prison, a cruel man who often colluded with the criminals in his custody.

6   In 1890 Chekhov undertook a grueling journey to the penal colony of the island of Sakhalin: the immediate outcome was eventually his book *Sakhalin Island*, denouncing the horrible treatment of the convicts, but in his fiction after 1891 Chekhov shows a greater distaste for authority, more sympathy for the oppressed, and skepticism about all political philosophies.

7   "Chelkash," a story Gorky wrote in 1895, is about a thief of that name who recruits a younger man, Gavrila, to help him rob goods from the docks to sell to ships anchored nearby. The two quarrel and Gavrila nearly murders Chelkash; out of scornful pride, Chelkash, when he recovers, throws all the money they have gained in Gavrila's face.

8   Vaska Pepel, a hereditary but penitent thief, is a central character in Gorky's play *The Lower Depths* (1902), set in a rooming house. The woman in charge of the rooming house pleads with him to murder her husband, but he refuses, partly because he is in love with her sister.

9   Benya Krik, the "King" of Jewish gangsters in Odessa, is a hero of Isaak Babel's *Odessa Stories* (1923–1924) and his play *Sunset* (1931). Despite a brief collaboration with Soviet forces, Benya is executed by them. Leonid Leonov's novel *The Thief* (1927) describes the life of Vekshin, a safecracker who eventually sees the error of his ways. Ilya Selvinsky's 1923 poem "Motke Malkhamoves" (literally, "angel of death") is about a bank robber claiming to have a bomb. Vera Inber's poem "Vaska Svist Behind Bars" of the 1920s is a semicomic portrait of a robber killed by a policeman. Veniamin Kaverin's novel *The End of the Hide-out* (1925) is about a gang of bank robbers who are arrested after a number of blunders. Ostap Bender, a con man of genius (who nevertheless fails in his search for wealth), is the hero of Ilya Ilf and Yevgeni Petrov's novels *The Twelve Chairs* (1928) and *The Golden Calf* (1931).

10   *The Stalin White Sea–Baltic Canal* (1934) was published as the testaments of some thirty-six writers to the redemption of "criminals," in an illustrated and finely produced blue-gray volume.

11   Nikolai Pogodin's play *The Aristocrats* and film *The Prisoners* (1935–36) portrayed a professional criminal, Kostia, "reforged" by hard labor on the White Sea canal.

12   *Timur and His Gang* is a well-known Soviet children's book by Arkady Gaidar.

13 Lev Sheinin was an NKVD interrogator who also wrote popular stories about crime and detection.

14 Nikolai Pogodin's play *The Aristocrats*.

15 Here Shalamov is describing the way thieves behave once they are in prison or in the camps.

16 A "political" was a prisoner convicted under article 58 of the Soviet Criminal Code, whose subsections listed all forms of anti-Soviet activity from disrespectful political utterances to spying and high treason.

17 These are women's names applied to gangsters' catamites.

18 The Serpantinka, or Serpantinnaya, named for the serpentine road leading to it, was a camp designated primarily for executions.

19 Cascarilla is the hero of Umberto Notari's novel *The Three Thieves* (1911) and of the Soviet film *The Three Million Trial* (1926).

20 "Navarino smoke and flame" describe the color of a tailcoat worn by Chichikov, the hero of Gogol's *Dead Souls*.

21 From "The Bear Cub," a song of anonymous origin, composed just before the 1917 revolution and made famous in a revision and setting by Aleksandr Galich in the 1980s.

22 This was an Odessa folk song about a bandit; in 1967 the song became famous in Vladimir Vysotsky's version. The identity of the thief Gorbachevsky is unknown.

23 Lines from Aleksandr Galich's "The Bear Cub."

24 The term is the title Pasternak gave to one of his longer poems.

25 This is a term in Russian billiards and cards for making a bet in which the winner gets five times the stake (one "transport" equals four "couches").

26 *Skushan* instead of *s kushem*. See chapter VIII of *The Island of Sakhalin*.

27 Shalamov is mistaken: however, there is a titular Councilor Shtoss in Mikhail Lermontov's unfinished story "Faro" (*shtoss* in Russian; faro is a variety of poker).

28 In Aleksandr Pushkin's story "The Queen of Spades" (1834), German, the protagonist, is determined to use any means, occult or violent, to get the secret of three winning cards; Chekalinsky is his gambling partner.

29 Lermontov's poem *The Tambov Treasurer's Wife*, now existing only with the censor's deletions, tells of an old treasurer staking his wife when he has lost all his possessions at cards.

30 Possibly this is a reference to Gilbert Keith Chesterton's essay "The Case for Hermits" in *The Well and the Shadows* (1935), where Chesterton argues, "If men do not have Solitude, they go mad."

31 The Wasserman test (now superseded) was devised in 1906 as the first blood test capable of detecting antibodies to syphilis.

32 *The Monrepo Refuge* (ca. 1870) was a satirical novel by Mikhail Saltykov-Shchedrin, describing an idyllic spa-like resort.

33 Salvarsan, an injectable mix of arsenobenzol, was the most effective treatment for syphilis before the discovery of antibiotics. It came into use in 1910.

34 Marshal Konstantin Rokossovsky (1896–1968), of Polish aristocratic origin, was one of a very few senior officers to survive Stalin's purges of 1937 and 1938: released in 1940, he showed exceptional talent and courage not only in fighting the Germans but in defying Stalin's orders. One reason for his success was that he did not care about his soldiers' past.

35 Piotr Vershigora was a partisan officer. He wrote his epic book in the 1950s.

36 Anton Makarenko (1888–1939) was famous for his work in the 1930s on reforming juvenile delinquents, and his books on the subject.

37 Voronko was a Belarusian partisan who figures in the semifictional memoirs of the partisan leader Piotr Vershigora.

38 Nikolai Krylenko was the People's Commissariat for Justice in the first half of the 1930s (he was shot in 1938): the "rubber band" was the principle of variable sentencing. Andrei Vyshinsky was the prosecutor for Stalin's show trials (and later became the Soviet foreign minister).

39 Nikolai Yevreinov (1879–1953) was a brilliant theater director; Luigi Pirandello (1867–1936) was a major Italian playwright.

40 Archive No. 3 was the name of the department that kept count of prisoner deaths in the camps.

41 The aphorism attributed to Nestor Makhno (1888–1934), the leader of the Greens or Anarchists in the Russian Civil War, was "Hit the Reds until they turn white, hit the Whites until they turn red."

42 Sheinin's story tells how President Édouard Herriot had his watch stolen and then returned during a visit to the Hermitage in Leningrad.

43 In the 1850s and '60s, Pierre Alexis Ponson du Terrail wrote several novels with Rocambole as the protagonist: at first a villain serving and then killing the dastardly Sir Williams, Rocambole, after a spell in prison, becomes a mastermind and chivalrous hero.

44 From Heinrich Heine's poem "Vitzliputzli" about the Aztec god of that name.

45 Yevgeni Baratynsky (1800–1844) was a major Russian lyrical poet.

46 Nikolai Nekrasov (1821–1878) was the most popular poet of the 1860s in Russia: his poems expressed sympathy for the poor, and "The Railway"

was famous for its insistence that Russia's new railways were built on the bones of its laborers. Aleksei Konstantinovich Tolstoy (1817–75) was a poet and playwright specializing in historical and religious themes: his "Vasili Shibanov," composed as a folk ballad, tells of Prince Kurbsky's Shibanov, a servant sent to deliver a denunciation to Ivan the Terrible and therefore tortured to death. Tolstoy's novel *The Silver Prince* was Russia's most popular historical novel: its hero stands up for justice in the court of Ivan the Terrible.

47 For English and Russian texts of "Smash and Grab," see Anna Pilkington, *The Garnett Book of Russian Folk and Anonymous Verse* (London: Garnett Press, 2015), 331.

48 The monasteries of the Solovetsky Islands in the White Sea were turned into concentration camps in the 1920s. Many intellectuals and former members of the gentry were exiled and murdered there. As well as plays, a number of songs, often ironic and literate, were composed by the prisoners; which one Shalamov had in mind is unknown.

49 Leonid Utiosov (1895–1982), a singer, actor, and composer, was famous for his songs and films about Odessa. "From the Odessa Jail" is one of his best-known songs.

50 Eugène Vidocq was a French detective of the early nineteenth century; Monsieur Lecoq was a fictional detective in novels by Émile Gaboriau; Vanka Kain, a Russian bandit and later a thief catcher, was sent to Siberia in 1755.

51 The primer *An Honest Mirror of Youth* was published by Peter the Great in 1717. One of the first modern Russian textbooks, composed by the bishop of Ryazan and Murom, with the help of James Bruce, the tsar's counselor, and also based on the writings of Erasmus, it was a tutorial in literacy, numeracy, morals, and religion. It was still in print and use at the end of the nineteenth century.

52 Akhun Babayev was a prominent party boss in Uzbekistan.

53 For English and Russian text of a version of this song, "The Safe," see Pilkington, *The Garnett Book of Russian Folk and Anonymous Verse*, 332–34.

54 Printed matter was largely unavailable to prisoners. They relied on oral memory for songs and verses, while the "novels" that criminals forced intellectuals to recite to them were versions improvised from what the reciter could remember of his reading.

55 *The Viazemsky Princes* was an oral novel based on historical fact and fiction about the court of Ivan the Terrible; *The Jack of Hearts Club* was the story of a real, notorious conspiracy of Russian banknote forgers in the

1870s, and a number of journalists embroidered the accounts of those who were convicted and those who escaped justice.

56 Vladimir Korolenko (1853–1921) was a prolific radical writer who was at one time exiled to Siberia; Lev Tolstoy graphically denounced the Russian judicial system and Siberian prison conditions in his novel *Resurrection*; Vera Figner (1852–1942) was a revolutionary whose memoirs reflect a life mostly spent in prison; Nikolai Morozov (1854–1946) was a revolutionary who served twenty-three years in Russia's worst prisons: his many works describe his experiences.

57 The Fedorovites were a Christian sect founded by Fedor Rybalkin in Voronezh Province in the early 1920s; they announced that the coming of the Antichrist was imminent. They were arrested in 1929.

58 A reference to the lines in Pushkin's narrative poem *The Gypsies*: "God's bird does not know / Care or labor…"

59 Khlestakov is the boastful impostor who deceives all the other characters in Gogol's comedy *The Government Inspector* (1836).

60 The Semperante theater existed in Moscow from 1917 to 1938.

61 Arkadi Adamov (1920–1991) was a Soviet writer of detective stories who revived the genre in the 1950s.

62 Count Xavier de Montépin (1823–1902) was an enormously prolific (and sometimes plagiarizing) French novelist.

63 *Bel Ami* (1885), Guy de Maupassant's best-known novel, is the story of Georges Duroy, a mediocre ex-soldier, journalist, and womanizer who ruthlessly exploits women and colleagues to get to the top of his profession.

64 The literary critic and children's poet Kornei Chukovsky (1882–1969) was well known for his 1922 biography and 1952 study of the poet Nikolai Nekrasov.

65 Emmanuel Kaminka and Irakli Andronikov were famous Soviet reciters on both the stage and television.

66 Anton Krechet is a noble thief, a Russian Robin Hood, in a series of novels begun in 1909 and written by a series of drunken hacks, usually known collectively under the pseudonym Mikhail Raskatov.

67 For reasons unknown, the word "forty" became gangster code for "let's have a cigarette."

BOOK FIVE: THE RESURRECTION OF THE LARCH

1 Alphonse Bertillon (1853–1914) was a forensic scientist who identified the bones of the murdered prince Andrei Bogoliubsky (1111–1174).

2   Nikolai Muralov (1877–1937) was an Old Bolshevik who distinguished himself in the Civil War in 1919 but later sided with Trotsky against Stalin and was ousted from positions of power. Despite expressing penitence, he was shot for Trotskyism.

3   Many Russian Christians were sectarians who dissented from the official Orthodox Church; they were regarded as politically dangerous and were repressed, especially those who refused to recognize any temporal authority.

4   Anton Makarenko, see Book Four, note 36.

5   In 1937 the Communist International (the "Club," or Komintern) in Moscow was subjected to severe repressions and many foreign communists were arrested and shot; Komintern was formally wound up in 1939, when Stalin agreed to a pact with Hitler.

6   "Oh my lobby" is an old and still-popular Russian folk song, with many variant texts. The singer acts as a seller of beer and spirits trying to attract customers.

7   General Heinz Guderian (1888–1954) was a very successful and much-feared commander of German tank divisions fighting the Soviets in World War II.

8   "Metal No. 1" means the gold mines, Kolyma's most valuable resource.

9   Specialists were people with professional qualifications (especially military) whose work was so necessary to the Soviet state that their tsarist allegiances were, for a time, overlooked.

10 Guliai-Pole ("Go-free Field") is a former Cossack village in southeastern Ukraine, which in 1917 Makhno made the center of his "anarcho-communist" republic.

11 Engineer Kipreyev and the events in this story are based on the physicist Georgi Demidov (1908–1987), whose own stories of Kolyma, *Chùdnaya Planeta* (Wondrous Planet), were not published until 2008.

12 Igor Kurchatov (1903–1960) was a physicist: he is considered the father of the Soviet atom bomb.

13 Chifir is tea brewed strongly (a large matchboxful of finely ground leaves, triple brewed, per cup) and drunk on an empty stomach; it is a hunger suppressant and a powerful, addictive stimulant.

14 Lend-lease was an arrangement made from 1941 to 1945 by the United States government with its allies in the war against Germany and Japan, by which supplies of armaments and food were delivered, primarily to Great Britain and the Soviet Union, often on credit but sometimes without the expectation of repayment.

15 James Forrestal, the United States secretary of the navy and later secretary of defense and an adviser to Presidents Roosevelt and Truman, opposed the use of the atomic bomb on Japan, fearing it would benefit the Soviet Union. He died (probably by suicide) later, however, in 1949.

16 In the 1930s, whenever there was a breakdown or accident in a major Soviet factory, it was normal for the factory engineers to be convicted for deliberately "wrecking" machinery. Such individuals were convicted as "wreckers."

17 "We're not slaves. Slaves aren't us" was in the first Soviet primer (1919–1921), which was used not only in schools but also to teach illiterate adults. The saying became popular because in the original Russian if the last space is removed the last two words mean "slaves are mute."

18 In Balzac's novel of 1831, *The Wild Ass's Skin*, a magical donkey skin shrinks every time that it grants its owner a wish, but the owner's own health dwindles.

19 Shalamov was mistaken. The People's Will was a revolutionary-socialist group that succeeded in 1881 in assassinating Tsar Alexander II. Nikolai Shelgunov (1824–1891) was an ethnologist and, along with his wife, had strong radical sympathies. He was persecuted at times, but never belonged to the People's Will. Another Shelgunov (unrelated to Nikolai), Vasili (1867–1939), was a member of Lenin's Social-Democratic Party, and subsequently a Bolshevik; he was remarkable for dying of natural causes.

20 Cyrano de Bergerac was a real French novelist (1619–1655) but is more famous as the hero of a play of 1897 by Edmond Rostand, in which Cyrano, in love with his cousin Roxane, believes he is too ugly to win her love and has his handsome friend Christian woo her on his behalf. Only after Christian dies in battle and Roxane enters a convent does Cyrano win her love, and then he dies.

21 Vlasov's men were Soviet soldiers recruited from German prisoner-of-war camps to fight in the Russian Liberation Army alongside the Germans all over Europe. After the war, some were executed and many were sent to the Gulag. General Andrei Vlasov (born 1901) was hanged in Moscow in 1946.

22 Shigalov, a character in Dostoyevsky's novel *The Devils*, is an extreme revolutionary theorist who believes in revolutionaries killing one another as a bonding exercise.

23 Nikolai Yezhov (1895–1940) became Stalin's henchman when he took charge of the NKVD. He was the architect of the Great Terror of 1937–38, which sent innocent victims, often chosen at random, to some seven hundred thousand executions and at least two million Gulag sentences.

24 Lavrenti Beria (1899–1953) took charge of the NKVD in 1939 and proved his versatility by organizing wartime military production and producing the Soviet atomic bomb. He survived Stalin but was shot by his politburo comrades, chiefly for his newly found political liberalism.

25 On August 25, 1906, Prime Minister Piotr Stolypin's dacha was blown up by Socialist Revolutionaries. His children were injured and twenty-eight other people were killed. Russia's most effective (and ruthless) reformer, Stolypin was assassinated in 1911 by a revolutionary with connections to the secret police.

26 Khamovniki (a medieval weavers' quarter) and Presnia are two central Moscow areas that suffered greatly from Stalin's "modernizing" bulldozers in the late 1920s and '30s, with the loss of many ancient monuments.

27 Sophia Perovskaya (born 1853) was one of the chief organizers of the People's Will and of the assassination of Tsar Alexander II. She was hanged in 1881.

28 Semion Frank (1877–1950) was a Russian philosopher particularly influential in the 1900s. Hostile to Marxism, he defended human freedom and eventually espoused Russian Orthodoxy.

29 Anatolii Aleksandrovich Kalashnikov (1888–1953), the son of a railway worker, became a socialist in 1906, specializing in distributing propaganda and explosives.

30 Sergei Koridze (1887–1956), also known as Morchadze, a close friend of the poet Mayakovsky, was famous for assisting convicted women terrorists to escape.

31 The ninth wave (*deviatyi val*) in Russian legend is the wave in a storm that sinks the ship; in describing art, the term suggests a similar power.

32 Boris Savinkov was a Socialist Revolutionary politician and later an émigré agent; he was killed in 1925, probably on Stalin's orders.

33 Yevno Azef (1869–1918) was a minor criminal who became a leading Socialist Revolutionary terrorist. He organized the assassination of Grand Duke Sergey in 1903. Yet since 1892 he had been a secret police agent and denounced many of his comrades. He was exposed in 1908, but fled to Germany. In 1915 he was imprisoned in Berlin as a Russian agent. He died of kidney disease. Nikolai Tatarov (1877–1906), the son of a priest, was a Socialist Revolutionary who in 1904 became a secret police agent. He was denounced by Azef and stabbed to death by another party member.

34 A famous lane in central Moscow.

35 Robert Bruce Lockhart (1887–1970) was a British diplomat who in 1918 sought to find an accommodation with the Bolsheviks; he was arrested by

the Soviet secret police as a spy. His *Memoirs of a British Agent* make entertaining but not wholly reliable reading.

36 The story is narrated by an engineer who, at the inauguration of a bridge he has built, finds himself ignored in favor of an actress, his mistress, who happens to be present.

37 The miners of the Don basin were the victims of the first Soviet show trial in 1928; they were falsely accused, along with German technical advisers, of wrecking and sabotage on behalf of foreign governments and underground political parties. Thanks to an international scandal, two of the Germans were acquitted and none of the miners was executed.

38 The regime department set out the degrees of severity or leniency to be observed in each particular type of camp or prison.

39 When Mikhail Sholokhov published his novel *Quiet Flows the Don* in 1928 at the age of twenty-two, critics suspected that he had plagiarized the text. In 1929 a commission dismissed these allegations; they arose again in 1937–1939; criticism of Sholokhov was at one point identified with Trotskyism, since Trotsky had tried to ban the work. There are no official records of anyone convicted under article 58 being accused of slandering Sholokhov, but the accusation is plausible. The authenticity of *Quiet Flows the Don* was generally accepted when a manuscript was discovered in 1999, but the argument that this manuscript is just a plagiarist's copy is still strong.

40 Leonid Ramzin (1887–1948), in exchange for testifying for the prosecution at a show trial in 1930, was allowed to continue his career as an engineer; Aleksei Ochkin (1886–1952), despite his Socialist Revolutionary past, was a surgeon in the Kremlin hospital; it is not clear to which Boyarshinov or Boyarshinova Shalamov is referring.

41 The khans of the Crimean Khanate (ca. 1340–1784) were always chosen from the Girei family, descended from Genghis Khan.

42 Prime Minister Piotr Stolypin, who took firm action against revolutionaries, was from 1906 associated with railway carriages for transporting large numbers of peasants and convicts. The railway carriages were adapted from cattle carriages.

43 Aleksandr Suvorov (1730–1800) was the greatest of Catherine the Great's generals. The Devil's Bridge was a key bridge in Switzerland, crossed by Suvorov's army in 1799.

44 In June 1928 the geologist Yuri Bilibin (1901–1952) headed a prospecting expedition, including Valentin Tsaregradsky (1902–1990), to Kolyma. With enormous difficulties, they devised a route to the future goldfields of the peninsula.

45 Ivan Michurin (1855–1935), even though he did not believe in genetics, was a successful plant hybridizer known for his varieties of fruits and vegetables.

46 Cannon (in Russian, Pushka) cigarettes were popular in the USSR from around 1926. They were advertised with the slogan: "Our cannons fire even in peacetime."

47 Maria Fiodorovna Andreyeva (1868–1953) was a leading actress of the Moscow Art Theater; at one time Maxim Gorky's partner, she later became a Soviet representative in Germany.

48 As a city just over a hundred kilometers from Moscow, Aleksandrov was the residence for many persons convicted and then released, but not rehabilitated.

49 In the novella, Whites use captured Bolsheviks as slave labor to extract salt.

50 A legendary figure supposed to have attempted flight during the reign of Ivan the Terrible.

51 The artist Vladimir Tatlin made *Letatlin*, a wooden ornithopter, in 1929.

52 Otto Lilienthal, an aeronautical constructor, died in 1896 after his glider crashed.

53 Dolgorukova was an eighteenth-century writer who followed her husband into exile in Siberia, where he was executed.

BOOK SIX: THE GLOVE, OR, KOLYMA STORIES II

1 Ilse Koch, the wife of the commandant of Buchenwald concentration camp, made gloves from the skins of the tattooed prisoners she killed.

2 Ménière's syndrome is a disease of the inner ear causing vertigo and deafness.

3 The spa Talaya ("Thawed Valley"), known for its therapeutic mud, is a ten-hour bus ride from Magadan. It is still in operation.

4 See *Kolyma Stories: Volume I* (New York: New York Review Books, 2018), 179–97.

5 A reference to a line from Henry Wadsworth Longfellow's *Song of Hiawatha*: "Came the Choctaws and Comanches..."

6 Johann Kaspar Lavater and Cesare Lombroso both promoted theories that predicted criminality or psychopathology from the dimensions and proportions of a subject's skull.

7 Shalamov's first version, discarded from his fair copy of this story, then continued: "He was horribly worried. After all, he had missed two whole classes of political study, and Zybalova, the secretary of the Communist

Youth organization, gave the second lieutenant the reprimand he deserved. He had trouble begging his Komsomol boss Galina not to enter anything into Postnikov's personal file; then the second lieutenant left, blushing, apologizing, and having trouble getting his arm into the sleeve of his nice new greatcoat. For a formal visit the second lieutenant was wearing a new uniform and a brand-new gold medal that read 'For Excellent Service' was trembling on his tunic. I couldn't work out whether Postnikov had gotten his medal for the hands of the Arkagala fugitive or whether the medal was earned for earlier heroic exploits of a similar kind."

8   Fermi was the creator of the world's first nuclear reactor.

9   A Dr. Krivitsky, mentioned in memoirs by other political prisoners, was formerly deputy commissar for the aviation industry.

10   Mikalojus Čiurlionis (1875–1911) was a Lithuanian symbolist, largely an abstract painter, but also a composer and writer, and effectively the founder of modern Lithuanian culture.

11   The Special Department in Soviet and Russian punishment camps was (and still is) responsible for seeing that the prison or camp regime is being adhered to.

12   SMERSH, an abbreviation of the Russian for "death to spies," was a group of counterintelligence organizations during World War II whose main remit was to identify and punish Soviet citizens suspected of collaborating with the Germans.

13   The Russian name for Antal Hidas, a Hungarian poet and translator, the son-in-law of the revolutionary Béla Kun. He was arrested along with Kun but was not shot. He died in Budapest in 1980.

14   "Wall newspapers," sheets of newsprint or typed newsletters in glass wall cases, were common in Soviet times, especially when paper was in short supply.

15   D. M. Zuyev-Insarov, an influential graphologist, was the author of *Handwriting and Personality*, published in Moscow in 1926.

16   In chess a8 and h8 are the corner squares in which the black castles start.

17   German Lopatin (1845–1918) was the Russian translator of Karl Marx's *Das Kapital*. His son Bruno was executed by the NKVD in 1938.

18   Paganel is the absentminded professor in Jules Verne's novel *In Search of the Castaways* (1867–1868).

19   Levan Ghoghoberidze was a Soviet diplomat who was executed in 1937.

20   Anastas Mikoyan (1895–1978) was the least-detested member of Stalin's politburo. His survival "from Ilyich Lenin to Ilyich Brezhnev without a

stroke or paralysis" was considered miraculous. An English version of his memoirs, *The Path of Struggles*, was published in 1988.

21 December 14, 1825, was the date of the failed coup by young army officers hoping to stop the coronation of Tsar Nicolas I. Five of the rebels were hanged, and hundreds were sent to Siberia, where many were joined by their wives, and even former nannies.

22 A song with words by Samuil Marshak (translated from the English nursery rhyme "For want of a nail, the shoe was lost") about a horseshoe whose missing nail is responsible for the death of the cavalry commander and the invasion of a foreign army.

23 Marina Ladynina was an actress and Ivan Pyryev, her husband, was a film director (she was the star and he was the director of *The Tractor Drivers*, a musical comedy).

24 In Russian, the "Hamburg Account," based on Hanseatic commercial practice, meant an absolute, unprejudiced scale of values. *The Hamburg Account* is also the title of a famous book of essays by the critic Viktor Shklovsky.

25 Wiener, a professor at the Massachusetts Institute of Technology and the American founder of cybernetics, was much respected in the USSR.

26 M.M. Slepniov (1896–1955) and M.T. Gromov (1899–1985) made record long-distance flights of eleven thousand kilometers in 1934, and in 1937 flew from Moscow to the North Pole.

27 In November 1933, the *Cheliuskin* was stuck for five months in Arctic ice before being crushed. Almost everybody aboard survived in improvised barracks on an ice floe and the group was rescued by a series of daring airplane flights.

28 Nikolai Podvoisky was briefly the People's Commissariat for War and later the People's Commissariat for Sport.

29 The opening line of Gogol's play *The Government Inspector*, when the mayor tells his officials that an inspector is on his way.

30 Professor Bitsch of Düsseldorf produced a version of Joseph Itten's "color circle."

31 In the 1890s the Italian doctor Scipione Riva-Rocci invented the sphygmomanometer to measure blood pressure.

32 Mikhail Beideman was a Russian lieutenant who went to Italy to fight with Garibaldi in 1860. On his return he was secretly convicted of intending to assassinate the tsar; he was imprisoned for twenty years and then died in a psychiatric hospital.

OTHER NEW YORK REVIEW CLASSICS

For a complete list of titles, visit www.nyrb.com or write to:
Catalog Requests, NYRB, 435 Hudson Street, New York, NY 10014

RENATA ADLER Speedboat*
ROBERT AICKMAN Compulsory Games*
KINGSLEY AMIS Lucky Jim*
IVO ANDRIĆ Omer Pasha Latas*
EVE BABITZ I Used to Be Charming: The Rest of Eve Babitz*
VICKI BAUM Grand Hotel*
FRANS G. BENGTSSON The Long Ships*
WALTER BENJAMIN The Storyteller Essays*
ALEXANDER BERKMAN Prison Memoirs of an Anarchist
MIRON BIAŁOSZEWSKI A Memoir of the Warsaw Uprising*
INÈS CAGNATI Free Day*
LESLEY BLANCH Journey into the Mind's Eye: Fragments of an Autobiography*
MALCOLM BRALY On the Yard*
ROBERT BRESSON Notes on the Cinematograph*
DAVID R. BUNCH Moderan*
JOHN HORNE BURNS The Gallery
DON CARPENTER Hard Rain Falling*
LEONORA CARRINGTON Down Below*
EILEEN CHANG Little Reunions*
ANTON CHEKHOV Peasants and Other Stories
DRISS CHRAÏBI The Simple Past*
JEAN-PAUL CLÉBERT Paris Vagabond*
ALBERT COSSERY Proud Beggars*
ASTOLPHE DE CUSTINE Letters from Russia*
JÓZEF CZAPSKI Inhuman Land: Searching for the Truth in Soviet Russia, 1941-1942*
ANTONIO DI BENEDETTO Zama*
ALFRED DÖBLIN Berlin Alexanderplatz*
THOMAS FLANAGAN The Year of the French*
BENJAMIN FONDANE Existential Monday: Philosophical Essays*
MAVIS GALLANT Paris Stories*
WILLIAM H. GASS On Being Blue: A Philosophical Inquiry*
GE FEI The Invisibility Cloak
JEAN GENET Prisoner of Love
FRANÇOISE GILOT Life with Picasso*
NATALIA GINZBURG Family Lexicon*
NIKOLAI GOGOL Dead Souls*
JEAN GIONO A King Alone*
NIKOLAI GOGOL Dead Souls*
ALICE GOODMAN History Is Our Mother: Three Libretti*
PAUL GOODMAN Growing Up Absurd: Problems of Youth in the Organized Society*
JULIEN GRACQ Balcony in the Forest*
HENRY GREEN Back*
VASILY GROSSMAN Life and Fate*
VASILY GROSSMAN Stalingrad*
PETER HANDKE Short Letter, Long Farewell
ELIZABETH HARDWICK The Collected Essays of Elizabeth Hardwick*
WOLFGANG HERRNDORF Sand*

* *Also available as an electronic book.*